CALLING THE WIND

Liza in High Cotton by Romare Bearden.
(Courtesy of the estate of Romare Bearden, A.C.A Galleries, New York.)

Books by Clarence Major

Calling the Wind:
Twentieth-Century African-American Short Stories

Parking Lots

Fun & Games

Painted Turtle: Woman with Guitar

Such Was the Season

My Amputations

Emergency Exit

Reflex and Bone Structure

No

All-Night Visitors

Surfaces and Masks

Some Observations of a Stranger at Zuni
in the Latter Part of the Century

Inside Diameter: The France Poems

The Syncopated Cakewalk

The Cotton Club

Private Line

Symptoms & Madness

Dictionary of Afro-American Slang

The Dark and Feeling

The New Black Poetry

CALLING
THE
WIND

**Twentieth-Century
African-American Short Stories**

Edited and with an introduction by
CLARENCE MAJOR

HarperPerennial
A Division of HarperCollinsPublishers
An Edward Burlingame Book

CALLING THE WIND. Copyright © 1993 by Clarence Major. All rights reserved. Printed in the United States of America. No part of this book may be used or reproduced in any manner whatsoever without written permission except in the case of brief quotations embodied in critical articles and reviews. For information address HarperCollins Publishers, Inc., 10 East 53rd Street, New York, NY 10022.

HarperCollins books may be purchased for educational, business, or sales promotional use. For information, please write: Special Markets Department, HarperCollins Publishers, Inc., 10 East 53rd Street, New York, NY 10022.

Designed by C. Linda Dingler

Library of Congress Cataloging-in-Publication Data
Calling the wind: twentieth-century African-American short stories/
    edited by Clarence Major.—1st ed.
        p. cm.
    "An Edward Burlingame book."
    ISBN 0-06-018337-3 (cloth)—ISBN 0-06-098201-2 (paper)
    1. Short stories, American—Afro-American authors. 2. Afro-
Americans—Fiction. I. Major, Clarence.
PS647.A35C35 1992
813'.0108896073—dc20   92-52620

93 94 95 96 97 CC/HC 10 9 8 7 6 5 4 3 2 1
93 94 95 96 97 CC/HC 10 9 8 7 6 5 4 3 2   (pbk.)

Contents

Acknowledgments   xi

Introduction by Clarence Major   xiii

Editor's Note   xxvii

Charles Chesnutt, The Goophered Grapevine (1899)   1

Paul Laurence Dunbar, The Ingrate (1900)   12

Jessie Fauset, Mary Elizabeth (1919)   18

Jean Toomer, Esther (1923)   25

Marita Bonner, The Hands: A Story (1925)   30

Nella Larsen, Sanctuary (1930)   34

Claude McKay, Truant (1932)   39

Arna Bontemps, A Summer Tragedy (1933)   50

Rudolph Fisher, Miss Cynthie (1933)   58

Zora Neale Hurston, The Gilded Six-Bits (1933)   69

Chester Himes, Headwaiter (1938)   79

Richard Wright, Bright and Morning Star (1938)   94

Dorothy West, Jack in the Pot (1940)   123

Ralph Ellison, Flying Home (1944)   135

Langston Hughes, Who's Passing for Who? (1952)   151

William Melvin Kelley, The Only Man on Liberty Street (1956)   155

James Baldwin, Come Out the Wilderness (1958)   163

Ann Petry, Has Anybody Seen Miss Dora Dean? (1958)   182

Junius Edwards, Mother Dear and Daddy (1962)   196

John Stewart, Blues for Pablo (1962)   205

John A. Williams, Son in the Afternoon (1962)   220

Robert Boles, What's Your Problem? (1964)   226

Henry Dumas, The Distributors (1964)   232

Rosa Guy, Wade (1965)   242

Diane Oliver, Key to the City (1965)   251

LeRoi Jones/Amiri Baraka, The Alternative (1967)   261

Paule Marshall, To Da-Duh, in Memoriam (1967)   275

Charles Wright, A New Day (1967)   284

Samuel R. Delany, Night and the Loves of Joe Dicostanzo (1968)   289

Cyrus Colter, The Lookout (1970)   305

Ernest J. Gaines, A Long Day in November (1971)   311

Toni Cade Bambara, The Lesson (1972)   348

James Alan McPherson, The Story of a Scar (1973)   355

Ellease Southerland, Soldiers (1973)   366

Alice Walker, Roselily (1973)   370

Gayl Jones, White Rat (1975)   374

Edgar Nkose White, Loimos (1975)   381

Charles Johnson, The Education of Mingo (1977)   389

Clarence Major, Scat (1979)   399

Cecil M. Brown, Now Is the Time (1981)   405

John Edgar Wideman, Damballah (1981)   421

Gloria Naylor, Kiswana Browne (1982)   428

Toni Morrison, "Recitatif" (1983)   438

Jamaica Kincaid, Girl (1984)   454

Henry Van Dyke, Chitterling (1985)   456

Colleen J. McElroy, Jesus and Fat Tuesday (1987)   466

Ann Allen Shockley, The World of Rosie Polk (1987)   480

Reginald McKnight, Mali Is Very Dangerous (1988)   498

Don Belton, Her Mother's Prayers on Fire (1989)   508

Hal Bennett, Wings of the Dove (1989)   517

CONTENTS / ix

Larry Duplechan, Zazoo (1989)   524

Trey Ellis, Guess Who's Coming to Seder (1989)   534

John McCluskey, Jr., Top of the Game (1989)   539

Richard Perry, Going to Meet Aaron (1989)   552

Tina McElroy Ansa, Willie Bea and Jaybird (1990)   558

Michelle Cliff, Screen Memory (1990)   566

Percival Everett, Age Would Be That Does (1990)   578

Al Young, Going for the Moon (1990)   584

Terry McMillan, Quilting on the Rebound (1991)   597

Biographical Notes   609

Acknowledgments

My friend and agent, Susan Bergholz, read all the drafts of the introduction and all the evolving selections for a period of five years. I am deeply grateful for her smart and constructive criticism. Her careful reading sent me back again and again to the task of making this anthology as fine as I possibly could.

I am also extremely lucky to have had Kathy Banks, my friend and editor at HarperCollins, working with me during the final stages. Her sensitive reading and intelligent advice made an enormous difference to the final shape of the book. She has my deep appreciation. Thanks also to Ed Burlingame for his support and encouragement and to Christa Weil.

And my gratitude for help or encouragement also goes to the following people: Edwin J. Rivers, J. J. Phillips, John McCluskey, Mrs. Blanche R. Oliver, Carl Cowl, Al Young, Ishmael Reed, Charles Johnson, John Stewart, Ann Allen Shockley and my wife, Pamela Major.

Introduction

V. F. Calverton, in the introduction to his landmark *Anthology of American Negro Literature* (1929), said that the Negro "gave to whatever [cultural forms] he took [from the West] a new style and a new interpretation." This collection is an example of how African Americans have done that with the short story.

Short stories, I discovered early in my teaching career, worked well as tools for learning. Over the years I tested many stories by black writers in the classroom. At a certain point, it seemed natural to collect in book form those most interesting, effective, and successful with students. One Chinese student, for example, discovered in a Richard Wright story a whole world that reminded him of the life of his grandparents in China. A young woman of Irish-German descent, concerned about the rights of women, saw in Zora Neale Hurston's "The Gilded Six-Bits," Dorothy West's "Jack in the Pot," Toni Cade Bambara's "The Lesson," and Cyrus Colter's "The Lookout," the means to a strategy for discussing the relation between women, money, and power. A Mexican-American, at the end of one of my courses, told me most of the stories, in one way or another, gave him insight into the behavior of members of his own family and community. Time and again I saw evidence of how these stories turned students on and, in some cases, even changed their lives.

Although the short story has roots in the oral traditions of any number of ancient civilizations, its beginnings as a formal literary genre in America are usually traced to Nathaniel Hawthorne, Washington Irving, and Edgar Allan Poe, who began consciously to develop and define the short story as a written form.

Poe laid out a blueprint: The short story was a "prose narrative" that necessarily had its own "magnitude": ordinarily, one should be able to read a short story in, say, half an hour. In any case, it shouldn't take a reader more than two hours to finish, for the idea was to create "a single effect." According to Poe, an "air of consequence or causation" must pervade the short story for it to work impressively. This was achieved through strict observance of certain principles of composition, as described in his essay "The Philosophy of Composition" and elsewhere:

Nothing is more clear than that every plot worth the name must be elaborated to its denouement before anything be attempted with the pen. It is only with the denouement constantly in view that we can give a plot its indispensable air of consequence, or causation, by making the incidents, and especially the tone at all points, tend to the development of the intention.

Poe's prescription amounts to a kind of tightrope walking for both the writer (in the process of construction) and the reader (in the process of reinventing the story as his or her own). The successful traditional short story aims for effect while creating its own universe, with emphasis on the complete unity— especially the tonal unity—of its parts. But by the 1920s the idea of the short story as an exemplary thing with strict adherence to a single effect or single dramatic pattern—especially to the point of sacrificing plausibility—began to be challenged.

During that period the notion of an abstract, ideal model of the short story, insofar as it existed in Poe's and Hawthorne's days, began to lose ground as a working referent. The form opened up as readers and writers alike turned to the short story to fulfill all kinds of needs. Some saw stories as paradigms of their own experience. Others appreciated the psychological or spiritual illumination they found in them. Still others enjoyed the short story on a purely aesthetic level—as an artful play of language, a shimmer of verbal energy made visible. And many turned to the form to explore—some might say escape to—fascinating worlds vastly different from their own.

The modern American short story, then, came to be defined as any effective short prose piece built on a series of repeated verbal signs, images, and symbols, adding up to a subject matter—which, at its simplest level, refers to the most frequent activity in the story—while what we call *theme* emerges as a recurrent commentary, either straightforward or imagistic, on the quality or meaning of that activity. But every good short story presents its own magic, and it usually defies formula. It creates its own reality. This is not to say that stories have no bearing on the reader's (or writer's) reality; one of the first things I tend to say to a literature class is, "I think we can begin from the assumption that storytelling is vital to human health. It gives us workable metaphors for our lives." And one of my purposes here is to gather a group of stories that offer a wide range of workable metaphors for the ways we live.

My own discovery of African-American writers happened during my last year of elementary school in Chicago. The discovery didn't take place in a classroom, and it occurred long after I had developed a love for reading and had been reading on my own—books I wanted to read, like J. D. Salinger's *The Catcher in the Rye* and *Eight Stories,* for example—and not simply stories I had to read for classes.

I suspected there were writers whose cultural heritage was similar to my own, but we never had occasion to read any in class, even though most of my teachers were themselves of the same heritage. To most Americans, even college-educated Americans, African-American literature was invisible. Even now, I still hear many of my students—most of them white—express surprise when they discover African-American writers other than Richard Wright, James Baldwin, and Alice Walker.

This is despite the unmistakable influence of other black cultural forms—such as blues and jazz and popular black idioms—on American culture in general, and despite the fact that the African-American literary anthology has had a relatively long publishing history. Those collections published in the 1920s, 1930s, and 1940s are now classic landmarks and historical keys to the cultural and artistic temperament of their moments in time. Although many of them are filled with works that Richard Wright, in his essay "Blueprint for Negro Writing," called "humble novels, poems and plays, prim and decorous ambassadors who went a-begging to white America," they nevertheless brought together the scattered and neglected—often privately published—efforts of Negro writers whose work might otherwise have been lost. They asserted and reasserted the presence of African-American stories, poems, plays, and essays, keeping important names and works before an intensely interested, if relatively small, American reading audience.

I came across such anthologies around the same time I discovered Richard Wright's *Native Son* and Chester Himes's *The Third Generation.* A whole new world of cultural interpretation opened up. I soon was reading William Gardner Smith's *The Stone Face* and James Baldwin's *Go Tell It on the Mountain.* Inspired by the example of these works, I was soon trying to write my own stories.

African-American writers have practiced the short story form with vigor, skill, and originality since the beginning. Like writers of European descent—writers such as Hemingway, Faulkner, Katherine Anne Porter, and Flannery O'Connor—writers of African descent found the form unusually suitable for capturing highly focused moments in the life of a vast and complex country. But average American readers, if they know anything at all about African-American literature, usually hold a view of it fashioned by the politics of race and media stereotypes. It's a view based largely on myths and assumptions about African Americans handed down generation after generation, not only among Anglo-Americans but among almost all ethnic groups in this country. In her story "Recitatif," Toni Morrison deliberately sets out to deny readers any access to such racial stereotyping. As she points out in her wonderful little book *Playing in the Dark* (1992), the story was "an experiment in the removal of all racial codes from a narrative about two characters of different races for whom racial identity is crucial." The writers gathered in this book collectively challenge the tendency Morrison set out to circumvent: the tendency to stereotype the Other.

This is the first trade anthology composed exclusively of twentieth-century African-American short stories since Langston Hughes's *The Best Short Stories by Negro Writers: An Anthology from 1899 to the Present,* published in 1967. In making the selections, I wanted to include stories that met Poe's definition of the short story as well as stories that effectively *defied* not just his definition but other conventions. I wanted both to indicate the full diversity of African-American work over the years and to show how the work of black writers has evolved, along with "mainstream" work, from earlier, formal practices of the genre to the present. But because of the complex history of this country, it is important to examine, at least briefly, some of the factors—elementary as they may be—that make up not just the literary but the social and political context in which this particular selection exists.

First, what *is* an African American? For that matter, what is an American? And if this selection represents "ethnic" literature, what is "ethnic" literature?

If asked to describe an American, most people around the world would almost reflexively describe a white person from North America. Whiteness in North America, however, is primarily a matter of *not being black.* In an essay titled "Our Greatest Gift to America," published in Calverton's 1929 anthology (pp. 410–412), journalist and novelist George S. Schuyler gives a stinging definition of white America and how it got that way:

It is fairly well established, I think, that our [black] presence in the Great Republic has been of incalculable psychological value to the masses of white citizens. Descendants of convicts, serfs and half-wits, with the rest have been buoyed up and greatly exalted by being constantly assured of their superiority to all other races and their equality with each other. On the stages of a thousand music halls, they have had their vanity tickled by blackface performers parading the idiocies of mythical black roustabouts and rustics. Between belly-cracking guffaws they have secretly congratulated themselves on the fact that they are not like these buffoons. Their books and magazines have told them, or insinuated, that morality, beauty, refinement and culture are restricted to Caucasians. On every hand they have seen smokes endeavoring to change from black to white, and from kinky hair to straight, by means of deleterious chemicals, and constantly they hear the Negroes urging each other to do this and that "like white folks." Nor do the crackers fail to observe, either, that pink epidermis is as highly treasured among blacks as in Nordic America, and that the most devastating charge that one Negro can make against another is that "he acs just like a nigger." Anything excellent they hear labeled by the race conscious Negroes as "like white folks," nor is it unusual for them, while loitering in the Negro ghetto, to hear black women compared to Fords, mulatto women to Cadillacs and white women to Packards. With so much flattery it is no wonder that the Caucasians have a very high opinion of themselves and attempt to live up to the lofty niche in which the Negroes have placed them. We should not marvel that every white elevator operator, school teacher and bricklayer identifies himself with Shakespeare, Julius Caesar, Napoleon, Newton, Edison, Wagner, Tennyson and Rembrandt as creators of their great civilization. As a result we have our American society, where everybody who sports a pink color believes himself to be the equal of all other whites by virtue of his lack of skin pigmentation, and his classic Caucasian features. . . . It is not surprising then, that democracy has worked better in this country than elsewhere. This belief in the equality of all white folks—making skin color the gauge of worth and the measure of citizenship rights—has caused the lowest to strive to become among the highest. Because of this great ferment, America has become the Utopia of the material world; the land of hope and opportunity. Without the transplanted African in their midst to bolster up the illusion, America would have unquestionably been a very different place; but instead the shine has served as a mudsill upon which all white people alike can stand and reach toward the stars. I submit that here is the gift par excellence of the Negro in America. To spur ten times our number on the great heights of achievement; to spare the nation the enervating presence of a destructive social caste system, such as exists elsewhere, by substituting a color caste system that roused the hope and pride of teeming millions of ofays—this indeed is a gift of which we can well be proud.

Despite the fact that Schuyler's tone is bitingly satiric and the words were written sixty-three years ago, his thesis—"Without the transplanted African in their midst to bolster up the illusion, America would have unquestionably been a very different place"—agrees completely with Toni Morrison's analysis. In *Playing in the Dark* (p. 65), Morrison says:

The presence of black people is inherent, along with gender and family ties, in the earliest lesson every child is taught regarding his or her distinctiveness. Africanism is inextricable from the definition of Americanness—from its origins on through its integrated or disintegrating twentieth-century self.

In other words, the very presence of an Other (in this case a dark, contrasting Other) helps to shape the popular (white) definition of an American self. This dark other presence, again in Morrison's words (p. 17), has a profoundly complex function:

Through the simple expedient of demonizing and reifying the range of color on a palette, American Africanism makes it possible to say and not say, to inscribe and erase, to escape and engage, to act out and act on, to historicize and render timeless.

It provides a way of contemplating chaos and civilization, desire and fear, and a mechanism for testing the problems and blessings of freedom.

This white image, contrasted against the black Other, is in fact only a mythic American. The American presence is so varied and so complex that exchange and conflict between the black image and the white image tend absurdly to diminish the richness of a network of ethnic cultures that truly is the American human landscape. Most individuals in these groups feel some sense of doubleness, feel their otherness *and* their Americanness. One indication of an internal struggle can be seen in their tendency to hyphenate the names signaling the two different selves—African-American, Native-American, Asian-American, Mexican-American, and so on.

W. E. B. Du Bois, in *The Souls of Black Folk* (1903), wrote (p. 45):

It is a peculiar sensation, this double-consciousness, this sense of always looking at one's self through the eyes of others, of measuring one's soul by the tape of a world that looks on in amused contempt and pity. One ever feels his twoness—an American, a Negro; two souls, two thoughts, two unreconciled strivings; two warring ideals in one dark body; whose dogged strength alone keeps it from being torn asunder.

Since Americans all, originally, came from somewhere else, this doubleness, as Jack Hicks points out in *In the Singer's Temple* (1981; p. 84),

lies at the heart of the American experience. At best an uneasy and shifting peace. To stress one's national and ethnic origins and culture or to conceive oneself as purely an American, cut from the ties of people and past—these are truly warring ideals, the poles of total assimilation and the supreme isolation of place, race, and class that have generated the tension defining our national struggles.

So to some degree doubleness describes the condition of all Americans, whether or not they know it.

Some researchers argue that since Anglo-Americans and descendants of Western Europe constitute this new, invented "white American" that Toni Morrison talks about, they set the agenda for the culture of the country. However, no human activity is ever that simple. The idea of being American is still new to even "white" Americans.

Among the many theories about the origins of Anglo-American feelings of selfhood is one that centers on social and cultural transformations made by the Puritans of New England. But the Puritans present only one example of many such transformations, in the colonies and afterward. Very likely a national sense of identity did not take hold on a massive scale until after World War I. Apparently, at that point, a sense of self among Americans was enforced—from the outside—by the enormous pressure of this worldwide action, which served at least to show Americans what they had in common and how they were different from peoples of other countries.

Television, it seems to me, became the other source of solidifying an American sense of selfhood. But that is another story.

The African-American journey to selfhood was always deeply ironic. Africans and people of African descent were subjected to legal and illegal slavery in the "land of liberty." And this "new world" was already an old world long inhabited by peoples—commonly called Indians—the Africans immediately identified with, especially in the Deep South. It's little wonder that such a historical experience would produce an ethnic population whose writers seemed instinctively to write stories with irony at their core.

If we can call any literature ethnic—that is, if it can be defined in cultural terms—then we can say it's the element of regionalism in the work that opens it to such a definition. I use the word "regionalism" with its connotations of the homespun, the local, the rural, the provincial, the narrow; even the unrefined. Werner Sollers, in *Beyond Ethnicity* (Oxford, 1986), uses the word "parochialism" to imply the same sort of limitations. Sollers says, "Ethnic writing is equated with parochialism and ethnic writers who are not parochial are classified not as ethnic but as 'wholly' American." He goes on to say that

a broader and more inclusive definition of ethnic literature is helpful: works written by, about, or for persons who perceive themselves, or were perceived by others, as members of ethnic groups, including even nationally and internationally popular writings by "major" authors and formally intricate and modernist texts.

William Boelhower, in *Through the Looking Glass* (1984), argues that *all* American literature is ethnic. In other words, Boelhower seems to suggest that no American personality is so generic that it has lost ethnic memory of a previous cultural life in Europe or Africa or China or India or South America or somewhere else.

When we say Americans live in a multi-ethnic or poly-ethnic society, we are acknowledging the truth of Hicks's comments on doubleness. The writers represented here grew up with a strong sense of it. Cultural doubleness is common among ethnic groups throughout the world. America, Russia, Yugoslavia, Italy, and other relatively recent federations are filled with peoples with divided cultural—to say nothing of political—allegiances. Cultural homogenization—such as it exists anywhere—is usually the byproduct of power seeking and plunder.

Just as irony is a key to the African-American experience, so it is an important device in African-American literature. While all good fiction is, on one level or another, ironic, many of the stories here pointedly deal with situations that appear to be one thing but are revealed in the end to be another—as in James Alan McPherson's "The Story of a Scar" (1973). In other instances the subtext of a story may all along be something quite different from what the story appears to say on the surface—as in Chesnutt's "The Goophered Grapevine" (1899) and Ralph Ellison's "Flying Home" (1944). These stories might also be read as allegories or parodies or satire, but in each case they partake of situational irony. That is, the ironic incident makes a moral judgment about—and effectively manipulates—the temporal or social context of the model incident, even as the ironic incident is measured against its model or ideal. In other words, an ironic situation usually comes into focus when juxtaposed to what we believe to be a stable, recognizable, predictable—and therefore usually preferred—reality.

Chesnutt's, Ellison's, and McPherson's stories share another device: Each incorporates a story told within the story. All three are therefore, among other things, about storytelling.

"The Goophered Grapevine," a parody of the plantation story, is about talking and listening, and its theme is deception—deceptive talking, deceptive listening. The outer, framing story is in the apparently authoritative but ultimately unreliable narrative voice of a young liberal white man from the North named John. The inner story, told by Uncle Julius—which, on the surface, seems to lack credibility—by contrast gains an ironic authority even as the old ex-slave insists that the visitors from up North really are not required to believe what he's about to tell them. Uncle Julius's aim is to make the visitors feel comfortable with their assumed prejudices, and he clearly reinforces any possible stereotypes they might hold about his people by going on to say that all Negroes love possum, chicken, and watermelon. Paul Laurence Dunbar called this act "wearing the mask."

Uncle Julius talks first about the plantation owner's struggle to keep the slaves from eating the scuppernong grapes the master grows to make wine; in order to accomplish his goal the owner, Mr. McAdoo, finally resorts to hiring a conjure woman called Aunt Peggy. The second part of Julius's story involves McAdoo's purchase of an elderly slave named Henry, who defies the goopher and eats the summer grapes but does not suffer the expected consequences. Using one of Aunt Peggy's potions made from the sap of the grapevine, Henry is instead transformed into a strong young man. Leave it to McAdoo to find in this a fine business opportunity: He sells Henry at a high price. Winter comes, Henry turns into an old man again, and thereupon McAdoo buys him back cheap. The slaveholder keeps this up for a number of years. Each spring Henry becomes young again; McAdoo sells him while he's strong and vigorous and then buys him back in the winter when he's old and bent. In this way the slaveholder increases his wealth.

Of course Uncle Julius's story is an entertaining attempt to dissuade John from buying the McAdoo plantation with its conjured fields: neglected since the Civil War ended a few years before, the plantation is Julius's home, pathetic as it may be. But the shrewd old man's story of the plantation's heyday is also a celebration of the African-American tall tale and a satire of the nostalgic and sentimental stories about slave and slaveholder relations so popular during Reconstruction. And while Uncle Julius does not leave any noticeable impression on John, John's wife, Annie, recognizes Uncle Julius's humanity and courage and is renewed by them.

In Ellison's "Flying Home," set in the 1940s, a young black man named Todd crashes his fighter plane in a white man's field. He's discovered by an old black man and a boy. The story lends itself to many different critical approaches and has literary roots in a number of ancient stories—of the death and rebirth of the phoenix, in the Icarus and Daedalus story of ill-fated flight, and in the biblical stories of the Fall as well as of the Prodigal Son. In its ironic structure, it bears a resemblance to Chesnutt's story of forty-five years before.

Jefferson, the narrator of the inner story, seems at the opening to be a simpleminded, childlike old man, much like Uncle Julius. Nevertheless it is his folksy wisdom that becomes the means by which Todd, the protagonist, rediscovers his abandoned cultural self. Jefferson begins with the story of the buzzard. In African-American folklore, the buzzard is a wily popular totem, a bird that manages to survive on dead things, things others do not want, and he is often unjustly reviled for it. The buzzard story sheds light on Todd's story in a number of ways. As a fighter pilot Todd is a symbol of death; he has also been given second-class treatment by the military establishment he's attempted to serve. And in Jefferson's opinion, he is a creature who has ranged too far from home and from the security of his own cultural identity.

It is old Jefferson who turns out to be the educated young man's teacher and deliverer; through him Todd is finally lifted from his fall, literally and spiritually, and delivered back to the bosom of his culture. As a phoenix he is brought up out of sleep, out of a dream of a "bird of flaming gold," and the end of the story suggests that in this transformation Todd's sense of himself will undergo a dramatic positive change.

Like "Flying Home," McPherson's "The Story of a Scar" is also about a conversation between two black people of different classes—the narrator, who considers himself to be a man of taste, and a woman with a scarred face. When they meet in a doctor's waiting room and he asks her about the scar, the two launch themselves into a "capping" exchange. He sees her as a foolish woman who's wasted her time on a no-good roughneck of a man, a view that is psychologically oppressive and insulting. In Zora Neale Hurston's words, he sees her as "the mule of the world."

She is, however, well aware of the narrator's condescension, and she challenges him every step of the way in order to get her own story told. She has been involved with two men who work with her at the post office: one, Billy, is supposed to be a good, responsible adult; the other, Teddy, an apparent no-account. So firm are the narrator's negative assumptions about the scarred woman and how she has come to be so wounded that at first we assume he's reading her correctly. We also assume that she is misjudging the narrator when she tells him how intolerant, narrow-minded, and stubbornly set in his ways he is.

By the end we have changed our minds about both of them. We see she is on target; he has completely—and viciously—misjudged her. In the reader's eyes, she vindicates herself by forcing the narrator to confront his prejudiced view of her. But the narrator's pretensions turn out to be so uncomfortably close to those of her attacker that we doubt he will ultimately be changed by what the story of the scar has to teach.

Although irony is a strong element in these stories, others utilize even bolder ironic strokes. In "The Ingrate" (1900), for example, Paul Laurence Dunbar demonstrates how a slaveholder's generosity in teaching his slave to write is simply another form of exploitation in a threadbare disguise. We quickly see a wide gap between the apparent reality of the situation and what the slaveholder professes to be the case. Even so, when the slave uses his new skills to escape bondage, the slaveholder feels betrayed. Similarly, in John Edgar Wideman's "Damballah" (1981), another slaveholder convinces himself that he has been wronged when the protagonist refuses to submit to a life of slavery. In both cases, self-deception leads to self-righteous indignation.

Most of the stories here can be read and appreciated for their varied and rich manipulations of verbal and structural irony, but they can also, of course, be appreciated from any number of angles. Some groupings suggest themselves immediately: Zora Neale Hurston's "The Gilded Six-Bits" (1933), Dorothy West's "Jack in the Pot" (1940), Cyrus Colter's "The Lookout" (1970), and Toni Cade Bambara's "The Lesson" (1972) are all wise stories about the power of money. Jean Toomer's "Esther" (1923) and Chester Himes's "The Head-waiter" (1938) are stories about the individual in conflict with himself or herself, or with his or her surroundings. Jessie Fauset's "Mary Elizabeth" (1919), Langston Hughes's "Who's Passing for Who?" (1952), William Melvin Kelley's "The Only Man on Liberty Street" (1956), and John A. Williams's "Son in the Afternoon" (1962) play on the complex psychology of gender, race, and class differences. Each of these stories records some particulars of the black experience. Each also bears witness to the social and political sensibility of its time.

The African-American short story is a product of a specific culture, but not one that developed in isolation. This more or less self-contained black culture would have evolved in America with or without legal segregation to coerce it.

Its evolution was an act of survival. Founded on sacred and secular foundations, black culture interacted with the larger mainstream along lines acceptable primarily to the mainstream. This history of separateness—or, to put it more harshly, alienation and segregation—alone justifies the act of gathering the writings of writers who, whether loosely or narrowly, can be called African-American.

These writers, then, are men and women whose visions were shaped by growing up somewhere in the United States or, if they were born elsewhere, by living as black people in this country. Their differences are as important as what they share. In an essay titled "Remembering Richard Wright" (*Going to the Territory*, 1986), Ralph Ellison makes an important point about the role of geography in the shaping of "fate." Ellison points out that because he grew up in the Southwest, he and Wright, who grew up in the Southeast, were "divided by geography and a difference of experience based thereupon."

If the social experiences of black Americans vary from region to region, the historical stages vary as much, and it's important to remember the aesthetic and social philosophies, the complexity, of each period of African-American literature. These have been defined as Antebellum (1853–1865), Postbellum (1865–1902), the period of the Old Guard (1902–1917), the Harlem Renaissance (1917–1929), and the period of Social Protest (1929–1959).

While each period had its overriding concerns, two social and political tendencies were more or less always present in African-American thought, and both were addressed to the problem of racial oppression. One was the quest for justice through racial integration with Anglo-Americans. The other was the quest for justice through geographical and/or psychological separation from Anglo-Americans. Both tendencies found expression in slave narratives and in essays, novels, poems, and short stories.

African-American artists in many media have given explicit or subtle expression to these concerns, usually maintaining a high level of artistic excellence and avoiding the mere business of chronicling offenses. Those concerns are vividly displayed in the short stories of the various periods represented here.

Writers of the Antebellum period, such as William Wells Brown and Martin R. Delany, were primarily concerned with informing a white audience of the injustices of slavery and racial oppression. These writers were absolutely sure they understood the meaning of freedom, understood it in the same way enslaved folk had understood its importance since the beginning of civilization. They hoped to find a humane way to tell white readers, preferably sympathetic white readers, about the crime of human bondage. A certain paradox lay in this, and many of the early works were prefaced with apologetic notes to the reader—shallow attempts to sugarcoat the just complaint.

The Postbellum period—which corresponds roughly with Reconstruction (1865–1877) and its promise of social and cultural prosperity—produced writers such as Paul Laurence Dunbar, Charles Chesnutt, Sutton Griggs, W. E. B. Du Bois, and others. These writers continued the attempt to educate a Eurocentric reading audience about the racial nightmare in which those of African descent lived. But they also began to write with the assumption that black consciousness and black culture were significant, self-evident entities in the world, deserving of respect.

The African-American short story formally begins with Dunbar and Chesnutt. Chesnutt's "The Goophered Grapevine" and Dunbar's "The Ingrate" speak directly to the social, psychological, and legal problems of black people before the turn of the century. W. E. B. Du Bois and others spill over into the next period, that of the Old Guard. By 1917 the Old Guard represented rather conservative ideas and ideals about African-American culture in general. The contrast between their positions and those of the next generation—the Harlem Renaissance—is as sharp as a blade of light pouring down through a stained glass window. The aesthetic and political stance of Rudolph Fisher, Zora Neale Hurston, Jean Toomer, Claude McKay, Nella Larsen, Wallace Thurman, and Langston Hughes is well described by Hughes in his famous essay, "The Negro Artist and the Racial Mountain," published in *The Nation*, June 23, 1926. In part, Hughes says (p. 694):

An artist must be free to choose what he does, certainly, but he must also never be afraid to do what he might choose. . . . We younger Negro artists who create now intend to express our individual dark-skinned selves without fear of shame. If white people are pleased we are glad. If they are not, it doesn't matter. We know we are beautiful. And ugly too. The tom-tom cries and the tom-tom laughs. If colored people are pleased we are glad. If they are not, their displeasure doesn't matter either. We build our temples for tomorrow, strong as we know how, and we stand on top of the mountain, free within ourselves.

That statement and the whole essay was, in effect, a manifesto and a declaration of independence. It was also a strike against what Hughes called the "smug Negro middle class."

The period I call Social Protest includes the Depression years of the 1930s and reaches into the 1940s and 1950s. Richard Wright was and is the best-known black writer of this time. It was characterized by the rise of a healthy intellectual curiosity on the social and cultural Left. To many black writers, Marxism or some form of socialism looked, at least for a while, like a viable solution to the economic problems black people and the rest of the nation faced. More important, the advent of a truly classless society would inevitably mean an end to racism.

But political rifts in the nation as a whole widened through the 1960s, and by the end of the decade Black (Cultural) Nationalism began to replace the integrative impulse of the earlier era of protest. Separation from Anglo-American culture was not simply the only route to justice, it was itself the goal. While the political agenda of many of the poets and playwrights of the nationalist period caused them to create what now looks like the work of ideologues, few black fiction writers completely fell into step.

Du Bois said that all art is propaganda, but propaganda is not necessarily art. When the Black Nationalist theory of culture was applied to fiction, it was done in the narrowest possible—to use a currently popular word—Afrocentric terms, and it tended to be an uncomfortable fit. The spirit of Black Nationalism, with its reactionary and conservative tendencies, was challenged by the diversity of such writers as Samuel R. Delany, Alice Walker, Henry Van Dyke, Ernest J. Gaines, James Alan McPherson, Paule Marshall, Charles Wright, John Edgar Wideman, and Al Young. These and other writers were creating an eclectic body of work that many critics took as a sign of a second "New Negro" Renaissance.

Again, in retrospect, it's possible to see that before the 1960s, African-American writers of fiction more often than not chose race as their theme and racial conflict as their subject matter. They were primarily interested in the effects of white racism on the lives of black people, but by the mid-1970s that was no longer the case. In the past two decades, black American artists have continued to be concerned with racial conflict, with racism, and with the rich ironies of American history and culture in what is oversimplified as the Black Experience, but they probe beyond its merely political aspects to find the roots that link their experience to all human experience.

These novelists and poets and playwrights and short story writers have probed the "human universals" through the cultural particulars. Ralph Ellison, in the 1982 introduction (p. xx) to the thirtieth anniversary edition of *Invisible Man* (1952), brings this impulse into focus in one neat sentence:

[My] task was one of revealing the human universals hidden within the plight of one who was born black and American, and not only as a means of conveying my personal vision of possibility, but as a way of dealing with the sheer rhetorical challenge involved in communicating across our barriers of race and religion, class, color and region—barriers which consist of the many strategies of division that were designed, and still function, to prevent what would otherwise have been a more or less natural recognition of the reality of black and white fraternity.

Tied into the web of assumptions and half-truths that make up an American's sense of reality is a denial of the history of actual black and white relations, intimate and otherwise, in this land. The possible "fraternity" Ellison speaks of is further eclipsed by this historical denial of the importance of black people in the shaping of white American reality and identity. Toni Morrison, again, makes the point well (*Playing in the Dark,* p. 44):

I want to suggest that . . . autonomy, authority, newness and difference, absolute power . . . not only became the major themes and presumptions of American literature, but that each one is made possible by, shaped by, activated by a complex awareness and employment of a constituted Africanism. It was this Africanism, deployed as rawness and savagery, that provided the staging ground and arena for the elaboration of the quintessential American identity.

Part of the American reality is, as James Baldwin often pointed out, that black people and white people in America are kissing cousins. Many of these short stories stand as testimony to that truth, to that troubled bond—troubled because the first time an enslaver forced himself upon his slave, though he failed to recognize it (or his own barbarism), he was acknowledging the slave's humanity, that which he officially denied. From that moment on, the failure of slavery was assured.

And, irony on irony, the denial of kinship is so sternly expressed both in public life and in mainstream literature that the denial warps the American psyche. This exchange and conflict has been a great double-edged challenge facing the serious American writer for nearly two centuries, and it remains so to this day.

C.M.

Editor's Note

This anthology is one in a tradition of anthologies, books that have helped to fill the gaps in what is undeniably a significant body of work produced by African-American poets, essayists, and fiction writers during the history of this country. Among the outstanding collections of black literature that appeared over the first four decades of this century were Alain Locke's *New Negro: An Interpretation* (1925); the *Anthology of American Negro Literature* (1929) edited by V. F. Calverton; Countee Cullen's *Caroling Dusk: An Anthology of Verse by Negro Poets* (1927); *Negro: An Anthology* (1934), collected and edited by Nancy Cunard; Arna Bontemps's *Golden Slippers: An Anthology of Negro Poetry* (1941); and Rosey E. Pool and Eric Walrond's *Black and Unknown Bards* (1958). Many of these are, unfortunately, out of print.

Later, in the sixties and seventies, there was another flurry of anthologies. Many of these were edited along thematic or historical lines; a few were put together on the basis of region. By the 1970s and 1980s, gender became a category, and there was a belated and much-welcomed rush of anthologies devoted to work by black women, several edited by Mary Helen Washington. Among the later collections—a number of them still in print—were Herbert Hill's *Soon, One Morning* (1963); Arthur P. Davis and Saunders Redding's *Cavalcade: Negro American Writing from 1760 to the Present* (1971); John A. Williams's *Beyond the Angry Black* (1966) and *Amistad* (1970) (with Charles Harris); Robert Hayden's *Afro-American Literature: An Introduction* (1971); Darwin T. Turner's *Black American Literature* (1970); Ishmael Reed's *Nineteen Necromancers from Now* (1970); Arna Bontemps's *American Negro Poetry* (1982); Langston Hughes's *The Best Short Stories by Negro Writers* (1967); Woodie King's *Black Short Story Anthology* (1972); John H. Clarke's *American Negro Short Stories* (1966); Abraham Chapman's *Black Voices* (1968) and *New Black Voices* (1972); LeRoi Jones and Larry Neal's *Black Fire* (1968); Houston A. Baker, Jr.'s *Black Literature in America* (1971); my own *The New Black Poetry* (1969); and, more recently, Terry McMillan's excellent *Breaking Ice: An Anthology of Contemporary Black Writers* (1990).

CALLING THE WIND

The Goophered Grapevine

Charles Chesnutt

1899

Some years ago my wife was in poor health, and our family doctor, in whose skill and honesty I had implicit confidence, advised a change of climate. I shared, from an unprofessional standpoint, his opinion that the raw winds, the chill rains, and the violent changes of temperature that characterized the winters in the region of the Great Lakes tended to aggravate my wife's difficulty, and would undoubtedly shorten her life if she remained exposed to them. The doctor's advice was that we seek, not a temporary place of sojourn, but a permanent residence, in a warmer and more equable climate. I was engaged at the time in grape-culture in northern Ohio, and, as I liked the business and had given it much study, I decided to look for some other locality suitable for carrying it on. I thought of sunny France, of sleepy Spain, of Southern California, but there were objections to them all. It occurred to me that I might find what I wanted in some one of our own Southern States. It was a sufficient time after the war for conditions in the South to have become somewhat settled; and I was enough of a pioneer to start a new industry, if I could not find a place where grape-culture had been tried. I wrote to a cousin who had gone into the turpentine business in central North Carolina. He assured me, in response to my inquiries, that no better place could be found in the South than the State and neighborhood where he lived; the climate was perfect for health and, in conjunction with the soil, ideal for grape-culture; labor was cheap, and land could be bought for a mere song. He gave us a cordial invitation to come and visit him while we looked into the matter. We accepted the invitation, and after several days of leisurely travel, the last hundred miles of which were up a river on a sidewheel steamer, we reached our destination, a quaint old town, which I shall call Patesville, because, for one reason, that is not its name. There was a red brick market-house in the public square, with a tall tower, which held a four-faced clock that struck the hours, and from which there pealed out a curfew at nine o'clock. There were two or three hotels, a courthouse, a jail, stores, offices, and all the appurtenances of a county seat and a commercial emporium; for while Patesville numbered only four or five thousand inhabitants, of all shades of complexion, it was one of the principal towns in North Carolina, and had a considerable trade in cotton and naval stores. This business activity was not immediately apparent to my unaccustomed eyes. Indeed, when I first saw the town, there brooded over it a calm that seemed almost sabbatic in its restfulness, though I learned later on that underneath its somnolent exterior the deeper currents of life—love and hatred, joy and despair, ambition and avarice, faith and friendship—flowed not less steadily than in livelier latitudes.

We found the weather delightful at that season, the end of summer, and were hospitably entertained. Our host was a man of means and evidently regarded our visit as a pleasure, and we were therefore correspondingly at our ease, and in a position to act with the coolness of judgment desirable in making so radical a change in our lives. My cousin placed a horse and buggy at our disposal, and himself acted as our guide until I became somewhat familiar with the country.

I found that grape-culture, while it had never been carried on to any great extent, was not entirely unknown in the neighborhood. Several planters thereabouts had attempted it on a commercial scale, in former years, with greater or less success; but like most Southern industries, it had felt the blight of war and had fallen into desuetude.

I went several times to look at a place that I thought might suit me. It was a plantation of considerable extent that had formerly belonged to a wealthy man by the name of McAdoo. The estate had been for years involved in litigation between disputing heirs, during which period shiftless cultivation had well-nigh exhausted the soil. There had been a vineyard of some extent on the place, but it had not been attended to since the war, and had lapsed into utter neglect. The vines—here partly supported by decayed and broken-down trellises, there twining themselves among the branches of the slender saplings which had sprung up among them—grew in wild and unpruned luxuriance, and the few scattered grapes they bore were the undisputed prey of the first comer. The site was admirably adapted to grape-raising; the soil, with a little attention, could not have been better; and with the native grape, the luscious scuppernong, as my main reliance in the beginning, I felt sure that I could introduce and cultivate successfully a number of other varieties.

One day I went over with my wife to show her the place. We drove out of the town over a long wooden bridge that spanned a spreading millpond, passed the long whitewashed fence surrounding the county fairground, and struck into a road so sandy that the horse's feet sank to the fetlocks. Our route lay partly up hill and partly down, for we were in the sand-hill country; we drove past cultivated farms, and then by abandoned fields grown up in scrub-oak and short-leaved pine, and once or twice through the solemn aisles of the virgin forest, where the tall pines, well-nigh meeting over the narrow road, shut out the sun, and wrapped us in cloistral solitude. Once, at a crossroads, I was in doubt as to the turn to take, and we sat there waiting ten minutes—we had already caught some of the native infection of restfulness—for some human being to come along who could direct us on our way. At length a little negro girl appeared, walking straight as an arrow, with a piggin full of water on her head. After a little patient investigation, necessary to overcome the child's shyness, we learned what we wished to know, and at the end of about five miles from the town reached our destination.

We drove between a pair of decayed gateposts—the gate itself had long since disappeared—and up a straight sandy lane, between two lines of rotting rail fence, partly concealed by jimsonweeds and briers, to the open space where a dwelling-house had once stood, evidently a spacious mansion, if we might judge from the ruined chimneys that were still standing, and the brick pillars on which the sills rested. The house itself, we had been informed, had fallen a victim to the fortunes of war.

We alighted from the buggy, walked about the yard for a while, and then wandered off into the adjoining vineyard. Upon Annie's complaining of weariness I led the way back to the yard, where a pine log, lying under a spreading elm, afforded a shady though somewhat hard seat. One end of the log was already occupied by a venerable-looking colored man. He held on his knees a hat full of grapes, over which he was smacking his lips with great gusto, and a pile of grapeskins near him indicated that the performance was no new thing. We approached him at an angle from the rear, and were close to him before he perceived us. He respectfully rose as we drew near, and was moving away, when I begged him to keep his seat.

"Don't let us disturb you," I said. "There is plenty of room for us all."

He resumed his seat with somewhat of embarrassment. While he had been standing, I had observed that he was a tall man, and, though slightly bowed by the weight of years, apparently quite vigorous. He was not entirely black, and this fact, together with the quality of his hair, which was about six inches long and very bushy, except on the top of his head, where he was quite bald, suggested a slight strain of other than negro blood. There was a shrewdness in his eyes, too, which was not altogether African, and which, as we afterwards learned from experience, was indicative of a corresponding shrewdness in his character. He went on eating the grapes, but did not seem to enjoy himself quite so well as he had apparently done before he became aware of our presence.

"Do you live around here?" I asked, anxious to put him at his ease.

"Yas, suh. I lives des ober yander, behine de nex' san'-hill, on de Lumberton plank-road."

"Do you know anything about the time when this vineyard was cultivated?"

"Lawd bless you, suh, I knows all about it. Dey ain' na'er a man in dis settlement w'at won' tell you ole Julius McAdoo 'uz bawn en raise' on dis yer same plantation. Is you de Norv'n gemman w'at's gwine ter buy de ole vimya'd?"

"I am looking at it," I replied; "but I don't know that I shall care to buy unless I can be reasonably sure of making something out of it."

"Well, suh, you is a stranger ter me, en I is a stranger ter you, en we is bofe strangers ter one anudder, but 'f I 'uz in yo' place, I wouldn' buy dis vimya'd."

"Why not?" I asked.

"Well, I dunno whe'r you b'lieves in cunj'in'er not—some er de w'ite folks don't, er says dey don't—but de truf er de matter is dat dis yer ole vimya'd is goophered."

"Is what?" I asked, not grasping the meaning of this unfamiliar word.

"Is goophered—cunju'd, bewitch'."

He imparted this information with such solemn earnestness, and with such an air of confidential mystery, that I felt somewhat interested, while Annie was evidently much impressed, and drew closer to me.

"How do you know it is bewitched?" I asked.

"I wouldn' spec' fer you ter b'lieve me 'less you know all 'bout de fac's. But ef you en young miss dere doan' min' lis'nin' ter a ole nigger run on a minute er two w'ile you er restin', I kin 'splain to you how it all happen'."

We assured him that we would be glad to hear how it all happened, and he began to tell us. At first the current of his memory—or imagination—seemed somewhat sluggish; but as his embarrassment wore off, his language flowed more freely, and the story acquired perspective and coherence. As he became more and more absorbed in the narrative, his eyes assumed a dreamy expression, and he seemed to lose sight of his auditors, and to be living over again in monologue his life on the old plantation.

"Ole Mars Dugal' McAdoo," he began, "bought dis place long many years befo' de wah, en I 'member well w'en he sot out all dis yer part er de plantation in scuppernon's. De vimes growed monst'us fas', en Mars Dugal' made a thousan' gallon er scuppernon' wine eve'y year.

"Now, ef dey's an'thing a nigger lub, nex' ter 'possum, en chick'n, en watermillyums, it's scuppernon's. Dey ain' nuffin dat kin stan' up side'n de scuppernon' fer sweetness; sugar ain't a suckumstance ter scuppernon'. W'en de season is nigh 'bout ober, en de grapes begin ter swivel up des a little wid de wrinkles er ole age—w'en de skin git sof' en brown—den de scuppernon' make you smack yo' lip en roll yo' eye en wush fer mo'; so I reckon it ain' very 'stonishin' dat niggers lub scuppernon'.

"Dey wuz a sight er niggers in de naberhood er de vimya'd. Dere wuz ole Mars Henry Brayboy's niggers, en ole Mars Jeems McLean's niggers, en Mars Dugal's own niggers; den dey wuz a settlement er free niggers en po' buckrahs down by de Wim'l'ton Road, en Mars Dugal' had de only vimya'd in de naberhood. I reckon it ain' so much so nowadays, but befo' de wah, in slab'ry times, a nigger didn' mine goin' fi' er ten mile in a night, w'en dey wuz sump'n good ter eat at de yuther een'.

"So atter a w'ile Mars Dugal' begin ter miss his scuppernon's. Co'se he 'cuse de niggers er it, but dey all 'nied it ter de las'. Mars Dugal' sot spring guns en steel traps, en he en de oberseah sot up nights once't er twice't, tel one night Mars Dugal'—he 'uz a monst'us keerless man—got his leg shot full er cow-peas. But somehow er 'nudder dey couldn' nebber ketch none er de niggers. I dunner how it happen, but it happen des like I tell you, en de grapes kep' on a-goin' des de same.

"But bimeby ole Mars Dugal' fix up a plan ter stop it. Dey wuz a cunjuh 'oman livin' down 'mongs' de free niggers on de Wim'l'ton Road, en all de darkies fum Rockfish ter Beaver Crick wuz feared er her. She could wuk de mos' powerfulles' kin' er goopher—could make people hab fits, er rheumatiz, er make 'em des dwinel away en die; en dey say she went out ridin' de niggers at night, fer she wuz a witch 'sides bein' a cunjuh 'oman. Mars Dugal' hearn 'bout Aun' Peggy's doin's, en begun ter 'flect whe'r er no he couldn' git her ter he'p him keep de niggers off'n de grapevimes. One day in de spring er de year, ole miss pack up a basket er chick'n en poun'-cake, en a bottle er scuppernon' wine, en Mars Dugal' tuk it in his buggy en driv ober ter Aun' Peggy's cabin. He tuk de basket in, en had a long talk wid Aun' Peggy.

"De nex' day Aun' Peggy come up ter de vimya'd. De niggers seed her slippin' 'roun', en dey soon foun' out what she 'uz doin' dere. Mars Dugal' had hi'ed her ter goopher de grapevimes. She sa'ntered 'roun' 'mongs' de vimes, en tuk a leaf fum dis one, en a grape-hull fum dat one, en a grape-seed fum anudder one; en den a little twig fum here, en a little pinch er dirt fum dere—en put it all in a big black bottle, wid a snake's toof en a speckle hen's gall en some ha'rs fum a black cat's tail, en den fill de bottle wid scuppernon' wine. W'en she got de goopher all ready en fix', she tuk'n went out in de woods en buried it under de root uv a red oak tree, en den come back en tole one er de niggers she done goopher de grapevimes, en a'er a nigger w'at eat dem grapes 'ud be sho ter die inside'n twel' mont's.

"Atter dat de niggers let de scuppernon's 'lone, en Mars Dugal' did n' hab no 'casion ter fine no mo' fault; en de season wuz mos' gone, w'en a strange gemman stop at de plantation one night ter see Mars Dugal' on some business; en his coachman, seein' de scuppernon's growin' so nice en sweet, slip 'roun' behine de smokehouse en et all de scuppernon's he could hole. Nobody didn' notice it at de time, but dat night, on de way home, de gemman's hoss runned away en kill' de coachman. W'en we hearn de noos, Aun' Lucy, de cook, she up'n say she seed de strange nigger eat'n' er de scuppernon's behine de smoke-house; en den we knowed de goopher had b'en er wukkin'. Den one er de nigger chilluns runned away fum de quarters one day, en got in de scuppernon's, en died de nex' week. W'ite folks say he die' er de fevuh, but de niggers knowed it wuz de goopher. So you k'n be sho de darkies did n' hab much ter do wid dem scuppernon' vimes.

"W'en de scuppernon' season 'uz ober fer dat year, Mars Dugal' foun' he had made fifteen hund'ed gallon er wine; en one er de niggers hearn him laffin' wid de oberseah fit ter kill, en sayin' dem fifteen hund'ed gallon er wine wuz monst'us good intrus' on de ten dollars he laid out on de vimya'd. So I 'low ez he paid Aun' Peggy ten dollars fer to goopher de grapevimes.

"De goopher did n' wuk no mo' tel de nex' summer, w'en 'long to'ds de middle er de season one er de fiel' han's died; en ez dat lef' Mars Dugal' sho't er han's, he went off ter town fer ter buy anudder. He fotch de noo nigger home wid 'im. He wuz er ole nigger, er de color er a gingy-cake, en ball ez a hoss-apple on de top er his head. He wuz a peart ole nigger, do', en could do a big day's wuk.

"Now it happen dat one er de niggers on de nex' plantation, one er ole Mars Henry Brayboy's niggers, had runned away de day befo', en tuk ter de swamp, en ole Mars Dugal' en some er de yuther nabor w'ite folks had gone out wid dere guns en dere dogs fer ter he'p 'em hunt fer de nigger; en de han's on our own plantation wuz all so flusterated dat we fuhgot ter tell de noo han' 'bout de goopher on de scuppernon' vimes. Co'se he smell de grapes en see de vimes, an atter dahk de fus' thing he done wuz ter slip off ter de grapevimes 'dout sayin' nuffin ter nobody. Nex' mawnin' he tole some er de niggers 'bout de fine bait er scuppernon' he et de night befo'.

"W'en dey tole 'im 'bout de goopher on de grapevimes, he 'uz dat tarrified dat he turn pale, en look des like he gwine ter die right in his tracks. De oberseah come up en axed w'at 'uz de matter; en w'en dey tole 'im Henry be'n eatin' er de scuppernon's en got de goopher on 'im, he gin Henry a big drink er w'iskey, en 'low dat de nex' rainy day he take 'im ober ter Aun' Peggy's, en see ef she would n' take de goopher off'n him, seein' ez he didn' know nuffin erbout it tel he done et de grapes.

"Sho nuff, it rain de nex' day, en de oberseah wen ober ter Aun' Peggy's wid Henry. En Aun' Peggy say dat bein' ez Henry did n' know 'bout de goopher, en et de grapes in ign'ance er de conseq'ences, she reckon she mought be able fer ter take de goopher off'n him. So she fotch out er bottle wid some cunjuh medicine in it, en po'd some out in a go'd fer Henry ter drink. He manage ter git it down; he say it tas'e like w'iskey wid sump'n bitter in it. She 'lowed dat 'ud keep de goopher off'n him tel de spring; but w'en de sap begin ter rise in de grapevimes he ha' ter come en see her ag'in, en she tel him w'at e's ter do.

"Nex' spring, w'en de sap commence ter rise in de scuppernon' vime, Henry tuk a ham one night. Whar'd he git de ham? *I* doan know; dey wa'n't no hams on de plantation 'cep'n' w'at 'uz in de smokehouse, but *I* never see

Henry 'bout de smokehouse. But ez I wuz a-sayin', he tuk de ham ober ter Aun' Peggy's; en Aun' Peggy tole 'im dat w'en Mars Dugal' begin ter prune de grapevimes, he mus' go en take 'n scrape off de sap whar it ooze out'n de cut een's er de vimes, en 'n'int his ball head wid it; en ef he do dat once't a year de goopher wouldn' wuk agin 'im long ez he done it. En bein' ez he fotch her de ham, she fix' it so he kin eat all de scuppernon' he want.

"So Henry 'n'int his head wid de sap out'n de big grapevime des ha'fway 'twix' de quarters en de big house, en de goopher nebber wuk agin him dat summer. But de beatenes' thing you eber see happen ter Henry. Up ter dat time he wuz ez ball ez a sweeten 'tater, but des ez soon ez de young leaves begun ter come out on de grapevimes, de ha'r begun ter grow out on Henry's head, en by de middle er de summer he had de bigges' head er ha'r on de plantation. Befo' dat, Henry had tol'able good ha'r 'roun' de aidges, but soon ez de young grapes begun ter come, Henry's ha'r begun to quirl all up in little balls, des like dis yer reg'lar grapy ha'r, en by de time de grapes got ripe his head look des like a bunch er grapes. Combin' it didn' do no good; he wuk at it ha'f de night wid er Jim Crow[1] en think he git it straighten' out, but in de mawnin' de grapes 'ud be dere des de same. So he gin it up, en tried ter keep de grapes down by havin' his ha'r cut sho't.

"But dat wa'n't de quares' thing 'bout de goopher. When Henry come ter de plantation, he wuz gittin' a little ole an stiff in de j'ints. But dat summer he got des ez spry en libely ez any young nigger on de plantation; fac', he got so biggity dat Mars Jackson, de oberseah, ha' ter th'eaten ter whip 'im ef he didn' stop cuttin' up his didos en behave hisse'f. But de mos' cur'ouses' thing happen' in de fall, when de sap begin ter go down in de grapevimes. Fus', when de grapes 'uz gethered, de knots begun ter straighten out'n Henry's ha'r; en w'en de leaves begin ter fall, Henry's ha'r 'mence ter drap out; en when de vimes 'uz bar', Henry's head wuz baller 'n it wuz in de spring, en he begin ter git ole en stiff in de j'ints ag'in, en paid no mo' 'tention ter de gals dyoin' er de whole winter. En nex' spring, w'en he rub de sap on ag'in, he got young ag'in, en so soopl en libely dat none er de young niggers on de plantation couldn' jump, ner dance, ner hoe ez much cotton ez Henry. But in de fall er de year his grapes 'mence ter straighten out, en his j'ints ter git stiff, en his ha'r drap off, en de rheumatiz begin ter wrastle wid 'im.

"Now, ef you'd 'a' knowed ole Mars Dugal' McAdoo, you'd 'a' knowed dat it ha' ter be a mighty rainy day when he could n' fine sump'n fer his niggers ter do, en it ha' ter be a mighty little hole he could n' crawl thoo, en ha' ter be a monst'us cloudy night when a dollar git by him in de dahkness; en w'en he see how Henry git young in de spring en ole in de fall, he 'lowed ter hisse'f

---

[1] A small card, resembling a currycomb in construction, and used by negroes in the rural districts instead of a comb.

ez how he could make mo' money out'n Henry dan by wukkin' him in de cotton fiel'. 'Long de nex' spring, atter de sap 'mence ter rise, en Henry 'n'int 'is head en sta'ted fer ter git young en soopl, Mars Dugal' up 'n tuk Henry ter town, en sole 'im fer fifteen hunder' dollars. Co'se de man w'at bought Henry didn' know nuffin 'bout de goopher, en Mars Dugal' didn' see no 'casion fer ter tell 'im. Long to'ds de fall, w'en de sap went down, Henry begin ter git ole ag'in same ez yuzhal, en his noo marster begin ter git skeered les'n he gwine ter lose his fifteen-hunder'-dollar nigger. He sent fer a mighty fine doctor, but de med'cine did n' 'pear ter do no good; de goopher had a good holt. Henry tole de doctor 'bout de goopher, but de doctor des laff at 'im.

"One day in de winter Mars Dugal' went ter town, en wuz santerin' 'long de Main Street, when who should he meet but Henry's noo marster. Dey said 'Hoddy,' en Mars Dugal' ax 'im ter hab a seegyar; en atter dey run on awhile 'bout de craps en de weather, Mars Dugal' ax 'im, sorter keerless, like ez ef he des thought of it—

" 'How you like de nigger I sole you las' spring?'

"Henry's marster shuck his head en knock de ashes off'n his seegyar.

" 'Spec' I made a bad bahgin when I bought dat nigger. Henry done good wuk all de summer, but sence de fall set in he 'pears ter be sorter pinin' away. Dey ain' nuffin pertickler de matter wid 'im—leastways de doctor say so—'cep'n' a tech er de rheumatiz; but his ha'r is all fell out, en ef he don't pick up his strenk mighty soon, I spec' I'm gwine ter lose 'im.'

"Dey smoked on awhile, en bimeby ole mars say, 'Well, a bahgin's a bahgin, but you en me is good fren's, en I doan wan' ter see you lose all de money you paid fer dat nigger; en ef w'at you say is so, en I ain't 'sputin' it, he ain't wuf much now. I 'spec's you wukked him too ha'd dis summer, er e'se de swamps down here don't agree wid de san'-hill nigger. So you des lemme know, en ef he gits any wusser I'll be willin' ter gib yer five hund'ed dollars fer 'im en take my chances on his livin'.'

"Sho 'nuff, when Henry begun ter draw up wid de rheumatiz en it look like he gwine ter die fer sho, his noo marster sen' fer Mars Dugal', en Mars Dugal' gin him what he promus, en brung Henry home ag'in. He tuk good keer uv 'im dyoin' er de winter—give 'im w'iskey ter rub his rheumatiz, en terbacker ter smoke, en all he want ter eat—'caze a nigger w'at he could make a thousan' dollars a year off'n didn' grow on eve'y huckleberry bush.

"Nex' spring, w'en de sap ris en Henry's ha'r commence' ter sprout, Mars Dugal' sole 'im ag'in, down in Robeson County dis time; en he kep' dat sellin' business up fer five year er mo'. Henry nebber say nuffin 'bout de goopher ter his noo marsters, 'caze he know he gwine ter be tuk good keer uv de nex' winter, w'en Mars Dugal' buy him back. En Mars Dugal' made 'nuff money off'n Henry ter buy anudder plantation ober on Beaver Crick.

"But 'long 'bout de een' er dat five year dey come a stranger ter stop at de plantation. De fus' day he 'uz dere he went out wid Mars Dugal' en spent all de mawnin' lookin' ober de vimya'd, en atter dinner dey spent all de evenin' playin' kya'ds. De niggers soon 'skiver dat he wuz a Yankee, en dat he come down ter Norf C'lina fer ter l'arn de w'ite folks how to raise grapes en make wine. He promus Mars Dugal' he c'd make de grapevimes b'ar twice't ez many grapes, en dat de noo winepress he wuz a-sellin' would make mo' d'n twice't ez many gallons er wine. En ole Mars Dugal' des drunk it all in, des 'peared ter be bewitch' wid dat Yankee. W'en de darkies see dat Yankee runnin' 'roun' de vimya'd en diggin' under de grapevimes, dey shuk dere heads en 'lowed dat dey feared Mars Dugal' losin' his min'. Mars Dugal' had all de dirt dug away fum under de roots er all de scuppernon' vimes, an' let 'em stan' dat away fer a week er mo'. Den dat Yankee made de niggers fix up a mixtry er lime en ashes en manyo, en po' it 'roun' de roots er de grapevimes. Den he 'vise Mars Dugal' fer ter trim de vimes close't, en Mars Dugal' tuck 'n done eve'ything de Yankee tole him ter do. Dyoin' all er dis time, mind yer, dis yer Yankee wuz libbin' off'n de fat er de lan' at de big house, en playin' kya'ds wid Mars Dugal' eve'y night; en dey say Mars Dugal' los' mo'n a thousan' dollars dyoin' er de week dat Yankee wuz a-ruinin' de grapevimes.

"W'en de sap ris nex' spring, ole Henry 'n'inted his head ez yuzhal, en his ha'r 'mence' ter grow des de same ez it done eve'y year. De scuppernon' vimes growed monst's fas', en de leaves wuz greener en thicker dan dey eber be'n dyoin' my rememb'ance; en Henry's ha'r growed out thicker dan eber, en he 'peared ter git younger 'n younger, en soopler 'n soopler; en seein' ez he wuz sho't er han's dat spring, havin' tuk in consid'able noo groun', Mars Dugal' 'cluded he would n' sell Henry 'tel he git de crap in en de cotton chop'. So he kep' Henry on de plantation.

"But 'long 'bout time fer de grapes ter come on de scuppernon' vimes, dey 'peared ter come a change ober 'em; de leaves withered en swivel up, en de young grapes turn' yaller, en bimeby eve'ybody on de plantation could see dat de whole vimya'd wuz dyin'. Mars Dugal' tuk'n water de vimes en done all he could, but 't wa'n' no use: dat Yankee had done bus' de watermillyum. One time de vimes picked up a bit, en Mars Dugal' 'lowed dey wuz gwine ter come out ag'in; but dat Yankee done dug too close under de roots, en prune de branches too close ter de vime, en all dat lime en ashes done burn' de life out'n de vimes, en dey des kep' a-with'in' en a-swivelin'.

"All dis time de goopher wuz a-wukkin'. When de vimes sta'ted ter wither, Henry 'mence ter complain er his rheumatiz; en when de leaves begin ter dry up, his ha'r 'mence ter drap out. When de vimes fresh up a bit, Henry 'd git peart ag'in, en when de vimes wither ag'in, Henry 'd git ole ag'in, en des kep' gittin' mo' en mo' fitten fer nuffin; he des pined away, en pined away, en fine'ly tuk ter his cabin; en when de big vime whar he got de sap ter 'n'int his head withered en turned yaller en died, Henry died too—des went out sorter like a cannel. Dey did n't 'pear ter be nuffin de matter wid 'im, 'cep'n' de rheumatiz, but his strenk des dwinel away 'tel he did n' hab ernuff lef' ter draw his bref. De goopher had got de under holt, en th'owed Henry dat time fer good en all.

"Mars Dugal' tuk on might'ly 'bout losin' his vimes en his nigger in de same year; en he swo' dat ef he could git holt er dat Yankee he'd wear 'im ter a frazzle en den chaw up de frazzle; en he'd done it, too, for Mars Dugal' 'uz a monst'us brash man w'en he once git started. He sot de vimya'd out ober ag'in, but it wuz th'ee er fo' year befo' de vimes got ter b'arin' any scupper-non's.

"W'en de wah broke out, Mars Dugal' raise' a comp'ny, en went off ter fight de Yankees. He say he wuz mighty glad dat wah come, en he des want ter kill a Yankee fer eve'y dollar he los' 'long er dat grape-raisin' Yankee. En I 'spec' he would 'a' done it, too, ef de Yankees hadn' s'picioned sump'n, en killed him fus'. Atter de s'render ole miss move ter town, de niggers all scattered 'way fum de plantation, en de vimya'd ain' be'n cultervated sence."

"Is that story true?" asked Annie doubtfully, but seriously, as the old man concluded his narrative.

"It's des ez true ez I'm a-settin' here, miss. Dey's a easy way ter prove it: I kin lead de way right ter Henry's grave ober yander in de plantation buryin'-groun'. En I tell yer w'at, marster, I wouldn n' 'vise you to buy dis yer ole vimya'd, 'caze de goopher's on it yit, en dey ain' no tellin' w'en it's gwine ter crap out."

"But I thought you said all the old vines died."

"Dey did 'pear ter die, but a few un 'em come out ag'in, en is mixed in 'mongs' de yuthers. I ain' skeered ter eat de grapes, 'caze I knows de old vimes fum de noo ones; but wid strangers dey ain' no tellin' w'at mought happen. I wouldn' 'vise yer ter buy dis vimya'd."

I bought the vineyard, nevertheless, and it has been for a long time in a thriving condition, and is often referred to by the local press as a striking illustration of the opportunities open to Northern capital in the development of Southern industries. The luscious scuppernong holds first rank among our grapes, though we cultivate a great many other varieties, and our income from grapes packed and shipped to the Northern markets is quite considerable. I have not noticed any developments of the goopher in the vineyard, although I have a mild suspicion that our colored assistants do not suffer from want of grapes during the season.

I found, when I bought the vineyard, that Uncle Julius had occupied a cabin on the place for many years, and derived a respectable revenue from the

The Ingrate

Paul Laurence Dunbar

1900

I

Mr. Leckler was a man of high principle. Indeed, he himself had admitted it at times to Mrs. Leckler. She was often called into counsel with him. He was one of those large-souled creatures with a hunger for unlimited advice, upon which he never acted. Mrs. Leckler knew this, but like the good, patient little wife that she was, she went on paying her poor tribute of advice and admiration. Today her husband's mind was particularly troubled—as usual, too, over a matter of principle. Mrs. Leckler came at his call.

"Mrs. Leckler," he said, "I am troubled in my mind. I—in fact, I am puzzled over a matter that involves either the maintaining or relinquishing of a principle."

"Well, Mr. Leckler?" said his wife interrogatively.

"If I had been a scheming, calculating Yankee, I should have been rich now; but all my life I have been too generous and confiding. I have always let principle stand between me and my interests." Mr. Leckler took himself all too seriously to be conscious of his pun, and went on: "Now this is a matter in which my duty and my principles seem to conflict. It stands thus: Josh has been doing a piece of plastering for Mr. Eckley over in Lexington, and from what he says, I think that city rascal has misrepresented the amount of work to me and so cut down the pay for it. Now, of course, I should not care, the matter of a dollar or two being nothing to me; but it is a very different matter when we consider poor Josh." There was deep pathos in Mr. Leckler's tone. "You know Josh is anxious to buy his freedom, and I allow him a part of whatever he makes; so you see it's he that's affected. Every dollar that he is cheated out of cuts off just so much from his earnings, and puts further away his hope of emancipation."

If the thought occurred to Mrs. Leckler that, since Josh received only about one tenth of what he earned, the advantage of just wages would be quite as much her husband's as the slave's, she did not betray it, but met the naïve reasoning product of the neglected grapevines. This, doubtless, accounted for his advice to me not to buy the vineyard, though whether it inspired the goopher story I am unable to state. I believe, however, that the wages I paid him for his services as coachman, for I gave him employment in that capacity, were more than an equivalent for anything he lost by the sale of the vineyard.

with the question, "But where does the conflict come in, Mr. Leckler?"

"Just here. If Josh knew how to read and write and cipher—"

"Mr. Leckler, are you crazy!"

"Listen to me, my dear, and give me the benefit of your judgment. This is a very momentous question. As I was about to say, if Josh knew these things, he could protect himself from cheating when his work is at too great a distance for me to look after it for him."

"But teaching a slave—"

"Yes, that's just what is against my principles. I know how public opinion and the law look at it. But my conscience rises up in rebellion every time I think of that poor black man being cheated out of his earnings. Really, Mrs. Leckler, I think I may trust to Josh's discretion and secretly give him such instructions as will permit him to protect himself."

"Well, of course, it's just as you think best," said his wife.

"I knew you would agree with me," he returned. "It's such a comfort to take counsel with you, my dear!" And the generous man walked out onto the veranda, very well satisfied with himself and his wife, and prospectively pleased with Josh. Once he murmured to himself, "I'll lay for Eckley next time."

Josh, the subject of Mr. Leckler's charitable solicitations, was the plantation plasterer. His master had given him his trade, in order that he might do whatever such work was needed about the place; but he became so proficient in his duties, having also no competition among the poor whites, that he had grown to be in great demand in the country thereabout. So Mr. Leckler found it profitable, instead of letting him do chores and field work in his idle time, to hire him out to neighboring farms and planters. Josh was a man of more than ordinary intelligence; and when he asked to be allowed to pay for himself by working overtime, his master readily agreed—for it promised more work to be done, for which he could allow the slave just what he pleased. Of course, he knew now that when the black man began to cipher this state of affairs would be changed; but it would mean such an increase of profit from the outside that he could afford to give up his own little peculations. Anyway, it would be many years before the slave could pay the two thousand dollars, which price he had set upon him. Should he approach that figure, Mr. Leckler felt it just possible that the market in slaves would take a sudden rise.

When Josh was told of his master's intention, his eyes gleamed with pleasure, and he went to his work with the zest of long hunger. He proved a remarkably apt pupil. He was indefatigable in doing the tasks assigned him. Even Mr. Leckler, who had great faith in his plasterer's ability, marveled at the speed which he had acquired the three R's. He did not know that on one of his many trips a free negro had given Josh the rudimentary tools of learning, and that ever since the slave had been adding to his store of learning by poring over signs and every bit of print that he could spell out. Neither was Josh so indiscreet as to intimate to his benefactor that he had been anticipated in his good intentions.

It was in this way, working and learning, that a year passed away, and Mr. Leckler thought that his object had been accomplished. He could safely trust Josh to protect his own interests, and so he thought that it was quite time that his servant's education should cease.

"You know, Josh," he said, "I have already gone against my principles and against the law for your sake, and of course a man can't stretch his conscience too far, even to help another who's being cheated; but I reckon you can take care of yourself now."

"Oh, yes, suh, I reckon I kin," said Josh.

"And it wouldn't do for you to be seen with any books about you now."

"Oh, no, suh, su't'n'y not." He didn't intend to be seen with any books about him.

It was just now that Mr. Leckler saw the good results of all he had done, and his heart was full of a great joy, for Eckley had been building some additions to his house and sent for Josh to do the plastering for him. The owner admonished his slave, took him over a few examples to freshen his memory, and sent him forth with glee. When the job was done, there was a discrepancy of two dollars in what Mr. Eckley offered for it and the price which accrued from Josh's measurements. To the employer's surprise, the black man went over the figures with him and convinced him of the incorrectness of the payment—and the additional two dollars were turned over.

"Some o' Leckler's work," said Eckley, "teaching a nigger to cipher! Close-fisted old reprobate—I've a mind to have the law on him."

Mr. Leckler heard the story with great glee. "I laid for him that time—the old fox." But to Mrs. Leckler he said, "You see, my dear wife, my rashness in teaching Josh to figure for himself is vindicated. See what he has saved for himself."

"What did he save?" asked the little woman indiscreetly.

Her husband blushed and stammered for a moment, and then replied, "Well, of course, it was only twenty cents saved to him, but to a man buying his freedom every cent counts; and after all, it is not the amount, Mrs. Leckler, it's the principle of the thing."

"Yes," said the lady meekly.

II

Unto the body it is easy for the master to say, "Thus far shalt thou go, and no farther." Gyves, chains, and fetters will enforce that command. But what master shall say unto the mind, "Here do I set the limit of your acquisition. Pass it not"? Who shall put gyves upon the intellect, or fetter the movement of thought? Joshua Leckler, as custom denominated him, had tasted of the forbidden fruit, and his appetite had grown by what it fed on. Night after night he crouched in his lonely cabin, by the blaze of a fat pine brand, poring over the few books that he had been able to secure and smuggle in. His fellow servants alternately laughed at him and wondered why he did not take a wife. But Joshua went on his way. He had no time for marrying or for love; other thoughts had taken possession of him. He was being swayed by ambitions other than the mere fathering of slaves for his master. To him his slavery was deep night. What wonder, then, that he should dream, and that through the ivory gate should come to him the forbidden vision of freedom? To own himself, to be master of his hands, feet, of his whole body—something would clutch at his heart as he thought of it, and the breath would come hard between his lips. But he met his master with an impassive face, always silent, always docile; and Mr. Leckler congratulated himself that so valuable and intelligent a slave should be at the same time so tractable. Usually intelligence in a slave meant discontent; but not so with Josh. Who more content than he? He remarked to his wife: "You see, my dear, this is what comes of treating even a nigger right."

Meanwhile the white hills of the North were beckoning to the chattel, and the north winds were whispering to him to be a chattel no longer. Often the eyes that looked away to where freedom lay were filled with a wistful longing that was tragic in its intensity, for they saw the hardships and the difficulties between the slave and his goal and, worst of all, an iniquitous law—liberty's compromise with bondage, that rose like a stone wall between him and hope—a law that degraded every free-thinking man to the level of a slave catcher. There it loomed up before him, formidable, impregnable, insurmountable. He measured it in all its terribleness, and paused. But on the other side there was liberty; and one day when he was away at work, a voice came out of the woods and whispered to him "Courage!"—and on that night the shadows beckoned him as the white hills had done, and the forest called to him, "Follow."

"It seems to me that Josh might have been able to get home tonight," said Mr. Leckler, walking up and down his veranda, "but I reckon it's just possible that he got through too late to catch a train." In the morning he said, "Well, he's not here yet; he must have had to do some extra work. If he doesn't get here by evening, I'll run up there."

In the evening, he did take the train for Joshua's place of employment, where he learned that his slave had left the night before. But where could he have gone? That no one knew, and for the first time it dawned upon his master that Josh had run away. He raged; he fumed; but nothing could be done until morning, and all the time Leckler knew that the most valuable slave on his plantation was working his way toward the North and freedom. He did not go back home, but paced the floor all night long. In the early dawn he hurried out, and the hounds were put on the fugitive's track. After some nosing around they set off toward a stretch of woods. In a few minutes they came yelping back, pawing their noses and rubbing their heads against the ground. They had found the trail, but Josh had played the old slave trick of filling his tracks with cayenne pepper. The dogs were soothed and taken deeper into the wood to find the trail. They soon took it up again, and dashed away with low bays. The scent led them directly to a little wayside station about six miles distant. Here it stopped. Burning with the chase, Mr. Leckler hastened to the station agent. Had he seen such a negro? Yes, he had taken the northbound train two nights before.

"But why did you let him go without a pass?" almost screamed the owner.

"I didn't," replied the agent. "He had a written pass, signed James Leckler, and I let him go on it."

"Forged, forged!" yelled the master. "He wrote it himself."

"Humph!" said the agent. "How was I to know that? Our niggers round here don't know how to write."

Mr. Leckler suddenly bethought him to hold his peace. Josh was probably now in the arms of some northern abolitionist, and there was nothing to be done now but advertise; and the disgusted master spread his notices broadcast before starting for home. As soon as he arrived at his house, he sought his wife and poured out his griefs to her.

"You see, Mrs. Leckler, this is what comes of my goodness of heart. I taught that nigger to read and write, so that he could protect himself—and look how he uses his knowledge. Oh, the ingrate, the ingrate! The very weapon which I give him to defend himself against others he turns upon me. Oh, it's awful—awful! I've always been too confiding. Here's the most valuable nigger on my plantation gone—gone, I tell you—and through my own kindness. It isn't his value, though, I'm thinking so much about. I could stand his loss, if it wasn't for the principle of the thing, the base ingratitude he has shown me. Oh, if I ever lay hands on him again!" Mr. Leckler closed his lips and clenched his fist with an eloquence that laughed at words.

Just at this time, in one of the underground railway stations, six miles north of the Ohio, an old Quaker was saying to Josh, "Lie still—thee'll be perfectly safe there. Here comes John Trader, our local slave catcher, but I will parley with him and send him away. Thee need not fear. None of thy brethren who have come to us have ever been taken back to bondage.—Good evening, Friend Trader!" and Josh heard the old Quaker's smooth voice roll on, while he lay back half smothering in a bag, among other bags of corn and potatoes.

It was after ten o'clock that night when he was thrown carelessly into a wagon and driven away to the next station, twenty-five miles to the northward. And by such stages, hiding by day and traveling by night, helped by a few of his own people who were blessed with freedom, and always by the good Quakers wherever found, he made his way into Canada. And on one never-to-be-forgotten morning he stood up, straightened himself, breathed God's blessed air, and knew himself free!

III

To Joshua Leckler this life in Canada was all new and strange. It was a new thing for him to feel himself a man and to have his manhood recognized by the whites with whom he came into free contact. It was new, too, this receiving the full measure of his worth in work. He went to his labor with a zest that he had never known before, and he took a pleasure in the very weariness it brought him. Ever and anon there came to his ears the cries of his brethren in the South. Frequently he met fugitives who, like himself, had escaped from bondage; and the harrowing tales that they told him made him burn to do something for those whom he had left behind him. But these fugitives and the papers he read told him other things. They said that the spirit of freedom was working in the United States, and already men were speaking out boldly in behalf of the manumission of the slaves; already there was a growing army behind that noble vanguard, Sumner, Phillips, Douglass, Garrison. He heard the names of Lucretia Mott and Harriet Beecher Stowe, and his heart swelled, for on the dim horizon he saw the first faint streaks of dawn.

So the years passed. Then from the surcharged clouds a flash of lightning broke, and there was the thunder of cannon and the rain of lead over the land. From his home in the North he watched the storm as it raged and wavered, now threatening the North with its awful power, now hanging dire and dreadful over the South. Then suddenly from out the fray came a voice like the trumpet tone of God to him: "Thou and thy brothers are free!" Free, free, with the freedom not cherished by the few alone, but for all that had been bound. Free, with the freedom not torn from the secret night, but open to the light of heaven.

When the first call for colored soldiers came, Joshua Leckler hastened down to Boston, and enrolled himself among those who were willing to fight to maintain their freedom. On account of his ability to read and write and his general intelligence, he was soon made an orderly sergeant. His regiment had already taken part in an engagement before the public roster of this band of Uncle Sam's niggers, as they were called, fell into Mr. Leckler's hands. He ran his eye down the column of names. It stopped at that of Joshua Leckler, Sergeant, Company F. He handed the paper to Mrs. Leckler with his finger on the place.

"Mrs. Leckler," he said, "this is nothing less than a judgment on me for teaching a nigger to read and write. I disobeyed the law of my state and, as a result, not only lost my nigger, but furnished the Yankees with a smart officer to help them fight the South. Mrs. Leckler, I have sinned—and been punished. But I am content, Mrs. Leckler; it all came through my kindness of heart—and your mistaken advice. But, oh, that ingrate, that ingrate!"

Mary Elizabeth

Jessie Fauset

1919

Mary Elizabeth was late that morning. As a direct result, Roger left for work without telling me good-bye, and I spent most of the day fighting the headache which always comes if I cry.

For I cannot get a breakfast. I can manage a dinner—one just puts the roast in the oven and takes it out again. And I really excel in getting lunch. There is a good delicatessen near us, and with dainty service and flowers, I get along very nicely. But breakfast! In the first place, it's a meal I neither like nor need. And I never, if I live a thousand years, shall learn to like coffee. I suppose that is why I cannot make it.

"Roger," I faltered, when the awful truth burst upon me and I began to realize that Mary Elizabeth wasn't coming, "Roger, couldn't you get breakfast downtown this morning? You know last time you weren't so satisfied with my coffee."

Roger was hostile. I think he had just cut himself, shaving. Anyway, he was horrid.

"No, I can't get my breakfast downtown!" He actually snapped at me. "Really, Sally, I don't believe there's another woman in the world who would send her husband out on a morning like this on an empty stomach. I don't see how you can be so unfeeling."

Well, it wasn't "a morning like this," for it was just the beginning of November. And I had only proposed his doing what I knew he would have to do eventually.

I didn't say anything more, but started on that breakfast. I don't know why I thought I had to have hotcakes! The breakfast really was awful! The cakes were tough and gummy and got cold one second, exactly, after I took them off the stove. And the coffee boiled, or stewed, or scorched, or did whatever the particular thing is that coffee shouldn't do. Roger sawed at one cake, took one mouthful of the dreadful brew, and pushed away his cup.

"It seems to me you might learn to make a decent cup of coffee," he said icily. Then he picked up his hat and flung out of the house.

I think it is stupid of me, too, not to learn how to make coffee. But, really, I'm no worse than Roger is about lots of things. Take "Five Hundred." Roger knows I love cards, and with the Cheltons right around the corner from us and as fond of it as I am, we could spend many a pleasant evening. But Roger will not learn. Only the night before, after I had gone through a whole hand with him, with hearts as trumps, I dealt the cards around again to imaginary opponents and we started playing. Clubs were trumps, and spades led. Roger, having no spades, played triumphantly a Jack of Hearts and proceeded to take the trick.

"But, Roger," I protested, "you threw off."

"Well," he said, deeply injured, "didn't you say hearts were trumps when you were playing before?"

And when I tried to explain, he threw down the cards and wanted to know what difference it made; he'd rather play casino, anyway! I didn't go out and slam the door.

But I couldn't keep from crying this particular morning. I not only value Roger's good opinion, but I hate to be considered stupid.

Mary Elizabeth came in about eleven o'clock. She is a small, weazened woman, very dark, somewhat wrinkled, and a model of self-possession. I wish I could make you see her, or that I could reproduce her accent, not that it is especially colored—Roger's and mine are much more so—but her pronunciation, her way of drawing out her vowels, is so distinctively Mary Elizabethan!

I was ashamed of my red eyes and tried to cover up my embarrassment with sternness.

"Mary Elizabeth," said I, "you are late!" Just as though she didn't know it.

"Yas'm, Mis' Pierson," she said composedly, taking off her coat. She didn't remove her hat—she never does until she has been in the house some two or three hours. I can't imagine why. It is a small, black, dusty affair, trimmed with black ribbon, some dingy white roses, and a sheaf of wheat. I give Mary Elizabeth a dress and hat now and then, but, although I recognize the dress from time to time, I never see any change in the hat. I don't know what she does with my ex-millinery.

"Yas'm," she said again, and looked comprehensively at the untouched breakfast dishes and the awful viands, which were still where Roger had left them.

"Looks as though you'd had to git breakfast yoreself," she observed brightly. And went out in the kitchen and ate all those cakes and drank that unspeakable coffee! Really she did, and she didn't warm them up either.

I watched her miserably, unable to decide whether Roger was too finicky or Mary Elizabeth a natural-born diplomat.

"Mr. Gales led me an awful chase last night," she explained. "When I got home yistiddy evenin', my cousin whut keeps house fer me (!) tole me Mr. Gales went out in the mornin' en hadn't come back."

"Mr. Gales," let me explain, is Mary Elizabeth's second husband, an octogenarian, and the most original person, I am convinced, in existence.

"Yas'm," she went on, eating a final cold hotcake, "en I went to look fer 'im, en had the whole perlice station out all night huntin' 'im. Look like they wusn't never goin' to find 'im. But I ses, 'Jes' let me look fer enough en long enough en I'll find 'im,' I ses, en I did. Way out Georgy Avenue, with the hat on ole Mis' give 'im. Sent it to 'im all the way fum Chicaga. He's had it fifteen years—high silk beaver. I knowed he wusn't goin' too fer with that hat on.

"I went up to 'im, settin' by a fence all muddy, holdin' his hat on with both hands. En I ses, 'Look here, man, you come erlong home with me, en let me put you to bed.' En he come jest as meek! No-o-me, I knowed he wusn't goin' fer with ole Mis' hat on."

"Who was old 'Mis,' Mary Elizabeth?" I asked her.

"Lady I used to work fer in Noo York," she informed me. "Me en Rosy, the cook, lived with her fer years. Old Mis' was turrible fond of me, though her en Rosy used to querrel all the time. Jes' seemed like they couldn't git erlong. 'Member once Rosy run after her one Sunday with a knife, en I kep 'em apart. Reckon Rosy musta bin right put out with ole Mis' that day. By en by her en Rosy move to Chicaga, en when I married Mr. Gales, she sent 'im that hat. That old white woman shore did like me. It's so late, reckon I'd better put off sweepin' tel termorrer, ma'am."

I acquiesced, following her about from room to room. This was partly to get away from my own doleful thoughts—Roger really had hurt my feelings—but just as much to hear her talk. At first I used not to believe all she said, but after I investigated once and found her truthful in one amazing statement, I capitulated.

She had been telling me some remarkable tale of her first husband and I was listening with the stupefied attention to which she always reduces me. Remember she was speaking of her first husband.

"En I ses to 'im, I ses, 'Mr. Gale—' "

"Wait a moment, Mary Elizabeth," I interrupted, meanly delighted to have caught her for once. "You mean your first husband, don't you?"

"Yas'm," she replied. "En I ses to 'im, 'Mr. Gale, I ses—' "

"But, Mary Elizabeth," I persisted, "that's your second husband, isn't it—Mr. Gale?"

She gave me her long-drawn "No-o-me! My first husband was Mr. Gale and my second is Mr. *Gales.* He spells his name with a Z, I reckon. I ain't never see it writ. Ez I wus sayin', I ses to Mr. Gale—"

And it was true! Since then I have never doubted Mary Elizabeth.

She was loquacious that afternoon. She told me about her sister, "where's got a home in the country and where's got eight children." I used to read Lucy Pratt's stories about little Ephraim or Ezekiel, I forget his name, who always said "where's" instead of "who's," but I never believed it really till I heard Mary Elizabeth use it. For some reason or other she never mentions her sister without mentioning the home too. "My sister where's got a home in the country" is her unvarying phrase.

"Mary Elizabeth," I asked her once, "does your sister live in the country, or does she simply own a house there?"

"Yas'm," she told me.

She is fond of her sister. "If Mr. Gales wus to die," she told me complacently, "I'd go to live with her."

"If he should die," I asked her idly, "would you marry again?"

"Oh, no-o-me!" She was emphatic. "Though I don't know why I shouldn't, I'd come by it hones'. My father wus married four times."

That shocked me out of my headache. "Four times, Mary Elizabeth, and you had all those stepmothers!" My mind refused to take it in.

"Oh, no-o-me! I always lived with Mamma. She was his first wife."

I hadn't thought of people in the state in which I had instinctively placed Mary Elizabeth's father and mother as indulging in divorce, but as Roger says slangily, "I wouldn't know."

Mary Elizabeth took off the dingy hat. "You see, Papa and Mamma—" the ineffable pathos of hearing this woman of sixty-four, with a husband of eighty, use the old childish terms!

"Papa and Mamma wus slaves, you know, Mis' Pierson, and so of course they wusn't exackly married. White folks wouldn't let 'em. But they wus awf'ly in love with each other. Heard Mamma tell erbout it lots of times, and how Papa wus the han'somest man! Reckon she wus long erbout sixteen or seventeen then. So they jumped over a broomstick, en they wus jes as happy! But not long after I come erlong, they sold Papa down South, and Mamma never see him no mo' fer years and years. Thought he was dead. So she married again."

"And he came back to her, Mary Elizabeth?" I was overwhelmed with the woefulness of it.

"Yas'm. After twenty-six years. Me and my sister where's got a home in the country—she's really my half-sister, see, Mis' Pierson—her en Mamma en my stepfather en me wus all down in Bumpus, Virginia, workin' fer some white folks, and we used to live in a little cabin, had a front stoop to it. En one day an ole cullud man come by, had a lot o' whiskers. I'd saw him lots of times there in Bumpus, lookin' and peerin' into every cullud woman's face. En jes' then my sister she call out, 'Come here, you Ma'y Elizabeth,' en that old man stopped, en he looked at me en he looked at me, en he ses to me, 'Chile, is yo' name Ma'y Elizabeth?'

"You know, Mis' Pierson, I thought he wus jes' bein' fresh, en I ain't paid no 'tention to 'im. I ain't sed nuthin' ontel he spoke to me three or four times, en then I ses to 'im, 'Go 'way fum here, man, you ain't got no call to be fresh with me. I'm a decent woman. You'd oughta be ashamed of yoreself, an ole man like you.' "

Mary Elizabeth stopped and looked hard at the back of her poor wrinkled hands.

"En he says to me, 'Daughter,' he ses, jes' like that, 'daughter,' he ses, 'hones' I ain't bein' fresh. Is yo' name shore enough Ma'y Elizabeth?"

"En I tole him, 'Yas'r.'

" 'Chile,' he ses, 'whar is yo' daddy?'

" 'Ain't got no daddy,' I tole him peart-like. 'They done tuk 'im away fum me twenty-six years ago, I wusn't but a mite of a baby. Sol' 'im down the river. My mother often talks about it.' And, oh, Mis' Pierson, you shoulda see the glory come into his face!

" 'Yore mother!' he ses, kinda out of breath. 'Yore mother! Ma'y Elizabeth, whar is your mother?'

" 'Back thar on the stoop,' I tole 'im. 'Why, did you know my daddy?'

"But he didn't pay no 'tention to me, jes' turned and walked up the stoop whar Mamma wus settin'! She was feelin' sorta porely that day. En you oughta see me steppin' erlong after 'im.

"He walked right up to her and giv' her one look. 'Oh, Maggie,' he shout out, 'oh, Maggie! Ain't you know me? Maggie, ain't you know me?'

"Mamma look at 'im and riz up outa her cheer. 'Who're you,' she ses, kinda trimbly, 'callin' me Maggie thata way? Who're you?'

"He went up real close to her; then, 'Maggie,' he ses jes' like that, kinda sad 'n tender, 'Maggie!' And hel' out his arms.

"She walked right into them. 'Oh,' she ses, 'it's Cassius! It's Cassius! It's my husban' come back to me! It's Cassius!' They wus like two mad people.

"My sister Minnie and me, we jes' stood and gawped at 'em. There they wus, holding on to each other like two pitiful childrun, en he tuk her hands and kissed 'em.

" 'Maggie,' he ses, 'you'll come away with me, won't you? You gona take me back, Maggie? We'll go away, you en Ma'y Elizabeth en me. Won't we, Maggie?'

"Reckon my mother clean fergot my stepfather. 'Yes, Cassius,' she ses, 'we'll go away.' And then she sees Minnie, en it all comes back to her. 'Oh, Cassius,' she ses, 'I cain't go with you, I'm married again, en this time fer real. This here gal's mine and three boys, too, and another chile comin' in November!' "

"But she went with him, Mary Elizabeth," I pleaded. "Surely she went with him after all those years. He really was her husband."

I don't know whether Mary Elizabeth meant to be sarcastic or not. "Oh, no-o-me, Mamma couldn't a done that. She wus a good woman. Her ole master, whut done sol' my father down river, brung her up too religious fer that, en anyways, Papa was married again, too. Had his fourth wife there in Bumpus with 'im."

The unspeakable tragedy of it!

I left her and went up to my room, and hunted out my dark-blue serge dress which I had meant to wear again that winter. But I had to give Mary Elizabeth something, so I took the dress down to her.

She was delighted with it. I could tell she was, because she used her rare and untranslatable expletive.

"Haytian!" she said. "My sister where's got a home in the country, got a dress looks somethin' like this, but it ain't as good. No-o-me. She got hers to wear at a friend's weddin'—gal she was riz up with. Thet gal married well, too, lemme tell you; her husband's a Sunday School sup'rintender."

I told her she needn't wait for Mr. Pierson, I would put dinner on the table. So off she went in the gathering dusk, trudging bravely back to her Mr. Gales and his high silk hat.

I watched her from the window till she was out of sight. It had been such a long time since I had thought of slavery. I was born in Pennsylvania, and neither my parents nor grandparents had been slaves; otherwise I might have had the same tale to tell as Mary Elizabeth, or, worse yet, Roger and I might have lived in those black days and loved and lost each other and futilely, damnably, met again like Cassius and Maggie.

Whereas it was now, and I had Roger and Roger had me.

How I loved him as I sat there in the hazy dusk. I thought of his dear, bronze perfection, his habit of swearing softly in excitement, his blessed stupidity. Just the same I didn't meet him at the door as usual, but pretended to be busy. He came rushing to me with the *Saturday Evening Post,* which is more to me than rubies. I thanked him warmly, but aloofly, if you can get that combination.

We ate dinner almost in silence for my part. But he praised everything—the cooking, the table, my appearance.

After dinner we went up to the little sitting-room. He hoped I wasn't tired—couldn't he fix the pillows for me? So!

I opened the magazine and the first thing I saw was a picture of a woman gazing in stony despair at the figure of a man disappearing around the bend of the road. It was too much. Suppose that were Roger and I! I'm afraid I sniffled. He was at my side in a moment.

"Dear loveliest! Don't cry. It was all my fault. You aren't any worse about coffee than I am about cards! And anyway, I needn't have slammed the door!

Forgive me, Sally. I always told you I was hard to get along with. I've had a horrible day—don't stay cross with me, dearest."

I held him to me and sobbed outright on his shoulder. "It isn't you, Roger," I told him, "I'm crying about Mary Elizabeth."

I regret to say he let me go then, so great was his dismay. Roger will never be half the diplomat that Mary Elizabeth is.

"Holy smokes!" he groaned. "She isn't going to leave us for good, is she?"

So then I told him about Maggie and Cassius. "And oh, Roger," I ended futilely, "to think that they had to separate after all those years, when he had come back, old and with whiskers!" I didn't mean to be so banal, but I was crying too hard to be coherent.

Roger had got up and was walking the floor, but he stopped then aghast.

"Whiskers!" he moaned. "My hat! Isn't that just like a woman?" He had to clear his throat once or twice before he could go on, and I think he wiped his eyes.

"Wasn't it the"—I really can't say what Roger said here—"wasn't it the darndest hard luck that when he did find her again, she should be married? She might have waited."

I stared at him astounded. "But, Roger," I reminded him, "he had married three other times; he didn't wait."

"Oh—!" said Roger, unquotably. "Married three fiddlesticks! He only did that to try to forget her."

Then he came over and knelt beside me again. "Darling, I do think it is a sensible thing for a poor woman to learn how to cook, but I don't care as long as you love me and we are together. Dear loveliest, if I had been Cassius"—he caught my hands so tight that he hurt them—"and I had married fifty times and had come back and found you married to someone else, I'd have killed you, killed you."

Well, he wasn't logical, but he was certainly convincing.

So thus, and not otherwise, Mary Elizabeth healed the breach.

Esther

Jean Toomer

1923

I

Nine.

Esther's hair falls in soft curls about her high-cheekboned chalk-white face. Esther's hair would be beautiful if there were more gloss to it. And if her face were not prematurely serious, one would call it pretty. Her cheeks are too flat and dead for a girl of nine. Esther looks like a little white child, starched, frilled, as she walks slowly from her home towards her father's grocery store. She is about to turn in Broad from Maple Street. White and black men loafing on the corner hold no interest for her. Then a strange thing happens. A clean-muscled, magnificent, black-skinned Negro, whom she had heard her father mention as King Barlo, suddenly drops to his knees on a spot called the Spittoon. White men, unaware of him, continue squirting tobacco juice in his direction. The saffron fluid splashes on his face. His smooth black face begins to glisten and to shine. Soon, people notice him, and gather round. His eyes are rapturous upon the heavens. Lips and nostrils quiver. Barlo is in a religious trance. Town folks know it. They are not startled. They are not afraid. They gather round. Some beg boxes from the grocery stores. From old McGregor's notion shop. A coffin case is pressed into use. Folks line the curbstones. Businessmen close shop. And Banker Warply parks his car close by. Silently, all await the prophet's voice. The sheriff, a great florid fellow whose leggings never meet around his bulging calves, swears in three deputies. "Wall, y cant never tell what a nigger like King Barlo might be up t." Soda bottles, five fingers full of shine, are passed to those who want them. A couple of stray dogs start a fight. Old Goodlow's cow comes flopping up the street. Barlo, still as an Indian fakir, has not moved. The town bell strikes six. The sun slips in behind a heavy mass of horizon cloud. The crowd is hushed and expectant. Barlo's under jaw relaxes, and his lips begin to move.

"Jesus has been awhisperin strange words deep down, O way down deep, deep in my ears."

Hums of awe and of excitement.

"He called me to His side an said, 'Git down on your knees beside me, son, Ise gwine t whisper in your ears.' "

An old sister cries, "Ah, Lord."

" 'Ise agwine t whisper in your ears,' He said, and I replied, 'Thy will be done on earth as it is in heaven.' "

"Ah, Lord. Amen. Amen."

"An Lord Jesus whispered strange good words deep down, O way down deep, deep in my ears. An He said, 'Tell em till you feel your throat on fire.' I saw a vision. I saw a man arise, an he was big an black an powerful—"

Someone yells, "Preach it, preacher, preach it!"

"—but his head was caught up in th clouds. An while he was agazin at th heavens, heart filled up with th Lord, some little white ant biddies came and tied his feet to chains. They led him t th coast, they led him t th sea, they led him across th ocean an they didnt set him free. The old coast didnt miss him, an th new coast wasnt free, he left the old-coast brothers, t give birth t you an me. O Lord, great God Almighty, t give birth t you an me."

Barlo pauses. Old gray mothers are in tears. Fragments of melodies are being hummed. White folks are touched and curiously awed. Off to themselves, white and black preachers confer as to how best to rid themselves of the vagrant, usurping fellow. Barlo looks as though he is struggling to continue. People are hushed. One can hear weevils work. Dusk is falling rapidly, and the customary store lights fail to throw their feeble glow across the gray dust and flagging of the Georgia town. Barlo rises to his full height. He is immense. To the people he assumes the outlines of his visioned African. In a mighty voice he bellows:

"Brothers an sisters, turn your faces t th sweet face of the Lord, an fill your hearts with glory! Open your eyes an see th dawnin of th mornin light! Open your ears—"

Years afterwards Esther was told that at that very moment a great, heavy, rumbling voice actually was heard. That hosts of angels and of demons paraded up and down the streets all night. That King Barlo rode out of town astride a pitch-black bull that had a glowing gold ring in its nose. And that old Limp Underwood, who hated niggers, woke up next morning to find that he held a black man in his arms. This much is certain: an inspired Negress, of wide reputation for being sanctified, drew a portrait of a black madonna on the courthouse wall. And King Barlo left town. He left his image indelibly upon the mind of Esther. He became the starting point of the only living patterns that her mind was to know.

II

Sixteen.

Esther begins to dream. The low evening sun sets the windows of McGregor's notion shop aflame. Esther makes believe that they really are aflame. The town fire department rushes madly down the road. It ruthlessly shoves black and white idlers to one side. It whoops. It clangs. It rescues from the second-story window a dimpled infant which she claims for her own. How had she come by it? She thinks of it immaculately. It is a sin to think of it immaculately. She must dream no more. She must repent her sin. Another dream comes. There is no fire department. There are no heroic men. The fire starts. The loafers on the corner form a circle, chew their tobacco faster, and squirt juice just as fast as they can chew. Gallons on top of gallons they squirt upon the flames. The air reeks with the stench of scorched tobacco juice. Women, fat chunky Negro women, lean scrawny white women, pull their skirts up above their heads and display the most ludicrous underclothes. The women scoot in all directions from the danger zone. She alone is left to take the baby in her arms. But what a baby! Black, singed, woolly, tobacco-juice baby—ugly as sin. Once held to her breast, miraculous thing: its breath is sweet and its lips can nibble. She loves it frantically. Her joy in it changes the town folks' jeers to harmless jealousy, and she is left alone.

Twenty-two.

Esther's schooling is over. She works behind the counter of her father's grocery store. "To keep the money in the family," so he said. She is learning to make distinctions between the business and the social worlds. "Good business comes from remembering that the white folks dont divide the niggers, Esther. Be just as black as any man who has a silver dollar." Esther listlessly forgets that she is near white, and that her father is the richest colored man in town. Black folk who drift in to buy lard and snuff and flour of her call her a sweet-natured, accommodating girl. She learns their names. She forgets them. She thinks about men. "I dont appeal to them. I wonder why." She recalls an affair she had with a little fair boy while still in school. It had ended in her shame when he as much as told her that for sweetness he preferred a lollipop. She remembers the salesman from the North who wanted to take her to the movies that first night he was in town. She refused, of course. And he never came back, having found out who she was. She thinks of Barlo. Barlo's image gives her a slightly stale thrill. She spices it by telling herself his glories. Black. Magnetically so. Best cotton picker in the county, in the state, in the whole world for that matter. Best man with his fists, best man with dice, with a razor. Promoter of church benefits. Of colored fairs. Vagrant preacher. Lover of all the women for miles and miles around. Esther decides that she loves him. And with a vague sense of life slipping by, she resolves that she will tell him so, whatever people say, the next time he comes to town. After the making of this resolution, which becomes a sort of wedding cake for her to tuck beneath her pillow and go to sleep upon, she sees nothing of Barlo for five years. Her hair thins. It looks like the dull silk on puny corn ears. Her face pales until it is the color of the gray dust that dances with dead cotton leaves.

III

Esther is twenty-seven.

Esther sells lard and snuff and flour to vague black faces that drift in her store to ask for them. Her eyes hardly see the people to whom she gives change. Her body is lean and beaten. She rests listlessly against the counter, too weary to sit down. From the street someone shouts, "King Barlo has come back to town." He passes her window, driving a large new car. Cut-out open. He veers to the curb and steps out. Barlo has made money on cotton during the war. He is as rich as anyone. Esther suddenly is animate. She goes to her door. She sees him at a distance, the center of a group of credulous men. She hears the deep-bass rumble of his talk. The sun swings low. McGregor's windows are aflame again. Pale flame. A sharply dressed white girl passes by. For a moment Esther wishes that she might be like her. Not white; she has no need for being that. But sharp, sporty, with get-up about her. Barlo is connected with that wish. She mustnt wish. Wishes only make you restless. Emptiness is a thing that grows by being moved. "I'll not think. Not wish. Just set my mind against it." Then the thought comes to her that those purposeless, easygoing men will possess him, if she doesnt. Purpose is not dead in her, now that she comes to think of it. That loose women will have their arms around him at Nat Bowle's place tonight. As if her veins are full of fired sun-bleached southern shanties, a swift heat sweeps them. Dead dreams, and a forgotten resolution are carried upward by the flames. Pale flames. "They shant have him. Oh, they shall not. Not if it kills me they shant have him." Jerky, aflutter, she closes the store and starts home. Folks lazing on store windowsills wonder what on earth can be the matter with Jim Crane's gal, as she passes them. "Come to remember, she always was a little off, a little crazy, I reckon." Esther seeks her own room and locks the door. Her mind is a pink mesh bag filled with baby toes.

Using the noise of the town clock striking twelve to cover the creaks of her departure, Esther slips into the quiet road. The town, her parents, most everyone is sound asleep. This fact is a stable thing that comforts her. After sundown a chill wind came up from the west. It is still blowing, but to her it is a steady, settled thing like the cold. She wants her mind to be like that. Solid, contained, and blank as a sheet of darkened ice. She will not permit herself to notice the peculiar phosphorescent glitter of the sweet-gum leaves. Their movement would excite her. Exciting, too, the recession of the dull familiar homes she knows so well. She doesnt know them at all. She closes her eyes, and holds them tightly. Wont do. Her being aware that they are closed recalls her purpose. She does not want to think of it. She opens them. She turns now into the deserted business street. The corrugated iron canopies and mule- and horse-gnawed hitching posts bring her a strange composure. Ghosts of the commonplaces of her daily life take stride with her and become her companions. And the echoes of her heels upon the flagging are rhythmically monotonous and soothing. Crossing the street at the corner of McGregor's notion shop, she thinks that the windows are a dull flame. Only a fancy. She walks faster. Then runs. A turn into a side street brings her abruptly to Nat Bowle's place. The house is squat and dark. It is always dark. Barlo is within. Quietly she opens the outside door and steps in. She passes through a small room. Pauses before a flight of stairs down which people's voices, muffled, come. The air is heavy with fresh tobacco smoke. It makes her sick. She wants to turn back. She goes up the steps. As if she were mounting to some great height, her head spins. She is violently dizzy. Blackness rushes to her eyes. And then she finds that she is in a large room. Barlo is before her.

"Well, I'm sholy damned—skuse me, but what, what brought you here, lil milk-white gal?"

"You." Her voice sounds like a frightened child's that calls homeward from some point miles away.

"Me?"

"Yes, you Barlo."

"This aint th place fer y. This aint th place fer y."

"I know. I know. But I've come for you."

"For me for what?"

She manages to look deep and straight into his eyes. He is slow at understanding. Guffaws and giggles break out from all around the room. A coarse woman's voice remarks, "So thats how th dictie niggers does it." Laughs. "Mus give em credit fo their gall."

Esther doesnt hear. Barlo does. His faculties are jogged. She sees a smile, ugly and repulsive to her, working upward through thick licker fumes. Barlo seems hideous. The thought comes suddenly that conception with a drunken man must be a mighty sin. She draws away, frozen. Like a somnambulist she wheels around and walks stiffly to the stairs. Down them. Jeers and hoots pelter bluntly upon her back. She steps out. There is no air, no street, and the town has completely disappeared.

The Hands: A Story

Marita Bonner

1925

I saw his hands as soon as I skipped on the car at Vesey Avenue. Dark brown, gnarled, knotted, bumping arm, in quirky knots like old brown bark on a cherry tree.

I skipped on the car real quickly. I wanted to cry, so I skipped. Someone had hurt my feelings and I wanted to cry—but I would not. I stared at everyone opposite me.

I am not rude. I can stare at people without their noticing me. Women only glance at me in pity or in grim scorn. Men never see me; so I stare safely.

You see, I am tallish and my bones poke out in subduable angles. I have no complexion—no hair. Of course there are some features and something atop my head, but the one is not complexion and the other not hair. My clothes look well when they are not on me. I have good taste in selecting things but I cannot wear them well. Nothing seems to belong to me, nor I to anything. I guess I am merely unfortunately ugly.

There are games I have to play by myself when I feel particularly ugly, particularly unfortunate.

I tried them all as soon as I had sat in my seat, for tears were coming up from behind, from each side, and from below my eyes and I was breathing in quick rushes—with long pauses in between—around lumps in my throat that kept rising and sinking like mercury in a thermometer. I plunged headlong into my first game: Being-where-I-was-not. . . .

There was all around me a crushing dark forest with a crooked ribbon of water in its midst. There was a cheese-colored moon and a wind playing a flighty dance rhythm through the trees. Vines draped low to the water's edge and the cold black slender loops of snakes were strung like bracelets on the boughs of trees. Spicy flowers and fruit and the tanging odor of crushed green leaves and water, too, still in its basin. Snakes—and no people snakes. Where were the people? I in the forest and the forest peopled by snakes. . . .

* * *

One of the mercurial lumps caught my breath and choked me out of my game. I started unmolested and struggled over another lump into my second game: Christ-in-all-men.

The lumps were closer together now—almost consolidating. Christ-in-all-men.

In the woman in the corner with the purple-scarlet painted cheeks and the purple blotched lips and the hungry restless light, quick-snapping like fox-fire, in her eyes!

Maybe the tears were run together. I could not see Christ-in-all-men there.

Then I saw the hands: dark brown skin laid in thin gray-rimmed patches, like an alligator's back. Joints jutting like nodes on a bough; hands laid carefully, one on the other, on blue denim trousers.

Working hands. Hands that had toiled.

Christ-in-all-men. Christ, the carpenter.

Now the game could be played in earnest. . . .

He started to work when he was seven. Ran errands, lugged coal, lugged oil, lugged washing, sold papers. In the summer when the sun baked the flesh on your hands; in the winter when the blood stands still in your hands; when the wind blows.

Went to school sometimes and labored hard to keep the pen from wavering between the round-end fingers.

Worked after school. Labored as hard with shovel as with pencil. Ran elevators; shoveled coal; washed windows; scrubbed; dug.

Graduated from "grades" and "got a job."

Worked.

Up at five; swallowed coffee.

Slumbered downtown, through a city half asleep, half preparing to go to bed. Scraped square-toed across a wharf, across a plank, down into a ship.

A strange ship that never moved, never went anywhere. Just stood at the wharf like a Christmas toy, with its insides fractured. All around, other ships whisked, frittered, floated—according to their bulk—in and out.

This one stood unashamed and motionless while you shoveled and shoveled and shoveled until the step from bin to boiler seemed a pit in which your feet were fastened. Until the blood in your arms and the blood in your head met together and your heart seemed crowded out of it all.

Shoveled until sooty sweat stood in pools on the floor and shrank the few garments on your back into a back that shoved them off at once with the hard quiver of muscles. Shoveled and shoveled—until it was dinnertime.

Sometimes he washed his hands; sometimes he did not. Days there were when he went above; then there were days when he dragged to a pile of coal close by the bin and sat to eat.

Slices of bread, half a loaf thick. Slabs of meat too wide to swallow well. Cold coffee in a flanked bottle—something sweet at the end.

Perhaps a snatch of sleep; perhaps a friendly smoke—then the shovel.

The feel in the handle for the "good grip" and then from bin to boiler— from boiler to bin until six.

World in dim twilight when he went down; world in dim twilight when he came up.

Home. At first one narrow room with a trough bed, a jigsaw mirror, and a gas light with an asthmatic flaw in it. A light that sputtered and flickered to hide from the hateful brassy brown paper on the wall and the piece of shade at the window that was pretending to be what it wasn't.

He washed his hands now and spread Vaseline on spots where the skin wore thin. Then he set forth into a world deliciously dark now. To dance halls, where violins and pianos wooed melody, syncopation, and one another with a breathtaking seduction. Where made a deal wood floor glassy and an over-robust figure a pleasing armful and made your teeth show whether you would or not.

Shovels were shovels; with music, lights, perfume, and gay colors, a mere poke in the ribs worthy of a deep-seated laugh. A brown face, ashy with white powder and dyed with too-bright rouge, make your breath draw in twice to once coming out.

Sometimes he played at pool and cards.

Sometimes it was lodge night and he added new dignity as carefully as he adjusted his white apron.

At church he took collection, balancing the basket carefully between thumb and forefinger. One night in June there was a revival and all the lost found Christ and themselves. As usher he helped most of them to and from the forward bench—politely ministering, protecting, urging on at once.

One slight brown girl, crying as if she had truly melted in tears, wavered up from a back seat. His sturdy hands steadied her, and their strength only made her cry the more.

He guided her into a bench and looked down into her round, plump, seal-smooth face with its tilted eyes too far apart and a nose, flat and yet upturned. A face full of the strangely unrelated features found only in a race as marred by tampering, crossing, and back-crossing as the Negro.

"Don't worry, Christ ain't hard to find if you're looking for Him," the hands said.

"I'm afraid of everything! Life. Religion. Help me! Where is God? Where is Christ? Tell me! What shall I do to be saved?" pleaded the eyes.

Of course, it was but a second, but he felt very, very strong and knowing and weak and awkward all at the same time. He withdrew rapidly and came back to be sick just as rapidly after the service—and stayed.

Patted her arm one dazing night as she mouthed almost in a whisper, "I do."

Patted her when she trembled into the unspeakable uncertainty of birth.

Patted little brown cheeks, wreathed in smiles. Wiped snubbed brown noses and patted young heads flung carefree and unknowing, high.

Shoveled. Sometimes with soul out of the ship and at home. Shoveled desperately, almost frantic with fear lest they lay him off at the wrong time.

Shoveled the children out of two rooms into four. Out of grades into high school. Out of gingham and into crepe-de-chine.

Shoveled and dreamed about someday with its hours of ease; its house with a yard and garden; its plenty to eat; its plenty to drink and something in the bank to put "him and her away decent."

Shoveled, patted, soothed, smoothed, steadied souls welcoming back from the fearsome darkness of the unknown and Judgment.

Shoveled, patted, smoothed, smoothed—steadied.

Laid carefully one upon the other on a lap of blue denim.

Snakes, peopling the forest. Christ-in-all-men.

Which game, O God, must I play most? . . .

Sanctuary

Nella Larsen

1930

I

On the southern coast, between Merton and Shawboro, there is a strip of desolation some half a mile wide and nearly ten miles long between the sea and old fields of ruined plantations. Skirting the edge of this narrow jungle is a partly grown-over road which still shows traces of furrows made by the wheels of wagons that have long since rotted away or been cut into firewood. This road is little used, now that the state has built its new highway a bit to the west and wagons are less numerous than automobiles.

In the forsaken road a man was walking swiftly. But in spite of his hurry, at every step he set down his feet with infinite care for the night was windless and the heavy silence intensified each sound; even the breaking of a twig could be plainly heard. And the man had need of caution as well as haste.

Before a lonely cottage that shrank timidly back from the road the man hesitated a moment, then struck out across the patch of green in front of it. Stepping behind a clump of bushes close to the house, he looked in through the lighted window at Annie Poole, standing at her kitchen table mixing the supper biscuits.

He was a big, black man with pale brown eyes in which there was an odd mixture of fear and amazement. The light showed streaks of gray soil on his heavy, sweating face and great hands, and on his torn clothes. In his woolly hair clung bits of dried leaves and dead grass.

He made a gesture as if to tap on the window, but turned away to the door instead. Without knocking he opened it and went in.

II

The woman's brown gaze was immediately on him, though she did not move. She said, "You ain't in no hurry, is you, Jim Hammer?" It wasn't, however, entirely a question.

"Ah's in trubble, Mis' Poole," the man explained, his voice shaking, his fingers twitching.

"W'at you done done now?"

"Shot a man, Mis' Poole."

"Trufe?" The woman seemed calm. But the word was spat out.

"Yas'm. Shot 'im." In the man's tone was something of wonder, as if he himself could not quite believe that he had really done this thing which he affirmed.

"Daid?"

"Dunno, Mis' Poole. Dunno."

"White man o' niggah?"

"Cain't say, Mis' Poole. White man, Ah reckons."

Annie Poole looked at him with cold contempt. She was a tiny, withered woman—fifty, perhaps—with a wrinkled face the color of old copper, framed by a crinkly mass of white hair. But about her small figure was some quality of hardness that belied her appearance of frailty. At last she spoke, boring her sharp little eyes into those of the anxious creature before her.

"An' w'at am you lookin' foh me to do 'bout et?"

"Jes' lemme stop till dey's gone by. Hide me till dey passes. Reckon dey ain't fur off now." His begging voice changed to a frightened whimper. "Foh de Lawd's sake, Mis' Poole, lemme stop."

And why, the woman inquired caustically, should she run the dangerous risk of hiding him?

"Obadiah, he'd lemme stop ef he was to home," the man whined.

Annie Poole sighed. "Yas," she admitted, slowly, reluctantly, "Ah spec' he would. Obadiah, he's too good to youall no 'count trash." Her slight shoulders lifted in a hopeless shrug. "Yas, Ah reckon he'd do et. Emspecial' seein how he allus set such a heap o' store by you. Cain't see w'at foh, mahse'f. Ah shuah don' see nuffin' in you but a heap o' dirt."

But a look of irony, of cunning, of complicity passed over her face. She went on, "Still, 'siderin' all an' all, how Obadiah's right fon' o' you, an' how white folks is white folks, Ah'm a-gwine hide you dis one time."

Crossing the kitchen, she opened a door leading into a small bedroom, saying, "Git yo'se'f in dat dere feather baid an' Ah'm a-gwine put de clo's on de top. Don' reckon dey'll fin' you ef dey does look foh you in mah house. An Ah don' spec' dey'll go foh to do dat. Not lessen you been keerless an' let 'em smell you out gittin' hyah." She turned on him a withering look. "But you allus been triflin'. Cain't do nuffin propah. An' Ah'm a-tellin' you ef dey warn't white folks an' you a po' niggah, Ah shuah wouldn't be lettin' you mess up mah feather baid dis ebenin', 'cose Ah jes' plain don' want you hyah. Ah done kep' mahse'f outen trubble all mah life. So's Obadiah."

"Ah's powahful 'bliged to you, Mis' Poole. You shuah am one good 'oman. De Lawd'll mos' suttinly—"

Annie Poole cut him off. "Dis ain't no time foh all dat kin' o' fiddle-de-roll. Ah does mah duty as Ah sees et 'thout no thanks from you. Ef de Lawd had gib you a white face 'stead o'dat dere black one, Ah shuah would turn you out. Now hush yo' mouf an' git yo'se'f in. An' don' git movin' and scrunchin' undah dose covahs and git yo'se'f kotched in mah house."

Without further comment the man did as he was told. After he had laid his soiled body and grimy garments between her snowy sheets, Annie Poole carefully rearranged the covering and placed piles of freshly laundered linen on top. Then she gave a pat here and there, eyed the result, and, finding it satisfactory, went back to her cooking.

III

Jim Hammer settled down to the racking business of waiting until the approaching danger should have passed him by. Soon savory odors seeped in to him and he realized that he was hungry. He wished that Annie Poole would bring him something to eat. Just one biscuit. But she wouldn't, he knew. Not she. She was a hard one, Obadiah's mother.

By and by he fell into a sleep from which he was dragged back by the rumbling sound of wheels in the road outside. For a second fear clutched so tightly at him that he almost leaped from the suffocating shelter of the bed in order to make some active attempt to escape the horror that his capture meant. There was a spasm at his heart, a pain so sharp, so slashing that he had to suppress an impulse to cry out. He felt himself falling. Down, down, down. . . . Everything grew dim and very distant in his memory. . . . Vanished. . . . Came rushing back.

Outside there was silence. He strained his ears. Nothing. No footsteps. No voices. They had gone on then. Gone without even stopping to ask Annie Poole if she had seen him pass that way. A sigh of relief slipped from him. His thick lips curled in an ugly, cunning smile. It had been smart of him to think of coming to Obadiah's mother's to hide. She was an old demon, but he was safe in her house.

He lay a short while longer, listening intently, and, hearing nothing, started to get up. But immediately he stopped, his yellow eyes glowing like pale flames. He had heard the unmistakable sound of men coming toward the house. Swiftly he slid back into the heavy, hot stuffiness of the bed and lay listening fearfully.

The terrifying sounds drew nearer. Slowly. Heavily. Just for a moment he thought they were not coming in—they took so long. But there was a light knock and the noise of a door being opened. His whole body went taut. His feet felt frozen, his hands clammy, his tongue like a weighted, dying thing. His pounding heart made it hard for his straining ears to hear what they were saying out there.

"Ebenin', Mistah Lowndes." Annie Poole's voice sounded as it always did, sharp and dry.

There was no answer. Or had he missed it? With slow care he shifted his position, bringing his head nearer the edge of the bed. Still he heard nothing. What were they waiting for? Why didn't they ask about him?

Annie Poole, it seemed, was of the same mind. "Ah don' reckon youall done traipsed 'way out hyah jes' foh yo' healf," she hinted.

"There's bad news for you, Annie, I'm 'fraid." The sheriff's voice was low and queer.

Jim Hammer visualized him standing out there—a tall, stooped man, his white tobacco-stained mustache drooping limply at the ends, his nose hooked and sharp, his eyes blue and cold. Bill Lowndes was a hard one too. And white.

"W'atall bad news, Mistah Lowndes?" The woman put the question quietly, directly.

"Obadiah—" the sheriff began—hesitated—began again. "Obadiah—ah—er, he's outside, Annie. I'm 'fraid—"

"Shucks! You done missed. Obadiah, he ain't done nuffin', Mistah Lowndes. Obadiah!" she called stridently, "Obadiah! git hyah an' splain yo'se'f."

But Obadiah didn't answer, didn't come in. Other men came in. Came in with steps that dragged and halted. No one spoke. Not even Annie Poole. Something was laid carefully upon the floor.

"Obadiah, chile," his mother said softly, "Obadiah, chile." Then, with sudden alarm, "He ain't daid, is he? Mistah Lowndes! Obadiah, he ain't daid?"

Jim Hammer didn't catch the answer to that pleading question. A new fear was stealing over him.

"There was a to-do, Annie," Bill Lowndes explained gently, "at the garage back o' the factory. Fellow tryin' to steal tires. Obadiah heerd a noise an' run out with two or three others. Scared the rascal, all right. Fired off his gun an' run. We allow et to be Jim Hammer. Picked up his cap back there. Never was no 'count. Thievin' an' sly. But we'll git 'im, Annie. We'll git 'im."

The man huddled in the feather bed prayed silently. "Oh, Lawd! Ah didn't go to do et. Not Obadiah, Lawd. You knows dat. You knows et." And into his frenzied brain came the thought that it would be better for him to get up and go out to them before Annie Poole gave him away. For he was lost now. With all his great strength he tried to get himself out of the bed. But he couldn't.

"Oh, Lawd!" he moaned. "Oh, Lawd!" His thoughts were bitter and they ran through his mind like panic. He knew that it had come to pass as it said somewhere in the Bible about the wicked. The Lord had stretched out his hand and smitten him. He was paralyzed. He couldn't move hand or foot. He moaned again. It was all there was left for him to do. For in the terror of this new calamity that had come upon him he had forgotten the waiting danger which was so near out there in the kitchen.

His hunters, however, didn't hear him. Bill Lowndes was saying, "We been a-lookin' for Jim out along the old road. Figured he'd make tracks for Shawboro. You ain't noticed anybody pass this evenin', Annie?"

The reply came promptly, unwaveringly. "No, Ah ain't sees nobody pass. Not yet."

IV

Jim Hammer caught his breath.

"Well," the sheriff concluded, "we'll be gittin' along. Obadiah was a mighty fine boy. Ef they was all like him—I'm sorry, Annie. Anything I c'n do, let me know."

"Thank you, Mistah Lowndes."

With the sound of the door closing on the departing men, power to move came back to the man in the bedroom. He pushed his dirt-caked feet out from the covers and rose up, but crouched down again. He wasn't cold now, but hot all over and burning. Almost he wished that Bill Lowndes and his men had taken him with them.

Annie Poole had come into the room.

It seemed a long time before Obadiah's mother spoke. When she did there were no tears, no reproaches; but there was a raging fury in her voice as she lashed out. "Git outen mah feather baid, Jim Hammer, an' outen mah house, an' don' nevah stop thankin' you' Jesus he done gib you dat black face."

Truant

Claude McKay

1932

The warbling of a mother's melody had just ended, and the audience was in a sentimental state and ready for the scene that the curtain, slowly drawn, disclosed. A mother in calico print jigged on her knee a little baby, crooning the while some Gaelic folk-words. A colleen sat on a red-covered box, mending a chemise; sitting at her feet, a younger sister with a picture book. Three boys in shirtsleeves and patched pantaloons playing with a red-and-green train on a lacquer-black railroad. A happy family. An antique sitting room, torn wallpaper, two comic chairs, and the Holy Virgin on the mantelpiece. A happy family. Father, fat and round like a chianti bottle, skips into the picture, and up leap boys and girls and mother with baby. The Merry Mulligans!

The orchestra starts at the pointing baton. Squeaky-burlesque family singing. Dancing. Stunting. A performing wonder, that little baby. Charming family of seven. American-famous. The Merry Mulligans, beloved of all lovers of clean vaudeville.

With them the show finished. Barclay Oram and his wife, Rhoda, descended from Nigger Heaven, walked up to 50th Street, and caught the local subway train for Harlem. He took the slower train, hoping there would be seats and the passengers not jammed together as always.

Perhaps others had hoped for the same thing. The cars were packed. Rhoda broke up a piece of chewing gum and chewed. She had a large mouth, and she chewed the gum as if she were eating food, opening her mouth so wide that people could see the roof. When they were first married, Barclay had detested her way of chewing gum and told her so. But she replied that it was absurd to let a little thing like chewing gum irritate him.

"Oh, you brown baby!" she had cried, taking his face in her hands and kissing him with the perfumed flavor of her favorite chewing gum on her breath. . . .

"The show was pretty nice, eh?" said Rhoda.

"I am fed up with them; a cabaret in Harlem is better," replied Barclay.

"I don't think so. Anything downtown for a change is preferable to the cheap old colored shows. I'm dead sick of them."

She chewed the gum vigorously, dropping a few pointless phrases that were half swallowed up in the roar of the train though the enormous gut of the city and the strange staccato talk of voices half lifted above and half caught in the roar. Barclay gazed moodily at the many straphangers who were jammed together. None seemed standing on his feet. All seemed like fat bags and lean boxes piled up indiscriminately in a warehouse. Penned up like cattle, the standing closely pressing the seated passengers, kneading them with their knees and blotting out their sight, so that those who had been fortunate to find seats were as uncomfortable as those who had not.

"I thought we'd have a little air in this local box," he said.

"It'll be better at Seventy-second Street," she said. "Some of them will get out."

"And others will push in. New York City is swarming with people like a beehive."

"Getting thicker and thicker every day," she agreed.

At 135th Street they left the train. Rhoda, as usual, put her hand through her husband's arm as they walked home. The saloons, restaurants, candy stores of the avenue were crowded. The Chop Suey Palace was doing a good after-theater business.

"Might have some chop suey," suggested Barclay.

"Not tonight," she said. "Betsy's with the Howlands, and they might want to go to bed."

"Ah, yes!" He had forgotten about Betsy, their four-year-old child. Always he forgot about her. Never could he quite realize that he was the father of a family. A railroad waiter, although he was thirty-six, he always felt himself just a boy—a servant boy. His betters whom he served treated him always as a boy—often as a nice dog. And when he grew irritated and snapped, they turned on him as upon a bad dog. It was better for him, then, that, although he was a husband and father, he should feel like an irresponsible boy. Even when sometimes he grew sad, sullen, and disquieted, these were the moods of a boy. Rhoda bossed him a little and never took his moods seriously. . . .

They went straight home. Barclay lighted up the three-room apartment. Rhoda went across the hall to the Howlands' for Betsy. She brought the child in, sleeping on her breast, and bent down that Barclay might kiss her. Then she put her to bed in her little cot beside the dresser.

They had a little supper, cold chicken and beer. . . . They went to bed in the front room that they had made their bedroom. Another room was let to a railroad porter, and the dining room served for an eating and sitting room.

Rhoda undressed, rubbed her face and her limbs with cold cream, slipped on a long white gown with pink ribbon around the neck, and lay down against the wall. Barclay laid himself down beside her in his underclothes. During the first six months of their union he had slept regularly in pajamas. Then he ignored them and began sleeping in his underclothes, returning to the habit of his village boyhood. Rhoda protested at first. Afterward she accepted it quietly. . . .

Sleep, sweet sleep. . . .

The next morning Rhoda shook Barclay at five o'clock. "Oh, God!" He stretched himself, turned over, and rested his head on her breast.

"Time to get up," she said.

"Yes." He sighed. "God! I feel tired." He stretched his arms, touched, fondled her face, and fell into a slight doze.

Ten minutes more. Rhoda gave him a dig in the back with her knee and cried, "You just must get up, Barclay."

"All right." He turned out of bed. Six o'clock in the Pennsylvania Station for duty, that was life itself. A dutiful black boy among proud and sure white men, so that he could himself be a man in Harlem with purchasing power for wife, child, flat, movie, food, liquor. . . .

He went to the bathroom and washed. Dressed, he entered the dining room, opened a cabinet, and poured out a glass of whiskey. That peppered him up and opened his eyes wide. It was not necessary for Rhoda to make coffee. He would breakfast with the other waiters in the dining car. Mechanically he kissed her good-bye. She heard him close the door, and she moved over into the middle of the bed, comfortably alone, for an early-morning nap.

It was a disastrous trip for Barclay. On the dining car he was the first waiter and in charge of the pantry. As pantryman he received five dollars a month more than the other waiters. It was his job to get the stores (with the steward and chef) from the commissary. He was responsible for the stuff kept in the pantry. There were some waiters and cooks addicted to petty stealing: butter, cream, cheese, sugar, fruit. They stole for their women in New York. They stole for their women-on-the-side in the stopover cities. Always Barclay had to mount guard quietly. Between him and the raw-voiced, black-bull chef there was an understanding to watch out for the nimble-fingered among the crew. For if they were short in the checking up of the stores, the steward held them responsible. And the commissary held the streward responsible.

This trip Barclay had one of his moody-boy spells. He would not watch the pantry. Let the boys swipe the stuff. He had no pleasure waiting on the passengers. It was often a pleasure, something of an anticipated adventure, each day to meet new passengers, remark the temperature of their looks, and sometimes make casual conversation with a transient acquaintance. But today it was all wrong from the moment he observed them, impatient, crowding the corridor, and the rushing of the dining room as soon as the doors were opened. They filled him with loathing, made him sick of service. *Service.* A beautiful word fallen upon bad days. No place for true human service in these automatic-serving days.

Mechanically Barclay picked up the dimes and quarters that were left for service. For Rhoda and Betsy. It pleasured him when Rhoda wore pretty clothes. And Betsy loved him more each time he remembered to bring home colored bonbons. What was he going to do with the child? He wondered if he would be able to give her a good education like her mother's. And what would she do? Perhaps marry a railroad waiter like her mother and raise up children to carry on the great tradition of black servitude.

Philadelphia, Harrisburg, Altoona, Pittsburgh. No dice, no coon-can, this trip. His workmates coaxed. Nothing could lift him out of himself. He was a moody boy this trip. The afternoon of the fourth day from New York brought the dining car to Washington. Washington reminded Barclay of a grave. He had sharp, hammering memories of his university days there. For there he had fallen in love. . . .

He went up to 7th Street, loitering through the Negro district, stopping curiously before a house, leaning against a stoop, sniffing here and there like a stray hound. He went into a barrelhouse and drank a glass of whiskey. The place was sour-smelling, full of black men, dim and smoky, close but friendly warm.

The hour of his train's departure approached. Barclay continued drinking. He felt pleased with himself in doing something irregular. Oh, he had been regular for such a long time! A good waiter, an honest pantryman. Never once had he sneaked a packet of sugar or a pound of butter for his flat. Rhoda would have flung it in the street. He had never given to the colored girls who worked in the yards and visited the dining cars with their teasing smiles. Oh, it was hard to be responsible, hard to be regular.

What would the steward say about his being left in Washington? Maybe he would be drunk himself, for he was a regular souser. Barclay recalled the day when he got helplessly stewed on the Washington run, and the waiters managed the dining car, handed out checks, made change among themselves, and gave the best service they ever did as a crew. At Philadelphia an inspector hopped on the train and took charge of the service. The dining car was crowded. The steward half roused himself out of his stupor and came lurching through the jam of passengers in the corridor into the diner, to dispute the stewardship with the inspector.

"I'm in charge of this diner," he said in a nerve-biting, imey-wimey voice. "Give a man a chance; treat me like a gen'leman."

Tears trickled down his cheeks. He staggered and swayed in the corridor, blocking the entrance and exit of the guests. Like a challenged mastiff, the inspector eyed him, at the same time glancing quickly from the waiters to the amazed guests. Then he gripped the steward by the scruff of the collar and, with the help of the Pullman conductor, locked him up in a drawing room until the train reached New York.

The crew did not like the steward and hoped they would be rid of him at last. But he was back with them the next trip. The inspector was known as a hard guy, quick to report a waiter if a flask of gin were discovered in his locker. But it was different with the steward. Both men were peers, the inspector being a promoted steward.

"Well, I'm off duty, anyhow," murmured Barclay. He smiled and ordered another drink. The train must have passed Baltimore by then, on its way to New York. What waiter was waiting on the first two tables? "I should worry." He had the warm, luxurious feelings of a truant. He drank himself drunk.

"Something for a change. I've been regular too long. Too awfully regular," he mused.

He rocked heavily out of the barrelhouse to a little fried-chicken restaurant. He ate. His stomach appeased, his thoughts turned to a speakeasy. May as well finish the thing in style—be grandly irregular, he thought. He found a speakeasy. Bold-eyed chocolate girls, brown girls, yellow girls. Blues. Pianola blues, gramophone blues. Easy-queasy, daddy-mammy, honey-baby, brown-gal, black-boy, hot-dog blues. . . .

The next day he reported himself at the restaurant-car department in Washington and was sent home to New York. There at the commissary the superintendent looked him over and said, "Well, you're a case. You wanted a little time off, eh? Well, take ten days."

That was his punishment—ten idle days. He left the commissary walking on air. For three years he had worked on the railroad without taking a holiday. Why? He did not himself know. He had often yearned for a few entirely free days. But he had never had the courage to take them, not for fear of forfeiting the nominal wages, but the tips—his real wages. Nor had he wanted to lose his former dining car. He had liked his work pals there. A good crew teaming splendidly along together, respectful to and respected by the steward, who was a decent-minded man. Moreover, there was the flat with Rhoda and Betsy. Every day was precious, every tip necessary. . . . Ten days gratuitously thrust upon him with malicious intent. No wages-and-food, no tips. Let him cool his heels and tighten his belt. Yet he was happy, happy like a truant suspended from school.

Freedom! Ten days. What would he do with them? There would be parties. Rhoda loved parties. She had friends in New York who knew her when she was a schoolteacher. Whist. Dancing. Movies.

He nosed around the tenderloin district. When he first came to New York he had lived on 40th Street.

He met a pal he had once worked with as elevator boy in a department store. They drank two glasses of beer each and walked up to San Juan Hill.

When Barclay got home, Rhoda, in an orange evening dress, was just leaving for a party. They embraced.

"I phoned up the commissary yesterday and they said you were left in Washington. Bad boy!" She laughed. "Guess I'll fix you something to eat."

"Don't bother. I'm not hungry," said Barclay.

"All right. I'm going on to Mame Dixon's for whist and a little dancing afterward. You might dress up and come on down and have a little fun."

"Not tonight, honey. We'll have plenty of time to go around together. They gave me ten days."

"Ten days!" she cried. "The rent is due on Friday and the insurance on—on—ten days! But why did you get left, Barclay?"

"I don't know. Felt rotten the whole trip—tired, blue. Been too punctual all along. Just had to break the habit. Feel a little irresponsible."

"But you might get in bad with the company. How could you when there's Betsy and me to think of and our social position?"

She broke up a stick of chewing gum and vigorously chewed.

"Well, anyway, come on along to Mame's if you feel like it." She rolled the gum with her tongue. "But if you don't, you can bring Betsy over from the Howlands'."

Chewing, chewing, she went out.

"Killjoy," murmured Barclay. Riding on the subway from San Juan Hill to Harlem, he had been guessing chucklingly at what she would say. Perhaps: "All right, honey-stick, why slave every day? Let's play around together for ten days."

Chewing, chewing. Always chewing. Yet that mouth was the enchanting thing about her. . . . Her mouth. It made me marry her. Her skin was brown and beautiful. Like cat's fur, soft to the fingers. But it was not her fruit-ripe skin. It was her mouth that made me.

Ordinary her face would have been, if it were not for the full, large mouth that was mounted on the ample plane of her features like an exquisite piece of bas-relief.

He went across the hall to the Howlands' and brought back Betsy.

"Candy, Daddy, candy!" The happy brown thing clapped her hands and pulled at his pantaloons. He set her on his knee and gave her a little paper packet. He danced her up and down: "Betsy, wupsy, mupsy, pretsy, eatsy plentsy candy."

She wriggled off his knee with the packet and dropped the candies one by one into a small glass jar, gurgling over the colors and popping one into her mouth at intervals. She returned again to Barclay's knee, squeezing a brown rubber doll. For a while she made a rocking horse of him. Then she scratched her head and yawned. Barclay undressed her and put her in the crib.

"Betsy and me and our social position." That social position! Alone he brooded, moody, unreasonable. Resentment gripped his heart. He hated his love of Rhoda's mouth. He hated the flat and his pitiable "social position." He hated fatherhood. He resented the sleeping child.

"Betsy and me and—" Should he go on forever like that? Round the circle of the eastern field? New York, Boston, Buffalo, Pittsburgh, Harrisburg, Washington, Baltimore, Philadelphia, again New York.

Forever? Getting off nowhere?

Forever fated to the lifelong tasks of the unimaginative? Why was he, a West Indian peasant boy, held prisoner within the huge granite-gray walls of New York? Dreaming of tawny tasseled fields of sugar cane and silver-gray john towhits among clusters of green and glossy-blue berries of pimento. The husbands and fathers of his village were not mechanically driven servant boys. They were hardy, independent tillers of the soil or struggling artisans.

What enchantment had lured him away from the green intimate life that clustered round his village, the simple African-transplanted life of the West Indian hills? Why had he hankered for the hard-slabbed streets, the vertical towers, the gray complex life of this steel-tempered city? Stone and steel! Steel and stone! Mounting in heaven-pursuing magnificence. Feet piled upon feet, miles circling miles, of steel and stone. A tree seemed absurd and a garden queer in this iron-gray majesty of man's imagination. He was a slave to it. A part of him was in love with this piling grandeur. And that was why he was a slave to it.

From the bedroom came a slight stirring and a sleepy murmur of child language. Barclay was lost in the past. Step by step he retraced his life. . . . His feverlike hunger for book knowledge, for strange lands and great cities. His grand adolescent dream.

The evening of his departure from the village came back star-blue and clear. He had trudged many miles to the railroad with his bright-patterned carpet bag on his shoulder. For three years in the capital of his island he had worked in a rum warehouse. Happy. On the road to his beautiful dream. Later he had crossed over to Santiago in Cuba. And at twenty-five he had reached New York, found his strange land—a great city of great books.

Two years of elevator-running and switchboard-operating had glanced by like a magic arrow against the gaunt gray walls of the city. Time was a radiant servant working for his dream.

His dream, of course, was the Negro university. Now he remembered how he turned green cold like a cucumber when he was told that he could not enter the university course. Two years' preparatory work was needed. Undaunted, he had returned to New York and crammed for a year. And the next fall he swept through the entrance examinations.

For Barclay then the highroad to wisdom led necessarily by way of a university. It had never occurred to him that he might have also attained his goal in his own free, informal way.

He had been enchanted by the words: University, Seat of Learning. He had seen young men of the insular island villages returned from the native colleges. They all brought back with them a new style of clothes, a different accent, a new gait, the exciting, intoxicating smell of the city—so much more intriguing than the ever-fresh accustomed smell of the bright-green hill-valley village. Style and accent and exotic smell, all those attractive fruits of college training, fundamental forms of cultural life. Home study could not give him the stamp. . . . His disillusion had not embittered him. . . .

My college days were happy, he reflected. A symmetrical group of buildings, gray walls supporting in winter stout, dark-brown leafless creepers. An all-Negro body of students—men and women—of many complexions, all intensely active. The booklore was there, housed in a kind of Gothic building with a projecting façade resting on Grecian pillars. The names of Aristotle, Solon, Virgil, Shakespeare, Dante, and Longfellow were cut in the façade. The building was one of the many symbols, scattered over America and the world, summing up the dream of a great romantic king of steel.

Barclay found no romance in textbooks, of course. But he found plenty of it in the company of the jolly girls and chummy chaps of his widened acquaintance. And the barbaric steps of the turkey trot and the bunny hug (exciting dances of that period) he had found more enchanting than the library. He was amorously touched by the warm, intimate little dances he attended—the spontaneous outburst of group singing when the dancers were particularly drunk on a rich, tintinnabulating melody.

Then one day he was abruptly pulled up in his fantastic steps. No more money in the box. He had to wheel round about and begin the heavy steps of working his way through college.

The next fall he met Rhoda. It was at one of those molasses-thick Aframerican affairs that had rendered university life so attractive to him, at the home of a very generous fawn-brown widow who enjoyed giving a few students a nice time at her flat. The widow entertained her guests in a free kind of way. She did not belong to the various divisions that go to the making of nice Negro society, for she was merely the widow of a Pullman porter who had saved up his tips and paid up on a good insurance policy. She had been too fine for the nondiscriminating parlor-social sets and too secular for the prayer-meeting black ladies. So she had cleverly gone in for the non-snobbish young intellectuals— poor students who could not afford to put on airs.

Barclay recalled the warm roomful of young Negro men and girls. Copper and chocolate and fine anthracite, with here and there a dash of cream, all warmly dancing. One night he was attracted to Rhoda. He danced with her all the time and she was warm to him, loving to him. She was the first American girl with whom he began a steady intimacy. All the ardors of him were stirred to her, and simply, impetuously, he rushed into deep love, like a bee that darts too far into the heart of a flower and, unable to withdraw, dies at the bottom of the juice.

Rhoda, who had been earning her own living as a teacher, helped him, and the problem of money was lifted from his mind. Oh, he was very happy then! Books and parties and Rhoda. . . .

In the middle of his junior year she told him she was with child. They discussed whether she should have the child or operate it away. If she had it without being married, she would lose her job. He remembered a schoolteaching girl of his village who had tried to conceal her pregnancy and died under an operation in the city. The other girls, the free peasant girls, always bore their children when they were gotten with child. Perhaps it was better that way.

Rhoda was pleased that Barclay wanted the thing to develop in the natural way. She desired a child. She was at that vague age when some women feel that marriage is more than the grim pursuit of a career. So they went to New York together and got married.

But Barclay did not fully realize the responsibility, perhaps could not, of marriage. Never fully understood its significance.

Barclay remembered now that he was as keen as Rhoda for the marriage, carried away by the curiosity to take up a new role. There had been something almost of eagerness in his desire to quit the university. And it had seemed a beautiful gesture. Rhoda had helped him when he was in great need, and he felt splendid now to come to her support when she was incapacitated for work. He would have hated to see her drop down to menial tasks. As a Jack-of-all-trades he had met many refined colored girls having a rough time, jammed at the bottom of the common scramble to survive.

He had been happy that Rhoda was not pushed to leave Betsy in one of those dime dumps where poor colored children were guarded while their mothers worked, happy that from his job on the railroad he was earning enough for the family to live simply and comfortably.

About that job he had never taken serious thought. Where was it leading him? What was it making of his character? He had taken it as if he were acting in a play rather than working at a job. It met the necessary bill of being in love. For he was really in love with Rhoda. The autumn-leaf mellowness of her body. Her ripe-ripe accent and richness of laughter. And her mouth: the full form of it, its strength and beauty, its almost unbearable sweetness, magnetic, drawing, sensuous, exquisite, a dark pagan piece of pleasure. . . . How fascinated and enslaved he had been to what was now stale with chewing gum and banal remarks on "social position."

Barclay's attitude to the railroad was about the same toward the modern world in general. He had entered lightheartedly into the whirl and crash and crush, the grand babel of building, the suction and spouting, groaning and whining and breaking of steel—all the riotous, contagious movement around him.

He had entered into the rough camaraderie of the railroad with all the hot energy of youth. It was a rugged new experience that kindled his vagabonding mind and body. There was rude poetry in the roar and rush and rattle of trains, the sharp whistle of engines and racing landscapes, the charm of a desolate mining town and glimpses of faces lost as soon as seen. He had even tried to capture some of those fleeting piled-up images. Some he had read to his work-mates, which they appreciated, but teased him for writing:

We are out in the field, the vast wide-open field,
Thundering through from city to city
Where factories grow like jungle trees
Yielding new harvests for the world.
Through Johnstown glowing like a world aflame,
And Pittsburgh, Negro-black, brooding in iron smoke,
Philly's Fifteenth Street of wenches, speakeasies, and cops.
Out in the field, new fields of life
Where machines spin flowers like tropic trees
And coal and steel are blazing suns—
And darkly we wonder, night-wrapped in the light.

The steel-framed poetry of cities did not crowd out but rather intensified in him the singing memories of his village life. He loved both, the one complementing the other. Against the intricate stone-and-steel flights of humanity's mass spirit, misty in space and time, hovered the green charm of his village. Yellow-eyed and white-lidded Spanish needles coloring the grassy hillsides, barefooted black girls, straight like young sweetwoods, tramping to market with baskets of mangoes or star apples poised unsupported on their heads. The native cockish liquor juice of the sugar cane, fermented in bamboo joints for all-night carousal at wakes and tea meetings. Heavy drays loaded with new-made sugar, yams, and plantains, rumbling along the chalky country road away down and over the hills under the starshine and the hot-free love songs of the draymen.

He remembered all, regretting nothing, since his life was a continual fluxion from one state to another. His deepest regret was always momentary, arising from remaining in a rut after he had exhausted the experience.

Rhoda now seemed only another impasse into which he had drifted. Just a hole to pull out of again and away from the road, that arena of steel rushing him round and round in the same familiar circle. He had to evade it and be irresponsible again.

But there was the child and the Moral Law. The cold white law. Rhoda seemed more than he to be subject to it, with her constant preoccupation about social position.

Spiritually he was subject to another law. Other goals of strange barbaric glory claimed his allegiance, and not the grim frock-coated gentleman of the Moral Law of the land. The Invisible Law that upheld those magnificent machines and steel-spired temples and new cathedrals erected to the steel-flung traffic plan of man. Oh, he could understand and love the poetry of them, but not their law that held humanity gripped in fear.

His thought fell to a whisper within him. He could never feel himself more than a stranger within these walls. His body went through the mechanical process, but untamed, for his spirit was wandering far. . . .

Rhoda at the party and the child asleep. He could hear her breathing and wondered if it were breath of his breath. For he often felt to himself a breath of his own related to none. Suppose he should start now on the trail again with that strange burning thought. Related to none.

There were the Liberty Bonds in his trunk. Rhoda would need them. He remembered how he had signed for them. All the waiters herded together in one of the commissary rooms and lectured by one of the special war men.

"Buy a bond, boys. All you boys will buy a bond because you all believe in the Allied cause. We are in the war to make the world safe for Democracy. You boys on the railroad are enjoying the blessings of Democracy like all real Americans. Your service is inestimable. Keep on doing your part and do your best by buying a bond because you believe in the Allied cause and you want America to win the war and the banner of Democracy float over the world. Come on, take your bond."

For the Moral Law. Buy a bond.

Well, it was all right; he had subscribed. One way of saving money, although the bonds were worth so much less now. There was the bankbook with a couple hundred dollars. Leave that too. Insurance policies. Forget them.

He thought he heard the child stir. He dared not look. He clicked the door and stepped out. Where? Destination did not matter. Maybe his true life lay in eternal inquietude.

A Summer Tragedy

Arna Bontemps

1933

Old Jeff Patton, the black share farmer, fumbled with his bow tie. His fingers trembled and the high stiff collar pinched his throat. A fellow loses his hand for such vanities after thirty or forty years of simple life. Once a year, or maybe twice if there's a wedding among his kinfolks, he may spruce up; but generally fancy clothes do nothing but adorn the wall of the big room and feed the moths. That had been Jeff Patton's experience. He had not worn his stiff-bosomed shirt more than a dozen times in all his married life. His swallow-tailed coat lay on the bed beside him, freshly brushed and pressed, but it was as full of holes as the overalls in which he worked on weekdays. The moths had used it badly. Jeff twisted his mouth into a hideous toothless grimace as he contended with the obstinate bow. He stamped his good foot and decided to give up the struggle.

"Jennie," he called.

"What's that, Jeff?" His wife's shrunken voice came out of the adjoining room like an echo. It was hardly bigger than a whisper.

"I reckon you'll have to he'p me wid this heah bow tie, baby," he said meekly. "Dog if I can hitch it up."

Her answer was not strong enough to reach him, but presently the old woman came to the door, feeling her way with a stick. She had a wasted, dead-leaf appearance. Her body, as scrawny and gnarled as a string bean, seemed less than nothing in the ocean of frayed and faded petticoats that surrounded her. These hung an inch or two above the tops of her heavy unlaced shoes and showed little grotesque piles where the stockings had fallen down from her negligible legs.

"You oughta could do a heap mo' wid a thing like that'n me—beingst as you got yo' good sight."

"Looks like I oughta could," he admitted. "But ma fingers is gone democrat on me. I get all mixed up in the looking glass an' can't tell wicha way to twist the devilish thing."

Jennie sat on the side of the bed and old Jeff Patton got down on one knee while she tied the bow knot. It was a slow and painful ordeal for each of them in this position. Jeff's bones cracked, his knee ached, and it was only after a half dozen attempts that Jennie worked a semblance of a bow into the tie.

"I got to dress maself now," the old woman whispered. "These is ma old shoes an' stockings, and I ain't so much as unwrapped ma dress."

"Well, don't worry 'bout me no mo', baby," Jeff said. "That 'bout finishes me. All I gotta do now is slip on that old coat 'n ves' an' I'll be fixed to leave."

Jennie disappeared again through the dim passage into the shed room. Being blind was no handicap to her in that black hole. Jeff heard the cane placed against the wall beside the door and knew that his wife was on easy ground. He put on his coat, took a battered top hat from the bedpost, and hobbled to the front door. He was ready to travel. As soon as Jennie could get on her Sunday shoes and her old black silk dress, they would start.

Outside the tiny log house, the day was warm and mellow with sunshine. A host of wasps were humming with busy excitement in the trunk of a dead sycamore. Gray squirrels were searching through the grass for hickory nuts, and blue jays were in the trees, hopping from branch to branch. Pine woods stretched away to the left like a black sea. Among them were scattered scores of log houses like Jeff's, houses of black share farmers. Cows and pigs wandered freely among the trees. There was no danger of loss. Each farmer knew his own stock and knew his neighbor's as well as he knew his neighbor's children.

Down the slope to the right were the cultivated acres on which the colored folks worked. They extended to the river, more than two miles away, and they were today green with the unmade cotton crop. A tiny thread of a road, which passed directly in front of Jeff's place, ran through these green fields like a pencil mark.

Jeff, standing outside the door, with his absurd hat in his left hand, surveyed the wide scene tenderly. He had been forty-five years on these acres. He loved them with the unexplained affection that others have for the countries to which they belong.

The sun was hot on his head, his collar still pinched his throat, and the Sunday clothes were intolerably hot. Jeff transferred the hat to his right hand and began fanning with it. Suddenly the whisper that was Jennie's voice came out of the shed room.

"You can bring the car round front whilst you's waitin'," it said feebly. There was a tired pause; then it added, "I'll soon be fixed to go."

"A'right, baby," Jeff answered. "I'll get it in a minute."

But he didn't move. A thought struck him that made his mouth fall open. The mention of the car brought to his mind, with new intensity, the trip he and Jennie were about to take. Fear came into his eyes; excitement took his breath. Lord, Jesus!

"Jeff . . . oh, Jeff," the old woman's whisper called.

He awakened with a jolt. "Hunh, baby?"

"What you doin'?"

"Nuthin. Jes studyin'. I jes been turnin' things round'n round in ma mind."

"You could be gettin' the car," she said.

"Oh, yes, right away, baby."

He started round to the shed, limping heavily on his bad leg. There were three frizzly chickens in the yard. All his other chickens had been killed or stolen recently. But the frizzly chickens had been saved somehow. That was fortunate indeed, for these curious creatures had a way of devouring "poison" from the yard and in that way protecting against conjure and black luck and spells. But even the frizzly chickens seemed now to be in a stupor. Jeff thought they had some ailment; he expected all three of them to die shortly.

The shed in which the old T-model Ford stood was only a grass roof held up by four corner poles. It had been built by tremulous hands at a time when the little rattletrap car had been regarded as a peculiar treasure. And, miraculously, despite wind and downpour it still stood.

Jeff adjusted the crank and put his weight upon it. The engine came to life with a sputter and bang that rattled the old car from radiator to taillight. Jeff hopped into the seat and put his foot on the accelerator. The sputtering and banging increased. The rattling became more violent. That was good. It was good banging, good sputtering and rattling, and it meant that the aged car was still in running condition. She could be depended on for this trip.

Again Jeff's thought halted as if paralyzed. The suggestion of the trip fell into the machinery of his mind like a wrench. He felt dazed and weak. He swung the car out into the yard, made a half turn, and drove around to the front door. When he took his hands off the wheel, he noticed that he was trembling violently. He cut off the motor and climbed to the ground to wait for Jennie.

A few minutes later she was at the window, her voice rattling against the pane like a broken shutter.

"I'm ready, Jeff."

He did not answer, but limped into the house and took her by the arm. He led her slowly through the big room, down the step, and across the yard.

"You reckon I'd oughta lock the do'?" he asked softly.

They stopped and Jennie weighed the question. Finally she shook her head. "Ne' mind the do'," she said. "I don't see no cause to lock up things."

"You right," Jeff agreed. "No cause to lock up."

Jeff opened the door and helped his wife into the car. A quick shudder passed over him. Jesus! Again he trembled.

"How come you shaking so?" Jennie whispered.

"I don't know," he said.

"You mus' be scairt, Jeff."

"No, baby, I ain't scairt."

He slammed the door after her and went around to crank up again. The motor started easily. Jeff wished that it had not been so responsive. He would have liked a few more minutes in which to turn things around in his head. As it was, with Jennie chiding him about being afraid, he had to keep going. He swung the car into the little pencil-mark road and started off toward the river, driving very slowly, very cautiously.

Chugging across the green countryside, the small battered Ford seemed tiny indeed. Jeff felt a familiar excitement, a thrill, as they came down the first slope to the immense levels on which the cotton was growing. He could not help reflecting that the crops were good. He knew what that meant, too; he had made forty-five of them with his own hands. It was true that he had worn out nearly a dozen mules, but that was the fault of Old Man Stevenson, the owner of the land. Major Stevenson had the odd notion that one mule was all a share farmer needed to work a thirty-acre plot. It was an expensive notion, the way it killed mules from overwork, but the old man held to it. Jeff thought it killed a good many share farmers as well as mules, but he had no sympathy for them. He had always been strong, and he had been taught to have no patience with weakness in men. Women or children might be tolerated if they were puny, but a weak man was a curse. Of course, his own children—

Jeff's thought halted there. He and Jennie never mentioned their dead children any more. And naturally he did not wish to dwell upon them in his mind. Before he knew it, some remark would slip out of his mouth and that would make Jennie feel blue. Perhaps she would cry. A woman like Jennie could not easily throw off the grief that comes from losing five grown children within two years. Even Jeff was still staggered by the blow. His memory had not been much good recently. He frequently talked to himself. And, although he had kept it a secret, he knew that his courage had left him. He was terrified by the least unfamiliar sound at night. He was reluctant to venture far from home in the daytime. And that habit of trembling when he felt fearful was now far beyond his control. Sometimes he became afraid and trembled without knowing what had frightened him. The feeling would just come over him like a chill.

The car rattled slowly over the dusty road. Jennie sat erect and silent, with a little absurd hat pinned to her hair. Her useless eyes seemed very large, very white in their deep sockets. Suddenly Jeff heard her voice, and he inclined his head to catch the words.

"Is we passed Delia Moore's house yet?" she asked.

"Not yet," he said.

"You must be drivin' mighty slow, Jeff."

"We might just as well take our time, baby."

There was a pause. A little puff of steam was coming out of the radiator of the car. Heat wavered above the hood. Delia Moore's house was nearly half a mile away. After a moment Jennie spoke again.

"You ain't really scairt, is you, Jeff?"

"Nah, baby, I ain't scairt."

"You know how we agreed—we gotta keep on goin'."

Jewels of perspiration appeared on Jeff's forehead. His eyes rounded, blinked, became fixed on the road.

"I don't know," he said with a shiver. "I reckon it's the only thing to do."

"Hm."

A flock of guinea fowls, pecking in the road, were scattered by the passing car. Some of them took to their wings; others hid under bushes. A blue jay, swaying on a leafy twig, was annoying a roadside squirrel. Jeff held an even speed till he came near Delia's place. Then he slowed down noticeably.

Delia's house was really no house at all, but an abandoned store building converted into a dwelling. It sat near a crossroads, beneath a single black cedar tree. There Delia, a cattish old creature of Jennie's age, lived alone. She had been there more years than anybody could remember, and long ago had won the disfavor of such women as Jennie. For in her young days Delia had been gayer, yellower, and saucier than seemed proper in those parts. Her ways with menfolks had been dark and suspicious. And the fact that she had had as many husbands as children did not help her reputation.

"Yonder's old Delia," Jeff said as they passed.

"What she doin'?"

"Jes sittin' in the do'," he said.

"She see us?"

"Hm," Jeff said. "Musta did."

That relieved Jennie. It strengthened her to know that her old enemy had seen her pass in her best clothes. That would give the old she-devil something to chew her gums and fret about, Jennie thought. Wouldn't she have a fit if she didn't find out? Old evil Delia! This would be just the thing for her. It would pay her back for being so evil. It would also pay her, Jennie thought, for the way she used to grin at Jeff—long ago when her teeth were good.

The road became smooth and red, and Jeff could tell by the smell of the air that they were nearing the river. He could see the rise where the road turned and ran along parallel to the stream. The car chugged on monotonously. After a long silent spell, Jennie leaned against Jeff and spoke.

"How many bale o' cotton you think we got standin'?" she said.

Jeff wrinkled his forehead as he calculated.

"'Bout twenty-five, I reckon."

"How many you make las' year?"

"Twenty-eight," he said. "How come you ask that?"

"I's jes thinkin'," Jennie said quietly.

"It don't make a speck o' difference though," Jeff reflected. "If we get much or if we get little, we still gonna be in debt to Old Man Stevenson when he gets through counting up agin us. It's took us a long time to learn that."

Jennie was not listening to these words. She had fallen into a trancelike meditation. Her lips twitched. She chewed her gums and rubbed her gnarled hands nervously. Suddenly she leaned forward, buried her face in the nervous hands, and burst into tears. She cried aloud in a dry cracked voice that suggested the rattle of fodder on dead stalks. She cried aloud like a child, for she had never learned to suppress a genuine sob. Her slight old frame shook heavily and seemed hardly able to sustain such violent grief.

"What's the matter, baby?" Jeff asked awkwardly. "Why you cryin' like all that?"

"I's jes thinkin'," she said.

"So you the one what's scairt now, hunh?"

"I ain't scairt, Jeff. I's jes thinkin' 'bout leavin' eve'thing like this— eve'thing we been used to. It's right sad-like."

Jeff did not answer, and presently Jennie buried her face again and cried.

The sun was almost overhead. It beat down furiously on the dusty wagon-path road, on the parched roadside grass and the tiny battered car. Jeff's hands, gripping the wheel, became wet with perspiration; his forehead sparkled. Jeff's lips parted. His mouth shaped a hideous grimace. His face suggested the face of a man being burned. But the torture passed and his expression softened again.

"You mustn't cry, baby," he said to his wife. "We gotta be strong. We can't break down."

Jennie waited a few seconds, then said, "You reckon we oughta do it, Jeff? You reckon we oughta go 'head an' do it, really?"

Jeff's voice choked; his eyes blurred. He was terrified to hear Jennie say the thing that had been in his mind all morning. She had egged him on when he had wanted more than anything in the world to wait, to reconsider, to think things over a little longer. Now she was getting cold feet. Actually there was no need of thinking the question through again. It would only end in making the same painful decision once more. Jeff knew that. There was no need of fooling around longer.

"We jes as well to do like we planned," he said. "They ain't nothin' else for us now—it's the bes' thing."

Jeff thought of the handicaps, the near impossibility, of making another crop with his leg bothering him more and more each week. Then there was always the chance that he would have another stroke, like the one that had made him lame. Another one might kill him. The least it could do would be to leave him helpless. Jeff gasped—Lord, Jesus! He could not bear to think of being helpless, like a baby, on Jennie's hands. Frail, blind Jennie.

The little pounding motor of the car worked harder and harder. The puff of steam from the cracked radiator became larger. Jeff realized that they were climbing a little rise. A moment later the road turned abruptly and he looked down upon the face of the river.

"Jeff."

"Hunh?"

"Is that the water I hear?"

"Hm. Tha's it."

"Well, which way you goin' now?"

"Down this-a way," he said. "The road runs 'long 'side o' the water a lil piece."

She waited awhile calmly. Then she said, "Drive faster."

"A'right, baby," Jeff said.

The water roared in the bed of the river. It was fifty or sixty feet below the level of the road. Between the road and the water there was a long smooth slope, sharply inclined. The slope was dry, the clay hardened by prolonged summer heat. The water below, roaring in a narrow channel, was noisy and wild.

"Jeff."

"Hunh?"

"How far you goin'?"

"Jes a lil piece down the road."

"You ain't scairt, is you, Jeff?"

"Nah, baby," he said trembling. "I ain't scairt."

"Remember how we planned it, Jeff. We gotta do it like we said. Brave-like."

"Hm."

Jeff's brain darkened. Things suddenly seemed unreal, like figures in a dream. Thoughts swam in his mind foolishly, hysterically, like little blind fish in a pool within a dense cave. They rushed, crossed one another, jostled, collided, retreated, and rushed again. Jeff soon became dizzy. He shuddered violently and turned to his wife.

"Jennie, I can't do it. I can't." His voice broke pitifully.

She did not appear to be listening. All the grief had gone from her face. She sat erect, her unseeing eyes wide open, strained and frightful. Her glossy black skin had become dull. She seemed as thin, as sharp and bony, as a starved bird. Now, having suffered and endured the sadness of tearing herself away from beloved things, she showed no anguish. She was absorbed with her own thoughts, and she didn't even hear Jeff's voice shouting in her ear.

Jeff said nothing more. For an instant there was light in his cavernous brain. The great chamber was, for less than a second, peopled by characters he knew and loved. They were simple, healthy creatures, and they behaved in a manner that he could understand. They had quality. But since he had already taken leave of them long ago, the remembrance did not break his heart again. Young Jeff

Patton was among them, the Jeff Patton of fifty years ago who went down to New Orleans with a crowd of country boys to the Mardi Gras doings. The gay young crowd, boys with candy-striped shirts and roughed-brown girls in noisy silks, was like a picture in his head. Yet it did not make him sad. On that very trip Slim Burns had killed Joe Beasley—the crowd had been broken up. Since then Jeff Patton's world had been the Greenbriar Plantation. If there had been other Mardi Gras carnivals, he had not heard of them. Since then there had been no time; the years had fallen on him like waves. Now he was old, worn out. Another paralytic stroke (like the one he had already suffered) would put him on his back for keeps. In that condition, with a frail blind woman to look after him, he would be worse off than if he were dead.

Suddenly Jeff's hands became steady. He actually felt brave. He slowed down the motor of the car and carefully pulled off the road. Below, the water of the stream boomed, a soft thunder in the deep channel. Jeff ran the car onto the clay slope, pointed it directly toward the stream, and put his foot heavily on the accelerator. The little car leaped furiously down the steep incline toward the water. The movement was nearly as swift and direct as a fall. The two old black folks, sitting quietly side by side, showed no excitement. In another instant the car hit the water and dropped immediately out of sight.

A little later it lodged in the mud of a shallow place. One wheel of the crushed and upturned little Ford became visible above the rushing water.

Miss Cynthie

Rudolph Fisher

1933

For the first time in her life somebody had called her "madam." She had been standing, bewildered but unafraid, while innumerable Red Caps appropriated piece after piece of the baggage arrayed on the platform. Neither her brief seventy years' journey through life nor her long two days' travel northward had dimmed the live brightness of her eyes, which, for all their bewilderment, had accurately selected her own treasures out of the row of luggage and guarded them vigilantly. "These yours, madam?"

The biggest Red Cap of all was smiling at her. He looked for all the world like Doc Crinshaw's oldest son back home. Her little brown face relaxed; she smiled back at him.

"They got to be. You all done took all the others."

He laughed aloud. Then—"Carry 'em for you?"

She contemplated his bulk. "Reckon you can manage it—puny little feller like you?"

Thereupon they were friends. Still grinning broadly, he surrounded himself with her impedimenta, the enormous brown extension case on one shoulder, the big straw suitcase in the opposite hand, the carpetbag under one arm. She herself held fast to the umbrella. "Always like to have sump'm in my hand when I walk. Can't never tell when you'll run across a snake."

"There aren't any snakes in the city."

"There's snakes everywhere, chile."

They began the tedious hike up the interminable platform. She was small and quick. Her carriage was surprisingly erect, her gait astonishingly spry. She said:

"You liked to took my breath back yonder, boy, callin' me 'madam.' Back home everybody call me 'Miss Cynthie.' Even their chillun. Black folks, white folks too. 'Miss Cynthie.' Well, when you come up with that 'madam' o' yourn, I say to myself, 'Now, I wonder who that chile's a-grinnin' at? "Madam" stands for mist'ess o' the house, and I sho' ain' mist'ess o' nothin' in this hyeh New York.' "

"Well, you see, we call everybody 'madam.' "

"Everybody? Hm." The bright eyes twinkled. "Seem like that'd worry me some—if I was a man."

He acknowledged his slip and observed, "I see this isn't your first trip to New York."

"First trip any place, son. First time I been over fifty miles from Waxhaw. Only travelin' I've done is in my head. Ain' seen many places, but I's seen a passel o' people. Reckon places is pretty much alike after people been in 'em awhile."

"Yes, ma'am. I guess that's right."

"You ain' no reg'lar bag-toter, is you?"

"Ma'am?"

"You talk too good."

"Well, I only do this in vacation time. I'm still in school."

"You is. What you aimin' to be?"

"I'm studying medicine."

"You is?" She beamed. "Aimin' to be a doctor, huh? Thank the Lord for that. That's what I always wanted my David to be. My grandchile hyeh in New York. He's to meet me hyeh now."

"I bet you'll have a great time."

"Mussn't bet, chile. That's sinful. I tole him 'for' he left home, I say, 'Son, you the only one o' the chillun what's got a chance to amount to sump'm. Don't th'ow it away. Be a preacher or a doctor. Work yo' way up and don' stop short. If the Lord don' see fit for you to doctor the soul, then doctor the body. If you don't get to be a reg'lar doctor, be a tooth doctor. If you jes' can't make that, be a foot doctor. And if you don't get that fur, be a undertaker. That's the least you must be. That ain' so bad. Keep you acquainted with the house of the Lord. Always mind the house o' the Lord—whatever you do, do like a church steeple: aim high and go straight.' "

"Did he get to be a doctor?"

"Don' b'lieve he did. Too late startin', I reckon. But he's done succeeded at sump'm. Mus' be at least a undertaker, 'cause he started sendin' the home folks money, and he come home las' year dressed like Judge Pettiford's boy what went off to school in Virginia. Wouldn't tell none of us 'zackly what he was doin', but he said he wouldn't never be happy till I come and see for myself. So hyeh I is." Something softened her voice. "His mammy died befo' he knowed her. But he was always sech a good chile—" The something was apprehension. "Hope he is a undertaker."

They were mounting a flight of steep stairs leading to an exit gate, about which clustered a few people still hoping to catch sight of arriving friends.

Among these a tall young brown-skinned man in a light gray suit suddenly waved his panama and yelled, "Hey, Miss Cynthie!"

Miss Cynthie stopped, looked up, and waved back with a delighted umbrella. The Red Cap's eyes lifted too. His lower jaw sagged.

"Is that your grandson?"

"It sho' is," she said and distanced him for the rest of the climb. The grandson, with an abandonment that superbly ignored onlookers, folded the little woman in an exultant, smothering embrace. As soon as she could, she pushed him off with breathless mock impatience.

"Go 'way, you fool, you. Aimin' to squeeze my soul out my body befo' I can get a look at this place?" She shook herself into the semblance of composure. "Well. You don't look hungry, anyhow."

"Ho-ho! Miss Cynthie in New York! Can y' imagine this? Come on. I'm parked on Eighth Avenue."

The Red Cap delivered the outlandish luggage into a robin's-egg-blue open Packard with scarlet wheels, accepted the grandson's dollar and smile, and stood watching the car roar away up Eighth Avenue.

Another Red Cap came up. "Got a break, hey, boy?"

"Dave Tappen himself—can you beat that?"

"The old lady hasn't seen the station yet—starin' at him."

"That's not the half of it, bozo. That's Dave Tappen's grandmother. And what do you s'pose she hopes?"

"What?"

"She hopes that Dave has turned out to be a successful undertaker!"

"Undertaker? Undertaker!"

They stared at each other a gaping moment, then doubled up with laughter.

"Look—through there—that's the Chrysler Building. Oh, hellelujah! I meant to bring you up Broadway—"

"David—"

"Ma'am?"

"This hyeh wagon yourn?"

"Nobody else's. Sweet buggy, ain't it?"

"David—you ain't turned out to be one of them moonshiners, is you?"

"Moonshiners? Moon—Ho! No indeed, Miss Cynthie. I got a better racket 'n that."

"Better which?"

"Game. Business. Pick-up."

"Tell me, David. What is yo' racket?"

"Can't spill it yet, Miss Cynthie. Rather show you. Tomorrow night you'll know the worst. Can you make out till tomorrow night?"

"David, you know I always wanted you to be a doctor, even if 'twasn' nothin' but a foot doctor. The very leas' I wanted you to be was a undertaker."

"Undertaker! Oh, Miss Cynthie!—with my sunny disposition?"

"Then you ain' even a undertaker?"

"Listen, Miss Cynthie. Just forget 'bout what I am for a while. Must till tomorrow night. I want you to see for yourself. Tellin' you will spoil it. Now stop askin', you hear?—because I'm not answerin', I'm surprisin' you. And don't expect anybody you meet to tell you. It'll mess up the whole works. Understand? Now give the big city a break. There's the elevated train going up Columbus Avenue. Ain't that hot stuff?"

Miss Cynthie looked. "Humph!" she said. "'Tain' half high as that trestle two mile from Waxhaw."

She thoroughly enjoyed the ride up Central Park West. The stagger lights, the extent of the park, the high, close, kingly buildings, remarkable because their stoves cooled them in summer as well as heated them in winter, all drew nods of mild interest. But what gave her special delight was not these: it was that David's car so effortlessly sped past the headlong drove of vehicles racing northward.

They stopped for a red light; when they started again their machine leaped forward with a triumphant eagerness that drew from her an unsuppressed "Hot you, David! That's it!"

He grinned appreciatively. "Why, you're a regular New Yorker already."

"New York nothin'! I done the same thing fifty years ago—befo' I knowed they was a New York."

"What!"

" 'Deed so. Didn' I use to tell you 'bout my young mare, Betty? Chile, I'd hitch Betty up to yo' grandpa's buggy and pass anything on the road. Betty never knowed what another horse's dust smelt like. No 'ndeedy. Shuh, boy, this ain' nothin' new to me. Why that broke-down Fo'd you Uncle Jake's got ain' nothin'—nothin' but a sorry mess. Done got so slow I jes' won' ride in it—I declare I'd rather walk. But this hyeh thing, now, this is right nice." She settled back in complete, complacent comfort, and they sped on, swift and silent.

Suddenly she sat erect with abrupt discovery.

"David—well—bless my soul!"

"What's the matter, Miss Cynthie?"

Then he saw what had caught her attention. They were traveling up Seventh Avenue now, and something was miraculously different. Not the road; that was as broad as ever, wide, white, gleaming in the sun. Not the houses; they were lofty still, lordly, disdainful, supercilious. Not the cars; they continued to race impatiently onward, innumerable, precipitate, tumultuous. Something else, something at once obvious and subtle, insistent, pervasive, compelling.

"David—this mus' be Harlem!"

"Good Lord, Miss Cynthie!"

"Don' use the name of the Lord in vain, David."

"But I mean—gee!—you're no fun at all. You get everything before a guy can tell you."

"You got plenty to tell me, David. But don' nobody need to tell me this. Look a yonder."

Not just a change of complexion. A completely dissimilar atmosphere. Sidewalks teeming with leisurely strollers, at once strangely dark and bright. Boys in white trousers, berets, and green shirts, with slickened black heads and proud swagger. Bareheaded girls in crisp organdie dresses, purple, canary, gay scarlet. And laughter, abandoned strong Negro laughter, some falling full on the ear, some not heard at all, yet sensed—the warm life-breath of the tireless carnival to which Harlem's heart quickens in summer.

"This is it," admitted David. "Get a good eyeful. Here's 125th Street—regular little Broadway. And here's the Alhambra, and up ahead we'll pass the Lafayette."

"What's them?"

"Theaters."

"Theaters? Theaters. Humph! Look, David, is that a colored folks' church?" They were passing a fine gray-stone edifice.

"That? Oh. Sure it is. So's this one on this side."

"No! Well, ain' that fine? Splendid big church like that for colored folks."

Taking his cue from this, her first tribute to the city he said, "You ain't seen nothing yet. Wait a minute."

They swung left through a side street and turned right on a boulevard. "What do you think o' that?" And he pointed to the quarter-million-dollar St. Mark's.

"That a colored church, too?"

" 'Tain' no white one. And they built it themselves, you know. Nobody's hand-me-down gift."

She heaved a great happy sigh. "Oh, yes, it was a gift, David. It was a gift from on high." Then, "Look a hyeh—which a one you belong to?"

"Me? Why, I don't belong to any—that is, none o' these. Mine's over in another section. Y'see, mine's Baptist. These are all Methodist. See?"

"Mm. Uh-huh. I see."

They circled a square and slipped into a quiet narrow street overlooking a park, stopping before the tallest of the apartment houses in the single commanding row.

Alighting, Miss Cynthie gave this imposing structure one sidewise, upward glance, and said, "Y'all live like bees in a hive, don't y'? I boun' the women does all the work, too." A moment later, "So this is a elevator? Feel like I'm glory-bound sho' nuff."

Along a tiled corridor and into David's apartment. Rooms leading into rooms. Luxurious couches, easy chairs, a brown-walnut grand piano, gay-shaded floor lamps, paneled walls, deep rugs, treacherous glass-wood floors—and a smiling golden-skinned girl in a gingham housedress, approaching with out-stretched hands.

"This is Ruth, Miss Cynthie."

"Miss Cynthie!" said Ruth.

They clasped hands. "Been wantin' to see David's girl ever since he first wrote us 'bout her."

"Come—here's your room this way. Here's the bath. Get out of your things and get comfy. You must be worn out with the trip."

"Worn out? Worn out? Shuh. How you gon' get worn out on a train? Now if 'twas a horse, maybe, or Jake's no-count Fo'd—but a train—didn't but one thing bother me on that train."

"What?"

"When the man made them beds down, I jes' couldn' manage to undress same as home. Why, s'posin' sump'm bus' the train open, where'd you be? Naked as a jaybird in dewberry time."

David took in her things and left her to get comfortable. He returned, and Ruth, despite his reassuring embrace, whispered:

"Dave, you can't fool old folks—why don't you go ahead and tell her about yourself? Think of the shock she's going to get—at her age."

David shook his head. "She'll get over the shock if she's there looking on. If we just told her, she'd never understand. We've got to railroad her into it. Then she'll be happy."

"She's nice. But she's got the same ideas as all old folks—"

"Yeah—but with her you can change 'em. Specially if everything is really all right. I know her. She's for church and all, but she believes in good times too, if they're right. Why, when I was a kid—" He broke off. "Listen!"

Miss Cynthie's voice came quite distinctly to them, singing a jaunty little rhyme:

"Oh I danced with the gal with the hole in her stockin'
And her toe kep' a-kickin' and her heel kep' a-knockin'—

Come up, Jesse, and get a drink o' gin,
'Cause you near to heaven as you'll ever get ag'in'."

"She taught me that when I wasn't knee-high to a cricket," David said. Miss Cynthie still sang softly and merrily:

"Then I danced with the gal with the dimple in her cheek,
And if she'd 'a' kep' a-smilin', I'd 'a' danced for a week—"

"God forgive me," prayed Miss Cynthie as she discovered David's purpose the following night. She let him and Ruth lead her, like an early Christian martyr, into the Lafayette Theater. The blinding glare of the lobby produced a merciful self-anesthesia, and she entered the sudden dimness of the interior as involuntarily as in a dream. . . .

Attendants outdid each other for Mr. Dave Tappen. She heard him tell them, "Fix us up till we go on," and found herself sitting between Ruth and David in the front row of a lower box. A miraculous device of the devil, a motion picture that talked, was just ending. At her feet the orchestra was assembling. The motion picture faded out amid a scattered round of applause. Lights blazed and the orchestra burst into an ungodly rumpus.

She looked out over the seated multitude, scanning row upon row of illumined faces: black faces, white faces, yellow, tan, brown; bald heads, bobbed heads, kinky and straight heads; and upon every countenance, expectancy— scowling expectancy in this case, smiling in that, complacent here, amused there, commentative elsewhere, but everywhere suspense, abeyance, anticipa- tion.

Half a dozen people were ushered down the nearer aisle to reserved seats in the second row. Some of them caught sight of David and Ruth and waved to them. The chairs immediately behind them in the box were being shifted. "Hello, Tap!" Miss Cynthie saw David turn, rise, and shake hands with two men. One of them was large, bald, and pink, emanating good cheer; the other short, thin, sallow, with thick black hair and a sour mien. Ruth also acknowl- edged their greeting. "This is my grandmother," David said proudly. "Miss Cynthie, meet my managers, Lou and Lee Goldman." "Pleased to meet you," managed Miss Cynthie. "Great lad, this boy of yours," said Lou Goldman. "Great little partner he's got, too," added Lee. They also settled back expec- tantly.

"Here we go!"

The curtain rose to reveal a cotton field at dawn. Pickers in blue denim overalls, bandannas, and wide-brimmed straws, or in gingham aprons and sun- bonnets, were singing as they worked. Their voices, from clearest soprano to richest bass, blended in low concordances, first simply humming a series of harmonies, until, gradually, came words, like figures forming in mist. As the sound grew, the mist cleared, the words came round and full, and the sun rose, bringing light as if in answer to the song. The chorus swelled, the radiance grew, the two, as if emanating from a single source, fused their crescendos, till at last they achieved a joint transcendence of tonal and visual brightness.

"Swell opener," said Lee Goldman.

"Ripe," agreed Lou.

David and Ruth arose. "Stay here and enjoy the show, Miss Cynthie. You'll see us again in a minute."

"Go to it, kids," said Lou Goldman

"Yeah—burn 'em up." said Lee.

Miss Cynthie hardly noted that she had been left, so absorbed was she in the spectacle. To her, the theater had always been the antithesis of church. As the one was the refuge of righteousness, so the other was the stronghold of transgression. But this first scene awakened memories, captured and held her attention by offering a blend of truth and novelty. Having thus baited her interest, the show now proceeded to play it like the trout through swift-flowing waters of wickedness. Resist as it might, her mind was caught and drawn into the impious subsequences.

The very music that had just rounded out so majestically now distorted itself into ragtime. The singers came forward and turned to dancers; boys, a crazy swaying background, threw up their arms and kicked out their legs in a rhythmic jamboree; girls, an agile brazen foreground, caught their skirts up to their hips and displayed their copper calves, knees, thighs, in shameless, incredible steps. Miss Cynthie turned dismayed eyes upon the audience, to discover that mob of sinners devouring it all with fond satisfaction. Then the dancers separated and with final abandon flung themselves off the stage in both directions.

Lee Goldman commented through the applause, "They work easy, them babies."

"Yeah," said Lou. "Savin' the hot stuff for later."

Two black-faced cotton pickers appropriated the scene, indulging in dialogue that their hearers found uproarious.

"Ah'm tired."

"Ah'm hongry."

"Dis job jes' wears me out."

"Starves me to death."

"Ah'm so tired—you know what Ah'd like to do?"

"What?"

"Ah'd like to go to sleep and dream I was sleepin'."

"What good dat do?"

"Den I could wake up and still be 'sleep."

"Well, y'know what Ah'd like to do?"

"No. What?"

"Ah'd like to swaller me a hog and a hen."

"What good dat do?"

"Den Ah'd always be full o' ham and eggs."

"Ham? Shuh. Don't you know a hog has to be smoked 'fo' he's a ham?"

"Well, if I swaller him, he'll have a smoke all around him, won't he?"

Presently Miss Cynthie was smiling like everyone else, but her smile soon fled. For the comics departed, and the dancing girls returned, this time in scant travesties on their earlier voluminous costumes—tiny sunbonnets perched jauntily on one side of their glistening bobs, bandannas reduced to scarlet neck ribbons, waists mere brassieres, skirts mere gingham sashes.

And now Miss Cynthie's whole body stiffened with a new and surpassing shock; her bright eyes first widened with unbelief, then slowly grew dull with misery. In the midst of a sudden great volley of applause her grandson had broken through that bevy of agile wantons and begun to sing.

He too was dressed as a cotton picker, but a Beau Brummel among cotton pickers; his hat bore a pleated green band, his bandanna was silk, his overalls blue satin, his shoes black patent leather. His eyes flashed, his teeth gleamed, his body swayed, his arms waved, his words came fast and clear. As he sang, his companions danced a concerted tap, uniformly wild, ecstatic. When he stopped singing, he himself began to dance and, without sacrificing crispness of execution, seemed to absorb into himself every measure of the energy which the girls, now merely standing off and swaying, had relinquished.

"Look at that boy go," said Lee Goldman.

"He ain't started yet," said Lou.

But surrounding comment, Dave's virtuosity, the eager enthusiasm of the audience were all alike lost on Miss Cynthie. She sat with stricken eyes watching this boy whom she'd raised from a babe, taught right from wrong, brought up in the church, and endowed with her prayers, this child whom she had dreamed of seeing a preacher, a regular doctor, a tooth doctor, a foot doctor, at the very least an undertaker—sat watching him disport himself for the benefit of a sin-sick, flesh-hungry mob of lost souls, not one of whom knew or cared to know the loving kindness of God; sat watching a David she'd never foreseen, turned tool of the devil, disciple of lust, unholy prince among sinners.

For a long time she sat there watching with wretched eyes, saw portrayed on the stage David's arrival in Harlem, his escape from "old friends" who tried to dupe him; saw him working as a trap drummer in a nightclub, where he fell in love with Ruth, a dancer; not the gentle Ruth Miss Cynthie knew, but a wild and shameless young savage who danced like seven devils—in only a girdle and breastplates; saw the two of them join in a song-and-dance act that eventually made them Broadway headliners, an act presented *in toto* as the pre-finale of this show. And not any of the melodies, not any of the sketches, not all the comic philosophy of the tired-and-hungry duo, gave her figure a moment's relaxation or brightened the dull defeat in her staring eyes. She sat apart, alone in the box, the symbol, the epitome of supreme failure. Let the rest of the theater be riotous, clamoring for more and more of Dave Tappen, "Tap," the greatest tapster of all time, idol of uptown and downtown New York. For her, they were lauding simply an exhibition of sin which centered about her David.

"This'll run a year on Broadway," said Lee Goldman.

"Then we'll take it to Paris."

Encores and curtains with Ruth, and at last David came out on the stage alone. The clamor dwindled. And now he did something quite unfamiliar to even the most consistent of his followers. Softly, delicately, he begun to tap a routine designed to fit a particular song. When he had established the rhythm, he began to sing the song:

> "Oh I danced with the gal with the hole in her stockin'
> And her toe kep' a-kickin' and her heel kep' a-knockin'—
>
> Come up, Jesse, and get a drink o' gin,
> 'Cause you near to heaven as you'll ever get ag'in'—"

As he danced and sang this song, frequently smiling across at Miss Cynthie, a visible change transformed her. She leaned forward incredulously, listened intently, then settled back in limp wonder. Her bewildered eyes turned on the crowd, on those serried rows of shriftless sinners. And she found in their faces now an overwhelming curious thing: a grin, a universal grin, a gleeful and sinless grin such as not the nakedest chorus in the performance had produced. In a few seconds, with her own song, David had dwarfed into unimportance, wiped off their faces, swept out of their minds every trace of what had seemed to be sin; had reduced it all to mere trivial detail and revealed these revelers as a crowd of children, enjoying the guileless antics of another child. And Miss Cynthie whispered:

"Bless my soul! They didn' mean nothin'. . . . They jes' didn' see no harm in it—"

> "Then I danced with the gal with the dimple in her cheek,
> And if she'd 'a' kep' a-smilin', I'd 'a' danced for a week—
> "Come up, Jesse—"

The crowd laughed, clapped their hands, whistled. Someone threw David a bright yellow flower. "From Broadway!"

He caught the flower. A hush fell. He said:

"I'm really happy tonight, folks. Y'see this flower? Means success, don't it? Well, listen. The one who is really responsible for my success is here tonight with me. Now what do you think o' that?"

The hush deepened.

"Y'know, folks, I'm sump'm like Adam—I never had no mother. But I've got a grandmother. Down home everybody calls her Miss Cynthie. And everybody loves her. Take that song I just did for you. Miss Cynthie taught me that when I wasn't knee-high to a cricket. But that wasn't all she taught me. Far back as I can remember, she used to always say one thing: Son, do like a church steeple—aim high and go straight. And for doin' it"—he grinned, contemplating the flower—"I get this."

He strode across to the edge of the stage that touched Miss Cynthie's box. He held up the flower.

"So y'see, folks, this isn't mine. It's really Miss Cynthie's." He leaned over to hand it to her. Miss Cynthie's last trace of doubt was swept away. She drew a deep breath of revelation; her bewilderment vanished, her redoubtable composure returned, her eyes lighted up; and no one but David, still holding the flower toward her, heard her sharply whispered reprimand:

"Keep it, you fool. Where's yo' manners—givin' 'way what somebody give you?"

David grinned.

"Take it, tyro. What you tryin' to do—crab my act?"

Thereupon, Miss Cynthie, smiling at him with bright, meaningful eyes, leaned over without rising from her chair, jerked a tiny twig off the stem of the flower, then sat decisively back, resolutely folding her arms, with only a leaf in her hand.

"This'll do me," she said.

The finale didn't matter. People filed out of the theater. Miss Cynthie sat awaiting her children, her foot absently patting time to the orchestra's jazz recessional. Perhaps she was thinking, God moves in a mysterious way, but her lips were unquestionably forming the words:

—danced with the gal—hole in her stockin'—
—toe kep' a-kickin'—heel kep' a-knockin'.

The Gilded Six-Bits

Zora Neale Hurston

1933

It was a Negro yard around a Negro house in a Negro settlement that looked to the payroll of the G and G Fertilizer works for its support.

But there was something happy about the place. The front yard was parted in the middle by a sidewalk from gate to doorstep, a sidewalk edged on either side by quart bottles driven neck down into the ground on a slant. A mess of homey flowers planted without a plan but blooming cheerily from their helter-skelter places. The fence and house were whitewashed. The porch and steps scrubbed white.

The front door stood open to the sunshine so that the floor of the front room could finish drying after its weekly scouring. It was Saturday. Everything clean from the front gate to the privy house. Yard raked so that the strokes of the rake would make a pattern. Fresh newspaper cut in fancy edge on the kitchen shelves.

Missie May was bathing herself in the galvanized washtub in the bedroom. Her dark-brown skin glistened under the soapsuds that skittered down from her washrag. Her stiff young breasts thrust forward aggressively like broad-based cones with the tips lacquered in black.

She heard men's voices in the distance and glanced at the dollar clock on the dresser.

"Humph! Ah'm way behind time t'day! Joe gointer be heah 'fore Ah git mah clothes on if Ah don't make haste."

She grabbed the clean meal sack at hand and dried herself hurriedly and began to dress. But before she could tie her slippers, there came the ring of singing metal on wood. Nine times.

Missie May grinned with delight. She had not seen the big tall man come stealing in the gate and creep up the walk grinning happily at the joyful mischief he was about to commit. But she knew that it was her husband throwing silver dollars in the door for her to pick up and pile beside her plate at dinner. It was this way every Saturday afternoon. The nine dollars hurled into the open door, he scurried to a hiding place behind the cape jasmine bush and waited.

Missie May promptly appeared at the door in mock alarm.

"Who dat chunkin' money in mah do'way?" she demanded. No answer from the yard. She leaped off the porch and began to search the shrubbery. She peeped under the porch and hung over the gate to look up and down the road. While she did this, the man behind the jasmine darted to the chinaberry tree. She spied him and gave chase.

"Nobody ain't gointer be chunkin' money at me and Ah not do 'em nothin'," she shouted in mock anger. He ran around the house with Missie May at his heels. She overtook him at the kitchen door. He ran inside but could not close it after him before she crowded in and locked with him in a rough-and-tumble. For several minutes the two were a furious mass of male and female energy. Shouting, laughing, twisting, turning, tussling, tickling each other in the ribs: Missie May clutching onto Joe and Joe trying, but not too hard, to get away.

"Missie May, take yo' hand out mah pocket!" Joe shouted out between laughs.

"Ah ain't, Joe, not lessen you gwine gimme whateve' it is good you got in yo' pocket. Turn it go, Joe, do Ah'll tear yo' clothes."

"Go on, tear 'em. You de one dat pushes de needles round heah. Move yo' hand, Missie May."

"Lemme git dat paper sack out yo' pocket. Ah bet it's candy kisses."

"Tain't. Move yo' hand. Woman ain't got no business in a man's clothes nohow. Go way."

Missie May gouged way down and gave an upward jerk and triumphed.

"Unhhunh! Ah got it. It 'tis so candy kisses. Ah knowed you had somethin' for me in yo' clothes. Now Ah got to see whut's in every pocket you got."

Joe smiled indulgently and let his wife go through all of his pockets and take out the things that he had hidden there for her to find. She bore off the chewing gum, the cake of sweet soap, the pocket handkerchief as if she had wrested them from him, as if they had not been bought for the sake of this friendly battle.

"Whew! dat play-fight done got me all warmed up!" Joe exclaimed. "Got me some water in de kittle?"

"Yo' water is on de fire and yo' clean things is 'cross de bed. Hurry up and wash yo'self and git changed so we kin eat. Ah'm hongry." As Missie said this, she bore the steaming kettle into the bedroom.

"You ain't hongry, sugar," Joe contradicted her. "Youse jes' a little empty. Ah'm de one whut's hongry. Ah could eat up camp meetin', back off 'ssociation, and drink Jurdan dry. Have it on de table when Ah git out de tub."

"Don't you mess wid mah business, man. You git in yo' clothes. Ah'm a real wife, not no dress-and-breath. Ah might not look lak one, but if you burn me, you won't git a thing but wife ashes."

Joe splashed in the bedroom and Missie May fanned around in the kitchen. A fresh red-and-white checked cloth on the table. Big pitcher of buttermilk beaded with pale drops of butter from the churn. Hot fried mullet, crackling bread, ham hock atop a mound of string beans and new potatoes, and perched on the windowsill a pone of spicy potato pudding.

Very little talk during the meal but that little consisted of banter that pretended to deny affection but in reality flaunted it. Like when Missie May reached for a second helping of the tater pone, Joe snatched it out of her reach.

After Missie May had made two or three unsuccessful grabs at the pan, she begged, "Aw, Joe, gimme some mo' dat tater pone."

"Nope, sweetenin' is for us menfolks. Y'all pritty lil frail eels don't need nothin' lak dis. You too sweet already."

"Please, Joe."

"Naw, naw. Ah don't want you to git no sweeter than whut you is already. We goin' down de road a lil piece t'night, so you go put on yo' Sunday-go-to-meetin' things."

Missie May looked at her husband to see if he was playing some prank. "Sho nuff, Joe?"

"Yeah. We goin' to de ice-cream parlor."

"Where de ice-cream parlor at, Joe?"

"A new man done come heah from Chicago and he done got a place and took and opened it up for a ice-cream parlor, and bein' as it's real swell, Ah wants you to be one de first ladies to walk in dere and have some set-down."

"Do Jesus, Ah ain't knowed nothin' 'bout it. Who de man done it?"

"Mister Otis D. Slemmons, of spots and places—Memphis, Chicago, Jacksonville, Philadelphia, and so on."

"Dat heavyset man wid his mouth full of gold teeths?"

"Yeah. Where did you see 'im at?"

"Ah went down to de sto' tuh git a box of lye and Ah seen 'im standin' on de corner talkin' to some of de mens, and Ah come on back and went to scrubbin' de floor, and he passed and tipped his hat whilst Ah was scourin' de steps. Ah thought, Ah never seen *him* befo'."

Joe smiled pleasantly. "Yeah, he's up-to-date. He got de finest clothes Ah ever seen on a colored man's back."

"Aw, he don't look no better in his clothes than you do in yourn. He got a puzzlegut on 'im and he so chuckle-headed, he got a pone behind his neck."

Joe looked down at his own abdomen and said wistfully, "Wisht Ah had a build on me lak he got. He ain't puzzle-gutted, honey. He jes' got a corporation. Dat make 'm look lak a rich white man. All rich mens is got some belly on 'em."

"Ah seen de pitchers of Henry Ford and he's a spare-built man, and Rockefeller look lak he ain't got but one gut. But Ford and Rockefeller and dis Slemmons and all de rest kin be as many-gutted as dey please. Ah'm satisfied wid you jes' lak you is, baby. God took pattern after a pine tree and built you noble. Youse a pritty man, and if Ah knowed any way to make you mo' pritty still Ah'd take and do it."

Joe reached over gently and toyed with Missie May's ear. "You jes' say dat cause you love me, but Ah know Ah can't hold no light to Otis D. Slemmons. Ah ain't never been nowhere and Ah ain't got nothin' but you."

Missie May got on his lap and kissed him and he kissed back in kind. Then he went on.

"All de womens is crazy 'bout 'im everywhere he go."

"How you know dat, Joe?"

"He tole us so hisself."

"Dat don't make it so. His mouf is cut crossways, ain't it? Well, he kin lie jes' lak anybody else."

"Good Lawd, Missie! You womens sho is hard to sense into things. He's got a five-dollar gold piece for a stickpin and he got a ten-dollar gold piece on his watch chain and his mouf is jes' crammed full of gold teeths. Sho wisht it wuz mine. And whut make it so cool, he got money 'cumulated. And womens give it all to 'im."

"Ah don't see whut de womens see on 'im. Ah wouldn't give 'im a wink if de sheriff wuz after 'im."

"Well, he tole us how de white womens in Chicago give 'im all dat gold money. So he don't 'low nobody to touch it at all. Not even put dey finger on it. Dey tole 'im not to. You kin make 'miration at it, but don't tetch it."

"Whyn't he stay up dere where dey so crazy 'bout 'im?"

"Ah reckon dey done made 'im vast-rich and he wants to travel some. He say dey wouldn't leave 'im hit a lick of work. He got mo' lady people crazy 'bout him than he kin shake a stick at."

"Joe, Ah hates to see you so dumb. Dat stray nigger jes' tell y'all anything and y'all b'lieve it."

"Go 'head on now, honey, and put on yo' clothes. He talkin' 'bout his pritty womens—Ah want 'im to see *mine.*"

Missie May went off to dress and Joe spent the time trying to make his stomach punch out like Slemmons' middle. He tried the rolling swagger of the stranger, but found that his tall bone-and-muscle stride fitted ill with it. He just had time to drop back into his seat before Missie May came in dressed to go.

On the way home that night Joe was exultant. "Didn't Ah say ole Otis was swell? Can't he talk Chicago talk? Wuzn't dat funny whut he said when great big fat ole Ida Armstrong come in? He asted me, 'Who is dat broad wid de forte shake?' Dat's a new word. Us always thought forty was a set of figgers but he showed us where it means a whole heap of things. Sometimes he don't say forty, he jes' say thirty-eight and two, and dat mean de same thing. Know whut he tole me when Ah wuz payin' for our ice cream? He say, 'Ah have to hand it to you, Joe. Dat wife of yours is jes' thirty-eight and two. Yessuh, she's forte!' Ain't he killin'?"

"He'll do in case of a rush. But he sho is got uh heap uh gold on 'im. Dat's de first time Ah ever seed gold money. It lookted good on him sho nuff, but it'd look a whole heap better on you."

"Who, me? Missie May, youse crazy! Where would a po' man lak me git gold money from?"

Missie May was silent for a minute, then she said, "Us might find some goin' long de road some time. Us could."

"Who would be losin' gold money round heah? We ain't even seen none dese white folks wearin' no gold money on dey watch chain. You must be figgerin' Mister Packard or Mister Cadillac goin' pass through heah."

"You don't know whut been lost 'round heah. Maybe somebody way back in memorial times lost they gold money and went on off and it ain't never been found. And then if we wuz to find it, you could wear some 'thout havin' no gang of womens lak dat Slemmons say he got."

Joe laughed and hugged her. "Don't be so wishful 'bout me. Ah'm satisfied de way Ah is. So long as Ah be yo' husband, Ah don't keer 'bout nothin' else. Ah'd ruther all de other womens in de world to be dead than for you to have de toothache. Less we go to bed and git our night rest."

It was Saturday night once more before Joe could parade his wife in Slemmons' ice-cream parlor again. He worked the night shift and Saturday was his only night off. Every other evening around six o'clock he left home, and dying dawn saw him hustling home around the lake where the challenging sun flung a flaming sword from east to west across the trembling water.

That was the best part of life—going home to Missie May. Their white-washed house, the mock battle on Saturday, the dinner and ice-cream parlor afterwards, church on Sunday nights when Missie outdressed any woman in town—all, everything was right.

One night around eleven the acid ran out at the G. and G. The foreman knocked off the crew and let the steam die down. As Joe rounded the lake on his way home, a lean moon rode the lake in a silver boat. If anybody had asked Joe about the moon on the lake, he would have said he hadn't paid it any attention. But he saw it with his feelings. It made him yearn painfully for Missie. Creation obsessed him. He thought about children. They had been married for more than a year now. They had money put away. They ought to be making little feet for shoes. A little boy child would be about right.

He saw a dim light in the bedroom and decided to come in through the kitchen door. He could wash the fertilizer dust off himself before presenting himself to Missie May. It would be nice for her not to know that he was there until he slipped into his place in bed and hugged her back. She always liked that.

He eased the kitchen door open slowly and silently, but when he went to set his dinner bucket on the table he bumped it into a pile of dishes, and something crashed to the floor. He heard his wife gasp in fright and hurried to reassure her.

"Iss me, honey. Don't get skeered."

There was a quick, large movement in the bedroom. A rustle, a thud, and a stealthy silence. The light went out.

What? Robbers? Murderers? Some varmint attacking his helpless wife, perhaps. He struck a match, threw himself on guard, and stepped over the doorsill into the bedroom.

The great belt on the wheel of Time slipped and eternity stood still. By the match light he could see the man's legs fighting with his breeches in his frantic desire to get them on. He had both chance and time to kill the intruder in his helpless condition—half in and half out of his pants—but he was too weak to take action. The shapeless enemies of humanity that live in the hours of Time had waylaid Joe. He was assaulted in his weakness, like Samson awakening after his haircut. So he just opened his mouth and laughed.

The match went out and he struck another and lit the lamp. A howling wind raced across his heart, but underneath its fury he heard his wife sobbing and Slemmons pleading for his life. Offering to buy it with all that he had. "Please, suh, don't kill me. Sixty-two dollars at de sto'. Gold money."

Joe just stood. Slemmons looked at the window, but it was screened. Joe stood out like a rough-backed mountain between him and the door. Barring him from escape, from sunrise, from life.

He considered a surprise attack upon the big clown that stood there laughing like a chessy cat. But before his fist could travel an inch, Joe's own rushed out to crush him like a battering ram. Then Joe stood over him.

"Git into yo' damn rags, Slemmons, and dat quick."

Slemmons scrambled to his feet and into his vest and coat. As he grabbed his hat, Joe's fury overrode his intentions and he grabbed at Slemmons with his left hand and struck at him with his right. The right landed. The left grazed the front of his vest. Slemmons was knocked a somersault into the kitchen and fled through the open door. Joe found himself alone with Missie May, with the golden watch charm clutched in his left fist. A short bit of broken chain dangled between his fingers.

Missie May was sobbing. Wails of weeping without words. Joe stood, and after a while he found out that he had something in his hand. And then he stood and felt without thinking and without seeing with his natural eyes. Missie May kept on crying and Joe kept on feeling so much and not knowing what to do with all his feelings, he put Slemmons' watch charm in his pants pocket and took a good laugh and went to bed.

"Missie May, whut you cryin' for?"

"Cause Ah love you so hard and Ah know you don't love *me* no mo'."

Joe sank his face into the pillow for a spell; then he said huskily, "You don't know de feelings of dat yet, Missie May."

"Oh, Joe, honey, he said he wuz gointer give me dat gold money and he jes' kept on after me—"

Joe was very still and silent for a long time. Then he said, "Well, don't cry no mo', Missie May. Ah got yo' gold piece for you."

The hours went past on their rusty ankles, Joe still and quiet on one bed rail and Missie May wrung dry of sobs on the other. Finally the sun's tide crept upon the shore of night and drowned all its hours. Missie May with her face stiff and streaked towards the window saw the dawn come into her yard. It was day. Nothing more. Joe wouldn't be coming home as usual. No need to fling open the front door and sweep off the porch, making it nice for Joe. Never no more breakfast to cook; no more washing and starching of Joe's jumper-jackets and pants. No more nothing. So why get up?

With this strange man in her bed, she felt embarrassed to get up and dress. She decided to wait till he had dressed and gone. Then she would get up, dress quickly, and be gone forever beyond reach of Joe's looks and laughs. But he never moved. Red light turned to yellow, then white.

From beyond the no-man's-land between them came a voice. A strange voice that yesterday had been Joe's.

"Missie May, ain't you gonna fix me no breakfus'?"

She sprang out of bed. "Yeah, Joe. Ah didn't reckon you wuz hongry."

No need to die today. Joe needed her for a few more minutes anyhow.

Soon there was a roaring fire in the cookstove. Water bucket full and two chickens killed. Joe loved fried chicken and rice. She didn't deserve a thing and good Joe was letting her cook him some breakfast. She rushed hot biscuits to the table as Joe took his seat.

He ate with his eyes in his plate. No laughter, no banter.

"Missie May, you ain't eatin' yo' breakfus'."

"Ah don't choose none, Ah thank yuh."

His coffee cup was empty. She sprang to refill it. When she turned from the stove and bent to set the cup beside Joe's plate, she saw the yellow coin on the table between them.

She slumped into her seat and wept into her arms.

Presently Joe said calmly, "Missie May, you cry too much. Don't look back lak Lot's wife aud turn to salt."

The sun, the hero of every day, the impersonal old man that beams as brightly on death as on birth, came up every morning and raced across the blue dome and dipped into the sea of fire every evening. Water ran downhill and birds nested.

Missie knew why she didn't leave Joe. She couldn't. She loved him too much. But she could not understand why Joe didn't leave her. He was polite, even kind at times, but aloof.

There were no more Saturday romps. No ringing silver dollars to stack beside her plate. No pockets to rifle. In fact the yellow coin in his trousers was like a monster hiding in the cave of his pockets to destroy her.

She often wondered if he still had it, but nothing could have induced her to ask nor yet to explore his pockets to see for herself. Its shadow was in the house whether or no.

One night Joe came home around midnight and complained of pains in the back. He asked Missie to rub him down with liniment. It had been three months since Missie had touched his body and it all seemed strange. But she rubbed him. Grateful for the chance. Before morning, youth triumphed and Missie exulted. But the next day, as she joyfully made up their bed, beneath her pillow she found the piece of money with the bit of chain attached.

Alone to herself, she looked at the thing with loathing, but look she must. She took it into her hands with trembling and saw first thing that it was no gold piece. It was a gilded half dollar. Then she knew why Slemmons had forbidden anyone to touch his gold. He trusted village eyes at a distance not to recognize his stickpin as a gilded quarter, and his watch charm as a four-bit piece.

She was glad at first that Joe had left it there. Perhaps he was through with her punishment. They were man and wife again. Then another thought came clawing at her. He had come home to buy from her as if she were any woman in the long house. Fifty cents for her love. As if to say that he could pay as well as Slemmons. She slid the coin into his Sunday pants pocket and dressed herself and left his house.

Halfway between her house and the quarters she met her husband's mother, and after a short talk she turned and went back home. Never would she admit defeat to that woman who prayed for it nightly. If she had not the substance of marriage she had the outside show. Joe must leave *her*. She let him see she didn't want his old gold four-bits too.

She saw no more of the coin for some time though she knew that Joe could not help finding it in his pocket. But his health kept poor, and he came home at least every ten days to be rubbed.

The sun swept around the horizon, trailing its robes of weeks and days. One morning as Joe came in from work, he found Missie May chopping wood. Without a word he took the ax and chopped a huge pile before he stopped.

"You ain't got no business choppin' wood, and you know it."

"How come? Ah been choppin' it for de last longest."

"Ah ain't blind. You makin' feet for shoes."

"Won't you be glad to have a lil baby chile, Joe?"

"You know dat 'thout astin' me."

"Iss gointer be a boy chile and de very spit of you."

"You reckon, Missie May?"

"Who else could it look lak?"

Joe said nothing, but he thrust his hand deep into his pocket and fingered something there.

It was almost six months later Missie May took to bed and Joe went and got his mother to come wait on the house.

Missie May delivered a fine boy. Her travail was over when Joe came in from work one morning. His mother and the old women were drinking great bowls of coffee around the fire in the kitchen.

The minute Joe came into the room his mother called him aside.

"How did Missie May make out?" he asked quickly.

"Who, dat gal? She strong as a ox. She gointer have plenty mo'. We done fixed her wid de sugar and lard to sweeten her for de nex' one."

Joe stood silent awhile.

"You ain't ast 'bout de baby, Joe. You oughter be mighty proud cause he sho is de spittin' image of yuh, son. Dat's yourn all right. If you never git another one, dat un is yourn. And you know Ah'm mighty proud too, son, cause Ah never thought well of you marryin' Missie May cause her ma used tuh fan her foot round right smart and Ah been mighty skeered dat Missie May wuz gointer git misput on her road."

Joe said nothing. He fooled around the house till late in the day, then just before he went to work, he went and stood at the foot of the bed and asked his wife how she felt. He did this every day during the week.

On Saturday he went to Orlando to make his market. It had been a long time since he had done that.

Meat and lard, meal and flour, soap and starch. Cans of corn and tomatoes. All the staples. He fooled around town for a while and bought bananas and apples. Way after while he went around to the candy store.

"Hello, Joe," the clerk greeted him. "Ain't seen you in a long time."

"Nope, Ah ain't been heah. Been round in spots and places."

"Want some of them molasses kisses you always buy?"

"Yessuh." He threw the gilded half dollar on the counter. "Will dat spend?"

"Whut is it, Joe? Well, I'll be doggone! A gold-plated four-bit piece. Where'd you git it, Joe?"

"Offen a stray nigger dat come through Eatonville. He had it on his watch chain for a charm—goin' round making out iss gold money. Ha ha! He had a quarter on his tie pin and it wuz all golded up too. Tryin' to fool people. Makin' out he so rich and everything. Ha! Ha! Tryin' to tole off folkses' wives from home."

"How did you git it, Joe? Did he fool you too?"

"Who, me? Naw suh! He ain't fooled me none. Know whut Ah done? He come round me wid his smart talk. Ah hauled off and knocked 'im down and took his old four-bits way from 'im. Gointer buy my wife some good ole 'lasses kisses wid it. Gimme fifty cents' worth of dem candy kisses."

"Fifty cents buys a mighty lot of candy kisses, Joe. Why don't you split it up and take some chocolate bars, too. They eat good, too."

"Yessuh, dey do, but Ah wants all dat in kisses. Ah got a lil boy chile home now. Tain't a week old yet, but he kin suck a sugar tit and maybe eat one them kisses hisself."

Joe got his candy and left the store. The clerk turned to the next customer. "Wisht I could be like these darkies. Laughin' all the time. Nothin' worries 'em."

Back in Eatonville, Joe reached his own front door. There was the ring of singing metal on wood. Fifteen times. Missie May couldn't run to the door, but she crept there as quickly as she could.

"Joe Banks, Ah hear you chunkin' money in mah do'way. You wait till Ah got mah strength back and Ah'm gointer fix you for dat."

Headwaiter

Chester Himes

1938

When headwaiter Dick Small pushed through the service hall into the main dining room, he ran smack into an early dinner rush. The creased, careful smile adorning his brown face knotted slightly in self-reproach. He should have been there sooner.

For a brief instant he paused just inside the doorway, head cocked to one side as if deferentially listening. A hum of cultured voices engaged in leisurely conversation, the gentle clatter of silver on fine china, the slight scrape of a chair, the tinkle of ice in glasses, the aroma of hot coffee and savory, well-cooked food, the sight of unhurried dining and hurried service blended into an atmosphere ineffably dear to his heart; for directing the services of this dining room in a commendable manner was the ultimate aim of his life, and as much a part of him as the thin spot in his meticulously brushed hair or the habitual immaculateness of the tuxedo which draped his slight, spright frame.

But he could sense a hint of exasperation in the general mood with that surety of feeling which twenty years as headwaiter at the Park Manor Hotel had bestowed upon him, and his roving gaze searched quickly for flaws in the service inspiring it.

There was fat Mr. McLaughlin knuckling the table impatiently as he awaited—Dick was quite sure that it was broiled lobster that Mr. McLaughlin was so impatiently awaiting. And Mrs. Shipley was frowning with displeasure at the dirty dishes which claimed her elbow room as she endeavored to lean closer to her boon companion, Mrs. Hamilton, and impart in a theatrical whisper a choice morsel of spicy gossip—Dick had no doubt that it was both choice and spicy. When Mr. Lyons lifted his glass to take another sip of iced water, he found to his extreme annoyance that there was no more iced water to be sipped, and even from where he stood, Dick could see Mr. Lyons' forbearance abruptly desert him.

The white-jacketed, black-bowed waiters showed a passable alacrity, he observed without censure, but they were accomplishing very little. Direction was lacking. The captain, black and slow, plodded hither and yon in a stew of indecision.

Dick clapped his hands. "Fill those glasses for that deuce over there," he directed the busboy who had sprung to his side. "Take an ashstand to the party at that center table. Clear up those ladies." He left the busboy spinning in his tracks, turned to the captain who came rushing over. "I'll take it over now, son. You slip into a white jacket and bring in Mr. McLaughlin's lobster."

His presence was established and the wrinkles of exasperation ironed smoothly out.

The captain nodded and flashed white teeth, relieved. He turned away, turned back. "Mr. Erskine has a party of six for seven-thirty. I gave it to Pat. Here's the bill of fare." He gave Dick a scrawled slip of paper.

Dick pocketed the order, aware that this party was something in the way of an event, for Mr. Erskine had been the very first of the older residents who had sworn they would never set foot within the dining room again until the "obnoxious"—Mr. Erskine himself had employed the term—syncopatings of "Sonny" Jenkins and his body-rocking "Cotton Pickers" had been everlastingly removed. His glance strayed involuntarily to the band dais at the rear where until just the day before Sonny and his black, foot-stomping troubadours had held forth; but deprived of their colorful appearance and cannonading rhythms it had a skeletoned, abandoned look.

Well, after all it was the older residents like Mr. Erskine who comprised the firm foundation upon which the hotel so staunchly rested, he reflected, agreeing with them (although he would not have admitted it) that the noticeable absence of Sonny and his boys was more to be desired than their somewhat jarring presence.

But he quickly pigeonholed the thought, the press of duty making no allowances for idle reflection. He went straight to the setup and scanned it quickly, his head to one side. After a moment's careful study, he leaned across the table and aligned a fork, smoothed an infinitesimal wrinkle from the linen, shifted the near candlestick just a wee bit to the left; then he rocked back on his heels and allowed his eyes to smile. He was pleased.

Flawless service for discriminating guests evoked in him a complete satisfaction. And who among the many to whom he had catered during his twenty years at the Park Manor had ever showed a finer sense of discrimination than Mr. Erskine, he thought, or a broader sense of appreciation, he added with a glow.

He nodded commendation to Pat, tan and lanky, who was spooning ice cubes into the upturned glasses with slim, deft fingers; and Pat acknowledged it with his roguish smile.

"Here's the bill of fare, Pat," he said in his quick, crisp voice. "Put your cocktails on ice and have everything prepared by a quarter after seven." He glanced at the wall clock and noticed that it was forty-seven minutes after six.

He stepped away, circled an unoccupied table, and came back, frowning slightly. "This is Mrs. Van Denter's table, Pat. Did the captain select it?"

"Cap called the desk, chief," Pat explained. "They said Mrs. Van Denter had gone into the country to spend a week with her sister."

His breath oozed slowly out. "You know how stubborn she is. Been that way for twenty years to my knowledge, ever since her husband died and left her—" he caught himself and stopped abruptly. Gossiping with a waiter. Chagrin bit him lightly, putting snap into his voice. "Put your reserved card on, Pat. Always put your reserved card on first, then—"

The sight of Mrs. Van Denter coming through the entrance archway choked him. She made straight for her table, plowing aside everyone who got in her way. Tonight she looked slightly forbidding, her grayish, stoutish, sixtyish appearance rockier than ever and the tight seam of her mouth carrying an overload of obstinacy. At first glance he thought that she had had a martini too many, but as she lumbered closer with her elephantine directness, he decided that it came from her heart, not her stomach.

Perhaps she and her sister had had a rift, he was thinking as he bowed with more than his customary deference and inquired as to her health. "And how are you this evening, Mrs. Van Denter?" After a pause in which she did not reply he began his apology. "I am very sorry, Mrs. Van Denter, but the captain was under the impression that you were in the country—"

She brushed him aside and aimed her solid body for her table, on which Pat was just placing the reserved card. Dick turned quickly behind her, his mouth hanging slack. There was the hint of a race. But she won.

And for all of the iced glasses and party silver and crimped napkins and bowl of roses and engraved name cards at each plate; for all of the big black-lettered card which read RESERVED, staring up into her face, she reached for the nearest chair, pulled it out, planted her plump body into it with sickening finality, and reached for an iced glass.

Dick dropped a menu card before her and signaled Pat to take her order, his actions registering no more than a natural concern. He picked up the bowl of flowers and the reserved card and placed them on another table, then moved casually away. It was an era of change, he told himself. It made the old more stubborn and the young more reckless—he didn't know which were the more difficult to please. But here were Mrs. Hughes and her guest right beside him, who seemed to be pleased enough even if no one else was, he noted, with obvious enjoyment of the fact.

"How do you do, Mrs. Hughes," he addressed the stately, white-haired lady. "And this is your sister, Mrs. Walpole, of Boston, I am sure. We're delighted to have you with us again, Mrs. Walpole. I remember quite well when you visited us before."

Mrs. Hughes smiled cordially and Mrs. Walpole said, "I've been here several times before."

"But I was referring to your last visit; it was in August three years ago."

"What a remarkable memory," Mrs. Hughes murmured.

Dick was gratified; he prided himself upon his memory and when someone took notice of it he felt rewarded. Turning away he caught his tuxedoed reflection in a paneled mirror and the slightly disturbing thought came to him that the blue and gold decorations of this dining room were too ornate for the casual informality which now existed. A vague regret threaded his thoughts as he recalled the bygone age when dressing for dinner had been the rigid rule. It took a slight effort to banish such recollections and when he spoke again his voice was brusque.

"Clear that table," he ordered a busboy as if the busboy alone was to blame for the change of things.

Then a party of seven at a center table demanded his personal attention. "Good evening, Mr. and Mrs. Seedle," he greeted the elderly hosts, knowing that they considered the service lacking until he made his appearance. "And how is this young gentleman?" he inquired of their seven-year-old grandson.

"I'm all right, Dick," the boy replied, "but I ain't no gentleman 'cause Gramma just said so—"

"Arnold!" Mrs. Seedle rebuked.

"Why does Granpa eat onions, Dick?" the boy asked, not to be repressed, but Dick bowed a smiling departure without replying.

"So Gramma can find him in the dark," he heard Mr. Seedle elucidate, feeling that "Gramma" could very likely find him right then in the dark without the aid of onions, as lit as he was.

"Fill these glasses," he directed a busy waiter to hide his growing smile, then filled them himself before the waiter had a chance to protest.

"Pst, pst." He called a busboy, received no reply. He hurried across the floor, light lumping slightly on the irritation in his face, shook the boy's shoulder. "What's the matter with you, are you deaf?" he demanded.

"No sir, I—I—er—"

"Go get the salad tray," he snapped and hurried away in his loping walk to greet Mrs. Collar, eighty and cross, who hesitated undecidedly under the entrance archway.

"It's a rather nasty night, Mrs. Collar," he remarked by way of greeting, seating her in a corner nook. "It doesn't seem to be able to make up its mind whether to rain or sleet, but I feel that it will clear up by tomorrow."

Mrs. Collar looked up at him over the rim of her ancient spectacles. "That isn't any encouragement to me," she replied in her harsh, unconciliatory voice.

Confusion took the smoothness out of Dick's speech. "I am not really sure, er—rer, I wouldn't be surprised if it continued, er, being indefinite."

"You're indefinite enough yourself," she snapped, scanning the menu card.

He laughed deprecatingly, signaled to a youth less than a year out of prison to take her order. "I'd make a poor gambler," he confessed ruefully.

Her head jerked quickly up again. "You don't gamble, do you, Dick?" she asked sharply.

"No, Mrs. Collar, I do not gamble," said headwaiter Dick Small, gambling then his job at five hundred a month to give an ex-con another chance. "Nor do I employ any man who does."

"You couldn't tell if they did," she pointed out matter-of-factly. "Not unless you had every one of them shadowed night and day."

The indelibleness abandoned his smile. He turned away from her, annoyance tight in his throat, and greeted a sudden influx of diners. But before he had finished seating them the indulgence came back to him. Mrs. Collar was really a very nice old lady, he admitted to himself, and he liked her. She was like olives; you had to acquire a taste for her. And he sincerely hoped that she was pleased with the service.

But after all, Mrs. Collar was just one diner, and he had neither the time nor the inclination to analyze her disposition, for the dining room was rapidly filling with younger and more demanding guests.

It was an unusual weekday crowd, and search his mind as he would, he could not think of one reason for it. There were no conventions in town as he knew of, and there were no more than the usual dinner "specials." And then he had it, and he wondered why he had not thought of it before. It was no more or less than the return of the dissenters, recalled by the serene and comfortable knowledge that "Sonny" Jenkins and his "Cotton Pickers" had no longer to be endured.

A repressed snort of laughter pushed air through his nose. But this was no laughing time, really, he censored himself. It was a time for smooth, fast service. His reputation as a headwaiter and even the prestige of the hotel itself were dependent upon the guests being served with the least possible delay.

He started kitchenward to recruit more waiters from the room service department, he just simply must have more waiters, when somethiing about a busboy halted him. He glanced down, looked up again.

"What kind of shoe polish do you use, son?" he inquired disarmingly.

"Paste," the boy replied, unthinking.

He let his gaze drop meaningfully to the boy's unshined shoes. "Try liquid next time, son," he suggested.

The boy jumped with sudden guilt. Dick stepped quickly around him and passed from the dining room before the boy had a chance to reply.

In the service hall Dick bumped into a waiter gobbling a leftover steak, said pleasantly enough, "Food is like drink, son, it's a habit. There's no place in service for the glutton or the drunkard."

The waiter strangled, blew steak all over the floor, but Dick passed on without a backward glance.

Over by the elevator where the room service was stationed, a waiter lounged indolently by a serviced table and yelled at the closed elevator doors, "Knock knock!"

Dick drew up quietly behind him, heard the slightly muffled reply from within the elevator: "Who's there?"

"Mr. Small, the headwaiter," he said crisply.

The waiter who had been leaning so indolently by the serviced table jumped. His hand flew up and knocked over a glass of water on the clean linen. The elevator doors popped open, emitting two more waiters in an impressive hurry.

"If you fellows don't care to work—" Dick began, exceedingly unimpressed.

The first waiter hoisted the room service table on his shoulder and started into the elevator without a word. The other two stammered in unison, "Yes sir, no sir, er—rer—"

"Put down that table," Dick grated at the first waiter.

The waiter let it drop as if it was hot.

"All three of you go into the dining room and report to the captain," Dick ordered.

They scampered quickly off.

"Here, serve this dinner," Dick directed a busboy who had performed a magical appearance.

"But I don't, er, know, er—"

"Find out," Dick snapped, at the end of his patience.

When he returned to the dining room he noticed that patrons were still entering. He greeted an incoming couple, seated them, and took their order on note paper, being unable to locate an idle waiter.

A bellboy passed through from the kitchen. Dick stopped him. "Give this order to Howard," he directed.

"But I'm a bellboy," the boy objected.

Dick stood stock still and looked at him. "All stages of existence have their drawbacks, son," he began in a lazy, philosophical vein.

But the boy was not to be fooled. Dick had such a smooth way of telling a servant that he was fired. He took the note and hurried away in search of Howard.

Dick's quick sight scanned the side stand before he turned away, exploring for negligence, but the pitchers were filled and the butter was iced and the silver was neatly arranged in the drawers. He allowed a slight expression of commendation to come into his smile. The busboys whose duty it was to keep the side stands in order had earned stars in their crowns, although they would never know it if they waited for Dick Small, headwaiter, to tell them.

Dick turned back to his guests, feeling a benign omnipotence in caring for their needs. He was as the captain of a ship, he reflected, the master of this dining room and solely responsible for its service. He seemed to derive a becoming dignity from this responsibility.

These people were his passengers; he must feed and serve and humor them with an impartial respect. They were his life; they took up his time, his thoughts, his energy. He was interested in them, interested in their private lives and their individual prosperity. He knew them, knew about them. His most vital emotions absorbed their coloring from the emotions of these dining room patrons: when they were pleased, he was pleased; when they were hurt, he was hurt; when they failed or prospered in their respective endeavors, it had a personal bearing on the course of his life.

Each day when he stood looking over them, as now, he received some feeling which added to his life, although it seldom showed in the imperturbableness of his smile.

Now his gaze drifted slowly from face to face, reading the feelings and emotions of each with an uncanny perception.

There were Tommy and Jackie Rightmire, the polo-playing twins. And did they have healthy appetites? And several tables distant he noticed their sister dining with a Spanish nobleman whom he had never been quite able to admire.

And there were Mr. Andrews and Mrs. Winnings, engaged as was their custom of late in animated chatter as they dined in the dubious seclusion of a rear column. Crowding forty, both of them, he was quite sure, and as obviously in love with each other as a pair of doves. But if the slightest censure threaded his thoughts as his gaze moved slowly on, it did not show in the bland smoothness of his expression.

He wondered what would happen if Mrs. Andrews, forty-two and showing it, and reputedly very jealous of Mr. Andrews' affections, should choose this dining room in which to dine some evening and inadvertently bump into their tête-à-tête.

And coincidentally, as it happens even in masterpieces, Mrs. Andrews did. She came through the entrance archway at the front and beat a hard-heeled, determined path straight toward her spouse's table.

Dick's compelling thought was to deter catastrophe, for catastrophe indeed it would be, he sincerely felt, should Mrs. Andrews encounter Mr. Andrews in such an inexplicable predicament. He headed her off just in time.

"Right this way, Mrs. Andrews," he began, pulling a chair from a conspicuously placed center table.

"No, no, not that." She discarded with a gesture. "I want something—

remote, quiet. I'm expecting a friend." Her eyes dared him to think no more than that which she had explicitly stated.

"Then this will be just the ticket for you," he purred smoothly, seating her across the dining room from her husband with her back toward him and the column between them.

"Thank you, this will be just fine." She smiled, pleased, and he had the feeling of a golfer who has just scored a hole in one.

The voice of a waiter halted his casual strolling as he moved away from her. "Chief, see that old man over there at the window? The one with the white goatee?"

Dick did not look at the old man "with the white goatee," he looked very pointedly at the waiter slouching with propped elbows on the side stand and lacking in a proper respect for the hotel's patrons, not to mention the hotel's headwaiter.

"He says all a nigger needs is something to eat and someplace to sleep," the waiter continued, unaware of the pointedness of Dick's frown. "He says he knows 'cause he's got a plantation of them—"

"Do *you* see that table over there from which Mrs. Van Denter is now arising?" he cut in, a forced restraint blunting his voice.

"Yes sir," the waiter replied quickly, sensing his mistake.

"Well, service it for six," he directed, the displeasure breaking through his restraint.

"Yes *sir.*" The waiter was glad to be off.

Dick followed him over to Mrs. Van Denter's table and bowed to her again with that slightly exaggerated deference. "Was your dinner enjoyable, madam?" he inquired.

But dinner, enjoyable or not, had not softened the stone of Mrs. Van Denter's face. "Dick," she snapped, "I find your obsequiousness a bit repugnant." Then she plodded smilelessly away.

Dick admitted to himself with a sense of reproach that it had been a *faux pas* but he couldn't take time to explore into it further for he noticed that the table of two women needed clearing and he went in search of a busboy to clear it.

The boy, a greenhorn, approached timidly from the rear of the thin, reedy lady with the lashing voice and reached around her for her plate, taking great care not to disturb her. The lady saw the stealthily reaching hand, "the clutching hand" she might have said had she said it. Her sharp mouth went slack like a fish's. "Oh!" she gasped.

The boy grew panicky. He grabbed the plate as if to dash away with it, as indeed he did. The thin lady clutched the other rim and held on for dear life. There was a moment's tug of war. A chicken bone fell to the table. Then anger jerked the thin lady around in her chair.

"Let loose!" she shrilled.

And "let loose" the now thoroughly frightened boy most certainly did. He not only let loose but he jumped a full yard backward, his nostrils flaring like a winded horse's and his eyes white-rimmed in his black face.

"Always taking my plate before I'm finished," the thin lady added caustically.

But she had no further need to fear that particular boy taking her plate ever again, finished or not finished, for he didn't stop running until he was downstairs in the locker room changing into his street clothes. Dick sent the captain down to bring him back, but the boy had definitely resigned.

"Well, he wouldn't have made a waiter, anyway," he remarked. "He has an innate fear of white people which he couldn't overcome. It makes him nervous and panicky around them." But he was annoyed just the same.

A stag party of four in the rear offered a brief respite from peevish old ladies and frightened busboys. He noticed that a raised window beside them slashed wind across their table and hastened quickly in their direction, concern prodding him.

"Is there too much draft for you, gentlemen?" he inquired solicitously, pausing in a half bow. But on closer observation he saw that they were all strangers to him and slightly drunk and not gentlemen, after all.

They all stopped eating and ogled him. "That's a good-looking tux, boy," one remarked. "Where'd you get it? Steal it?"

"No sir, I purchased it—" he began restrainedly.

"What makes you black?" another cut in. A laugh spurted.

Anger broke loose in him then. It shook him like a squall. But his smile weathered it. When the breath had softened in his lungs he said politely, "God did, gentlemen," and moved away.

At a center table a high-pressure voice was saying, "Just talked to the governor at the capitol. He said—" It sounded unreal to Dick. He turned his glance obliquely, saw the latecomer sit opposite his comely, young wife. It was the wife who signed the checks, he recalled; and who was the woman he had seen him with the other day and had intended to remember?

But the sight of old Mr. Woodford standing in the entrance archway snapped his line of thought before Mnemosyne could come to his aid. He rushed to meet him. "And how are you this evening, Mr. Woodford, sir?" he asked, and then added without awaiting a reply, knowing there would be none, "Right this way, sir. I reserved your table for you." He had already noted that Mr. Woodford's table was unoccupied.

He received Mr. Woodford's grudging nod, led the way rearward, head cocked, arms swinging, recalling reluctantly the time when Mr. Woodford was genial and talkative and worth many millions—broke now since the stock market crash and glum, with slightly bloodshot eyes from drinking a little too much, he suspected.

When he turned away he caught the beckoning finger of old Mrs. Miller, a resident for many years at the Park Manor and a special friend of the Rumanian countess who resided there on her visits to America. He moved quickly toward her, his smile becoming more genuine, less careful.

"And when have you heard from our good friend, her highness, Mrs. Miller?" he inquired with assured familiarity.

"I was just going to tell you, Dick," she replied in a reedy, year-thinned voice. "I had a cablegram from her daughter just this afternoon."

"And when is she going to pay us another visit? Soon, I hope."

"Never, Dick," she quavered. "She died last week."

Dick went rigid. The brown of his face tinged ashily. Then he noticed that Mrs. Miller's eyes were red and swollen from crying and he upbraided himself for not having noticed immediately.

He could find no suitable words for the moment. He pitied her in a sincere, personal way, for he knew that the countess was the one person in all the world whom she considered as a friend. But he could not express his pity. He was only a headwaiter. He thought there was something sublime in her gallantry which would not let her grief prostrate her; and he knew the countess would have wished it so.

Oddly, for a fleeting instant he was a young black waiter in Atlantic City, thirty-six years ago. It was his afternoon off and he had seven dollars. The pretty brown girl beside him was saying, "I want the five-dollar one." It was a wedding ring, and she was to be his bride. Seven dollars—and now he was headwaiter at five hundred a month, had bought a seven-thousand-dollar home, had a few thousand in the bank. That afternoon seemed a long way behind.

He said aloud, a sincere depth of feeling in his voice, "We shall miss her so much, Mrs. Miller. The world can little spare the loss of one so fine."

And by that sincere tribute to one who was dead he earned for himself five thousand dollars in Mrs. Miller's will.

"Indeed we shall miss her, Dick," Mrs. Miller replied, barely able to stem the flow of tears.

When he moved away from her his actions were slowed, groggy, as if he had taken a severe beating. In a very short time he would pass the sixty mark. Sixty was old for a waiter in a busy hotel. He shook himself as if he were awaking from a bad dream, stepped forward with renewed pounce.

Perhaps he wasn't looking, perhaps he couldn't see. He bumped into a busboy with a loaded tray. China crashed on the tiled floor, silver rang. The sudden shatter shook the room. He patted the stooping boy on the shoulder, the unusual show of feeling leaving the boy slightly flustered, turned quickly away, head held high, refusing to notice the shattered crockery. And by his refusal to notice it he averted attention.

The ringing of the telephone in the corner brought relief to his thoughts. He hurried over, picked up the receiver. "Dining room, the headwaiter speaking," he said. Faint traces of emotion still lingered in his eyes.

Behind him a woman's husky voice was saying, "But Mildred is selfish. No matter what you give in material things, my dear, unless you give something of yourself—" He recognized the voice as Mrs. Porter's, of Porter Paints and Varnish. . . . The telephone began speaking and drew his attention.

He hooked the receiver, stuck a reserved sign on a table, started kitchenward to get a glass of water when the question jerked him up short like the snap of a noose.

"Boy, didn't you get a pardon from the penitentiary about a year back?"

The voices of the other three men and four women at the table stopped and hung rigidly suspended in an all-enveloping gasp. Motion froze as solid as the ice cubes tinkling in the glasses. Silence came in a tight clamp, restricting the breath.

But the waiter to whom the question had been addressed remained placid. "Yes sir," he replied.

Dick turned toward the party, brushing the apprehension from before him with a widespread gesture.

"First degree?" the voice persisted.

A woman said, "Oh!"

"Yes sir," the waiter repeated.

Dick entered the conversation then. "I engaged him, sir." He addressed the genial-faced man who had put the questions. "Turned out to be one of my best boys, too."

"Why?" the man wanted to know, more from curiosity than reprobation. "I imagine that the residents of the hotel here would resent it if they knew. I might myself."

"I felt that he was a good boy and that all he needed was another chance," Dick explained.

The man's eyes lingered a moment appraisingly upon Dick's face, then switched to the waiter's. "Let's give it to him," he decided, closing the incident. Ease came back into the diners and the dinner moved serenely on.

But the genial-faced man had earned Dick's everlasting gratefulness, although he would perhaps never know it.

Dick had forgotten that he was thirsty, drawn again into the maelstrom of duties confronting a headwaiter.

The rush gradually subsided. Dick was made aware of it by the actions of his waiters. They had begun to move about with that Negroid languor which bespoke liberal tips. He was reminded of the Negro of Mark Twain legend who said he didn't want to make a dime 'cause he had a dime. His smile was indulgent. He knew his boys.

His rapid sight counted twenty-one remaining diners. So he released the first shift of waiters with the ironic suggestion: "Don't disappoint your money, boys. Give it a break and spend it."

He watched their happy departure for a moment, knowing full well that they would be hanging over their favorite bars before the hour was passed; then his attention was drawn to a drunken party at a center table, overflow from the bar no doubt. The coarseness of their speech and actions spread a personal humiliation within him. He wanted to feel that his guests deserved the respect which he bestowed upon them.

Someone of the party made a risqué remark and everyone laughed. Everyone except one woman. She was looking at the lobster in front of her with mouth-twitching nausea. Then horror came into her face. "It moved! It moved!" she cried, voice rising hysterically. "It moved!" She backed away from the table, crying over and over again, "It moved!"

Dick stepped quickly forward, his careful smile forced, and whisked the platter of lobster from the table. "Is there something else you desire, madam?" he asked politely, presenting her with a menu.

A man swung leisurely from his seat and winked at him. "She desires a bit of air, that's all," he said.

A waiter smothered a laugh in a napkin.

"Take that napkin from your face!" Dick chastened with severe voice. "Get some side towels and use them, and don't ever let me catch you using a napkin in such a manner." His harshness was an outlet.

He moved toward the side windows, trying to stifle the buildup of emotion in the smoothness of his mind. The guests were always right and a waiter was always impersonal, in action and in thought, no matter what occurred: that was the one rigid tenet in the waiter's code. But platitudes helped him very little. He decided that he must be tired.

George, tall and sepia, passed him. He noticed that George needed new tuxedo trousers. But he didn't say anything because he knew that George had a high-yellow woman who took most of his money. And George knew what a waiter needed, anyway. He'd give him enough rope—

He was surprised to see that it was Mr. Upshaw whom George was serving. Mr. Upshaw had once said he didn't like "yellah niggers," as if they could help being yellow. Maybe Mr. Upshaw didn't consider George as being yellow. . . .

He thought no more about it for he had just noticed Mr. Spivat, half owner of the hotel, dining alone at a window table. He went over and spoke to him. "Nasty weather we're having, Mr. Spivat."

"Yes, it is, Dick," Mr. Spivat replied absently, scanning the stocks final.

The window behind Mr. Spivat drew Dick's gaze. He raised his sight into the dark night. Park foliage across the street was a thick blackness, looking slightly gummy in the wet sleet and rain. On a distant summit the museum was a chiseled stone block in white light, hanging from the starless night by invisible strings. Streetlights in the foreground showed a stone wall bordering the park, a strip of sidewalk, slushy pavement.

A car turned the corner, its headlights stabbing into the darkness. Motor purr sounded faintly as it passed, the red taillight bobbed lingeringly into the bog of distant darkness. Dick stared into the void after it, feeling very tired. He thought of a chicken farm in the country, where he could get off his feet. But he knew that he would never be satisfied away from a dining room.

When he turned back traces of weariness showed in the edges of his smile, making it ragged. But his eyes were as sharp as ever. They lingered a moment on the slightly hobbling figure of Bishop. A little stooped, Bishop was, a little paunched, a little gray, with a moon face and soiled eyes and rough skin of midnight blue. A good name, Bishop, a descriptive name, he thought with a half smile.

He noticed Bishop lurch once, so he followed him into the kitchen, overtook him at the pastry room, and spun him about, sniffing his breath. He caught the scent of mints and a very faint odor of alcohol.

"You haven't been drinking again, have you, Bishop?" he asked sharply. He liked Bishop, but Bishop would drink, and a drinking waiter could not be tolerated.

Bishop rolled his eyes and laughed to dispel such a horrid idea. "Nawsuh, chief. Been rubbin' my leg with rubbin' alcawl. Thass what you smell. My n'ritis is terrible bad, suh."

Dick nodded sympathetically. "You need to watch your diet, Bishop," he advised. "Go home when you serve that dessert."

Bishop bobbed, rubbing his hands together involuntarily. "Thank you, suh, Mistah Small."

Dick turned back into the dining room, followed by Bishop with coffee and cream. He stopped just inside the doorway, his gaze lingering on Bishop's limp.

But his frown was inspired by thoughts of his own wife more than by Bishop's limp. She was using an exceeding amount of money lately. He didn't want to start thinking unfair thoughts of her, that was the way so many marriages were broken up.

He caught himself and brought his mind back to the dining room. He tried to recall whether he had assigned Bishop to wait on Mr. Spivat. He certainly wouldn't have, he knew, had he known that Bishop was limping so badly, for Mr. Spivat was convinced, anyway, that all Negro waiters were drunkards; and Bishop did appear drunk.

It all happened so quickly that the picture was telescoped in his mind and his body started moving before thought directed its motions.

Bishop's right leg buckled as he placed the tiny pitcher of cream. He jackknifed forward on his knee. Cream flew in a thin sheet over the front of Mr. Spivat's dark blue suit.

Mr. Spivat blanched, then ripened like a russet apple. Insensate fury jerked him erect. His foot began motion as if to kick the kneeling figure, froze in knotted restraint.

Dick was there in three swift strides, applying a cold, damp towel to Mr. Spivat's suit. "Clean up, George," he directed the other waiter, trying to avert the drama which he felt engulfing them. "Sorry, Mr. Spivat, sir. The boy's got neuritis, it's very bad during this nasty weather. I'll lay him off until it gets better."

But neither could cold, damp towels help Mr. Spivat's suit, nor could expressions of sorrow allay the fury in his mind.

He mashed the words out between his clenched teeth. "Dick, see that this man gets his money, and if I ever see him in this hotel again I'll fire the whole bunch of you!" He wheeled and started walking jerkily from the room, his body moving as if it were being snatched along with slack strings. "Drunk!" he ground out.

Dick motioned Bishop from the dining room and followed behind. He had the checker make out a requisition for Bishop's pay, an even thirteen dollars. He couldn't meet the doglike plea of Bishop's eyes.

Bishop stood at a respectful distance, his shoulders drooping, his whole body sagging; very black, very wordless. Bishop had always liked Mr. Spivat, had liked serving him. He and Mr. Spivat used to discuss baseball during the summer months.

After a time he said irrelevantly, a slight protest in his voice, "I got seven kids."

Dick looked down at his feet, big feet they were, with broken arches from shouldering heavy trays on adamant concrete, big and flat and knotty. He felt in his pockets, discovered a twenty-dollar banknote. He pressed it into Bishop's hand.

Bishop said, "I wasn't drunk, chief," as if Dick might think he was.

Dick wanted to believe that, but he couldn't. Bishop as a rule did not eat mints; he didn't like sweets of any kind. But mints would help kill the odor of whiskey on his breath. Dick sighed. He knew that Bishop liked serving Mr. Spivat. There was very little of the likes and dislikes of all his waiters, of their family affairs and personal lives, that Dick did not know. But of them all, he sympathized most with Bishop.

But what could he do? Bishop would drink.

He said, "Accidents will happen, son. Yours just cost you your job. If there's anything I can ever do for you, anything in reason, let me know. And even if it isn't in reason, come and let me say so." He stood quite still for a moment. His face showed extreme weariness.

Then he shook it all from his mind. It required a special effort. He blinked his eyes clear of the picture of a dejected black face, donned his creased, careful smile and pushed through the service hall into the dining room. His head was cocked to one side as though he were deferentially listening.

Bright and Morning Star

Richard Wright

1938

I

She stood with her black face some six inches from the moist windowpane and wondered when on earth would it ever stop raining. It might keep up like this all week, she thought. She heard rain droning upon the roof and high up in the wet sky her eyes followed the silent rush of a bright shaft of yellow that swung from the airplane beacon in far-off Memphis. Momently she could see it cutting through the rainy dark; it would hover a second like a gleaming sword above her head, then vanish. She sighed, troubling, Johnny-Boys been trampin in this slop all day wid no decent shoes on his feet. . . . Through the window she could see the rich black earth sprawling outside in the night. There was more rain than the clay could soak up; pools stood everywhere. She yawned and mumbled: "Rains good n bad. It kin make seeds bus up thu the groun er it kin bog things down lika watah-soaked coffin." Her hands were folded loosely over her stomach and the hot air of the kitchen traced a filmy veil of sweat on her forehead. From the cookstove came the soft singing of burning wood and now and then a throaty bubble rose from a pot of simmering greens.

"Shucks, Johnny-Boy coulda let somebody else do all tha runnin in the rain. Theres others bettah fixed fer it than he is. But, naw! Johnny-Boy ain the one t trust nobody t do nothin. Hes gotta do it *all* hisself. . . ."

She glanced at a pile of damp clothes in a zinc tub. Waal, Ah bettah git t work. She turned, lifted a smoothing iron with a thick pad of cloth, touched a spit-wet finger to it with a quick, jerking motion: *smiiitz!* Yeah, its hot! Stooping, she took a blue work shirt from the tub and shook it out. With a deft twist of her shoulders she caught the iron in her right hand; the fingers of her left hand took a piece of wax from a tin box and a frying sizzle came as she smeared the bottom. She was thinking of nothing now; her hands followed a lifelong ritual of toil. Spreading a sleeve, she ran the hot iron to and fro until the wet cloth became stiff. She was deep in the midst of her work when a song rose up out of the far-off days of her childhood and broke through half-parted lips:

> *"Hes the Lily of the Valley, the Bright n Mawnin Star*
> *Hes the Fairest of Ten Thousan t mah soul . . ."*

A gust of wind dashed rain against the window. Johnny-Boy oughta c mon home n eat his suppah. Aw, Lawd! Itd be fine ef Sug could eat wid us tonight! Itd be like ol times! Mabbe aftah all it wont be long fo he comes back. Tha lettah Ah got from im las week said *Don give up hope. . . .* Yeah; we gotta live in hope. Then both of her sons, Sug and Johnny-Boy, would be back with her.

With an involuntary nervous gesture, she stopped and stood still, listening. But the only sound was the lulling fall of rain. Shucks, ain no usa me ackin this way, she thought. Every time they gits ready to hol them meetings Ah gits jumpity. Ah been a lil scared ever since Sug went t jail. She heard the clock ticking and looked. Johnny-Boys a *hour* late! He sho mus be havin a time doin all tha trampin, trampin thu the mud. . . . But her fear was a quiet one; it was more like an intense brooding than a fear; it was a sort of hugging of hated facts so closely that she could feel their grain, like letting cold water run over her hand from a faucet on a winter morning.

She ironed again, faster now, as if she felt the more she engaged her body in work the less she would think. But how could she forget Johnny-Boy out there on those wet fields rounding up white and black Communists for a meeting tomorrow? And that was just what Sug had been doing when the sheriff had caught him, beat him, and tried to make him tell who and where his comrades were. Po Sug! They sho musta beat the boy somethin awful! But, thank Gawd, he didnt talk! He ain no weaklin, Sug ain! Hes been lion-hearted all his life long.

That had happened a year ago. And now each time those meetings came around the old terror surged back. While shoving the iron a cluster of toiling days returned; days of washing and ironing to feed Johnny-Boy and Sug so they could do party work; days of carrying a hundred pounds of white folks' clothes upon her head across fields sometimes wet and sometimes dry. But in those days a hundred pounds was nothing to carry carefully balanced upon her head while stepping by instinct over the corn and cotton rows. The only time it had seemed heavy was when she had heard of Sug's arrest. She had been coming home one morning with a bundle upon her head, her hands swinging idly by her sides, walking slowly with her eyes in front of her, when Bob, Johnny-Boy's pal, had called from across the fields and had come and told her that the sheriff had got Sug. That morning the bundle had become heavier than she could ever remember.

And with each passing week now, though she spoke of it to no one, things were becoming heavier. The tubs of water and the smoothing iron and the bundle of clothes were becoming harder to lift, with her back aching so; and her work was taking longer, all because Sug was gone and she didn't know just when Johnny-Boy would be taken too. To ease the ache of anxiety that was swelling her heart, she hummed, then sang softly:

> *"He walks wid me, He talks wid me,*
> *He tells me Ahm His Own. . . ."*

Guiltily, she stopped and smiled. Looks like Ah jus cant seem t fergit them ol songs, no mattah how hard Ah tries. . . . She had learned them when she was a little girl living and working on a farm. Every Monday morning from the corn and cotton fields the slow strains had floated from her mother's lips, lonely and haunting; and later, as the years had filled with gall, she had learned their deep meaning. Long hours of scrubbing floors for a few cents a day had taught her who Jesus was, what a great boon it was to cling to Him, to be like Him and suffer without a mumbling word. She had poured the yearning of her life into the songs, feeling buoyed with a faith beyond this world. The figure of the Man nailed in agony to the Cross, His burial in a cold grave, His transfigured Resurrection, His being breath and clay, God and Man—all had focused her feelings upon an imagery which had swept her life into a wondrous vision.

But as she had grown older, a cold white mountain, the white folks and their laws, had swum into her vision and shattered her songs and their spell of peace. To her that white mountain was temptation, something to lure her from her Lord, a part of the world God had made in order that she might endure it and come through all the stronger, just as Christ had risen with greater glory from the tomb. The days crowded with trouble had enhanced her faith and she had grown to love hardship with a bitter pride; she had obeyed the laws of the white folks with a soft smile of secret knowing.

After her mother had been snatched up to heaven in a chariot of fire, the years had brought her a rough workingman and two black babies, Sug and Johnny-Boy, all three of whom she had wrapped in the charm and magic of her vision. Then she was tested by no less than God; her man died, a trial which she bore with the strength shed by the grace of her vision; finally even the memory of her man faded into the vision itself, leaving her with two black boys growing tall, slowly into manhood.

Then one day grief had come to her heart when Johnny-Boy and Sug had walked forth demanding their lives. She had sought to fill their eyes with her vision, but they would have none of it. And she had wept when they began to boast of the strength shed by a new and terrible vision.

But she had loved them, even as she loved them now; bleeding, her heart had followed them. She could have done no less, being an old woman in a strange world. And day by day her sons had ripped from her startled eyes her old vision, and image by image had given her a new one, different, but great and strong enough to fling her into the light of another grace. The wrongs and sufferings of black men had taken the place of Him nailed to the Cross; the meager beginnings of the party had become another Resurrection; and the hate of those who would destroy her new faith had quickened in her a hunger to feel how deeply her new strength went.

"Lawd, Johnny-Boy," she would sometimes say, "Ah just wan them white folks t try t make me tell *who* is *in* the party n who *ain!* Ah just wan em t try, n Ahll show em somethin they never thought a black woman could have!"

But sometimes like tonight, while lost in the forgetfulness of work, the past and the present would become mixed in her; while toiling under a strange star for a new freedom the old songs would slip from her lips with their beguiling sweetness.

The iron was getting cold. She put more wood into the fire, stood again at the window, and watched the yellow blade of light cut through the wet darkness. Johnny-Boy ain here yit. . . . Then, before she was aware of it, she was still, listening for sounds. Under the drone of rain she heard the slosh of feet in mud. Tha ain Johnny-Boy. She knew his long, heavy footsteps in a million. She heard feet come on the porch. Some woman. . . . She heard bare knuckles knock three times, then once. Thas some of them comrades! She unbarred the door, cracked it a few inches, and flinched from the cold rush of damp wind.

"Whos tha?"

"Its me!"

"Who?"

"Me, Reva!"

She flung the door open.

"Lawd, chile, c mon in!"

She stepped to one side and a thin, blond-haired white girl ran through the door; as she slid the bolt she heard the girl gasping and shaking her wet clothes. Somethings wrong! Reva wauldna walked a mile t mah house in all this slop fer nothin! Tha gals stuck onto Johnny-Boy. Ah wondah ef anything happened t im?

"Git on inter the kitchen, Reva, where its warm."

"Lawd, Ah sho is wet!"

"How yuh reckon yuhd be, in all tha rain?"

"Johnny-Boy ain here *yit?*" asked Reva.

"Naw! N ain no usa yuh worryin bout im. Jus yuh git them shoes off! Yuh wanna ketch yo deatha col?" She stood looking absently. Yeah; its somethin about the party er Johnny-Boy thas gone wrong. Lawd, Ah wondah ef her pa knows how she feels bout Johnny-Boy. "Honey, yuh hadnt oughta come out in sloppy weather like this."

"Ah had t come, An Sue."

She led Reva to the kitchen.

"Git them shoes off n git close t the stove so yuhll git dry!"

"An Sue, Ah got somethin t tell yuh. . . ."

The words made her hold her breath. *Ah bet its somethin bout Johnny-Boy!*

"Whut, honey?"

"The sheriff wuz by our house tonight. He come to see pa."

"Yeah?"

"He done got word from somewheres bout tha meetin tomorrow."

"Is it Johnny-Boy, Reva?"

"Aw, naw, An Sue! Ah ain hearda word bout him. Ain yuh seen im tonight?"

"He ain come home t eat yit."

"Where kin he be?"

"Lawd knows, chile."

"Somebodys gotta tell them comrades tha meetings off," said Reva. "The sheriffs got men watchin our house. Ah had t slip out t git here widout em followin me."

"Reva?"

"Hunh?"

"Ahma ol woman n Ah wans yuh t tell me the truth."

"Whut, An Sue?"

"Yuh ain tryin t fool me, is yuh?"

"*Fool* yuh?"

"Bout Johnny-Boy?"

"Lawd, naw, An Sue!"

"Ef theres anythin wrong just tell me, chile. Ah kin stan it."

She stood by the ironing board, her hands as usual folded loosely over her stomach, watching Reva pull off her water-clogged shoe. She was feeling that Johnny-Boy was already lost to her; she was feeling the pain that would come when she knew it for certain; and she was feeling that she would have to be brave and bear it. She was like a person caught in a swift current of water and knew where the water was sweeping her and did not want to go on but had to go on to the end.

"It ain nothin bout Johnny-Boy, An Sue," said Reva. "But we gotta do somethin er we'll all git inter trouble."

"How the sheriff know about tha meetin?"

"Thas whut pa wans t know."

"Somebody done turned Judas."

"Sho looks like it."

"Ah bet it wuz some of them new ones," she said.

"Its hard t tell," said Reva.

"Lissen, Reva, yuh oughta stay here n git dry, but yuh bettah git back n tell yo pa Johnny-Boy ain here n Ah don know when hes gonna show up. *Some*bodys gotta tell them comrades t stay erway from yo pas house."

She stood with her back to the window, looking at Reva's wide blue eyes. Po critter! Gotta go back thu all tha slop! Though she felt sorry for Reva, not once did she think that it would not have to be done. Being a woman, Reva was not suspect; she would *have* to go. It was just as natural for Reva to go back through the cold rain as it was for her to iron night and day, or for Sug to be in jail. Right now, Johnny-Boy was out there on those dark fields trying to get home. Lawd, don let em git im tonight! In spite of herself her feelings became torn. She loved her son and, loving him, she loved what he was trying to do. Johnny-Boy was happiest when he was working for the party, and her love for him was for his happiness. She frowned, trying hard to fit something together in her feelings: for her to try to stop Johnny-Boy was to admit that all the toil of years meant nothing; and to let him go meant that sometime or other he would be caught, like Sug. In facing it this way she felt a little stunned, as though she had come suddenly upon a blank wall in the dark. But outside in the rain were people, white and black, whom she had known all her life. Those people depended upon Johnny-Boy, loved him, and looked to him as a man and leader. Yeah; hes gotta keep on; he cant stop now. . . . She looked at Reva; she was crying and pulling her shoes back on with reluctant fingers.

"Whut yuh carryin on that way fer, chile?"

"Yuh done los Sug, now yuh sendin Johnny-Boy. . . ."

"Ah got t, honey."

She was glad she could say that. Reva believed in black folks and not for anything in the world would she falter before her. In Reva's trust and acceptance of her she had found her first feelings of humanity; Reva's love was her refuge from shame and degradation. If in the early days of her life the white mountain had driven her back from the earth, then in her last days Reva's love was drawing her toward it, like the beacon that swung through the night outside. She heard Reva sobbing.

"Hush, honey!"

"Mah brothers in jail too! Ma cries every day. . . ."

"Ah knows, honey."

She helped Reva with her coat; her fingers felt the scant flesh of the girl's shoulders. She don git ernuff t eat, she thought. She slipped her arms around Reva's waist and held her close for a moment.

"Now, yuh stop that crying."

"A-a-ah c-c-cant help it. . . ."

"Everythingll be awright; Johnny-Boyll be back."

"Yuh think so?"

"Sho, chile. Cos he will."

Neither of them spoke again until they stood in the doorway. Outside they could hear water washing through the ruts of the street.

"Be sho n send Johnny-Boy t tell the folks t stay erway from pas house," said Reva.

"Ahll tell im. Don yuh worry."

"Good-bye!"

"Good-bye!"

Leaning against the door jamb, she shook her head slowly and watched Reva vanish through the falling rain.

II

She was back at her board, ironing, when she heard feet sucking in the mud of the back yard: feet she knew from long years of listening were Johnny-Boy's. But tonight, with all the rain and fear, his coming was like a leaving, was almost more than she could bear. Tears welled to her eyes and she blinked them away. She felt that he was coming so that she could give him up; to see him now was to say good-bye. But it was a good-bye she knew she could never say; they were not that way toward each other. All day long they could sit in the same room and not speak; she was his mother and he was her son. Most of the time a nod or a grunt would carry all the meaning that she wanted to convey to him, or he to her. She did not even turn her head when she heard him come stomping into the kitchen. She heard him pull up a chair, sit, sigh, and draw off his muddy shoes; they fell to the floor with heavy thuds. Soon the kitchen was full of the scent of his drying socks and his burning pipe. Tha boys hongry! She paused and looked at him over her shoulder; he was puffing at his pipe with his head tilted back and his feet propped up on the edge of the stove; his eyelids drooped and his wet clothes steamed from the heat of the fire. Lawd, that boy gits mo like his pa every day he lives, she mused, her lips breaking in a slow faint smile. Hols tha pipe in his mouth just like his pa usta hol his. Wondah how they woulda got erlong ef his pa hada lived? They oughta liked each other, they so much alike. She wished there could have been other children besides Sug, so Johnny-Boy would not have to be so much alone. A man needs a woman by his side. . . . She thought of Reva; she liked Reva; the brightest glow her heart had ever known was when she had learned that Reva loved Johnny-Boy. But beyond Reva were cold white faces. Ef theys caught it means *death*. . . . She jerked around when she heard Johnny-Boy's pipe clatter to the floor. She saw him pick it up, smile sheepishly at her, and wag his head.

"Gawd, Ahm sleepy," he mumbled.

She got a pillow from her room and gave it to him.

"Here," she said.

"Hunh," he said, putting the pillow between his head and the back of the chair.

They were silent again. Yes, she would have to tell him to go back out into the cold rain and slop; maybe to get caught; maybe for the last time; she didn't know. But she would let him eat and get dry before telling him that the sheriff knew of the meeting to be held at Lem's tomorrow. And she would make him take a big dose of soda before he went out; soda always helped to stave off a cold. She looked at the clock. It was eleven. Theres time yit. Spreading a newspaper on the apron of the stove, she placed a heaping plate of greens upon it, a knife, a fork, a cup of coffee, a slab of cornbread, and a dish of peach cobbler.

"Yo suppahs ready," she said.

"Yeah," he said.

He did not move. She ironed again. Presently, she heard him eating. When she could no longer hear his knife tinkling against the edge of the plate, she knew he was through. It was almost twelve now. She would let him rest a little while longer before she told him. Till one er'clock, mabbe. Hes so tired. . . . She finished her ironing, put away the board, and stacked the clothes in her dresser drawer. She poured herself a cup of black coffee, drew up a chair, sat down and drank.

"Yuh almos dry," she said, not looking around.

"Yeah," he said, turning sharply to her.

The tone of voice in which she had spoken had let him know that more was coming. She drained her cup and waited a moment longer.

"Reva wuz here."

"Yeah?"

"She lef bout an hour ergo."

"Whut she say?"

"She said ol man Lem hada visit from the sheriff today."

"Bout the meetin?"

"Yeah."

She saw him stare at the coals glowing red through the crevices of the stove and run his fingers nervously through his hair. She knew he was wondering how the sheriff had found out. In the silence he would ask a wordless question and in the silence she would answer wordlessly. Johnny-Boys too trustin, she thought. Hes trying to make the party big n hes takin in folks fastern he kin git t know em. You cant trust ever white man yuh meet. . . .

"Yuh know, Johnny-Boy, yuh been takin in a lotta them white folks lately. . . ."

"Aw, ma!"

"But, Johnny-Boy . . ."

"Please, don talk t me bout tha now, ma."

Yuh ain t ol t lissen n learn, son," she said.

"Ah know whut yuh gonna say, ma. N yuh wrong. Yuh cant judge folks jus by how yuh feel bcount em n by how long yuh done knowed em. Ef we start tha we wouldnt have *no*body in the party. When folks pledge they word t be with us, then we gotta take em in. Wes too weak t be choosy."

He rose abruptly, rammed his hands into his pockets, and stood facing the window; she looked at his back in a long silence. She knew his faith; it was deep. He had always said that black men could not fight the rich bosses alone; a man could not fight with every hand against him. But he believes so hard hes blind, she thought. At odd times they had had these arguments before; always she would be pitting her feeling against the hard necessity of his thinking, and always she would lose. She shook her head. Po Johnny-Boy he don know. . . .

"But ain nona our folks tol, Johnny-Boy," she said.

"How yuh know?" he asked. His voice came low and with a tinge of anger. He still faced the window, and now and then the yellow blade of light flicked across the sharp outine of his black face.

"Cause Ah know em," she said.

"*Any*body mighta tol," he said.

"It wuznt nona *our* folks," she said again.

She saw his hand sweep in a swift arc of disgust.

"*Our* folks! Ma, who in Gawd's name is *our* folks?"

"The folks we wuz born n raised wid, son. The folks we *know!*"

"We can't make the party grow tha way, ma."

"It mighta been Booker," she said.

"Yuh don know."

". . . er Blattberg . . ."

"Fer Chrissakes!"

". . . er any of the fo-five others whut joined las week."

"Ma, yuh jus don wan me t go out tonight," he said.

"Yo ol ma wans yuh t be careful, son."

"Ma, when yuh start doubtin folks in the party, then there ain no end."

"Son, Ah knows ever black man n woman in this parta the county," she said, standing too. "Ah watched em grow up; Ah even helped birth n nurse some of em; Ah knows em *all* from way back. There ain none of em that *coulda* tol! The folks Ah know jus don open they dos n ast death t walk in! Son, it wuz some of them *white* folks! Yuh jus mark mah word n wait n see!"

"Why is it gotta be *white* folks?" he asked. "Ef they tol, then theys jus Judases, thas all."

"Son, look at whuts befo yuh."

He shook his head and sighed.

"Ma, Ah done tol yuh a hundred times. Ah can't see white n Ah cant see black," he said. "Ah sees rich men n Ah sees po men."

She picked up his dirty dishes and piled them in a pan. Out of the corners of her eyes she saw him sit and pull on his wet shoes. Hes goin! When she put the last dish away he was standing fully dressed, warming his hands over the stove. Jus a few mo minutes now n he'll be gone, like Sug, mabbe. Her throat tightened. This black man's fight takes *ever*thin! Looks like Gawd put us in this worl jus t beat us down!

"Keep this, ma," he said.

She saw a crumpled wad of money in his outstretched fingers.

"Naw, yuh keep it. Yuh might need it."

"It ain mine, ma. It berlongs t the party."

"But, Johnny-Boy, yuh might hafta go erway!"

"Ah kin make out."

"Don fergit yosef too much, son."

"Ef Ah don come back theyll need it."

He was looking at her face and she was looking at the money.

"Yuh keep tha," she said slowly. "Ahll give em the money."

"From where?"

"Ah got some."

"Where yuh git it from?"

She sighed.

"Ah been savin a dollah a week fer Sug ever since hes been in jail."

"Lawd, ma!"

She saw the look of puzzled love and wonder in his eyes. Clumsily, he put the money back into his pocket.

"Ahm gone," he said.

"Here; drink this glass of soda watah."

She watched him drink, then put the glass away.

"Waal," she said. "Take the stuff outta yo pockets!"

She lifted the lid of the stove and he dumped all the papers from his pockets into the fire. She followed him to the door and made him turn round.

"Lawd, yuh tryin to maka revolution n yuh cant even keep yo coat buttoned." Her nimble fingers fastened his collar high around his throat. "There!"

He pulled the brim of his hat low over his eyes. She opened the door and with the suddenness of the cold gust of wind that struck her face, he was gone. She watched the black fields and the rain take him, her eyes burning. When the last faint footstep could no longer be heard, she closed the door, went to her bed, lay down, and pulled the cover over her while fully dressed. Her feelings coursed with the rhythm of the rain: Hes gone! Lawd, Ah *know* hes gone! Her blood felt cold.

III

She was floating in a gray void somewhere between sleeping and dreaming and then suddenly she was wide awake, hearing and feeling in the same instant the thunder of the door crashing in and a cold wind filling the room. It was pitch black and she stared, resting on her elbows, her mouth open, not breathing, her ears full of the sound of tramping feet and booming voices. She knew at once: They lookin fer im! Then, filled with her will, she was on her feet, rigid, waiting, listening.

"The lamps burnin!"

"Yuh see her?"

"Naw!"

"Look in the kitchen!"

"Gee, this place smells like niggers!"

"Say, somebody's here er been here!"

"Yeah; theres fire in the stove!"

"Mabbe hes been here n gone?"

"Boy, look at these jars of jam!"

"Niggers make good jam!"

"Git some bread!"

"Heres some cornbread!"

"Say, lemme git some!"

"Take it easy! Theres plenty here!"

"Ahma take some of this stuff home!"

"Look, heres a pota greens!"

"N some hot cawffee!"

"Say, yuh guys! C mon! Cut it out! We didn't come here for a feas!"

She walked slowly down the hall. They lookin fer im, but they ain got im yit! She stopped in the doorway, her gnarled black hands as always folded over her stomach, but tight now, so tightly the veins bulged. The kitchen was crowded with white men in glistening raincoats. Though the lamp burned, their flashlights still glowed in red fists. Across her floor she saw the muddy tracks of their boots.

"Yuh white folks git outta mah house!"

There was quick silence; every face turned toward her. She saw a sudden movement, but did not know what it meant until something hot and wet slammed her squarely in the face. She gasped, but did not move. Calmly, she wiped the warm greasy liquor of greens from her eyes with her left hand. One of the white men had thrown a handful of greens out of the pot at her.

"How they taste, ol bitch?"

"Ah ast yuh t git outta mah house!"

She saw the sheriff detach himself from the crowd and walk toward her.

"Now, Anty . . ."

"White man, don yuh *Anty* me!"

"Yuh ain got the right sperit!"

"Sperit hell! Yuh git these men outta mah house!"

"Yuh ack like yuh don like it!"

"Naw, Ah don like it, n yuh knows dam wall Ah don!"

"Whut yuh gonna do bout it?"

"Ahm tellin yuh t git outta mah house!"

"Gittin sassy?"

"Ef telling yuh t git outta mah house is sass, then Ahm sassy!"

Her words came in a tense whisper; but beyond, back of them, she was watching, thinking, judging the men.

"Listen, Anty." The sheriff's voice came soft and low. "Ahm here t hep yuh. How come yuh wanna ack this way?"

"Yuh ain never heped yo *own* sef since yuh been born," she flared. "How kin the likes of yuh hep me?"

One of the white men came forward and stood directly in front of her.

"Lissen, nigger woman, yuh talkin t *white* men!"

"Ah don care who Ahm talkin t!"

"Yuhll wish some day yuh did!"

"Not t the likes of yuh!"

"Yuh need somebody t teach yuh how t be a good nigger!"

"*Yuh* cant teach it t me!"

"Yuh gonna change yo tune."

"Not longs mah bloods warm!"

"Don git smart now!"

"Yuh git outta mah house!"

"Spose we don go?" the sheriff asked.

They were crowded around her. She had not moved since she had taken her place in the doorway. She was thinking only of Johnny-Boy as she stood there giving and taking words; and she knew that they, too, were thinking of Johnny-Boy. She knew they wanted him, and her heart was daring them to take him from her.

"Spose we don go?" the sheriff asked again.

"Twenty of yuh runnin over one ol woman! Now, ain yuh white men glad yuh so brave?"

The sheriff grabbed her arm.

"C mon, now! Yuh done did ernuff sass for one night. Wheres tha nigger son of yos?"

"Don yuh wished yuh knowed?"

"Yuh wanna git slapped?"

"Ah ain never seen one of you kind tha wuznt too low fer—"

The sheriff slapped her straight across her face with his open palm. She fell back against a wall and sank to her knees.

"Is tha whut white men do t nigger women?"

She rose slowly and stood again, not even touching the place that ached from his blow, her hands folded over her stomach.

"Ah ain never seen one of yo kind tha wuznt too low fer—"

He slapped her again; she reeled backward several feet and fell on her side. "Is tha whut we too low t do?"

She stood before him again, dry-eyed, as though she had not been struck. Her lips were numb and her chin was wet with blood.

"Aw, let her go! Its the nigger we wan!" said one.

"Wheres that nigger son of yos?" the sheriff asked.

"Find im," she said.

"By Gawd, ef we hafta find im we'll kill im!"

"He wont be the only nigger yuh ever killed," she said.

She was consumed with a bitter pride. There was nothing on this earth, she felt then, that they could not do to her but that she could take. She stood on a narrow plot of ground from which she would die before she was pushed. And then it was, while standing there feeling warm blood seeping down her throat, that she gave up Johnny-Boy, gave him up to the white folks. She gave him up because they had come tramping into her heart demanding him, thinking they could get him by beating her, thinking they could scare her into making her tell where he was. She gave him up because she wanted them to know that they could not get what they wanted by bluffing and killing.

"Wheres this meetin gonna be?" the sheriff asked.

"Don yuh wish yuh knowed?"

"Ain there gonna be a meetin?"

"How come yuh astin me?"

"There *is* gonna be a meeting," said the sheriff.

"Is it?"

"Ah gotta great mind t choke it outta yuh!"

"Yuh so smart," she said.

"We ain playin wid yuh!"

"Did Ah say yuh wuz?"

"Tha nigger son of yos is erroun here somewheres n we aim t find him," said the sheriff. "Ef yuh tell us where he is n ef he talks, mabbe he'll git off easy. But ef we hafta find im, we'll kill im! Ef we hafta find im, then yuh git a sheet t put over im in the mawnin, see? Git yuh a sheet, cause hes gonna be dead!"

"He won't be the only nigger yuh ever killed," she said again.

The sheriff walked past her. The others followed. Yuh didn't git whut yuh wanted! she thought exultingly. N yuh ain gonna *never* git it! Hotly, something ached in her to make them feel the intensity of her pride and freedom; her heart groped to turn the bitter hours of her life into words of a kind that would make them feel that she had taken all they had done to her in her stride and could still take more. Her faith surged so strongly in her she was all but blinded. She walked behind them to the door, knotting and twisting her fingers. She saw them step to the muddy ground. Each whirl of the yellow beacon revealed glimpses of slanting rain. Her lips moved, then she shouted.

"Yuh didn't git whut yuh wanted! N yuh ain gonna nevah git it!"

The sheriff stopped and turned; his voice came low and hard.

"Now, by Gawd, thas ernuff outta yuh!"

"Ah know when Ah done said ernuff!"

"Aw, naw, yuh don!" he said. "Yuh don know when yuh done said ernuff, but Ahma teach yuh ternight!"

He was up the steps and across the porch with one bound. She backed into the hall, her eyes full on his face.

"Tell me when yuh gonna stop talkin!" he said, swinging his fist.

The blow caught her high on the cheek; her eyes went blank; she fell flat on her face. She felt the hard heel of his wet shoes coming into her temple and stomach.

"Lemme hear yuh talk some mo!"

She wanted to, but could not; pain numbed and choked her. She lay still and somewhere out of the gray void of unconsciousness she heard someone say: *aw fer chrissakes leave her erlone its the nigger we wan.* . . .

IV

She never knew how long she had lain huddled in the dark hallway. Her first returning feeling was of a nameless fear crowding the inside of her, then a deep pain spreading from her temple downward over her body. Her ears were filled with the drone of rain and she shuddered from the cold wind blowing through the door. She opened her eyes and at first saw nothing. As if she were imagining it, she knew she was half lying and half sitting in a corner against a wall. With difficulty she twisted her neck and what she saw made her hold her breath—a vast white blur was suspended directly above her. For a moment she could not tell if her fear was from the blur or if the blur was from her fear. Gradually the blur resolved itself into a huge white face that slowly filled her vision. She was stone still, conscious really of the effort to breathe, feeling somehow that she existed only by the mercy of that white face. She had seen it before; its fear had gripped her many times; it had for her the fear of all the white faces she had ever seen in her life. *Sue.* . . . As from a great distance, she heard her name being called. She was regaining consciousness now, but the fear was coming with her. She looked into the face of a white man, wanting to scream out for him to go, yet accepting his presence because she felt she had to. Though some remote part of her mind was active, her limbs were powerless. It was as if an invisible knife had split her in two, leaving one half of her lying there helpless, while the other half shrank in dread from a forgotten but familiar enemy. *Sue its me Sue its me* . . . Then all at once the voice came clearly.

"Sue, its me! Its Booker!"

And she heard an answering voice speaking inside of her, Yeah, its Booker. . . . The one whut jus joined. . . . She roused herself, struggling for full consciousness; and as she did so she transferred to the person of Booker the nameless fear she felt. It seemed that Booker towered above her as a challenge to her right to exist upon the earth.

"Yuh awright?"

She did not answer; she started violently to her feet and fell.

"Sue, yuh hurt!"

"Yah," she breathed.

"Where they hit yuh?"

"Its mah head," she whispered.

She was speaking even though she did not want to; the fear that had hold of her compelled her.

"They beat yuh?"

"Yeah."

"Them bastards! Them Gawddam bastards!"

She heard him saying it over and over; then she felt herself being lifted.

"Naw!" she gasped.

"Ahma take yuh t the kitchen!"

"Put me down!"

"But yuh cant stay here like this!"

She shrank in his arms and pushed her hands against his body; when she was in the kitchen she freed herself, sank into a chair, and held tightly to its back. She looked wonderingly at Booker. There was nothing about him that should frighten her so, but even that did not ease her tension. She saw him go to the water bucket, wet his handkerchief, wring it, and offer it to her. Distrustfully, she stared at the damp cloth.

"Here; put this on yo forehead. . . ."

"Naw!"

"C mon; itll make yuh feel bettah!"

She hesitated in confusion. What right had she to be afraid when someone was acting kindly as this toward her? Reluctantly, she leaned forward and pressed the damp cloth to her head. It helped. With each passing minute she was catching hold of herself, yet wondering why she felt as she did.

"What happened?"

"Ah don know."

"Yuh feel bettah?"

"Yeah."

"Who all wuz here?"

"Ah don know," she said again.

"Yo head still hurt?"

"Yeah."

"Gee, Ahm sorry."

"Ahm awright." She sighed and buried her face in her hands.

She felt him touch her shoulder.

"Sue, Ah got some bad news fer yuh. . . ."

She knew; she stiffened and grew cold. It had happened; she stared dry-eyed, with compressed lips.

"Its mah Johnny-Boy," she said.

"Yeah, Ahm awful sorry t halfta tell yuh this way. But Ah thought yuh oughta know. . . ."

Her tension eased and a vacant place opened up inside of her. A voice whispered, Jesus, hep me!

"W-w-where is he?"

"They got im out to Foleys Woods tryin t make im tell who the others is."

"He ain gonna tell," she said. "They just as wall kill im, cause he ain gonna nevah tell."

"Ah hope he don," said Booker. "But he didnt hava chance t tell the others. They grabbed im jus as he got t the woods."

Then all the horror of it flashed upon her; she saw flung out over the rainy countryside an array of shacks where white and black comrades were sleeping; in the morning they would be rising and going to Lem's; then they would be caught. And that meant terror, prison, and death. The comrades would have to be told; she would have to tell them; she could not entrust Johnny-Boy's work to another, and especially not to Booker as long as she felt toward him as she did. Gripping the bottom of the chair with both hands, she tried to rise; the room blurred and she swayed. She found herself resting in Booker's arms.

"Lemme go!"

"Sue, yuh too weak t walk!"

"Ah gotta tell em!" she said.

"Set down, Sue! Yuh hurt! Yuh sick!"

When seated, she looked at him helplessly.

"Sue, lissen! Johnny-Boys caught. Ahm here. Yuh tell me who they is n Ahll tell em."

She stared at the floor and did not answer. Yes; she was too weak to go. There was no way for her to tramp all those miles through the rain tonight. But should she tell Booker? If only she had somebody like Reva to talk to! She did not want to decide alone; she must make no mistake about this. She felt Booker's fingers pressing on her arm and it was as though the white mountain was pushing her to the edge of a sheer height; she again exclaimed inwardly, Jesus, hep me! Booker's white face was at her side, waiting. Would she be doing right to tell him? Suppose she did not tell and then the comrades were caught? She could not ever forgive herself for doing a thing like that. But maybe she was wrong; maybe her fear was what Johnny-Boy had always called "jus foolishness." She remembered his saying, Ma we can't make the party grow ef we start doubtin everybody. . . .

"Tell me who they is, Sue, n Ahll tell em. Ah jus joined n Ah don know who they is."

"Ah don know who they is," she said.

"Yuh *gotta* tell me who they is, Sue!"

"Ah told yuh Ah don know."

"Yuh *do* know! C mon! Set up n talk!"

"Naw!"

"Yuh wan em all t git *killed?*"

She shook her head and swallowed. Lawd, Ah don blieve in this man!

"Lissen, Ahll call the names n yuh tell me which ones is in the party n which ones ain, see?"

"Naw!"

"Please, Sue!"

"Ah don know," she said.

"Sue, yuh ain doin right by em. Johnny-Boy wouldn't wan yuh t be this way. Hes out there holdin up his end. Les hol up ours. . . ."

"Lawd, Ah don know. . . ."

"Is yuh scareda me cause Ahm *white?* Johnny-Boy ain like tha. Don let all the work we done go fer nothin."

She gave up and bowed her head in her hands.

"Is it Johnson? Tell me, Sue!"

"Yeah," she whispered in horror, a mounting horror of feeling herself being undone.

"Is it Green?"

"Yeah."

"Murphy?"

"Lawd, Ah don know!"

"Yuh gotta tell me, Sue!"

"Mistah Booker, please leave me erlone. . . ."

"Is it Murphy?"

She answered yes to the names of Johnny-Boy's comrades; she answered until he asked her no more. Then she thought, How he know the sheriffs men is watchin Lems house? She stood up and held onto her chair, feeling something sure and firm within her.

"How yuh know about Lem?"

"Why . . . how Ah know?"

"Whut yuh doin here this tima night? How yuh know the sheriff got Johnny-Boy?"

"Sue, don yuh blieve in me?"

She did not, but she could not answer. She stared at him until her lips hung open; she was searching deep within herself for certainty.

"You meet Reva?" she asked.

"Reva?"

"Yeah, Lems gal?"

"Oh, yeah. Sho, Ah met Reva."

"She tell yuh?"

She asked the question more of herself than of him; she longed to believe.

"Yeah," he said softly. "Ah reckon Ah oughta be goin t tell em now."

"Who?" she asked. "Tell *who?*"

The muscles of her body were stiff as she waited for his answer; she felt as though life depended upon it.

"The comrades," he said.

"Yeah." She sighed.

She did not know when he left; she was not looking or listening. She just suddenly saw the room empty and from her the thing that had made her fearful was gone.

V

For a space of time that seemed to her as long as she had been upon the earth, she sat huddled over the cold stove. One minute she would say to herself, They both gone now, Johnny-Boy n Sug. . . . Mabbe Ahll never see em ergin. Then a surge of guilt would blot out her longing. "Lawd, Ah shouldna tol!" she mumbled. "But no man kin be so lowdown as t do a thing like tha. . . ." Several times she had an impulse to try to tell the comrades herself; she was feeling a little better now. But what good would that do? She had told Booker the names. He jus couldnt be a Judas t po folks like us. . . . He *couldnt!*

"An Sue!"

Thas Reva! Her heart leaped with an anxious gladness. She rose without answering and limped down the dark hallway. Through the open door, against the background of rain, she saw Reva's face lit now and then to whiteness by the whirling beams of the beacon. She was about to call, but a thought checked her. Jesus, hep me! Ah gotta tell her bout Johnny-Boy. . . . Lawd, Ah can't!

"An Sue, yuh there?"

"C mon in, chile!"

She caught Reva and held her close for a moment without speaking.

"Lawd, Ahm sho glad yuh here," she said at last.

"Ah thought somethin had happened t yuh," said Reva, pulling away. "Ah saw the do open. . . . Pa told me to come back n stay wid yuh tonight. . . ." Reva paused and started. "W-w-whuts the mattah?"

She was so full of having Reva with her that she did not understand what the question meant.

"Hunh?"

"Yo neck . . ."

"Aw, it ain nothin, chile. C mon in the kitchen."

"But theres blood on yo neck!"

"The sheriff wuz here. . . ."

"Them fools! Whut they wanna bother yuh fer? Ah could kill em! So hep me Gawd, Ah could!"

"It ain nothin," she said.

She was wondering how to tell Reva about Johnny-Boy and Booker. Ahll wait a lil while longer, she thought. Now that Reva was here, her fear did not seem as awful as before.

"C mon, lemme fix yo head. An Sue. Yoh hurt."

They went to the kitchen. She sat silent while Reva dressed her scalp. She was feeling better now; in just a little while she would tell Reva. She felt the girl's finger pressing gently upon her head.

"Tha hurt?"

"A lil, chile."

"Yuh po thing!"

"It ain nothin."

"Did Johnny-Boy come?"

She hesitated.

"Yeah."

"He done gone t tell the others?"

Reva's voice sounded so clear and confident that it mocked her. Lawd, Ah cant tell this chile. . . .

"Yuh told im, didn't yuh, An Sue?"

"Y-y-yeah. . . ."

"Gee! Thas good! Ah told pa he didnt hafta worry ef Johnny-Boy got the news. Mabbe thingsll come out awright."

"Ah hope. . . ."

She could not go on; she had gone as far as she could. For the first time that night she began to cry.

"Hush, An Sue! Yuh awways been brave. Itll be awwright!"

"Ain nothin awwright, chile. The worls jus too much fer us. Ah reckon."

"Ef you cry that way itll make me cry."

She forced herself to stop. Naw, Ah cant carry on tha way in fronta Reva. . . . Right now she had a deep need for Reva to believe in her. She watched the girl get pine knots from behind the stove, rekindle the fire, and put on the coffeepot.

"Yuh wan some cawffee?" Reva asked.

"Naw, honey."

"Aw, c mon, An Sue."

"Jusa lil, honey."

"Thas the way to be. Oh, say, Ah fergot," said Reva, measuring out spoonsful of coffee. "Pa told me t tell yuh t watch out fer tha Booker man. Hes a stool."

She showed not one sign of outward movement or expression, but as the words fell from Reva's lips she went limp inside.

"Pa tol me soon as Ah got back home. He got word from town. . . ."

She stopped listening. She felt as though she had been slapped to the extreme outer edge of life, into a cold darkness. She knew now what she had felt when she had looked up out of her fog of pain and had seen Booker. It was the image of all the white folks, and the fear that went with them, that she had seen and felt during her lifetime. And again, for the second time that night, something she had felt had come true. All she could say to herself was, Ah didnt like im! Gawd knows, Ah didn't! Ah told Johnny-Boy it wuz some of them white folks. . . .

"Here; drink yo cawffee. . . ."

She took the cup; her fingers trembled, and the steaming liquid spilt onto her dress and leg.

"Ahm sorry, An Sue!"

Her leg was scalded, but the pain did not bother her.

"Its awright," she said.

"Wait; lemme put some lard on tha burn!"

"It don hurt."

"Yuh worried bout somethin."

"Naw, honey."

"Lemme fix yuh so mo cawffee."

"Ah don wan nothin now, Reva."

"Waal, buck up. Don be tha way. . . ."

They were silent. She heard Reva drinking. No; she would not tell Reva; Reva was all she had left. But she had to do something, some way, somehow. She was undone too much as it was; and to tell Reva about Booker or Johnny-Boy was more than she was equal to; it would be too coldly shameful. She wanted to be alone and fight this thing out with herself.

"Go t bed, honey. Yuh tired."

"Naw, Ahm awright, An Sue."

She heard the bottom of Reva's empty cup clank against the top of the stove. Ah *got* t make her go t bed! Yes; Booker would tell the names of the comrades to the sheriff. If she could only stop him some way! That was the answer, the point, the star that grew bright in the morning of new hope. Soon, maybe half an hour from now, Booker would reach Foleys Woods. Hes boun t go the long way, cause he don know no short cut, she thought. Ah could wade the creek n beat im there. . . . But what would she do after that?

"Reva, honey, go t bed. Ahm awright. Yuh need res."

"Ah ain sleepy, An Sue!"

"Ah knows whuts bes fer yuh, chile. Yuh tired n wet."

"A wanna stay up wid yuh."

She forced a smile and said, "Ah don think they gonna hurt Johnny-Boy. . . ."

"Fer *real*, An Sue?"

"Sho, honey."

"But Ah wanna wait up wid yuh."

"Thas mah job, honey. Thas whut a mas fer, t wait up fer her chullun."

"Good night, An Sue."

"Good night, honey."

She watched Reva pull up and leave the kitchen; presently she heard the shucks in the mattress whispering, and she knew that Reva had gone to bed. She was alone. Through the cracks of the stove she saw the fire dying to gray ashes; the room was growing cold again. The yellow beacon continued to flit past the window and the rain still drummed. Yes, she was alone; she had done this awful thing alone; she must find some way out, alone. Like touching a festering sore, she put her finger upon that moment when she had shouted her defiance to the sheriff, when she had shouted to feel her strength. She had lost Sug to save others; she had let Johnny-Boy go to save others; and then in a moment of weakness that came from too much strength she had lost all. If she had not shouted to the sheriff, she would have been strong enough to have resisted Booker; she would have been able to tell the comrades herself. Something tightened in her as she remembered and understood the fit of fear she had felt on coming to herself in the dark hallway. A part of her life she thought she had done away with forever had had hold of her then. She had thought the soft, warm past was over; she had thought that it did not mean much when now she sang: "Hes the Lily of the Valley, the Bright n Mawnin Star. . . ." The days when she had sung that song were the days when she had not hoped for anything on this earth, the days when the cold mountain had driven her into the arms of Jesus. She had thought that Sug and Johnny-Boy had taught her to forget Him, to fix her hope upon the fight of black men for freedom. Through the gradual years she had believed and worked with them, had felt strength shed from the grace of their terrible vision. That grace had been upon her when she had let the sheriff slap her down; it had been upon her when she had risen time and again from the floor and faced him. But she had trapped herself with her own hunger; to water the long dry thirst of her faith, her pride had made a bargain which her flesh could not keep. Her having told the names of Johnny-Boy's comrades was but an incident in a deeper horror. She stood up and looked at the floor while call and counter-call, loyalty and counter-loyalty struggled in her soul. Mired she was between two abandoned worlds, living, but dying without the strength of the grace that either gave. The clearer she felt it the fuller did something well up from the depths of her for release; the more urgent did she feel the need to fling into her black sky another star, another hope, one more terrible vision to give her the strength to live and act. Softly and restlessly she walked about the kitchen, feeling herself naked against the night, the rain, the world; and shamed whenever the thought of Reva's love crossed her mind. She lifted her empty hands and looked at her writhing fingers. Lawd, whut kin Ah do now? She could still wade the creek and get to Foley's Woods before Booker. And then what? How could she manage to see Johnny-Boy or Booker? Again she heard the sheriff's threatening voice: Git yuh a sheet, cause hes gonna be dead! The sheet! Thas it, the *sheet!* Her whole being leaped with will; the long years of her life bent toward a moment of focus, a point. Ah kin go wid mah sheet! Ahll be doin whut he said! Lawd Gawd in Heaven, Ahma go lika nigger woman wid mah windin sheet t git mah dead son! But then what? She stood straight and smiled grimly; she had in her heart the whole meaning of her life; her entire personality was poised on the brink of a total act. Ah know! Ah *know!* She thought of Johnny-Boy's gun in the dresser drawer. Ahll hide the gun in the sheet n go aftah Johnny-Boy's body. . . . She tiptoed to her room, eased out the dresser drawer, and got a sheet. Reva was sleeping; the darkness was filled with her quiet breathing. She groped in the drawer and found the gun. She wound the gun in the sheet and held them both under her apron. Then she stole to the bedside and watched Reva. Lawd, hep her! But mabbe shes bettah off. This had t happen sometime. . . . She n Johnny-Boy couldna been together in this here South . . . n Ah couldn't tell her bout Booker. Itll come out awright n she wont nevah know. Reva's trust would never be shaken. She caught her breath as the shucks in the mattress rustled dryly; then all was quiet and she breathed easily again. She tiptoed to the door, down the hall, and stood on the porch. Above her the yellow beacon whirled through the rain. She went over muddy ground, mounted a slope, stopped and looked back at her house. The lamp glowed in her window, and the yellow beacon that swung every few seconds seemed to feed it with light. She turned and started across the fields, holding the gun and sheet tightly, thinking, Po Reva . . . po critter . . . shes fas ersleep. . . .

VI

For the most part she walked with her eyes half shut, her lips tightly compressed, leaning her body against the wind and the driving rain, feeling the pistol in the sheet sagging cold and heavy in her fingers. Already she was getting wet; it seemed that her feet found every puddle of water that stood between the corn rows.

She came to the edge of the creek and paused, wondering at what point was it low. Taking the sheet from under her apron, she wrapped the gun in it so that her finger could be upon the trigger. Ahll cross here, she thought. At first she did not feel the water; her feet were already wet. But the water grew cold as it came up to her knees; she gasped when it reached her waist. Lawd, this creeks high! When she had passed the middle, she knew that she was out of danger. She came out of the water, climbed a grassy hill, walked on, turned a bend, and saw the lights of autos gleaming ahead. Yeah; theys still there! She hurried with her head down. Wonda did Ah beat im here? Lawd, Ah *hope* so! A vivid image of Booker's white face hovered a moment before her eyes and a surging will rose up in her so hard and strong that it vanished. She was among the autos now. From nearby came the hoarse voices of the men.

"Hey, yuh!"

She stopped, nervously clutching the sheet. Two white men with shotguns came toward her.

"Whut in hell yuh doin out here?"

She did not answer.

"Didn't yuh hear somebody speak t yuh?"

"Ahm comin aftah mah son," she said humbly.

"Yo *son?*"

"Yessuh."

"Whut yo son doin out here?"

"The sheriff's got im."

"Holy Scott! Jim, its the niggers ma!"

"What yuh got there?" asked one.

"A sheet."

"A *sheet?*"

"Yessuh."

"Fer whut?"

"The sheriff tol me t bring a sheet t git his body."

"Waal, waal . . ."

"Now, ain tha somethin?"

The white men looked at each other.

"These niggers sho love one ernother," said one.

"N tha ain no lie," said the other.

"Take me t the sheriff," she begged.

"Yuh ain givin us *orders,* is yuh?"

"Nawsuh."

"We'll take yuh when wes good n ready."

"Yessuh."

"So yuh wan his body?"

"Yessuh."

"Waal, he ain dead yit."

"They gonna kill im," she said.

"Ef he talks they wont."

"He ain gonna talk," she said.

"How yuh know?"

"Cause he ain."

"We got ways of makin niggers talk."

"Yuh ain got no way fer im."

"You thinka lot of that black Red, don yuh?"

"Hes mah son."

"Why don yuh teach im some sense?"

"Hes mah son," she said again.

"Lissen, ol nigger woman, yuh stand there wid yo hair white. Yuh got bettah sense than t blieve tha niggers kin make a revolution. . . ."

"A black republic," said the other one, laughing.

"Take me t the sheriff," she begged.

"Yuh his ma," said one. "Yuh kin make im talk n tell whos in this thing wid im."

"He ain gonna talk," she said.

"Don yuh wan im t live?"

She did not answer.

"C mon, les take her t Bradley."

They grabbed her arms and she clutched hard at the sheet and gun; they led her toward the crowd in the woods. Her feelings were simple; Booker would not tell; she was there with the gun to see to that. The louder became the voices of the men the deeper became her feeling of wanting to right the mistake she had made; of wanting to fight her way back to solid ground. She would stall for time until Booker showed up. Oh, ef theyll only lemme git close t Johnny-Boy! As they led her near the crowd she saw white faces turning and looking at her and heard a rising clamor of voices.

"Whos tha?"

"A nigger woman!"

"Whut she doin out here?"

"This is his ma!" called one of the men.

"Whut she want?"

"She brought a sheet t cover his body!"

"He ain dead yit!"

"They tryin t make im talk!"

"But he will be dead soon ef he don open up!"

"Say, look! The niggers ma brought a sheet t cover up his body!"

"Now, ain tha sweet?"

"Mabbe she wans t hol a prayer meetin!"

"Did she git a preacher?"

"Say, go git Bradley!"

"O.K.!"

The crowd grew quiet. They looked at her curiously; she felt their cold eyes trying to detect some weakness in her. Humbly, she stood with the sheet covering the gun. She had already accepted all that they could do to her.

The sheriff came.

"So yuh brought you sheet, hunh?"

"Yessuh," she whispered.

"Looks like them slaps we gave yuh learned yuh some sense, didnt they?"

She did not answer.

"Yuh don need tha sheet. Yo son ain dead yit," he said, reaching toward her.

She backed away, her eyes wide.

"Naw!"

"Now, lissen, Anty!" he said. "There ain no use in yuh ackin a fool! Go in there n tell tha nigger son of yos t tell us whos in this wid im, see? Ah promise we wont kill im ef he talks. We'll let him git outta town."

"There ain nothin Ah kin tell im," she said.

"Yuh wan us t kill im?"

She did not answer. She saw someone lean toward the sheriff and whisper.

"Bring her erlong," the sheriff said.

They led her to a muddy clearing. The rain streamed down through the ghostly glare of the flashlights. As the men formed a semicircle she saw Johnny-Boy lying in a trough of mud. He was tied with rope; he lay hunched and one side of his face rested in a pool of black water. His eyes were staring questioningly at her.

"Speak t im," said the sheriff.

If she could only tell him why she was here! But that was impossible; she was close to what she wanted and she stared straight before her with compressed lips.

"Say, nigger!" called the sheriff, kicking Johnny-Boy. "Here's yo ma!"

Johnny-Boy did not move or speak. The sheriff faced her again.

"Lissen, Anty," he said. "Yuh got mo say wid im than anybody. Tell im t talk n hava chance. Whut he wanna pertect the other niggers n white folks fer?"

She slid her finger about the trigger of the gun and looked stonily at the mud.

"Go t him," said the sheriff.

She did not move. Her heart was crying out to answer the amazed question in Johnny-Boy's eyes. But there was no way now.

"Wall, yuhre astin fer it. By Gawd, we gotta way to *make* yuh talk t im," he said, turning away. "Say, Tim, git one of them logs n turn that nigger upside-down n put his legs on it!"

A murmur of assent ran through the crowd. She bit her lips; she knew what that meant.

"Yuh wan yo nigger son crippled?" she heard the sheriff ask.

She did not answer. She saw them roll the log up; they lifted Johnny-Boy and laid him on his face and stomach, then they pulled his legs over the log. His kneecaps rested on the sheer top of the log's back and the toes of his shoes pointed groundward. So absorbed was she in watching that she felt that it was she who was being lifted and made ready for torture.

"Git a crowbar!" said the sheriff.

A tall, lank man got a crowbar from a nearby auto and stood over the log. His jaws worked slowly on a wad of tobacco.

"Now, its up t yuh, Anty," the sheriff said. "Tell the man what t do!"

She looked into the rain. The sheriff turned.

"Mabbe she think wes playin. Ef she don say nothin, then break em at the kneecaps!"

"O.K., Sheriff!"

She stood waiting for Booker. Her legs felt weak; she wondered if she would be able to wait much longer. Over and over she said to herself, Ef he come now Ahd kill em both!

"She ain saying nothin, Sheriff!"

"Waal, Gawddammit, let im have it!"

The crowbar came down and Johnny-Boy's body lunged in the mud and water. There was a scream. She swayed, holding tight to the gun and sheet.

"Hol im! Git the other leg!"

The crowbar fell again. There was another scream.

"Yuh break em?" asked the sheriff.

The tall man lifted Johnny-Boy's legs and let them drop limply again, dropping rearward from the kneecaps. Johnny-Boy's body lay still. His head had rolled to one side and she could not see his face.

"Jus lika broke sparrow wing," said the man, laughing softly.

Then Johnny-Boy's face turned to her; he screamed.

"Go way, ma! Go way!"

It was the first time she had heard his voice since she had come out to the woods; she all but lost control of herself. She started violently forward, but the sheriff's arm checked her.

"Aw naw! Yuh had yo chance!" He turned to Johnny-Boy. "She kin go ef yuh talk."

"Mistah, he ain gonna talk," she said.

"Go way, ma!" said Johnny-Boy.

"Shoot im! Don make im suffah so," she begged.

"He'll either talk or he'll never hear yuh ergin," the sheriff said. "Theres other things we kin do t im."

She said nothing.

"What yuh come here fer, ma?" Johnny-Boy sobbed.

"Ahm gonna split his eardrums," the sheriff said. "Ef yuh got anythin t say t im yuh bettah say it *now!*"

She closed her eyes. She heard the sheriff's feet sucking in mud. Ah could save im! She opened her eyes; there were shouts of eagerness from the crowd as it pushed in closer.

"Bus em, Sheriff!"

"Fix im so he can't hear!"

"He knows how t do it, too!"

"He busted a Jew boy tha way once!"

She saw the sheriff stoop over Johnny-Boy, place his flat palm over one ear, and strike his fist against it with all his might. He placed his palm over the other ear and struck again. Johnny-Boy moaned, his head rolling from side to side, his eyes showing white amazement in a world without sound.

"Yuh wouldn't talk t im when yuh had the chance," said the sheriff. "Try n talk now."

She felt warm tears on her cheeks. She longed to shoot Johnny-Boy and let him go. But if she did that they would take the gun from her, and Booker would tell who the others were. Lawd, hep me! The men were talking loudly now, as though the main business was over. It seemed ages that she stood there watching Johnny-Boy roll and whimper in his world of silence.

"Say, Sheriff, heres somebody lookin fer yuh!"

"Who is it?"

"Ah don know!"

"Bring em in!"

She stiffened and looked around wildly, holding the gun tight. Is tha Booker? Then she held still, feeling that her excitement might betray her. Mabbe Ah kin shoot em both; mabbe Ah kin shoot *twice!* The sheriff stood in front of her, waiting. The crowd parted and she saw Booker hurrying forward.

"Ah know em all, Sheriff!" he called.

He came full into the muddy clearing where Johnny-Boy lay.

"Yuh mean yuh got the names?"

"Sho! The ol nigger—"

She saw his lips hang open and silent when he saw her. She stepped forward and raised the sheet.

"Whut—"

She fired, once; then, without pausing, she turned, hearing them yell. She aimed at Johnny-Boy, but they had their arms around her, bearing her to the ground, clawing at the sheet in her hand. She glimpsed Booker lying sprawled in the mud, on his face, his hands stretched out before him; then a cluster of yelling men blotted him out. She lay without struggling, looking upward through the rain at the white faces above her. And she was suddenly at peace; they were not a white mountain now; they were not pushing her any longer to the edge of life. Its awright. . . .

"She shot Booker!"

"She hada gun in the sheet!"

"She shot im right thu the head!"

"Whut she shoot im fer?"

"Kill the bitch!"

"Ah *thought* somethin wuz wrong bout her!"

"Ah wuz fer givin it t her from the firs!"

"Thas whut yuh git fer treatin a nigger nice!"

"Say, Bookers dead!"

She stopped looking into the white faces, stopped listening. She waited, giving up her life before they took it from her; she had done what she wanted. Ef only Johnny-Boy. . . . She looked at him, he lay looking at her with tired eyes. Ef she could only tell im! But he lay already buried in a grave of silence.

"Whut yuh kill im fer, hunh?"

It was the sheriff's voice; she did not answer.

"Mabbe she wuz shootin at yuh, Sheriff?"

"Whut yuh kill im fer?"

She felt the sheriff's foot come into her side; she closed her eyes.

"Yuh black bitch!"

"Let her have it!"

"Yuh reckon she foun out bout Booker?"

"She mighta."

"Jesus Chris, whut yuh dummies *waitin* on!"

"Yeah, kill her!"

"Kill em *both!*"

"Let her know her nigger sons dead firs!"

She turned her head toward Johnny-Boy; he lay looking puzzled in a world beyond the reach of voices. At leas he can't hear, she thought.

"C mon, let im have it!"

She listened to hear what Johnny-Boy could not. They came, two of them, one right behind the other; so close together that they sounded like one shot. She did not look at Johnny-Boy now; she looked at the white faces of the men, hard and wet in the glare of the flashlights.

"Yuh hear tha, nigger woman?"

"Did that surprise im? Hes in hell now wonderin whut hit im!"

"C mon! Give it t her, Sheriff!"

"Lemme shoot her, Sheriff! It wuz mah pal she shot!"

"Awright, Pete! Thas fair ernuff!"

She gave up as much of her life as she could before they took it from her. But the sound of the shot and the streak of fire that tore its way through her chest forced her to live again, intensely. She had not moved, save for the slight jarring impact of the bullet. She felt the heat of her own blood warming her cold, wet back. She yearned suddenly to talk. "Yuh didn't git whut yuh wanted! N yuh ain gonna nevah git it! Yuh didn't kill me; Ah come here by mahsef. . . ." She felt rain falling into her wide-open, dimming eyes and heard faint voices. Her lips moved soundlessly. *Yuh didnt git yuh didnt yuh didnt. . . .* Focused and pointed she was, buried in the depths of her star, swallowed in its peace and strength; and not feeling her flesh growing cold, cold as the rain that fell from the invisible sky upon the doomed living and the dead that never dies.

Jack in the Pot

Dorothy West

1940

When she walked down the aisle of the theater, clutching the money in her hand, hearing the applause and laughter, seeing, dimly, the grinning black faces, she was trembling so violently that she did not know how she could ever regain her seat.

It was unbelievable. Week after week she had come on Wednesday afternoon to this smelly, third-run neighborhood movie house, paid her dime, received her beano card, and gone inside to wait through an indifferent feature until the houselights came on and a too-jovial white man wheeled a board onto the stage and busily fished in a bowl for numbers.

Today it had happened. As the too-jovial white man called each number, she found a corresponding one on her card. When he called the seventh number and explained dramatically that whoever had punched five numbers in a row had won the jackpot of fifty-five dollars, she listened in smiling disbelief that there was that much money in his pocket. It was then that the woman beside her leaned toward her and said excitedly, "Look, lady, you got it!"

She did not remember going down the aisle. Undoubtedly her neighbor had prodded her to her feet. When it was over, she tottered dazedly to her seat and sat in a dreamy stupor, scarcely able to believe her good fortune.

The drawing continued, the last dollar was given away, the theater darkened, and the afternoon crowd filed out. The little gray woman, collecting her wits, followed them.

She revived in the sharp air. Her head cleared and happiness swelled in her throat. She had fifty-five dollars in her purse. It was wonderful to think about.

She reached her own intersection and paused before Mr. Spiro's general market. Here she regularly shopped, settling part of her bill fortnightly out of her relief check. When Mr. Spiro put in inferior stock because most of his customers were poor-paying reliefers, she had wanted to shop elsewhere. But she could never get paid up.

Excitement smote her. She would go in, settle her account, and say good-bye to Mr. Spiro forever. Resolutely she turned into the market.

Mr. Spiro, broad and unkempt, began to boom heartily, from behind the counter. "Hello, Mrs. Edmunds."

She lowered her eyes and asked diffidently, "How much is my bill, Mr. Spiro?"

He recoiled in horror. "Do I worry about your bill, Mrs. Edmunds? Don't you pay something when you get your relief check? Ain't you one of my best customers?"

"I'd like to settle," said Mrs. Edmunds breathlessly.

Mr. Spiro eyed her shrewdly. His voice was soft and insinuating. "You got cash, Mrs. Edmunds? You hit the number? Every other week you give me something on account. This week you want to settle. Am I losing your trade? Ain't I always treated you right?"

"Sure, Mr. Spiro," she answered nervously. "I was telling my husband just last night, ain't another man treats me like Mr. Spiro. And I said I wished I could settle my bill."

"Gee," he said triumphantly. "It's like I said. You're one of my best customers. Worrying about your bill when I ain't even worrying. I was telling your investigator"—he paused significantly—"when Mr. Edmunds gets a job, I know I'll get the balance. Mr. Edmunds got himself a job maybe?"

She was stiff with fright. "No, I'd have told you right off, and her too. I ain't one to cheat on relief. I was only saying how I wished I could settle. I wasn't saying that I was."

"Well, then, what you want for supper?" Mr. Spiro asked soothingly.

"Loaf of bread," she answered gratefully, "two pork chops, one kinda thick, can of spaghetti, little can of milk."

The purchases were itemized. Mrs. Edmunds said good night and left the store. She felt sick and ashamed, for she had turned tail in the moment that was to have been her triumph over tyranny.

A little boy came toward her in the familiar rags of the neighborhood children. Suddenly Mrs. Edmunds could bear no longer the intolerable weight of her mean provisions.

"Little boy," she said.

"Ma'am?" He stopped and stared at her.

"Here." She held out the bag to him. "Take it home to your mama. It's food. It's clean."

He blinked, then snatched the bag from her hands and turned and ran very fast in the direction from which he had come.

* * *

Mrs. Edmunds felt better at once. Now she could buy a really good supper. She walked ten blocks to a better neighborhood, and the cold did not bother her. Her misshapen shoes were winged.

She pushed inside a resplendent store and marched to the meat counter. A porterhouse steak caught her eye. She could not look past it. It was big and thick and beautiful.

The clerk leaned toward her. "Steak, moddom?"

"That one."

It was glorious not to care about the cost of things. She bought mushrooms, fresh peas, cauliflower, tomatoes, a pound of good coffee, a pint of real cream, a dozen dinner rolls, and a maple walnut layer cake.

The winter stars were pricking the sky when she entered the dimly lit hallway of the old-law tenement in which she lived. The dank smell smote her instantly after the long walk in the brisk, clear air. The Smith boy's dog had dirtied the hall again. Mr. Johnson, the janitor, was mournfully mopping up.

"Evenin', Mis' Edmunds, ma'am," he said plaintively.

"Evening," Mrs. Edmunds said coldly. Suddenly she hated Mr. Johnson. He was so humble.

Five young children shared the uninhabitable basement with him. They were always half sick, and he was always neglecting his duties to tend to them. The tenants were continually deciding to report him to the agent and then at the last moment deciding not to.

"I'll be up tomorrow to see 'bout them windows, Mis' Edmunds, ma'am. My baby kep' frettin' today, and I been so busy doctorin'."

"Those children need a mother," said Mrs. Edmunds severely. "You ought to get married again."

"My wife ain' daid," cried Mr. Johnson, shocked out of his servility. "She's in that T.B. home. Been there two years and 'bout on the road to health."

"Well," said Mrs. Edmunds inconclusively, and then added briskly, "I been waiting weeks and weeks for them window strips. Winter's half over. If the place was kept warm—"

"Yes'm, Mis' Edmunds," he said hastily, his bloodshot eyes imploring. "It's that ol' furnace. I done tol' the agent time and again, but they ain' fixin' to fix up this house 'long as you all is relief folks."

The steak was sizzling on the stove when Mr. Edmunds' key turned in the lock of the tiny three-room flat. His step dragged down the hall. Mrs. Edmunds knew what that meant: "No man wanted." Two years ago Mr. Edmunds had begun, doggedly, to canvas the city for work, leaving home soon after breakfast and rarely returning before supper.

Once he had had a little stationery store. After losing it, he had spent his small savings and sold or pawned every decent article of furniture and clothing before applying for relief. Even so, there had been a long investigation while he and his wife slowly starved. Fear had been implanted in Mrs. Edmunds. Thereafter she was never wholly unafraid. Mr. Edmunds had had to stand by and watch his wife starve. He never got over being ashamed.

Mr. Edmunds stood in the kitchen doorway, holding his rain-streaked hat in his knotted hand. He was forty-nine, and he looked like an old man.

"I'm back," he said. "Cooking supper."

It was not a question. He seemed unaware of the intoxicating odors.

She smiled at him brightly. "Smell good?"

He shook suddenly with the cold that was still in him. "Smells like always to me."

Her face fell in disappointment, but she said gently, "You oughtn't to be walking 'round this kind of weather."

"I was looking for work," he said fiercely. "Work's not going to come knocking."

She did not want to quarrel with him. He was too cold, and their supper was too fine.

"Things'll pick up in the spring," she said soothingly.

"Not for me," he answered gloomily. "Look how I look. Like a bum. I wouldn't hire me myself."

"What you want me to do about it?" she asked furiously.

"Nothing," he said with wry humor, "unless you can make money, and make me just about fifty dollars."

She caught her breath and stared at his shabbiness. She had seen him look like this so long that she had forgotten that clothes would make a difference.

She nodded toward the stove. "That steak and all. Guess you think I got a fortune. Well, I won a little old measly dollar at the movies."

His face lightened, and his eyes grew soft with affection. "You shouldn't have bought a steak," he said. "Wish you'd bought yourself something you been wanting. Like gloves. Some good warm gloves. Hurts my heart when I see you with cold hands."

She was ashamed, and wished she knew how to cross the room to kiss him. "Go wash," she said gruffly. "Steak's 'most too done already."

It was a wonderful dinner. Both of them had been starved for fresh meat. Mrs. Edmunds' face was flushed, and there was color in her lips, as if the good blood of the meat had filtered through her skin. Mr. Edmunds ate a pound and a half of the two-pound steak, and his hands seemed steadier with each sharp thrust of the knife.

Over coffee and cake they talked contentedly. Mrs. Edmunds wanted to tell the truth about the money, and waited for an opening.

"We'll move out of this hole someday soon," said Mr. Edmunds. "Things won't be like this always." He was full and warm and confident.

"If I had fifty dollars," Mrs. Edmunds began cautiously, "I believe I'd move tomorrow. Pay up these people what I owe and get me a fit place to live in."

"Fifty dollars would be a drop in the bucket. You got to have something coming in steady."

He had hurt her again. "Fifty dollars is more than you got," she said meanly.

"It's more than you got too," he said mildly. "Look at it like this. If you had fifty dollars and made a change, them relief folks would worry you like a pack of wolves. But say, f' instance, you had fifty dollars and I had a job, we could walk out of here without a howdy-do to anybody."

It would have been anticlimactic to tell him about the money. She got up. "I'll do the dishes. You sit still."

He noticed no change in her and went on earnestly, "Lord's bound to put something in my way soon. We don't live human. I never see a paper 'cept when I pick one up in the subway. I ain't had a cigarette in three years. We ain't got a radio. We don't have no company. All the pleasure you get is a ten-cent movie one day a week. I don't even get that."

Presently Mrs. Edmunds ventured, "You think the investigator would notice if we got a little radio for the bedroom?"

"Somebody got one to give away?" His face was eager.

"Maybe."

"Well, seeing how she could check with the party what give it to you, I think it would be all right."

"Well, ne' mind—" Her voice petered out.

It was his turn to try. "Want to play me a game of cards?"

He had not asked her for months. She cleared her throat.

"I'll play a hand or two."

He stretched luxuriously. "I feel so good. Feeling like this, bet I'll land something tomorrow."

She said very gently, "The investigator comes tomorrow."

He smiled quickly to hide his disappointment. "Clean forgot. It don't matter. That meal was so good it'll carry me straight through Friday."

She opened her mouth to tell him about the jackpot, to promise him as many meals as there was money. Suddenly someone upstairs pounded on the radiator for heat. In a moment someone downstairs pounded. Presently their side of the house resounded. It was maddening. Mrs. Edmunds was bitterly aware that her hands and feet were like ice.

" 'Tisn't no use," she cried wildly to the walls. She burst into tears. " 'Tisn't nothing no use."

Her husband crossed quickly to her. He kissed her cheek. "I'm going to make all this up to you. You'll see."

By half-past eight they were in bed. By quarter to nine Mrs. Edmunds was quietly sleeping. Mr. Edmunds lay staring at the ceiling. It kept coming closer.

Mrs. Edmunds waked first and decided to go again to the grand market. She dressed and went out into the street. An ambulance stood in front of the door. In a minute an intern emerged from the basement, carrying a bundled child. Mr. Johnson followed, his eyes more bleary and bloodshot than ever.

Mrs. Edmunds rushed up to him. "The baby?" she asked anxiously.

His face worked pitifully. "Yes, ma'am, Mis' Edmunds. Pneumonia. I heard you folks knockin' for heat last night but my hands was too full. I ain't forgot about them windows, though. I'll be up tomorrow bright and early."

Mr. Edmunds stood in the kitchen door. "I smell meat in the morning?" he asked incredulously. He sat down, and she spread the feast: kidneys and omelet, hot buttered rolls, and strawberry jam. "You mind," he said happily, "explaining this mystery? Was that dollar of yours made out of elastic?"

"It wasn't a dollar like I said. It was five. I wanted to surprise you."

She did not look at him and her voice was breathless. She had decided to wait until after the investigator's visit to tell him the whole truth about the money. Otherwise they might both be nervous and betray themselves by their guilty knowledge.

"We got chicken for dinner," she added shyly.

"Lord, I don't know when I had a piece of chicken."

They ate, and the morning passed glowingly. With Mr. Edmunds' help, Mrs. Edmunds moved the furniture and gave the flat a thorough cleaning. She liked for the investigator to find her busy. She felt less embarrassed about being on relief when it could be seen that she occupied her time.

The afternoon waned. The Edmundses sat in the living room, and there was nothing to do. They were hungry but dared not start dinner. With activity suspended, they became aware of the penetrating cold and the rattling windows. Mr. Edmunds began to have that wild look of waiting for the investigator.

Mrs. Edmunds suddenly had an idea. She would go and get a newspaper and a package of cigarettes for him.

At the corner, she ran into Mr. Johnson. Rather, he ran into her, for he turned the corner with his head down and his gait as unsteady as if he had been drinking.

"That you, Mr. Johnson?" she said sharply.

He raised his head, and she saw that he was not drunk.

"Yes, ma'am, Mis' Edmunds."

"The baby—is she worse?"

Tears welled out of his eyes. "The Lord done took her."

Tears stood in her own eyes. "God knows I'm sorry to hear that. Let me know if there's anything I can do."

"Thank you, Mis' Edmunds, ma'am. But ain't nothin' nobody can do. I been pricin' funerals. I can get one for fifty dollars. But I been to my brother, and he ain't got it. I been everywhere. Couldn't raise no more than ten dollars." He was suddenly embarrassed. "I know all you tenants is on relief. I wasn't fixin' to ask you all."

"Fifty dollars," she said strainedly, "is a lot of money."

"God'd have to pass a miracle for me to raise it. Guess the city'll have to bury her. You reckon they'll let me take flowers?"

"You being the father, I guess they would," she said weakly.

When she returned home the flat was a little warmer. She entered the living room. Her husband's face brightened.

"You bought a paper!"

She held out the cigarettes. "You smoke this kind?" she asked lifelessly.

He jumped up and crossed to her. "I declare I don't know how to thank you! Wish that investigator'd come. I sure want to taste them."

"Go ahead and smoke," she cried fiercely. "It's none of her business. We got our rights same as working people."

She turned into the bedroom. She was utterly spent. Too much had happened in the last twenty-four hours.

"Guess I'll stretch out for a bit. I'm not going to sleep. If I do drop off, listen out for the investigator. The bell needs fixing. She might have to knock."

At half-past five Mr. Edmunds put down the newspaper and tiptoed to the bedroom door. His wife was still asleep. He stood for a moment in indecision, then decided it was long past the hour when the investigator usually called and went down the hall to the kitchen. He wanted to prepare supper as a surprise. He opened the window, took the foodstuffs out of the crate that in winter served as icebox, and set them on the table.

The doorbell tinkled faintly.

He went to the door and opened it. The investigator stepped inside. She was small and young and white.

"Good evening, miss," he said.

"I'm sorry to call so late," she apologized. "I've been busy all day with an evicted family. But I knew you were expecting me, and I didn't want you to stay in tomorrow."

"You come on up front, miss," he said. "I'll wake up my wife. She wasn't feeling so well and went to lie down."

She saw the light from the kitchen, and the dark rooms beyond.

"Don't wake Mrs. Edmunds," she said kindly, "if she isn't well. I'll just sit in the kitchen for a minute with you."

He looked down at her, but her open, honest face did not disarm him. He braced himself for whatever was to follow.

"Go right on in, miss," he said.

He took the dish towel and dusted the clean chair. "Sit down, miss."

He stood facing her with a furrow between his brows, and his arms folded. There was an awkward pause. She cast about for something to say and saw the table.

"I interrupted your dinner preparations."

His voice and his face hardened for the blow.

"I was getting dinner for my wife. It's chicken."

"It looks like a nice one," she said pleasantly.

He was baffled. "We ain't had chicken once in three years."

"I understand," she said sincerely. "Sometimes I spend my whole salary on something I want very much."

"You ain't much like an investigator," he said in surprise. "One we had before you woulda raised Ned." He sat down suddenly, his defenses down. "Miss, I been wanting to ask you this for a long time. You ever have any men's clothes?"

Her voice was distressed. "Every once in a while. But with so many people needing assistance, we can only give them to our employables. But I'll keep your request in mind."

He did not answer. He just sat staring at the floor, presenting an adjustment problem. There was nothing else to say to him.

She rose. "I'll be going now, Mr. Edmunds."

"I'll tell my wife you was here, miss."

A voice called from the bedroom. "Is that you talking?"

"It's the investigator lady," he said. "She's just going."

Mrs. Edmunds came hurrying down the hall, the sleep in her face and tousled hair.

"I was just lying down, ma'am. I didn't mean to go to sleep. My husband should've called me."

"I didn't want him to wake you."

"And he kept you sitting in the kitchen."

She glanced inside to assure herself that it was sufficiently spotless for the fine clothes of the investigator. She saw the laden table and felt so ill that water welled into her mouth.

"The investigator lady knows about the chicken," Mr. Edmunds said quickly. "She—"

"It was only five dollars," his wife interrupted, wringing her hands.

"Five dollars for a chicken?" The investigator was shocked and incredulous.

"She didn't buy that chicken out of none of your relief money," Mr. Edmunds said defiantly. "It was money she won at a movie."

"It was only five dollars," Mrs. Edmunds repeated tearfully.

"We ain't trying to conceal nothing," Mr. Edmunds snarled. He was cornered and fighting. "If you'd asked me how we come by the chicken, I'd have told you."

"For God's sake, ma'am, don't cut us off," Mrs. Edmunds moaned. "I'll never go to another movie. It was only ten cents. I didn't know I was doing wrong." She burst into tears.

The investigator stood tense. They had both been screaming at her. She was tired and so irritated that she wanted to scream back.

"Mrs. Edmunds," she said sharply, "get hold of yourself. I'm not going to cut you off. That's ridiculous. You won five dollars at a movie and you bought some food. That's fine. I wish my family could win five dollars for food."

She turned and tore out of the flat. They heard her stumbling and sobbing down the stairs.

"You feel like eating?" Mrs. Edmunds asked dully.

"I guess we're both hungry. That's why we got so upset."

"Maybe we'd better eat, then."

"Let me fix it."

"No." She entered the kitchen. "I kinda want to see you just sitting and smoking a cigarette."

He sat down and reached in his pocket with some eagerness. "I ain't had one yet." He lit a cigarette, inhaled, and felt better immediately.

"You think," she said bleakly, "she'll write that up in our case?"

"I don't know, dear."

"You think they'll close our case if she does?"

"I don't know that neither, dear."

She clutched the sink for support. "My God, what would we do?"

The smoke curled around him luxuriously. "Don't think about it till it happens."

"I got to think about it. The rent, the gas, the light, the food."

"They wouldn't hardly close our case for five dollars."

"Maybe they'd think it was more."

"You could prove it by the movie manager."

She went numb all over. Then suddenly she got mad about it.

It was nine o'clock when they sat down in the living room. The heat came up grudgingly. Mrs. Edmunds wrapped herself in her sweater and read the funnies. Mr. Edmunds was happily inhaling his second cigarette. They were both replete and in good humor.

The window rattled and Mr. Edmunds looked around at it lazily. "Been about two months since you asked Mr. Johnson for weatherstrips."

The paper shook in her hand. She did not look up. "He promised to fix it this morning, but his baby died."

"His baby! You don't say!"

She kept her eyes glued to the paper. "Pneumonia."

His voice filled with sympathy. He crushed out his cigarette. "Believe I'll go down and sit with him awhile."

"He's not there," she said hastily. "I met him when I was going to the store. He said he'd be out all evening."

"I bet the poor man's trying to raise some money."

She let the paper fall in her lap and clasped her hands to keep them from trembling. She lied again, as she had been lying steadily in the past twenty-four hours, as she had not lied before in all her life.

"He didn't say nothing to me about raising money."

"Wasn't no need to. Where would you get the first five cents to give him?"

"I guess," she cried jealously, "you want me to give him the rest of my money."

"No," he said. "I want you to spend what little's left on yourself. Me, I wish I had fifty dollars to give him."

"As poor as you are," she asked angrily, "you'd give him that much money? That's easy to say when you haven't got it."

"I look at it this way," he said simply. "I think how I'd feel in his shoes."

"You got your own troubles," she argued heatedly. "The Johnson baby is better off dead. You'd be a fool to put fifty dollars in the ground. I'd spend my fifty dollars on the living."

"Tain't no use to work yourself up," he said. "You ain't got fifty dollars, and neither have I. We'll be quarreling in a minute over make-believe money. Let's go to bed."

Mrs. Edmunds waked at seven and tried to lie quietly by her husband's side, but lying still was torture. She dressed and went into the kitchen and felt too listless to make her coffee. She sat down at the table and dropped her head on her folded arms. No tears came. There was only the burning in her throat and behind her eyes.

She sat in this manner for half an hour. Suddenly she heard a man's slow tread outside her front door. Terror gripped her. The steps moved on down the hall, but for a moment her knees were water. When she could control her trembling, she stood up and knew that she had to get out of the house. It could not contain her and Mr. Johnson.

She walked quickly away from her neighborhood. It was a raw day, and her feet and hands were beginning to grow numb. She felt sorry for herself. Other people were hurrying past in overshoes and heavy gloves. There was fifty-one dollars in her purse. It was her right to do what she pleased with it. Determinedly she turned into the subway.

In a downtown department store she rode the escalator to the dress department. She walked up and down the rows of lovely garments, stopping to finger critically, standing back to admire.

A salesgirl came toward her, looking straight at her with soft, expectant eyes.

"Do you wish to be waited on, madam?"

Mrs. Edmunds opened her mouth to say yes, but the word would not come. She stared at the girl stupidly. "I was just looking," she said.

In the shoe department, she saw a pair of comfort shoes and sat down timidly in a fine leather chair.

A salesman lounged toward her. "Something in shoes?"

"Yes, sir. That comfort shoe."

"Size?" His voice was bored.

"I don't know," she said.

"I'll have to measure you," he said reproachfully. "Give me your foot." He sat down on a stool and held out his hand.

She dragged her eyes up to his face. "How much you say those shoes cost?"

"I didn't say. Eight dollars."

She rose with acute relief. "I ain't got that much with me."

She retreated unsteadily. Something was making her knees weak and her head light.

Her legs steadied. She went quickly to the down escalator. She reached the third floor and was briskly crossing to the next down escalator when she saw the little dresses. A banner screamed that they were selling at the sacrifice price of one dollar. She decided to examine them.

She pushed through the crowd of women and emerged triumphantly within reach of the dresses. She searched carefully. There were pinks and blues and yellows. She was looking for white. She pushed back through the crowd. In her careful hands lay a little white dress. It was spun gold and gossamer.

Boldly she beckoned a salesgirl. "I'll take this, miss," she said.

All the way home she was excited and close to tears. She was in a fever to see Mr. Johnson. She would let the regret come later. A child lay dead and waiting burial.

She turned her corner at a run. Going down the rickety basement stairs, she prayed that Mr. Johnson was on the premises.

She pounded on his door and he opened it. The agony in his face told her instantly that he had been unable to borrow the money. She tried to speak, and her tongue tripped over her eagerness.

Fear took hold of her and rattled her teeth. "Mr. Johnson, what about the funeral?"

"I give the baby to the student doctors."

"Oh, my God, Mr. Johnson! Oh, my God!"

"I bought her some flowers."

She turned and went blindly up the stairs. Drooping in the front doorway was a frost-nipped bunch of white flowers. She dragged herself up to her flat. Once she stopped to hide the package under her coat. She would never look at that little white dress again. The ten five-dollar bills were ten five-pound stones in her purse. They almost hurled her backward.

She turned the key in her lock. Mr. Edmunds stood at the door. He looked rested and confident.

"I been waiting for you. I just started to go."

"You had any breakfast?" she asked tonelessly.

"I made some coffee. It was all I wanted."

"I shoulda made some oatmeal before I went out."

"You have on the big pot time I come home. Bet I'll land something good," he boasted. "You brought good luck in this house. We ain't seen the last of it." He pecked her cheek and went out, hurrying as if he were late for work.

She plodded into the bedroom. The steam was coming up fine. She sank down on the side of the bed and unbuttoned her coat. The package fell on her lap. She took the ten five-dollar bills and pushed them between a fold of the package. It was burial money. She could never use it for anything else. She hid the package under the mattress.

Wearily she buttoned up her coat and opened her purse again. It was empty, for the few cents remaining from her last relief check had been spent indiscriminately with her prize money.

She went into the kitchen to take stock of her needs. There was nothing left from their feasts. She felt the coffeepot. It was still hot, but her throat was too constricted for her to attempt to swallow.

She took her paper shopping bag and started out to Mr. Spiro's.

Flying Home

Ralph Ellison

1944

When Todd came to, he saw two faces suspended above him in a sun so hot and blinding that he could not tell if they were black or white. He stirred, feeling a pain that burned as though his whole body had been laid open to the sun which glared into his eyes. For a moment an old fear of being touched by white hands seized him. Then the very sharpness of the pain began slowly to clear his head. Sounds came to him dimly. *He done come to.* Who are they? he thought. *Naw, he ain't, I coulda sworn he was white.* Then he heard clearly:

"You hurt bad?"

Something within him uncoiled. It was a Negro sound.

"He's still out," he heard.

"Give 'im time. . . . Say, son, you hurt bad?"

Was he? There was that awful pain. He lay rigid, hearing their breathing and trying to weave a meaning between them and his being stretched painfully upon the ground. He watched them warily, his mind traveling back over a painful distance. Jagged scenes, swiftly unfolding as in a movie trailer, reeled through his mind, and he saw himself piloting a tail-spinning plane and landing and falling from the cockpit and trying to stand. Then, as in a great silence, he remembered the sound of crunching bone, and now, looking up into the anxious faces of an old Negro man and a boy from where he lay in the same field, the memory sickened him and he wanted to remember no more.

"How you feel, son?"

Todd hesitated, as though to answer would be to admit an inacceptable weakness. Then, "It's my ankle," he said.

"Which one?"

"The left."

With a sense of remoteness he watched the old man bend and remove his boot, feeling the pressure ease.

"That any better?"

"A lot. Thank you."

He had the sensation of discussing someone else, that his concern was with some far more important thing, which for some reason escaped him.

"You done broke it bad," the old man said. "We have to get you to a doctor."

He felt that he had been thrown into a tailspin. He looked at his watch; how long had he been here? He knew there was but one important thing in the world, to get the plane back to the field before his officers were displeased.

"Help me up," he said. "Into the ship."

"But it's broke too bad—"

"Give me your arm!"

"But, son . . ."

Clutching the old man's arm he pulled himself up, keeping his left leg clear, thinking, I'd never make him understand, as the leather-smooth face came parallel with his own.

"Now, let's see."

He pushed the old man back, hearing a bird's insistent shrill. He swayed giddily. Blackness washed over him, like infinity.

"You best sit down."

"No, I'm O.K."

"But, son. You jus' gonna make it worse. . . ."

It was a fact that everything in him cried out to deny, even against the flaming pain in his ankle. He would have to try again.

"You mess with that ankle they have to cut your foot off," he heard.

Holding his breath, he started up again. It pained so badly that he had to bite his lips to keep from crying out and he allowed them to help him down with a pang of despair.

"It's best you take it easy. We gon' git you a doctor."

Of all the luck, he thought. Of all the rotten luck, now I have done it. The fumes of high-octane gasoline clung in the heat, taunting him.

"We kin ride him into town on old Ned," the boy said.

Ned? He turned, seeing the boy point toward an ox team browsing where the buried blade of a plow marked the end of a furrow. Thoughts of himself riding an ox through the town, past streets full of white faces, down the concrete runways of the airfield made swift images of humiliation in his mind. With a pang he remembered his girl's last letter. "Todd," she had written, "I don't need the papers to tell me you had the intelligence to fly. And I have always known you to be as brave as anyone else. The papers annoy me. Don't you be contented to prove over and over again that you're brave or skillful just because you're black, Todd. I think they keep beating that dead horse because they don't want to say why you boys are not yet fighting. I'm really disappointed, Todd. Anyone with brains can learn to fly, but then what? What about using it, and who will you use it for? I wish, dear, you'd write about this. I sometimes think they're playing a trick on us. It's very humiliating. . . ." He wiped cold sweat from his face, thinking, What does she know of humiliation? She's never been down South. Now the humiliation would come. When you must have them judge you, knowing that they never accept your mistakes as your own but hold it against your whole race—that was humiliation. Yes, and humiliation was when you could never be simply yourself, when you were always a part of this old black ignorant man. Sure, he's all right. Nice and kind and helpful. But he's not you. Well, there's one humiliation I can spare myself.

"No," he said, "I have orders not to leave the ship. . . ."

"Aw," the old man said. Then, turning to the boy, "Teddy, then you better hustle down to Mister Graves and get him to come—"

"No, wait!" he protested before he was fully aware. Graves might be white. "Just have him get word to the field, please. They'll take care of the rest."

He saw the boy leave, running.

"How far does he have to go?"

"Might' nigh a mile."

He rested back, looking at the dusty face of his watch. But now they know something has happened, he thought. In the ship there was a perfectly good radio, but it was useless. The old fellow would never operate it. That buzzard knocked me back a hundred years, he thought. Irony danced within him like the gnats circling the old man's head. With all I've learned I'm dependent upon this "peasant's" sense of time and space. His leg throbbed. In the plane, instead of time being measured by the rhythms of pain and a kid's legs, the instruments would have told him at a glance. Twisting upon his elbows he saw where dust had powdered the plane's fuselage, feeling the lump form in his throat that was always there when he thought of flight. It's crouched there, he thought, like the abandoned shell of a locust. I'm naked without it. Not a machine, a suit of clothes you wear. And with a sudden embarrassment and wonder he whispered, "It's the only dignity I have. . . ."

He saw the old man watching, his torn overalls clinging limply to him in the heat. He felt a sharp need to tell the old man what he felt. But that would be meaningless. If I tried to explain why I need to fly back, he'd think I was simply afraid of white officers. But it's more than fear . . . a sense of anguish clung to him like the veil of sweat that hugged his face. He watched the old man, hearing him humming snatches of a tune as he admired the plane. He felt a furtive sense of resentment. Such old men often came to the field to watch the pilots with childish eyes. At first it had made him proud; they had been a meaningful part of a new experience. But soon he realized they did not understand his accomplishments and they came to shame and embarrass him, like the distasteful praise of an idiot. A part of the meaning of flying had gone then, and he had not been able to regain it. If I were a prizefighter I would be more human, he thought. Not a monkey doing tricks, but a man. They were pleased simply that he was a Negro who could fly, and that was not enough. He felt cut off from them by age, by understanding, by sensibility, by technology, and by his need to measure himself against the mirror of other men's appreciation. Somehow he felt betrayed, as he had when as a child he grew to discover that his father was dead. Now for him any real appreciation lay with his white officers; and with them he could never be sure. Between ignorant black men and condescending whites, his course of flight seemed mapped by the nature of things away from all needed and natural landmarks. Under some sealed orders, couched in ever more technical and mysterious terms, his path curved swiftly away from both the shame the old man symbolized and the cloudy terrain of white men's regard. Flying blind, he knew but one point of landing, and there he would receive his wings. After that the enemy would aprpeciate his skill and he would assume his deepest meaning, he thought sadly, neither from those who condescended nor from those who praised without understanding, but from the enemy who would recognize his manhood and skill in terms of hate. . . .

He sighed, seeing the oxen making queer, prehistoric shadows against the dry brown earth.

"You just take it easy, son," the old man soothed. "That boy won't take long. Crazy as he is about airplanes."

"I can wait," he said.

"What kinda airplane you call this here'n?"

"An Advanced Trainer," he said, seeing the old man smile. His fingers were like gnarled dark wood against the metal as he touched the low-slung wing.

" 'Bout how fast can she fly?"

"Over two hundred an hour."

"Lawd! That's so fast I bet it don't seem like you moving!"

Holding himself rigid, Todd opened his flying suit. The shade had gone and he lay in a ball of fire.

"You mind if I take a look inside? I was always curious to see. . . ."

"Help yourself. Just don't touch anything."

He heard him climb upon the metal wing, grunting. Now the questions would start. Well, so you don't have to think to answer. . . .

He saw the old man looking over into the cockpit, his eyes bright as a child's.

"You must have to know a lot to work all these here things."

He was silent, seeing him step down and kneel beside him.

"Son, how come you want to fly way up there in the air?"

Because it's the most meaningful act in the world . . . because it makes me less like you, he thought.

But he said, "Because I like it, I guess. It's as good a way to fight and die as I know."

"Yeah? I guess you right," the old man said. "But how long you think before they gonna let you all fight?"

He tensed. This was the question all Negroes asked, put with the same timid hopefulness and longing that always opened a greater void within him than that he had felt beneath the plane the first time he had flown. He felt light-headed. It came to him suddenly that there was something sinister about the conversation, that he was flying unwillingly into unsafe and uncharted regions. If he could only be insulting and tell this old man who was trying to help him to shut up!

"I bet you one thing . . ."

"Yes?"

"That you was plenty scared coming down."

He did not answer. Like a dog on a trail the old man seemed to smell out his fears, and he felt anger bubble within him.

"You sho' scared me. When I seen you coming down in that thing with it a-rollin' and a-jumpin' like a pitchin' hoss, I thought sho' you was a goner. I almost had me a stroke!" He saw the old man grinning, "Ever'thin's been happening round here this morning, come to think of it."

"Like what?" he asked.

"Well, first thing I know, here come two white fellers looking for Mister Rudolph, that's Mister Graves's cousin. That got me worked up right away."

"Why?"

"Why? 'Cause he done broke outa the crazy house, that's why. He liable to kill somebody," he said. "They oughta have him by now, though. Then here you come. First I think it's one of them white boys. Then doggone if you don't fall outa there. Lawd, I'd done heard about you boys but I haven't never seen one o' you-all. Cain't tell you how it felt to see somebody what look like me in a airplane!"

The old man talked on, the sound streaming around Todd's thoughts like air flowing over the fuselage of a flying plane. You were a fool, he thought, remembering how before the spin the sun had blazed bright against the billboard signs beyond the town, and how a boy's blue kite had bloomed beneath him, tugging gently in the wind like a strange, odd-shaped flower. He had once flown such kites himself and tried to find the boy at the end of the invisible cord. But he had been flying too high and too fast. He had climbed steeply away in exultation. Too steeply, he thought. And one of the first rules you learn is that if the angle of thrust is too steep the plane goes into a spin. And then, instead of pulling out of it and going into a dive you let a buzzard panic you. A lousy buzzard!

"Son, what made all that blood on the glass?"

"A buzzard," he said, remembering how the blood and feathers had sprayed back against the hatch. It had been as though he had flown into a storm of blood and blackness.

"Well, I declare! They's lots of 'em around here. They after dead things. Don't eat nothing what's alive."

"A little bit more and he would have made a meal out of me," Todd said grimly.

"They bad luck, all right. Teddy's got a name for 'em, calls 'em jimcrows." The old man laughed.

"It's a damned good name."

"They the damnedest birds. Once I seen a hoss all stretched out like he was sick, you know. So I hollers, 'Gid up from there, suh!' Just to make sho! An' doggone, son, if I don't see two ole jimcrows come flying right up outa that hoss's insides! Yessuh! The sun was shinin' on 'em and they couldn't a been no greasier if they'd been eating barbecue."

Todd thought he would vomit, his stomach quivered.

"You made that up," he said.

"Nawsuh! Saw him just like I see you."

"Well, I'm glad it was you."

"You see lots a funny things down here, son."

"No, I'll let you see them," he said.

"By the way, the white folks round here don't like to see you boys up there in the sky. They ever bother you?"

"No."

"Well, they'd like to."

"Someone always wants to bother someone else," Todd said. "How do you know?"

"I just know."

"Well," he said defensively, "no one has bothered us."

Blood pounded in his ears as he looked away into space. He tensed, seeing a black spot in the sky, and strained to confirm what he could not clearly see.

"What does that look like to you?" he asked excitedly.

"Just another bad luck, son."

Then he saw the movement of wings with disappointment. It was gliding smoothly down, wings outspread, tail feathers gripping the air, down swiftly— gone behind the green screen of trees. It was like a bird he had imagined there; only the sloping branches of the pines remained, sharp against the pale stretch of sky. He lay barely breathing and stared at the point where it had disappeared, caught in a spell of loathing and admiration. Why did they make them so disgusting and yet teach them to fly so well?

"It's like when I was up in heaven," he heard, starting. The old man was chuckling, rubbing his stubbled chin.

"What did you say?"

"Sho', I died and went to heaven . . . maybe by time I tell you about it they be done come after you."

"I hope so," he said wearily.

"You boys ever sit around and swap lies?"

"Not often. Is this going to be one?"

"Well, I ain't so sho', on account of it took place when I was dead." The old man paused, "That wasn't no lie 'bout the buzzards, though."

"All right," he said.

"Sho' you want to hear 'bout heaven?"

"Please," he answered, resting his head upon his arm.

"Well, I went to heaven and right away started to sproutin' me some wings. Six good ones, they was. Just like them the white angels had. I couldn't hardly believe it. I was so glad that I went off on some clouds by myself and tried 'em out. You know, 'cause I didn't want to make a fool outa myself the first thing. . . ."

It's an old tale, Todd thought. Told me years ago. Had forgotten. But at least it will keep him from talking about buzzards.

He closed his eyes, listening.

"First thing I done was to git up on a low cloud and jump off. And doggone, boy, if them wings didn't work! First I tried the right; then I tried the left; then I tried 'em both together. Then Lawd, I started to move on out among the folks. I let 'em see me. . . ."

He saw the old man gesturing flight with his arms, his face full of mock pride as he indicated an imaginary crowd, thinking, It'll be in the newspapers.

"So I went out and found me some colored angels—somehow I didn't believe I was an angel till I seen a real black one, ha, yes! Then I was sho'—but they tole me I better come down 'cause us colored folks had to wear a special kin' a harness when we flew. That was how come they wasn't flyin'. Oh, yes, an' you had to be extra strong for a black man even, to fly with one of them harnesses. . . ."

This is a new turn, Todd thought. What's he driving at?

"So I said to myself, I ain't gonna be bothered with no harness! Oh, naw! 'Cause if God let you sprout wings you oughta have sense enough not to let nobody make you wear something what gits in the way of flyin'. So I starts to flyin'. Heck, son." He chuckled, his eyes twinkling. "You know I had to let eve'ybody know that old Jefferson could fly good as anybody else. And I could too, fly smooth as a bird! I could even loop-the-loop—only I had to make sho' to keep my long white robe down roun' my ankles. . . ."

Todd felt uneasy. He wanted to laugh at the joke, but his body refused, as of an independent will. He felt as he had as a child when after he had chewed a sugar-coated pill which his mother had given him, she had laughed at his efforts to remove the terrible taste.

"Well," he heard, "I was doing all right till I got to speeding. Found out I could fan up a right strong breeze, I could fly so fast. I could do all kin'sa stunts too. I started flying up to the stars and divin' down and zooming roun' the moon. Man, I like to scare the devil outa some ole white angels. I was raisin' hell. Not that I meant any harm, son. But I was just feeling good. It was so good to know I was free at last. I accidentally knocked the tips offa some stars and they tell me I caused a storm and a coupla lynchings down here in Macon County—though I swear I believe them boys what said that was making up lies on me. . . ."

He's mocking me, Todd thought angrily. He thinks it's a joke. Grinning down at me. . . . His throat was dry. He looked at his watch; why the hell didn't they come? Since they had to, why? You got yourself into it, Todd thought. Like Jonah in the whale.

"One day I was flying down one of them heavenly streets, justa throwin' feathers in everybody's face. An' ole Saint Peter called me in. Said, 'Jefferson, tell me two things, what you doin' flyin' without a harness, an' how come you flyin' so fast?' So I tole him I was flyin' without a harness 'cause it got in my way, but I couldn'ta been flyin' so fast, 'cause I wasn't usin' but one wing. Saint Peter said, 'You wasn't flyin' with but one wing?' 'Yessuh,' I says, scared-like. So he says, 'Well, since you got sucha extra fine pair of wings you can leave off yo' harness awhile. But from now on none of that there one-wing flyin', 'cause you gittin' up too damn much speed!' "

And with one mouth full of bad teeth you're making too damned much talk, thought Todd. Why don't I send him after the boy? His body ached from the hard ground, and seeking to shift his position he twisted his ankle and hated himself for crying out.

"It gittin' worse?"

"I . . . I twisted it," he groaned.

"Try not to think about it, son. That's what I do."

He bit his lip, fighting pain with counter-pain as the voice resumed its rhythmical droning. Jefferson seemed caught in his own creation.

"After all that trouble I just floated roun' heaven in slow motion. But I forgot, like colored folks will do, and got to flyin' with one wing again. This time I was restin' my old broken arm and got to flyin' fast enough to shame the devil. I was comin' so fast, Lawd, I got myself called befo' ole Saint Peter again. He said, 'Jeff, didn't I warn you 'bout that speedin'?' 'Yessuh,' I says, 'but it was an accident.' He looked at me sad-like and shook his head and I knowed I was gone. He said, 'Jeff, you and that speedin' is a danger to the heavenly community. If I was to let you keep on flyin', heaven wouldn't be nothin' but uproar. Jeff, you got to go!' Son, I argued and pleaded with that old white man, but it didn't do a bit of good. They rushed me straight to them pearly gates and gimme a parachute and a map of the state of Alabama."

Todd heard him laughing so that he could hardly speak, making a screen between them upon which his humiliation glowed like fire.

"Maybe you'd better stop awhile," he said, his voice unreal.

"Ain't much more." Jefferson laughed. "When they gimme the parachute, ole Saint Peter ask me if I wanted to say a few words before I went. I felt so bad I couldn't hardly look at him, specially with all them white angels standin' around. Then somebody laughed and made me mad. So I tole him, 'Well, you done took my wings. And you puttin' me out. You got charge of things so's I can't do nothin' about it. But you got to admit just this: While I was up here I was the flyinest sonofabitch what ever hit heaven!'"

At the burst of laughter Todd felt such an intense humiliation that only great violence would wash it away. The laughter which shook the old man like a boiling purge set up vibrations of guilt within him which not even the intricate machinery of the plane would have been adequate to transform, and he heard himself screaming, "Why do you laugh at me this way?"

He hated himself at that moment, but he had lost control. He saw Jefferson's mouth fall open, "What?"

"Answer me!"

His blood pounded as though it would surely burst his temples and he tried to reach the old man and fell, screaming.

"Can I help it because they won't let us actually fly? Maybe we are a bunch of buzzards feeding on a dead horse, but we can hope to be eagles, can't we? Can't we?"

He fell back, exhausted, his ankle pounding. The saliva was like straw in his mouth. If he had the strength he would strangle this old man. This grinning, gray-headed clown who made him feel as he felt when watched by the white officers at the field. And yet this old man had neither power, prestige, rank, nor technique. Nothing that could rid him of this terrible feeling. He watched him, seeing his face struggle to express a turmoil of feeling.

"What you mean, son? What you talking 'bout?"

"Go away. Go tell your tales to the white folks."

"But I didn't mean nothing like that. I . . . I wasn't tryin' to hurt your feelings. . . ."

"Please. Get the hell away from me!"

"But I didn't, son. I didn't mean all them things a-tall."

Todd shook as with a chill, searching Jefferson's face for a trace of the mockery he had seen there. But now the face was somber and tired and old. He was confused. He could not be sure that there had ever been laughter there, that Jefferson had ever really laughed in his whole life. He saw Jefferson reach out to touch him and shrank away, wondering if anything except the pain, now causing his vision to waver, was real. Perhaps he had imagined it all.

"Don't let it get you down, son," the voice said pensively.

He heard Jefferson sigh wearily, as though he felt more than he could say. His anger ebbed, leaving only the pain.

"I'm sorry," he mumbled.

"You just wore out with pain, was all. . . ."

He saw him through a blur, smiling. And for a second he felt the embarrassed silence of understanding flutter between them.

"What you was doin' flyin' over this section, son? Wasn't you scared they might shoot you for a cow?"

Todd tensed. Was he being laughed at again? But before he could decide, the pain shook him and a part of him was lying calmly behind the screen of pain that had fallen between them, recalling the first time he had ever seen a plane. It was as though an endless series of hangars had been shaken ajar in the air base of his memory and from each, like a young wasp emerging from its cell, arose the memory of a plane.

The first time I ever saw a plane I was very small and planes were new in the world. I was four and a half and the only plane that I had ever seen was a model suspended from the ceiling of the automobile exhibit at the State Fair. But I did not know that it was only a model. I did not know how large a real plane was, or how expensive. To me it was a fascinating toy, complete in itself, which my mother said could only be owned by rich little white boys. I stood rigid with admiration, my head straining backwards as I watched the gray little plane describing arcs above the gleaming tops of the automobiles. And I vowed that, rich or poor, someday I would own such a toy. My mother had to drag me out of the exhibit, and not even the merry-go-round, the Ferris wheel, or the racing horses could hold my attention for the rest of the fair. I was too busy imitating the tiny drone of the plane with my lips, and imitating with my hands the motion, swift and circling, that it made in flight.

After that I no longer used the pieces of lumber that lay about our backyard to construct wagons and autos . . . now it was used for airplanes. I built biplanes, using pieces of board for wings, a small box for the fuselage, another piece of wood for the rudder. The trip to the fair had brought something new into my small world. I asked my mother repeatedly when the fair would come back again. I'd lie in the grass and watch the sky, and each fighting bird became a soaring plane. I would have been good a year just to have seen a plane again. I became a nuisance to everyone with my questions about airplanes. But planes were new to the old folks, too, and there was little that they could tell me. Only my uncle knew some of the answers. And better still, he could carve propellers from pieces of wood that would whirl rapidly in the wind, wobbling noisily upon oiled nails.

I wanted a plane more than I'd wanted anything; more than I wanted the red wagon with rubber tires, more than the train that ran on a track with its train of cars. I asked my mother over and over again.

"Mamma?"

"What do you want, boy?" she'd say.

"Mamma, will you get mad if I ask you?" I'd say.

"What do you want now? I ain't got time to be answering a lot of fool questions. What do you want?"

"Mamma, when you gonna get me one?" I'd ask.

"Get you one what?" she'd say.

"You know, Mamma, what I been asking you. . . ."

"Boy," she'd say, "if you don't want a spanking you better come on an' tell me what you talking about so I can get on with my work."

"Aw, Mamma, you know. . . ."

"What I just tell you?" she'd say.

"I mean when you gonna buy me a airplane?"

"*Airplane!* Boy, is you crazy? How many times I have to tell you to stop that foolishness? I done told you them things cost too much. I bet I'm gon' wham the living daylight out of you if you don't quit worrying me 'bout them things!"

But this did not stop me, and a few days later I'd try all over again.

Then one day a strange thing happened. It was spring, and for some reason I had been hot and irritable all morning. It was a beautiful spring. I could feel it as I played barefoot in the backyard. Blossoms hung from the thorny black locust trees like clusters of fragrant white grapes. Butterflies flickered in the sunlight above the short new dew-wet grass. I had gone in the house for bread and butter and coming out I heard a steady unfamiliar drone. It was unlike anything I had ever heard before. I tried to place the sound. It was no use. It was a sensation like that I had when searching for my father's watch, heard ticking unseen in a room. It made me feel as though I had forgotten to perform some task that my mother had ordered . . . then I located it, overhead. In the sky, flying quite low and about a hundred yards off, was a plane! It came so slowly that it seemed barely to move. My mouth hung wide; my bread and butter fell into the dirt. I wanted to jump up and down and cheer. And when the idea struck I trembled with excitement. "Some little white boy's plane's done flew away and all I got to do is stretch out my hands and it'll be mine!" It was a little plane like that at the fair, flying no higher than the eaves of our roof. Seeing it come steadily forward I felt the world grow warm with promise. I opened the screen and climbed over it and clung there, waiting. I would catch the plane as it came over and swing down fast and run into the house before anyone could see me. Then no one could come to claim the plane. It droned nearer. Then when it hung like a silver cross in the blue directly above me I stretched out my hand and grabbed. It was like sticking my finger through a soap bubble. The plane flew on, as though I had simple blown my breath after it. I grabbed again, frantically, trying to catch the tail. My fingers clutched the air and disappointment surged tight and hard in my throat. Giving one last desperate grasp, I strained forward. My fingers ripped from the screen. I was falling. The ground burst hard against me. I drummed the earth with my heels and when my breath returned, I lay there bawling.

My mother rushed through the door.

"What's the matter, chile! What on earth is wrong with you?"

"It's gone! It's gone!"

"What gone?"

"The airplane . . ."

"Airplane?"

"Yessum, jus' like the one at the fair. . . . I . . . I tried to stop it an' it kep' right on going. . . ."

"When, boy?"

"Just now," I cried, through my tears.

"Where it go, boy, what way?"

"Yonder, there. . . ."

She scanned the sky, her arms akimbo and her checkered apron flapping in the wind as I pointed to the fading plane. Finally she looked down at me, slowly shaking her head.

"It's gone! It's gone!" I cried.

"Boy, is you a fool?" she said. "Don't you see that there's a real airplane 'stead of one of them toy ones?"

"Real?" I forgot to cry. "Real?"

"Yass, real. Don't you know that thing you reaching for is bigger'n a auto? You here trying to reach for it and I bet it's flying 'bout two hundred miles higher'n this roof." She was disgusted with me. "You come on in this house before somebody else sees what a fool you done turned out to be. You must think these here lil ole arms of you'n is mighty long. . . ."

I was carried into the house and undressed for bed and the doctor was called. I cried bitterly, as much from the disappointment of finding the plane so far beyond my reach as from the pain.

When the doctor came I heard my mother telling him about the plane and asking if anything was wrong with my mind. He explained that I had had a fever for several hours. But I was kept in bed for a week and I constantly saw the plane in my sleep, flying just beyond my fingertips, sailing so slowly that it seemed barely to move. And each time I'd reach out to grab it I'd miss, and through each dream I'd hear my grandma warning:

> Young man, young man,
> Yo' arms too short
> To box with God. . . .

"Hey, son!"

At first he did not know where he was and looked at the old man, pointing, with blurred eyes.

"Ain't that one of you-all's airplanes coming after you?"

As his vision cleared he saw a small black shape above a distant field, soaring through waves of heat. But he could not be sure, and with the pain he feared that somehow a horrible recurring fantasy of being split in twain by the whirling blades of a propeller had come true.

"You think he sees us?" he heard.

"See? I hope so."

"He's coming like a bat outa hell!"

Straining, he heard the faint sound of a motor and hoped it would soon be over.

"How you feeling?"

"Like a nightmare," he said.

"Hey, he's done curved back the other way!"

"Maybe he saw us," he said. "Maybe he's gone to send out the ambulance and ground crew." And, he thought with despair, maybe he didn't even see us. "Where did you send the boy?"

"Down to Mister Graves," Jefferson said. "Man what owns this land."

"Do you think he phoned?"

Jefferson looked at him quickly.

"Aw sho'. Dabney Graves is got a bad name on accounta them killings, but he'll call though. . . ."

"What killings?"

"Them five fellers . . . ain't you heard?" he asked with surprise.

"No."

"Everybody knows 'bout Dabney Graves, especially the colored. He done killed enough of us."

Todd had the sensation of being caught in a white neighborhood after dark.

"What did they do?" he asked.

"Thought they was men," Jefferson said. "An' some he owed money, like he do me. . . ."

"But why do you stay here?"

"You black, son."

"I know, but—"

"You have to come by the white folks, too."

He turned away from Jefferson's eyes, at once consoled and accused. And I'll have to come by them soon, he thought with despair. Closing his eyes, he heard Jefferson's voice as the sun burned blood-red upon his lips.

"I got nowhere to go," Jefferson said, "an' they'd come after me if I did.

But Dabney Graves is a funny fellow. He's all the time making jokes. He can be mean as hell, then he's liable to turn right around and back the colored against the white folks. I seen him do it. But me, I hates him for that more'n anything else. 'Cause just as soon as he gits tired helping a man he don't care what happens to him. He just leaves him stone cold. And then the other white folks is double hard on anybody he done helped. For him it's just a joke. He don't give a hilla beans for nobody—but hisself. . . .''

Todd listened to the thread of detachment in the old man's voice. It was as though he held his words arm's length before him to avoid their destructive meaning.

"He'd just as soon do you a favor and then turn right around and have you strung up. Me, I stays outa his way 'cause down here that's what you gotta do."

If my ankle would only ease for a while, he thought. *The closer I spin toward the earth the blacker I become,* flashed through his mind. Sweat ran into his eyes, and he was sure that he would never see the plane if his head continued whirling. He tried to see Jefferson; what was it that Jefferson held in his hand? It was a little black man, another Jefferson! A little black Jefferson that shook with fits of belly laughter while the other Jefferson looked on with detachment. Then Jefferson looked up from the thing in his hand and turned to speak, but Todd was far away, searching the sky for a plane in a hot dry land on a day and age he had long forgotten. He was going mysteriously with his mother through empty streets where black faces peered from behind drawn shades and someone was rapping at a window and he was looking back to see a hand and a frightened face frantically beckoning from a cracked door and his mother was looking down the empty perspective of the street and shaking her head and hurrying him along and at first it was only a flash he saw and a motor was droning as through the sun-glare he saw it gleaming silver as it circled and he was seeing a burst like a puff of white smoke and hearing his mother yell, Come along, boy, I got no time for them fool airplanes, I got no time; and he saw it a second time, the plane flying high, and the burst appeared suddenly and fell slowly, billowing out and sparkling like fireworks and he was watching and being hurried along as the air filled with a flurry of white pinwheeling cards that caught in the wind and scattered over the rooftops and into the gutters and a woman was running and snatching a card and reading it and screaming and he darted into the shower, grabbing as in winter he grabbed for snowflakes and bounding away at his mother's, Come on here, boy! Come on, I say! and he was watching as she took the card away, seeing her face grow puzzled and turning taut as her voice quavered, "Niggers Stay Away from the Polls," and died to a moan of terror as he saw the eyeless sockets of a white hood staring at him from the card and above he saw the plane spiraling gracefully, agleam in the sun like a fiery sword. And seeing it soar he was caught, transfixed between a terrible horror and a horrible fascination.

The sun was not so high now, and Jefferson was calling, and gradually he saw three figures moving across the curving roll of the field.

"Look like some doctors, all dressed in white," said Jefferson.

They're coming at last, Todd thought. And he felt such a release of tension within him that he thought he would faint. But no sooner did he close his eyes than he was seized and he was struggling with three white men who were forcing his arms into some kind of coat. It was too much for him, his arms were pinned to his sides and as the pain blazed in his eyes, he realized that it was a straitjacket. What filthy joke was this?

"That oughta hold him, Mister Graves," he heard.

His total energies seemed focused in his eyes as he searched their faces. That was Graves; the other two wore hospital uniforms. He was poised between two poles of fear and hate as he heard the one called Graves saying, "He looks kinda purty in that there suit, boys. I'm glad you dropped by."

"This boy ain't crazy, Mister Graves," one of the others said. "He needs a doctor, not us. Don't see how you led us way out here anyway. It might be a joke to you, but your cousin Rudolph liable to kill somebody. White folks or niggers, don't make no difference."

Todd saw the man turn red with anger. Graves looked down upon him, chuckling.

"This nigguh belongs in a straitjacket too, boys. I knowed that the minit Jeff's kid said something 'bout a nigguh flyer. You all know you cain't let the nigguh git up that high without his going crazy. The nigguh brain ain't built right for high altitudes. . . ."

Todd watched the drawling red face, feeling that all the unnamed horror and obscenities he had ever imagined stood materialized before him.

"Let's git outa here," one of the attendants said.

Todd saw the other reach toward him, realizing for the first time that he lay upon a stretcher as he yelled, "Don't put your hands on me!"

They drew back, surprised.

"What's that you say, nigguh?" asked Graves.

He did not answer and thought that Graves's foot was aimed at his head. It landed on his chest and he could hardly breathe. He coughed helplessly, seeing Graves's lips stretch taut over his yellow teeth, and tried to shift his head. It was as though a half-dead fly was dragging slowly across his face and a bomb seemed to burst within him. Blasts of hot, hysterical laughter tore from his chest, causing his eyes to pop, and he felt that the veins in his neck would surely burst. And then a part of him stood behind it all, watching the surprise in Graves's red face and his own hysteria. He thought he would never stop, he would laugh himself to death. It rang in his ears like Jefferson's laughter and he looked for him, centering his eyes desperately upon his face, as though somehow he had become his sole salvation in an insane world of outrage and humiliation. It brought a certain relief. He was suddenly aware that although his body was still contorted it was an echo that no longer rang in his ears. He heard Jefferson's voice with gratitude.

"Mister Graves, the army done tole him not to leave his airplane."

"Nigguh, army or no, you gittin' off my land! That airplane can stay 'cause it was paid for by taxpayers' money. But you gittin' off. An' dead or alive, it don't make no difference to me."

Todd was beyond it now, lost in a world of anguish.

"Jeff," Graves said, "you and Teddy come and grab holt. I want you to take this here black eagle over to that nigguh airfield and leave him."

Jefferson and the boy approached him silently. He looked away, realizing and doubting at once that only they could release him from his overpowering sense of isolation.

They bent for the stretcher. One of the attendants moved toward Teddy.

"Think you can manage it, boy?"

"I think I can, suh," Teddy said.

"Well, you better go behind then, and let yo' pa go ahead so's to keep that leg elevated."

He saw the white men walking ahead as Jefferson and the boy carried him along in silence. Then they were pausing and he felt a hand wiping his face; then he was moving again. And it was as though he had been lifted out of his isolation, back into the world of men. A new current of communication flowed between the man and boy and himself. They moved him gently. Far away he heard a mockingbird liquidly calling. He raised his eyes, seeing a buzzard poised unmoving in space. For a moment the whole afternoon seemed suspended, and he waited for the horror to seize him again. Then like a song within his head he heard the boy's soft humming and saw the dark bird glide into the sun and glow like a bird of flaming gold.

Who's Passing for Who?

Langston Hughes

1952

One of the great difficulties about being a member of a minority race is that so many kindhearted, well-meaning bores gather around to help. Usually, to tell the truth, they have nothing to help with, except their company—which is often appallingly dull.

Some members of the Negro race seem very well able to put up with it, though, in these uplifting years. Such was Caleb Johnson, colored social worker, who was always dragging around with him some nondescript white person or two, inviting them to dinner, showing them Harlem, ending up at the Savoy—much to the displeasure of whatever friends of his might be out that evening for fun, not sociology.

Friends are friends and, unfortunately, overearnest uplifters are uplifters—no matter what color they may be. If it were the white race that was ground down instead of Negroes, Caleb Johnson would be one of the first to offer Nordics the sympathy of his utterly inane society, under the impression that somehow he would be doing them a great deal of good.

You see, Caleb, and his white friends too, were all bores. Or so we who lived in Harlem's literary bohemia during the "Negro Renaissance" thought. We literary ones considered ourselves too broad-minded to be bothered with questions of color. We liked people of any race who smoked incessantly, drank liberally, wore complexion and morality as loose garments, and made fun of anyone who didn't do likewise. We snubbed and high-hatted any Negro or white luckless enough not to understand Gertrude Stein, *Ulysses*, Man Ray, the theremin, Jean Toomer, or George Antheil. By the end of the 1920s Caleb was just catching up to Dos Passos. He thought H. G. Wells good.

We met Caleb one night in Small's. He had three assorted white folks in tow. We would have passed him by with but a nod had he not hailed us enthusiastically, risen, and introduced us with great acclaim to his friends, who turned out to be schoolteachers from Iowa, a woman and two men. They appeared amazed and delighted to meet all at once two Negro writers and a black painter in the flesh. They invited us to have a drink with them. Money being scarce with us, we deigned to sit down at their table.

The white lady said, "I've never met a Negro writer before."

The two men added, "Neither have we."

"Why, we know any number of *white* writers," we three dark bohemians declared with bored nonchalance.

"But Negro writers are much more rare," said the lady.

"There are plenty in Harlem," we said.

"But not in Iowa," said one of the men, shaking his mop of red hair.

"There are no good *white* writers in Iowa either, are there?" we asked superciliously.

"Oh, yes, Ruth Suckow came from there."

Whereupon we proceeded to light in upon Ruth Suckow as old hat and to annihilate her in favor of Kay Boyle. The way we flung names around seemed to impress both Caleb and his white guests. This, of course, delighted us, though we were too young and too proud to admit it.

The drinks came and everything was going well, all of us drinking and we three showing off in a highbrow manner, when suddenly at the table just behind us a man got up and knocked down a woman. He was a brownskin man. The woman was blond. As she rose he knocked her down again. Then the red-haired man from Iowa got up and knocked the colored man down.

He said, "Keep your hands off that white woman."

The man got up and said, "She's not a white woman. She's my wife."

One of the waiters added, "She's not white, sir, she's colored."

Whereupon the man from Iowa looked puzzled, dropped his fists, and said, "I'm sorry."

The colored man said, "What are you doing up here in Harlem anyway, interfering with my family affairs?"

The white man said, "I thought she was a white woman."

The woman, who had been on the floor, rose and said, "Well, I'm not a white woman, I'm colored, and you leave my husband alone."

Then they both lit in on the gentleman from Iowa. It took all of us and several waiters, too, to separate them. When it was over the manager requested us to kindly pay our bill and get out. He said we were disturbing the peace. So we all left. We went to a fish restaurant down the street. Caleb was terribly apologetic to his white friends. We artists were both mad and amused.

"Why did you say you were sorry," said the colored painter to the visitor from Iowa, "after you'd hit that man—and then found out it wasn't a white woman you were defending, but merely a light-colored woman who looked white?"

"Well," answered the red-haired Iowan, "I didn't mean to be butting in if they were all the same race."

"Don't you think a woman needs defending from a brute, no matter what race she may be?" asked the painter.

"Yes, but I think it's up to you to defend your own women."

"Oh, so you'd divide up a brawl according to races, no matter who was right?"

"Well, I wouldn't say that."

"You mean you wouldn't defend a colored woman whose husband was knocking her down?" asked the poet.

Before the visitor had time to answer, the painter said, "No! You just got mad because you thought a black man was hitting a *white* woman."

"But she *looked* like a white woman," countered the man.

"Maybe she was just passing for colored," I said.

"Like some Negroes pass for white," Caleb interposed.

"Anyhow, I don't like it," said the colored painter, "the way you stopped defending her when you found out she wasn't white."

"No, we don't like it," we all agreed except Caleb.

Caleb said in extenuation, "But Mr. Stubblefield is new to Harlem."

The red-haired white man said, "Yes, it's my first time here."

"Maybe Mr. Stubblefield ought to stay out of Harlem," we observed.

"I agree," Mr. Stubblefield said. "Good night."

He got up then and there and left the café. He stalked as he walked. His red head disappeared into the night.

"Oh, that's too bad," said the white couple who remained. "Stubby's temper just got the best of him. But explain to us, are many colored folks really as fair as that woman?"

"Sure, lots of them have more white blood than colored, and pass for white."

"Do they?" said the lady and gentleman from Iowa.

"You never read Nella Larsen?" we asked.

"She writes novels," Caleb explained. "She's part white herself."

"Read her," we advised. "Also read the *Autobiography of an Ex-Colored Man.*" Not that we had read it ourselves—because we paid but little attention to the older colored writers—but we knew it was about passing for white.

We all ordered fish and settled down comfortably to shocking our white friends with tales about how many Negroes there were passing for white all over America. We were determined to *épater le bourgeois* real good via this white couple we had cornered, when the woman leaned over the table in the midst of our dissertations and said, "Listen, gentlemen, you needn't spread the word, but me and my husband aren't white either. We've just been *passing* for white for the last fifteen years."

"What?"

"We're colored too, just like you," said the husband. "But it's better passing for white because we make more money."

Well, that took the wind out of us. It took the wind out of Caleb, too. He thought all the time he was showing some fine white folks Harlem—and they were as colored as he was!

Caleb almost never cursed. But this time he said, "I'll be damned!"

Then everybody laughed. And laughed! We almost had hysterics. All at once we dropped our professionally self-conscious "Negro" manners, became natural, ate fish, and talked and kidded freely like colored folks do when there are no white folks around. We really had fun then, joking about that red-haired guy who mistook a fair colored woman for white. After the fish we went to two or three more night spots and drank until five o'clock in the morning.

Finally we put the light-colored people in a taxi heading downtown. They turned to shout a last good-bye. The cab was just about to move off, when the woman called to the driver to stop.

She leaned out the window and said with a grin, "Listen, boys! I hate to confuse you again. But, to tell the truth, my husband and I aren't really colored at all. We're white. We just thought we'd kid you by passing for colored a little while—just as you said Negroes sometimes pass for white."

She laughed as they sped off toward Central Park, waving. "Good-bye!"

We didn't say a thing. We just stood there on the corner in Harlem dumbfounded—not knowing now *which* way we'd been fooled. Were they really white—passing for colored? Or colored—passing for white?

Whatever race they were, they had had too much fun at our expense—even if they did pay for the drinks.

The Only Man on Liberty Street

William Melvin Kelley

1956

She was squatting in the front yard, digging with an old brass spoon in the dirt, which was an ocean to the islands of short yellow grass. She wore a red-and-white checkered dress, which hung loosely from her shoulders and obscured her legs. It was early spring and she was barefoot. Her toes stuck out from under the skirt. She could not see the man yet, riding down Liberty Street, his shoulders square, the duster he wore spread back over the horse's rump, a carpetbag tied with a leather strap to his saddle horn and knocking against his leg. She could not see him until he had dismounted and tied his horse to a small black iron Negro jockey and unstrapped the bag. She watched now as he opened the wooden gate, came into the yard, and stood, looking down at her, his face stern, almost gray beneath the brim of his wide hat.

She knew him. Her mother called him Mister Herder and had told Jennie that he was Jennie's father. He was one of the men who came riding down Liberty Street in their fine black suits and starched shirts and large dark ties. Each of these had a house to go to, into which, in the evening usually, he would disappear. Only women and children lived on Liberty Street. All of them were Negroes. Some of the women were quite dark, but most were coffee color. They were all very beautiful. Her mother was light. She was tall, had black eyes, and black hair so long she could sit on it.

The man standing over her was the one who came to her house once or twice a week. He was never there in the morning when Jennie got up. He was tall, and thin, and blond. He had a short beard that looked as coarse as the grass beneath her feet. His eyes were blue, like Jennie's. He did not speak English very well. Jennie's mother had told her he came from across the sea, and Jennie often wondered if he went there between visits to their house.

"Jennie? Your mother tells me that you ask why I do not stay at night. Is so?"

She looked up at him. "Yes, Mister Herder." The hair under his jaw was darker than the hair on his cheeks.

He nodded. "I stay now. Go bring your mother."

She left the spoon in the dirt and ran into the house, down the long hall, dark now because she had been sitting in the sun. She found her mother standing over the stove, a great black lid in her left hand, a wooden spoon in her right. There were beads of sweat on her forehead. She wore a full black skirt and a white blouse. Her one waist-length braid hung straight between her shoulder blades. She turned to Jennie's running steps.

"Mama? That man? My father? He in the yard. He brung a carpetbag."

First her mother smiled, then frowned, then looked puzzled. "A carpetbag, darling?"

"Yes, Mama."

She followed her mother through the house, pausing with her at the hall mirror, where the woman ran her hand up the back of her neck to smooth stray black hair. Then they went onto the porch, where the man was now seated, surveying the tiny yard and the dark green hedge that enclosed it. The carpetbag rested beside his chair. Her mother stood with her hands beneath her apron, staring at the bag. "Mister Herder?"

He turned to them. "I will not go back this time. No matter what. Why should I live in that house when I must come here to know what home is?" He nodded sharply as if in answer to a question. "So! I stay, I give her that house. I will send her money, but I stay here."

Her mother stood silently for an instant, then turned to the door. "Dinner'll be on the table in a half hour." She opened the screen door. The spring whined and cracked. "Oh." She let go the door and picked up the carpetbag. "I'll take this on up." She went inside. As she passed, Jennie could see she was smiling again.

After that, Jennie's mother became a celebrity on Liberty Street. The other women would stop her to ask about the man. "And he staying for good, Josie?"

"Yes."

"You have any trouble yet?"

"Not yet."

"Well, child, you make him put that there house in your name. You don't want to be no Sissie Markham. That white woman come down the same day he died and moved Sissie and her children right into the gutter. You get that house put in your name. You hear?"

"Yes."

"How is it? It different?"

Her mother would look dazed. "Yes, it different. He told me to call him Maynard."

The other women were always very surprised.

At first, Jennie too was surprised. The man was always there in the morning and sometimes even woke her up. Her mother no longer called him Mister Herder, and at odd times, though still quite seldom, said, No. She had never before heard her mother say no to anything the man ever said. It was not long before Jennie was convinced that he actually was her father. She began to call him Papa.

Daily now a white woman had been driving by their house. Jennie did not know who she was or what she wanted but, playing in the yard, would see the white woman's gray buggy turn the corner and come slowly down the block, pulled by a speckled horse that trudged in the dry dust. A Negro driver sat erect in his black uniform, a whip in his fist. The white woman would peer at the house as if looking for an address or something special. She would look at the curtained windows, looking for someone, and sometimes even at Jennie. The look was not kind or tender, but hard and angry as if she knew something bad about the child.

Then one day the buggy stopped, the Negro pulling gently on the reins. The white woman leaned forward, spoke to the driver, and handed him a small pink envelope. He jumped down, opened the gate, and without looking at Jennie, his face dark and shining, advanced on the porch, up the three steps, which knocked hollow beneath his boots, opened the screen door, and twisted the polished brass bell key in the center of the open winter door.

Her mother came, drying her hands. The Negro reached out the envelope and her mother took it, looking beyond him for an instant at the buggy and the white woman, who returned her look coldly. As the Negro turned, her mother opened the letter and read it, moving her lips slightly. Then Jennie could see the twinkling at the corners of her eyes. Her mother stood framed in the black square of doorway, tall, fair, the black hair swept to hide her ears, her eyes glistening.

Jennie turned back to the white woman now and saw her lean deeper into her seat. Then she pulled forward. "Do you understand what I will have them do?" She was shouting shrilly and spoke like Jennie's father. "You tell him he has got one wife! You are something different!" She leaned back again, waved her gloved hand, and the buggy lurched down the street, gained speed, and jangled out of sight around the corner.

Jennie was on her feet and pounding up the stairs. "Mama?"

"Go play, Jennie. Go on now, *play!*" Still her mother stared straight ahead, as if the buggy and the white woman remained in front of the house. She still held the letter as if to read it. The corners of her eyes were wet. Then she turned and went into the house. The screen door clacked behind her.

At nights now Jennie waited by the gate in the yard for her father to turn the corner, walking. In the beginning she had been waiting too for the day he would not turn the corner. But each night he came, that day seemed less likely to come. Even so, she was always surprised to see him. When she did, she would wave, timidly, raising her hand only to her shoulder, wiggling only her fingers, as if to wave too wildly would somehow cause the entire picture of his advancing to collapse as only a slight wind would be enough to disarrange a design of feathers.

That night too she waved and saw him raise his hand high over his head, greeting her. She backed away when he reached the gate so he might open it, her head thrown way back, looking up at him.

"Well, my Jennie, what kind of day did you have?"

She only smiled, then remembered the white woman. "A woman come to visit Mama. She come in a buggy and give her a letter too. She made Mama cry."

His smile fled. He sucked his tongue, angry now. "We go see what is wrong. Come." He reached for her hand.

Her mother was in the kitchen. She looked as if she did not really care what she was doing or how, walking from pump to stove, stove to cupboard in a deep trance. The pink envelope was on the table.

She turned to them. Her eyes were red. Several strands of hair stuck to her temples. She cleared her nose and pointed to the letter. "She come today."

Her father let go Jennie's hand, picked up the letter, and read it. When he was finished he took it to the stove and dropped it into the flame. There was a puff of smoke before he replaced the lid. He shook his head. "She cannot make me go back, Josephine."

Her mother fell heavily into a wooden chair, beginning to cry again. "But she's white, Maynard."

He raised his eyebrows like a priest or a displeased schoolteacher. "Your skin is whiter."

"My mother was a slave."

He threw up his hands, making fists. "Your mother did not ask to be a slave!" Then he went to her, crouched on his haunches before her, speaking quietly. "No one can make me go back."

"But she can get them to do what she say." She turned her gaze on Jennie, but looked away quickly. "You wasn't here after the war. But I seen things. I seen things happen to field niggers that . . . I was up in the house; they didn't bother me. My own father, General Dewey Willson, he stood on a platform in the center of town and promised to keep the niggers down. I was close by." She took his face in her hands. "Maynard, maybe you better go back, leastways—"

"I go back—dead! You hear? Dead. These children, these cowardly children in their masks will not move me! I go back dead. That is all. We do not discuss it." And he was gone. Jennie heard him thundering down the hall, knocking against the table near the stairs, going up to the second floor.

Her mother was looking at her now, her eyes even more red than before, her lips trembling, her hands active in her lap. "Jennie?"

"Yes, Mama." She took a step toward her, staring into the woman's eyes.

"Jennie, I want you to promise me something and not forget it."

"Yes, Mama." She was between her mother's knees, felt the woman's hands clutching her shoulders.

"Jennie, you'll be right pretty when you get grown. Did you know that? Promise me you'll go up north. Promise me if I'm not here when you get eighteen, you'll go north and get married. You understand?"

Jennie was not sure she did. She could not picture the North, except that she had heard once it was cold and white things fell from the sky. She could not picture being eighteen and her mother not being there. But she knew her mother wanted her to understand and she lied. "Yes, Mama."

"Repeat what I just said."

She did. Her mother kissed her mouth, the first time ever.

From the kitchen below came their voices. Her father's voice sounded hard, cut short; Jennie knew he had made a decision and was sticking to it. Her mother was pleading, trying to change his mind. It was July the Fourth, the day of the shooting match.

She dressed in her Sunday clothes and, coming downstairs, heard her mother. "Maynard, please don't take her." She was frantic now. "I'm begging you. Don't take that child with you today."

"I take her. We do not discuss it. I take her. Those sneaking cowards in their masks . . ." Jennie knew now what they were talking about. Her father had promised to take her to the shooting match. For some reason, her mother feared there would be trouble if Jennie went downtown. She did not know why her mother felt that way, except that it might have something to do with the white woman, who continued to ride by their house each morning, after her father had left for the day. Perhaps her mother did not want to be alone in the house when the white woman drove by in her gray buggy, even though she had not stopped the buggy since the day, two months ago, when the Negro had given her mother the pink envelope.

But other strange things had happened after that. In the beginning she and her mother, as always before, had gone downtown to the market, to shop amid the bright stalls brimming with green and yellow vegetables and brick-red meats, tended by dark country Negroes in shabby clothes and large straw hats. It would get very quiet when they passed, and Jennie would see the Negroes look away, fear in their eyes, and knots of white men watching, sometimes giggling. But the white women in fine clothes were the most frightening; sitting on the verandas or passing in carriages, some even coming to their windows, they would stare angrily as if her mother had done something terrible to each one personally, as if all these white women could be the one who drove by each morning. Her mother would walk through it all, her back straight, very like her father's, the bun into which she wove her waist-length braid on market days gleaming dark.

In the beginning they had gone to the suddenly quiet market. But now her mother hardly set foot from the house, and the food was brought to them in a carton by a crippled Negro boy, who was coming just as Jennie and her father left the house that morning.

Balancing the carton on his left arm, he removed his ragged hat and smiled. "Morning, Mister Herder. Good luck at the shooting match, sir." His left leg was short and he seemed to tilt.

Her father nodded. "Thank you, Felix. I do my best."

"Then you a sure thing, Mister Herder." He replaced his hat and went on around the house.

Walking, her hand in her father's, Jennie could see some of the women of Liberty Street peering out at them through their curtains.

Downtown was not the same. Flags and banners draped the verandas; people wore their best clothes. The square had been roped off, a platform set up to one side, and New Marsails Avenue, which ran into the square, had been cleared for two blocks. Far away down the avenue stood a row of cotton bales onto which had been pinned oilcloth targets. From where they stood, the bull's-eyes looked no bigger than red jawbreakers.

Many men slapped her father on the back and, furtively, looked at her with a kind of clinical interest. But mostly they ignored her. The celebrity of the day was her father, and unlike her mother he was very popular. Everyone felt sure he would win the match; he was the best shot in the state.

After everyone shot, the judge came running down from the targets, waving his arms. "Maynard Herder. Six shots, and you can cover them all with a good gob of spit!" He grabbed her father's elbow and pulled him toward the platform, where an old man with white hair and beard, wearing a gray uniform trimmed with yellow, waited. She followed them to the platform steps, but was afraid to go any farther because now some women had begun to look at her as they had at her mother.

The old man made a short speech, his voice deep but coarse, grainy-sounding, and gave her father a silver medal in a blue velvet box. Her father turned and smiled at her. She started up the steps toward him, but just then the old man put his hand on her father's shoulder.

People had begun to walk away from the streets leading out of the square. There was less noise now, but she could not hear the first words the old man said to her father.

Her father's face tightened into the same look she had seen the day the letter came, the same as this morning in the kitchen. She went halfway up the stairs, stopped.

The old man went on. "You know I'm no meddler. Everybody knows about Liberty Street. I had a woman down there myself . . . before the war."

"I know that." The words came out of her father's face, though his lips did not move.

The old man nodded. "But, Maynard, what you're doing is different."

"She's your own daughter."

"Maybe that's why. . . ." The old man looked down the street, toward the cotton bales and the targets. "But she's a nigger. And now the talking is taking an ugly turn, and the folks talking are the ones I can't hold."

Her father spoke in an angry whisper. "You see what I do to that target? You tell those children in their masks I do that to the forehead of any man . . . or woman . . . that comes near her or my house. You tell them."

"Maynard, that wouldn't do any real good *after* they'd done something to her." He stopped, looked at Jennie, and smiled. "That's my only granddaughter, you know." His eyes clicked off her. "You're a man who knows firearms. You're a gunsmith. I know firearms too. Pistols and rifles can do lots of things, but they don't make very good doctors. Nobody's asking you to give her up. Just go back home. That's all. Go back to your wife."

Her father turned away, walking fast, came down the stairs, and grabbed her hand. His face was red as blood between the white of his collar and the straw yellow of his hair.

They slowed after a block, paused in a small park with green trees shading several benches and a statue of a stern-faced young man in uniform, carrying pack and rifle. "We will sit."

She squirmed up onto the bench beside him. The warm wind smelled of salt from the Gulf of Mexico. The leaves were a dull, low tambourine. Her father was quiet for a long while.

Jennie watched birds bobbing for worms in the grass near them, then looked at the young stone soldier. Far off but, from where she viewed it, just over the soldier's hat, a gliding sea gull dived suddenly behind the rooftops. That was when she saw the white man, standing across the street from the park, smiling at her. There were other white men with him, some looking at her, others at the man, all laughing. He waved to her. She smiled at him, though he was the kind of man her mother told her always to stay away from. He was dressed as poorly as any Negro. From behind his back, he produced a brown rag doll, looked at her again, then grabbed the doll by its legs and tore it part way up the middle. Then he jammed his finger into the rip between the doll's legs. The other men laughed uproariously.

Jennie pulled her father's sleeve. "Papa? What he doing?"

"Who?" Her father turned. The man repeated the show and her father bolted to his feet, yelling, "I will kill you! You hear? I will kill you for that!"

The men only snickered and ambled away.

Her father was red again. He had clenched his fists; now his hands were white like the bottoms of fishes. He sighed, shook his head, and sat down. "I cannot kill everybody." He shook his head again, then leaned forward to get up. But first he thrust the blue velvet medal box into her hand. It was warm from his hand, wet and prickly. "When you grow up, you go to the North like your mother tells you. And you take this with you. It is yours. Always remember I gave it to you." He stood. "Now you must go home alone. Tell your mother I come later."

That night, Jennie tried to stay awake until he came home, until he was there to kiss her good night, his whiskers scratching her cheek. But all at once there was sun at her window and the sound of carts and wagons grating outside in the dirt street. Her mother was quiet while the two of them ate. After breakfast, Jennie went into the yard to wait for the gray buggy to turn the corner, but for the first morning in many months, the white woman did not jounce by, peering at the house, searching for someone or something special.

Come Out the Wilderness

James Baldwin

1958

Paul did not yet feel her eyes on him. She watched him. He went to the window, peering out between the slats in the venetian blinds. She could tell from his profile that it did not look like a pleasant day. In profile, all of the contradictions that so confounded her seemed to be revealed. He had a boy's long, rather thin neck, but it supported a head that seemed even more massive than it actually was because of its plantation of thickly curling black hair, hair that was always a little too long or else, cruelly, much too short. His forehead was broad and high, but this austerity was contradicted by a short, blunt, almost ludicrously upturned nose. And he had a large mouth and very heavy, sensual lips, which suggested a certain wry cruelty when turned down but looked like the mask of comedy when he laughed. His body was really excessively black with hair, which proved, she said, since Negroes were generally less hairy than whites, which race, in fact, had moved farthest from the ape. Other people did not see his beauty, which always mildly astonished her—it was like thinking that the sun was ordinary. He was sloppy about the way he stood and sat, that was true, and so his shoulders were already beginning to be round. And he was a poor man's son, a city boy, and so his body could not really remind anyone of a Michelangelo statue as she—"fantastically," he said—claimed; it did not have that luxury or that power. It was economically tense and hard and testified only to the agility of the poor, who are always dancing one step ahead of the devil.

He stepped away from the window, looking worried. Ruth closed her eyes. When she opened them, he was disappearing away from her down the short black hall that led to the bathroom. She wondered what time he had come in last night; she wondered if he had a hangover; she heard the water running. She thought that he had probably not been home long. She was very sensitive to his comings and goings and had often found herself abruptly upright and wide awake a moment after he, restless at two-thirty in the morning, had closed the door behind him. Then there was no more sleep for her. She lay there on a bed that inexorably became a bed of ashes and hot coals, while her imagination dwelt on every conceivable disaster, from his having forsaken her for another woman to his having somehow ended up in the morgue. And as the night faded from black to gray to daylight, the telephone began to seem another presence in the house, sitting not far from her like a great, malevolent black cat that might, at any moment, with one shrill cry, scatter her life like dismembered limbs all over this tiny room. There were places she could have called, but she would have died first. After all—he had only needed to point it out once; he would never have occasion to point it out again—they were not married. Often she had pulled herself out of bed, her loins cold and all her body trembling, and gotten dressed and had coffee and gone to work without seeing him. But he would call her in the office later in the day. She would have had several stiff drinks at lunch and so could be very offhand over the phone, pretending that she had only supposed him to have gotten up a little earlier than herself that morning. But the moment she put the receiver down she hated him. She made herself sick with fantasies of how she would be revenged. Then she hated herself; thinking into what an iron maiden of love and hatred he had placed her, she hated him even more. She could not help feeling that he treated her this way because of her color, because she was a colored girl. Then her past and her present threatened to engulf her. She knew she was being unfair, she could not help it; she thought of psychiatry; she saw herself transformed, at peace with the world, herself, her color, with the male of indeterminate color she would have found. Always, this journey round her skull ended with tears, resolutions, prayers, with Paul's face, which then had the power to reconcile her even to the lowest circle of hell.

After work, on the way home, she stopped for another drink, or two or three; bought Sen-Sen to muffle the odor; wore the most casually glowing of smiles as he casually kissed her when she came through the door.

She knew that he was going to leave her. It was in his walk, his talk, his eyes. He wanted to go. He had already moved back, crouching to leap. And she had no rival. He was not going to another woman. He simply wanted to go. It would happen today, tomorrow, three weeks from today; it was over, she could do nothing about it; neither could she save herself by jumping first. She had no place to go, she only wanted him. She had tried hard to want other men, and she was still young, only twenty-six, and there was no real lack of opportunity. But all she knew about other men was that they were not Paul.

Through the gloom of the hallway he came back into the room and, moving to the edge of the bed, lit a cigarette. She smiled up at him.

"Good morning," she said. "Would you light one for me, too?"

He looked down at her with a sleepy and slightly shamefaced grin. Without a word he offered her his freshly lit cigarette, lit another, and then got into bed, shivering slightly.

"Good morning," he said then. "Did you sleep well?"

"Very well," she said lightly. "Did you? I didn't hear you come in."

"Ah, I was very quiet," he said teasingly, curling his great body toward her and putting his head on her breast. "I didn't want to wake you up. I was afraid you'd hit me with something."

She laughed. "What time *did* you come in?"

"Oh"—he raised his head, dragging on his cigarette, and half frowned, half smiled—"about an hour or so ago."

"What did you do? Find a new after-hours joint?"

"No. I ran into Cosmo. We went over to his place to look at a couple new paintings he's done. He had a bottle, we sat around."

She knew Cosmo and distrusted him. He was about forty, and he had had two wives; he did not think women were worth much. She was sure that Cosmo had been giving Paul advice as to how to be rid of her; she could imagine, or believed she could, how he had spoken about her, and she felt her skin tighten. At the same moment she became aware of the warmth of Paul's body.

"What did you talk about?" she asked.

"Oh. Painting. His paintings, my paintings, all God's chillun's paintings."

During the day, while she was at work, Paul painted in the back room of this cramped and criminally expensive Village apartment where the light was bad and where there was not really room enough for him to step back and look at his canvas. Most of his paintings were stored with a friend. Still, there were enough, standing against the wall, piled on top of the closet and on the table, for a sizable one-man show. "If they were any good," said Paul, who worked very hard. She knew this despite the fact that he said so rather too often. She knew, by his face, his distance, his quality, frequently, of seeming to be like a spring, unutterably dangerous to touch. And by the exhaustion, different in kind from any other, with which he sometimes stretched out in bed.

She thought—of course—that his paintings were very good, but he did not take her judgment seriously. "You're sweet, funnyface," he sometimes said, "but, you know, you aren't really very bright." She was scarcely at all mollified by his adding, "Thank heaven. I hate bright women."

She remembered, now, how stupid she had felt about music all the time she had lived with Arthur, a man of her own color who had played a clarinet. She was still finding out today, so many years after their breakup, how much she had learned from him—not only about music, unluckily. If I stay on this merry-go-round, she thought, I'm going to become very accomplished, just the sort of girl no man will ever marry.

She moved closer to Paul, the fingers of one hand playing with his hair. He lay still. It was very silent.

"Ruth," he said finally, "I've been thinking. . . ."

At once she was all attention. She drew on her cigarette, her fingers still drifting through his hair, as though she were playing with water.

"Yes?" she prompted.

She had always wondered, when the moment came, if she would make things easy for him or difficult. She still did not know. He leaned up on one elbow, looking down at her. She met his eyes, hoping that her own eyes reflected nothing but calm curiosity. He continued to stare at her and put one hand on her short, dark hair. Then, "You're a nice girl," he said irrelevantly, and leaned down and kissed her.

With a kiss! she thought.

"My father wouldn't think so," she said, "if he could see me now. What is it you've been thinking?"

He still said nothing but only looked down at her, an expression in his eyes that she could not read.

"I've been thinking," he said, "that it's about time I got started on that portrait of you. I ought to get started right away."

She felt, very sharply, that his nerve had failed him. But she felt, too, that his decision now to do a portrait of her was a means of moving far enough away from her to be able to tell her the truth. Also, he had always said that he could do something wonderful with her on canvas—it would be foolish to let the opportunity pass. Cosmo had probably told him this. She had always been flattered by his desire to paint her, but now she hoped that he would suddenly go blind.

"Anytime," she said, and could not resist, "Am I to be part of a gallery?"

"Yeah. I'll probably be able to sell you for a thousand bucks," he said, and kissed her again.

"That's not a very nice thing to say," she murmured.

"You're a funny girl. What's not nice about a thousand dollars?" He leaned over her to put out his cigarette in the ashtray near the bed; then took hers and put it out, too. He fell back against her and put his hand on her breast.

She said tentatively, "Well, I suppose if you do it often enough, I could stop working."

His arms tightened, but she did not feel that this was due entirely to desire; it might be said that he was striving now to distract her. "If I do *what* enough?" He grinned.

"Now, now." She smiled. "You just said that I was a nice girl."

"You're one of the nicest girls I ever met," said Paul soberly. "Really you are. I often wonder . . ."

"You often wonder what?"

"What's going to become of you."

She felt like a river trying to run two ways at once: she felt herself shrinking from him, yet she flowed toward him, too; she knew he felt it. "But as long as you're with me," she said, and she could not help herself, she felt she was about to cry; she held his face between her hands, pressing yet closer against him. "As long as you're with me." His face was white, his eyes glowed; there was a war in him, too. Everything that divided them charged, for an instant, the tiny space between them. Then the veils of habit and desire covered both their eyes.

"Life is very long," said Paul at last. He kissed her. They both sighed. And slowly she surrendered, opening up before him like the dark continent, made mad and delirious and blind by the entry of a mortal as bright as the morning, as white as milk.

When she left the house, he was sleeping. Because she was late for work and because it was raining, she dropped into a cab and was whirled out of the streets of the Village—which still suggested, at least, some faint memory of the individual life—into the grim publicities of midtown Manhattan. Blocks and squares and exclamation marks, stone and steel and glass as far as the eye could see; everything towering, lifting itself against, though by no means into, heaven. The people, so surrounded by heights that they had lost any sense of what heights were, rather resembled, nevertheless, these gray rigidities and also resembled, in their frantic motion, people fleeing a burning town. Ruth, who was not so many years removed from trees and earth, had felt in the beginning that she would never be able to live on an island so eccentric; she had, for example, before she arrived, dreamed of herself as walking by the river. But apart from the difficulties of realizing this ambition, which were not inconsiderable, it turned out that a lone girl walking by the river was simply asking to be victimized by both the disturbers and the defenders of the public peace. She retreated into the interior, and this dream was abandoned—along with others. For her as for most of Manhattan, trees and water ceased to be realities; the nervous, trusting landscape of the city began to be the landscape of her mind. And soon her mind, like life on the island, seemed to be incapable of flexibility, of moving outward, could only shriek upward into meaningless abstractions or drop downward into cruelty and confusion.

She worked for a life insurance company that had only recently become sufficiently progressive to hire Negroes. This meant that she worked in an atmosphere so positively electric with interracial goodwill that no one ever dreamed of telling the truth about anything. It would have seemed, and it quite possibly would have been, a spiteful act. The only other Negro there was male, a Mr. Davis, who was very highly placed. He was an expert, it appeared, in some way about Negroes and life insurance, from which Ruth had ungenerously concluded that he was the company's expert on how to cheat more Negroes out of more money and not only remain within the law but also be honored with a plaque for good race relations. She often—but not always—took dictation from him. The other girls, manifesting a rough, girl-scoutish camaraderie that made the question of their sincerity archaic, found him "marvelous" and wondered if he had a wife. Ruth found herself unable to pursue these strangely overheated and yet eerily impersonal speculations with anything like the indicated vehemence. Since it was extremely unlikely that any of these girls would ever even go dancing with Mr. Davis, it was impossible to believe that they had any ambition to share his couch, matrimonial or otherwise, and yet, lacking this ambition, it was impossible to account for their avidity. But they were all incredibly innocent and made her ashamed of her body. At the same time it demanded, during their maddening coffee breaks, a great deal of willpower not to take Paul's photograph out of her wallet and wave it before them, saying, *You'll never lay a finger on Mr. Davis. But look what I took from you!* Her face at such moments allowed them to conclude that she was planning to ensnare Mr. Davis herself. It was perhaps this assumption, despite her phone calls from Paul, that allowed them to discuss Mr. Davis so freely before her, and they also felt, in an incoherent way, that these discussions were proof of their democracy. She did not find Mr. Davis "marvelous," though she thought him good looking enough in a square, stocky, gleaming, black-boyish sort of way.

Near her office, visible from her window and having the air of contraband in Caesar's marketplace, was a small gray chapel. An ugly neon cross jutted out above the heads of passersby, proclaiming JESUS SAVES. Today, as the lunch hour approached and she began, as always, to fidget, debating whether she should telephone Paul or wait for Paul to telephone her, she found herself staring in some irritation at this cross, thinking about her childhood. The telephone rang and rang, but never for her; she began to feel the need of a drink. She thought of Paul sleeping while she typed and became outraged; then thought of his painting and became maternal; thought of his arms and paused to light a cigarette, throwing the most pitying of glances toward the girl who shared her office, who still had a crush on Frank Sinatra. Nevertheless, the sublimatory tube still burning, the smoke tickling her nostrils, and the typewriter bell clanging at brief intervals like signals flashing by on a railroad track, she relapsed into bitterness, confusion, fury: for she was trapped. Paul was a trap. She wanted a man of her own, and she wanted children, and all she could see for herself today was a lifetime of typing while Paul slept or a lifetime of typing with no Paul. And she began rather to envy the stocky girl with the crush on Frank Sinatra, since she would settle one day, obviously, for a great deal less and probably turn out children as Detroit turned out cars and never sigh for an instant for what she had missed, having indeed never, and especially with a lifetime of moviegoing behind her, missed anything.

JESUS SAVES. She began to think of the days of her innocence. These days had been spent in the South, where her mother and father and older brother remained. She had an older sister, married and with several children, in Oakland, and a baby sister who had become a small-time nightclub singer in New Orleans. There were relatives of her father's living in Harlem, and she was sure that they wrote to him often complaining that she never visited them. They, like her father, were earnest churchgoers, though, unlike her father, their religion was strongly mixed with an opportunistic respectability and with ambitions to better society and their own place in it, which her father would have scorned. Their ambitions vitiated in them what her father called the "true" religion, and what remained of this religion, which was principally vindictiveness, prevented them from understanding anything whatever about those concrete northern realities that made them at once so obsequious and so venomous.

Her innocence. It was many years ago. She remembered their house, so poor and plain, standing by itself, apart from other houses, as nude and fragile on the stony ground as an upturned cardboard box. And it was nearly as dark inside as it might have been beneath a box; it leaked when the rain fell, froze when the wind blew, could scarcely be entered in July. They tried to coax sustenance out of a soil that had long ago gone out of the business. As time went on, they grew to depend less and less on the soil and more on the oyster boats, and on the wages and leftovers brought home by their mother, and then herself, from the white kitchens in town. And her mother still struggled in these white kitchens, humming sweet hymns, tiny, mild-eyed, and bent, her father still labored on the oyster boats; after a lifetime of labor, should they drop dead tomorrow, there would not be a penny for their burial clothes. Her brother, still unmarried, nearing thirty now, loitered through the town with his dangerous reputation, drinking and living off the women he murdered with his lovemaking. He made her parents fearful, but they reiterated in each letter that they had placed him, and all of their children, in the hands of God. Ruth opened each letter in guilt and fear, expecting each time to be confronted with the catastrophe that had at last overtaken her kin; anticipating, too, with a selfish annoyance that added to her guilt, the enforced and necessary journey back to her home in mourning; the survivors gathered together to do brief honor to the dead, whose death was certainly, in part, attributable to the indifference of the living. She often wrote her brother asking him to come north, and asked her sister in Oakland to second her in this plea. But she knew that he would not come north—because of her. She had shamed him and embittered him; she was one of the reasons he drank.

Her mother's song, which she doubtless still hummed each evening as she walked the old streets homeward, began with the question, *How did you feel when you come out the wilderness?*

And she remembered her mother, half humming, half singing, with a steady, tense beat that would have made any blues singer sit up and listen (though she thought it best not to say this to her mother):

"Come out the wilderness,
Come out the wilderness.
How did you feel when you

come out the wilderness,
    Leaning on the Lord?"

And the answers were many: *Oh, my soul felt happy!* or *I shouted hallelujah!* or *I do thank God!*

Ruth finished her cigarette, looking out over the stone-cold, hideous New York streets, and thought with a strange new pain of her mother. Her mother had once been no older than she, Ruth, was today, she had probably been pretty, she had also wept and trembled and cried beneath the rude thrusting that was her master and her life, and children had knocked in her womb and split her as they came crying out. Out, and into the wilderness: she had placed them in the hands of God. She had known nothing but labor and sorrow, she had had to confront, every day of her life, the everlasting, nagging, infinitesimal details, it had clearly all come to nothing; how could she be singing still?

JESUS SAVES. She put out her cigarette, and a sense of loss and disaster wavered through her like a mist. She wished, in that moment, from the bottom of her heart, that she had never left home. She wished that she had never met Paul. She wished that she had never been touched by his whiteness. She should have found a great, slow, black man, full of laughter and sighs and grace, a man at whose center there burned a steady, smokeless fire. She should have surrendered to him and been a woman, and had his children, and found, through being irreplaceable, despite whatever shadows life might cast, peace that would enable her to endure.

She had left home practically by accident: it had been partly due to her brother. He had grown too accustomed to thinking of her as his prized, adored little sister to recognize the changes that were occurring within her. This had had something to do with the fact that his own sexual coming of age had disturbed his peace with her—he would, in good faith, have denied this, which did not make it less true. When she was seventeen, her brother had surprised her alone in a barn with a boy. Nothing had taken place between herself and this boy, though there was no saying what might not have happened if her brother had not come in. She, guilty though she was in everything but the act, could scarcely believe and had not, until today, ever quite forgiven his immediate leap to the obvious conclusion. She began screaming before he hit her; her father had had to come running to pull her brother off the boy. And she had shouted their innocence in a steadily blackening despair, for the boy was too badly beaten to be able to speak, and it was clear that no one believed her. She bawled at last, "Goddammit, I wish I had, I wish I had. I might as well of done it!" Her father slapped her. Her brother gave her a look and said, "You dirty . . . you dirty . . . you black and dirty—" Then her mother had had to step between her father and her brother. She turned and ran and sat down for a long time in the darkness on a hillside, by herself, shivering. And she felt dirty; she felt that nothing would ever make her clean.

After this she and her brother scarcely spoke. He had wounded her so deeply she could not face his eyes. Her father dragged her to church to make her cry repentance, but she was as stubborn as her father; she told him she had nothing to repent. And she avoided them all, which was exactly the most dangerous thing that could have happened, for when she met the musician, Arthur, who was more than twenty years older than she, she ran away to New York with him. She lived with him for more than four years. She did not love him all that time. She simply did not know how to escape his domination. He had never made the big time himself, and he therefore wanted her to become a singer; and perhaps she had ceased to love him when it became clear that she had no talent whatever. He was very disappointed, but he was also very proud, and he made her go to school to study shorthand and typing, and made her self-conscious about her accent and her grammar, and took great delight in dressing her. Through him, she got over feeling that she was black and unattractive, and as soon as this happened, she was able to leave him. In fleeing Harlem and her relatives there, she drifted downtown to the Village where, eventually, she found employment as a waitress in one of those restaurants with candles on the tables. Here, after a year or so and several increasingly disastrous and desperate liaisons, she met Paul.

The telephone rang several desks away from her, and at the same instant she was informed that Mr. Davis wanted her in his office. She was sure that it was Paul telephoning, but she picked up her pad and walked into Mr. Davis's cubbyhole. Someone picked up the receiver, cutting off the bell, and she closed the door of Mr. Davis's office behind her.

"Good morning," she said.

"Good morning," he answered. He looked out of his window. "Though, between you and me, I've seen better mornings. This morning ain't half trying."

They both laughed, self-consciously amused and relieved by his "ain't."

She sat down, her pencil poised, looking at him questioningly.

"How do you like your job?" he asked her.

She had not expected his question, which she immediately distrusted and resented, suspecting him, on no evidence whatever, of acting now as a company spy.

"It's quite pleasant," she said in a guarded, ladylike tone, and stared hypnotically at him as though she believed that he was about to do her mischief by magical means and she had to resist his spell.

"Are you intending to be a career girl?"

He was giving her more attention this morning than he ever had before, with the result that she found herself reciprocating. A tentative friendliness wavered in the air between them. She smiled. "I guess I ought to say that it depends on my luck."

He laughed—perhaps rather too uproariously, though, more probably, she had merely grown unaccustomed to his kind of laughter. Her brother bobbed briefly to the surface of her mind.

"Well," he said, "does your luck seem likely to take you out of this office anytime in the near future?"

"No," she said, "it certainly doesn't look that way," and they laughed again. But she wondered if he would be laughing if he knew about Paul.

"If you don't mind my saying so, then," he said, "*I'm* lucky." He quickly riffled some papers on his desk, putting on a business air as rakishly as she had seen him put on his hat. "There's going to be some changes made around here—I reckon you have heard that." He grinned. Then, briskly: "I'm going to be needing a secretary. Would you like it? You get a raise"—he coughed—"in salary, of course."

"Why, I'd love it," she heard herself saying before she had had time for the bitter reflection that this professional advance probably represented the absolute extent of her luck. And she was ashamed of the thought, which she could not repress, that Paul would probably hang on a little longer if he knew she was making more money.

She resolved not to tell him and wondered how many hours this resolution would last.

Mr. Davis looked at her with an intentness almost personal. There was a strained, brief silence. "Good," he said at last. "There are a few details to be worked out, like getting me more office space"—they both smiled—"but you'll be hearing directly in a few days. I only wanted to sound you out first." He rose and held out his hand. "I hope you're going to like working with me," he said. "I think I'm going to like working with you."

She rose and shook his hand, bewildered to find that something in his simplicity had touched her very deeply. "I'm sure I will," she said gravely. "And thank you very much." She reached backward for the doorknob.

"Miss Bowman," he said sharply—and paused. "Well, if I were you, I wouldn't mention it yet to"—he waved his hand uncomfortably—"the girls out there." Now he really did look rather boyish. "It looks better if it comes from the front office."

"I understand," she said quickly.

"Also, I didn't ask for you out of any—racial—considerations," he said. "You just seemed the most *sensible* girl available."

"I understand," she repeated; they were both trying not to smile. "And thank you again." She closed the door of his office behind her.

"A man called you," said the stocky girl. "He said he'd call back."

"Thank you," Ruth said. She could see that the girl wanted to talk, so she busily studied some papers on her desk and retired behind the noise of her typewriter.

The stocky girl had gone out to lunch, and Ruth was reluctantly deciding that she might as well go too, when Paul called again.

"Hello. How's it going up there?"

"Dull. How are things down there? Are you out of bed already?"

"What do you mean, already?" He sounded slightly nettled and was trying not to sound that way, the almost certain signal that a storm was coming. "It's nearly one o'clock. I got work to do too, you know."

"Yes. I know." But neither could she quite keep the sardonic edge out of her voice.

There was a silence.

"You coming straight home from work?"

"Yes. Will you be there?"

"Yeah. I got to go uptown with Cosmo this afternoon, talk to some gallery guy. Cosmo thinks he might like my stuff."

"Oh"—thinking *Damn Cosmo!*—"that's wonderful, Paul. I hope something comes of it."

Nothing whatever would come of it. The gallery owner would be evasive— *if* he existed, if they ever got to his gallery—and then Paul and Cosmo would get drunk. She would hear, while she ached to be free, to be anywhere else, *with* anyone else, from Paul, all about how stupid art dealers were, how incestuous the art world had become, how impossible it was to *do* anything—his eyes, meanwhile, focusing with a drunken intensity, his eyes at once arrogant and defensive.

Well. Most of what he said was true, and she knew it; it was not his fault. *Not his fault.* "Yeah. I sure hope so. I thought I'd take up some of my watercolors, some small sketches—you know, all the most *obvious* things I've got."

This policy did not, empirically, seem to be as foolproof as everyone believed, but she did not know how to put her uncertain objections into words. "That sounds good. What time have you got to be there?"

"Around three. I'm meeting Cosmo now for lunch."

"Oh"—lightly—"why don't you two, just this once, order your lunch before you order your cocktails?"

He laughed, too, and was clearly no more amused than she. "Well, Cosmo'll be buying, he'll have to, so I guess I'll leave it up to him to order."

Touché. Her hand, holding the receiver, shook. "Well, I hope you two make it to the gallery without falling flat on your faces."

"Don't worry." Then, in a rush—she recognized the tone before she understood the words; it was his you-can't-say-I-haven't-been-honest-with-you tone: "Cosmo says the gallery owner's got a daughter."

I hope to God she marries you, she thought. I hope she marries you and takes you off to Istanbul forever where I will never have to hear of you again, so I can get a breath of air, so I can get out from under.

They both laughed, a laugh conspiratorial and sophisticated, like the whispered whiskey laughter of a couple in a nightclub. "Oh?" she said. "Is she pretty?"

"She's probably a pig. She's had two husbands already, both artists."

She laughed again. "Where has she buried the bodies?"

"Well"—really amused this time but also rather grim—"one of them ended up in the booby hatch and the other turned into a fairy and was last seen dancing with some soldiers in Majorca."

Now they laughed together, and the wires between them hummed, almost, with the stormless friendship they both hoped to feel for each other someday. "A powerful pig. Maybe you *better* have a few drinks."

"You see what I mean? But Cosmo says she's not such a fool about painting."

"She doesn't seem to have much luck with painters. Maybe you'll break the jinx."

"Maybe. Wish me luck. It sure would be nice to unload some of my stuff on somebody."

You're doing just fine, she thought. "Will you call me later?"

"Yeah. Around three-thirty, four o'clock, as soon as I get away from there."

"Right. Be good."

"You, too. Good-bye."

"Good-bye."

She put down the receiver, still amused and still trembling. After all, he had called her. But he would probably not have called her if he were not actually nourishing the hope that the gallery owner's daughter might find him interesting; in that case he would have to tell Ruth about her, and it was better to have the way prepared. Paul was always preparing the way for one unlikely exploit or flight or another; it was the reason he told Ruth "everything." To tell everything is a very effective means of keeping secrets. Secrets hidden at the heart of midnight are simply waiting to be dragged to the light, as, on some unlucky high noon, they always are. But secrets shrouded in the glare of candor are bound to defeat even the most determined and agile inspector, for the light is always changing and proves that the eye cannot be trusted. So Ruth knew about Paul nearly all there was to know, knew him better than anyone else on earth ever had or probably ever would, only—she did not know him well enough to stop him from being Paul.

While she was waiting for the elevator, she realized, with mild astonishment, that she was actually hoping that the gallery owner's daughter would take Paul away. This hope resembled the desperation of someone suffering from a toothache who, in order to bring the toothache to an end, was almost willing to jump out of a window. But she found herself wondering if love really ought to be like a toothache. Love ought—she stepped out of the elevator, really wondering for a moment which way to turn—to be a means of being released from guilt and terror. But Paul's touch would never release her. He had power over her not because she was free but because she was guilty. To enforce his power over her he had only to keep her guilt awake. This did not demand malice on his part, it scarcely demanded perception—it only demanded that he have, as, in fact, he overwhelmingly did have, an instinct for his own convenience. His touch, which should have raised her, lifted her roughly only to throw her down hard; whenever he touched her, she became blacker and dirtier than ever; the loneliest place under heaven was in Paul's arms.

And yet—she went into his arms with such eagerness and such hope. She had once thought herself happy. Was this because she had been proud that he was white? But it was she who was insisting on these colors. Her blackness was not Paul's fault. Neither was her guilt. She was punishing herself for something, a crime she could not remember. *You dirty . . . you black and dirty . . .*

She bumped into someone as she passed the cigar stand in the lobby and, looking up to murmur, "Excuse me," recognized Mr. Davis. He was stuffing cigars into his breast pocket—though the gesture was rather like that of a small boy stuffing his pockets with cookies, she was immediately certain that they were among the most expensive cigars that could be bought. She wondered what he spent on his clothes—it looked like a great deal. From the crown of rakishly tilted, deafeningly conservative hat to the tips of his astutely dulled shoes, he glowed with a very nearly vindictive sharpness. There were no flies on Mr. Davis. He would always be the best-dressed man in *any*body's lobby.

He was just about the last person she wanted to see. But perhaps his lunch hour was over and he was coming in.

"Miss Bowman!" He gave her a delighted grin. "Are you just going to lunch?"

He made her want to laugh. There was something so incongruous about finding that grin behind all that manner and under all those clothes.

"Yes," she said. "I guess you've had your lunch?"

"*No*, I ain't had no lunch," he said. "I'm hungry just like you." He paused. "I be delighted to have your company, Miss Bowman."

Very courtly, she thought, amused, and the smile is extremely wicked. Then she realized that she was pleased that a man was *being* courtly with her, even if only for an instant in a crowded lobby, and at the same instant made the discovery that what was so widely referred to as a "wicked" smile was really only the smile, scarcely ever to be encountered anymore, of a man who was not afraid of women.

She thought it safe to demur. "Please don't think you have to be polite."

"I'm never polite about food," he told her. "Almost drove my mamma crazy." He took her arm. "I know a right nice place nearby." His stride and his accent made her think of home. She also realized that he, like many Negroes of his uneasily rising generation, kept in touch, so to speak, with himself by deliberately affecting, whenever possible, the illiterate speech of his youth. "We going to get on real well, you'll see. Time you get through being *my* secretary, you likely to end up with Alcoholics Anonymous."

The place "nearby" turned out to be a short taxi ride away, but it was, as he had said, "right nice." She doubted that Mr. Davis could possibly eat there every day, though it was clear that he was a man who liked to spend money.

She ordered a dry martini and he a bourbon on the rocks. He professed himself astonished that she knew what a dry martini was. "I thought you was a country girl."

"I *am* a country girl," she said.

"No, no," he said, "no more. You a country girl who came to the city, and that's the dangerous kind. Don't know if it's safe, having you for my secretary."

Underneath all this chatter she felt him watching her, sizing her up.

"Are you afraid your wife will object?" she asked.

"You ought to be able to look at me," he said, "and tell that I ain't got a wife."

She laughed. "So you're *not* married. I wonder if I should tell the girls in the office?"

"I don't care what you tell them," he said. Then: "How do you get along with them?"

"We get along fine," she said. "We don't have much to talk about except whether or not you're married, but that'll probably last until you *do* get married, and then we can talk about your wife."

But thinking *For God's sake let's get off this subject,* she added, before he could say anything, "You called me a country girl. Aren't you a country boy?"

"I am," he said, "but *I* didn't change my drinking habits when I come north. If bourbon was good enough for me down yonder, it's good enough for me up here."

"*I* didn't have any drinking habits to change, Mr. Davis," she told him. "I was too young to be drinking when I left home."

His eyes were slightly questioning, but he held his peace, while she wished that she had held hers. She concentrated on sipping her martini, suddenly remembering that she was sitting opposite a man who knew more about why girls left home than could be learned from locker-room stories. She wondered if he had a sister and tried to be amused at finding herself still so incorrigibly old-fashioned. But he did not, really, seem to be much like her brother. She met his eyes again.

"Where I come from," he said, with a smile, "*nobody* was too young to be drinking. Toughened them up for later life," and he laughed.

By the time lunch was over she had learned that he was from a small town in Alabama, was the youngest of three sons (but had no sisters), had gone to college in Tennessee, was a reserve officer in the Air Force. He was thirty-two. His mother was living, his father was dead. He had lived in New York for two years but was beginning, now, to like it less than he had in the beginning.

"At first," he said, "I thought it would be fun to live in a city where didn't nobody know you and you didn't know nobody and where, look like, you could do just anything you was big and black enough to do. But you get tired not knowing nobody, and there ain't really that many things you want to do alone."

"Oh, but you must have friends," she said, "uptown."

"I don't live uptown. I live in Brooklyn. Ain't *nobody* in Brooklyn got friends."

She laughed with him but distrusted the turn the conversation was taking. They were walking back to the office. He walked slowly as though in deliberate opposition to the people around them, although they were already a little late—at least *she* was late, but since she was with one of her superiors, it possibly didn't matter.

"Where do you live?" he asked her. "Do you live uptown?"

"No," she said, "I live downtown on Bank Street." And after a moment: "That's in the Village, Greenwich Village."

He grinned. "Don't tell me you studying to be a writer or a dancer or something?"

"No. I just found myself there. It used to be cheap."

He scowled. "Ain't nothing cheap in this town no more, not even the necessities."

His tone made clear to which necessities he referred, and she would have loved to tease him a little, just to watch him laugh. But she was beginning, with every step they took, to be a little afraid of him. She was responding to him with parts of herself that had been buried so long she had forgotten they existed. In his office that morning, when he shook her hand, she had suddenly felt a warmth of affection, of nostalgia, of gratitude even—and again in the lobby—he had somehow made her feel safe. It was his friendliness that was so unsettling. She had grown used to unfriendly people.

Still, she did not *want* to be friends with him; still less did she desire that their friendship should ever become anything more. Sooner or later he would learn about Paul. He would look at her differently then. It would not be—so much—because of Paul as a man, perhaps not even Paul as a white man. But it would make him bitter, it would make her ashamed for him to see how she was letting herself be wasted—for Paul, who did not love her.

This was the reason she was ashamed and wished to avoid the scrutiny of Mr. Davis. She was doing something to herself—out of shame?—that he would be right in finding indefensible. She was punishing herself. For what? She looked sideways at his black Sambo profile under the handsome lightweight Dobbs hat and wished she could tell him about it, that he would turn his head, holding it slightly to one side, and watch her with those eyes that had seen and that had learned to hide so much. Eyes that had seen so many girls like her taken beyond the hope of rescue, while all the owner of the eyes could do—perhaps she wore Paul the way Mr. Davis wore his hat. And she looked away from him, half smiling and yet near tears, over the furious streets on which, here and there, like a design, colored people also hurried, thinking, *And we were slaves here once.*

"Do you like music?" he asked her abruptly. "I don't necessarily mean Carnegie Hall."

Now was the time to stop him. She had only to say, Mr. Davis, I'm living with someone. It would not be necessary to say anything more than that.

She met his eyes. "Of course I like music," she said faintly.

"Well, I know a place I'd like to take you one of these evenings after work. Not going to be easy, being *my* secretary."

His smile forced her to smile with him. But, "Mr. Davis," she said, and stopped. They were before the entrance to their office building.

"What's the matter?" he asked. "You forget something?"

"No." She looked down, feeling big, black, and foolish. "Mr. Davis," she said, "you don't know anything about me."

"You don't know anything about me, either," he said.

"That's not what I mean," she said.

He sounded slightly angry. "I ain't asked you nothing yet," he said. "Why can't you wait till you're asked?"

"Well," she stammered, "it may be too late by then."

They stared at each other for a moment. "Well," he said, "if it turns out to be too late, won't be nobody to blame but me, will it?"

She stared at him again, almost hating him. She blindly felt that he had no right to do this to her, to cause her to feel such a leap of hope, if he was only, in the end, going to give her back all of her shame.

"You know what they say down home," she said slowly. "If you don't know what you doing, you better ask somebody." There were tears in her eyes.

He took her arm. "Come on in this house, girl," he said. "We got insurance to sell."

They said nothing to each other in the elevator on the way upstairs. She wanted to laugh, and she wanted to cry. He, ostentatiously, did not watch her; he stood next to her, humming "Rocks in My Bed."

She waited all afternoon for Paul to telephone, but although, perversely enough, the phone seemed never to cease ringing, it never rang for her. At five-fifteen, just before she left the office, she called the apartment. Paul was not there. She went downstairs to a nearby bar and ordered a drink and called again at a quarter to six. He was not there. She resolved to have one more drink and leave this bar, which she did, wandering a few blocks north to a bar frequented by theater people. She sat in a booth and ordered a drink and at a quarter to seven called again. He was not there.

She was in a reckless, desperate state, like flight. She knew that she could not possibly go home and cook supper and wait in the empty apartment until his key turned in the lock. He would come in, breathless and contrite—or else, truculently, *not* contrite—probably a little drunk, probably quite hungry. He would tell her where he had been and what he had been doing. Whatever he told her would probably be true—there are so many ways of telling the truth! And whether it was true or not did not matter, and she would not be able to reproach him for the one thing that *did* matter: that he had left her sitting in the house alone. She could not make this reproach because, after all, leaving women sitting around in empty houses had been the specialty of all men for ages. And, for ages, when the men arrived, women bestirred themselves to cook supper—luckily, it was not yet common knowledge that many a woman had narrowly avoided committing murder by calmly breaking a few eggs.

She wondered where it had all gone to—the ease, the pleasure they had had together once. At one time their evenings together, sitting around the house, drinking beer or reading or simply laughing and talking, had been the best part of all their days. Paul, reading or walking about with a can of beer in his hand, talking, gesturing, scratching his chest; Paul, stretched out on the sofa, staring at the ceiling; Paul, cheerful, with that lowdown, cavernous chuckle and that foolish grin; Paul, grim, with his mouth turned down and his eyes burning; Paul doing anything whatever. Paul with his eyelids sealed in sleep, drooling and snoring. Paul lighting her cigarette, touching her elbow, talking, talking, talking, in his million ways, to her, had been the light that lighted up her world. Now it was all gone, it would never come again, and that face which was like the heavens was darkening against her.

These present days, after supper, when the chatter each used as a cover began to show dangerous signs of growing thinner, there would be no choice but sleep. She might, indeed, have preferred a late movie or a round of the bars, lights, noise, other people, but this would scarcely be Paul's desire, already tired from his day. Besides—after all, she had to face the office in the morning. Eventually, therefore, bed; perhaps he or she or both of them might read awhile; perhaps there would take place between them what had sometimes been described as the act of love. Then sleep, black and dreadful, like a drugged state, from which she would be rescued by the scream of the alarm clock or the realization that Paul was no longer in bed.

Ah. Her throat ached with tears of fury and despair. In the days before she had met Paul men had taken her out, she laughed a lot, she had been young. She had not wished to spend her life protecting herself, with laughter, against men she cared nothing about; but she could not go on like this either, drinking in random bars because she was afraid to go home; neither could she guess what life might bring her when Paul was gone.

She wished that she had never met him. She wished that he, or she, or both of them were dead. And for a moment she really wished it, with a violence that frightened her. Perhaps there was always murder at the very heart of love; the strong desire to murder the beloved so that one could at last be assured of privacy and peace and be as safe and unchanging as the grave. Perhaps this was why disasters, thicker and more malevolent than bees, circled Paul's head whenever he was out of her sight. Perhaps in those moments when she had believed herself willing to lay down her life for him she had not only been presenting herself with a metaphor for her peace, his death; death, which would be an inadequate revenge for the color of his skin, for his failure, by not loving her, to release her from the prison of her own.

The waitress passed her table, and Ruth ordered another drink. After this drink she would go. The bar was beginning to fill up, mostly, as she judged, with theater people, some of them, possibly, on their way to work, most of them drawn here by habit and hope. For the past few moments, without realizing it, she had been watching a lean, pale boy at the bar, whose curly hair leaned electrically over his forehead like a living, awry crown. Something about him, his stance, his profile, or his grin, prodded painfully at her attention. But it was not that he reminded her of Paul. He reminded her of a boy she had known briefly a few years ago, a very lonely boy who was now a merchant seaman, probably, wherever he might be on the globe at this moment, whoring his unbearably unrealized, mysteriously painful life away. She had been fond of him, but loneliness in him had been like a cancer, it had really unfitted him for human intercourse, and she had not been sorry to see him go. She had not thought of him for years; yet, now, this stranger at the bar, whom she was beginning to recognize as an actor of brief but growing reputation, abruptly brought him back to her; brought him back encrusted, as it were, with the anguish of the intervening years. She remembered things she had forgotten and wished that she had been wiser then—then she smiled at herself, wishing she were wiser now.

Once, when he had done something to hurt her, she told him, trying to be calm but choked and trembling with rage, "Look. This is the twentieth century. We're not down on a plantation, you're not the master's son, and I'm not the black girl you can just sleep with when you want to and kick about as you please!"

His face, then, had held something, held many things—bitterness, amusement, fury; but the startling element was pain, his pain, with which she now invested the face of the actor at the bar. It made her wish that she had held her tongue.

"Well," he said at last, "I guess I'll get on back to the big house and leave you down here with the pickaninnies."

They had seen each other a few times thereafter, but that was really the evening on which everything had ended between them.

She wondered if that boy had ever found a home.

The actor at the bar looked toward her briefly, but she knew he was not seeing her. He looked at his watch, frowned, she saw that he was not as young as he looked; he ordered another drink and looked downward, leaning both elbows on the bar. The dim lights played on the crown of his hair. He moved his head slightly, with impatience, upward, his mouth slightly open, and in that instant, somehow, his profile was burned into her mind. He reminded her then of Paul, of the vanished boy, of others she had seen and never touched, of an army of boys—boys forever!—an army she feared and hated and loved. In that gesture, that look upward, with the light so briefly on his face, she saw the bones that held his face together and the sorrow beginning to corrode his brow, the blood beating like butterfly wings against the cage of his heavy neck. But there was no name for something blind, cruel, lustful, lost, intolerably vulnerable in his eyes and mouth. She knew that in spite of everything, his color, his power, or his coming fame, he was lost. He did not know what had happened to his life. And never would. This was the pain she had seen on the face of that boy so long ago, and it was this that had driven Paul into her arms, and now away. The sons of the masters were roaming the world, looking for arms to hold them. And the arms that might have held them—could not forgive.

A sound escaped her; she was astonished to realize it was a sob. The waitress looked at her sharply. Ruth put some money on the table and hurried out. It was dark now, and the rain that had been falling intermittently all day spangled the air and glittered all over the street. It fell against her face and mingled with her tears, and she walked briskly through the crowds to hide from them and from herself the fact that she did not know where she was going.

Has Anybody Seen
Miss Dora Dean?

Ann Petry

1958

One afternoon last winter, when the telephone rang in my house in Wheeling, New York, I started not to answer it; it was snowing, I was reading a book I had been waiting for weeks to get hold of, and I did not want to be disturbed. But it seemed to me that the peals of the bell were longer, more insistent than usual, so I picked up the phone and said, "Hello."

It was Peter Forbes—and neither that name nor any other is the actual one—and he was calling from Bridgeport. He said abruptly, and wheezily, for he is an asthmatic, "Ma is terribly ill. Really awfully sick."

He paused, and I said I was very sorry. His mother, Sarah Forbes, and my mother had grown up together in a black section of Bridgeport.

Peter said, "She's got some dishes she wants you to have. So will you come as soon as you can? Because she is really very sick."

I had heard that Sarah, who was in her seventies, was not well, but I was startled to learn that she was "terribly ill," "really very sick." I said, "I'll come tomorrow. Will that be all right?"

"No, no," he said. "Please come today. Ma keeps worrying about these dishes. So will you please come—well, right away? She is really terribly, terribly ill."

Knowing Sarah as well as I did, I could understand his insistence. Sarah had an unpleasant voice; it was a querulous, peevish voice. When she was angry or irritated, or wanted you to do something that you did not want to do, she talked and talked and talked, until finally her voice seemed to be pursuing you. It was like a physical pursuit from which there was no escape.

I said, "I'll leave right away," and hung up.

It took me three hours to drive from Wheeling to Bridgeport, though the distance is only forty-five miles. But it is forty-five miles of winding road—all hills and sharp curves. The slush in the road was beginning to freeze, and the windshield wiper kept getting stuck; at frequent intervals I had to stop the car and get out and push the snow away so that the wiper could function again.

During that long, tedious drive, I kept thinking about Sarah and remembering things about her. It was at least two years since I had seen her. But before that, over a period of twenty years, I had seen her almost every summer, because Peter drove over to Wheeling to go fishing, and his mother came too. She usually accompanied him whenever he went out for a ride. He would leave her at my house, so that she could visit with me while he and his two boys went fishing.

I thoroughly enjoyed these visits, for Sarah could be utterly charming when she was so minded. She was a tall woman with rather bushy black hair that had a streak of gray near the front. Her skin was a wonderful reddish brown color and quite unwrinkled, in spite of her age. She would have been extremely attractive if she hadn't grown so fat. All this fat was deposited on her abdomen and behind. Her legs had stayed thin, and her feet were long and thin, and her head, neck, and shoulders were small, but she was huge from waist to knee. In silhouette, she looked rather like a pouter pigeon in reverse. Her legs were not sturdy enough to support so much weight, and she was always leaning against doors, or against people, for support. This gave her an air of helplessness, which was completely spurious. She had a caustic sense of humor, and though she was an old woman, if something struck her as being funny, she would be seized by fits of giggling just as if she were a very young and silly girl.

I knew a great deal about Sarah Forbes. This knowledge stemmed from a long-distance telephone call that she made to my mother thirty-three years ago, when I was nine years old. I overheard my mother's side of the conversation. I can still repeat what she said, word for word, even imitating the intonation, the inflection of her voice.

In those days we lived in the building that housed my father's drugstore, in Wheeling. Our kitchen was on the ground floor, behind the store, and the bedrooms were upstairs, above it. Just as other children sat in the family living room, I sat in the drugstore—right near the front window on a bench when the weather was cold, outside on the wooden steps that extended across the front of the building when the weather was warm. Sitting outside on those splintery steps, I could hear everything that went on inside. In summer, the big front door of the store stayed wide open all day, and there was a screen door with fancy scrollwork on all the wooden parts. There were windows on either side of the door. On each window my father had painted his name in white letters with the most wonderful curlicues and flourishes, and under it the word DRUGGIST. On one window it said COLD SODA, and on the other window ICE CREAM, and over the door it said DRUG STORE.

Whether I sat inside the store or outside it, I had a long, sweeping view of the church, the church green, and the street. The street was as carefully composed as a painting: tall elm trees, white fences, Federal houses.

If I was sitting outside on the steps, listening to what went on in the store, no one paid any attention to me, but if I was sitting inside on the bench near the window, my mother or my father would shoo me out whenever a customer reached the really interesting part of the story he was telling. I was always being shooed out until I discovered that if I sat motionless on the bench, with a book held open in front of me, and did not glance up, everyone forgot about me. Occasionally, someone would stop right in the middle of a hair-raising story, and then my father would say, "Oh, she's got her nose in a book. She's just like she's deaf when she's got her nose in a book. You can say anything you want to and she won't hear a word." It was like having a permanent season ticket in a theater where there was a continuous performance and the same play was never given twice.

My special interest in Sarah dates from a rainy afternoon when I was sitting inside the store. It was a dull afternoon—no customers, nothing, just the busy sound of rain dripping from the eaves, hitting the wooden steps. The wall telephone rang, and my mother, wiping her hands on her apron, came to answer it from the kitchen, which was just behind the prescription room of the store. Before she picked up the receiver, she said, "That's a long-distance call. I can tell by the way the operator is ringing. That's a long-distance call."

I sat up straight, I picked up my book, and I heard the tinkling sound of money being dropped in at the other end. Then I heard my mother saying, "Why, Sarah, how are you? . . . What? What did you say? . . . Found him? Found him where?" She listened. "Oh, no!" She listened again. "Oh, my dear! Why, how dreadful! Surely an accident. You think—!" A longer period of listening. "Oh, no. Why that's impossible. Nobody would deliberately—" She didn't finish what she was going to say, and listened again. "A letter? Forbes left a letter? Tear it up! You mustn't let anyone know that—" There was a long pause. "But you must think of Peter. These things have an effect on—Excuse me."

She turned and looked at me. I had put the book down on the bench, and I was staring straight at her, breathing quite fast and listening so intently that my mouth was open.

She said, "Go out and play."

I kept staring at her, not moving, because I was trying to figure out what in the world she and Sarah Forbes had been discussing. What had happened that no one must know about?

She said again, her voice rising slightly, "Go out and play."

So I went the long way, through the back of the store and the prescription room and the kitchen, and I slammed the back door, and then I edged inside the prescription room again, very quietly, and I heard my mother say, "He must have had a heart attack and fallen right across the railroad tracks just as the train was due. That's the only possible explanation. And, Sarah, burn that letter. Burn it up!" She hung up the phone, and then she said to herself, "How dreadful. How perfectly dreadful!"

Whether Sarah took my mother's advice and burned Forbes' letter I do not know, but it became common knowledge that he had committed suicide, and his death was so reported in the Bridgeport newspapers. His body had been found on the railroad tracks near Shacktown, an outlying, poverty-stricken section of Bridgeport, where the white riffraff lived and the lowest brothels were to be found. He was the only person that my father and my mother and my aunts had ever known who had killed himself, and they talked about him endlessly— not his suicide but his life as they had known it. His death seemed to have put them on the defensive. They sounded as though he had said to them, "This life all of us black folk lead is valueless; it is disgusting, it is cheap, it is contemptible, and I am throwing it away, so that everyone will know exactly what I think of it." They did not say this, but they sounded perplexed and uneasy whenever they spoke of Forbes, and they seemed to feel that if they could pool their knowledge of him they might be able to reach some acceptable explanation of why he had killed himself. I heard Forbes and Sarah discussed, off and on, all during the period of my growing up.

I never saw Forbes. The Wingates, an enormously wealthy white family for whom he worked, had stopped coming to Wheeling before I was born, and he had stopped coming there too. But I heard him described so often that I knew exactly what he looked like, how he sounded when he talked, what kind of clothes he wore. He was a tall, slender black man. He was butler, social secretary, gentleman's gentleman. When Mr. Wingate became ill, he played the role of male nurse. Then, after Mr. Wingate's death, he ran the house for Mrs. Wingate. He could cook, he could sew, he could act as coachman if necessary; he did all the buying and all the hiring.

The Wingates were summer residents of Wheeling. Their winter home was in Bridgeport. In Wheeling, they owned what they called a cottage; it was an exact replica of an old Southern mansion—white columns, long graveled driveways, carefully maintained lawns, brick stables, and all within six hundred feet of Long Island Sound.

During the summer, Forbes rode a bicycle over to my father's drugstore every pleasant afternoon. He said he needed the exercise. Whenever I heard my family describing Forbes, I always thought how dull and uninteresting he must have been. There would never be anything unexpected about him, never anything unexplained. He would always move exactly as he was supposed to when someone pulled the proper strings. He was serious, economical, extremely conservative—a tall, elegant figure in carefully pressed black clothes and polished shoes. His voice was slightly effeminate, his speech very precise. Mrs. Wingate was an Episcopalian and so was Forbes.

But one day when my father was talking about Forbes, some six months after his death, he suddenly threw his head back and laughed. He said, "I can see him now, bicycling down the street, with those long legs of his pinched up in those straight tight pants he wore, pumping his legs up and down, and whistling 'Has Anybody Seen Miss Dora Dean?' with his coattails flying in the wind. I can see him now." And he laughed again.

At the time, I could not understand why my father should have found this funny. Years later, I learned that the tune Forbes whistled was one that Bert Williams and George Walker, a memorable team of black comedians, had made famous along with their cakewalk. They were singing "Dora Dean" in New York in about 1896. Dora Dean, the girl of the song, played the lead in a hit show called *The Creole Show,* which was notable for a chorus of sixteen beautiful brown girls. I suppose it amused my father to think that Forbes, who seemed to have silver polish in his veins instead of good red blood, should be whistling a tune that suggested cakewalks, beautiful brown girls, and ragtime.

Mrs. Wingate's name entered into the discussions of Forbes because he worked for her. It was usually my mother who spoke of Mrs. Wingate, and she said the same thing so often that I can quote her: "Mrs. Wingate always said she simply couldn't live without Forbes. She said he planned the menus, he checked the guest lists, he supervised the wine cellar—he did everything. Remember how she used to come into the store and say he was her mind, her heart, her hands? That was a funny thing to say, wasn't it?" There would be a pause, and then she would say, "Wasn't it too bad that she let herself get so fat?"

It was from my mother that I learned what Mrs. Wingate looked like. She was short and blond, and her face looked like the face of a fat china doll—pink and white and round. She used rice powder and rouge to achieve this effect. She bought these items in our drugstore. The powder came wrapped in thin white paper with a self stripe, and the rouge came in little round cardboard boxes, and inside there was a round, hard cake of reddish powder and a tiny powder puff to apply it with. She must have used a great deal of rouge, because at least once during the summer she would send Forbes up to the drugstore with a carton filled with these little empty rouge boxes. He would put them on the counter, saying, in his careful, precise, high-pitched voice, "Mrs. Wingate thought you might be able to use these." My father said he dumped them on the pile of rubbish in back of the store, to be burned, wondering what in the world she thought he would or could use them for. They smelled of perfume, and the reddish powder had discolored them, even on the outside.

Mrs. Wingate grew fatter and fatter until, finally, getting her in and out of carriages, and then, during a later period, in and out of cars—even cars that were specially built—was impossible unless Forbes was on hand.

Forbes was lean, but he was wiry and tremendously strong. He could get Mrs. Wingate in and out of a carriage or a car without effort; at least he gave the illusion of effortlessness. My father said it was Mrs. Wingate who panted, who frowned, whose flesh quivered, whose forehead was dampened with sweat.

My father always ended his description of this performance by saying, "Remember how he used to have that white woman practically on his back? Yes, sir, practically on his back."

After I heard my father say that, I retained a curious mental picture of Forbes—a lean, wiry black man—carrying an enormously fat pink and white woman piggyback. He did not lean over or bend over under the woman's weight; he stood straight, back unbent, so that she kept sliding down, down, down, and as he carried this quivering, soft-fleshed Mrs. Wingate, he was whistling "Has Anybody Seen Miss Dora Dean?"

I don't know that Forbes was actually looking for a reasonable facsimile of Dora Dean, but he found one, and he fell in love with her when he was forty years old. That was in 1900. He was so completely the perfect servant, with no emotional ties of his own and no life of his own, that my family seemed to think it was almost shocking that his attention should have been diverted from his job long enough to let him fall in love.

But it must have been inevitable from the first moment he saw Sarah Trumbull. I have a full-length photograph of her taken before she was married. She might well have been one of those beautiful girls in *The Creole Show.* In the photograph, she has a young, innocent face—lovely eyes, and a pointed chin, and a very pretty mouth with a quirk at the corner that suggests a sense of humor. Her hair is slightly frizzy, and it is worn in a high, puffed-out pompadour, which serves as a frame for the small, exquisite face. She is wearing a shirtwaist with big, stiff sleeves, and a tight choker of lace around her throat. This costume makes her waist look tiny and her neck long and graceful.

My mother had been born in Bridgeport, and though she was older than Sarah, she had known her quite well. Sarah was the only child of a Baptist minister, and, according to my mother's rather severe standards, she was a silly, giggling girl with a reputation for being fast. She was frivolous, flirtatious. She liked to play cards, and played pinochle for money. She played the violin very well, and she used to wear a ring with a diamond in it on her little finger, and just before she started to play, she would polish it on her skirt, so that it would catch the light and wink at the audience. She had scandalized the people in her father's church because she played ragtime on the piano at dances, parties, and cakewalks. (I overheard my father say that he had always heard this called "whorehouse music"; he couldn't understand how it got to be "ragtime.")

Anyway, one night in 1900 Forbes had a night off and went to a dance in

New Haven, and there was Sarah Trumbull in a white muslin dress with violet ribbons, playing ragtime on the piano. And there was a cakewalk that night, and Forbes and Sarah were the winners. I found a yellowed clipping about it in one of my mother's scrapbooks—that's how I know what Sarah was wearing.

I have never seen a cakewalk but I have heard it described. About fourteen couples took part, and they walked in time to music—not in a circle but in a square, with the men on the inside. The participants were always beautifully dressed, and they walked with grace and style. It was a strutting kind of walk. The test of their skill lay in the way they pivoted when they turned the corners. The judges stopped the music at intervals and eliminated possibly three couples at a time. The most graceful couple was awarded a beautifully decorated cake, so that they had literally walked to win a cake.

In those days, Sarah Trumbull was tall, slender, and graceful, and John Forbes was equally tall, slender, and graceful. He was probably very solemn and she was probably giggling as they turned the corners in a cakewalk.

A year later, they were married in the Episcopal church (colored) in Bridgeport. Sarah was a Baptist and her father was a Baptist minister, but she was married in an Episcopal church. If this had been a prize fight, I would say that Mrs. Wingate won the first round on points.

When my family discussed Forbes, they skipped the years after his marriage and went straight from his wedding to Sarah Trumbull in an Episcopal church (colored) to his death, twenty-four years later. Because I knew so little of the intervening years, I pictured him as being as ageless as a highly stylized figure in a marionette show—black, erect, elegantly dressed, effeminate, temperamental as a cat. I had never been able to explain why our cats did the things they did, and since there did not seem to be any reasonable explanation for Forbes' suicide, I attributed to him the unreasonableness of a cat.

The conversations in which my parents conjectured why Forbes killed himself were inconclusive and repetitive. My mother would sigh and say that she really believed Forbes killed himself because Sarah was such a slovenly housekeeper—that he just couldn't bear the dirt and the confusion in which he had to live, because, after all, he was accustomed to the elegance of the Wingate mansion.

My father never quite agreed. He said, "Well, yes, except that he'd been married to Sarah for twenty years or so. Why should he suddenly get upset about dirt after all that time?"

Once, my mother pressed him for his point of view, and he said, "Maybe he was the type that never should have married."

"What do you mean by that?"

"Well, he'd worked for that Mrs. Wingate, and he waited too long to get married, and then he married a young girl. How old was Sarah—twenty, wasn't she? And he was forty at the time, and—"

"Yes, yes," my mother said impatiently. "But what did you mean when you said he was a type that never should have married?"

"Well, if he'd been another type of man, I would have said there was more than met the eye between him and Mrs. Wingate. But he was so ladylike there couldn't have been. Mrs. Wingate thought a lot of him, and he thought a lot of Mrs. Wingate. That's all there was to it—it was just like one of those lifetime friendships between two ladies."

" 'Between two ladies'!" my mother said indignantly. "Why, what a wicked thing to say! Forbes was— Well, I've never seen another man, white or black, with manners like his. He was a perfect gentleman."

"Too perfect," my father said dryly. "That type don't make good husbands."

"But something must have *happened* to make him kill himself. He was thrifty and hard-working and intelligent and honest. Why should he kill himself?"

My father tried to end the conversation. "It isn't good to keep talking about the dead like this, figuring and figuring about why they did something—it's like you were pulling at them, trying to pull them back. After all, how do you know but you might succeed in bringing them back? It's best to let them alone. Let Forbes alone. It isn't for nothing that they have that saying about let them rest in peace."

There was silence for a while. Then my mother said softly, "But I do wish I knew why he killed himself."

My father said, "Sarah told you he said in the letter he was tired of living. I don't believe that. But I guess we have to accept it. There's just one thing I'd like to know."

"What's that?"

"I keep wondering what he was doing in Shacktown. That seems a strange place for a respectable married man like Forbes. That's where all those barefooted foreign women live, and practically every one of those orange-crate houses they live in has a red light in the window. It seems like a strange part of the city for a respectable married man like Forbes to have been visiting."

By the time I was ten, Forbes' death had for me a kind of reality of its own—a theatrical reality. I used to sit on the steps in front of the drugstore and half close my eyes so that I could block out the church green and the picket fences and the elm trees and the big old houses, and I would pretend that I was looking at a play instead. I set it up in my mind's eye. The play takes place on the wrong side of the railroad tracks, where the land is all cinders, in a section where voluptuous, big-hipped foreign women go barefooted, wrap their heads and shoulders in brilliant red and green shawls, and carry bundles on their heads—that is, those who work. Those who do not work wear hats with so many feathers on them they look as if they had whole turkeys on their heads. The houses in this area are built entirely of packing cases and orange crates. There is the sound of a train in the distance, and a thin, carefully dressed black man, in a neat black suit and polished shoes, walks swiftly onstage and up the slight incline toward the railroad tracks—no path there, no road. It is a winter's night and cold. This is Forbes, and he is not wearing an overcoat.

As narrator for an imaginary audience, I used to say, "What is he doing in this part of town in his neat black suit and his starched white shirt? He could not possibly know anyone here in Shacktown, a place built of cinders and packing cases. Bleak. Treeless. No road here. What is he doing here? Where is he going?"

The train whistles, and Forbes walks up the embankment and lies down across the tracks. The train comes roaring into sight and it slices him in two— quickly, neatly. And the curtain comes down as a telephone rings in a drugstore miles away.

This picture of Forbes remained with me, unchanged; I still see him like that. But in the intervening years Sarah changed. My first distinct recollection of her was of a stout middle-aged woman with a querulous voice, which was always lifted in complaint. Her complaint centered on money—the lack of it, the importance of it. But even in middle age there were vestigial remains of the girl who scandalized the religious black folk of Bridgeport by pounding out whorehouse music on the piano, and who looked as though she had just stepped out of the chorus line of *The Creole Show:* the wonderful smooth reddish-brown skin, the giggle over which she seemed to have no control, and the flirtatious manner of a Gay Nineties beauty. The coyness and the fits of giggling she had as an old woman were relics of these mannerisms.

I got to Bridgeport just at dusk. As I rang the bell of the two-story frame house where Sarah lived, I remembered something. This was the house that Mrs. Wingate had given to Forbes and Sarah as a wedding present. They had lived in it together exactly three weeks, and then Forbes went back to live at the Wingate mansion. Mrs. Wingate had asked him to come back because she might want to go out at night, and how could she get in and out of a car without him? It would be very inconvenient to have to wait for him to come all the way from the other side of town. (The Wingate mansion was at the south end of the city, and the dark-brown two-story taxpayer was at the north end of the city.) Mrs. Wingate had said that Sarah would, of course, stay where she was. She increased Forbes' wages and promised to remember him most generously in her will.

"It was a funny thing," my mother once said. "You know, Sarah used to call Forbes by his first name, John, when he was courting her, and when they were first married. After he went back to live at Mrs. Wingate's, she called him Forbes. All the rest of his life, she called him by his last name, just as though she was talking to Mrs. Wingate's butler."

One of Peter Forbes' gangling boys—Sarah's younger grandson—opened the door, and I stopped thinking about the past. He was a nice-mannered, gentle-looking boy, tall and thin, his face shaped rather like Sarah's in the old photograph—a small-boned face. His skin was the same wonderful reddish-brown color. I wondered why he wasn't in school, and immediately asked him.

"I've finished," he said. "I finished last June. I'm eighteen and I'm going in the Army."

I said what most people say when confronted by evidence of the passage of time. "It doesn't seem possible."

He said, "Yeah, that's right," took a deep breath, and said, "Nana's in the bedroom. You'd better come right in."

He seemed to be affected by the same need for haste that had made his father urge me to come see Sarah right away. I did not pause even long enough to take my coat off; I followed him down a dark hall, trying to remember what his real name was. Sarah had brought Peter's children up. Peter had been married to a very nice girl, and they had two boys. The very nice girl left Peter after the second baby was born and never came back. Sarah had given nicknames to the boys; the older was called Boodie, and the younger was Lud. It was Lud who had answered the door. I could not remember anything but the nickname—Lud.

We entered a bedroom at the back of the house. The moment I saw Sarah, I knew that she was dying. She was sitting slumped over in a wheelchair. In the two years since I had seen her, she had become a gaunt old woman with terrible bruised shadows under her eyes, and she was so thin that she looked like a skeleton. Her skin, which had been that rich reddish brown, was now overlaid with gray.

Lud said, "Nana, she's here. She's come, Nana."

Sarah opened her eyes and nodded. The eyes that I had remembered as black and penetrating were dull and their color had changed; they were light brown. I bent over and kissed her.

"I'm not so bright today," she said, and the words came out slowly, as though she had to think about using the muscles of her throat, her tongue, her lips—had to think, even, before she breathed. After she finished speaking, she closed her eyes and she looked as though she were already dead.

"She isn't asleep," Lud said. "You just say something to her. She'll answer—won't you, Nana?"

Sarah did not answer. I took off my coat, for the heat in the room was unbearable, and I looked around for a place to put it and laid it on a chair, thinking that the room had not changed. It was exactly as I remembered it, and I had not been in it for twenty years. There was too much furniture, the windows were heavily curtained, there was a figured carpet on the floor, and a brass bed, a very beautiful brass bed; one of the walls was covered with framed photographs.

A white cat darted through the room, and I jumped, startled, remembering another white cat that used to dart through these same rooms—but that was twenty years ago. "That's surely not the same cat, Lud? The one you've always had?"

"We've had this one about three years."

"Oh. But the other cat was white, too, wasn't it? It was deaf and it had never been outside the house—isn't that right? And it had blue eyes."

"So's this one. He doesn't go outside. He's deaf and he's got blue eyes." Lud grinned and his face was suddenly lively and very young. "And he's white," he said, and then laughed out loud. "Nana calls him our white folks."

"What's the cat's name?"

"Willie."

That was the name of the other cat, the one I had known. And Willie, so Sarah Forbes had said (boasted, perhaps?)—Willie did not like men. I wondered if this cat did.

"Is he friendly?"

"No," Lud said.

"Doesn't like men," Sarah Forbes said. Her voice was strong and clear, and it had its old familiar querulousness. The boy and I looked at her in surprise. She seemed about to say something more, and I wondered what it was going to be, for there was a kind of malevolence in her expression.

But Peter Forbes came into the room and she did not say anything. We shook hands and talked about the weather, and I thought how little he had changed during the years I had known him. He is a tall, slender man, middle-aged now, with a shaggy head and a petulant mouth that has deeply etched lines at the corners.

At the sight of Peter, Sarah seemed to grow stronger. She sat up straight. "Wheel me out to the dining room," she ordered.

"Yes, Ma," he said obediently. The wheelchair made no sound. "You come, too," he said to me.

"There's some china . . ." Sarah's voice trailed off, and she was slumping again, almost onto one arm of the wheelchair, her arms, head, and neck absolutely limp. She looked like a discarded rag doll.

We stood in the dining room and looked at her, all three of us. I said, "I'd better go. She's not well enough to be doing this. She hasn't the strength."

"You can't go," Peter said, with a firmness that surprised me. "Ma has some dishes she wants you to have. She's been talking about them for days now. She won't give us a minute's peace until you have them. You've got to stay until she gives them to you." Then he added, very politely and quite winningly, "Please don't go."

So I stayed. The dining room was just as hot as the bedroom. It, too, was filled with furniture—a dining room set, three cabinets filled with china and glassware, a studio couch, and, in a bay window, a big aquarium with fish in it.

Willie, the white cat, ran into the room from the hall, clawed his way up the draperies at the bay window, and sat crouched on the cornice, staring into the fish tank. His round blue eyes kept following the movements of the fish, back and forth, back and forth.

"Doesn't he try to catch the fish?" I asked.

Lud said, "That's what he wants to do. But he can't get at them. So he just watches them."

"Why, that's terrible," I said. "Can't you—"

Sarah had straightened up again. "Open those doors," she said.

"Yes, Ma." Peter opened one of the china cabinets.

"Get my cane."

"Yes, Ma." He went into the bedroom and came back with a slender malacca cane. She took it from him in a swift snatching movement and, holding it and pointing with it, was transformed. She was no longer a hideous old woman dying slowly but an arrogant, commanding figure.

"That," she said, "and that," pointing imperiously to a shelf in the china cabinet where a tall chocolate pot stood, with matching cups and saucers, covered thick with dust.

"Get a carton and some newspapers." She pointed at Lud, and she jabbed him viciously in the stomach with the cane. He jumped, and said, "Oh, oo-ooh!" pain and outrage in his voice.

"Go get the carton," Peter said matter-of-factly.

While we waited for Lud to come back, Sarah seemed to doze. Finally, Peter sat down and motioned to me to sit down. He picked up a newspaper and began to read.

Something about the way Sarah had ordered him around set me to wondering what kind of childhood Peter had had. He must have been about twelve years old when Mrs. Wingate died and left thirty-five thousand dollars to Forbes.

With this money, Forbes took what he called a flyer in real estate; he acquired an equity in six tenement houses. My mother had disapproved. She distrusted the whole idea of mortgages and loans, and she felt that Forbes was gambling with his inheritance; if his tenants were unable to pay the rent, he would be unable to meet the interest on his notes and would lose everything.

During this period, Mother went to see Sarah fairly often and she always came away from these visits quite disturbed. She said that Sarah, who had at one time cared too much about her looks, now did not seem to care at all. The house was dreadful—confused and dusty. She said that Forbes had changed. He was still immaculate, but he was now too thin—bony—and his movements were jerky. He seemed to have a dreadful, almost maniacal urge to keep moving, and he would sit down, stand up, walk about the room, sit down again, get up, walk about again. At first she used to say that he was nervous, and then she amended this and enlarged it by saying he was distraught.

Mrs. Wingate had been dead exactly two years when Forbes committed suicide. Immediately, all of Sarah's friends predicted financial disaster for her. Forbes' money was tied up in heavily mortgaged real estate, and shortly after his death the Depression came along, with its eviction notices and foreclosures.

I glanced at Sarah, dozing in the wheelchair, her chin resting on her chest. At twenty, she had been a silly, giggling girl. And yet somewhere under the surface there must have been the makings of a cold, shrewd property owner, a badgering, browbeating fishwife of a woman who could intimidate drunks, evict widows and orphans—a woman capable of using an umbrella or a hatpin as a weapon. She had made regular weekly collections of rent, because she soon learned that if she went around only once a month, the rent money would have gone for food or for liquor or for playing the numbers. Peter went with her when she made her collections. He was tall, thin, and asthmatic and wore tweed knee pants and long stockings—a ridiculous costume for a boy in his teens.

It was during those years that Sarah perfected her technique of leaning against people and began to develop a whining voice. She began to get fat. Her behind seemed to swell up, but her legs stayed thin, like pipestems, so that she walked carefully. She was what my father called spindle-shanked.

I suppose she had to whine, to threaten, to cajole, perhaps cry, in order to screw the rent money out of her tenants; at any rate, she succeeded. Years later, she told Mother that she had not lost a single piece of property. She finally sold all of it except the two-story taxpayer where they lived. She said that the bank that held the mortgages and notes had congratulated her; they told her that no real estate operator in Bridgeport had been able to do what she had done—bring all his property through the Depression intact.

Sarah straightened up in the wheelchair and pointed with her cane. "That," she said. Peter hesitated. "That" seemed to be some white cups and saucers with no adornment of any kind. Sarah threatened Peter with the cane, and he took them out of the cabinet and put them on the table.

"Perfect," she said to me. "Six of them. All perfect. Belonged to my grandmother. Handed down. They're yours now. You hand them down."

I shook my head. "Wait a minute," I said, slowly and distinctly, in order to be sure she understood. "What about your grandsons? What about Lud and Boodie? These cups should belong to Lud and Boodie."

"They will run with whores," she said coldly. "Just like Peter does. Just like Forbes kept trying to do, only he couldn't. That's what he was after in Shack-town that time, and when he found he couldn't—just wasn't able to—he laid himself down on the railroad track." She paused for a moment. "I cried for three days afterward. For three whole days." She paused again. "I wasn't crying because of what happened to him. I was crying because of what had happened to me. To my whole life. My whole life."

I could not look at Peter. I heard him take a deep breath.

Sarah said, "Those cups are yours. I'm giving them to you so that I'll know where they are. I'll know who owns them. If they should stay here . . ." She shrugged.

Lud came back with the carton and a pile of newspapers and Sarah did not even glance in his direction. She said, "The chocolate cups belonged to a French king. Mrs. Wingate gave them to me for a wedding present when I married her Forbes. I want you to have them so that I'll know who owns them."

We wrapped the pieces of china separately, and put wads of crumpled newspaper in between as we packed the carton. Sarah watched us. Sometimes she half closed her eyes, but she kept looking until we had finished. After that, her head slumped and her breathing changed. It was light, shallow, with pauses in between. I could hear the thumping of her heart way across the room.

I said, "Good-bye, Sarah," and kissed the back of her neck, but she did not answer or move.

It was still snowing when Lud carried the carton out to the car for me, held the door open, and closed it after I got in. I thought he did it with a kind of gracefulness that he couldn't possibly have acquired from Peter; perhaps it was something inherited from Forbes, his grandfather.

Lud said, "Did those cups really belong to one of the kings of France?"

"Maybe. I really don't know. I wish you'd put them back in the house. This whole carton of china is more yours than it is mine. These things belonged to your grandmother and they should stay in your family."

"Oh, no," he said hastily, and he stepped away from the car. "I don't want them. What would I do with them? Besides, Nana's ghost would come back and bug me." He laughed uneasily. "And if Nana's ghost bugged anybody, they'd flip for sure."

When I got home, I washed the chocolate set, and having got rid of the accumulated dust of fifty years, I decided that it could easily have belonged to one of the kings of France. It was of the very old, soft-paste type of porcelain. It had been made in the Sèvres factory and it was exquisitely decorated in the lovely color known as rose pompadour.

I was admiring the shape of the cups when the telephone rang. It was Peter Forbes. He said, "Ma died in her sleep just a few minutes after you left."

Mother Dear and Daddy

Junius Edwards

1962

They came in the night while we slept. We knew they were coming, but not when, and we expected to see them when they did. We never thought that they would come at night. When we got up, well, when John, my brother, got up (he was always getting up early), when he got up, he looked out of the window and ran and jumped back in bed and shook me and called my name.

"Jim, Jim, they here. They here already. Wake up, Jim. They—"

"Hey, quit shaking me. I been woke long time."

"They here." He ran to the window. "Come on look."

He didn't have to tell me "come on look" because I was at the window when he got there, almost, anyway. They had come all right; we could see the cars parked in the yard, like big cats crouching, backs hunched, ready to attack.

"I'll go tell Mary, then," John said, and bolted out of the room as fast as you could blow out a coal-oil lamp.

While he was out telling our three sisters, I stood there at the window and counted the cars. There were five in all, besides our car, and they were all black and shiny as my plate whenever I got through eating red beans and rice. Our car sat over there by itself, dusty and dirty as one of those bums that come by all the time wanting a meal.

I stood there, leaning on the windowsill, with my right foot on top of my left foot, scratching my left foot with my toes, and looking at our car. I could feel my eyes burning, burning, and the tears coming and washing the burns, and me sucking my tongue because of the burning and trying not to make a sound. My body went cold, and inside it I could feel something surging up; not like being sick, this surging came up my whole body, my arms, too, and ended with my eyes burning. I fought to hold it back, keep it buried. Even when I was alone, I always fought it, always won and kept it down, even at times when it was sudden and fast and got to my eyes and burned like hot needles behind my eyelids, hot needles with legs running around trying to get past my eyelids and spill out on my cheeks; even then I kept it down.

I had fought it for two weeks and I was good at it and getting better. Maybe I was good at it because of that first day. I had not fought it then. I had let it come, right in front of Aunt Mabel; I let it come, not trying to stop it, control it; I let it come.

"What we going to do?" I asked Aunt Mabel, after it had come, had shaken me and left me as empty as an unfilled grave. "What we going to do, Aunt Mabel?"

"Lord knows, son. Lord knows," Aunt Mabel said, sitting in her rocker, moving, slow, back and forth, looking down at me, on my knees, my arms resting on her huge right thigh and my head turned up to her, watching that round face, her lips tight now, her head shaking side to side, and her eyes clouded, and me not understanding her answer, but thinking I should and not daring to ask again and feeling the question pounding my brain: What we going to do? What we going to do?

"The Lord giveth and the Lord taketh away."

But what we going to do? I could not understand Aunt Mabel. I did not know what her mumbling about the Lord had to do with this. All I knew was she had just told me Mother Dear and Daddy were dead. Mother Dear and Daddy were dead. Mother Dear and Daddy would not come back. Mother Dear and Daddy wouldn't take us home again. What we going to do?

"I want to go home. I want to go home," I screamed and got to my feet and ran to the door, realizing it was Aunt Mabel calling my name. I ran out to the yard where John and our sisters played, and right past them. I did not feel my feet move; I did not feel I owned a body. I wanted to get home. And hearing Aunt Mabel call my name, seeing houses, cars, people, trees, like one big thing made of windows, walls, wheels, heads, branches, arms and legs, and behind that one big thing, our house, with our car out front, and our yard and our tree, and then the big thing was gone and I was at our house, running up the steps across the porch, as fast as I could, straight to the screened door, *wham!* and I lay on my back on the porch looking up at the screen, at the imprints made in it by my head and hands and my right knee. I got right up and started banging on the door, trying to twist the knob.

"Mother Dear! Daddy! Mother Dear! Daddy!" I called as loud as I could and kept banging on the door. Then I ran to the back door and called again and banged and kicked the door. They did not come.

They would not come.

"Mother Dear! Daddy! It's me. Let me in. Open the door!"

They would not come.

I ran to the front, out to the street, and turned and looked up to their room and saw the shades were drawn just as they were drawn when Mother Dear and

Daddy took us over to Aunt Mabel's house to stay for the weekend while they went away fishing with cousin Bob.

I cupped my hands up to my mouth.

"Mother Dear. Daddy. Mother Dear! Daddy!"

I called, and called again and all the while I kept my eyes glued on that window, waiting. Any moment now, any second now, now, *now,* waited to see that white shade zoom up and then the window, and then Mother Dear and Daddy, both together, lean out, smiling, laughing, waving, calling my name, now, now, *now.*

They did not come.

They would not come. The shade stood still, stayed still, with the sun shining on it through the windowpane; stayed still, as if the sun were a huge nail shooting through the pane and holding it down. It did not go up. It would not go up.

They would not come.

I knew it. Suddenly, just like that, *snap,* I knew they would not come; could not come. The shades would stay still. I knew they would not come. I lowered my hands, my eyes darting from shaded window to shaded window, around the yard, under the house, searching—for what? I did not know, and then there was the car. My eyes were glued to the car, and I started over to it, slowly at first, and then I ran and I stopped short and pressed my head up against the glass in the front door beside the steering wheel. The glass was hot on my nose and lips and forehead, and burned them, but I did not care, I pressed harder, as if by doing so I could push right through the glass, not breaking it, but melting through it. Then, I felt as though I *was* inside, in my favorite spot up front with Daddy, and in back were Mother Dear and John and our sisters; Daddy whistling and the trees going by and the farms and green, green, green, and other cars, and Daddy starting to sing and all of us joining him singing "Choo-Choo Train to Town," even Jo Ann and Willie Mae, who had not learned the words yet, singing, singing, and ending laughing and feeling Daddy's hand on my head.

"Jim." I turned from the window, and it was Aunt Mabel's hand on my head.

"Come on, son." She took my right hand and led me up the street as if I were a baby just starting to walk.

"What we going to do, Aunt Mabel?"

"You got to be brave, Jim. You the oldest. You got to look out for your brother and sisters."

I decided then that I would not let my brother and sisters see me cry, ever. I was twelve years old and the oldest, and I had to take care of them.

"When can we go back home, Aunt Mabel?"

"I guess we ought to move over to your house while we wait for the family to get here," Aunt Mabel said. "It's bigger than mine and your clothes there."

I looked up at Aunt Mabel. I had not expected her to move back with us. I wanted only we children to move back home.

When we got back to Aunt Mabel's house I told John about the automobile accident and that Mother Dear and Daddy were dead. John was only eight, but he understood and he cried, and I understood just how he felt, so I left him alone.

The next day we moved back to our house. Aunt Mabel, too. Every time one of our sisters would ask for Mother Dear and Daddy we always said they were gone away. They were too young to understand about death.

Aunt Mabel told me that our uncles and aunts and grandparents were coming. I didn't know any of them. I remembered Christmas presents from them and Mother Dear and Daddy talking about them, but I had never seen them.

"They're good folks," Aunt Mabel said, "and it won't make no difference which one you all go to live with."

"But, Aunt Mabel. We going to stay home."

"You can't, son. You all too young to stay here by yourself, and I can't take care of you."

"I can take care of us, Aunt Mabel. I'm the oldest. I can take care of us."

Aunt Mabel smiled. "Bet you could, too. But you all need somebody to be a mama and a papa to you. You all got to go live with one of your aunts and uncles."

I knew right away that Aunt Mabel was right. I told John about it and we started trying to guess where we would go. The family was scattered all over, mostly in big cities like New York, Philadelphia, and Boston. Our grandfather on Daddy's side was in Texas. John and I couldn't decide what we liked best: Texas and horses or big cities and buildings. We talked about it every day while we waited for them to come, and now they were here.

I left the window and started to get dressed. John ran back into the room.

"Them won't wake up."

"They can sleep, then," I said. "Let's go see where the cars came from."

We got dressed and ran out to the yard and looked at the license plates. There were two from New York, two from Pennsylvania, and one from Massachusetts.

"None of them from Texas," I said.

"Which one you like best?" asked John.

"That one," I said, pointing to the one from Massachusetts. I liked it because it was the biggest one. The five of us could get in it without any trouble at all.

We examined each car carefully for an hour, and then Aunt Mabel called us and told us to come in the house.

"They all here," she said, "all that's coming, I guess. Now, you all be good so they'll like you."

I followed Aunt Mabel into the living room. I could feel John right behind me, up close, and I could hear his breathing.

"Here the boys," Aunt Mabel announced, and walked across the room and sat down.

John and I stopped at the door. Our sisters were lined up, side by side, in the middle of the room, smiling. I had heard voices before we came into the room, but now there was silence and all eyes were on us. They sat in a half circle in straight-back chairs, near the walls around the room. I looked at them. I stared at each face. Aunt Mabel and our sisters were the only smiling faces I saw. I didn't know about John, but right at that moment, I was scared. I wanted to turn and run away as fast as I could. I felt as if I had committed the worst crime and those faces hated me for it. Besides Aunt Mabel, there were five men and five women, all dressed in black. Each man had a black line above his upper lip. The two men who were fat had thick black lines and the other three had thinner ones. I didn't like the lines. Daddy never wore one and I always thought his face was cleaner and friendlier and happier than other men I had seen who wore them.

I noticed the features of these people right away. They were all like Mother Dear, Aunt Mabel, and our sisters, and they were pink rose. I knew they were Mother Dear's relatives. Daddy didn't have any brothers or sisters, and he used to tell John and me whenever we got into a fight with each other that we should be kind to each other because we were brothers and it was good to have a brother and that he wished he had had brothers and sisters. Mother Dear had plenty of brothers and sisters. She had three brothers, and I knew them right away as the three who weren't fat, and three sisters, Aunt Mabel, of course, and the two women who sat beside the fat men.

I stood there looking, staring at those faces that looked as if they had just taken straight castor oil. I looked at John, now standing at my right. He stood there with his mouth hanging open and his eyes straight ahead. I could tell he was scared and as soon as I knew he was scared, I wasn't scared any more and I wanted to tell him not to be scared because I wasn't going to let anything happen to him. Just when I was about to tell him, Aunt Mabel broke the silence.

"Come on over here next to your sisters," she said.

We shuffled over to where our sisters were and stood there like slaves on auction.

"They good children," Aunt Mabel said. "No trouble at all."

The others still kept quiet, except for whispers among themselves.

"Say your names, boys," Aunt Mabel said.

"James," I said.

"John," said John.

"We call James Jim," Aunt Mabel said, and smiled at me.

I looked at her. It was all right for her to call me Jim. Mother Dear and Daddy called me Jim. I looked back at those faces. I didn't want *them* to call me Jim.

"Well," Aunt Mabel said to them, "you all going to tell the boys your names?"

They introduced themselves to us, not smiling, not changing those castor oil expressions. Apparently they had already introduced themselves to our sisters.

"Mabel," one of the fat men said, "why don't you get these kids out of here so we can talk."

"Jim, you and the children go in the dining room," Aunt Mabel said, and when we were going, she added, "And close the door."

We went into the dining room and I closed the door. Our sisters sat down in the middle of the floor and played. John stood over them, watching, but when he saw me with my ear to the door, he came over and joined me. We faced each other with our heads pressed up against the door and we listened. The only voice I could recognize was Aunt Mabel's.

"Carol and I have thought this thing over, and we can see our way clear to take the girls," one of the men said.

"Now, wait a minute, Sam," another man said. "We thought we'd take *one* of the girls, at least."

Then for a minute it sounded as if they were all trying to get a word in. They talked all at the same time, even yelled. It sounded as if everyone wanted a girl.

"Lord have mercy. You mean you going to split them up? You mean they won't be together?"

"Five kids? Frankly, we can't afford two, but we'd be willing to take the three girls."

There was another minute of all of them trying to speak at the same time, at the top of their voices, each one wanting a girl.

"Why don't you all talk like people? I don't like to see them split up, but I guess five is too many for anybody, specially when they not your own."

"Then you understand that they'll have to be separated? There's no other way, and since we already have a son, we thought we would take one of the girls."

"Well," Aunt Mabel said, "look like to me you all want a girl. I didn't hear nobody say nothing about the boys yet."

There was silence. John and I pressed harder against the door. John's mouth was open, his bottom lip hanging, and he was staring at me hard. I could tell he was scared and I must have looked scared to him, so I closed my own mouth and tried to swallow. There was nothing to swallow and I had to open my mouth again and take a deep breath.

"Come to think of it, you all didn't say one word to them boys," Aunt Mabel said. "Why don't you all want boys?"

"We have a boy."

"We do too."

"Girls are easier."

"Boys are impossible."

"Lord have mercy."

"Listen, Mabel, you don't understand the situation."

"Don't get on your high horse with me. Talk plain."

"All right, Mabel. The fact is, the boys are—well—they're too, well, too much like the father."

"What?"

"You heard me. I know that's why *we* don't want one, and it's probably why the others here don't want one and it's no use avoiding it."

"Is that right? Is that why you all don't want one too?" Aunt Mabel asked. There was silence.

"Lord have mercy. I never heard such a thing in all my life. Your own sister's children, too."

"You don't understand, Mabel."

"No, I don't. Lord knows I don't. What you all doing up there? Passing? Huh? That what you doing? No. No. You couldn't be doing that. Even if you wanted to, you couldn't be doing that. You not that light that you can pass, none of you all. Lord have mercy. They too black for you. Your own sister's children."

John looked down at his hands, at the back of his hands, and then at me and down at our sisters and at his hands again.

"I never thought I'd live to see the day my own flesh and blood would talk like that, and all the trouble in the world. My own sisters and brothers," Aunt Mabel said.

"Mabel, you've been here in this town all your life. This town isn't the world. You don't know how it is."

John rubbed the back of his hand on his pants and looked at it again.

I kept listening.

"It's hard enough like it is without having these boys, having to always explain about them. You can see that, Mabel. Look at us, how light we are. We'd always have to explain to everyone they're our dead sister's boys and people who we don't explain to will jump to all kinds of conclusions. Socially, we'd be out too. No, Mabel. That's just the way it is and we can't do a thing about it. I, for one, have certain standards I want to live up to, and having these boys won't help."

"I never thought it. I never thought it."

"That's the way it is, Mabel. Those boys will do none of us any good."

John went over to where our sisters played and stood over them, examining them.

Aunt Mabel said, "So that's how come you didn't want her to get married. That's how come you tried to get her away from here."

John kneeled down and touched each one of our sisters. He looked at them and at his hand, at them and at his hand, and then to me. Then his eyes became shiny and he started batting his eyes and the sides of his face grew, his cheeks puffed way out, his mouth closed tight. He fought it all he could and I knew it was useless, he would not succeed. I could feel the same thing happening to me, but I held it back and concentrated on him, watched his swelling face until it exploded and thinking he might yell out, I rushed to him and got down on my knees and held him, held him close, just as Daddy would have, with my left arm around his back and my right hand behind his head, holding his head to my chest and felt his body shaking like a balloon when you let out the air and I listened to him groan like a whipped dog. I didn't say one word to him. I couldn't. I let him cry and I held him and watched our sisters and they suddenly realized he was crying and they came to us and helped me hold him and tried to get him to tell why he cried and when he would not tell they asked me and when I would not tell they stood there holding both of us until John got control of himself. He sat back on his heels and sobbed and the girls stepped back and watched him. I stood up and watched all of them. The girls stood there and watched him and waited, their faces alert, ready to run to him and help him. It was as if they knew, now, this was not a physical wound that made him cry, not a twisted arm, a stubbed toe, or a beating, and certainly not a cry that would make them laugh and yell "crybaby" at him. It was as if they knew it was a wound they had never had and that it was deeper than skin.

I heard the voices in the living room, louder now, and wilder, so I started back to my place at the door, but before I got there, John lost control again. We got to him at the same time and tried to hold him, but this time he pushed us away, fought us off, and got to his feet and ran into the living room. I got to my feet as fast as I could and ran after him into the living room. He was screaming now and when I ran into the living room, I stopped short at what I saw. John had run in and jumped in the lap of the first man he came to and he was there on his knees in the man's lap screaming and pounding the man's chest and face. The man pushed him off and John fell to the floor on his back and got right up and jumped in the man's lap again, still screaming, and pounded the man's chest and face with both his little fists.

"John, John, John!" I yelled, and ran to him and pulled him out of the man's lap, just in time, too, because the man swung at him backhanded, but I had John down and the man missed. John, still screaming, kicking, struggled with me, trying to get away from me so he could get back to the man.

"John, John!" I yelled, shaking him, trying to make him hear me. "John,

John!" But I could see he wasn't listening to me even though he was looking straight at me as I stood in front of him holding both of his arms and shouting his name. He only screamed.

Suddenly, I started walking backwards from him, holding his arms still, pulling him along with me until we were in the center of the room and then I smiled at him. "Come on, John, come on, John," I said, and laughed, laughed hard, looking into his eyes; I kept it up, laughed loud and harder still and felt my body shake from it. Then I saw John's face change, first a smile, then he broke into a laugh, too. I stared into his eyes and we laughed. We laughed. We laughed. We laughed. We threw our heads back and we laughed. We held each other's hands and danced round and round and laughed. Our sisters came and joined our dance. We formed a circle, all of us laughing, laughing, and we danced round and round. We were the only people in the world. We danced round and round and laughed and laughed.

"Hey," I said, "Choo-Choo Train, Choo-Choo Train" and they joined me:

"Choo-choo train, choo-choo train,
We going to take that choo-choo train,
Choo-choo train to town,
Choo-choo train,
Choo-choo train—"

Round and round, "Choo-choo train," louder and louder I sang, "CHOO-CHOO TRAIN, CHOO-CHOO TRAIN, CHOO-CHOO TRAIN TO TEXAS" round and round, "CHOO-CHOO TRAIN" until I realized what I had said and I screamed happily and said it again and again until they caught on and said it too. We went faster and faster and said it louder and louder, sounding like a choo-choo train: TEXAS, TEXAS, TEXAS, TEXAS, TEXAS. . . .

Blues for Pablo

John Stewart

1962

. . . asante, Miles . . .

Pablo had left his house at dawn that Thursday morning. He watched them kill four animals, stood by while they skinned the carcasses and emptied the hot entrails. In the dimly lit slaughterhouse where no foreign sound penetrated the thick walls save the churn of the outside refrigerating unit, his four men worked deliberately, jointing the dead bodies with precise movements, first into huge sides of beef, then into lesser and lesser cuts. There was not much talk amid the hacking sounds of hatchet and knife, the piercing scrape of the saw. When they spoke they used only short, sharp grunts, and they seldom looked at each other. They were good men. Like himself, they were Mexicans, and often Pablo felt like a father to them. With age he had grown heavy and slow, but they were young. They moved lightly, and with a seriousness that matched the meticulous black hair gummed down above their bloody white coats. When he took the knife and prepared to open his finger they all stopped, standing where they were with the heavy darkness in their eyes, silently joining him in the sacred moment as the blood fell in slow, thick drops onto the sawdust floor. After he wiped the knife they resumed working, their feet stirring the flakes, making his blood one with that of the dead animals, and when he was ready to leave, most of the beef already hung in cuts from the sharp iron hooks.

The sun was bright and hot as he emerged through the heavy doors, and as he started across the valley sweat began to form in slow drops all over his heavy face. The sweat came faster as he crossed over the railway tracks, walked under the freeway, and headed for the cluster of houses. There was not much shade from the afternoon sun. The houses rose square and low, their shadows lost against their own walls, and the scattered trees stood spare, dry from the summer heat. All along the narrow deserted streets across the valley he felt the finger throbbing with each pulse. It was a good feeling. It kept alive the moment when the knife had sliced in a quick, sharp pain to let the blood drip slowly down. That was a good moment. He gave, he did not lose. Each week he gave a few drops of blood, a little in gratefulness, a little to let their spirits know how great was his respect for the proud animals, but mostly to stir his own spirit into a strong compassion for everything alive.

His thick face impassively set in an unchanging expression, Pablo walked across the corner of City Terrace Drive with solid steps, admitting no vision of the old men sunning themselves on the bus-stop bench, the children with their dogs noisily prancing between the bakery and the store. He walked directly into the little library and, though he sweated freely, made no effort to stop the drops slipping from beneath his hat, streaking his dust-covered face.

"How are you today, Mr. Montez?" the lady clerk asked, not waiting to hear his answer, but going back between the shelves to return with the book. "We have a new one in," she said when she came back. "It's all about the last hours before he died. What a remarkable man! Would you like to have it?"

Pablo considered for several moments. He had no wish to disturb the ceremony of Thursday with new things, although something new was already introduced into his day. Shortly he would have to face the girl and her friend. "No," he said, shaking his head more than saying the word. The regular book with its smooth brown cover was part of Thursday. He liked the naked sword on the cover with the red cloth lapped over it. The slightly curved blade recalled a memory of days older than he himself, older than his father or grandfather. It produced visions of fierce naked men caked with sweat and dust receiving similar blades in their proud chests, fearlessly falling in the hot trampled sand, letting go life without a cry while their blood trickled red along the blade. Manolete was such a man. A man's life was only a preparation for the end of living, and when his end came, that torero let go fearlessly. Each week, through Manolete, Pablo reminded himself of his own fearlessness.

His finger still throbbed a little where the blood had dried in the narrow slit, and the clerk had already filled out the card when Pablo said, "Señora, could I take the book with me?"

"Oh, yes, of course. Prefer to read at home today?" She smiled, fixing her glasses. "My, you must know this book by heart by now." She started making another card. "Where is your friend, the young girl? She never comes in anymore."

"She is perhaps in school," Pablo said. The lady clerk had seen the friendship start, had often watched them mount the hill together, and as she kept pushing the glasses back on her nose, her face showed a readiness to discover his secrets.

In City Terrace Heights people were always ready to find out secrets, especially his. For all of his five years on the hill Pablo had managed to keep them at a distance and had, like his house, become an attraction. On the streets he could see the women stop and look, and he knew they talked of him. When he passed on, they'd turn and point at his house and go on talking—not the young ones, but the old wrinkled women who met to gossip when the evenings were warm. They were all Mexicans too, the people in the streets and the people in the little white houses, but he didn't know them and he had no wish to know them. The curious ones wanted to know him—like the lady clerk behind her glasses. He knew they talked about him and the girl; she didn't care, and Pablo didn't care either, except he wanted them to leave her alone, as they left him alone.

Leaving the library, Pablo walked to the broken old Jew selling papers across the street. Nobody talked about the Jew, nobody ever pointed at him, but he too was a proud man. As Pablo approached, the Jew left the narrow shade cast by his cardboard stand. His eyes seemed the only nourished things about his thin, sunken face, and they glittered strongly as he came out to meet Pablo. With all Pablo felt for the humped man in the baggy suit and greasy cap, there was no need for words. Pablo paid slowly for his paper, they shook hands, and the Jew turned back to his scanty shade.

Pablo went through the motions of Thursday with his usual heaviness. After getting the paper, he went to the store. He stepped right by the old men gathered on the bus-stop bench who were not waiting for any bus. Most of them were as dark as he, but they were bony and wrinkled. They were not as broken as the Jew, and they were not as proud. They sat switching the flies away, talking rapidly, while the wine bottle in a brown paper sack passed from hand to hand. They paid him no attention, and he paid them none. It was all the same for them. He felt a different compassion—they would all die wrong. They would dry up and die. They would have no blood to give and the spirits would remain asleep when they died. Pablo bought the wine and started home.

So far Thursday had gone as usual. He'd given his blood, he'd got the book, and he'd got the paper and wine. But as he drew nearer the house, the presence of the girl came down to meet him, and he could no longer put off thinking of the strange situation into which she had placed him.

It seemed a long time since the day when she had smiled and they had spoken for the first time. Before that, she used to be the unknown virgin of his Thursdays, because each time he went to the library she was there, her round face always intent over an open book. She wore her black hair loose, and it fell over her sweater, almost down to her waist. She was always in sweaters and skirts, and when they first met, her legs were covered with long socks. As Pablo thought of what she looked like in those days, he realized it was not even a year ago when she seemed such a child. She had later told him it was all because she had heard the women in the library talking about him, but the first time she spoke, she'd waited for him to come out and said, "Isn't it odd, our meeting at the library every Thursday?" In those days Pablo read his book at the library. He never brought it home. It was not easy to think of something to say, and he'd asked why did she come to the little place; the college must have a bigger library.

"I like the atmosphere," she'd replied. "When I walk down City Terrace, it's like being in Mexico. Of course I've never been there, but I have a feeling for the place. You know, when I sit near the window and watch all the Mexicans passing up and down—it's tremendously different from campus. It's like being in an entirely foreign country."

"For you, then, Mexico is a land of mystery?"

"Well, sort of. But I am sure I would like it. I like you. You are very Americanized, but I like you."

She was so simple then. So easily she said, "I like you," that Pablo had felt a great elation for many days afterwards, even though he only half believed her. With his greater years he knew liking someone was not such a simple thing. But she'd said it again when she came to the house. She was studying Spanish, and when she came they pretended not to know any English until he grew tired of her great accent and said it was too hard for him to remember so much Spanish. He offered her wine, and they drank. Then she came every Thursday, and after the Spanish, they'd drink wine and she would talk. It was nice to have her in the house. She was young and quick, and sometimes when she would sit as quietly as he for a long time, he could feel all the strain of the words she was holding back. It was good to feel that she did this for him. Everything was good, and the night when she came up through the rain there was nothing to do but to take her in.

It was a Thursday night. When he opened the door she stood holding a suitcase in one hand and some books in the other, with a few wet hairs sticking to her face and the skirt wrapped tight around her young legs. She had waited with a question on her face, until he'd motioned her in.

"It's cold outside," she said.

"Where are you going?" he asked, when he already knew the answer.

She grinned, "I've been put out. I've been put out in the rain. Can you imagine that?"

"Who would put you into the rain?"

He'd had visions of an angry father, or a mother who heard she came to his house, and when she said, "My friend," he'd suddenly realized that all the time he didn't know where she lived, or much else about her, except that she went to the college and came to his place every Thursday. When he found out her "friend" was the third man with whom she had lived it was a slight shock.

"Your friend, he doesn't want you anymore?"

"Well, actually, he wants to do as he pleases with me. I must come when he wants me to come and go when he wants me to go. I'm not his servant." She seemed to be enjoying being able to say that, and when she asked, "You don't mind my coming here, do you?" there was in her voice something which said she'd enjoy it just as much to say she wasn't his servant.

Yet in their five months together she was mostly very kind. She did strange things sometimes, and said even stranger things, but she'd brought something to the house that was never there before. From the first, she treated the house as though she'd known it all her life. She used it as he himself never had. She had books, and at night she used all the lights. She left her things, combs, hairpins, sometimes her clothes, wherever she dropped them, and always Pablo had to clean the kitchen after she cooked. But it was a special happiness to have her there—to see her leave on mornings with the books under her arms, and to have her come home on evenings, flinging things down and kicking her shoes off. They were like father and daughter for weeks, until one day they touched and he wanted to be her fourth man. After that happened, she said, "You're such a man. You've made me learn to love, Pablo, do you realize that? I'll never forget you."

At a curve in the up-winding road, Pablo stopped. The sun stabbed steadily at his back, and in his narrow hat he cast a stunted shadow that barely slipped over the road into the sandy bank. The dust still came, some of it floating higher, much of it falling on the short, dry grass that ran straggling back from the road. Ahead, the avocado tree, partly covered with dust also, waved thick branches outside the kitchen window. He was high up, and he looked steadily at the house above, but couldn't see if anyone was watching down. After he'd rested, Pablo took his eyes away, and gazing only at the loose dirt road, he started up the last steep rise trying not to breathe too heavily.

She was young and her tricks were sometimes very simple, but there were things about Rhoda that Pablo couldn't quite explain: like when her face said one thing and her body said another. She had several faces. Sometimes she was the smiling college girl; at other times she looked like a hard whore; or sometimes she could be as innocent as a virgin. In the beginning she had only one face, and after he became her man they spoke mostly with their bodies. That was sufficient. Pablo couldn't remember when the faces started, but with their coming a restlessness came to the house, and it showed sometimes in the way she talked.

"Where do you go every Thursday, Pablo?"

"I go to see my men. The men who work for me."

"You never told me you had men working for you." He'd remained silent. "Why don't you ever talk? I swear, it's always a pain to get anything out of you."

"You will not like to hear what my men do."

"What do they do?"

"They kill the bulls."

"Kill bulls! You mean in a bullfight?"

"Oh, no, in my slaughterhouse."

"You have a slaughterhouse? My God! I don't know what I'll find out about you next."

It was night while they talked, and Pablo had felt the distance grow between them on the bed. He talked about himself, hoping that what he said would bring her back nearer. He told her of the blood he gave each Thursday, about the book, and the paper, and the wine.

She was very curious. "Why do you read the same book over and over again?"

"He was a great man. He lived by the spirits, and when he died, his place with the greatest spirits was already waiting."

"Is that what you want to do? I mean when you die? I mean, is that what you want to happen to you when you die?"

"I already have a place. I have only to keep it."

"And that's what the blood's for?"

"Yes."

"But what do the paper and wine have to do with it?"

"The paper has nothing to do with it, except I buy from a Jew who is also a spiritual man. And the wine, it is nothing but wine. I drink, and feel happy that I am alive, and that I know where I am going when I die."

"You're such a man!" she'd exclaimed. She had come back nearer to him, Pablo could feel, even though her next words were hardly what he expected.

"Pablo, would you mind if I go to bed with other men?"

He'd grunted, neither yes nor no, because he was trying to understand what she wanted and to think what was good for her.

"I knew you wouldn't mind. You're such a man," she repeated. "I feel so free with you. Let us have an understanding, Pablo. If I have a man, I'll bring him here, and you can bring your women, too. I know you have other women; but that way there'll be nothing going on behind your back, nothing behind my back. And we can be real lovers." He'd grunted again, neither yes nor no. Sometimes she could be a woman, but that night she was a child.

He hadn't brought any women to the house; he hadn't needed any other women. Yet he wasn't very shocked when she said last night she was bringing a man to the house today. He was in his chair and she had come into his room. "I'm not really interested in him, I just think he'd be fun. Do you mind?" She was wearing her little girl's face. She held his hand and talked like a child reminding her father of a promise he'd made. He'd grunted, neither yes nor no, because there was nothing to say except he'd stay at the library all day.

But she said, "No, no. You must come home early, Pablo. You must be here."

The people in the valley all knew she lived there. They saw her through their windows each morning going down in her black skirt with books under her arm; and on evenings they saw her from their flat open porches as she came back.

From their steps and streets they would see whoever the strange man was who came up the narrow road.

Yet while she'd held his hand, pretending they'd for the time become just good friends, he felt he should do or say something to make her see how ignorant it was to play the whore while he was there. But her little girl's face was ready to call him jealous, and he didn't know how to make her use the face that would understand.

When he reached the house there were voices. Pablo sat on the top step and took off his hat. He put down the things he carried, then wiped the dust and sweat from his face. Inside the house he heard them laughing—Rhoda in her girlish voice and the man with a not much heavier tone. The hill was quiet when their voices faded, except for the sound of traffic below and the wind through the avocado tree. The cars and people he could see over on College Hill were tiny figures shifting in the bright sun between the red buildings and square patches of green. Pablo wasn't jealous, and he wasn't hurt that she should be with another man in his house, but he still thought she was making a great waste of herself with her game of faces and men.

When he heard them again she was talking in the voice that matched her whore's face. Pablo was very hot and tired. His finger with the dried blood caked in its rings throbbed slightly, and he felt a little awkward about going in because the man sounded so young.

Suddenly the kitchen door behind him opened. "Pablo," she called, "Pablo, don't sit out there. Come inside and meet Eddie." He picked up the wine and book and left the paper on the step. She held the door open, and as he walked by, "Ah, you brought the book. You'll read while I talk with Eddie? But you must meet him first."

Like his voice, Eddie was slight but firm. Not as dark as Pablo, his black hair fell heavy and straight, and his quick, easy movements as he left his seat made Pablo very aware of his own thickness. A constant smile tugged at the corners of Eddie's mouth all the while Rhoda was saying, "Eddie Pena, and this is Pablo . . . my roommate." She was smiling too as Eddie extended his slim hand. Pablo shook, slowly letting his eyes run over the young man again. Although he was slender, his muscles were well formed. He was perhaps no older than Rhoda, and he reminded Pablo very much of what he had looked like when he was young, except with his constant smile Eddie seemed more knowing than even Rhoda herself with her many faces. "Eddie's from Costa Rica," she was saying. "He's in my art class."

"So you are an artist?" Pablo asked.

"Eddie is a great artist," she said, bustling back into the kitchen. She wore the regular schoolgirl skirt and sweater, and her hair, braided in one long heavy pigtail, bounced down her back as she returned with the bottle of wine and glasses. The room was neater than usual. The regular heap of books and papers was cleared and the floor was swept clean of ashes. From the dusty window a streak of yellow sun ran the length of the room, and as they moved, the bare floor creaked slightly with every step. They took seats at the table, and Rhoda poured the wine. She kept the first glass for herself and offered the second to Pablo.

"No, Eddie," Pablo said, waving a hand at the young man.

"I do not drink, señor," Eddie said with a smile of satisfaction. Pablo took the wine and drank it in one draught.

"This is a very nice house," the boy said.

"Well, not pretty, but a good house," Pablo answered. He wasn't sure how he should talk to Eddie, but wished only to let the boy know there were no bad feelings.

"He built it himself," Rhoda said.

"Is that right, señor?"

"Yes, little by little. I wanted to have more rooms, but it is big enough."

"He got tired and stopped," Rhoda said.

"With four rooms, that's plenty when you are alone, is it not, señor?"

"One of these days Pablo is going to get a wife and start having children. That's what he was thinking about," she said. Eddie's smile slipped into a polite laugh, but Pablo sat hunched in his chair, not looking at the young man. "When are you going to get married, Eddie?" she asked.

"After a long time," he answered quickly. "After I've done something." He sat with the same ease Rhoda showed when she first came, an ease that Pablo couldn't feel with a strange man in the house.

"So you're an artist?" Pablo asked again.

"I told you," Rhoda said in her impatient girl's voice. "He's great."

"You paint?" Pablo asked.

"No, señor, I work with the clay," answered Eddie.

"He is a genius," she said. "You ought to see the crucifix he did."

"You did a crucifixion?" Pablo asked.

"A crucifix, señor. Christ hanging on the cross."

"You make a crucifixion out of clay?" Pablo said in his slow, heavy voice.

"He is a genius," she said again excitedly.

Pablo filled his glass from the bottle. "No, Eddie," he said. "A crucifixion out of clay, that is no good. Where is the blood?" The strong wine made his nose tingle, and Pablo drank until his glass was empty.

Eddie was saying, "The blood is in the clay. There was no cup under the cross, señor, all the blood fell into the ground." The boy was quick. Rhoda sat watching him with her whore's eyes, and Pablo felt little beads of sweat form on his own face again. He didn't hate the young man. He felt only a little sorry that such a boy could know how to get behind Rhoda's faces. Eddie had neither his knowledge nor his experience, but in his own young way he had a means of finding her out that Pablo didn't have. He could hurt, but Pablo could only protect her.

"Don't you think he's great?" she asked.

Pablo grunted and took some more wine. He pondered, considering if there was any truth in what Eddie said, while the two talked freely. Soon he was out of the conversation. They turned to him only when she asked support for her exclamations about things she herself had told him and then he would nod or shake his head without looking at either of them directly until they started talking again. They argued over strange names, Degas, Goya, and others, Rhoda putting on her college face and Eddie with his face serious and sharp, although his eyes never stopped smiling. Taking his lead from Rhoda, Pablo felt he was acting quite well like a father and was on the point of leaving the room when she said, "Pablo too has a deep artistic sense. He never talks, but it is there. Perhaps the greatest artistic sense I've ever known."

"Is he too an aesthete?" Eddie asked with a challenge in his voice. "Where is his work?"

"He used to be a matador!" she exclaimed.

Pablo felt very satisfied when he saw the expression that brought to Eddie's face. He looked at Rhoda and she was watching him with all the expectancy of a little girl.

"Did you change your name, señor? I never heard of Pablo."

Putting down his glass slowly, Pablo said, "You are too young." He had a strange feeling of contentment in being able to say so to Eddie with the girl listening. "In my work there is life and blood, not clay."

"Where did you enter the ring, señor?" the boy asked, still challenging.

"Mexico. I was born in Mexico." Pablo kept his voice even and deep, letting each word fall heavily into the room. "My first bull was in the great Plaza before thousands of people . . . when I too was young." He paused and the room was so quiet as the others waited that the hum of traffic from the distant freeway became noticeable. "But it is not nice the way people watch, the things they want from the fight. They see only the wrong things. You have been to the Plaza, Eddie?"

"Yes, señor," the boy said without lifting his face.

"What did you laugh at?"

"I do not laugh, señor, but the whole thing is silly. The man kills the bull, the bull kills the man, it is only a game with death. You are a quiet man but lucky to be sitting here at all."

Pablo pushed back his chair and stood up. The desire to let Eddie know what an unlearned boy he was took possession of Pablo. He tried to hold the folds of his body tight, even though his stomach fell, and his loose breasts made sagging heaps under his wrinkled suit. But he looked down on Eddie, and with his serious face said, "Silly things we see through silly eyes. A wise bull is not easy to understand, and neither is a man, Eddie. When the two face, it is a strange thing that happens. A man killed, a bull killed, yes; but the blood of it is a sacred thing." From the corner of his eye Pablo could see Rhoda watching him with her young face, silently supporting him, but he didn't lower his eyes. He held himself up high, as if in salutation to the fluttering trumpets of the Plaza, and went on. "Such a bull I had for my first time, Eddie, a wise bull. He knew I was not afraid. He was not afraid. And never once he came for the cloth; the body always. Low, with his eyes shut. Twice I moved, twice he came back faster. The third time I ran. They laughed, Eddie; you ever hear the whole Plaza laugh? They laughed because they thought I was a coward. The bull knew I was young. When he stood away from the barrera I saw him opening his black scornful eyes. To respect is not to be afraid, do you know that? You are a young man, but always remember, to respect is not to be afraid." Pablo stopped, and the traffic hum came again.

"You ran, señor?" Eddie asked quietly.

"Only the first time," replied Pablo from his height above the young man.

"You are a brave man." Eddie chuckled. "I admire you."

"Pablo is a brave man," Rhoda said, "like any great artist. It is the bravest thing I know for a man to cut himself each week."

"You cut yourself, señor?" Eddie asked, surprised and a little shocked.

"I give a little blood to the spirits. It is a small thing," Pablo said.

"He does," she said, "every Thursday at his own slaughterhouse."

"You keep a slaughterhouse?" Eddie asked with even greater surprise. "From a matador, you become a butcher, señor?"

"He doesn't kill," she said, "he just owns the place." They were both very quick, and talked with an ease that didn't have any dignity. Pablo put down his glass and picked up the book.

"You are a fine man, Señor Pablo. One day I will do you with my clay."

Pablo said nothing. He just left the room with all the stiff highness that he could manage.

"You will not need to cut yourself," Eddie called. "Remember already there is blood in my clay."

As Pablo left the two, he felt his finger throbbing slightly again, and for a short time it didn't matter that they were together, alone, free for Rhoda to make her faces with Eddie looking on like a smiling cat. He went to the bathroom and washed the brown dust from his skin and hair.

His own room had none of the yellow sun slanting through its bareness. The only decoration he had allowed himself was the parochial calendar nailed up above the bureau, with its lustful angel looking directly down at his bed. With a deliberate movement Pablo lifted the chair and placed it nearer the window. Then he sat down and, opening the book, started again at chapter four.

The torero was in the act of once more exhausting his third bull. He called for the sword and wiped it clean through the red cloth. With a fearless step he marched back to the center of the ring surrounded by the screaming Plaza. Suddenly through the sweaty stink and dust, he saw the fierce ancestors tumbling, one after the other, their exposed breasts spotted with the flowing blood. . . . Voices came again, loudly, from her room this time.

She talked freely, as though he was not in the house, and when Eddie tried to make her speak more softly she said, "It doesn't matter if he hears. We have an understanding." Eddie murmured something again, and she said in her rasping whore's voice, "You let him frighten you with his pretending to be a matador?" Eddie murmured again, and she said, "Heavens, no. He gets that out of a book he reads every Thursday." Eddie murmured. "Oh, yes, he cuts himself. Didn't you notice the finger he held away from his glass?" They talked on, her loud whore's voice answering Eddie's delicate murmurs. Pablo didn't wish to listen. It didn't matter if Eddie knew he was not a torero; he was in touch with the spirits—that made him as good as all toreros—but it was painful to hear her expose herself too easily. In her confiding in Eddie, she was really saying that he didn't have any right to protect her. It was very painful to hear her show Eddie how much she wished to be used. They fell silent, but the raspy words with which she'd answered Eddie's murmurs seemed to penetrate again and again into the room, blurring the vision of his mystic torero. He could no longer read, and his oneness with the bleeding ancestors was no longer real. Pablo stood up and looked out the window beyond which his house sent a dark shadow stretching up the hill. Quietly he pondered whether he should send them away or whether he should leave; but before he did either came the light swish of clothing, then all was quiet again, until the struggling moans began. Pablo didn't want to listen, but he couldn't trust himself to move because he was afraid his legs would carry him to her door. Then from the thick moans her little girl's voice cried out hoarsely, like a pig after its throat is cut. Again and again her cry sank into Pablo, but there was no sound from Eddie. The book fell. The feelings which ran through him moved much swifter than he could, and as her cries came faster and higher he lifted his heavy wounded hand and crashed it against the bureau. Blood squashed out of his finger, and after a moment, when the pain came warm and biting, he went back outside.

With his finger pulsing pain, Pablo sat again on the steps. From College Hill his eyes slipped down over the valley. Back among the gray warehouses was the cool, dim slaughterhouse with thick walls, and the sawdust floor that held his blood mingled with that of the bulls. Pablo picked it out. It was very far away, and seemed now to have no connection with his heavy, swollen finger stiff with the blood still sticky around the pulpy split. Down on City Terrace the old men still crowded on the bus-stop bench, and the Jew, quite small from where Pablo sat, still hopped about in front of his paper stand. The women were coming out now. One by one the low houses opened their doors, and out of their dark insides the women stepped, some with children on their hips, others walking idly with baskets; and when the sun finally slipped behind College Hill, the streets that were deserted when he crossed in the stinging afternoon heat were clustered with groups of dresses. If anyone had seen Eddie, the talk would spread, and they would wait, watching from below, guessing at what went on inside the house on the hillside.

Pablo made an army out of the great shadow of College Hill, starting its advance over the valley. Led by the tall college walls it inched on rapidly, covering the tracks and warehouses, climbing over City Terrace Avenue with its lounging men and gossiping women, moving steadily up his dust-smothered hill. It was a good army. It conquered without feeling, until all was gray. Shadows were not men, they had no weaknesses. But even as Pablo spurred the dusky march against daylight he still remembered Rhoda's wailing cries, felt still the terrible tenderness they'd opened in him.

She used to be beautiful, especially on mornings before her skin grew hot and the pimples made little red spots in her face. With her eyes then she could make his body lose its heaviness, snap hard, a firm support for her natural softness. Eddie had touched that softness, made her wail not in comfort but in fright. He couldn't hear what went on in her room from where he sat, but Pablo knew she must have cried like that several times over. Pablo didn't hate the young man, he just felt very sad that Rhoda was so easily free with the pitiful little girl cries, and for him had so many false faces.

He didn't hear them come until she said, "Isn't it beautiful?" When he looked around they were standing just behind him, and Rhoda with outstretched hand was pointing down at the valley, but Eddie's eyes were on him, smiling warmly with the contentment of a grateful guest. "Don't you think it's great?" she asked.

"It's very nice. You have an exquisite view here, Señor Pablo," Eddie said, still looking at Pablo, smiling.

"It's beautiful," she said again in her college girl's voice. "If you wait, you'll see how pretty it is when the lights come on." They weren't looking at the valley, they were looking at the college. "It's a great place," she said, talking with no hint of the crying wail in her voice.

"It is a nice place, but not great," Eddie said, and once again they argued in school-like voices, as if nothing had taken place in the bed next to Pablo's room. Even when she held Eddie's arm Pablo felt there was no private meaning in her touch. There was a hardness about both of them. Her hair was plaited tighter than before, and, like her breasts, her face pointed sharp and hard in the gray dusk. He turned his eyes away.

"Listen to the leaves," she said, "listen. Nothing on this hill whispers as tenderly as that. When I'm alone, I sit and pretend they're talking to me."

The young man laughed. "Do the leaves talk to you too, Señor Pablo?"

But before Pablo could answer she said, "He doesn't have any tenderness. He's strong, and he knows beauty, but he doesn't have any tenderness."

"How can he know beauty and not have tenderness?" Eddie asked.

"Gauguin was not a tender man," she said.

"You are wrong, señorita; in Gauguin there was such a heart, he felt tenderness for the most grotesque things." They talked on. They ignored Pablo. Their voices went quickly, and they said many things about him as though he were not listening. He waited, and as they went back inside Eddie called, "You are a fine man, Señor Pablo. Next time I come I'll bring my clay." Pablo didn't hate the boy. He wanted Eddie to know that in his heart there was no hate. He stood up to say good-bye, but before he turned, the door was closed behind them both. Pablo sat down again. He thought of the many times he'd held her body next to his—he didn't have many words, but there was tenderness in those times. He sat remembering fiercely how after a night together she would awaken with the morning light on her round face, and sometimes with a smile, but always wordlessly, slip out of bed to dress for school. There was never any hard talking with him; he had a respect for what their bodies found together, and while they lay still, the spirits always came and stood at a safe distance watching.

It had grown too dark for Pablo to see who was watching from below, but he knew there were people out in the warm streets watching Eddie as the boy bobbed down the hill, straight and blacker than the dark slope. Together she and the young man had laughed at him. He knew. They were young and fast, but they had never felt the hot pain of a knife and watched their blood run. They laughed at his imaginary bull, but she had never seen a bull die or smelled the hot insides as they were emptied out. A man was not much different. The low houses had already lighted up their square windows, and Pablo watched until Eddie disappeared toward the foot of the hill. He couldn't hear her stirring, but he waited, half hoping she would join him on the step. When after some time she didn't, Pablo went in.

She was seated at the table with one of her books opened beside the half-empty wine bottle. She didn't look up, and Pablo remained in the kitchen. After a few moments he found that he was hungry, but when he started to get out meat for dinner she left the table, saying, "Don't, Pablo, I'll cook dinner." She gripped the saucepan that he held, but he didn't let it go immediately.

She let her hand fall and said, "Are you angry with me?"

Pablo grunted and shook his head. He wasn't sure what he felt about her.

She held his sleeve and spoke with her little girl face, "Did you like Eddie?" Pablo didn't answer. "What's the matter with you?" she asked. Pablo put down the saucepan and she followed him into the living room. "What's the matter? Did I do something wrong?"

"Do you like Eddie?" he asked.

"Why, I don't know—it's not a matter of liking him. Is that what's worrying you? Why don't you say what's worrying you?"

"He is very hard," Pablo said.

"Well, what do you think I am?"

She had looked hard out in the gray light, but now that Eddie was gone her face and breasts no longer pointed like sharp rocks. Pablo searched for what he wanted to say. "You are soft. Inside you are very soft." That wasn't really what he meant. She laughed. "Eddie . . . is not good for you." It was very difficult to say what he had in mind.

"You're jealous," she burst out. "Pablo, you're jealous."

"Together we have been with the greatest spirits."

She refused to understand. "I never thought I could make you jealous."

"That is for children," Pablo snapped. "A man is never jealous."

"Then what are you talking about?"

"I heard you cry out. Eddie hurt you."

"I always cry like that. Eddie can't hurt me . . . besides, what were you doing listening to the cries I made?"

"You're a child. You do not know what you are doing."

"If all you have to do is listen to what goes on in my room, then all I can say is I'm ashamed for you."

"I was not listening. I heard."

"Such an old ass . . . do you know what you're doing? You with your phony toreros and your bleeding finger? You don't fool me." Her breasts went up and down quickly, and there was no falseness in her shining face. "What are you trying to do, put me out? Well, I can go. I'll find a place." She went to her room.

Where Pablo stood was filled with the smell of open wine; it was warm inside the house, and the freeway noise came like a steady drone. Yet already the place seemed empty. It was a heavy thing to do, but after a few moments Pablo followed her.

The door was open, and she sat on the bed with her knees together, her chin propped on her hands. As he approached, she looked up and he stopped. There were things he wanted to say, but they were hard to find.

She spoke first.

"Do you love me, Pablo?" He could only stand silently, watching her. She came to her feet. "You never tell me, Pablo—you never tell me anything. Why don't you talk?"

He remembered how quickly she and Eddie could talk. "Words don't come quickly when a man's old."

She came to him. "But I'm very young, Pablo. Would you forgive me if I'm very young sometimes?"

He put his arms around her, and she gave in against him.

"We can talk without words, can't we, Pablo?"

He grunted softly.

After he had supported her for a few moments she said, "Pablo, when will we go to Mexico? I want to see real bulls. You always say they are so beautiful . . . let's see them together, alive and real . . . and a real torero."

"You are very ignorant," he said.

"I know, I know. I am so stupid. Remember the first time how you had to hold my arms . . . you made me so helpless."

Pablo remembered well. She was never helpless. She had fought hard like a wild dog, until he was sweating and tired. Then she had said she didn't mean to fight. But there was nothing really hard about her as she leaned on him. He was much harder.

"You could be so strong," she said, starting to rub her body against his.

Son in the Afternoon

John A. Williams

1962

It was hot. I tend to be a bitch when it's hot. I goosed the little Ford over Sepulveda Boulevard toward Santa Monica until I got stuck in the traffic that pours from L.A. into the surrounding towns. I'd had a very lousy day at the studio.

I was—still am—a writer, and this studio had hired me to check scripts and films with Negroes in them to make sure the Negro moviegoer wouldn't be offended. The signs were already clear one day the whole of American industry would be racing pell-mell to get a Negro, showcase a spade. I was kind of a pioneer. I'm a *Negro* writer, you see. The day had been tough because of a couple of verbs—slink and walk. One of those Hollywood hippies had done a script calling for a Negro waiter to slink away from the table where a dinner party was glaring at him. I said the waiter should walk, not slink, because later on he becomes a hero. The Hollywood hippie, who understood it all because he had some colored friends, said it was essential to the plot that the waiter slink. I said you don't slink one minute and become a hero the next; there has to be some consistency. The Negro actor I was standing up for said nothing either way. He had played Uncle Tom roles so long that he had become Uncle Tom. But the director agreed with me.

Anyway . . . hear me out now. I was on my way to Santa Monica to pick up my mother, Nora. It was a long haul for such a hot day. I had planned a quiet evening: a nice shower, fresh clothes, and then I would have dinner at the Watkins and talk with some of the musicians on the scene for a quick taste before they cut to their gigs. After, I was going to the Pigalle down on Figueroa and catch Earl Grant at the organ, and still later, if nothing exciting happened, I'd pick up Scottie and make it to the Lighthouse on the Beach or to the Strollers and listen to some of the white boys play. I liked the long drive, especially while listening to Sleepy Stein's show on the radio. Later, much later of course, it would be home, back to Watts.

So you see, this picking up Nora was a little inconvenient. My mother was a maid for the Couchmans. Ronald Couchman was an architect, a good one I understood from Nora, who has a fine sense for this sort of thing; you don't work in some hundred-odd houses during your life without getting some idea of the way a house should be laid out. Couchman's wife, Kay, was a playgirl who drove a white Jaguar from one party to another. My mother didn't like her too much; she didn't seem to care much for her son, Ronald junior. There's something wrong with a parent who can't really love her own child, Nora thought. The Couchmans lived in a real fine residential section, of course. A number of actors lived nearby, character actors, not really big stars.

Somehow it is very funny. I mean that the maids and butlers knew every-thing about these people, and these people knew nothing at all about the help. Through Nora and her friends I knew who was laying whose wife, who had money and who *really* had money; I knew about the wild parties hours before the police, and who smoked marijuana, when, and where they got it.

To get to the Couchmans' driveway I had to go three blocks up one side of a palm-planted center strip and back down the other. The driveway bent gently, then swept back out of sight of the main road. The house, sheltered by slim palms, looked like a transplanted New England Colonial. I parked and walked to the kitchen door, skirting the growling Great Dane who was tied to a tree. That was the route to the kitchen door.

I don't like kitchen doors. Entering people's houses by them, I mean. I'd done this thing most of my life when I called at places where Nora worked to pick up the patched or worn sheets or the half-eaten roasts, the battered, tarnished silver—the fringe benefits of a housemaid. As a teenager I'd told Nora I was through with that crap; I was not going through anyone's kitchen door. She only laughed and said I'd learn. One day soon after, I called for her and without knocking walked right through the front door of this house and right on through the living room. I was almost out of the room when I saw feet behind the couch. I leaned over and there was Mr. Jorgensen and his wife making out like crazy. I guess they thought Nora had gone and it must have hit them sort of suddenly and they went at it like the hell bomb was due to drop any minute. I've been that way too, mostly in the spring. Of course, when Mr. Jorgensen looked over his shoulder and saw me, you know what happened. I was thrown out and Nora right behind me. It was the middle of winter, the old man was sick, and the coal bill three months overdue. Nora was right about those kitchen doors: I learned.

My mother saw me before I could ring the bell. She opened the door. "Hello," she said. She was breathing hard, like she'd been running or something. "Come in and sit down. I don't know *where* that Kay is. Little Ronald is sick, and she's probably out gettin' drunk again." She left me then and trotted back through the house, I guess to be with Ronnie. I hated the combination of her white nylon uniform, her dark brown face, and the wide streaks of gray in her hair. Nora had married this guy from Texas a few years after the old man had died. He was all right. He made out okay. Nora didn't have to work, but she just couldn't be still; she always had to be doing something. I suggested she quit work, but I had as much luck as her husband. I used to tease her about liking to be around those white folks. It would have been good for her to take an extended trip around the country visiting my brothers and sisters. Once she got to Philadelphia, she could go right out to the cemetery and sit awhile with the old man.

I walked through the Couchman home. I liked the library. I thought if I knew Couchman I'd like him. The room made me feel like that. I left it and went into the big living room. You could tell that Couchman had let his wife do that. Everything in it was fast, dartlike, with no sense of ease. But on the walls were several of Couchman's conceptions of buildings and homes. I guess he was a disciple of Wright. My mother walked rapidly through the room without looking at me and said, "Just be patient, Wendell. She should be here real soon."

"Yeah," I said, "with a snootful." I had turned back to the drawings when Ronnie scampered into the room, his face twisted with rage.

"Nora!" he tried to roar, perhaps the way he'd seen the parents of some of his friends roar at their maids. I'm quite sure Kay didn't shout at Nora, and I don't think Couchman would. But then no one shouts at Nora. "Nora, you come right back here this minute!" The little bastard shouted and stamped and pointed to a spot on the floor where Nora was supposed to come to roost. I have a nasty temper. Sometimes it lies dormant for ages, and at other times, like when the weather is hot and nothing seems to be going right, it's bubbling and ready to explode. "Don't talk to *my* mother like that, you little—!" I said sharply, breaking off just before I cursed. I wanted him to be large enough for me to strike. "How'd you like for me to talk to *your* mother like that?"

The nine-year-old looked up at me in surprise and confusion. He hadn't expected me say anything. I was just another piece of furniture. Tears rose in his eyes and spilled out onto his pale cheeks. He put his hands behind him, twisted them. He moved backwards, away from me. He looked at my mother with a "Nora, come help me" look. And sure enough, there was Nora, speeding back across the room, gathering the kid in her arms, tucking his robe together. I was too angry to feel hatred for myself.

Ronnie was the Couchmans' only kid. Nora loved him. I suppose that was the trouble. Couchman was gone ten, twelve hours a day. Kay didn't stay around the house any longer than she had to. So Ronnie had only my mother. I think kids should have someone to love, and Nora wasn't a bad sort. But somehow when the six of us, her own children, were growing up we never had her. She was gone, out scuffling to get those crumbs to put into our mouths and shoes for our feet and praying for something to happen so that all the space in between would be taken care of. Nora's affection for us took the form of rushing out into the morning's five o'clock blackness to wake some silly bitch and get her coffee; took form in her trudging five miles home every night instead of taking the streetcar to save money to buy tablets for us, to use at school, we said. But the truth was that all of us liked to draw and we went through a writing tablet in a couple of hours every day. Can you imagine? There's not a goddamn artist among us. We never had the physical affection, the pat on the head, the quick, smiling kiss, the "gimme a hug" routine. All of this Ronnie was getting.

Now he buried his little blond head in Nora's breast and sobbed. "There, there now," Nora said. "Don't you cry, Ronnie. Ol' Wendell is just jealous, and he hasn't much sense either. He didn't mean nuthin'."

I left the room. Nora had hit it, of course, hit it and passed on. I looked back. It didn't look so incongruous, the white and black together, I mean. Ronnie was still sobbing. His head bobbed gently on Nora's shoulder. The only time I ever got that close to her was when she trapped me with a bear hug so she could whale the daylights out of me after I put a snowball through Mrs. Grant's window. I walked outside and lit a cigarette. When Ronnie was in the hospital the month before, Nora got me to run her way over to Hollywood every night to see him. I didn't like that worth a damn. All right, I'll admit it: it did upset me. All that affection I didn't get, nor my brothers and sisters, going to that little white boy who, without a doubt, when away from her called her the names he'd learned from adults. Can you imagine a nine-year-old kid calling Nora a "girl," "our girl"? I spat at the Great Dane. He snarled and then I bounced a rock off his fanny. "Lay down, you bastard," I muttered. It was a good thing he was tied up.

I heard the low cough of the Jaguar slapping against the road. The car was throttled down, and with a muted roar it swung into the driveway. The woman aimed it for me. I was evil enough not to move. I was tired of playing with these people. At the last moment, grinning, she swung the wheel over and braked. She bounded out of the car like a tennis player vaulting over a net.

"Hi," she said, tugging at her shorts.

"Hello."

"You're Nora's boy?"

"I'm Nora's son." Hell, I was as old as she was; besides, I can't stand "boy."

"Nora tells us you're working in Hollywood. Like it?"

"It's all right."

"You must be pretty talented."

We stood looking at each other while the dog whined for her attention. Kay had a nice body and it was well tanned. She was high; boy, was she high. Looking at her, I could feel myself going into my sexy bastard routine; sometimes I can swing it great. Maybe it all had to do with the business inside.

Kay took off her sunglasses and took a good look at me. "Do you have a cigarette?"

I gave her one and lit it. "Nice tan," I said. Most white people I know think it's a great big deal if a Negro compliments them on their tans. It's a large laugh. You have all this volleyball about color, and come summer you can't hold the white folks back from the beaches, anyplace where they can get some sun. And of course the blacker they get, the more pleased they are. Crazy. If there is ever a Negro revolt, it will come during the summer and Negroes will descend upon the beaches around the nation and paralyze the country. You can't conceal cattle prods and bombs and pistols and police dogs when you're showing your birthday suit to the sun.

"You like it?" she asked. She was pleased. She placed her arm next to mine. "Almost the same color," she said.

"Ronnie isn't feeling well," I said.

"Oh, the poor kid. I'm so glad we have Nora. She's such a charm. I'll run right in and look at him. Do have a drink in the bar. Fix me one too, will you?" Kay skipped inside and I went to the bar and poured out two strong drinks. I made hers stronger than mine. She was back soon. "Nora was trying to put him to sleep and she made me stay out." She giggled. She quickly tossed off her drink. "Another, please?" While I was fixing her drink she was saying how amazing it was for Nora to have such a talented son. What she was really saying was that it was amazing for a servant to have a son who was not also a servant. "Anything can happen in a democracy," I said. "Servants' sons drink with madames and so on."

"Oh, Nora isn't a servant," Kay said. "She's part of the family."

Yeah, I thought. Where and how many times had I heard *that* before?

In the ensuing silence, she started to admire her tan again. "You think it's pretty good, do you? You don't know how hard I worked to get it." I moved close to her and held her arm. I placed my other arm around her. She pretended not to see or feel it, but she wasn't trying to get away either. In fact she was pressing closer and the register in my brain that tells me at the precise moment when I'm in, went off. Kay was *very* high. I put both arms around her and she put both hers around me. When I kissed her, she responded completely.

"Mom!"

"Ronnie, come back to bed," I heard Nora shout from the other room. We could hear Ronnie running over the rug in the outer room. Kay tried to get away from me, push me to one side, because we could tell that Ronnie knew where to look for his mom; he was running right for the bar, where we were. "Oh, please," she said, "don't let him see us." I wouldn't let her push me away. "Stop!" she hissed. "He'll *see* us!" We stopped struggling just for an instant, and we listened to the echoes of the word *see*. She gritted her teeth and renewed her efforts to get away.

Me? I had the scene laid right out. The kid breaks into the room, see, and sees his mother in this real wriggly clinch with this colored guy who's just shouted at him, see, and no matter how his mother explains it away, the kid has the image—the colored guy and his mother—for the rest of his life, see?

That's the way it happened. The kid's mother hissed under her breath, *"You're crazy!"* and she looked at me as though she were seeing me or something about me for the very first time. I'd released her as soon as Ronnie, romping into the bar, saw us and came to a full, open-mouthed halt. Kay went to him. He looked first at me, then at his mother. Kay turned to me, but she couldn't speak.

Outside in the living room my mother called, "Wendell, where are you? We can go now."

I started to move past Kay and Ronnie. I felt many things, but I made myself think mostly, *There, you little bastard, there.*

My mother thrust her face inside the door and said, "Good-bye, Mrs. Couchman. See you tomorrow. 'Bye, Ronnie."

"Yes," Kay said, sort of stunned. "Tomorrow." She was reaching for Ronnie's hand as we left, but the kid was slapping her hand away. I hurried quickly after Nora, hating the long drive back to Watts.

What's Your Problem?

Robert Boles

1964

I had been in my apartment only a few minutes. Summer had permeated everything. The office had been hot, and I was tired. I always am the first hour or so after work. I had taken off my shirt and shoes and was standing at my kitchen table finishing a game of solitaire before washing up. There was a light breeze, a warm one from the window, that felt good on the skin of my chest and back. Someone knocked on my door. Not knowing who it was, I put on and buttoned my shirt. Nadine would be coming over. That was something I was not too happy about—it meant forfeiting the night baseball game. Nevertheless, I was certain that it was not her. She would have used her key, unless, of course, she had lost it, which I very much doubted; Nadine never lost anything. While putting on my shoes, I called out, "Just a minute!"

It was the father of the boy who lived across the street from me. I didn't know the man well. I had moved from downtown Boston to this apartment only a few months before, one of several Negroes being quietly integrated. He had been friendly enough. I had had a drink with him and his wife in the early part of the summer. Gin and tonic. I don't drink gin often. We had sat on their front steps in the early evening. I remembered it well. Three boys had been fighting with their son. I had separated them and taken the boy home. The mother and father seemed appreciative, and afterward we talked a little. They were delighted to find out that I had read a book that they had. And after that, the boy decided he liked me and began paying me shy visits. I did nothing to discourage them.

The father looked now as if the summer sun had never touched him. Pale. Perhaps the dark-blue suit he was wearing had something to do with it. I apologized for my appearance and asked him to come in. He seemed surprised at my invitation, almost as if he felt he didn't warrant it. I wondered vaguely if he was going to accuse me of corrupting his son—I could think of no other reason for the visit. He was very nervous. He sat on the edge of the couch and looked at me intensely, a glimmer of a smile on his face. His eyes didn't stray, as most people's do when they enter a place unfamiliar to them.

"I'd offer you gin, but all I have is Scotch," I said to him.

He refused and leaned forward, putting his elbows on his spread knees and folding his hands.

"I can make some lemonade," I offered.

He smiled and shook his head, then stared at his hands.

I was about to excuse myself and get something cool to drink when he said quite suddenly, "Dreadful what's going on in the South! Cattle prods and all that."

"Yes, it is," I said cautiously. I wondered if he had come to soothe a guilty conscience. Perhaps he wanted to assure me that his heart was in the right place.

As ennui settled on me, he spoke again. "I was wondering if you could do something for me, Warner." His serious tone of voice did not match his facial expression. I would have laughed, but his calling me by my first name irritated me.

"What's your problem?" I asked him. I asked him straight out, as if I had known him for a good length of time.

He took a pillow from behind him and placed it at the other end of the couch and leaned back. His hands were on his thighs. I noticed how he lined his index fingers with the creases in his trousers. He looked at the floor. "Our son, Timothy," he said. "He's done something." He began to gesture with his hands. "I can't seem to talk to him. When I try, I don't get anywhere. And I was wondering if you could talk to him for us." He looked up at me.

I was standing with my forearm on the radiator—because it was cool. "I don't understand," I said.

"I know that he comes over here often to look at your things and play your mandolin," he said in justification, and pointed to the instrument hanging on the wall. "Is that it?"

"Yes, it is," I said. "I don't play it myself. I bought it in a pawnshop to use as a decoration."

"Yes, I see," he said. "And a very handsome decoration it is." He adjusted himself. "Actually, you know, Timothy is a bright boy." His words embarrassed him. "I can't understand why he's done a thing like this!"

"What has he done?" I asked. His forehead had begun to glisten with perspiration, so I offered him a drink again, and again he refused.

"As I was saying," he continued. "About two months ago, we bought him a dog. I mean, the boy is pretty lonely. He doesn't get along well with other children in the neighborhood. We thought it would be a good idea for him to have it."

When he paused, I said, "A little brown cocker spaniel."

"Yes," he said.

"I've seen it running around," I said, still wondering why he had come. It was at this point that I heard Nadine's footsteps on the landing. I moved toward the door.

"Today he put it in the washing machine," he said.

"That's one way to wash a dog," I said quickly. I was interested, but I excused myself and went to the door in order to catch her before she used her key.

Timothy's father put his hands beside him on the couch and waited.

I stepped out into the hallway. Nadine was coming around the newel post. She gave me a large smile, dropped her bag on the floor deliberately—part of a passionate game—and stretched out her arms in greeting. With my thumb, I indicated that someone was inside, then held the door open for her. She brushed her breasts across my arm as she entered. I was forced to smile.

My guest stood.

"This is Mr. Hudson," I said to Nadine. "A neighbor of mine." To him I said, "Mr. Hudson, this is Nadine James."

They shook hands cordially. I believe that he blushed. When he sat down again, she asked me if there was any coffee in the coffeepot. I told her that I didn't think there was. She asked us if we wanted some. Timothy's father refused, as I thought he would. Maybe he thought that my dishes weren't clean. But I said yes, to make certain that she would leave the room. I was pretty sure, though, that she asked for that reason.

"Iced?" she asked.

"Yes," I said. "Good idea."

After she had gone. Timothy's father spoke in modulated tones. "I'm disturbing you."

"Not at all," I said. "I'll be glad to do whatever I can."

He looked toward the kitchen. "I wouldn't want to take you away from a previous engagement."

"Don't be ridiculous," I said. Again my tone was perhaps too intimate. "She comes over often and cooks for me. I do a very bad job of it."

"I undestand," he said.

"I don't quite know what your problem is," I told him.

"The boy killed the dog!" he said to me. "He's much too old to be doing things like that! He knows better. I have him in his room now. I can't make him out. He hasn't cried or said a word. He looks at me as if he doesn't have an idea what I'm talking about."

I decided then that I did not want to get involved, but it was too late to back out. "Just what do you want me to do?" I asked.

"Talk to him," he said. "Just talk to him."

I agreed by nodding my head, then went into the kitchen.

Nadine had put the coffeepot on the stove and was sitting reading a magazine. She had cleared the table. "I must tell you about the dream I had last night!" she said.

I was rude. "What have you done with my cards?" I demanded.

"I'm sorry," she said.

"Forget it," I said. "I wouldn't have won anyway."

My reproach had hurt her. I hadn't meant it to. "I'm sorry," I said. "I've been living alone for too long."

She smiled sweetly, not to forgive me but to tell me that she understood. I think she realized that the man sitting in my living room was getting on my nerves.

I kissed her. She became very serious. When we separated, I held her at arm's length. "I have to go out for a little while," I said. "I'll explain it all to you when I get back." I asked her if we needed anything from the store. She said no.

"Have we got any cognac left?"

"We're all out of it," she said.

"I'll bring a bottle."

I went back into the living room and told Timothy's father that I would be with him right away, and went to get a jacket. When I returned, he was standing, ready to leave.

On the street, his manner changed.

There was an aura of confidence and an air of casual broadmindedness about him. "She's a lovely girl," he said.

"She is, isn't she," I replied.

As we walked, the street lamps came on. It was suddenly evening.

Before we entered his house, he apologized again and said that he regretted having to take the matter outside of the immediate family.

I told him that I would help him as much as possible.

"The dog is still in the washing machine," he told me. "My wife saw Tim standing there. She went up to see what was fascinating him so. Of course, she pulled out the plug immediately. It happened just before I came home."

When we entered his house, his demeanor changed again. He became an angry father, secure in his household. As we started for the second floor, he planted his feet heavily on the treads in the dark stairwell. I followed him. I heard a door being pulled open. His wife, wearing a faded red apron, came out onto the landing to meet us. She smiled warmly and shook my hand. Her eyes showed that she had been crying.

I was not particularly moved by their dilemma, but I felt odd being in their home during a period of strain. I was terribly aware that I was on the second floor of a house, with space beneath me. They took me through the dining room and into the kitchen, then opened the lid of the washing machine. It was not necessary for them to show me proof. I felt they were treating me as if I were a washing-machine repairman and responsible for their difficulties.

The dog was dead. The water was still. Clothes were suspended in it. I couldn't see all of the poor dead thing. One of his ears seemed to be floating, and the hairs rooted to its skin were extended in the water.

Timothy's mother became upset, wept again, and left the room. In the harsh light, her tears made her seem ugly; the wet spots emphasized different parts of her face.

Timothy's father removed his jacket and placed it on the back of one of the kitchen chairs. He sat down and pointed to a chair at the opposite side of the table. His gesture was authoritative.

"I'll stand, thank you," I said, beginning to resent him.

"I don't know what to do," he confessed. "What would you do if your son did something like this?"

"I don't have a son," I said.

"But if you did."

I thought of walking out. I was uncomfortable—an alien in their sphere. I didn't need him, or his wife, or his son, or his dead dog.

He pressed me for an answer.

"I'd make him bury it," I said.

"That's a good idea," he said. "Yes, yes. I want to teach him a lesson!" he added emphatically.

He continued in that vein, but I paid little attention to his words. The idea had come into my head that he was stalling for some reason or other. Then all at once I realized that he was squeamish about handling the dead dog, and that made him disgusting. After a while, he stopped talking, moistened his lips, and looked at me as if I were a priest. His wife, with a handkerchief in her hand and without the apron, came back into the room and stood by his side.

I had a good mind to walk out. I felt nothing for them; I felt only that I did not belong with them. I was not even very fond of Timothy. I didn't mind his being around, as long as he didn't get into all sorts of things. Only once or twice did I really think that I liked him. Those were the times when I was telling him fantastic stories and his large blue eyes seemed to glow. But then, people's eyes, if I really looked at them, always had some sort of effect on me.

Finally, I told Mr. Hudson that I did not know what to say.

His wife, tears beginning to form in her eyes, spoke to me very softly. "Perhaps if you can talk to him and find out the reason."

I was silent.

Her husband, thinking that I was properly touched, escorted her from the room and asked me to wait.

What he thought was true. She had seemed to be sincere—it was her crying. I lit a cigarette and sat at the table. It was an effort for me to keep my arms off it. Bad habits are hard to break. The top of the table was dirty, as if they had recently finished a meal, but there were no dishes. I assumed that it had been lunch—certainly not dinner—and began to think badly of her housekeeping. I stood up when I heard footsteps.

Timothy was ushered into the room by his father. Nothing was said to me. The father left and closed the door, with Timothy in front of it.

In that instant, I was torn between a terrible anger against the parents and an aching compassion for the boy. I don't think that any adult male can hate a boy, regardless of what he has done. "I'm sorry," I said to him very softly. "I have to leave." I did not want him to misconstrue my words, but I knew that he did. It could not be helped. We stood, looking at each other.

What would become of him? He was evidently quite a disturbed boy and belonged in a home somewhere. He rushed to me and hugged me to prevent my leaving. I stroked his yellow hair, removed his thin arms from around my waist, and made him sit in a chair. His mouth turned down at the corners.

I knelt before him and put my fist lightly to his jaw. "This is not my affair," I said softly. "It's between you and your parents. When this is all over, you can come to my house and play the mandolin some more. I'll buy you a book that will teach you all the chords. All right?"

The boy was silent.

"When's your birthday?" I asked him.

He was pouting, but he managed to say, "The twelfth of September."

"When that day comes," I said, "the mandolin will be yours."

I left the kitchen. His parents, who were sitting in the unlit dining room, stood when they saw me.

"This is none of my business," I said. My voice was calm but forceful. "I'd like to keep it that way."

It seemed that they had been prepared for my reaction.

"You'll have to get someone else to do your dirty work," I said.

The Distributors

Henry Dumas

1964

"We start at eight sharp," the foreman said to me, "but you and your friend be here at seven-thirty tomorrow so we can sign you up." We shook hands and I left.

A job at last. Kenny and I had spent the last three weeks looking. I found a phone in the corner restaurant to call him. He would be excited, even though it was only construction work. We had both wanted to spend the summer in the sun. School had drained all the blood out of us, anyway.

The line was busy, so I ordered a cup of coffee and sat down near the phone. Halfway through the cup I called again. Still busy. He must be calling ads in the paper, I thought.

A neatly dressed woman came into the restaurant. She and the waitress began talking.

". . . and it's saved me so much work. Honest, Sue, I just don't know what to do with all my time."

"Where's your father-in-law?" asked the waitress.

"It's amazing, Sue. That's taken care of too. And maybe he's better off. Even the baby rests good now." And she whispered in the waitress's ear, "They call it acceleration or something."

"Well, what's Fred think?"

"Oh, he's too crazy about the automatic memory cells to worry about that. You know it tells you everything you were thinking all day!"

"Yeah," said the waitress, "I've heard about it, but we can't pay for one right now."

"They're cheap," whispered the other woman.

"How much did you pay?"

"They have a special credit plan, and you don't have to pay unless you like it."

As I dialed Kenny's again I wondered what it was they were talking about.

The line was still busy. I decided to take a bus, because Kenny might be talking to Edna and on the phone a long time.

Mrs. Waspold came to the door.

"Hello, Carl," she said. "Kenneth is on the phone."

I knew he would be. I told her about the job possibility and that the foreman had said he could use two men for the summer. "Well," she said, "I don't think Kenny will like it. They just called him up for a job a little while ago."

I sat down in the living room, wondering who Kenny was talking to. From the kitchen Mrs. Waspold stirred about. A pot dropped and she became irritated. As I sat there I could hear a heavy wheezing coming from old Mr. Waspold's room. Kenny's grandfather was very sick and helpless. The chortling of his chest sounded like the dying sputters of an engine.

Just then Kenny came into the room.

"Hey, Carl, listen! Great news! How would you like to be a representative for American Dynamisms Incorporated?"

"What're you talking about?" I asked. His enthusiasm had taken me by surprise. He moved like a guy rushing to catch a train.

"Come on," he said, running to the door. "I'll tell you all about it on the way."

He got the keys to the family car. "Mother, if Edna calls tell her I'll be by to see her after the interview."

I followed Kenny out. We were halfway across town before he could settle down.

"Listen," he said. "Carl, baby, we're in!" We stopped for a red light, and among the people crossing was the same woman from the restaurant.

"I got both of us interviews."

"Doing what?" I asked.

"Well, I don't know exactly . . . using our college training, he told me. I talked with a Mr. Mortishan, and he promised us jobs making over a hundred dollars a week to start. Man, oh, man!"

"How certain is this, because I've already made arrangements for us to start at the construction company down Canal Road."

"Forget it, Carl. We're in. Mr. Mortishan said for us to come down immediately, and he'd sign us up for the whole summer. With raises!"

"Sounds too good to be true," I said. "But I'd like to know a little more about it."

"Well, what's the difference what we do? If we can make that much money starting out—"

"Wait," I interrupted. "Suppose we get hooked doing something we don't want?"

"Don't be silly. This is a big outfit."

"Who was the guy you talked to, and why can't we know what kind of a job we're being considered for?"

"Listen, Carl, I talked to the guy. He sounded okay to me. I'm not going to tell them how to run their business."

"Yeah," I said, "but I'd like to know what's the job."

Kenny became defensive. Ever since taking that course called "The Sociology of Management," he seemed to be tolerating me. Once he said that the course I was taking was totally useless.

"Where'd you get the tip about this place?" I asked. I had heard of American Dynamisms, but I couldn't remember where.

"Remember the guy who came around during exam week, sending kids places for jobs?"

I did recall a well-dressed, efficient-looking guy around the campus before graduation, recruiting seniors, but for what, nobody knew.

"This is his card," and he handed me a card. "Mr. Mortishan said to see no one but him, under any circumstances."

The card was the folding kind. On each section were bold letters in the center and small ones at the bottom.

STAY UNDER CARE KINDNESS EFFICIENCY OF R
Processing Card
DISTRIBUTING AMERICAN DYNAMISMS ABROAD
Rek-cording Card
SEND THE WHOLE FAMILY TO CAMP
Human Factor Card

Mr. Mortishan's name was not on it. I handed it back. Kenny parked the car in front of a deserted store three blocks from the river, behind a factory. Closed venetian blinds hung at the windows. We checked the address. No mistake. This was the place. The lettering on the door was plain and neat, just like the card.

We went in. Down a narrow hallway in front of us were double doors. They looked tight, but noises drifted through the place, as though coming out of the walls. A thin haze of cigarette smoke mixed with a stronger odor, possibly of cigar or burning wood or incense. Off the hallway were doors; the first one was extremely wide, as though it contained a gigantic piece of equipment that could not go through an ordinary door; the rest were shut. We didn't see anyone at the huge desk in the first room.

Strange music penetrated the walls. We heard voices, then a roar, as if people were cheering. The tempo of the music was one degree faster than any human could keep up with.

"What can I do with you?"

Standing in the hall behind us was a neatly dressed man with close-cut hair whose ready smile was wide, even, and precise.

"We have interviews with Mr. Mortishan. I just talked—"

"I'm sorry. Mr. Mortishan is very busy now. May I help you?"

"I have an interview at eleven," said Kenny.

"Fine. I'm Mr. Mortishan's assistant. Come down the hall to my office."

Kenny stood still. "I just talked to Mr. Mortishan on the phone a few minutes ago, and he warned me not to talk to anyone else, under any circumstances."

"Oh." The young man laughed. "I'm sorry, but you must forgive me. That was our Rek-cording. Mr. Mortishan is on an extended visit out of town. He will process in later. Won't you step into my office?"

Kenny looked at me, shrugged his shoulders, and went into the room.

"Not you." The young man halted me. The door slammed. From behind the double doors down the hall came the continued rise and fall of unintelligible sounds, like some kind of a meeting.

I went up the hall into the open room and sat down. I didn't know how long Kenny's interview would be. I looked for something to read. But there were no books, magazines, or pamphlets, only a picture hanging almost to the ceiling. I looked at it. What an odd place to hang a picture, I thought. Even more, what an odd picture. I couldn't tell if the thing was a multicolored machine or an Expressionist painting of an elongated peanut.

Just as I was beginning to examine the rest of the room, the picture began to move. I was not scared at first. What kind of a gag is this? I wondered. For a moment I thought the room was some kind of a psych testing lab, and if it was, Kenny and I were going through the test for hiring.

The picture moved down the wall, and as it moved, the wall opened in back of it, unzipping itself. I stood up. The noises increased, and before I could think of moving out of the room, the picture was touching the floor—flat on its face—and stepping out from behind it was a very fat man.

"Sit down, Carl," he said to me. He waddled around to the great desk. "I'm sorry to keep you gentlemen waiting."

"What kind of positions do you have open?" I asked.

"Stop," he said, lighting up a fat cigar. "Stop." He reached into his drawer and handed me a stack of forms, saying, "Fill these out first, then ask questions."

He picked up the phone and began dialing. I wondered if he were Mr. Mortishan. I didn't have a chance to say anything. He was talking and blowing smoke. After looking at the application, I knew that it would take almost two hours to finish. I wondered if Kenny was going through the same ordeal. The questions were routine, and as I hurried through them I could hear the fat man talking in a low voice on the phone about demonstrations and appointments and camps. He was watching me out of the corner of his eye. I hadn't noticed, but the picture was back in its place and the wall was closed.

All of a sudden I heard voices in the hall.

"Stop writing," the fat man said. "Go into the hall."

I got up and went out. The double doors were open, and the hall was filled with young men dressed in shirt sleeves and ties, milling about, drinking from cups. I saw Kenny just as the assistant was shoving a cup in his hand.

"Hey, Ken . . ." He didn't hear me. The men were moving back through the double doors. Behind me came several more, and I was swept into the room through the double doors. Inside was like an arena. I lost sight of Kenny. In the center of the floor was a large area that seemed like a threshing floor. It was sunken and worn in a circle. Around the room were hundreds of chairs. Some of them were occupied by fat-looking men sitting like dignified spectators. Their weights seemed to spread out over the seats, as though in a moment they would turn to lard and flood the floor.

"Selling is the business of every salesman! But our men distribute rather than sell. Rekcus sells himself! Rekcus Rekcus we adore! Rekcus Rekcus nothing more!" It was the assistant. He ran to the center of the floor, holding a metallic-looking suitcase in one hand and a torch in the other. He raised the torch and shouted, "Every person you meet is a potential customer. Consider him already owning a Rekcus. Never cross him off until—"

A bright light suddenly shone from the ceiling on the assistant; otherwise the place was still dim.

"—until we demonstrate and deliver him—"

A roar came up from the men, a frenzied sound, as if they were drunk.

"—Rekcus! And remember: D-A-D, Deliver American Dynamisms to your home! your job! your place of play!"

Someone shoved a cup toward my hand. I didn't want it, but rather than let it fall I received it, since the person was letting it go. I was about to taste it when the odor of some chemical hit me. I put the cup on a table and sat down in a chair, feeling a bit dizzy. The crowd was forming a circle around the speaker. I tried to spot Kenny. He was lost in the crowd, which began a mad chanting after periodic shouts by the assistant. It was crazy. I looked for the door.

Two men came over to me. A light shone in my face.

"We would like to demonstrate at your initiation ceremony," one of them said. The other one held the light steadily on my face.

I tried to dodge the light. "What're you talking about?"

"Don't you believe in the Rekcus principle of acceleration?"

"In the factors of humanoid control?"

"In simuldad?"

"Yes, distribution and demonstration simultaneously?"

"Do you have old parents?"

"Where is your appointment card?"

"Your initiation card?"

"What initiation?" I asked.

"Would you simuldad a Rekcus to your mother?"

"Your father?"

"Have you ever sold anything to a child?"

"Do you understand Rekcus dehumanization?"

"Are you ready to sell?"

"Who is your dadsponsor?"

"What?" I asked.

They looked at each other; then they jerked me off the chair and shoved me out into the room among the crowd, which seized me, spun me around, locked arms, and we all went frantically around the center of the floor. Sitting on an elongated bulletlike structure in the center of the room was the fat man. He was grinning at me. Then he pointed at Kenny. "Get him!"

They all descended on Kenny. He ran. Was he playing the game? I couldn't tell. One man tackled him waist high, bringing him down to the hard floor. The shrieks, shouts, and laughs grew louder and louder. Speeches were begun and not finished. Hot drinks were flung to the ceiling. Desperately I tried to find the door.

"Where do you think you're going?" The ready smile of the assistant greeted me.

I coughed. "Well, I was looking for the other fellow, Kenneth—"

He began to laugh hysterically, bending over several times. Kenny came limping over to me, a big grin on his face.

"Carl, we're in! We're accepted. All we gotta do is sell—I mean, simuldad—I mean—"

"REKCUS REKCUS WE ADORE! REKCUS REKCUS WE ADORE!"

They kept it up, and Kenny, his lips hesitating at first, then catching up with the words, broke away from me and skip-hobbled back across the room with a couple of young men running on either side of him, trying to trip him up. Then Kenny suddenly turned and hollered at me: "Carl! I told him I'll be your sponsor. You have to come to my initiation tonight. Your whole family is coming. At my house!"

"What?" I asked, but he didn't hear me. Suddenly the assistant stopped laughing, came over to me, looked me over, glanced at his watch, and said:

"Get out."

He spoke softly, but his words were like two knives stabbing, one on either side of my chest. The double doors opened in front of me. I stumbled over somebody, felt for the door, and was out. I waited. The doors closed and the shouting went on.

I hurried out to the car and sat in it, sweating. When I tried to go back in an hour later, the door was locked. I sat in the car for another hour, waiting for Kenny. Then I went to look for a phone. No one was at my house. I phoned Kenny's. No one answered. Mrs. Waspold was probably helping the old man to the bathroom. I ran back to the car. It was gone.

I phoned Edna, Kenny's girlfriend, to see if he was there. "Oh, Carl," she said, "Kenny was looking for you. He's on his way here. Congratulations on the job. You're coming to the demonstration tonight, aren't you?"

I held the phone away from me and stared at it briefly; finally I managed to say "Yes" and hung up.

Wandering through the park, I watched a softball game. After that I sat near the pond, watching the ducks paddling around. But even when I went home my head was ringing: *Rekcus Rekcus we adore. Rekcus Rekcus nothing more.*

After dinner I drove my folks to Kenny's house. The living room was filled with talking neighbors. Kenny rushed over to me.

"Carl, buddy, how do I look?" He had gotten a crew cut, a new suit, a manicure, had shaved so close he had nicked his chin, and he was smiling in a peculiar way.

"Sharp," I said. "But what's all this demonstration business about?"

"Ahhh," he said, looking at me with a doubtful frown, "then you didn't get *your* appointment yet?"

"I don't think I want anything from that place," I began, but Kenny wasn't paying attention. "What's the initiation for? I waited a couple of hours for you."

"I'm hired, Carl!" he said, racing off to answer the door. "I start selling tomorrow. My first contact will be your house. It has all been arranged."

Coming in and following Kenny to the center of the living room was the assistant. Kenny made a brief announcement. The excitement was high as everybody took seats and waited.

While Kenny was introducing him, Mr. Mortishan's assistant was setting up a metallic tube box.

"On behalf of American Dynamisms I want to thank you all for coming, and especially you, Mr. and Mrs. Waspold, for allowing us to use your home. Today we discovered Kenneth Waspold. D-A-D is looking for loyal, dedicated young men with bright futures and clear minds. We think we found another one in Kenny." He smiled, executed a turn, saying, "Now to the point of the meeting."

He pointed to Mr. Hendy, sitting nearby. "Come here, sir." Mr. Hendy got up. "Put your hand here." Mr. Hendy did it. "Squeeze." A narrow tube began to rise from the strange-looking case. Mr. Mortishan's assistant seized it and put it close to Mr. Hendy's ear. "Continue squeezing." After a minute of this Mr. Hendy looked astonished, faced the audience with a look of paralysis, opened his mouth, and speechlessly turned red in the face.

"Incredible . . ." he mumbled and stumbled to his seat.

The assistant went around the room with the same procedure, next with Mr. Hendy's wife, then Kenny's father and mother, and after each person had a chance they all were gasping with amazement.

I sat in the corner. A curious fear held me there. Not once had he looked at me, and when it finally came my turn—since I was the last—a quiet fell on everybody.

"You had your chance this afternoon?" He wasn't asking me a question, as it sounded. Rather, he was telling me.

The guests began asking him questions. My only question was, What had they heard and felt? But he didn't give them a chance to overwhelm him. "We believe firmly in letting our products sell themselves. That's why we never high-pressure our customers. Ladies and gentlemen, there is no product more capable of selling itself than Rekcus! You have just met Rekcus!"

Kenny was wide-eyed, taking it all in. No doubt he thought he would use the same procedure at my house. The neighbors were awed. My folks seemed very receptive.

"Have you ever met a machine like this one?" he asked. The people shook their heads. "You have seen nothing yet!" He pressed a button, and the machine began to enlarge itself. Sections opened and closed, fitting with other parts. It stopped. It looked like a metallic peanut. When he pushed another button, the machine began to hum as a handle came out; the assistant seized it and pushed the machine around the floor for five minutes in a vacuum-cleaninglike motion.

"Examine your floor," he said to Mrs. Waspold.

"Oh!" she exclaimed, after careful examination.

The women began buzzing. The assistant went through several other miraculous demonstrations: cleaning and washing dishes without soap and water, air-conditioning and moisture control, dry-laundering without removing linen from bed, massaging, electric cooking, and more.

"Ladies and gentlemen, there is nothing Rekcus can't do in the home!"

He demonstrated for the men. The machine began ejecting tools, gadgets, and supplies. It was a workshop in itself: a radio, a TV, a phonograph, a fan, a movie projector, and more. I couldn't believe it, and I began looking for him to make mistakes, like a magician does once in a while.

But he was polished in every way, a master salesman. The machine did all the work. Both were perfect.

After an hour of breathtaking feats, the machine began to expand by itself, unfolding like a crib. I could see soft blankets inside.

"Would you like to put your baby in the crib?" he asked a woman with a newborn child. "I assure you, the child will be the better for it."

Smiling, the woman placed the baby in the machine. "He's going to cry," she frowned. Once down, the tiny baby began to whimper, then cry.

Mr. Mortishan's assistant just stood there with a ready, even smile.

The machine hummed and began a liquid motion back and forth. An arm appeared and cuddled the baby. A bottle leaped up. Music and the sound of a woman's voice—very much like the mother's—calmed the baby. It stopped crying and closed its eyes, sucking away.

"Ladies and gentlemen, you have seen nothing! I speak the truth. There is no machine like this one. You can't buy it in the stores, you can't see it in the shops, but you can own one without any money down. You have just seen it *perform.* Now see it *live.* "

The machine grew again until it was about six feet, standing on wiry metal legs four feet from the floor.

"I want a volunteer. If you have been suffering from backache, heart trouble, rheumatism, hardening of the arteries, sinus, colds, flu, fevers, high and low blood pressure, gland trouble, liver infections, kidney ailments, lung trouble, overweight, underweight, headache, ulcers, sores, boils, cavities, tumors, and old age, then come. If your spirits are deflated, no pep, no get-up-and-go, no zoom, no desire to do anything but sleep it off, if you have longed to travel to distant shores in search of a utopia and bliss, if you need a doctor, then come, I want a volunteer.

"Ladies and gentlemen, D-A-D will go even further for you. You have heard many hot-line salesmen attempt to force something on you that you don't need. If you are in what you think is good health, you might want a change of disposition. Modern psychology has taught our scientists that there are many of us normal people who desire to experience the difficult aspects of living. Rekcus and our scientists have discovered a unique method: cytoplasmic acceleration of metabolic processes. Through C-A-M-P and psychotherapy we can induce any malady known or unknown to man.

"I repeat: if you're suffering from aches and pains of body and mind, youth, old age, come. I want one volunteer!"

Several people got up, but old Mr. Waspold was being led up by Kenny's father. He was so old and helpless that he had been kept in his room during the demonstration. He mumbled things to himself as Mr. Waspold and Mr. Hendy helped him into the machine. He lay down immediately as if he were back in bed.

"The Rekcus is both a dehumanizer and a humanizer, two-in-one, a truly amazing machine. Right here I hold in my hand the simple program card that will set the vitalizers to charge the patient."

A lid slid over the sleeping old man. The machine looked like an overgrown bullet. He inserted the card. A humming sound filled the room, and the old man's voice could be heard chuckling. Then it grew higher and higher, as if it were going back in time. Soon it was whimpering like a baby. The people buzzed and talked to each other.

Suddenly the lid opened.

The assistant motioned them to come. From where I was I could see the old man's face. It was the same, but the inside of the machine had been dressed up with silk, and the old man's clothes had been changed to suit and tie.

"He's resting well," a voice said.

When it came my turn to look, the lid closed, and the assistant said to me out of the corner of his mouth, "You get out."

Kenny's grandfather hadn't moved. The people were poking him and exclaiming.

"This machine is not only accurate in telling the body's time, it is practical. It *does* something about the body's time. And it is very cheap if you want to get another Rekcus. . . ."

I left and sat in the car. Tall buildings blocked the moon. *Oh, you don't have to pay unless you like it. Fred's too crazy about it to think. Get out, get in, get out. Rekcus will help you. Get out, Rekcus will get you.* I left the keys in the car and walked home, thinking I hoped I got there before Kenny.

"Well," said the foreman the next morning, "did the other guy find a better job?"

"No," I said.

"What? Is he sick?"

"Yes," I said. "He's sick."

"Well, I can't wait. I'll have to get another guy in his place."

"Yes," I said. "He's very sick."

Wade

Rosa Guy

1965

"Come back for the funeral, Wade, come back." They had got stinko, he and Uncle Dan and Willie Earl, and Uncle Dan had held him in his arms and cried, because Wade was going to the army. Willie Earl had wished him luck, all smug and contented, because he was a longshoreman and would not be called. He was happy at the thought that while Wade and a lot of suckers were risking their lives, falling dead by the hundreds, he would be making that long money putting in hours and hours of overtime.

It hadn't made any difference to Wade, though. The way he saw it, it took a war to get him off Lenox Avenue, and as long as Uncle Sam was paying the bills, he would go for the ride, sit out his time, then make it back to his family. He was no hero and he wasn't going to try to prove anything. That was why he promised Uncle Dan he would be back.

But life, even when it doesn't have a hell of a lot of meaning, is never that simple. He had been given a gun and forced to kill people he never knew, for reasons that he gave less than a damn about. But for the first time in his life he made friends outside his family and laughed and joked with guys he would never have thought of laughing and joking with before. They were a special brand of guys, though. They had to be special to form a special kind of joke, that wasn't so funny as it was tough, to hide the hurt and relief that got to you when, after walking and laughing with a guy one minute, you saw his guts blown open the next.

There were other kinds: there were the guys who got scared and tried to dig holes to hide in, as though the holes would last the duration; and there were those who pissed and messed all over themselves; and there were those who did all those things and still came up with jokes. Then there were the special few, mean and evil—some said even half crazy. Maybe they had lived too long curled up behind their eyes; they laughed and joked all the while. Some called them ignorant, but there were times he had seen them leading the leaders.

It was out there, lying in one of those foxholes after the invasion of Normandy, that he looked upward and saw the sky and realized that in all his years in Harlem he had not ever really seen a star. He got to looking up at the sky every chance he got, studying the stars and the moon and thinking of his life back in Harlem. He got to thinking in some vague way that he might not go back after his bit, that maybe he might start looking for new horizons, shake out his mind and see what he might be able to do with it. It might be that he was still brilliant, still the whiz kid.

But even with all this going around in his mind he looked out for home and Mumma. Faith had at last landed a job, not as secretary, but with the shortage of workers they had begun to hire Negroes in department stores as salesladies, and with the allotment and all the extra money he didn't need while he was in combat, he figured she must be doing better than she had ever done in her life. He played crap and blackjack and sent home all his winnings, asking Mumma to save him a part of it, telling her he had plans, big plans, a lot he wanted to do in the future. Even after he met Michele he kept sending Mumma money and making sure that things at home were always under control.

He didn't as a rule go for ofays, even the broads, but there wasn't much else you could do over there, except if you wanted a WAC, and the way he looked at it, anything American had to wait until he could do no better. It wasn't that chicks over there were not like chicks all over. They went to bed with a guy and thought they had a club, always pulling more out of him than he was willing to give.

That was something that he made up his mind one day to investigate: what did they think they had between their legs that inspired dreams? Even the lowest whores he ever went with had the strange idea that all they had to do was spread out one time and they had themselves a fish—hook, line, and sinker. Yet a lot of studs went for it, laying their leave around as though they were in some screwing paradise, leaving all their money behind to go back behind the lines to finish their dreaming.

Michele wasn't like that. She was colorless all the way through to her soul. It wasn't that she was bad-looking, she just had a face that had seen a hell of a lot and couldn't be impressed any more. Before she got into his bed, she said "l'argent." And he had to pay up. Then she lay there not moving until he had finished. That got him mad as hell. Her eyes were not friendly, not unfriendly, just empty.

When she started out the door, he got in her way and said "l'argent" again, and he paid her and this time it was the same. By then he was boiling. The next time he stepped into her way and she said "l'argent" he shook his head. She made to pass around him but he stood solidly still. She looked into his eyes and realized that it was useless. She shrugged and went to sit on the bed.

He didn't let her up for a week. At first her stony silence, her hostility, got to him and he met scorn with scorn. He pulled her hair, slapped her face, pushed her around with his feet. She never changed expression, just looked at him from eyes that said she was used to it. After the third day of bread, cheese, and wine, which he had a hustling kid bring to the door, and Michele, he became as gentle as a lamb.

He tried like hell to get one word out of her, one expression of softness, of warmth. By the end of the week, he was blubbering like a nine-month baby starting to be weaned. He got up one morning and she was gone.

He began to feel the bottomless depths of his loneliness. It was not new to him. Being in this strange country far away from his family had only released the familiar sensation that he had known so long ago. Maybe since the time Big Willie died, maybe when he and Faith had been put away, he couldn't exactly remember but it had seemed like always. He lay looking out at a shaft of sunlight playing on a line of clothes across the cluttered court from his room, wondering what he would do with the rest of his leave. The idea of another chick left him unmoved.

He heard a slight sound at the door and looking around saw her entering the room, her arms full of groceries. She went about fixing a long-overdue meal while he stood in the middle of the floor turning around stupidly, following her movements around the room. He wanted to cry more than anything, but when she stood before him all he could do was take her in his arms.

They lived together for the rest of his leave, and all the weekends while he was stationed in France, and they might have been happy except that happiness is one of those words that have meaning only in a dictionary.

It had been one of those evenings when a whole day had gone by without a blemish and they were at the very top of their spirits. Maybe they were a little drunk, but he knew that Michele had started looking downright pretty to him. They had reached the point in their relationship when their eyes gave out messages. He didn't know whether he was in love. It wasn't the same feeling he had for Gay but it was more comfortable. Somewhere along the line, he had stopped trying to prove anything.

Being in France was just about the best of it. Sure, they had been the liberators and so everyone looked up to them, but it was much more than that. It was as though a weight had dropped off your shoulders, this being away from home. You got aboard the metro and sat down and the feeling of intruding didn't dig into you, making you tense and belligerent. You walked on the streets jostling people or being jostled by them without your hair standing up at the back of your neck. Being able to argue with a cabdriver over a sou and get cussed out with you returning the compliment, and it was only that sou you argued about. It was slow getting used to—that you were a man and not a special kind of man.

It was funny as hell, the light feeling that came over you when you fully realized that at home a whole country had been standing solidly on your shoulders, looking at you upside down, and you had been trying to move and get around, acting like a normal man, with that weight on your shoulders. You went around pretending, and telling yourself and shouting out loud to anyone who would listen that you were like all other men. But it wasn't true! How could it be true with all that weight upon you? You had to be different. Wade started thinking of the reasons studs back home talked so loud especially in White areas. It was to try to convince the White man that he wasn't really on your shoulder, even when *he* knew it was a lie. The reason why, when he came out of the subway in Harlem, he could push out his chest and make his back a little straighter, wishing he could hide forever in the glowing tide of pure people.

Being away from the scene made you feel as a bird must feel when he could just spread his wings and soar. And when he thought of making it permanent, he didn't think of bringing Michele home and sealing her in his prison. He was finished with prisons. After all this crap was over he would go home and settle Mumma, get the money she was holding for him, and make it back to Paris. He knew it wasn't so easy as he was thinking, but then life was never easy.

So they were almost happy when they stepped into the café, because they had been reading all kinds of things and meanings in each other's faces and they were, as the French say, *d'accord.* He had heard a loud singing before they entered but the tune had not penetrated their togetherness. As he and Michele sat at their table, he heard the song dying out and a loud silence rose to hit him and he knew that they had stumbled into and were about to be drowned by the atmosphere of the good old U.S.A. That was when the notes of the song started echoing and reechoing deep down inside of him: *I wish I was in the land of cotton.* "Dixie."

When he saw the group of White officers his first impulse was to quit the scene. They must have begun early because they obviously had pushed everyone else out of the joint by their loudness. It was funny how much louder they were in France than were their Black brothers. Wade wanted just to be gone and forget that he had trespassed into U.S. territory, but not backing down from the bastards had become a way of life with him.

They had run Big Willie over the Mason and Dixon Line; they had got his own backsides torn up by Mumma when he stepped out of his boundaries; they had been responsible for making him a jailbird at age eleven; had succeeded in keeping him in his own private world in Harlem, U.S.A. But Paris, France was everybody's playground, and he wasn't about to start running here. They had better believe that.

Wade called the waiter with a nonchalance he was far from feeling, looking around at the same time to size up what he might have to put up with. His heart almost paused in its beating as he saw a big, red-faced captain, the hate stinking out through every pore in his body and oozing out of his eyes through the glassy drunken stare that he slobbered over them. Some of his buddies tried to pull him back into what they probably thought was a balling time, and Wade hoped they'd succeed, but the fool wasn't having any.

Michele sipped her drink without realizing anything was wrong, but the waiters had that quiet look on their faces, and they got busy with a hundred little things, trying to get the cat's intention wiped off his face. Wade, too, calm as anything, tried to level a stare of warning to the cat, letting him know he was no turkey, that there were limits he never went beyond, that he had no gods, hoping the cat was sober enough to read it. But he wasn't.

"Well, look at what we got here, an African monkey all dressed up like an honest-to-goodness U.S. soldier," he shouted across the room.

There was relief in the knowledge that Michele did not speak English, yet it didn't make him feel like a whole human being, worth a damn. He was exposed for what he was. An American. A Black American.

"Boy, do you know what we would do to you if we had you back home?"

Wade looked over to their table because he had the feeling that the captain had stood up and he wondered what was keeping him from approaching their table. It was a chick. She was trying to persuade him to sit back down. Cute as hell, too. The kind of chick who would make an army of mouths pucker, but that thing in the captain was a hell of a lot bigger than her charms. Even when she managed to drag him back down, Wade knew it was only a matter of time before he would be up again.

Wade drank up and ordered another, wishing that his good intentions toward Michele would make him get up and take her out of there, but this thing between him and the captain seemed bigger than all the chicks in the joint.

Michele realized that something was going on by this time, and she sipped her drink, waiting for her cue. This chick had lived! She didn't fear a thing. He smiled across at her, thinking how wonderful it was having her with him, because he realized, sitting across from her, that the abuse she had lived through as a woman made her his equal.

The men with the captain started leaving. It seemed that he had killed the hell out of their party. A few stayed on because they were too stoned to move, sitting with their heads on the table, their bodies wavering, undecided whether they should fall off their seats. The captain's chick sat on, a puzzled frown pleating her brow as though she were trying to figure what more she could add to her charms. But the next time Wade's gaze traveled the room, she must have come to the amazing revelation: nothing. She had gone and there the captain was, still staring at them.

Wade poured all of his attention into his drink, and into that quiet waiting look in Michele's eyes, but every pore in his body stood at attention, and when the captain finally rose and staggered toward them, it was as though every pore got to marching, doing a military drill right down his back. But he never moved his gaze from Michele's, sat smiling quietly, reassuringly, at her.

Then the captain was swaying over their table, holding onto the edge for support, leering down at Michele drunkenly. "Where I come from," he said, "ladies don't drink with niggers, so you must be a whore."

Michele must have recognized the word "whore," because her face went suddenly blank. Wade could have kicked himself for not taking her out of there sooner as he saw the weeks of pleasure, the days of happiness emptying out of her eyes. Yet he never let the smile leave his face, or his eyelashes give a blink, as he called the waiter and paid him. Then he was ready.

Rising slowly to his feet, Wade gave Michele enough time to take a few significant steps toward the door. Then passing in front of the captain, he said in a hard whisper loud enough only to penetrate the captain's drunkenness, making sure that no one else heard, "Where you come from, captain, your mothers have to fuck our fathers to know what a prick is. You don't call that prostitution, you call that destitution."

Leading Michele through the door, he hurriedly pressed some money into her hand, telling her to get a cab. Then leaving her standing near the curb, he walked slowly down the street.

There was no guesswork about it. The captain *had* to follow Wade just as steel has to follow a magnet. It was there, bigger than the two of them, that American thing that tied them together, like a sickness that neither one could do anything about. Wade knew instinctively just when the captain staggered out of the café. He stopped to make sure the captain saw him. From then on it was a matter of timing. He walked slowly enough for the drunk to think he was catching him, and every time Wade thought the captain might be ready to lunge, he quickened his steps, leading him directly down the street that he and Michele had traveled earlier, laughing and being happy, on their stroll through the Bois.

It had turned chilly, with a damp raw sharp wind cutting through even the thickness of the heavy army coat, but that didn't stop the captain. It probably only cleared his head, for his steps became steady and Wade didn't have to keep stopping so often in order to lead his quarry deeper and deeper into the Bois.

A hazy moon lit their way into the woods, and Wade hoped that for a little while longer the blond-haired, blue-eyed captain would not get the idea that he was being taken. But the whiskey plus the fact that he was a good three inches taller than Wade was enough to keep him brave.

Wade walked on, and finding a cluster of trees that caused deep shadows he ducked into them, waiting silently, holding his breath, not daring to look out but praying that the turkey wouldn't miss him and walk back the other way. But he came on, passing the spot where Wade stood, peering through the darkness, puzzle and disappointment showing over him as though he had really lost a good thing.

Wade stepped out of the shadow behind him. "Captain, you looking for me?"

The captain spun around, breathing heavily. Then, seeing Wade, he sneered, "Yeah, I'm looking for big-mouth Black Sambo. That's you, ain't it?"

"At your service, captain."

"I just want you to repeat one more time what you said back there in that café. Just one more time."

"I said, captain, that your mother fucked my father so she could know the feel of a man. And that's why you are here, captain; you want to feel a hot rod up your ass, too. You are just like your goddamn mother."

The captain started pulling off his coat, and that was a damn-fool thing to do. Wade let him have it just like that. He didn't believe in fooling around with a stud he knew he had to beat. He had no intention of getting hurt for nothing. The captain did not get to his feet again until he had rid himself of his coat, a point that was not lost on Wade—that the cat sobered easily or maybe he was not so drunk as he made out. When he jumped to his feet again, he bore no resemblance to the staggering fool who had wavered before Wade a minute before. But Wade, his coat thrown aside too, was waiting.

This time Wade clasped his hands and brought them down, first on one side of the captain's neck, staggering him, then on the other side of his neck, then with his fists full in his face. The captain fell back against a tree and Wade kept at him with both hands to his face and head until he slid to the ground dazed. But the captain wasn't ready to give up, and made his unsteady way to his feet, holding onto the tree for support. Before he could get fully onto his feet or lift his head, Wade clasped his hands again and let him have one with all his strength at the back of his neck.

By this time the captain must have realized that he wasn't being taken by a pushover, and maybe the idea was coming to him that he didn't have a chance. But he was a game stud. He had fallen on his stomach. Now he crawled around on his hands and knees until he found Wade's feet, then pulled himself slowly upward. Wade waited to hear whether he wanted to say something, but obviously the captain didn't, because he went right into balling his hands into fists again. This time Wade wasted him.

Months afterward, Wade tried to think back to what was in his mind at that time, but try as he would, nothing came. Maybe it was that other him curled up behind his eyes, coming out alive, violently alive, determined, determined as hell to even some score, there in the Bois in France, in that little shaft of light allowed by the moon. Later he thought of getting into trouble, possibly of getting caught, but at the time nothing was on his mind but beating the hell out of the stud.

He heard a little movement not too far away and, looking up, saw Michele. There she was just standing, saying nothing, as though this scene were routine in her life. A rush of love that he had never felt before overcame him because of her calm, her way of looking at punishment and seeing it because she was part of the whole ugly stinking scene. She wasn't going to make any more of it than that. She had passed from player to spectator and all she wanted was a chance to live a little, to breathe, without paying any more dues. That was what he wanted too.

He realized suddenly that he was twenty-two years old and had lived and become old without ever having been young, without ever being able to breathe, never feeling free or light of heart, or being what other people called "happy." Now suddenly he wanted to be young, to breathe, to live.

"Now," he said, out of breath, panting, pulling the limp form of the captain up by the collar of his jacket. "Now, mother-fucker, say 'I'm sorry.' Apologize, you low-down Mississippi cracker, for all of those things you said and all of those things you meant to say, if you only had the chance."

The captain looked up into Wade's eyes, his thickened face turning up into a sickly smile, his blue eyes cleared of the drunken haze, blazing clearly in that tiny shaft of moonlight. Fear for his very life glistened there, but it did not hide or erase the hatred that poured out of him. "You still," the captain gasped painfully through his bloody lips, "ain't nothing but a goddamn nigger."

Wade's anger rose like some terrible thing, hardly a part of him, bigger and mightier than he, pushing the man to the ground. Then using his foot he kicked his face, stomping where he knew the head should be, feeling the crushing of bones beneath his shoe, then bearing down on his heels, grinding and grinding until he felt nothing but a mass of pulp under the heel of his boot. Anger spent, Wade leaned weakly against the tree wiping his face, trying to get his mind together; but somehow he wasn't able to function. Dazed, he kept looking down, and if it hadn't been for Michele pulling on him, insisting, "*Chéri*, we must go. We must go," he might have stood against the tree the rest of the night.

But as he pulled himself up to follow her, he realized that he didn't want to leave the body out here just like that and it was more, much more, than the fear of having the body traced to him: he had been shaken to his very soul by the intensity of the man's hatred of him; but he had also been shaken by his own hatred of the man, of his reaction brought on by this hatred. It was *madness*, this thing that had tied them together out here in this senseless battle, but it was *their* madness and should not be aired to the world. It was a sickness that was a part of both of their lives from the time they were on their mother's milk, but it was a private sickness, something that ought not to be shown.

He found himself suddenly understanding the colored cats who lied and bragged about how important they were back at home and how real gone things were for them back in the States. He knew now that they had to prove they were like all the world's peoples. That the quotation, "From dust you came and to dust you will return" had to have the same meaning for them as for all. That there was nothing written up in the Bible or any other goddamn book that said, "From dust you come, you will live like dust, and dust you will forever be." A man had to feel that in all this crap there had to be something working for him—a soul—and home was like having a soul. You were fighting and working like hell for it, saying in effect that you were willing to give your life for it, and where did you stand? What were you, if it were all a lie?

They began a frantic searching around the neighborhood near the Bois, and it was strange they were not seen, they were so busy trying to keep out of the way of gendarmes and the military police. But finally, they found a shovel. Wade forced Michele to leave him, making her promise she would wait in the room for him—something she consented reluctantly to do.

He insisted, not because it would not have been easier with another hand to break through the earth, nor did the thought of having her implicated enter his mind. Strangely enough he simply wanted to be alone with his fellow American there under the Paris sky, where they had played out their battle of hatred.

He dug a damned decent grave and dragged the cat into it, putting his coat and hat over him, bowed his head—he didn't know why, he didn't pray—then covered the body with the earth. When he had finished, he stood awhile trying to think but found nothing to think about. He had killed men, since the war, for whom he had felt much more: a little savagery if the cat had a mean, set face; a little awe if he had a poetic face; a little regret if he had a young face; and relief when it was a close call. But here, at first, he felt nothing. He listened to the insects, the brush of branches hitting against branches; smelled the brownness, the sweetness of the freshly turned earth, but felt nothing.

Then suddenly it came: the sense of being unshackled, the lightness of heart that he must have read about somewhere. He moved his feet as though they had really been in chains; then he threw back his head and laughed.

He almost skipped out of the woods, shovel in hand. Skipping and feeling what it meant to be gay and happy and really free for the first time in his entire life. He took the shovel home and gave it to Michele as a souvenir. Then he asked her to marry him. He was sure that he would never live in the States. He had got the man off his back and he wanted to keep him off.

Funny thing, he and Michele never discussed the shovel or that night. It was as though it never happened, only it had, and it had changed the hell out of him. They spoke of the day he had to leave and when he intended to come back, the house they intended to build right outside Paris, and the babies they intended to have. And when she spoke, Michele got to laughing, and it surprised him how young she looked. He even began looking at himself in the mirror, and funny thing, he looked young too.

Key to the City

Diane Oliver

1965

"Nora, want to eat your breakfast with me?" Her mother's starched uniform swished as she walked to the door.

"All right, Mama, I'm getting up now." She watched her mother push aside the curtain that separated her bedroom from the hallway. Then she swung both feet to the edge of the bed and stood up. The little girl who slept beside her did not stir as Nora pulled on her blue jeans and tiptoed from the room.

In the kitchen her mother already sat at the table. "Babycake still asleep?" she asked. "That child ought to be completely worn out getting ready for this trip. You'd think we'd been to Chicago and back."

Nora slipped her egg from the skillet to the plate. "At least Mattie isn't so much trouble," she said, "but the two of them sure don't help my packing."

"I wish I could help, but Mrs. Anderson is not going to let me off early."

"She still mad about you leaving?"

Her mother nodded and Nora watched the wrinkles around her mouth deepen into soft brown folds. "Time for me to be leaving." She looked at the battered alarm clock on the center of the table. "Listen, honey, be sure and get the eggs before the girls get up. The chickens deserve a little bit of peace." She picked up her handbag from the kitchen chair and walked out the door.

Nora rinsed her plate in the kitchen sink and, taking the wicker basket from on top the icebox, opened the screen door. Immediately the hens scurried around her, giggling with cackles as they flapped across the front yard. She looked down at the basket in her hand. Here she was gathering eggs like she did every day of her life, and tomorrow the family was leaving for Chicago.

Her daddy had a good part-time job, he said, but he'd gotten so busy he no longer had time to write, not even to send a card for her graduation. She felt strange knowing she would see him in a few hours. Tomorrow morning she and Mattie and Mama and Babycake planned to ride all the way from Still Creek to Chicago without ever leaving the bus except when they all had to go to the bathroom.

Mama probably would have a time with Babycake. Her little sister got sick whenever she rode for a long time, and they couldn't wash her very well in those bus station bathrooms. She knew her daddy would meet them at the downtown Chicago bus station; he would be awfully glad to see them. A lot of people around Still Creek said he'd left them and wasn't going to send for them or even see them again. She had known better. If he said he would send for his family, he would. Besides, when he first married her mama, he promised they'd get away to Chicago. Which was really why Mama took on another job instead of staying home with the kids. With both of them working full time, she figured she could save some money.

At their graduation exercises, the principal had announced the two members of the class who would go on to college. Nora's going to college was the reason they were moving. Her parents said she could go to a branch of the city college practically free and finish up her education. They had planned to move "one of these days" for as long as she could remember.

Nora could repeat their special family formula backwards, frontwards, and even sideways. They had talked about it ever since she was a little girl. Mama and Daddy would get jobs up north, and with the money she herself could earn, she would eventually get through college. Then she would put Mattie through, and Mattie would see that Babycake graduated. And of course if any other sisters or brothers came along, they would do the same thing for them.

She waved to Mrs. McAuley, who was hanging out clothes next door. Her wash, like their family's, was conspicuous with the absence of a man's blue work shirts. Nora wondered if Mr. McAuley would ever come home, but the neighborhood's early morning sounds blotted out the memory of him. Behind the chicken coop she could hear the grinding noise of Mr. Johnson's tractor. How funny to think that in a few hours she would no longer hear that familiar sound. Leaving was just a day away, and even thinking about it made her throat feel a little funny.

By the time the eggs were gathered and set up high on top of the icebox, Mama had long since been off to work. Nora made Mattie and Babycake mayonnaise and egg sandwiches for breakfast. After they were through eating, she tried to persuade the two little girls to play house outside. But in an hour they were tired and wanted to help her.

"Go on, Mattie, go back outdoors and play." She tried to keep her impatience from showing.

"But we don't got nothing to play with," Mattie said, determined not to leave. "Margie and Tanker-Belle are all packed up, and you said we won't see them again until we get there."

Mattie's brown eyes began watering as if she were going to cry. Margie and

Tanker-Belle were the two dolls of the family. Tanker-Belle had been one of those fancy toaster-cover dolls that some well-meaning aunt on Mama's side had sent as a Christmas gift. Which would have been nice, but they didn't have a toaster.

Mattie had practically confiscated the doll and for reasons known only to Mattie had named her Tanker-Belle. She had spent most of her time since Christmas in the Pretend House back of the pecan tree. Tanker-Belle was rather frayed, after having spent several nights in the rain.

Now Nora explained to the little girls that at last the doll was going to have a nice long rest. She had packed Tanker-Belle immediately after breakfast while Mattie was busy with something else. She was now inside the big roasting pan with the dictionary and the kitchen forks. But Mattie insisted that she knew Tanker-Belle was lonesome inside the turkey pan.

"I'll tell you what, Mattie," Nora said as she tried to comfort the sobbing child. "Look on my dresser and get a nickel out of the blue bag. You go find Babycake and you all walk up to Mr. James' store for a double orange popsicle. Then go play in the Pretend House until lunchtime."

"Can I, Nora! Oh, can I?" Mattie's smile stopped the tears running down her cheeks. She raced out of the little hallway, jumping over boxes, and through the bedroom door for a nickel. In a second she was calling Babycake and the two little girls started up the road.

Five dollars and ninety-five cents' worth of graduation money was left. Nora kept a mental record of her savings since June. Her habit of saving was a reaction, she guessed. Her father had all the good intentions in the world but whenever they needed money he never had enough. That was one reason why her mother had taken the responsibility of moving the family.

She stooped down and began cramming some books in another cardboard box, in a hurry to move on to something else. By the time the little girls were finished with the popsicle, it would be time for their naps. Nora tied a string around the box and made a double knot. If she could just have an hour by herself, she could finish the packing.

She had begun scrubbing the kitchen floor when suddenly a noise that sounded like a rock hitting the wire of the chicken coop made her drop the rag and run to the back door.

"Babycake, you and Mattie stop bothering the chickens. We won't get any eggs if you keep on; what's wrong with you all anyway?"

"Babycake wants all the popsicle, Nora. And you gave it to me, didn't you, Nora?"

By the time Mattie explained about the popsicle and how Babycake had gotten angry and thrown a rock at the chickens, Babycake was crying. Mattie, upon seeing Babycake's tears, had begun crying herself and Nora stood there, outdone. Here she was faced with two squealing little girls and her with all that work to do.

"I can tell," she said firmly, "that it's time for two naps. Give me the popsicle and you can eat it after you've had a nap." She marched her sisters through the back door, stopped to deposit the ice cream on the kitchen table, and continued toward the bedroom. While she undressed her sisters, the popsicle lay forgotten.

In a quarter of an hour Babycake was asleep. Mattie, who was ready to get up again, decided she was not sleepy and began singing to herself. Nora had to stop packing again and tell her to be quiet. She didn't notice the popsicle until she saw the sticky orange drops on her clean kitchen floor. She wiped off the table and floor and swallowed what was left of the dripping orange popsicle. There was no getting around it, she'd have to spend another nickel for some more ice cream.

Nora worked all evening, sorting clothes, folding linen, and packing kitchen utensils. Finally, the boxes were ready to go.

In the morning the smell of freshly fried chicken lingered throughout the house. The two fryers Mama had killed last night plus the one Mrs. McAuley brought over would last them the time the trip would take. In the bottom of the lunch basket were three sweet potato pies and a brown bag full of the Georgia peaches that grew wild in their back yard.

According to the schedule propped on an empty milk bottle on the kitchen table, in a half hour everybody would be ready to pile in the Edwards car for the bus station. The Edwardses were going to keep all the house furnishings in their barn until Mama sent for the furniture.

The two big beds already had been dismantled and Mattie's roll-away cot was folded up near the front door. Nora walked from the hall into the living room. The whole house looked so empty, even her father's postcards were missing from the mantel over the fireplace. Suddenly she smiled. All of the furniture was covered with old newspapers their neighbors had saved, and four layers of the *Still Creek Bugle* couldn't possibly revive the sagging sofa cushions.

By seven-thirty Babycake had been freshly washed and ironed for the trip. She was commanded to sit still on the front stoop and announce the Edwardses' arrival. Mattie, who also had been dared to get dirty, kept her company. The two little girls sat on the first step, facing the swing tied to the pine tree. Their sliding feet had trampled the bits of grass growing beneath the rope, and scattered in the yard were a few green weeds the chickens had not pecked away.

Babycake reached over and gave the potted Christmas cactus a good-bye pat. The leaves were shiny because she had poured water over them this morning—Mama insisted the plant be clean when Mrs. Edwards carried the pot home.

All at once there was a honk from the horn and a long lanky boy, the oldest of the Edwards boys, was running up the steps.

"Pop says are y'all ready yet?" Without giving them a chance to answer he started piling boxes in the trunk of the car. Babycake and Mattie were so scared they would get dirty and get left they did everything Nora told them to do.

"Mattie, pick up the little shoe box. . . . Babycake, make sure we got the lunch. No, I'll take care of the lunch, you pick up the hatbox over there." Their little house had never been so cluttered and then so empty. Come to think of it, their neighborhood seldom had seen such excitement.

Everybody in Still Creek was at the bus station to see the Murrays off. There was no need to ask how they'd gotten there. Those few people who had cars drove down and piled in as many neighbors as they could. Uncle Ben, Aunt Mabel's husband, was one of those who had walked the three quarters of a mile to the bus station. Mabel had caught a ride. Anyway, they were all there, a mass of black humanity overflowing the little waiting room marked COLORED.

In one corner of one half of Still Creek Bus Terminal, Mattie sat on an upright box as Aunt Mabel gave her pigtails a quick brushing. When she had tied each end with a bright yellow ribbon, Mabel thumped Mattie on the neck and pushed her off the box toward her mama's voice that attempted to round up the family.

Nora saw Aunt Mabel trying to catch Uncle Ben's eye. Mabel began to speak above the noise in the room.

"Haven't been this many people here since they brought that Jackson boy's body home," she said, "the one who was killed overseas three years ago."

While Uncle Ben and Aunt Mabel discussed the community gatherings at the station during the last five years, Mama was getting ready to buy their tickets. Somebody got up so she could sit down and count out the money for four one-way tickets to Chicago.

Mattie was hanging over her shoulders, wide-eyed. "Mama," she breathed, "are we rich?"

"Hush, child, I'm trying to count." When she had counted out the correct amount of money four times, she tied what was left into a handkerchief and put it in the blue denim purse, which in turn went into her genuine imitation leather cowhide bag. Still counting silently, she made her way to the ticket window. When the man had given her the tickets and counted out the change, Nora felt like giving a glorious hallelujah of relief. At times like this she always felt something wrong was going to happen. She could imagine the fare going up and them without enough money, having to go back home.

With Mama talking to Aunt Mabel, Nora slipped out of the side door for a final look at her home town. The Georgia landscape was shallow and dull and, to her eyes that had seen no other part of the country, beautiful. Even this early in the morning a thickness had settled over the countryside, covering everything with a film of fine red dust. She fingered the purse inside her pocket. Six dollars she had now—Mrs. Edwards had given her a dime to buy some candy in case she got hungry on the way.

The sound of voices inside the waiting room reached her ears. She could hear Aunt Mabel crying, louder and louder. The voices seemed to reach out and carry her with them. The bus—the bus must have come. Quickly she shut her purse and ran back toward the waiting room.

Sure enough, there was her mother frantically hugging and kissing everybody and thanking them for all the good things they had done for the Murrays. Mattie was pulling Mama's hand and begging her to hurry up before they got left. Seeing Nora, her mother beckoned her to come and get Mattie and Babycake for a final trip to the bathroom.

By the time everybody had been pushed out of the waiting room, the men had most of the luggage stored underneath the bus. Then began the last-minute hugging and kissing and gift-giving all over again. Nora felt a dollar bill pressed into her hand. She couldn't help the tears; Uncle Ben really didn't have any money to spare. She bent over and kissed the old man on his cheek.

The bus driver checked his watch and in a dry, matter-of-fact voice announced that anybody who was leaving with him had better hurry up and get on because he was driving in exactly two shakes. Finally the steel door closed. In the rear of the bus, their noses pressed against the windowpanes, the four Murrays waved good-bye to friends and neighbors and to Still Creek, Georgia, "the original home of fine Georgia peaches."

After hours of riding, Nora lost track of the towns they passed. Still Creek seemed so far away and the slight jogging of the bus no longer made her head ache. The whole trip had become a kaleidoscope of sounds and colors. The small towns surrounded with ranch-style houses and green lawns were loose fragments she counted, like turning storybook pages in her mind.

At the next rest stop, Nora decided to stretch her legs in the bus aisle. Mama herself took the little girls inside for a glass of milk and a trip to the bathroom. When the bus started again, she began telling a fairy tale to Mattie and then suddenly the accident occurred. Little Babycake had stuffed herself with too much sweet potato custard and she lost all her dinner on the back seat of the bus. They tried to clean up the seat with some old waxed paper, but they couldn't clean and pay attention to Babycake too.

Babycake started crying. Her stomach hurt and she wanted to go home. Mama tried to hush her, but the more she patted, the more Babycake cried. By the time the sourness had spread throughout the bus, Mama sent Nora up to the bus driver to ask him if he would stop and let Babycake get her stomach settled.

Nora stood up and held on to the seats, cautiously walking up the aisle, toward the back of the bus driver's gray-blue suit. After hours of riding, the jacket still looked freshly pressed, and he didn't even glance up in the mirror as she approached the driver's seat.

"My little sister's sick," she explained. "If she could get some air, my mother said she might feel better." She held on to the pole near the front steps, facing the back of the driver's gray head.

Muttering something unintelligible, he said no. He had lost enough time and would be stopping soon anyway. They would just have to wait like everybody else.

While she was standing in the aisle, the bus picked up speed and turned a sharp curve. Nora felt herself fall against two elderly women and although the bus was air-conditioned, one was struggling trying to raise the window.

"Niggers," she whispered, her voice grating, colliding with the growl of the motor.

Nora was not certain she had heard the woman speak, but even thinking of the word hurt her ears. Nobody'd ever called her a nigger to her face before. At least never with such anger. She looked into the woman's eyes, seeing the fierce look her father often described as belonging to white people. Fierceness that was hatred. She was conscious of the bus moving, jerking to a stop, and then moving again, but she heard nothing except the woman's words. It was as if the words formed an invisible cloak and only by pushing it away with her thoughts did she keep from being smothered.

She wanted to see her father now—have him take his wife and children from this horrible bus and put them down where they did not have to move ever again. What if . . . no, he would not do that, not after he talked so badly about Mr. McAuley deserting his family six months after they met him in Chicago. The McAuleys stayed in the city not even a year; in December they had come home. Even with the extra money allotted them because of Mr. McAuley's disappearance they did not have enough money to eat. She dared not even think.

Nora never knew how many rest stops the bus made. Once as she turned toward the window she realized the daylight had changed into darkness. She even forgot to watch for the sign telling them they had crossed the Illinois state line. Mattie wanted to play Cookie Jar, but she could not concentrate on the hand clapping for trying not to remember those words. Nora was almost asleep when the bus turned into an entrance, pulled up to the curb, and stopped.

Because there were so many bundles to carry out, they were the last people getting off the bus. Babycake was the first one to see him. She caught hold of Mama's hand, yelling, "Here we are, here we are," and started to run across the terminal to the man in the black trenchcoat. Nora had to hold her back. The man Babycake saw was not their father. He was a little too tall, and when he passed the family, he just looked at them strangely.

They stood outside the big glass door with the little packages, waiting and looking through each crowd of people, but no one came.

"You people need help or something?" a woman asked. She walked as if she knew every inch of the ground surrounding the terminal. "If you need a taxi, I'll show you where to stand."

Nora shook her head. "No, thank you, we're waiting for someone." Her eyes dropped to the pavement and for a while she was conscious only of shoes, so many different colors, passing, all walking by them. After fifteen minutes and two "May I help you's" Mama guided them through the revolving door and to a bench in the middle of the station.

"That way he can see us when he comes," she said, sitting down on the bench. Nora again braided Mattie and Babycake's hair and then there was nothing to do but wait.

Oh, why hadn't he come? He was supposed to be here; they had sent the letter last Friday. She had told him the exact time of their arrival. Twice she'd written it out.

Now Babycake was getting sleepy again. "Where's Daddy?" she asked, "Aren't we there now?"

"Hush up." Her mother motioned for Nora to unlace Babycake's shoes. "Maybe he can't find us," she whispered above the little girls' heads.

An hour passed. Nora stood. "Where you going?" Mattie asked. "Don't you get lost from us too."

"To check the luggage, it won't take long." Nora began walking down the side of the terminal, near the shiny cigarette machine and past the magazine rack. Everything glittered with a metallic glow but the fluorescent lighting only emphasized the emptiness within her. She looked up and saw an overhead panel advertising a course in shorthand—gt-gd-jb. . . . Then she met Elizabeth Taylor's gaze beneath the sign pointing to the telephone booth.

At once she was aware of what had happened. He was working overtime and had overslept. She had the apartment building's telephone number from one of his first letters. She would call and whoever answered would tell her where to reach him and then he would come get them. With sticky fingers she loosened a dime from her money collection and lifted the receiver. The phone rang once, and a voice answered.

"McConnell's Drug Store—Hello? This is McConnell's Drug Store."

"Please," Nora whispered, "could I speak with Mr. Joseph Murray?"

"Sorry, miss, but no Joe Murray works here."

"Are you sure, don't you know him?"

"No, lady, but if you want to wait I'll check the list of people working in the building."

Then he was back too soon, and he was sorry, no Murray was even listed there.

Nora emerged from the booth and stood at the lockers, wondering if she should look outside, when she felt someone bump into her. She turned quickly, into a woman tugging on a small boy. "Excuse me," the woman murmured, pushing the boy ahead of her.

Abruptly pulling away, Nora ran toward the doors out to the sidewalk into the darkness. She tried to brush the air from her face, but the fingers slightly touching her eyelashes came away damp. She stood outside, her eyes tightly closed, trying not to see them, all three of them huddled on that bench. Then her cheeks were dry.

Nora went back to the station bench and whispered to her mother, who was sitting quietly, Babycake's head nestled in her lap.

"Mama? Oh, Mama, did you know all the time?"

Her mother shook her head and reached for her daughter's hand.

"I couldn't know for sure," she said. "We had to work toward something. Don't you see? We wouldn't have ever gotten out if we didn't work toward something." Her voice was sad and quiet, as if she might slowly start humming Babycake to sleep.

"What are we going to do, Mama? They're bound to make us move out of here sometimes."

"We'll just stay right in this spot," she said, covering Babycake with a coat, "just in case." She turned her face toward the suitcases and Nora, seeing that her mother might cry, was sorry she had asked.

"Tomorrow we can call the Welfare people. Somebody there can help us find a place to go." Her mother spoke with her eyes fixed on the travel posters on the far side of the room.

That they never before had had to ask for help made no difference to Nora. She felt that they were pieces in a giant jigsaw puzzle, oddly shaped blobs that would never be put together. Here was her mother sitting so quietly, not letting anything upset her. But then that was not so difficult to do, she herself was not conscious of feeling anything. He loved them, he had to. After all, they were his, but sometimes loving became a burden. And if he had met them at the bus station, perhaps they would have become that to him. But they were supposed to be a family, weren't they? She was no longer certain.

Stepping over the suitcases piled near the bench holding Babycake, Nora began sorting bundles. She looked at the clock on the terminal wall; the silvery hands seemed fixed. Strange that it was morning already; outside the sky was still dark.

She'd probably have to babysit for a while, until Mama found a job and a place to leave the little girls during the day. She began fingering the string around the boxes. Today was Saturday and Mattie and Babycake's Sunday dresses would need ironing, but she'd worry about that later. Their hair ribbons did not have to be pressed, if she could ever remember where they were.

Slowly Nora put down the box. Her shoulders slid down the back of the bench. She couldn't press anything. She couldn't even remember where they had packed the iron.

The Alternative

LeRoi Jones/Amiri Baraka

1967

This may not seem like much, but it makes a difference. And then there are those who prefer to look their fate in the eyes.

—Camus, Between Yes and No

The leader sits straddling the bed, and the night, tho innocent, blinds him. (Who is our flesh. Our lover, marched here from where we sit now sweating and remembering. Old man. Old man, find me, who am your only blood.)

Sits straddling the bed under a heavy velvet canopy. Homemade. The door opened for a breeze, which will not come through the other heavy velvet hung at the opening. (Each thread a face, or smell, rubbed against himself with yellow glasses and fear at their exposure. Death. Death. They (the younger students) run by screaming. Tho impromptu. Tho dead, themselves.

The leader, at his bed, stuck with 130 lbs. black meat sewed to failing bone. A head with big red eyes turning senselessly. Five toes on each foot. Each foot needing washing. And hands that dangle to the floor, tho the boy himself is thin small washed out, he needs huge bleak hands that drag the floor. And a head full of walls and flowers. Blinking lights. He is speaking.

"Yeh?" The walls are empty, heat at the ceiling. Tho one wall is painted with a lady. (Her name now. In large relief, a faked rag stuck between the chalk marks of her sex. Finley. Teddy's Doris. There sprawled where the wind fiddled with the drying cloth. Leon came in and laughed. Carl came in and hid his mouth, but he laughed. Teddy said, "Aw, Man."

"Come on, Hollywood. You can't beat that. Not with your years. Man,

you're a schoolteacher 10 years after weeping for this old stinking bitch. And
hit with a aspirin bottle (myth says)."

The leader is sprawled, dying. His retinue walks into their comfortable cells.
"I have duraw-ings," says Leon, whimpering now in the buses from Chicago.
Dead in a bottle. Floats out of sight, until the Africans arrive with love and
prestige. "Niggers." They say. "Niggers." Be happy your ancestors are recognized in this burg. Martyrs. Dead in an automat, because the boys had left. Lost
in New York, frightened of the burned lady, they fled into those streets and sang
their homage to the Radio City.

The leader sits watching the window. The dried orange glass etched with
the fading wind. (How many there then? 13 Rue Madeleine. The Boys Club.
They give, what he has given them. Names. And the black cloth hung on the
door swings back and forth. One pork chop on the hot plate. And how many
there. Here, now. Just the shadow, waving its arms. The eyes tearing or staring
blindly at the dead street. These same who loved me all my life. These same
I find my senses in. Their flesh a wagon of dust, a mind conceived from all minds.
A country, of thought. Where I am, will go, have never left. A love, of love. And
the silence the question posed each second. "Is this my mind, my feeling. Is this
voice something heavy in the locked streets of the universe. Dead ends. Where
their talk (these nouns) is bitter vegetable." That is, the suitable question rings
against the walls. Higher learning. That is, the moon through the window clearly
visible. The leader in seersucker, reading his books. An astronomer of sorts.
"Will you look at that? I mean, really, now, fellows. Cats!" (Which was Smitty
from the City's entree. And him the smoothest of you American types. Said,
"Cats. Cats. What's goin' on?" The debate.

The leader's job (he keeps it still, above the streets, summers of low smoke,
early evening drunk and wobbling thru the world. He keeps it, baby. You dig?)
was absolute. "I have the abstract position of watching these halls. Walking up
the stairs giggling. Hurt under the cement steps, weeping . . . is my only task.
Tho I play hockey with the broom & wine bottles. And am the sole martyr of
this cause. A.B., Young Rick, T.P., Carl, Hambrick, Li'l' Cholley, Phil. O.K. All
their knowledge "Flait! More! Way!" The leader's job . . . to make attention
for the place. Sit along the sides of the water or lay quietly back under his own
shooting vomit, happy to die in a new gray suit. Yes. "And what not."

How many here now? Danny. (Brilliant dirty curly Dan, the m.d.) Later,
now, where you off to, my man. The tall skinny farmers, lucky to find sales and
shiny white shoes. Now made it socially against the temples. This "hotspot"
Darien drunk teacher blues . . . "and she tried to come on like she didn't even
like to fuck. I mean, you know the kind. . . ." The hand extended, palm upward.
I place my own in yours. That cross, of feeling. Willie, in his grinning grave,
has it all. The place, of all souls, in their greasy significance. An armor, like the

smells drifting slowly up Georgia. The bridge players change clothes, and descend. Carrying home the rolls.

Jimmy Lassiter, first looie. A vector. What is the angle made if a straight line is drawn from the chapel, across to Jimmy, and connected there, to me, and back up the hill again? The angle of progress. "I was talkin' to ol' Mordecai yesterday in a dream, and it's me sayin' 'dig, baby, why don't you come off it?' You know."

The line, for Jimmy's sad and useless horn. And they tell me (via phone, letter, accidental meetings in the Village. "Oh he's in med school and married and lost to you, hombre." Ha. They don't dig completely where I'm at. I have him now, complete. Though it is a vicious sadness cripples my fingers. Those blue and empty afternoons I saw him walking at my side. Criminals in that world. Complete heroes of our time. (Add Allen to complete an early splinter group. Muslim heroes with flapping pants. Raincoats. Trolley car romances.)

And it's me making a portrait of them all. That was the leader's job. Alone with them. (Without them. Except beautiful faces shoved out the window, sunny days, I ran to meet my darkest girl. Ol' Doll. "Man, that bitch got a goddamn new car." And what not. And it's me sayin' to her, Baby, knock me a kiss.

Tonight the leader is faced with decision. Brown had found him drunk and weeping among the dirty clothes. Some guy with a crippled arm had reported to the farmers (a boppin' gang gone social. Sociologists, artistic arbiters of our times). This one an athlete of mouselike proportions. "You know," he said, his withered arm hung stupidly in the rayon suit, "that cat's nuts. He was sittin' up in that room last night with dark glasses on . . . with a yellow bulb . . . pretendin' to read some abstract shit." (Damn, even the color wrong. Where are you now, hippie, under this abstract shit. Not even defense. That you remain forever in that world. No light. Under my fingers. That you exist alone, as I make you. Your sin, a final ugliness to you. For the leopards, all thumbs jerked toward the sand.) "Man, we do not need cats like that in the frat." (Agreed.)

Tom comes in with two big bottles of wine. For the contest. An outing. "Hugh Herbert and W. C. Fields will now indian wrestle for ownership of this here country!" (Agreed.) The leader loses . . . but is still the leader because he said some words no one had heard of before. (That was after the loss.)

Yng Rick has fucked someone else. Let's listen. "Oh, man, you cats don't know what's happenin'." (You're too much, Rick. Much too much. Like Larry Darnell in them ol' italian schools. Much too much.) "Babes" he called them (a poor project across from the convents: Baxter Terrace. Home of the enemy. We stood them off. We Cavaliers. And then, even tho Johnny Boy was his hero. Another midget placed on the purple. Early leader, like myself. The fight of gigantic proportions to settle all those ancient property disputes would have been between us. Both weighing close to 125. But I avoided that like the plague, and managed three times to drive past him with good hooks without incident. Whew, I said to Love. Whew. And Rick, had gone away from them, to school. Like myself. And now, strangely, for the Gods are white our teachers said, he found himself with me. And all the gold and diamonds of the crown I wore he hated. Though, the new wine settled, and his social graces kept him far enough away to ease the hurt of serving a hated master. Hence "babes," and the constant reference to his wiggling flesh. Listen.

"Yeh. Me and Chris had these D.C. babes at their cribs." (Does a dance step with the suggestive flair.) "Oooooo, that was some good box."

Tom knew immediately where that bit was at. And he pulled Rick into virtual madness . . . lies at least. "Yeh, Rick. Yeh? You mean you got a little Jones, huh? Was it good?" (Tom pulls on Rick's sleeve like Laurel and Rick swings.)

"Man, Tom, you don't have to believe it, baby. It's in here now!" (points to his stomach).

The leader stirs. "Hmm, that's a funny way to fuck." Rick will give a boxing demonstration in a second.

Dick Smith smiles. "Wow, Rick, you're way," extending his hand, palm upward. "And what not," Dick adds, for us to laugh. "O.K., you're bad." (At R's crooked jab.) "Huh, this cat always wants to bust somebody up, and what not. Hey, baby, you must be frustrated or something. How come you don't use up all that energy on your babes . . . and what not?"

The rest there, floating empty nouns. Under the sheets. The same death as the crippled fag. Lost with no defense. Except they sit now, for this portrait . . . in which they will be portrayed as losers. Only the leader wins. Tell him that.

Some guys playing cards. Some talking about culture, i.e., the leader had a new side. (Modesty denies.) They sit around, in real light. The leader in his green glasses, fidgeting with his joint. Carl, in a brown fedora, trims his toes and nails. Spars with Rick. Smells his foot and smiles. Brady reads, in his silence, a crumpled black dispatch. Shorter's liver smells the hall and Leon slams the door, waiting for the single chop, the leader might have to share. The door opens, two farmers come in, sharp in orange suits. The hippies laugh, and hide their youthful lies. "Man, I was always hip. I mean, I knew about Brooks Brothers when I was 10." (So sad we never know the truth. About that world, until the bones dry in our heads. Young blond governors with their "dads" hip at the age of 2. That way. Which, now, I sit in judgment of. What I wanted those days with the covers of books turned toward the audience. The first nighters. Or dragging my two forwards to the Music Box to see Elliot Nugent. They would say, these dead men, laughing at us, "The natives are restless," stroking their gouty feet. Gimme culture, culture, culture, and *Romeo and Juliet* over the emerson.

How many there now? Make it 9. Phil's cracking the books. Jimmy Jones and Pud, two D.C. boys, famous and funny, study "zo" at the top of their voices. "Hemiptera," says Pud. "Homoptera," says Jimmy. "Weak as a bitch," says Phil. "Both your knowledges are flait."

More than 9. Mazique, Enty, operating now in silence. Right hands flashing down the cards. "Uhh!" In love with someone, and money from home. Both perfect, with curly hair. "Uhh! Shit, Enty, hearts is trumps."

"What? Ohh, shit!"

"Uhh!," their beautiful hands flashing under the single bulb.

Hambrick comes with liquor. (A box of fifths, purchased with the fantastic wealth of his father's six shrimp shops.) "You cats caint have all this goddam booze. Brown and I got dates, that's why, and we need some for the babes."

Brown has hot dogs for five. Franks, he says. "Damn, Cholley, you only get a half of frank . . . and you take the whole motherfucking thing."

"Aww, man, I'll pay you back." And the room, each inch, is packed with lives. Make it 12 . . . all heroes, or dead. Indian chiefs, the ones not waging their wars, like Clark, in the legal mist of Baltimore. A judge. Old Clark. You remember when we got drunk together and you fell down the stairs. Or that time you fell in the punch bowl, puking, and let that sweet yellow ass get away? Boy, I'll never forget that, as long as I live. (Having died seconds later, he talks thru his rot.) Yeh, boy, you were always a card. (White man talk. A card. Who the hell says that, except that branch office with no culture.) Piles of bullion, and casual violence. To the mind. Nights they kick you against the buildings. Communist homosexual nigger. "Aw man, I'm married and got two kids."

What could be happening? Some uproar. "FUCK YOU, YOU FUNNY-LOOKING SUNAFABITCH."

"Me? Funny-looking? Oh, wow. Will you listen to this little pointy head bastard calling *me* funny-looking. Hey, Everett. Hey Everett! Who's the funniest looking . . . me or Keyes?"

"Aww, both you cats need some work. Man, I'm trying to read."

"Read? What? You gettin' into them books, huh? Barnes is whippin' your ass, huh? I told you not to take Organic . . . as light as you are."

"Shit. I'm not even thinking about Barnes. Barnes can kiss my ass."

"Shit. You better start thinking about him, or you'll punch right out. They don't need lightweights down in the valley. Ask Ugly Wilson."

"Look, Tom, I wasn't bothering you."

"Bothering me? Wha's the matter with you, ol' Jimmy. Commere, boy, lemme rub your head."

"Man, you better get the hell outa here."

"What? . . . Why? What you gonna do? You can't fight, you little funny-looking buzzard."

"Hey, Tom, why you always bothering ol' Jimmy Wilson. He's a good man."

"Oh, oh, here's that little light-ass Dan sticking up for Ugly again. Why you like him, huh? Cause he's the only cat uglier than you? Huh?"

"Tom's the worst-looking cat on campus calling me ugly."

"Well, you are. Wait, lemme bring you this mirror so you can see yourself. Now, what you think. You can't think anything else."

"Aww, man, blow, will you?"

The pork chop is cooked and little Charlie is trying to cut a piece off before the leader can stop him. "Ow, goddam."

"Well, who told you to try to steal it, jive ass."

"Hey, man, I gotta get somea that chop."

"Gimme some, Ray."

"Why don't you cats go buy something to eat. I didn't ask anybody for any of those hot dogs. So get away from my grease. Hungry-ass spooks."

"Wait a minute, fella. I know you don't mean Young Rick."

"Go ask one of those D.C. babes for something to eat. I know they must have something you could sink your teeth into."

Pud and Jimmy Jones are wrestling under Phil's desk.

A.B. is playin' the dozen with Leon and Teddy. "Teddy, are your momma's legs as crooked as yours?"

"This cat always wants to talk about people's mothers! Country bastard."

Tom is pinching Jimmy Wilson. Dan is laughing at them.

Enty and Mazique are playing bridge with the farmers. "Uhh! Beat that, jew boy!"

"What the fuck is trumps?"

The leader is defending his pork chop from Cholley, Rick, Brady, Brown, Hambrick, Carl, Dick Smith, (S from the City has gone out catting.)

"Who is it?"

A muffled voice, under the uproar. "It's Mister Bush."

"Bush? Hey, Ray . . . Ray."

"Who is it?"

Plainer. "Mister Bush." (Each syllable pronounced and correct as a soft southern american can.) Innocent VIII in his bedroom shoes. Gregory at Canossa, raging softly in his dignity and power. "Mister Bush."

"Ohh, shit. Get that liquor somewhere. O.K., Mr. Bush, just a second. . . . Not there, asshole, in the drawer."

"Mr. McGhee, will you kindly open the door."

"Ohh, shit, the hot plate. I got it." The leader turns a wastepaper basket upside-down on top of the chop. Swings open the door. "Oh, Hello, Mister Bush. How are you this evening?" About 15 boots sit smiling toward the door. Come in, Boniface. What news of Luther? In unison, now.

"Hi. . . . Hello. . . . How are you, Mister Bush?"

"Uh, huh." He stares around the room, grinding his eyes into their various hearts. An unhealthy atmosphere, this America. "Mr. McGhee, why is it if there's noise in this dormitory it always comes from this room?" Aww, he knows. He wrote me years later in the air force that he knew, even then.

"What are you running here, a boys' club?" (That's it.) He could narrow his eyes even in that affluence. Put his hands on his hips. Shove that stomach at you as proof he was an authority of the social grace . . . a western man, no matter the color of his skin. How To? He was saying, this is not the way. Don't act like that word. Don't fail us. We've waited for all you handsome boys too long. Erect a new world, of lies and stocking caps. Silence, and a reluctance of memory. Forget the slow grasses, and flame, flame in the valley. Feet bound, dumb eyes begging for darkness. The bodies moved with the secret movement of the air. Swinging. My beautiful grandmother kneels in the shadow weeping. Flame, flame in the valley. Where is it there is light? Where, this music rakes my talk?

"Why is it, Mr. McGhee, when there's some disturbance in this building, it always comes from here?" (Aww, you said that. . . .)

"And what are all you other gentlemen doing in here? Good night, there must be twenty of you here! Really, gentlemen, don't any of you have anything to do?" He made to smile, Ha, I know some of you who'd better be in your rooms right now hitting those books . . . or you might not be with us next semester. Ha.

"O.K., who is that under that sheet?" (It was Enty, a student dormitory director, hiding under the sheets, flat on the leader's bed.) "You, sir, whoever you are, come out of there, hiding won't do you any good. Come out!" (We watched the sheet, and it quivered. Innocent raised his finger.) "Come out, sir!" (The sheet pushed slowly back. Enty's head appeared. And Bush more embarrassed than he.) "Mr. Enty! My assistant dormitory director, good night. A man of responsibility. Go-od night! Are there any more hiding in here, Mr. McGhee?"

"Not that I know of."

"Alright, Mr. Enty, you come with me. And the rest of you had better go to your rooms and try to make some better grades. Mr. McGhee, I'll talk to you tomorrow morning in my office."

The leader smiles. "Yes." (Jive ass.)

Bush turns to go, Enty following sadly. "My God, what's that terrible odor . . . something burning." (The leader's chop, and the wastepaper, under the basket, starting to smoke.) "Mr. McGhee, what's that smell?"

"Uhhh" (come on, baby). "Oh, it's Strothers' kneepads on the radiator! (Yass) They're drying."

"Well, Jesus, I hope they dry soon. Whew! And don't forget, tomorrow morning, Mr. McGhee, and you other gentlemen had better retire, it's 2 in the morning!" The door slams. Charlie sits where Enty was. The bottles come out. The basket is turned right side up. Chop and most of the papers smoking. The leader pours water onto the mess and sinks to his bed.

"Damn. Now I have to go hungry. Shit."

"That was pretty slick, Ugly, the kneepads! Why don't you eat them, they look pretty done."

The talk is to that. That elegance of performance. The rite of lust, or self-extinction. Preservation. Some leave, and a softer uproar descends. Jimmy Jones and Pud wrestle quietly on the bed. Phil quotes the *Post*'s sport section on Willie Mays. Hambrick and Brown go for franks. Charlie scrapes the "burn" off the chop and eats it alone. Tom, Dan, Ted, and the leader drink and manufacture lives for each person they know. We know. Even you. Tom, the lawyer. Dan, the lawyer. Ted, the high-school teacher. All their proper ways. And the leader, without cause or place. Except talk, feeling, guilt. Again, only those areas of the world make sense. Talk. We are doing that now. Feeling: that too. Guilt. That inch of wisdom, forever. Except he sits reading in green glasses. As, "No, no, the utmost share/Of my desire shall be/Only to kiss that air/That lately kissèd thee."

"Uhh! What's trumps, dammit!"

As, "Tell me not, Sweet, I am unkind,/That from the nunnery/Of thy chaste breast and quiet mind/To war and arms I fly."

"You talking about a lightweight mammy-tapper, boy, you really king."

Oh, Lucasta, find me here on the bed, with hard pecker and dirty feet. Oh, I suffer, in my green glasses, under the canopy of my loves. Oh, I am drunk and vomity in my room, with only Charlie Ventura to understand my grace. As, "Hardly are those words out when a vast image out of *Spiritus Mundi*/Troubles my sight: somewhere in sands of the desert/A shape with lion body and the head of a man/A gaze blank and pitiless as the sun,/Is moving its slow thighs, while all about it/Reel shadows of the indignant desert birds."

Primers for dogs who are learning to read. Tinkle of European teacups. All longing, speed, suffering. All adventure, sadness, stink, and wisdom. All feeling, silence, light. As, "Crush, O sea, the cities with their catacomb-like corridors/ And crush eternally the vile people,/The idiots, and the abstemious, and mow down, mow down/With a single stroke the bent backs of the shrunken harvest!"

"Damn, Charlie, We brought back a frank for everybody . . . now you want two. Wrong sunafabitch!"

"Verde que te quiero verde./Verde viento. Verdes ramas./El barco sobre la mar/y el caballo en la montaña."

"Hey, man, I saw that ol' fagit Bobby Hutchens down in the lobby with a real D.C. queer. I mean a real way-type sissy."

"Huh, man, he's just another *actor* . . . hooo."

"That cat still wearing them funny-lookin' pants?"

"Yeh, and orange glasses. Plus, the cat always needs a haircut, and what not."

"Hey, man, you cats better cool it . . . you talkin' about Ray's main man. You dig?"

"Yeh. I see this cat easin' around corners with the cat all the time. I mean, talkin' some off-the-wall shit, too, baby."

"Yeh. Yeh. Why don't you cats go fuck yourselves or something hip like that, huh?"

"O.K., ugly Tom, you better quit inferring that shit about Ray. What you trying to say, ol' pointy head is funny or somthing?"

"Funny . . . how the sound of your voice . . . thri-ills me. Strange. . . . " (The last à la King Cole.)

"Fuck you cats and your funny-looking families too."

A wall. With light at the top, perhaps. No, there is light. Seen from both sides, a gesture of life. But always more than is given. An abstract infinitive. To love. To lie. To want. And that always . . . to want. Always, more than is given. The dead scramble up each side . . . words or drunkenness. Praise, to the flesh. Rousseau, Hobbes, and their betters. All move, from flesh to love. From love to flesh. At that point under the static light. It could be Shostakovich in Charleston, South Carolina. Or in the dull windows of Chicago, an unread volume of Joyce. Some black woman who will never hear the word *Negress* or remember your name. Or a thin preacher who thinks your name is Stephen. A wall. Oh, Lucasta.

"Man, you cats don't know anything about Hutchens. I don't see why you talk about the cat and don't know the first thing about him."

"Shit. If he ain't funny . . . Skippy's a punk."

"How come you don't say that to Skippy?"

"Our Own Boy, Skippy Weatherson. All-coon fullback for 12 years."

"You tell him that!"

"Man, don't try to change the subject. This cat's trying to keep us from talking about his boy Hutchens."

"Yeh, mammy-rammer. What's happenin', McGhee, ol' man?"

"Hooo. Yeh. They call this cat Dick Brown. Hoooo!"

Rick moves to the offensive. The leader in his book, or laughs. "Aww, man, that cat ain't my boy. I just don't think you cats ought to talk about people you don't know anything about! Plus, that cat probably gets more ass than any of you silly-ass motherfuckers."

"Hee. That Ray sure can pronounce that word. I mean he don't say mutha' like most folks . . . he always pronounces the mother *and* the fucker, so proper. And it sure makes it sound nasty." (A texas millionaire talking.)

"Hutchens teachin' the cat how to talk . . . that's what's happening. Ha. In exchange for services rendered!"

"Wait, Tom. Is it you saying that Hutchens and my man here are into some funny shit?"

"No, man. It's you saying that. It was me just inferring, you dig?"

"Hey, why don't you cats just get drunk in silence, huh?"

"Hey, Bricks, what was Hutchens doin' downstairs with that cat?"

"Well, they were just coming in the dormitory, I guess. Hutchens was signing in, that's all."

"Hey, you dig . . . I bet he's takin' that cat up to his crib."

"Yeh, I wonder what they into by now. Huh! Probably suckin' the shit out of each other."

"Aww, man, cool it, willya. . . . Damn!"

"What's the matter, Ray, you don't dig love?"

"Hey, it's young Rick saying that we oughta go up and dig what's happenin' up there?"

"Square motherfucker!"

"*Votre mère!*"

"*Votre mère noir!*"

"Boy, these cats in French One think they hip!"

"Yeh, let's go up and see what those cats are doing."

"Tecch, aww, shit. Damn, you some square cats, wow! Cats got nothing better to do than fuck with people. Damn!"

Wall. Even to move, impossible. I sit, now, forever where I am. No further. No farther. Father, who am I to hide myself? And brew a world of soft lies.

Again. "Verde que te quiero verde." Green. Read it again, Il Duce. Make it build some light here . . . where there is only darkness. Tell them "Verde, que te quiero verde." I want you Green. Leader, the paratroopers will come for you at noon. A helicopter low over the monastery. To get you out.

But my country. My people. These dead souls, I call my people. Flesh of my flesh.

At noon, Il Duce. Make them all et ceteras. Extras. The soft strings behind the final horns.

"Hey, Ray, you comin' with us?"

"Fuck you cats. I got other things to do."

"Damn, now the cat's trying to pretend he can read Spanish."

"Yeh . . . well, let's go see what's happening, cats."

"Cats. Cats. Cats. . . . What's happenin'?"

"Hey, Smitty! We going upstairs to peep that ol' sissy Hutchens. He's got some big-time D.C. faggot in there with him. You know, we figured it'd be better than 3-D."

"Yeh? That's pretty hip. You not coming, Ray?"

"No, man . . . I'm sure you cats can peep in a keyhole without me."

"Bobby's his main man, that's all."

"Yeh, mine and your daddy's."

Noise. Shouts, and Rick begs them to be softer. For the circus. Up the creaking stairs, except Carl and Leon, who go to the freshman dorm to play Ping-Pong . . . and Ted who is behind in his math.

The 3rd floor of Park Hall, an old 19th-century philanthropy, gone to seed. The missionaries' words dead & hung useless in the air. "Be clean, thrifty, and responsible. Show the anti-Christs you're ready for freedom and God's true word." Peasants among the mulattoes, and the postman's son squats in his glasses shivering at his crimes.

"Hey, which room is his?"

"Three Oh Five."

"Hey, Tom, how you know the cat's room so good? This cat must be sneaking too."

"Huhh, yeh!"

"O.K., Rick, just keep walking."

"Here it is."

"Be cool, bastard. Shut up." They stood and grinned. And punched each other. Two bulbs in the hall. A window at each end. One facing the reservoir, the other, the fine-arts building where Professor Gorsun sits angry at jazz. "Goddamn it none of that nigger music in my new building. Culture. Goddamn it, ladies and gentlemen, line up and be baptized. This pose will take the hurt away. We are white and featureless under this roof. Praise God, from whom all blessings flow!"

"Bobby. Bobby, baby."

"Huh?"

"Don't go blank on me like that, baby. I was saying something."

"Oh, I'm sorry . . . I guess I'm just tired or something."

"I was saying, how can you live in a place like this? I mean, really, baby, this place is nowhere. Whew. It's like a jail or something eviler."

"Yes, I know."

"Well, why don't you leave it then. You're much too sensitive for a place like this. I don't see why you stay in this damn school. You know, you're really talented."

"Yeh, well, I figured I have to get a degree, you know. Teach or something, I suppose. There's not really much work around for spliv actors."

"Oh, Bobby, you ought to stop being so conscious of being colored. It really is not fashionable. Ummm. You know you have beautiful eyes."

"You want another drink, Lyle?"

"Ugg. Oh, that cheap bourbon. You know I have some beautiful wines at home. You should try drinking some good stuff for a change. Damn, Bob, why don't you just leave this dump and move into my place? There's certainly enough room. And we certainly get along. Ummm. Such beautiful eyes and hair too."

"Hah. How much rent would I have to pay out there. I don't have penny the first!"

"Rent? No, no . . . you don't have to worry about that. I'll take care of all that. I've got one of those gooood jobs, honey. U.S. guvment."

"Oh? Where do you work?"

"The P.O. with the rest of the fellas. But it's enough for what I want to do. And you wouldn't be an expense. Hmmp. Or would you? You know you have the kind of strong masculine hands I love. Like you could crush anything you wanted. Lucky I'm on your good side. Hmmp."

"Well, maybe at the end of this semester I could leave. If the offer still holds then."

"Still holds? Well, why not? We'll still be friends then, I'm certain. Ummm. Say, why don't we shut off that light. Umm. Let me do it. There. . . . You know I loved you in Jimmy's play, but the rest of those people are really just kids. You were the only person who really understood what was going on. You have a strong maturity that comes through right away. How old are you, Bobby?"

"Nineteen."

"Oh, baby . . . that's why your skin is so soft. Yes. Say, why wait until the end of the semester . . . that's two months away. I might be dead before that, you know. Umm."

The wind moves thru the leader's room, and he sits alone, under the drooping velvet, repeating words he does not understand. The yellow light burns. He turns it off. Smokes. Masturbates. Turns it on. Verde, verde. Te quiero. Smokes. And then to his other source. "Yma's brother," Tom said when he saw it. "Yma Sumac, Albert Camus. Man, nobody wants to go by their right names no more. And a cat told me that chick ain't really from Peru. She was born in Brooklyn, man, and her name's Camus too. Amy Camus. This cat's name is probably Trebla Sumac, and he ain't French he's from Brooklyn too. Yeh. Ha!"

In the dark the words are anything. "If it is true that the only paradise is that which one has lost, I know what name to give that something tender and inhuman which dwells within me today."

"Oh, shit, fuck it. Fuck it." He slams the book against the wall, and empties

Hambrick's bottle. "I mean, why?" Empties bottle. "Shiiit."

When he swings the door open the hall above is screams. Screams. All their voices, even now right here. The yellow glasses falling on the stairs, and broken. In his bare feet. "Shiit. Dumb-ass cats!"

"Rick, Rick, what's the cat doing now?"

"Man, be cool. Ha, the cat's kissin' Hutchens on the face, man. Um-uh-mm. Yeh, baby. Damn, he's puttin' his hands all over the cat. Aww, rotten motherfuckers!"

"What's happening?"

"Bastards shut out the lights!"

"Damn."

"Gaw-uhd damn!"

"Hey, let's break open the door."

"Yeh, HEY, YOU CATS, WHAT'S HAPPENING IN THERE, HUH?"

"Yeh. Hee, hee. OPEN UP, FAGGOTS!"

"Wheee! HEY, LET US IN, GIRLS!"

Ricky and Jimmy run against the door, the others screaming and jumping, doors opening all along the hall. They all come out, screaming as well. "LET US IN. HEY, WHAT'S HAPPENIN', BABY!" Rick and Jimmy run against the door, and the door is breaking.

"Who is it? What do you want?" Bobby turns the light on, and his friend, a balding queer of 40, is hugged against the sink.

"Who are they, Bobby? What do they want?"

"Bastards. Damn if I know. GET OUTA HERE, AND MIND YOUR OWN DAMN BUSINESS, YOU CREEPS. Creeps. Damn. Put on your clothes, Lyle!"

"God, they're trying to break the door down, Bobby. What do they want? Why are they screaming like that?"

"GET THE HELL AWAY FROM THIS DOOR, GODDAMN IT!"

"YEH, YEH. WE SAW WHAT YOU WAS DOIN', HUTCHENS. OPEN THE DOOR AND LET US GET IN ON IT."

"WHEEEEEE! HIT THE FUCKING DOOR, RICK! HIT IT!"

And at the top of the stairs the leader stops, the whole hall full of citizens. Doctors, judges, first negro directors of welfare chain, morticians, chemists, ad men, fighters for civil rights, all admirable, useful men. "BREAK THE FUCKIN' DOOR OPEN, RICK! YEH!"

A wall. Against it, from where you stand, the sea stretches smooth for miles out. Their voices distant thuds of meat against the sand. Murmurs of insects. Hideous singers against your pillow every night of your life. They are there now, screaming at you.

"Ray, Ray, come on, man, help us break this faggot's door!"

"Yeh, Ray, come on!"

"Man, you cats are fools. Evil stupid fools!"

"What? Man, will you listen to this cat."

"Listen, hell, let's get this door. One more smash and it's in. Come on, Brady, let's break the fuckin' thing."

"Yeh, come on, you cats, don't stand there listenin' to that pointy-head clown, he just don't want us to pop his ol' lady!"

"YEH, YEH. LET'S GET IN THERE. HIT IT HIT IT!"

"Goddamn it. Goddamn it, get the fuck out of here. Get outa here. Damn it, Rick, you sunafabitch, get the hell outa here. Leave the cat alone!"

"Man, don't push me like that, you lil' skinny ass. I'll bust your jaw for you."

"Yeh? Yeh? Yeh? Well, you come on, you lyin' ass. This cat's always talking about all his 'babes' and all he's got to do is sneak around peeping in keyholes. You big lying asshole . . . all you know how to do is bullshit and jerk off!"

"Fuck you, Ray."

"Your ugly-ass mama."

"Shiit. You wanna go round with me, baby?"

"Come on. Come on, big time cocksman, come on!"

Rick hits the leader full in the face, and he falls backwards across the hall. The crowd follows screaming at this new feature.

"Aww, man, somebody stop this shit. Rick'll kill Ray!"

"Well, you stop it, man."

"O.K., O.K., cut it out. Cut it out, Rick. You win, man. Leave the cat alone. Leave him alone."

"Bad Rick . . . Bad Rick, Bad-ass Rick!"

"Well, man, you saw the cat fuckin' with me. He started the shit!"

"Yeh . . . tough cat!"

"Get up, Ray."

And then the door does open and Bobby Hutchens stands in the half-light in his shower shoes, a broom in his hands. The boys scream and turn their attention back to Love. Bald Lyle is in the closet. More noise. More lies. More prints in the sand, away, or toward some name. I am a poet. I am a rich famous butcher. I am the man who paints the gold balls on the tops of flagpoles. I am, no matter, more beautiful than anyone else. And I have come a long way to say this. Here. In the long hall, shadows across my hands. My face pushed hard against the floor. And the wood, old and protestant. And their voices, all these other selves screaming for blood. For blood, or whatever it is fills their noble lives.

To Da-Duh, in Memoriam

Paule Marshall

1967

"Oh Nana! all of you is not involved in this evil business Death,
Nor all of us in life."

—Lebert Bethune, *"At My Grandmother's Grave"*

I did not see her at first, I remember. For not only was it dark inside the crowded disembarkation shed in spite of the daylight flooding in from outside, but standing there waiting for her with my mother and sister I was still somewhat blinded from the sheen of tropical sunlight on the water of the bay which we had just crossed in the landing boat, leaving behind us the ship that had brought us from New York lying in the offing. Besides, being only nine years of age at the time and knowing nothing of islands I was busy attending to the alien sights and sounds of Barbados, the unfamiliar smells.

I did not see her, but I was alerted to her approach by my mother's hand, which suddenly tightened around mine, and looking up I traced her gaze through the gloom in the shed until I finally made out the small, purposeful, painfully erect figure of the old woman headed our way.

Her face was drowned in the shadow of an ugly rolled-brim brown felt hat, but the details of her slight body and of the struggle taking place within it were clear enough—an intense, unrelenting struggle between her back which was beginning to bend ever so slightly under the weight of her eighty-odd years and the rest of her which sought to deny those years and hold that back straight, keep it in line. Moving swiftly toward us (so swiftly it seemed she did not intend stopping when she reached us but would sweep past us out the doorway which opened onto the sea and like Christ walk upon the water!), she was caught between the sunlight at her end of the building and the darkness inside—and for a moment she appeared to contain them both: the light in the long severe old-fashioned white dress she wore which brought the sense of a past that was still alive into our bustling present and in the snatch of white at her eye; the darkness in her black high-top shoes and in her face which was visible now that she was closer.

It was as stark and fleshless as a death mask, that face. The maggots might have already done their work, leaving only the framework of bone beneath the ruined skin and deep wells at the temple and jaw. But her eyes were alive, unnervingly so for one so old, with a sharp light that flicked out of the dim clouded depths like a lizard's tongue to snap up all in her view. Those eyes betrayed a child's curiosity about the world, and I wondered vaguely seeing them, and seeing the way the bodice of her ancient dress had collapsed in on her flat chest (what had happened to her breasts?), whether she might not be some kind of child at the same time that she was a woman, with fourteen children, my mother included, to prove it. Perhaps she was both, both child and woman, darkness and light, past and present, life and death—all the opposites contained and reconciled in her.

"My Da-duh," my mother said formally and stepped forward. The name sounded like thunder fading softly in the distance.

"Child," Da-duh said, and her tone, her quick scrutiny of my mother, the brief embrace in which they appeared to shy from each other rather than touch, wiped out the fifteen years my mother had been away and restored the old relationship. My mother, who was such a formidable figure in my eyes, had suddenly with a word been reduced to my status.

"Yes, God is good," Da-duh said with a nod that was like a tic. "He has spared me to see my child again."

We were led forward then, apologetically, because not only did Da-duh prefer boys but she also liked her grandchildren to be "white," that is, fair-skinned; and we had, I was to discover, a number of cousins, the outside children of white estate managers and the like, who qualified. We, though, were as black as she.

My sister, being the older, was presented first. "This one takes after the father," my mother said and waited to be reproved.

Frowning, Da-duh tilted my sister's face toward the light. But her frown soon gave way to a grudging smile, for my sister with her large mild eyes and little broad winged nose, with our father's high-cheeked Barbadian cast to her face, was pretty.

"She's goin' be lucky," Da-duh said and patted her once on the cheek. "Any girl child that takes after the father does be lucky."

She turned then to me. But oddly enough she did not touch me. Instead, leaning close, she peered hard at me, and then quickly drew back. I thought I saw her hand start up as though to shield her eyes. It was almost as if she saw not only me, a thin truculent child who it was said took after no one but myself, but something in me which for some reason she found disturbing, even threatening. We looked silently at each other for a long time there in the noisy shed, our gaze locked. She was the first to look away.

"But Adry," she said to my mother and her laugh was cracked, thin, apprehensive. "Where did you get this one here with this fierce look?"

"We don't know where she came out of, my Da-duh," my mother said, laughing also. Even I smiled to myself. After all, I had won the encounter. Da-duh had recognized my small strength—and this was all I ever asked of the adults in my life then.

"Come, soul," Da-duh said and took my hand. "You must be one of those New York terrors you hear so much about."

She led us, me at her side and my sister and mother behind, out of the shed into the sunlight that was like a bright driving summer rain and over to a group of people clustered beside a decrepit lorry. They were our relatives, most of them from St. Andrews although Da-duh herself lived in St. Thomas, the women wearing bright print dresses, the colors vivid against their darkness, the men rusty black suits that encased them like straitjackets. Da-duh, holding fast to my hand, became my anchor as they circled round us like a nervous sea, exclaiming, touching us with their calloused hands, embracing us shyly. They laughed in awed bursts: "But look Adry got big-big children!"/"And see the nice things they wearing, wristwatch and all!"/"I tell you, Adry has done all right for sheself in New York. . . ."

Da-duh, ashamed at their wonder, embarrassed for them, admonished them the while. "But oh, Christ," she said, "why you all got to get on like you never saw people from 'Away' before? You would think New York is the only place in the world to hear wunna. That's why I don't like to go anyplace with you St. Andrews people, you know. You all ain't been colonized."

We were in the back of the lorry finally, packed in among the barrels of ham, flour, cornmeal, and rice and the trunks of clothes that my mother had brought as gifts. We made our way slowly through Bridgetown's clogged streets, part of a funereal procession of cars and open-sided buses, bicycles, and donkey carts. The dim little limestone shops and offices along the way marched with us, at the same mournful pace, toward the same grave ceremony—as did the people, the women balancing huge baskets on top their heads as if they were no more than hats they wore to shade them from the sun. Looking over the edge of the lorry I watched as their feet slurred the dust. I listened, and their voices, raw and loud and dissonant in the heat, seemed to be grappling with each other high overhead.

Da-duh sat on a trunk in our midst, a monarch amid her court. She still held my hand, but it was different now. I had suddenly become her anchor, for

I felt her fear of the lorry with its asthmatic motor (a fear and distrust, I later learned, she held of all machines) beating like a pulse in her rough palm.

As soon as we left Bridgetown behind, though, she relaxed, and while the others around us talked she gazed at the canes standing tall on either side of the winding marl road. "C'dear," she said softly to herself after a time. "The canes this side are pretty enough."

They were too much for me. I thought of them as giant weeds that had overrun the island, leaving scarcely any room for the small tottering houses of sun-bleached pine we passed or the people, dark streaks as our lorry hurtled by. I suddenly feared that we were journeying, unaware that we were, toward some dangerous place where the canes, grown as high and thick as a forest, would close in on us and run us through with their stiletto blades. I longed then for the familiar: for the street in Brooklyn where I lived, for my father who had refused to accompany us ("Blowing out good money on foolishness," he had said of the trip), for a game of tag with my friends under the chestnut tree outside our aging brownstone house.

"Yes, but wait till you see St. Thomas canes," Da-duh was saying to me. "They's canes father, bo." She gave a proud arrogant nod. "Tomorrow, God willing, I goin' take you out in the ground and show them to you."

True to her word Da-duh took me with her the following day out into the ground. It was a fairly large plot adjoining her weathered board and shingle house and consisting of a small orchard, a good-sized canepiece, and behind the canes, where the land sloped abruptly down, a gully. She had purchased it with Panama money sent her by her eldest son, my uncle Joseph, who had died working on the canal. We entered the ground along a trail no wider than her body and as devious and complex as her reasons for showing me her land. Da-duh strode briskly ahead, her slight form filled out this morning by the layers of sacking petticoats she wore under her working dress to protect her against the damp. A fresh white cloth, elaborately arranged around her head, added to her height and lent her a vain, almost roguish air.

Her pace slowed once we reached the orchard, and glancing back at me occasionally over her shoulder, she pointed out the various trees.

"This here is a breadfruit," she said. "That one yonder is a papaw. Here's a guava. This is a mango. I know you don't have anything like these in New York. Here's a sugar apple." (The fruit looked more like artichokes than apples to me.) "This one bears limes. . . ." She went on for some time, intoning the names of the trees as though they were those of her gods. Finally, turning to me, she said, "I know you don't have anything this nice where you come from." Then, as I hesitated: "I said I know you don't have anything this nice where you come from. . . ."

"No," I said and my world did seem suddenly lacking.

Da-duh nodded and passed on. The orchard ended and we were on the narrow cart road that led through the canepiece, the canes clashing like swords above my cowering head. Again she turned and, her thin muscular arms spread wide, her dim gaze embracing the small field of canes, she said—and her voice almost broke under the weight of her pride, "Tell me, have you got anything like these in that place where you were born?"

"No."

"I din' think so. I bet you don't even know that these canes here and the sugar you eat is one and the same thing. That they does throw the canes into some damn machine at the factory and squeeze out all the little life in them to make sugar for you all so in New York to eat. I bet you don't know that."

"I've got two cavities and I'm not allowed to eat a lot of sugar."

But Da-duh didn't hear me. She had turned with an inexplicably angry motion and was making her way rapidly out of the canes and down the slope at the edge of the field which led to the gully below. Following her apprehensively down the incline amid a stand of banana plants whose leaves flapped like elephant's ears in the wind, I found myself in the middle of a small tropical wood—a place dense and damp and gloomy and tremulous with the fitful play of light and shadow as the leaves high above moved against the sun that was almost hidden from view. It was a violent place, the tangled foliage fighting each other for a chance at the sunlight, the branches of the trees locked in what seemed an immemorial struggle, one both necessary and inevitable. But despite the violence, it was pleasant, almost peaceful in the gully, and beneath the thick undergrowth the earth smelled like spring.

This time Da-duh didn't even bother to ask her usual question, but simply turned and waited for me to speak.

"No," I said, my head bowed. "We don't have anything like this in New York."

"Ah," she cried, her triumph complete. "I din' think so. Why, I've heard that's a place where you can walk till you near drop and never see a tree."

"We've got a chestnut tree in front of our house," I said.

"Does it bear?" She waited. "I ask you, does it bear?"

"Not anymore," I muttered. "It used to, but not anymore."

She gave the nod that was like a nervous twitch. "You see," she said. "Nothing can bear there." Then, secure behind her scorn, she added, "But tell me, what's this snow like that you hear so much about?"

Looking up, I studied her closely, sensing my chance, and then I told her, describing at length and with as much drama as I could summon not only what snow in the city was like, but what it would be like here, in her perennial summer kingdom.

". . . And you see all these trees you got here," I said. "Well, they'd be bare. No leaves, no fruit, nothing. They'd be covered in snow. You see your canes. They'd be buried under tons of snow. The snow would be higher than your head, higher than your house, and you wouldn't be able to come down into this here gully because it would be snowed under. . . ."

She searched my face for the lie, still scornful but intrigued. "What a thing, huh?" she said finally, whispering it softly to herself.

"And when it snows you couldn't dress like you are now," I said. "Oh, no, you'd freeze to death. You'd have to wear a hat and gloves and galoshes and ear muffs so your ears wouldn't freeze and drop off, and a heavy coat. I've got a Shirley Temple coat with fur on the collar. I can dance. You wanna see?"

Before she could answer I began, with a dance called the Truck which was popular back then in the 1930s. My right forefinger waving, I trucked around the nearby trees and around Da-duh's awed and rigid form. After the Truck I did the Suzy-Q, my lean hips swishing, my sneakers sidling zigzag over the ground. "I can sing," I said and did so, starting with "I'm Gonna Sit Right Down and Write Myself a Letter," then, without pausing, "Tea For Two," and ending with "I Found a Million Dollar Baby in a Five and Ten Cent Store."

For long moments afterward Da-duh stared at me as if I were a creature from Mars, an emissary from some world she did not know but which intrigued her and whose power she both felt and feared. Yet something about my perform-ance must have pleased her, because bending down she slowly lifted her long skirt and then, one by one, the layers of petticoats until she came to a drawstring purse dangling at the end of a long strip of cloth tied round her waist. Opening the purse she handed me a penny. "Here," she said half smiling against her will. "Take this to buy yourself a sweet at the shop up the road. There's nothing to be done with you, soul."

From then on, whenever I wasn't taken to visit relatives, I accompanied Da-duh out into the ground, and alone with her amid the canes or down in the gully I told her about New York. It always began with some slighting remark on her part: "I know they don't have anything this nice where you come from," or "Tell me, I hear those foolish people in New York does do such and such. . . ." But as I answered, re-creating my towering world of steel and concrete and machines for her, building the city out of words, I would feel her give way. I came to know the signs of her surrender: the total stillness that would come over her little hard dry form, the probing gaze that like a surgeon's knife sought to cut through my skull to get at the images there, to see if I were lying; above all, her fear, a fear nameless and profound, the same one I had felt beating in the palm of her hand that day in the lorry.

Over the weeks I told her about refrigerators, radios, gas stoves, elevators, trolley cars, wringer washing machines, movies, airplanes, the cyclone at Coney Island, subways, toasters, electric lights: "At night, see, all you have to do is flip this little switch on the wall and all the lights in the house go on. Just like that. Like magic. It's like turning on the sun at night."

"But tell me," she said to me once with a faint mocking smile, "do the white people have all these things too or it's only the people looking like us?"

I laughed, "What d'ya mean," I said. "The white people have even better." Then: "I beat up a white girl in my class last term."

"Beating up white people!" Her tone was incredulous.

"How you mean!" I said, using an expression of hers. "She called me a name."

For some reason Da-duh could not quite get over this and repeated in the same hushed, shocked voice, "Beating up white people now! Oh, the Lord, the world's changing up so I can scarce recognize it anymore."

One morning toward the end of our stay, Da-duh led me into a part of the gully that we had never visited before, an area darker and more thickly overgrown than the rest, almost impenetrable. There in a small clearing amid the dense bush, she stopped before an incredibly tall royal palm which rose cleanly out of the ground and, drawing the eye up with it, soared high above the trees around it into the sky. It appeared to be touching the blue dome of sky, to be flaunting its dark crown of fronds right in the blinding white face of the late morning sun.

Da-duh watched me a long time before she spoke, and then she said very quietly, "All right, now, tell me if you've got anything this tall in that place you're from."

I almost wished, seeing her face, that I could have said no. "Yes," I said. "We've got buildings hundreds of times this tall in New York. There's one called the Empire State Building that's the tallest in the world. My class visited it last year and I went all the way to the top. It's got over a hundred floors. I can't describe how tall it is. Wait a minute. What's the name of that hill I went to visit the other day, where they have the police station?"

"You mean Bissex?"

"Yes, Bissex. Well, the Empire State Building is way taller than that."

"You're lying now!" she shouted, trembling with rage. Her hand lifted to strike me.

"No, I'm not," I said. "It really is; if you don't believe me I'll send you a picture postcard of it soon as I get back home so you can see for yourself. But it's way taller than Bissex."

All the fight went out of her at that. The hand poised to strike me fell limp to her side, and as she stared at me, seeing not me but the building that was taller than the highest hill she knew, the small stubborn light in her eyes (it was the same amber as the flame in the kerosene lamp she lit at dusk) began to fail. Finally, with a vague gesture that even in the midst of her defeat still tried to dismiss me and my world, she turned and started back through the gully, walking slowly, her steps groping and uncertain, as if she were suddenly no longer sure of the way, while I followed, triumphant yet strangely saddened, behind.

The next morning I found her dressed for our morning walk but stretched out on the Berbice chair in the tiny drawing room where she sometimes napped during the afternoon heat, her face turned to the window beside her. She appeared thinner and suddenly indescribably old.

"My Da-duh," I said.

"Yes, nuh," she said. Her voice was listless and the face she slowly turned my way was, now that I think back on it, like a Benin mask, the features drawn and almost distorted by an ancient abstract sorrow.

"Don't you feel well?" I asked.

"Girl, I don't know."

"My Da-duh, I goin' boil you some bush tea," my aunt, Da-duh's youngest child, who lived with her, called from the shed roof kitchen.

"Who tell you I need bush tea?" she cried, her voice assuming for a moment its old authority. "You can't even rest nowadays without some malicious person looking for you to be dead. Come, girl." She motioned me to a place beside her on the old-fashioned lounge chair. "Give us a tune."

I sang for her until breakfast at eleven, all my brash irreverent Tin Pan Alley songs, and then just before noon we went out into the ground. But it was a short, dispirited walk. Da-duh didn't even notice that the mangoes were beginning to ripen and would have to be picked before the village boys got to them. And when she paused occasionally and looked out across the canes or up at her trees, it wasn't as if she were seeing them but something else. Some huge, monolithic shape had imposed itself, it seemed, between her and the land, obstructing her vision. Returning to the house she slept the entire afternoon on the Berbice chair.

She remained like this until we left, languishing away the mornings on the chair at the window, gazing out at the land as if it were already doomed; then, at noon, taking the brief stroll with me through the ground during which she seldom spoke, and afterward returning home to sleep till almost dusk sometimes.

On the day of our departure she put on the austere, ankle-length white dress, the black shoes, and brown felt hat (her town clothes, she called them), but she did not go with us to town. She saw us off on the road outside her house and in the midst of my mother's tearful protracted farewell, she leaned down and whispered in my ear, "Girl, you're not to forget now to send me the picture of that building, you hear."

By the time I mailed her the large colored picture postcard of the Empire State Building she was dead. She died during the famous '37 strike which began shortly after we left. On the day of her death England sent planes flying low over the island in a show of force—so low, according to my aunt's letter, that the downdraft from them shook the ripened mangoes from the trees in Da-duh's orchard. Frightened, everyone in the village fled into the canes. Except Da-duh. She remained in the house at the window, so my aunt said, watching as the planes came swooping and screaming like monstrous birds down over the village, over her house, rattling her trees and flattening the young canes in her field. It must have seemed to her lying there that they did not intend pulling out of their dive, but like the hard-back beetles which hurled themselves with suicidal force against the walls of the house at night, those menacing silver shapes would hurl themselves in an ecstasy of self-immolation onto the land, destroying it utterly.

When the planes finally left and the villagers returned they found her dead on the Berbice chair at the window.

She died and I lived, but always, to this day even, within the shadow of her death. For a brief period after I was grown I went to live alone, like one doing penance, in a loft above a noisy factory in downtown New York and there painted seas of sugarcane and huge swirling Van Gogh suns and palm trees striding like brightly plumed Tutsi warriors across a tropical landscape, while the thunderous tread of the machines downstairs jarred the floor beneath my easel, mocking my efforts.

A New Day

Charles Wright

1967

"I'm caught. Between the devil and the deep blue sea." Lee Mosely laughed and made a V for victory sign and closed the front door against a potpourri of family voices, shouting good wishes and tokens of warning.

The late, sharp March air was refreshing and helped cool his nervous excitement, but his large hands were tight fists in his raincoat pockets. All morning he had been socking one fist into the other, running around the crowded, small living room like an impatient man waiting for a train, and had even screamed at his mother, who had recoiled as if he had sliced her heart with a knife. Andy, his brother-in-law, with his whine of advice: "Consider . . . Brother . . ."

Consider your five stair-step children. Consider the sweet brown babe switching down the subway steps ahead of me. What would she say? Lee wondered.

Of course, deep down in his heart, he wanted the job, wanted it desperately. The job seemed to hold so much promise, and really he was getting nowhere fast, not a goddamn place in the year and seven weeks that he had been shipping clerk at French-American Hats. But that job, too, in the beginning had held such promise. He remembered how everyone had been proud of him.

Lee Mosely was a twenty-five-year-old Negro whose greatest achievement had been the fact that he had graduated twenty-fourth in his high school class of one hundred and twenty-seven. This new job that he was applying for promised the world, at least as much of the world as he expected to get in one hustling lifetime. But he wouldn't wear his Ivy League suits and unloosen his tie at ten in the morning for coffee and doughnuts. He would have to wear a uniform and mouth a grave Yes mam and No mam. What was worse, his future boss was a Southern white woman, and he had never said one word to a Southern white woman in his life, had never expected to either.

"It's honest work, ain't it?" his mother had said. "Mrs. Davies ain't exactly a stranger. All our people down home worked for her people. They were might good to us and you should be proud to work for her. Why, you'll even be going overseas, and none of us ain't been overseas except Joe and that was during the big war. Lord knows, Mrs. Davies pays well."

Lee had seen her picture once in the *Daily News,* leaving the opera, furred and bejeweled, a waxen little woman with huge gleaming eyes, who faced the camera with pouting lips as if she were on the verge of spitting. He had laughed because it seemed strange to see a society woman posing as if she were on her way to jail.

Remembering, he laughed now and rushed up the subway steps at Columbus Circle.

Mrs. Maude T. Davies had taken a suite in a hotel on Central Park South for the spring, a spring that might well be two weeks or a year. Lee's Aunt Ella in South Carolina had arranged the job, a very easy job. Morning and afternoon drives around Central Park. The hotel's room service would supply the meals, and Lee would personally serve them. The salary was one hundred and fifty dollars a week, and it was understood that Lee could have the old custom-built Packard on days off.

"Lord," Lee moaned audibly and sprinted into the servants' entrance of the hotel.

Before ringing the doorbell, he carefully wiped his face with a handkerchief that his mother had ironed last night and inspected his fingernails, cleared his throat, and stole a quick glance around the silent, silk-walled corridor.

He rang the doorbell, whispered "Dammit," because the buzzing sound seemed as loud as the sea in his ears.

"Come in," a husky female voice shouted, and Lee's heart exploded in his ears. His armpits began to drip.

But he opened the door manfully and entered like a boy who was reluctant to accept a gift, his highly polished black shoes sinking into layers of apple-green carpet.

He raised his head slowly and saw Mrs. Davies sitting in a yellow satin wing chair, bundled in a mink coat and wearing white gloves. A flowered scarf was tied neatly around her small oval head.

"I'm Lee Mosely. Sarah's boy. I came to see about a job."

Mrs. Davies looked at him coldly and then turned toward the bedroom.

"Muffie," she called, and then sat up stiffly, clasping her gloved hands. "You go down to the garage and get the car. Muffie and I will meet you in the lobby."

"Yes mam," Lee said, executing a nod that he prayed would serve as a polite bow. He turned smartly like a soldier and started for the door.

Muffie, a Yorkshire terrier bowed in yellow satin, trotted from the bedroom and darted between Lee's legs. His bark was like an old man coughing. Lee moaned, "Lord," and noiselessly closed the door.

He parked the beige Packard ever so carefully and hopped out of the car as Mrs. Davies emerged from the hotel lobby.

Extending his arm, he assisted Mrs. Davies from the curb.

"Thank you," she said sweetly. "Now, I expect you to open and close the car door but I'm no invalid. Do you understand?"

"Yes mam. I'm sorry."

"Drive me through the park."

Muffie barked. Lee closed the door and then they drove off as the sun skirted from behind dark clouds.

There were many people in the park and it was like a spring day except for the chilled air.

"We haven't had any snow in a long time," Lee said, making conversation. "Guess spring's just around the corner."

"I know that," Mrs. Davies said curtly.

And that was the end of their conversation until they returned to the hotel, twenty minutes later.

"Put the car away," Mrs. Davies commanded. "Don't linger in the garage. The waiter will bring up lunch shortly and you must receive him."

Would the waiter ever come? Lee wondered, pacing the yellow- and white-tiled serving pantry. Should he or Mrs. Davies phone down to the restaurant? The silence and waiting was unbearable. Even Muffie seemed to be barking impatiently.

The servant entrance bell rang and Mrs. Davies screamed, "Lee!" and he opened the door quickly and smiled at the pale blue-veined waiter, who did not return the smile. He had eyes like a dead fish, Lee thought, rolling in the white covered tables. There was a hastily scrawled note which read: *Miss Davies food on top. Yours on bottom.*

Grinning, Lee took his tray from under the bottom shelf and was surprised to see two bottles of German beer. He set his tray on the pantry counter and took a quick peep at Mrs. Davies's tossed salad, one baby lamb chop. There was a split of champagne in a small ice bucket.

"Lord," he marveled, and rolled the white-covered table into the living room.

"Where are you eating, mam?" Lee asked, pleased because his voice sounded so professional.

"Where?" Mrs. Davies boomed. "In this room, boy!"

"But don't you have a special place?" Lee asked, relieved to see a faint smile on the thin lips.

"Over by the window. I like the view. It's almost as pretty as South

Carolina. Put the yellow wing over there too. I shall always dine by the window unless I decide otherwise. Understand?"

"Yes mam." Lee bowed and rolled the table in front of the floor-to-ceiling wall of windows. Then he rushed over and picked up the wing chair as if it were a loaf of bread.

He seated Mrs. Davies and asked gravely, "Will that be all, mam?"

"Of course!"

Exiting quickly, Lee remembered what his Uncle Joe had said about V-day. "Man. When they tell us the war is over, I just sat down in the foxhole and shook my head."

And Lee Mosely shook his head and entered the serving pantry, took a deep breath of relief which might well have been a prayer.

He pulled up a leather-covered fruitwood stool to the pantry counter and began eating his lunch of fried chicken, mashed potatoes, gravy, and tossed salad. He marveled at the silver domes covering the hot, tasty food, amused at his distorted reflection in the domes. He thanked God for the food and the good job. True, Mrs. Davies was sharp-tongued, a little funny, but she was nothing like the Southern women he had seen in the movies and on television and had read about in magazines and newspapers. She was not a part of Negro legends, of plots, deeds, and mockery. She was a wealthy woman named Mrs. Maude T. Davies.

Yeah, that's it, Lee mused in the quiet and luxury and warmth of the serving pantry.

He bit into a succulent chicken leg and took a long drink of the rich, clear-tasting German beer.

And then he belched. Mrs. Maude T. Davies screamed, "Nigger!"

I still have half a chicken leg left, Lee thought. He continued eating, chewing very slowly, but it was difficult to swallow. The chicken seemed to set on the valley of his tongue like glue.

So there was not only the pain of digesting but the quicksand sense of rage and frustration, and something else, a nameless something that had always started ruefully at the top of his skull like a windmill.

He knew he had heard *that* word, although the second lever of his mind kept insisting loudly that he was mistaken.

So he continued eating with difficulty his good lunch.

"Nigger boy!" Mrs. Davies repeated, a shrill command, strangely hot and tingling like the telephone wire of the imagination, the words entering through the paneled pantry door like a human being.

Lee Mosely sweated very hard summer and winter. Now he felt his blood congeal, freeze, although his anger, hot and dry, came bubbling to the surface. Saliva doubled in his mouth and his eyes smarted. The soggy chicken was still wedged on his tongue and he couldn't swallow it or spit it out. He had never cried since becoming a man and thought very little of men who cried. But for the love of God, what could he do to check his rage, helplessness?

"Nigger!" Mrs. Davies screamed again, and he knew that some evil white trick had come at last to castrate him. He had lived with this feeling for a long time, and it was only natural that his stomach and bowels grumbled as if in protest.

And then like the clammy fear that evaporates at the crack of day, Lee's trembling left hand picked up the bottle of beer and he brought it to his lips and drank. He sopped the bread in the cold gravy. He lit a cigarette and drank the other bottle of German beer.

A few minutes later, he got up and went into the living room.

Mrs. Davies was sitting very erect and elegant in the satin chair and had that snotty *Daily News* photograph expression, Lee thought bitterly.

"Mrs. Davies," he said politely, clearly, "did you call me?"

"Yes," Mrs. Maude T. Davies replied, like a jaded professional actress. Her smile was warm, pleased, amused. "Lee, you and I are going to get along very well together. I like people who think before they answer."

Night and the Loves of Joe Dicostanzo

Samuel R. Delany

1968

She was weeping, banally, in the moonlight.

He was annoyed, but contented himself with taking her luxuriant red hair (really rather mousy before the huge ivory disk balancing on the carbon-paper forest) and changing it to black. Then he coughed.

She turned from the balustrade. Tears rolled under her jaw. Two, like inexhaustible pearls, reappeared from the shadow on her neck. She *was* beautiful.

"Joey . . . ?" She whispered so softly he recognized his name only because that was what she must say.

He looked at his dirty knuckles against the top of the wall, then stepped forward, letting his fist roll. The open zipper on his sleeve jingled.

The breeze cast her hair forward from her shoulder, and her eyes (he would leave them green; green in the moonlight. Stunning) flicked down to perceive the change. "Oh, Joey. . . ."

He wondered if she appreciated it. No matter. He stuck his hands into his back pockets. The left one was torn.

"You're getting . . . tired of me, aren't you?"

"Jesus, Morgantha—" he said.

The breeze, for a moment, became a wind, and his chin and toes got cold. He curled his toes through the dust. He couldn't curl his chin, so he dropped it into the collar of his turtleneck.

She wore only the green gossamer, fastened at her shoulder with a cluster of gold scorpions. Her left breast, bare, taunted the moon.

He said, "Morgantha, you know you're a real—" and then just chewed on his back teeth and made fists inside his jeans.

"Joey—" She spoke with sudden eagerness, backing to the edge of the puddle so that her heels touched the heels of her reflection. "You know, I could be an awful lot of help to you. I really could, if you'd let me. I could tell you so much, about things you'd really like to know. Like why the clocks in the East Wing never read later than three. Or what's in the locked chamber that grumbles and thumps so. Joey, there's a little one-eyed boy coming to try and—"

"Oh, cut it out, Morgantha!" and felt his anger surge. He tried to stop. But it was too late because the emotion was what did it. There was no ritualized gesture, no motion of control.

Morgantha stepped backwards. Not a ripple: she fell straight down while her reflection shot straight up. For one moment reality and image were joined at the waist like a queen on some grotesque playing card. Then there was only the green gauze settling, darkening here and there.

Regret had grown to pain in his belly and along the back of his neck, even before the anger peeled away. He lunged forward, grabbed up the wet shift, as if he might somehow retract, retrieve, recall. . . .

Gold insects scurried from the dripping folds, splashed through the shallows to trail dark curves over the flags. He danced back from their scrabblings. A baker's dozen of them, at least!

As he pranced from the largest, he saw the smallest stop beside his other foot, curl its tail, and deliver its sting straight into his instep.

He howled and hopped.

Satisfied, the vengeful beasts scurried away, disappearing into the crevices of the masonry, climbing over the wall or merely flickering out in the shadow.

With a bellow he flung the wet cloth. It stuck on the wall, fold on fold opening down the rock. He turned and hobbled across the roof, the dust first softening under his wet feet, then gritty, then just cool and dry. And the *throb, throb, throb.*

When he got to the doorway, he dug out his crusty handkerchief, pawed through for a clean spot, took off his rimless glasses, and scrubbed at the lenses (*jingle, jingle, jingle:* the zipper fasteners on his leather jacket). When he slipped the wire hooks back under the hair clutching his ears, he realized he'd only managed to fog part of the glass so that the moon and the few lit windows in farther towers had all grown luminous penumbras. And his foot hurt.

He picked up his unicycle and kicked unenthusiastically at the starter. The third time, which hurt the most, the motor coughed its hot breath against his pants. He manhandled it around toward the dark portal, put one leg over the seat, folded his arms, swayed a bit for balance. Then he picked up his other foot, leaned forward, and caromed down the spiral steps. At each turn, as he racketed around the tower, a narrow window flung a handful of moonlight in his eyes.

Between, was all darkness and thunder.

* * *

Joey halted halfway along the East Wing's northwest corridor on the seventh floor.

The motor stopped roaring, purred instead. He got off and frowned at the line of depressed piling that ran back along the maroon carpeting into the lithic dark.

He dragged the unicycle over to lean it on the wall. "Hey!"

"Joey?"

"I'm coming in."

"I'll be there in a minute if you'll just—"

But Joey strode up the three steps in the narrow alcove, punched the wooden door with both fists; it flew in.

The grandfather clock in the niche in the floor-to-ceiling bookshelf said twenty to three.

"You know, you're a real pain," Maximillian said. "If I were only a fraction meaner than I am, I'd drop you back into whatever bad dream you came out of."

"Try it." Joey sat in the leather wing chair in front of the desk.

Maximillian pushed aside two mounds of books and regarded Joey through his black plastic frames. His fingers meshed into a big veined knot between olive corduroy. "What's the matter now? And get your feet off my desk."

Joey put his feet on the floor again. "I just got rid of Morgantha."

"Why don't you go somewhere else and complain about your love life?" Maximillian leaned back and put his own loafers up. Two volumes dropped. And his heel had tapped the crystal paperweight, which rolled forward and nearly—

Joey caught it.

"Thanks," Maximillian said.

Before he put it back, Joey looked into the flashings and crystal glister. Below the reflected points from the candles set about the room, there was a rippling as of water, beyond a darkness that could have been the edge of a bridge; also, something that might have been shrubbery, and in it: a face under lots of hair with a . . . black rag over one eye.

Joey's attention was broken by a rumbling downstairs that ended in a double thump. The flames in their luminous waxen collars shook.

Maximillian put his feet down. Both he and Joey looked at the floor.

A gold scorpion ran from beneath the desk, dodged about one of the fallen books that stood open on its spine, and disappeared behind a pedestal on which sat the stained bust of a nameless patriarch.

"Eh . . . what's this?" Joey asked, hefting the crystal.

"Oh." Maximillian's eyes came up. His brows lowered. "Usually it shows the view through the front gate over the bridge."

"That's what I thought it was." Suddenly Joey turned and hurled the crystal.

It *thwumped* the thick hanging, which expelled a wall of dust that broke apart: great gray dragons fragmented into medium-sized vultures that finally vanished as small bats. The crystal thudded to the two-foot mound of tapestry on the floor and *churrrrred* across the planks to the side of the desk.

Maximillian picked it up and leaned on his elbows to examine it. After a while he said, "You really are upset about this Morgantha business, huh?" He put down the crystal, took out his meerschaum, and tamped it in the baboon's-head humidor beside him. The yellow eyes glanced up, blinked twice, then crossed again to contemplate the flat, black, perpetually damp-looking nose. Actually, Joey knew, it was shellac. "Well, go on, Joey. Talk about it."

"Max," Joey said, "you are a figment of my imagination. Why don't you admit it?"

"Because you are a figment of mine." Maximillian sucked the flaming flower from the match. After several bubbly explosions he caressed the ocher bowl with his thumb. "I'd rather talk about Morgantha. You're not really going to go through this again?"

"Yes, I am."

"Joey, look—"

"Max, I've finally got it figured out. One day, a long time ago, I decided to make something I couldn't unmake. I was very lonely. I wanted someone around as different from me as possible. So I made a Maximillian; and I made one I couldn't get rid of. Then I made myself forget having made it. . . ."

"Oh, really, Joey! I made you. And I remember perfectly well making you. I remember before you were here; and I remember even before that."

"Because I *willed* you to have those memories, don't you see?"

"Joey, look: everything about you is preposterous. The way you clatter up and down the steps, and that outlandish outfit. How could you possibly be real?"

"Because you could never conceive of making anything that preposterous, Max. You've told me so a dozen times. How could you?"

"That is a very good question."

"If you made me like you say, then why can't you unmake me, the way I unmade Morgantha?"

"I have more self-control than you, for one thing."

"Because you can't! You can't! You can't! I get you furious a dozen times a week. Believe me, if you could unmake me, I'd have been gone long ago." He sat forward energetically. "I make and unmake things all the time. But I've never actually seen you make anything at all."

"I've told you before, I don't think it's something to be abused."

"You're just trying to keep me from getting really mad and unmaking you."

"Quote you back at yourself," Maximillian said dryly. "Just try."

"I have. It never works."

The hands on the grandfather clock had swung around with amazing stealth to two minutes of.

"What's more, I've given you the only explanation that accounts for why it doesn't."

Maximillian sighed. "I remember distinctly making you. You have no memory at all of making me. By all the laws of economy and logic—"

Joey flung his hand out. "Do you see anything around here either logical or economical?"

"That's not the same—"

"Could you make a rock so heavy you couldn't lift it?"

"Of course I could. And that's not the same thing at all as making a rock I couldn't unmake if I happened to see it falling toward me from a balcony."

"Max." Joey clapped his hands in frustration. "Do you realize I've never seen you outside this *room?*"

"All my needs are provided for here or in the chambers adjoining."

"Come out with me now."

"I'm busy."

"You can't come out. I made you so you'd always be in this one room."

"Absurd. Every couple of days I go for a walk in some of the lower corridors."

"And every time I come here, you're always sitting behind that desk, no matter what time of the day or night. I've never caught you out. Not even to take a leak."

"All the more reason to believe I made you. I never summon you—I suppose I do it unconsciously, because I must admit I occasionally develop a certain fondness for you *in absentia*—while I'm taking a walk, a nap, or a . . . leak."

Joey just grunted. "What are you reading anyway?"

"Puffins." He picked up his current volume. "R. M. Lockley. Perfectly delightful book. If you promise to take good care of it, I'll lend it to—"

"Max, you've got to come with me! There's something outside. Morgantha told me just before I got rid of her. There's something outside that's trying to get *in!*" He lowered his voice theatrically. "Over the moat!"

Maximillian's laughter burst out with an introductory sound Joey would have sworn was a *pop.* "Go fight your own delusions."

"It's not one of mine, it's one of yours!"

"Cut it out," Maximillian said and picked up Lockley. "You really do make me angry sometimes, you know? You've got to learn to take the responsibility for what's yours and stop trying to assume the glory for what's not."

"Such as?"

The book flapped down on the table. *"You,* for one thing. *Me,* for another!"

"Damn it, Max—" In frustration Joey stalked across the room. He turned back, but his outrage was trapped by an occasionally recurrent stutter.

Maximillian had folded his arms and was glaring. The hands of the grandfather clock had crept back to quarter of.

Joey slammed the door.

The direct way to the moat took Joey roaring and bouncing down another flight of steps and off through a stone corridor whose ceiling was so low he had to hold his head down.

Fires flickered behind iron cages set in niches on his left. As he passed the black studded door of the locked chamber on his right—a five-by-five square recessed in the rougher wall—he could not be sure (it may have been vibrations from the engine, as his muffler had fallen off two weeks before), but he thought the door rattled as he shot by. He swung his vehicle around into another stairwell.

Fists bagging his jacket pockets even further, and meerschaum chirping, Maximillian shortly went for a walk in the remoter levels to ponder his origins. His certainty over the matter, alas, could only be assumed in the security of his study. The further away he wandered (and he did take at least one goodly stroll every other day), the greater grew his doubt. What he talked of to Joey—and he was fairly certain Joey knew it—was a period some years back when through overwork, fatigue, and the ever-mounting pressure from the discovery in one of the lumber rooms of a slightly damp eleventh edition of the *Encyclopaedia Britannica* which threatened to decompose before he got all thirty-seven volumes read, he had hallucinated a time in which he had created not only Joey but all the rooms, books, staircases, and chambers, vacant, furnished, or locked; as well as the briny water around them and the brackish woods beyond. Before that, his memories were a little hazy. The only thing certain about that time was that Joey had been there, and the castle, and the wood.

He had been walking in darkness for some time when he became aware that the echo of his footsteps was returning over a very long distance.

Far above him and fifty feet to the right was a small rectangle of moonlight cut by bars. Equally far below him, and left, a luminous pearl flickered on shifting waters. And there was a distant *plash, plash, plash.* He had wandered onto one of the stone arches that spanned the castle's immense cistern. As he came down the steps (there were no rails on either side), a dim light resolved into one of the iron cages where the oil still flickered, lighting the wet, high wall as though it were made of mica.

He reached the crumbling ledge and entered a very narrow corridor, where more fires were caged by the doorway. After thirty feet the rough walls gave way to dressed stone. And the ceiling was a little higher. A little further and the dirt floor slipped beneath plank.

A chair had been placed at a bend. The carved black rungs had nearly pulled from their pegs. The leather cushion had cracked away at the corners and seemed to be stuffed with cardboard. But it was a chair.

A little further still, and the corridor had heaved itself out to respectable breadth and width. There were, irregularly, doors on the left and, quite regularly, windows on the right.

One reason Maximillian did not venture from his study more frequently was the feeling of being observed that grew with the distance. Joey must be spying on him—that was his rationalization. Alas, Joey had never given Maximillian the slightest inkling that he had observed any of his wanderings. Both spying and reticence were entirely alien to Joey's character as Maximillian perceived it. But Maximillian still nurtured the possibility as a hope.

Between dark drapes a wing of moonlight fell over an immense painting. The surface was nearly black with dirt and overvarnishing. The frame was an eight-inch width of gilded leaves, shells, and birds. Max stopped to gaze into the murky umbers stained to teak.

Behind the frame the canvas had come loose from its stretchers at one corner. A texture here from a brush stroke, there something that was either color or glare from the moon; was that a pale highlight or a scar where the underpainting and layered glazes had cracked from the white-lead sizing?

Maximillian looked left, where a crystal candelabra rewired for electricity had about half the bulbs working. He looked to the right where the chair sat in the corridor's elbow.

He faced the canvas again and cleared his throat.

"Agent XMQ7-34, calling Supervisor 86th Sector, Precinct B. Please come in. Please come in. This is Agent, eh . . . XMQ7-34 calling Supervisor of the—"

"Supervisor here. What's the report?"

"The experiment is progressing nicely, sir. The subject is responding well to the evocation of paranoid projection."

"Good."

"He's moving through the prescribed stages exactly on schedule."

"Very fine."

"The psychic tensions have practically webbed in the life force; it awaits only your orders before we move on to the final phase."

"Oh, yes. Excellent. Splendid. But tell me, Agent XMQ7-34, how do you find yourself holding up under all this?"

"To tell the truth, it's a little hard on me, Chief. You know, it's funny, but I'm really becoming sort of fond of the subject . . . I mean, in a way."

"I'm afraid, Agent XMQ7-34, it's a process I'm familiar with. They try so hard, put up such a battle, that you can't help developing a certain respect for the little buggers."

"That's it, Chief." Maximillian began to laugh. "That's it exactly. . . ."

Laughter from the canvas joined his, merged with it, was absorbed by it, till Maximillian's rang alone. He was unable to keep up the charade any longer.

He glanced down the hall hoping to catch sight of Joey's head pulling back around the corner. But the audience for whom he conjured his voice was, as usual, absent.

As Maximillian turned from the painting, for one moment the vast surface cleared of moon glare:

A small window near the top; on a narrow stone bridge two figures struggled in the shadow of the wall, high above black water. One of the figures was naked.

But Maximillian had already taken another step; again reflected light blotted the surface. Frowning, he moved to one side, forward, back, but could not find the spot again where the subject cleared.

Finally he turned and walked toward the chandelier.

Through blue hangings that curtained the open door came the sound of gentle converse. Occasionally a man's or woman's laughter segregated itself.

Maximillian frowned again.

It had been almost a year since he had been in this hall. His last visit had been on an evening when he had been particularly depressed. A disastrous idea, he had known it wouldn't work; still, he had made a party.

He had left early, fleeing back to his study and his books. As he stood there now, he realized he could not recall ever consciously unmaking the gathering. The voices chattered on.

He looked at the electrified chandelier. The black extension cord he had run to the other chandelier inside to light the party room still hung down to the rug, curled twice, and snaked off between the hangings.

His apprehension deepened. The party had been formal. He was wearing only his baggy corduroys. Suddenly, perhaps too suddenly, he pushed through the drapery onto the small balcony.

"Maximillian! Oh, there, I told you he'd be back. Steve, Bert, Ronny, Max is back. Didn't I say he wouldn't run off and just desert us forever?"

"Well, you certainly took your time, boy. It's almost twenty-five to three."

"Come on down from there and have a martini."

"Oh, Karl, it's much too late in the evening for martinis. Max wants something stronger than that."

"Are you feeling any better, honey? You looked a sight when you ran out of here."

"Oh, Max was just having one of his moods, weren't you, Max darling?"

He held the railing and gazed down into the room.

"I think he still looks sort of green around the gills."

"All he needs is a drink. Max, come on down here and have a drink."

He opened his mouth, his tongue stumbling; he tried to think of something witty to toss before his descent.

"Max? Max! I *am* glad you came back, really. It wasn't something I said, was it? Tell me it wasn't something I said. I was only kidding, Max. Really I—"

"Come on, Sheila. Let it go."

"Max, Ronny just told me the funniest story. Come on, Ronny, tell Max the one you just told me. The one about—well, you know!"

"Oh, yes, you've got to hear this one. Gracie laughed so much she lost her shoe. Gracie, did you ever get your shoe back? I saw Oliver doing something with it over there behind the piano."

"Max? Oh, come on, Max! You're not going to run out on us again, are you?"

"Of course he's not. He just got here, right, Max? Max . . . ?"

"Oh, don't pay him any mind. You know how Max is. He'll be back."

Maximillian stopped in the corridor. His palms were moist. As he opened his fingers, they cooled. For one moment he tried to summon up the will to unmake what was inside.

The hangings swung. The conversation burbled and wound. A woman laughed. More conversation. A man laughed.

He felt terribly drained. The necessary anger that would erase it all was stifled in him. He swallowed, and was surprised by the breaking sound from his throat.

Hands in his jacket pockets, he hurried down the hall.

The gate's beams, vertical and cross, creaked up into the stone. Joey looked out on the bridge. The trees beyond the shrubbery wrinkled and rolled. A moment later the surface of the water reticulated like foil. And terror divided the focus of his senses into some great fly's eye through which the whole vision before him was suddenly fragmented and absurd. Then the ordinary fear with which he could cope returned.

He stepped from the stone floor to the wooden bridge, paused for a moment with his hand on the seven-inch links of the draw chain, till he remembered it was caked in grease. He looked at the black smears on his fingers, wiped them on his jean thigh, and put both hands in his back pockets without checking again: it would take soap. And water. . . .

Something moved in the shrubbery at the head of the bridge. Squinting through the fogged lens, Joey stepped forward. The forest roared softly. The wind flattened the leather jacket to his side; zippers tinkled.

A figure darted forward, gained the boards, and came up short as though it had expected no hindrance.

Joey snatched his hand from his pockets so fast his knuckles stung: he heard more threads go in the left one.

The boy was naked.

Crouched.

Balanced on the balls of his feet.

Hands to the side.

His hair, black as rags of the night itself, whipped and snapped at one shoulder.

"What do you want?" Joey demanded over the wind.

A black cloth was tied down around the left eye.

The right one, huge and yellow, blinked.

"Come on," Joey said. "What do you want?"

The boy blinked again. Then he laughed, a skinny sound that twisted out like barbed wire through dry pine needles. His arms came back to his sides. He took another step.

Joey said, "You better get away from here."

The boy said, "Hello, Joey."

"You better get away from here now," Joey repeated. "What do you want?"

There were cuts and scratches on the boy's shins and feet. He held his head slightly to the side in order to see. "Can I come inside, Joey?" and the following laughter was all breath. It sounded terribly wet.

"No. You can't. What do you want?"

"Aw, come on." Another step. The boy stuck out his hand. "I'll tell you when we get inside."

Joey took the hand to shake. "You can't come in." Joey's hand was thick, dry, and gritty.

"Yes, I can." The boy's was long and moist. And he was still laughing.

"You get on out of here." But physical contact, unpleasant as it was, made the child less threatening. The eye rag was knotted across his left ear. A splatter of acne wounds made their red galaxy on his jaw. "Get off the bridge." Joey tried to pull his hand away. The fingers stiffened around his own. "Now come *on*—" He shook his hand. The hand holding his swung with his shaking. "Hey!" Now Joey pulled back in earnest.

The boy laughed and pulled against him. He was very strong.

Joey leaned back and grabbed his own wrist with his free hand. The boy leaned too. His free hand waved behind him. The boy's foot touched Joey's; his toes were wet and cold with night water.

The boy grinned.

Joey jerked, slipped, yanked.

Then the boy released all pressure.

Joey staggered backward, almost tripped on the sill, went back three more steps, and sat down.

The boy stood over him, his grip still firm.

The gate creaked down. The splintered stumps of the vertical beams thudded into puddles that had collected in the worn depressions, sending dark rills through the checkered moonlight.

"Told you I could get in."

Something ran out into the pale square where the boy stood, paused to raise its glittering barb, thought better, and scurried off. Joey felt a sympathetic throb in his instep.

"You know what I want?"

As Joey pushed to his feet, the boy helped him with a tug. Joey narrowed his eyes; the boy released his hand.

"I'm going to unlock that room upstairs. I'm going to push back the door, and whatever is inside is going to come out."

"Huh?"

"What do you think will happen once it's let out?"

"What out?"

The boy suddenly giggled and rubbed his wrist across his mouth. "Joey, you know . . ." He looked around the dim hall. ". . . Maybe the clocks in the East Wing will get on with their business at last. Perhaps you and Maximillian will decide you don't want to live here any more, and move away into the forest. Interesting to think about, isn't it?"

Joey tried to focus his discomfort.

The boy's vocal expression suddenly changed. "I've got to try and unlock it. Take me up there, Joey. All you have to do is show me the door. I'll do the rest. I'll let it out, and then I can go. It'll be simple. Show me where the chamber is. Once I open the door, I'll go away and leave you alone. . . ."

"No." Joey wanted to give his refusal full voice. But it came out in a rasping hiss. He turned in the echoing hall (the discomfort focused was terror) and ran through the nearest doorway.

"Joey . . . !"

He scrambled down the ill-lit steps. At the bottom he turned to see the silhouetted figure, a hand on either wall, starting after him.

Joey missed the next step. His heel struck full on the stone and jarred him to the head. But he was running again.

He swung under an archway, knowing steps would take him shortly, up, up where the locked chamber waited. Desperately he tried to think of somewhere, someplace, some direction to—

He crossed a grate and felt his feet press momentarily between cold bars. The steps were close.

"Joey . . . ?"

He practically fell up them, trying to recall some turnoff, some cross passage to take him away. He scrambled over the length of the hallway in his memory. It opened directly into the low stone corridor not three yards away from the recessed square, five by five.

He remembered the conduit the same moment he passed it. And he was on his knees, lugging away the heavy cover. He shoved the circular hatch from him and heard it clanging down the steps, *ka-tang, tang, tang,* for all the world like his unicycle.

"Hey, what the—!" from behind him.

Joey lunged through the opening. His back and shoulders scraped the sides and roof.

"Joey, you shouldn't have done that—"

He had to crawl with his forearms flat. His own breath raged in echo around his ears. There was water on the floor. And much more softly, at a distinctly different rhythm, somebody else was breathing.

His head tapped the plate on the other end in blackness. He shoved with his shoulder. For a moment it stuck—

". . . Joey?"

—and that was terrible.

Then it pushed away. The *thud* of the fall was duller than he expected. He scrambled out over the metal plate and crouched on all fours on a rug.

As he stood he saw a sideways **H** of light between the double doors just ahead of him. Behind him was the sound of scrabbling. He pushed the doors apart, lurched out, and was practically blind after his crawl through the darkness.

"Oh, I say there—"

"I told Sheila. I told her, I don't think anyone could have blamed her. I mean, after all—"

"Oliver! Come out from under there!"

"Leave him alone, Bert. You know how Oliver is—oh, pardon me!"

"Hey, I didn't see you come in! Are you all right? Here, let me get you a martini."

"For God's sake, Steve, it's too late in the evening for—"

"Dreadfully sorry. Did I bump into you?"

". . . Joey?"

"Say, I bet you haven't heard this one. Ronny, tell this young man that story about—"

As he pushed forward, Joey felt the electrical cord catch around his ankle. The chandelier shook overhead.

"Hey, watch it there! Better keep your eyes in front of you, young fellow."

The cord pulled free: the room dropped into darkness deep as the conduit's.

"You're sure I can't get you something? If not a martini, perhaps—"

"I think you're being terribly hard on him, Karl."

"After all, he has been under a great deal of pressure, you know."

"All *I* know is that if anyone had said that to me, I would have scratched his eyes out!"

"Joey?"

"Oliver? Is that you under there? Hey, are you all right? Oliver?"

Joey was clambering up the steps toward the little balcony.

"After I've gone and mixed this, doesn't anybody want it? Would you—"

"Joey . . . ?"

He beat at the hangings. Then, suddenly, he was through and into the hallway.

He stepped over the extension cord and hurried up the corridor. The air was dusty with moonlight.

By a huge gilt frame he turned to look behind him. For a moment the glare cleared from the blackened varnish: two figures struggled through a richly appointed room filled with men and women in evening dress. One of the figures was naked.

And someone was pushing aside the blue hangings back in the doorway.

Joey turned again and ran down the hall. At the bend, he punched the wall by the chair. Again he looked back.

"Joey, are you taking me in the right direction? You're sure now this is the way? If you take me there, then I can let it out and leave you alone. You know, you can't lose me. You think you'll just take me around in circles, don't you? But that's not going to work. You'll make a mistake, turn down the wrong hall, and there we'll be, won't we?"

Joey felt the arm of the chair move under his hand. He glanced down: the whole frame swayed, about to collapse.

"Lead on! Right this way to the locked chamber. Is it down there, Joey?"

Joey started along the hall again. He was holding his breath, he realized. He let it out with an aching gasp and sucked in another.

"Right behind you, Joey."

The walls were no longer paneled, but merely dressed stone. And there were no more windows. He had barely noted this when the ceiling dropped to within a foot of his head.

"This long-way-around business is a real waste of time, Joey. Why don't you just give up and show me the quick way, nice and simple?"

The walls were closer too. He moved forward in slow-motion hysteria. Pebbles chewed the soles of his feet. The niched flames flickered. For a moment he had a vision of the hall diminishing to the size of the conduit.

He stopped, because suddenly he was standing in an echoing hollow that stretched out and up into dimness that became blackness and still went on.

"Which way do we go now?"

Joey jumped, because the voice was practically at his elbow. He was thinking about running, was running—

A weight landed on his back. Joey staggered forward, zippers going like chimes. There was the sound of breath, roaring loud; then a sharp pain below his ear.

Joey's shriek vaulted about the echoing cistern. The boy had bitten. Joey went forward, clawing up the stairs. The weight released, and Joey ran ten more steps before he realized he was on one of the bridges. He turned to see the boy again, in silhouette from the fires on the ledge.

"Go on, Joey." The boy was breathing hard. "That was just to show you I'm losing patience, though."

Joey backed up another step.

The boy came on two.

At the next step pale light caught in Joey's eyes. High, very high above him was a window, broken by bars and filled with moonlight. The beam lit three of the chipped steps before falling over the edge to flicker on the misty ripplings far, so terribly far below. Joey backed up another four steps.

"You know I really am losing my taste for all of this crawling around in the dark." The liquescent breathing lisped among the sounds of dripping. "When are you going to cut this out and show me the chamber? I think I'm going to have to teach you another lesson." Then the figure was racing forward.

Joey saw him pass through the shaft. The face was creased with rage about the yellow eye. Joey whirled, started up, stumbled immediately. He went down on his hands.

At the same time he heard a high shriek. And something struck his back, slipped to the side—It jerked him hugely to the side. Joey went flat, clutching the steps, cheek pressed against the crumblings.

And the shrieking.

Joey bit the corner of the stone and cried and kicked violently. An amazing weight was hanging from below his waist. There was the sound of ripping cloth. And then there wasn't any more weight.

The splash cut out the core of the sound. The echo grew quieter, and then even quieter. It may have been the reverberation from his own sobs, but the echo didn't quite stop.

After a while he pushed himself up and walked down. He halted at the beginning of the moonlight's wash.

There was a dark smear to the step's edge. At one end a golden carapace was crushed flat, along with clotted maroon.

Stung and slipping, the boy must have leaped for Joey only to catch his back pocket. Joey ran his hand over the stubble of threads on his buttock. Then, jingling softly, he stepped around the moonlit stain.

When he reached the ledge, he was holding his breath again. When he let it out, the echo still came back like shrieking.

The grandfather clock showed less than five minutes to three.

The baboon's eyes uncrossed from the gleaming nose, rolled to the left, then to the right. The lips lifted from the yellow teeth. The humidor gave up a sound for all the world like someone clearing his throat:

"Agent XMQ7-34, calling Supervisor 86th Sector, Precinct B. Please come in. Please come in. This is, eh . . . Agent XMQ7-34 calling Supervisor of the—"

"Supervisor here," the marble patriarch announced from his pedestal. "What's the report?"

"The experiment is progressing nicely, sir. The subject is responding well to the evocation of—"

"Yes, of course," interrupted the bust. "I know, I know: but you just can't help respecting the little buggers. Oh, yes, yes, I know about all that."

Their mounting laughter was cut off by rumblings from the chamber beneath, punctuated by three distinct *thwumps,* the second much louder than either the first or third.

The baboon rolled his eyes around to observe the grandfather clock just as Maximillian opened the door: seventeen minutes past two.

Maximillian had been back from his walk almost half an hour and was making fair progress in his comparison of Apollinaire's *Le Poète Assassiné* with the Padgett translation when the whine of Joey's unicycle came shuddering through the door.

I tell you truly, brethren, Padgett had rendered, *there are few spectacles that do not put the soul in danger. I know of only one place*—Maximillian looked up, frowning. The familiar whine became a familiar roar—*one place you can go fearlessly and that is*—Maximillian closed the book as the motor coughed to silence.

"Max!" The door banged back against the bookshelf as Joey bounded forward. "Max, it almost got in! But I led it on a wild-goose chase! Into the cistern. And it tripped and fell into the—oh, Max!"

"What are you talking about?"

Joey was gasping between each clutch of words. "It wanted to open the locked chamber! Let it out! But I wouldn't let it." He grabbed the edge of the desk. "Max, don't make any more of those! Please, Max, please don't ever make any more."

Maximillian shook his head. He wished Joey wouldn't barge in on him. He was beginning to wish it more than anything else. "Make what?"

"Ones like *that!*"

"God damn it, Joey, will you get *out* of here!" He was standing now, astounded at his own anger, aware that the tics in the muscles of his face were his own winces at the volume of his voice.

Joey backed to the door. He made three forays into some word or other but kept jamming on the letter *b.* Then he fled the room.

Maximillian sat down while the unicycle thundered outside, and couldn't find his place in Padgett at all.

* * *

Clacketing up the tower steps, he didn't care if Max didn't know what he had just saved them from. And he didn't care if Max never lent him another book forever and ever. And he didn't care if Max never went out of his old study anyway. And if he got mad enough, Max better watch out, because he *would* unmake him.

He reached the sill and rolled out on the tower roof. He caught himself on the stone wall as the cycle sagged, got off, and positioned his machine against the door jamb.

A small moon winked overhead between running clouds. The puddle rippled by the balustrade as the wind unrolled across the roof and swayed through his hair so that it tickled his forehead.

He didn't care if he never saw Max again. He would make a beautiful, sweet, interesting girl who would do everything he said, and would never talk back to him, and be very much in love. With him. He'd make this one colored. And maybe she'd be able to play songs on the autoharp. Yes, she'd have a nice voice, and would sing to him after dinner, and be as dark and as warm as the shadows in the hallways in the remoter levels.

He picked the green shift off the wall. Then he sat down and leaned against the rock. He held the gauze around his fists, bent his face to touch his chin to it. It was practically dry, now, and cool.

He tried to think about the interesting colored girl. But it was chilly and his thoughts kept drifting. The flags were cold on his feet and through the seat of his pants (he didn't wear underwear any more), and soon he would zip his jacket closed over his sweater. When he squinted, the stuff on his right lens made the reflected moon explode on the waters beside him in a shower of silent silver needles. And he was tired, almost tired enough to sleep, right there, but first he would think some more about the girl until he would hear her voice behind him, calling him: Joey? Joey . . . ?

In another tower a clock chimed three. He started to his knees, looked out over the wall. But the chimes had sounded from the West Wing, where the clocks were all perfectly normal anyway.

"Joey?"

The Lookout

Cyrus Colter

1970

Wild torrents of snow darkened the view ahead as, its windshield wipers laboring, the Buick crept down the street into the blizzard. The young woman inside leaned forward over the steering wheel trying to see out through the foggy glass. Alone, she wore a blue winter coat, white gloves on her brown hands, and was bareheaded. She glanced at her watch; it was one-forty-five. "They'll start getting there around two," she told herself. It was Saturday afternoon. She hoped she'd be lucky enough to get just the right parking spot—one from which she would see without being seen. The swirling snow would help. She turned left to circle the block in order to park across the street from Laura's big house on Woodlawn Avenue.

It was a sense of compulsion that had sent Mildred out of the house into the bad weather, leaving her husband and two boys to think up some Saturday diversion for themselves. She hadn't said where she was going, which, in itself, was a little unusual. But Wes was so agreeable, so easygoing . . . sometimes she wished to God he weren't! The boys would have questions, though. . . .

Coming now from the opposite direction, Mildred eased her car into the well-chosen space, lifting a resolute chin to find the curb almost hidden in the drifting snow. After turning off the motor, she felt in her purse for a cigarette. She was a handsome woman of thirty-eight, with smooth coppery skin and soft hair blandished by a chic haircut. Her serious turn of mind and self-possession blended in rather naturally with her recent moodiness and, with her cool good looks, created a curiously sensual amalgam. Mashing the red-hot dash lighter against the cigarette end, she blew a jet of pearl-gray smoke against the windshield and then settled back to wait.

Woodlawn was a wide residential street. Traffic was especially light today, with the bad weather. As she sat smoking, Mildred realized how tense and uneasy she was. It was a risky foolish thing she was doing—one of those catty women going into Laura Font's bridge luncheon could see and recognize her.

That would be bad, she knew, for recently she had made a quietly desperate effort at indifference; she had been careful not to show any awareness that she had not kept pace with her former friends. To be caught here now would be the fatal admission. She could hardly withstand the urge to reach for the ignition key and start the motor. But she wouldn't—she couldn't.

It had been only by sheer coincidence in a telephone talk that she learned of Laura's party in the first place. And now, having spent the whole morning mustering the courage to come, she must hazard staying at least long enough to see who went in and what they were wearing—at least until she'd seen Janice, the guest of honor, arrive. She wasn't parked directly in front of Laura's anyway, but down the street a bit. No one would see her through the sifting veil of snow. But if they did! If they did, they'd wonder, of course, why she didn't come in. And after a while, when she didn't, they'd know she wasn't invited. Still, she must take the chance.

She had heard of Laura's huge fireplace, and she knew she'd have it blazing today for all those vain, lucky women. Yes, vain—because of the financial strain they constantly kept their husbands under to outdo each other in the trappings of success. And lucky too—for the husbands, despite all, had somehow borne up physically. It *was* luck—she knew now you could never tell beforehand whether a man "had it" or not.

When Wes came out of the university, everyone said he was going places, and they said the same later on, when they were married. For the first five years he *had* grown; he was ambitious for big things. Then something happened—the plateau; he stopped maturing. And now, after fifteen years, he had what *he* considered a good job with the insurance company he'd started out with. He was content to go to the football games in the fall, and for the rest of the year to have in a few cronies periodically for poker in front of his tidy bar. Lately, to her secret disgust, he had been watching the late TV movies. He had long ago left the supervision of the two boys completely to her, and sometimes she found she had three boys on her hands instead of two.

Mildred sat and waited and watched the snow. The houses in the area were large and well back from the street; to Mildred, they were remote and ghostly in the white swirl. A small delivery truck with large letters on its side reading BRISTOL PASTRIES pulled up from the other direction and stopped in front of Laura's. The young driver climbed out with a package held carefully in both hands and carried it around to a rear door. Yes, the cake, thought Mildred. She lit another cigarette and drew the smoke in hungrily.

Laura's success had surprised everybody. She had taken little Herbie, who it was true was very bright in school, and she had somehow urged him to the top. Now Herbie—with his kinky red hair and blue eyes—was an outstanding physician; he had his own clinic and staff of doctors. And Laura, herself, had everything to go with her station in life—a stately stone house (owned formerly by a wealthy Jewish family), a Mercedes-Benz car for herself, and two house servants. For a girl whose father had been a postman, she had done well indeed. In school Laura hadn't been nearly as good-looking as she, Mildred, and at the University of Illinois, she didn't go out with the popular fellows that Mildred knew. She was humble, and Mildred proud—proud of Wes, who was slender and handsome then, and who reveled in the smoldering traces of jealousy Mildred always tried to hide. Looking back, it was all so incredibly fantastic!

Soon a Ford station wagon came down the other side of the street toward her. It slowed and pulled to the curb in front of Laura's. Mildred put the window down a little and saw a mousy-looking young woman in a scanty broadtail jacket get out. She gasped. Hilda Simpson!—married to a pharmacist. Even Wes made more money than Ted Simpson! But Hilda's father had been a classics professor at Fisk University. That made the difference—*her* father was a caterer. Mildred smiled to herself. Hilda *would* be the first one there, so glad to be invited. And imagine anyone wearing a broadtail jacket in this weather instead of a warm cloth coat. You couldn't impress *that* crowd with broadtail.

The snow was coming down more slowly now, in big spinning flakes. Mildred started the motor for a few seconds to let the windshield wipers clear the glass. Soon a Lincoln Continental drew up slowly from behind and parked just ahead of her. She tensed. Two women got out from different sides of the car, closed the doors, and, talking, started across the street toward Laura's big iron gate. Mildred gently exhaled a cloud of smoke. Both were light-skinned, and the one who had driven the car was beautiful. Mildred didn't know her, but recognized the other one as Mae Todd, the old-maid high school principal. She watched the two women mount Laura's stone steps. Suddenly it came to her. The beautiful one must be Evelyn Todd, Dr. Herman Todd's new wife and Mae's new sister-in-law. Mildred smiled again, knowing that old Mrs. Todd, the doctor's jealous first wife, must surely be turning over about now—out there in Burr-Oak Cemetery. So that was the beauty from Boston, so *soignée* in her casual-style Matara Alaskan seal and plum-colored suede pumps worn bravely in the snow. Mildred sat and watched them enter through the big arched door.

The impulse to leave gripped her, but she tried to ignore it. She leaned forward and glanced at her face in the rearview mirror, and then sat back, absently pulling at a ravel in her glove. She knew if she left now she'd miss seeing Janice arrive—lucky Janice, home from New York just to be feted by the elite. Was this the same girl who grew up with Mildred, stayed whole weekends at her house, and so often double-dated with her? Janice had roomed with her all during their junior and senior years at Illinois. She knew Janice had been in Chicago since Tuesday; last year when she came home she'd at least phoned. How callous could you get? But *her* husband was a successful publisher, and husbands were the key to everything.

No one arrived now for ten minutes. Then two new Cadillacs followed by a Plymouth came down the other side of the street toward her, all moving slowly in the accumulated snow. The Cadillacs plowed over to the curb near Laura's car, and the Plymouth went on. There was the slow indecisive parking by women, a clambering out of silk and mink, and a slamming of heavy car doors. Mildred, jittery, sat back from the car window and watched. It was Sadie Tate and her gang—a cruel, vicious coterie of social brigands. All boasted northern university degrees and light skins. There were no black or dark brown women among these vocal members of the NAACP, Mildred knew—these implacable foes of discrimination. She watched Sadie lead them slowly up the wide stone steps. Sadie, over the years, had consumed so many hors d'oeuvres and martinis that she was now barrel-shaped. A sense of awe held Mildred—this was a life she could never know. It was too late. She lit another cigarette and tried to relax by tilting her head far back and blowing the smoke up against the ceiling.

Then the cars all seemed to come at once. Mildred was frightened, for it had almost stopped snowing. The guests were pulling up from both directions now and hunting parking space. Soon a big beige Imperial eased up from behind and was opposite her car window before she knew it. She fell back terrified. The car stopped. There were three women in the front seat, and a man wearing a chauffeur's cap sitting in the back. He got out and opened the right front door for the women. Mildred recognized the first one out—Nan Hawthorne, well off, and snob of snobs. Then she saw only the long legs of the next woman sliding out, but she knew that it was Janice. She was laughing as she got an assist from the chauffeur, and then, waiting for Betty Bond, the driver, to be helped out, she stooped over and brushed a fluff of snow from her ankle. All three were soon talking and laughing again as they stood waiting for the chauffeur to pull off and let them cross the street. Suddenly Janice glanced around toward Mildred's car. Fear congealed her. But Janice hadn't seen—she was too busily amused at something Nan Hawthorne was saying. The three then crossed the street abreast, tall Janice in the middle.

Janice was wearing a soft, rippling, full-length mink. Mildred watched her proud carriage. She'd never known Janice to look patrician before. Her legs were still too skinny, but she was dressed so tastefully that her thin body lent elegance to the finished impression she made. And she looked terribly happy, Mildred thought—for there'd be other parties, you could see. Where tonight, for instance? To Sadie's? Mildred had heard that the men servants at Sadie's wore mauve jackets. Maybe Nan Hawthorne, who abhorred large cocktail parties, would have in a favored few. Or Betty Bond might be giving something—a dinner, perhaps. Each occasion would be smart and lavish and cultivated.

Just then Audrey Johnson, mannish as ever, drove up in an Oldsmobile station wagon, looking for a place to park. Audrey was one of the very few in that group who was still nice to Mildred, but she had always had her doubts about Audrey.

Two boys trudged by in the snow, one dragging a sled. They were about the age of Mildred's boys. She spent a good deal of her time nowadays thinking about her sons and what they'd make of themselves. She hoped they'd turn out to be real men, with a passionate pride in accomplishment—still, not at a sacrifice in tenderness to their wives. And then, as always lately, her thoughts turned inward. She could testify that the woman should never be stronger than the man. Only calamity ensued. She knew that her incessant yearning for the life she'd seen today was futile.

She'd tried hard to manage herself accordingly; no fair-minded person would deny that. Yet, here she sat, in this snowy lookout, like a member of the FBI. It was insane. If only she hadn't found out about Janice being in town! It had set her back and jarred her resolve. They had been so close once. She used to tell Janice what she ought and ought not do. She wondered if she ever thought about it now. Perhaps Janice laughed at the thought. She had a perfect right to, certainly; but she'd no doubt forgotten it all. Probably no impression remained—not even of Mildred. It was just as well. . . .

She mashed out her cigarette and started the motor. There was only one thing she was sure of now: she didn't want to go home. And she wouldn't—at least for a while. Then, in plain view, she pulled away from the curb, no longer caring who saw her, and drove off. But there was no place to go—yes, perhaps to Mama's, but no place else. Poor, uncomprehending Mama—who thought "Millie" was "doing simply grand." Wesley was so wonderful to her. "They've got *everything*—an automatic dishwasher and a *stereo*. Goodness! I would've thought I was a queen! But Millie now thinks nothing of it."

On Fifty-fifth Street Mildred pulled over in front of a liquor store. She'd take along a fifth of hundred-proof bourbon, and she and Mama could make some good strong Manhattans. She went in and bought the whiskey, and it was only as she drove away that she remembered the drinks would start Mama talking, blubbering probably about Charlie, Mildred's aimless brother. She hadn't considered that. On such occasions Mama could get pretty loathsome. But it would be better than going home. And she herself could have a half dozen Manhattans—even more, if they were required—until she would yearn for nothing. Mama didn't give a damn. . . .

She was operating the car instinctively now, stopping for red lights by seeming automation. It had stopped snowing completely, and she regretted this. She had always loved the snow; it made the world look so unreal and insubstantial. Dreams had a better chance of coming true in a world of unreality. Sometimes she went out walking alone in the falling snow, feeling the strange urge to be caught up in it somehow and made dizzy, completely out of her head, by its crazy, swirling madness. But sooner or later the snowing always stopped—as it had today—and she had nothing to do but to return to earth with a cold and bitter heart.

A Long Day in November

Ernest J. Gaines

1971

I

Somebody is shaking me but I don't want to get up, because I'm tired and I'm sleepy and I don't want to get up now. It's warm under the cover here, but it's cold up there and I don't want to get up now.

"Sonny?" I hear. I don't know who's calling me, but it must be Mama. She's shaking me by the foot. She's got my ankle through the cover. "Wake up, honey," she says. "I want you to get up and wee-wee."

"I don't want to wee-wee, Mama," I say.

"Come on," she says, shaking me. "Come on. Get up for Mama."

"It's cold up there," I say.

"Come on," she says. "Mama won't let her baby get cold."

I pull the sheet and blanket from under my head and push them back over my shoulder. I feel the cold and I try to cover up again, but Mama grabs the cover before I get it over me. Mama is standing side the bed looking down at me smiling.

"I'm cold, Mama," I say.

"Mama go'n wrap his little coat 'round her baby," she says.

She gets my coat off the chair and puts it on me, and then she fastens some of the buttons.

"Now," she says. "See? You warm."

I gape and look at Mama. She hugs me real hard and rubs her face against my face. My mama's face is warm and soft, and it feels good.

"Come on," she says.

I get up but I can still feel that cold floor. I get on my knees and look under the bed for my pot.

"See it?" Mama says.

"Uh-uh."

"I bet you didn't bring it in," she says.

"I left it on the chicken coop," I say.

"Well, go to the back door," Mama says. "Hurry up before you get cold."

We go in the kitchen and Mama cracks open the door for me. I can see the fence back of the house and I can see the little pecan tree over by the toilet. I can see the big pecan tree over by the other fence by Miss Viola Brown's house. Miss Viola Brown must be sleeping because it's late at night. I bet you nobody else in the quarters up now. I bet you I'm the only little boy up.

I get my tee-tee and I wee-wee fast and hard, because I don't want to get cold. Mama latches the door when I get through wee-weeing and we go back in the front.

"Sonny?" she says.

"Hunh?"

"Tomorrow morning when you get up, me and you leaving here, hear?"

"Where we going?" I ask.

"We going to Grandma," Mama says.

"We leaving us house?" I ask.

"Yes," she says.

"Daddy leaving too?"

"No." she says. "Just me and you."

"Daddy don't want to leave?"

"I don't know what your daddy wants," Mama says. "But he don't want me. And we leaving, hear?"

"Uh-huh," I say.

"I'm tired of it," Mama says.

"Hunh?"

"You won't understand, honey," Mama says. "You too young still."

"I'm getting cold, Mama," I say.

"All right," she says.

I get back in bed and Mama pulls the cover up over me. She leans over and kisses me on the jaw, and then she goes back to her bed. I hear the spring when she gets in the bed, then I hear her crying.

"Mama?" I call.

She don't answer me.

"Mama?" I call her.

"Go to sleep, baby," she says.

I don't call her no more but I keep listening. I listen for a long time, but I don't hear nothing no more. I feel myself going back to sleep. . . .

Billy Joe Martin's got the tire and he's rolling it in the road, and I run to the gate to look at him. I want to go out in the road, but Mama don't want me to play out there like Billy Joe Martin and the other children. . . . Lucy's playing side the house. She's jumping rope with—I don't know who that is. I go side the house and play with Lucy. Lucy beats me jumping rope. The rope keeps on hitting me on the leg. But it don't hit Lucy on the leg. Lucy jumps too high for it. . . . Me and Billy Joe Martin shoots marbles and I beat him shooting. . . . Mama's sweeping the gallery and knocking the dust out of the broom on the side of the house. Mama keeps on knocking the broom against the wall. Got plenty dust in the broom. Somebody's beating on the door. Mama, somebody's beating on the door. Somebody's beating on the door, Mama.

"Amy, please let me in," I hear.

Somebody's beating on the door, Mama. Mama, somebody's beating on the door.

"Amy, honey? Honey, please let me in."

I push the cover back and listen. I hear Daddy beating on the door.

"Mama," I say. "Mama, Daddy's knocking on the door. He wants to come in."

"Go back to sleep, Sonny," Mama says.

"Daddy's out there," I say. "He wants to come in."

"Go back to sleep, I told you," Mama says.

It gets quiet for a little while, and then Daddy says, "Sonny?"

"Hunh?"

"Come open the door for your daddy."

"Mama go'n whip me if I get up," I say.

"I won't let her whip you," Daddy says. "Come and open the door like a good boy."

I push the cover back and I sit up and look over at Mama's bed. Mama's under the cover and she's quiet like she's sleeping. I get out of my bed real quiet and go unlatch the door for Daddy.

"Look what I brought you and your mama," he says.

"What?" I ask.

Daddy takes a paper bag out of his jumper pocket. I dip my hand down in it and get a handful of candy.

"Get back in that bed, Sonny," Mama says.

"I'm eating candy," I say.

"Get back in that bed like I told you," Mama says.

"Daddy's up with me," I say.

"You heard me, boy?"

"You can take your candy with you," Daddy says. He follows me to the bed and tucks the cover under me, then he goes back to their bed.

"Honey?" he says.

"Don't touch me," Mama says.

"Honey?" Daddy says.

"Get your hands off me," Mama says.

"Honey?" Daddy says. Then he starts crying. He cries a good little while, and then he stops. I don't chew on my candy while Daddy's crying but when he stops I chew on another piece.

"Go to sleep, Sonny," he says.

"I want to eat my candy," I say.

"Hurry then. You got to go to school tomorrow."

I put another piece in my mouth and chew on it.

"Honey?" I hear Daddy saying. "Honey, you go'n wake me up to go to work?"

"I do hope you stop bothering me," Mama says.

"Wake me up round four-thirty, hear, honey?" Daddy says. "I can cut 'bout six tons tomorrow. Maybe seven."

Mama don't say nothing to Daddy, and I feel sleepy again. I finish chewing my last piece of candy and I turn on my side. I feel like I'm going away. . . .

I run around the house in the mud, and I feel the mud between my toes. The mud is soft and I like to play in the mud. I try to get out the mud, but I can't get out. I'm not stuck in the mud, but I can't get out. Lucy can't come over and play in the mud because her mama don't want her to catch a cold. . . . Billy Joe Martin shows me his dime and puts it back in his pocket. Mama bought me a pretty little red coat and I show it to Lucy. But I don't let Billy Joe Martin put his hand on it. Lucy can touch it all she wants, but I don't let Billy Joe Martin put his hand on it. . . . Me and Lucy get on the horse and ride up and down the road. The horse runs fast, and me and Lucy bounce on the horse and laugh. . . . Mama and Daddy and Uncle Al and Grandma's sitting by the fire talking. I'm outside shooting marbles, but I hear them. I don't know what they talking about, but I hear them. I hear them. I hear them. I hear them.

"Honey, you let me oversleep," Daddy says. "Look here, it's going on seven."

"You ought to been thought about that last night," Mama says.

"Honey, please," Daddy says. "Don't start a fuss right off this morning."

"Then don't open your mouth," Mama says.

"Honey, the car broke down," Daddy says. "What was I suppose to do—it broke down on me. I just couldn't walk away and not try to fix it."

Mama's quiet.

"Honey," Daddy says. "Don't be mad with me. Come on, now."

"Don't touch me," Mama says.

"Honey, I got to go to work. Come on."

"I mean it," she says.

"Honey, how can I work without touching you? You know I can't do a day's work without touching you some."

"I told you not to put your hands on me," Mama says. I hear her slap Daddy on the hand. "I mean it," she says.

"Honey," Daddy says. "This is Eddie, your husband."

"Go back to your car," Mama says. "Go rub 'gainst it. You ought to be able to find a hole in it somewhere."

"Honey, you oughtn't talk like that in the house," Daddy says. "What if Sonny hear you?"

I stay quiet and I don't move because I don't want them to know I'm woke.

"Honey, listen to me," Daddy says. "From the bottom of my heart I'm sorry. Now come on."

"I told you once," Mama says. "You not getting on me. Go get on your car."

"Honey, respect the child," Daddy says.

"How come you don't respect him?" Mama says. "How come you don't come home sometime and respect him? How come you don't leave the car 'lone and come home and respect him? How come you don't respect him? You the one needs to respect him."

"I told you it broke down," Daddy says. "I was coming home when it broke down. I even had to leave it out on the road. I made it here quick as I could."

"You can go back quick as you can, for all I care."

"Honey, you don't mean that," Daddy says. "I know you don't mean that. You just saying that 'cause you mad."

Mama's quiet.

"Honey?" Daddy says.

"I hope you let me go back to sleep, Eddie," Mama says.

"Honey, don't go back to sleep," Daddy says, "when I'm in this kind of fix."

"I'm getting up," Mama says. "Damn all this."

I hear the spring mash down on the bed boards, then I hear Mama walking across the floor, going back in the kitchen.

"Oh, Lord," Daddy says. "Oh, Lord. The suffering a man got to go through in this world. Sonny?" he says.

"Don't wake that baby up," Mama says from the door.

"I got to have somebody to talk to," Daddy says. "Sonny?"

"I told you not to wake him up," Mama says.

"You don't want to talk to me," Daddy says, "I need somebody to talk to. Sonny?" he says.

"Hunh?"

"See what you did?" Mama says. "You woke him up, and he ain't going back to sleep."

Daddy comes to the bed and sits beside me. He looks down at me and passes his hand over my head.

"You love your daddy, Sonny?" he says.

"Uh-huh."

"Please love me," Daddy says.

I look up at Daddy and he looks at me, and then he just falls down on me and starts crying.

"A man needs somebody to love him," he says.

"Get love from what you give love," Mama says, back in the kitchen. "You love your car. Go let it love you back."

Daddy shakes his face in the cover.

"The suffering a man got to go through in this world," he says. "Sonny, I hope you never have to go through all this."

Daddy lays there side me a long time. I can hear Mama back in the kitchen. I hear her putting some wood in the stove, and then I hear her lighting the fire. I hear her pouring some water in the teakettle, and I hear when she sets the kettle on the stove.

Daddy raises up and wipes his eyes. He looks at me and shakes his head, and then he goes and puts on his overalls.

"It's a hard life," he says. "Hard, hard. One day, Sonny—you too young right now—but one day you'll know what I mean."

"Can I get up, Daddy?"

"Better ask your mama," Daddy says.

"Can I get up, Mama?" I call.

Mama don't answer me.

"Mama?" I call.

"Your pa standing in there," Mama says. "He the one woke you up."

"Can I get up, Daddy?"

"Sonny, I got enough troubles right now," Daddy says.

"I want get up and wee-wee," I say.

"Get up," Mama says. "You go'n worry me till I let you get up anyhow."

I push the cover back and hurry and get in my clothes. Daddy ties my shoes for me, and we go back in the kitchen and stand side the stove. When Mama sees me she just looks at me a minute, then she goes out in the yard and gets my pot. She holds it to let me wee-wee, then she carries it in the front room.

"Freezing," Daddy says. "Lord."

He rubs his hands together and pours up some water in the basin. After he washes his face, he washes my face; then me and him sit at the table and eat. Mama don't eat with us.

"You love your daddy?" Daddy says.

"Uh-huh," I say.

"That's a good boy," he says. "Always love your daddy."

"I love Mama, too. I love her more than I love you."

"You got a good little mama," Daddy says. "I love her, too. She the only thing keep me going—counting you too, of course."

I look at Mama standing side the stove, warming.

"Well, I better get going," Daddy says. "Maybe if I work hard I'll get me a couple tons."

Daddy gets up from the table and goes in the front room. He comes back with his jumper and his hat on.

"I'm leaving, honey," he says.

Mama don't answer Daddy.

"Honey, tell me 'Bye, old dog' or something," Daddy says. "Just don't stand there."

Mama still don't answer him, and Daddy jerks his cane knife out the wall and goes on out.

"Hurry up, honey," Mama says. "We going to Mama."

I finish eating and I go in the front room where Mama is. Mama's pulling a big bundle from under the bed. "What's that?" I ask.

"Us clothes," she says.

"We go'n take us clothes to Grandma?"

"I'm go'n try," Mama says. "Find your cap."

I get my cap and fasten it, and I come back and look at Mama standing in front of the looking glass. I can see her face in the glass, and look like she want cry. She comes from the dresser and looks at the big bundle of clothes on the floor.

"Where's your pot?" she says. "Get it."

I get the pot from under the bed and go and dump the wee-wee out.

"Come on," Mama says.

She drags the big bundle of clothes out on the gallery and I shut the door. Mama squats down and puts the bundle on her head, and then she stands up and me and her go down the steps. Soon's I get out in the road I can feel the wind. It's strong and it's blowing in my face. My face is cold and one of my hands is cold.

I look up and I see the tree in Grandma's yard. We go little farther and I see the house. I run up ahead of Mama and hold the gate open for her. After she goes in I let the gate slam.

Spot starts barking soon's he sees me. He runs down the steps at me and I let him smell the pot. Spot follows me and Mama back to the house.

"Grandma," I call.

"Who that out there?" Grandma asks.

"Me," I say.

"What you doing out there in all that cold for, boy?" Grandma says. I hear her coming to the door fussing. She opens the door and looks at me and Mama.

"What you doing here with all that?" she asks.

"I'm leaving him, Mama," Mama says.

"Eddie?" Grandma says. "What he done you now?"

"I'm just tired of it," Mama says.

"Come in here out that cold," Grandma says. "Walking out there in all that weather. . . ."

We go inside and Mama drops the big bundle of clothes on the floor. I go to the fire and warm my hands. Mama and Grandma come to the fire and Mama stands at the other end of the fireplace and warms her hands.

"Now what that no-good nigger done done?" Grandma asks.

"Mama, I'm just tired of Eddie running up and down the road in that car," Mama says.

"He beat you?" Grandma asks.

"No, he didn't beat me," Mama says. "Mama, Eddie didn't get home till after two this morning. Messing 'round with that old car somewhere out on the road all night."

"I warned you 'bout that nigger," Grandma says. "Even 'fore you married him. I sung at you and sung at you. I said, 'Amy, that nigger ain't no good. A yellow nigger with a gap like that 'tween his front teeth ain't no good.' But you wouldn't listen."

"Can me and Sonny stay here?" Mama asks.

"Where else can y'all go?" Grandma says. "I'm your mom, ain't I? You think I can put you out in the cold like he did?"

"He didn't put me out, Mama, I left," Mama says.

"You finally getting some sense in your head," Grandma says. "You ought to been left that nigger before you ever married him."

Uncle Al comes in the front room and looks at the bundle of clothes on the floor. Uncle Al's got on his overall, and got just one strap hooked. The other strap's hanging down his back.

"Fix that thing on you," Grandma says. "You not in a stable."

Uncle Al fixes his clothes and looks at me and Mama at the fire.

"Y'all had a round?" he asks Mama.

"Eddie and that car again," Mama says.

"That's all they want these days," Grandma says. "Cars. Why don't they marry them cars? No. When they got their troubles, they come running to the womenfolks. When they ain't got no troubles and when their pockets full of money they run jump in the car. I told you that when you was working to help him pay for it."

Uncle Al stands side me on the fireplace, and I lean against him and look at the steam coming out of a piece of wood. I get tired of Grandma fussing all the time.

"Y'all moving in with us?" Uncle Al asks.

"For a few days," Mama says. "Then I'll try to find another place somewhere in the quarters."

"Freddie's still there," Grandma says.

"Mama, please," Mama says.

"Why not?" Grandma says. "He always loved you."

"Not in front of him," Mama says.

Mama leaves the fireplace and goes to the bundle of clothes. I can hear her untying the bundle.

"Ain't it 'bout time you was leaving for school?" Uncle Al asks.

"I don't want to go," I say. "It's too cold."

"It's never too cold for school," Mama says. "Warm up good and let Uncle Al button your coat for you."

I get closer to the fire and I feel the fire on my pants. I turn around and warm my back. I turn again, and Uncle Al leans over and buttons up my coat. Uncle Al's smoking a pipe and it almost gets in my face.

"You want take a 'tato with you?" Uncle Al says.

"Uh-huh."

Uncle Al gets a potato out of the ashes and knocks all the ashes off it and puts it in my pocket.

"Now, you ready," he says.

"And be sure to come back here when you get out," Mama says, giving me my book. "Don't go back home now."

I go out on the gallery and feel the wind in my face. Oh, I hate the winter; oh, I hate it. Soon's I come in the road, I see Lucy. Lucy sees me and waits for me. I run where she is.

"Hi," I say.

"Hi," she says. And we walk to school together.

II

It's warm inside the schoolhouse. Bill made a big fire in the heater, and I can hear it roaring up the pipes. I look out the window and I can see the smoke flying cross the yard. Bill sure knows how to make a good fire. Bill's the biggest boy in school, and he always makes the fire for us.

Everybody's studying their lesson, but I don't know mine. I wish I knowed it, but I don't. Mama didn't teach me my lesson last night, and she didn't teach it to me this morning, and I don't know it.

Bob and Rex in the yard. Rex is barking at the cow. I don't know what all this other reading is. I see Rex again, and I see the cow again. But I don't know what all the rest of it is.

Bill comes up to the heater and I look up and see him putting another piece of wood in the fire. He goes back to his seat and sits down side Juanita. Miss Hebert looks at Bill when he goes back to his seat. I look in my book at Bob and Rex. Bob's got on a white shirt and blue pants. Rex is a German police dog. He's white and brown. Mr. Bouie's got a dog just like Rex. He don't bite though. He's a good dog. But Mr. Guerin old dog'll bite you, though. I seen him this morning when me and Mama was going down to Grandma's house.

I ain't go'n eat dinner at us house, because me and Mama don't stay there no more. I'm go'n eat at Grandma's house. I don't know where Daddy go'n eat dinner. He must be go'n cook his own dinner.

I can hear Bill and Juanita back of me. They whispering to each other, but I can hear them. Juanita's some pretty. I hope I was big so I could love her. But I better look at my lesson and don't think about other things.

"First grade," Miss Hebert says.

We go up to the front and sit down on the bench. Miss Hebert looks at us and makes a mark in her rollbook. She puts the rollbook down and comes over to the bench where we at.

"Does everyone know his lesson today?" she asks.

"Yes, ma'am," Lucy says, louder than anybody else in the whole school-house..

"Good," Miss Hebert says. "And I'll start with you today, Lucy. Hold your book in one hand and begin."

" 'Bob and Rex are in the yard,' " Lucy reads. " 'Rex is barking at the cow. The cow is watching Rex.' "

"Good," Miss Hebert says. "Point to barking."

Lucy points.

"Good," Miss Hebert says. "Shirley Ann, let's see how well you can read."

I look in the book at Bob and Rex. Rex is barking at the cow. The cow is looking at Rex.

"William Joseph," Miss Hebert says.

I'm next; I'm scared. I don't know my lesson and Miss Hebert go'n whip me. Miss Hebert don't like you when you don't know your lesson. Mama ought to been teached me my lesson, but she didn't. . . . Bob and Rex . . .

"Eddie," Miss Hebert says.

I don't know my lesson. I don't know my lesson. I don't know my lesson. I feel warm. I'm wet. I hear the wee-wee dripping on the floor. I'm crying. I'm crying because I wee-wee on myself. My clothes wet. Lucy and them go'n laugh at me. Billy Joe Martin and them go'n tease me. I don't know my lesson. I don't know my lesson. I don't know my lesson.

"Oh, Eddie, look what you did," I think I hear Miss Hebert saying. I don't know if she's saying this, but I think I hear her say it. My eyes shut and I'm crying. I don't want look at none of them, because I know they laughing at me.

"It's running under that bench there now," Billy Joe Martin says. "Look out for your feet back there. It's moving fast."

"William Joseph," Miss Hebert says. "Go over there and stand in that corner. Turn your face to the wall and stay there until I tell you to move. Eddie," she says to me, "go stand by the heater."

I don't move, because I'll see them, and I don't want to see them.

"Eddie," Miss Hebert says.

But I don't answer her, and I don't move.

"Bill," Miss Hebert says.

I hear Bill coming up to the front and then I feel him taking me by the hand and leading me away. I walk with my eyes shut. Me and Bill stop at the heater, because I can feel the fire. Then Bill takes my book and leaves me standing there.

"Juanita," Miss Hebert says. "Get a mop, will you. Please."

I hear Juanita going to the back, and then I hear her coming back to the front. The fire pops in the heater, but I don't open my eyes. Nobody's saying anything, but I know they all watching me.

When Juanita gets through mopping she takes the mop back, and I hear Miss Hebert going on with the lesson. When she gets through with the first graders, she calls the second graders up here.

Bill comes up to the heater and puts another piece of wood in the fire.

"Want to turn around?" he asks me.

I don't answer him, but I got my eyes open now and I'm looking down at the floor. Bill turns me around so I can dry the back of my pants. He pats me on the shoulder and goes back to his seat.

After Miss Hebert gets through with the second graders, she tells the children they can go out for recess. I can hear them getting their coats and hats. When all of them leave, I raise my head.

"Eddie," Miss Hebert says.

I turn and see her sitting behind her desk. And I see Billy Joe Martin standing in the corner with his face to the wall.

"Come up to the front," Miss Hebert says.

I go up there looking down at the floor, because I know she's go'n whip me now.

"William Joseph," Miss Hebert says. "You may leave."

Billy Joe Martin runs and gets his coat, then he runs outside to shoot marbles. I stand in front of Miss Hebert's desk with my head down.

"Look up," she says.

I raise my head and look at Miss Hebert. She's smiling, and she don't look mad.

"Now," she says. "Did you study your lesson last night?"

"Yes, ma'am," I say.

"I want the truth now," she says. "Did you?"

I oughtn't story in the churchhouse, but I'm scared Miss Hebert go'n whip me.

"Yes, ma'am," I say.

"Did you study it this morning?" she asks.

I feel a big knot coming up in my throat and I feel like I'm go'n cry again. I'm scared Miss Hebert go'n whip me, that's why I story to her.

"You didn't study your lesson, did you?" she says.

I shake my head. "No, ma'am."

"You didn't study it last night either, did you?"

"No, ma'am," I say. "Mama didn't have time to help me. Daddy wasn't home. Mama didn't have time to help me."

"Where is your father?" Miss Hebert asks.

"Cutting cane."

"Here on the place?"

"Yes, ma'am," I say.

Miss Hebert looks at me, then she gets out a pencil and starts writing on a piece of paper. I look at her writing and I look at the clock and the strap on her desk. I can hear the clock ticking. I hear Billy Joe Martin and them shooting marbles outside. I can hear Lucy and them jumping rope, and some more children playing patty-cake.

"I want you to give this to your mother or your father when you get home," Miss Hebert says. "This is only a little note saying I would like to see them sometime when they aren't too busy."

"We don't live home no more," I say.

"Oh?" Miss Hebert says. "Did you move?"

"Me and Mama," I say. "But Daddy didn't."

Miss Hebert looks at me, then she writes some more on the note. She puts her pencil down and folds the note up.

"Be sure you give this to your mother," she says. "Put it in your pocket and don't lose it."

I take the note from Miss Hebert, but I don't leave the desk.

"Do you want to go outside?" she asks.

"Yes, ma'am."

"You may leave," she says.

I go over and get my coat and cap, and then I go out in the yard. I see Billy Joe Martin and Charles and them shooting marbles over by the gate. I don't go over there because they'll tease me. I go side the schoolhouse and look at Lucy and them jumping rope. Lucy's not jumping right now.

"Hi, Lucy," I say.

Lucy looks over at Shirley and they laugh. They look at my pants and laugh.

"You want a piece of potato?" I ask Lucy.

"No," Lucy says. "And you not my boyfriend no more, neither."

I look at Lucy and I go stand side the wall in the sun. I peel my potato and eat it. And look like soon's I get through, Miss Hebert comes to the front and says recess is over.

We go inside, and I go to the back and take off my coat and cap. Bill comes back there and hangs the things up for us. I go over to Miss Hebert's desk and Miss Hebert gives me a book. I go back to my seat and sit down side Lucy.

"Hi, Lucy," I say.

Lucy looks at Shirley and Shirley puts her hand over her mouth and laughs. I feel like getting up from there and socking Shirley in the mouth, but I know Miss Hebert'll whip me. Because I got no business socking people after I done wee-wee on myself. I open my book and look at my lesson so I don't have to look at none of them.

III

It's almost dinnertime, and when I get home I'm not coming back here either, now. I'm go'n stay there. I'm go'n stay right there and sit by the fire. Lucy and them don't want play with me, and I'm not coming back up here. Miss Hebert go'n touch that little bell in a little while. She getting ready to touch it right now.

Soon's Miss Hebert touch the bell all the children run go get their hats and coats. I unhook my coat and drop it on the bench till I put my cap on. Then I put my coat on, and I get my book and leave.

I see Bill and Juanita going out the schoolyard, and I run and catch up with them. Time I get there I hear Billy Joe Martin and them coming up behind me.

"Look at that baby," Billy Joe Martin says.

"Piss on himself," Ju-Ju says.

"Y'all leave him alone," Bill says.

"Baby, baby, piss on himself," Billy Joe Martin sings.

"What'd I say?" Bill says.

"Piss on himself," Billy Joe Martin sings.

"Wait," Bill says. "Let me take my belt off."

"Good-bye, piss pot," Billy Joe Martin says. Him and Ju-Ju run down the road. They spank their hindparts with their hands and run like horses.

"They just bad," Juanita says.

"Don't pay them no mind," Bill says. "They'll leave you 'lone."

We go on down the road and Bill and Juanita hold hands. I go to Grandma's gate and open it. I look at Bill and Juanita going down the road. They walking close together, and Juanita done put her head on Bill's shoulder. I like to see Bill and Juanita like that. It makes me feel good. But when I go in the yard I don't feel good no more. I know old Grandma go'n start fussing. Spot runs down the walk with me. I put my hand on his head and me and him go back to the gallery. I make him stay on the gallery, because Grandma don't want him inside. I pull the door open and I see Grandma and Uncle Al sitting by the fire. I look for my mama, but I don't see her.

"Where Mama?" I ask Uncle Al.

"In the kitchen," Grandma says. "But she talking to somebody."

I go back to the kitchen.

"Come back here," Grandma says.

"I want see my mama now," I say.

"You'll see her when she come out," Grandma says.

"I want see my mama now," I say.

"Don't you hear me talking to you, boy?" Grandma hollers at me.

"What's the matter?" Mama asks. Mama comes out of the kitchen and Mr. Freddie Jackson comes out of there too. I hate Mr. Freddie Jackson. I never did like him. He always trying to be 'round my mama.

"That boy don't listen to nobody," Grandma says.

"Hi, Sonny," Mr. Freddie Jackson says.

I look at him standing there, but I don't speak to him. And I take the note out of my pocket and hand it to Mama.

"What's this?" Mama says.

"Miss Hebert sent it."

Mama unfolds the note and takes it to the fireplace to read it. I can see Mama's mouth working. When she gets through reading, she folds the note up again.

"She want to see me or Eddie sometime when we free," Mama says. "Sonny been doing pretty bad in his class."

"I can just see that nigger husband of yours in a schoolhouse," Grandma says.

"Mama, please," Mama says.

Mama helps me off with my coat and I go to the fireplace and stand side Uncle Al. Uncle Al pulls me between his legs and holds my hand out to the fire.

"Well?" I hear Grandma saying.

"You know how I feel 'bout her," Mr. Freddie Jackson says. "My house open to her and Sonny any time she want to come there."

"Well?" Grandma says.

"Mama, I'm still married to Eddie," Mama says.

"You mean you still love that yellow thing," Grandma says. "That's what you mean, ain't it?"

"I didn't say that," Mama says. "What would people say, out one house and in another one the same day?"

"Who care what people say?" Grandma says. "Let people say what they big 'nough to say. You looking out for yourself, not what people say."

"You understand, don't you, Freddie?" Mama says.

"I believe I do," he says. "But like I say, Amy. Any time. You know that."

"And there ain't no time like right now," Grandma says. "You can take that bundle of clothes down there for her."

"Let her make up her own mind, Rachel," Uncle Al says. "She can make up her own mind."

"If you know what's good for you, you better keep out of this," Grandma says. "She my daughter and if she ain't got sense enough to look out for herself

I have. What you want to do, go out in the field cutting sugarcane in the morning?"

"I don't mind it," Mama says.

"You done forgot how hard cutting sugarcane is?" Grandma says. "You must be done forgot."

"I ain't forgot," Mama says. "But if the other women can do it, I suppose I can do it too."

"Now you talking back," Grandma says.

"I'm not talking back, Mama," Mama says. "I just feel that it ain't right to leave one house and go to another house the same day. That ain't right in nobody's book."

"Maybe she's right, Mrs. Rachel," Mr. Freddie Jackson says.

"Her trouble is she still in love with that albino," Grandma says. "That's what your trouble is. You ain't satisfied 'less he got you doing all the work while he rip and run up and down the road with his other nigger friends. No, you ain't satisfied."

Grandma goes back in the kitchen fussing. After she leaves the fire everything gets quiet. Everything stays quiet a minute, then Grandma starts singing her church hymn.

"Why did you bring your book home?" Mama says.

"Miss Hebert say I can stay home if I want," I say. "We had us lesson already."

"You sure she said that?" Mama says.

"Uh-huh."

"I'm go'n ask her, you know."

"She said it," I say.

Mama don't say no more, but I know she still looking at me, and I don't look at her. Then Spot starts barking outside and everybody looks that way. But nobody don't move. Spot keeps barking, and I go to the door to see what he's barking at. I see Daddy coming up the walk. I pull the door and go back to the fireplace.

"Daddy coming, Mama," I say.

"Wait," Grandma says, coming out the kitchen. "Let me talk to that nigger. I'll give him a piece of my mind."

Grandma goes to the door and pushes it open. She stands in the door and I hear Daddy talking to Spot. Then Daddy comes up to the gallery.

"Amy in there, Mama?" Daddy says.

"She is," Grandma says.

I hear Daddy coming up the steps.

"And where you think you going?" Grandma asks.

"I want speak to her," Daddy says.

"Well, she don't want speak to you," Grandma says. "So you might's well go right on back down them steps and march right straight out of my yard."

"I want speak to my wife," Daddy says.

"She ain't your wife no more," Grandma says. "She left you."

"What you mean she left me?" Daddy says.

"She ain't up at your house no more, is she?" Grandma says. "That look like a good 'nough sign to me that she done left."

"Amy?" Daddy calls.

Mama don't answer. She's looking down in the fire. I don't feel good when Mama's looking like that.

"Amy?" Daddy calls.

Mama still don't answer him.

"You satisfied?" Grandma says.

"You the one trying to make Amy leave me," Daddy says. "You ain't never liked me. From the starting you didn't like me."

"That's right, I never did," Grandma says. "You yellow, you got a gap 'tween your teeth, and you ain't no good. You want me to say more?"

"You always wanted her to marry somebody else," Daddy says.

"You right again," Grandma says.

"Amy?" Daddy calls. "You can hear me, honey?"

"She can hear you," Grandma says. "She standing right there by that fireplace. She can hear you good's I can hear you. And I can hear you too good for comfort."

"I'm going in there," Daddy says. "She got somebody in there and I'm going in there and see."

"You take one more step toward my door," Grandma says, "and it'll need a undertaker to collect the pieces. So help me God I'll get that butcher knife and chop on your tail till I can't see tail to chop on. You the kind of nigger who like to rip and run up and down the road in your car long's you got a dime, but when you get broke and your belly get empty you run to your wife. You just take one more step to this door, and I bet you somebody'll be crying at your funeral. If you know anybody who care that much for you, you old yellow dog."

Daddy is quiet awhile, then I hear him crying. I don't feel good, because I don't like to hear Daddy and Mama crying. I look at Mama but she's looking down in the fire.

"You never like me," Daddy says.

"You said that before," Grandma says. "And I repeat: No, I never liked you, don't like you, and never will like you. Now get out my yard 'fore I put the dog on you."

"I want see my boy," Daddy says. "I got a right to see my boy."

"In the first place, you ain't got no right in my yard," Grandma says.

"I want see my boy," Daddy says. "You might be able to keep me from seeing my wife, but you and nobody else can keep me from seeing my son. Half of him is me."

"You ain't leaving?" Grandma asks Daddy.

"I want see my boy," Daddy says. "And I'm go'n see my boy."

"Wait," Grandma says. "Your head hard. Wait till I come back. You go'n see all kind of boys."

Grandma comes back inside and goes to Uncle Al's room. I look towards the wall and I can hear Daddy moving on the gallery. I hear Mama crying and I look at her. I don't want to see my mama crying and I lay my head on Uncle Al's knee and I want to cry.

"Amy, honey," Daddy calls. "Ain't you coming up home and cook me something to eat? It's lonely up there without you, honey. You don't know how lonely it is without you. I can't stay up there without you, honey. Please come home. . . ."

I hear Grandma coming out of Uncle Al's room and I look at her. Grandma's got Uncle Al's shotgun and she's putting a shell in it.

"Mama," Mama screams.

"Don't worry," Grandma says. "I'm go'n shoot over his head. I ain't go'n have them sending me to pen for a good-for-nothing nigger like that."

"Mama, don't," Mama says. "He might hurt himself."

"Good," Grandma says. "Save me the trouble of doing it for him."

Mama runs to the wall. "Eddie, run," she screams. "Mama got the shot-gun."

I hear Daddy going down the steps. I hear Spot running after him barking. Grandma knocks the door open with the gun barrel and shoots. I hear Daddy hollering.

"Mama, you didn'?" Mama says.

"I shot two miles over that nigger head," Grandma says. "Long-legged coward."

We all run out on the gallery and I see Daddy out in the road crying. I can see the people coming out on the galleries. They looking at us and they looking at Daddy. Daddy's standing out in the road crying.

"Boy, I would've like to seen old Eddie getting out of this yard," Uncle Al says.

Daddy's walking up and down the road in front of the house and he's crying.

"Let's go back inside," Grandma says. "We won't be bothered with him for a while."

It's cold and me and Uncle Al and Grandma go back inside. Mr. Freddie Jackson and Mama come back in little later.

"Oh, Lord," Mama says.

Mama starts crying and he takes Mama in his arms. Mama lays her head on his shoulder, but she just keeps her head there a little and she moves. "Can I go lay cross your bed, Uncle Al?" she says.

"Sure," Uncle Al says.

I watch Mama going to Uncle Al's room.

"Well, I better be going," he says.

"Freddie," Grandma calls him, from the kitchen.

"Yes, ma'am?" he says.

"Come here a minute," Grandma says.

He goes back in the kitchen where Grandma is. I get between Uncle Al's legs and look at the fire. Uncle Al rubs my head with his hand. He comes out of the kitchen and goes in Uncle Al's room where Mama is. He must be sitting down on the bed because I can hear the spring.

"Y'all come on and eat," Grandma tells me and Uncle Al.

Me and Uncle Al do like she say, because if we don't she go'n start fussing. And Lord knows I don't want hear no more fussing.

When I get through eating, I tell Uncle Al I want go back to the toilet. I don't want go back there for truth; I want go out in the yard and see if Daddy's still out there.

Soon's I come on the gallery I see him. He's standing by the gate looking at the house. He beckons for me to come to the gate, and I go out there. Daddy grabs me like I might run away from him and hugs me real tight.

"You still love your daddy, Sonny?" he asks me.

"Uh-huh."

Daddy hugs me and kisses me on the face.

"I love my baby," he says, "I love my baby. Where your mama?"

"Laying cross Uncle Al bed in his room," I say. "And Mr. Freddie Jackson in there, too."

Daddy pushes me away and looks at me real hard. "Who else in there?" he asks. "Who else?"

"Just them," I say. "Uncle Al in Grandma's room by the fire, and Grandma's in the kitchen."

"Oh, Lord," Daddy says. "Oh, Lord, have mercy." He turns his head and starts crying. Then he looks at me again. "This ain't right. I bet you it ain't nobody but your grandma. It's her, ain't it?"

"Uh-huh. She sent him in there."

"Oh, Lord," Daddy says. "And right in front of her little grandson—and in daylight, too." He looks at me real sad and holds me to him again. I can feel his pocket button against my face. "Come on, Sonny," he says.

"Where we going?"

"Madame Toussaint," he says. "I hate it, but I got to."

He takes my hand and me and him walk away. When we cross the railroad tracks, I see the people cutting cane. No matter how far you look you don't see nothing but cane.

"Get me a piece of cane, Daddy," I say.

"Sonny, please," he says. "I'm thinking."

"I want a piece of two-ninety," I say.

Daddy turns my hand loose and jumps over the ditch. He finds a piece of two-ninety and jumps back over. Daddy takes out a little knife and peels the cane with it. He gives me a round and he cuts him off a round and chews it. I like two-ninety cane. It's soft and sweet and got plenty juice in it.

"I want another piece," I say.

Daddy cuts me off another round and hands it to me.

"I'll be glad when you big enough to peel your own cane," he says.

"I can peel my own cane now," I say.

Daddy breaks me off three joints and hands it to me. I peel the cane with my teeth. Two-ninety cane is soft and it's easy to peel.

Me and Daddy go round the bend, then I can see Madame Toussaint's house. Madame Toussaint got a old house, and look like it wants to fall down any minute. I'm scared of Madame Toussaint. Billy Joe Martin say Madame Toussaint's a witch, and he said one time he seen Madame Toussaint riding a broom.

Daddy pulls Madame Toussaint little old broken-down gate open and we go in the yard. Me and Daddy go far as the steps, but we don't go up on the gallery. Madame Toussaint got plenty trees round her house—little trees and big trees; and she got moss hanging from every tree. I move closer so Daddy can hold my hand.

"Madame Toussaint?" Daddy calls.

Madame Toussaint don't answer. Like she ain't there.

"Madame Toussaint?" Daddy calls again.

"Who that?" Madame Toussaint answers.

"Me," Daddy says. "Eddie Howard and his little boy Sonny."

"What you want?" Madame Toussaint calls from in her house.

"I want talk to you," Daddy says. "I need little advise on something."

I hear a dog bark three times in the house. He must be a big dog because he sure's got a heavy voice. Madame Toussaint comes to the door and cracks it open.

"Can I come in?" Daddy says.

"Come on in," Madame Toussaint says.

Me and Daddy go up the steps and Madame Toussaint opens the door for us. Madame Toussaint's a little bitty little old lady and her face the color of cowhide. I look at Madame Toussaint and I walk close side Daddy. Me and Daddy go in the house and Madame Toussaint shuts the door and comes back to her fireplace. She sits down in her big old rocking chair and looks at me and

Daddy. I look round Daddy's leg at Madame Toussaint, but I let Daddy hold my hand.

"I need some advise, Madame Toussaint," Daddy says.

"Your wife left you," Madame Toussaint says.

"How you know?" Daddy asks.

"That's all you men come back here for," Madame Toussaint says. "That's how I know."

"Yes," Daddy says. "She done left and staying with another man already."

"She left," Madame Toussaint says. "But she's not staying with another man."

"Yes, she is," Daddy says.

"She's not," Madame Toussaint says. "You trying to tell me my business?"

"No, ma'am," Daddy says.

"I should hope not," Madame Toussaint says.

Madame Toussaint ain't got but three old rotten teeth in her mouth. I bet you she can't peel no cane with them old rotten teeth. I bet you they'd break off in a hard piece of cane.

"I need advise, Madame Toussaint," Daddy says.

"You got money?" Madame Toussaint asks.

"I got some," Daddy says.

"How much?" she asks Daddy. She's looking up at Daddy like she don't believe him.

Daddy turns my hand loose and sticks his hand down in his pocket. He gets all his money out his pocket and leans over the fire to see how much he's got. I see some matches and a piece of string and some nails in Daddy's hand. I reach for the piece of string and Daddy taps me on the hand.

"I got about seventy-five cents," Daddy says. "Counting pennies and all."

"My price is three dollars," Madame Toussaint says.

"I can cut you a load of wood," Daddy says. "Or make grocery for you. I'll do anything in the world if you can help me, Madame Toussaint."

"Three dollars," Madame Toussaint says. "I got all the wood I'll need this winter. Enough grocery to last me till summer."

"But this all I got," Daddy says.

"When you get more, come back," Madame Toussaint says.

"But I want my wife back now," Daddy says. "I can't wait till I get more money."

"Three dollars is my price," Madame Toussaint says. "No more, no less."

"But can't you give me just a little advise for seventy-five cents?" Daddy says. "Seventy-five cents' worth? Maybe I can start from there and figure something out."

"Give me the money," Madame Toussaint says. "But don't complain to me if you're not satisfied."

"Don't worry," Daddy says. "I won't complain. Anything to get her back home."

Daddy leans over the fire again and picks the money out of his hand. Then he reaches it to Madame Toussaint.

"Give me that little piece of string, too," Madame Toussaint says. "It might come in handy sometime in the future. Wait," she says. "Run it across the boy's face three times, then pass it to me behind your back."

"What's that for?" Daddy asks.

"Just do like I say," Madame Toussaint says.

"Yes, ma'am," Daddy says. Daddy turns to me. "Hold still a second," he says. He rubs the little old dirty piece of cord over my face and then sticks his hand behind his back.

Madame Toussaint reaches in her pocket and takes out her pocketbook. She opens it and puts the money in. She opens another little compartment and stuffs the string down in it. Then she snaps the pocketbook and puts it back in her pocket. She picks up three little green sticks she got tied together and starts poking in the fire with them.

"What's the advise?" Daddy asks.

Madame Toussaint don't say nothing.

"Madame Toussaint?" Daddy says.

Madame Toussaint still don't answer him—she just looks down in the fire. Her face is red from the fire. I get scared of Madame Toussaint. She can ride all over the plantation on her broom. Billy Joe Martin seen her one night riding cross the houses. She was whipping her broom with three switches.

Madame Toussaint raises her head and looks at Daddy. Her eyes's big and white, and I get scared of her. I hide my face side Daddy's leg.

"Give it up," I hear her say.

"Give what up?" Daddy says.

"Give it up," she says.

"What?" Daddy says.

"Give it up," she says.

"I don't even know what you talking 'bout," Daddy says. "How can I give up something and I don't know what it is?"

"I said it three times," Madame Toussaint says. "No more, no less. Up to you now to follow it through from there."

"Follow what from where?" Daddy says. "You said three little old words. 'Give it up.' I don't know no more now than I knowed before I come here."

"I told you you wasn't go'n be satisfied," Madame Toussaint says.

"You want me to be satisfied with just three little old words?" Daddy says.

"You can leave," Madame Toussaint says.

"What?" Daddy says. "You mean I give you seventy-five cents for three words? A quarter a word? And I'm leaving? Uh-uh."

"Rollo?" Madame Toussaint says.

I see Madame Toussaint's big old black dog get up out of the corner and come where she is. Madame Toussaint starts patting him on the head.

"Two dollars and twenty-five cents more and you get all the advise you need," Madame Toussaint says.

"Can't I get you a load of wood and fix your house for you or something?" Daddy says.

"I don't want my house fixed and I don't need no more wood," Madame Toussaint says. "I got three loads of wood just three days ago from a man who didn't have money. Before I know it I'll have wood piled up all over my yard."

"Can't I do anything?" Daddy asks.

"You can leave," Madame Toussaint says. "I ought to have somebody else dropping around pretty soon. Lately I've been having men dropping in three times a day. All of them just like you. What they can do to make their wives love them more. What they can do to keep their wives from running around with some other man. What they can do to make their wives give in. What they can do to make their wives scratch their backs. What they can do to make their wives look at them when they talking. Get out of my house before I put the dog on you. You been here too long for seventy-five cents."

Madame Toussaint's big old black dog gives three loud barks that makes my head hurt. Madame Toussaint pats him on the head to calm him down.

"Come on, Sonny," Daddy says.

I let Daddy take my hand and we go out of the house. It's freezing outside.

"What was them words again?" Daddy asks me.

"Hunh?"

"What she said when she looked up out the fire?" Daddy asks.

"I was scared," I say. "Her face was red and her eyes got big and white. I was scared. I had to hide my face."

"Didn't you hear what she told me?" Daddy asks.

"She told you three dollars," I say.

"I mean when she looked up, Sonny," Daddy says.

"She said 'Give it up,'" I say.

"Yes," Daddy says. "'Give it up.' Give what up? I don't even know what she's talking 'bout. I hope she don't mean give you and Amy up. She ain't that crazy. I don't know nothing else she can be talking 'bout. You don't know, do you?"

"Uh-uh," I say.

"'Give it up,'" Daddy says. "'Give it up.' I wonder who them other men was she was speaking of. Charles and his wife had a fight the other week. It might be him. Frank Armstrong and his wife had a round couple weeks back. It might be him. I wonder what kind of advise she gived them. No, I'm sure that can't help me out. I just need three dollars. Three dollars is the only thing go'n make her talk."

"I want another piece of cane," I say.

"No," Daddy says. "You'll be peeing in bed all night tonight."

"Me and Mama go'n stay at Grandma house tonight," I say.

"Please be quiet, Sonny," Daddy says. "I got enough troubles on my mind. Don't add more, please."

I stay quiet after this, and I can see people cutting cane all over the field. I can see more people loading cane on a wagon.

"Come on," Daddy says. "I got to get me a few dollars some kind of way."

Daddy carries me cross the ditch on his back. I look down at the stubbles where the people done cut the cane. Them rows some long. Plenty cane's lying on the ground. I can see cane all over the field. Me and Daddy go over where the people cutting cane.

"How come you ain't working this evening?" a man asks Daddy.

"Charlie around anywhere?" Daddy asks the man.

"Farther over," the man says. "Hi, youngster."

"Hi," I say.

Me and Daddy go cross the field, and I can hear Mr. Charlie singing. Mr. Charlie stops his singing when he sees me and Daddy. He chops the top off a armful of cane and throws it cross the row. Mr. Charlie's cutting cane all by himself.

"Hi, Brother Howard," Mr. Charlie says.

"Hi," Daddy says. Daddy squats down and let me slide off his back.

"Hi there, little Brother Sonny," Mr. Charlie says.

"Hi," I say.

"That's good," Mr. Charlie says. "How you this beautiful day, Brother Howard?"

"I'm fine," Daddy says. "Charlie, I want to know if you can spare me 'bout three dollars till Saturday."

"Sure, Brother Howard," Mr. Charlie says. "You mind telling me just why you need it? I don't mind lending a good Brother anything long's I know he ain't throwing it away."

"I want to pay Madame Toussaint for some advise," Daddy says.

"Trouble, Brother?" Mr. Charlie asks.

"Amy done left me, Charlie," Daddy says. "I need some advise. I just got to get her back."

"I know what you mean, Brother," Mr. Charlie says. "I had to visit Madame—you won't carry this no farther, huh?"

"Of course not."

"Just the other week I had to take a little trip back there to consult her," Mr. Charlie says.

"What was wrong?" Daddy asks.

"Little misunderstanding between me and Sister Laura," Mr. Charlie says.

"She helped?" Daddy asks.

"Told me to stop spending so much time in church and little more time at home." Mr. Charlie says. "I couldn't see that. You know as far back as I can go in my family, my people been good church members."

"I know that," Daddy says.

" 'Just slack up a little bit,' she tole me. 'Go twice a week, and spend the rest of the time at home.' I'm following her advise, Brother Howard, and I wouldn't be a bit surprise if there ain't a little Charlie next summer sometime."

"Charlie, you old dog," Daddy says.

Mr. Charlie laughs.

"I'll be doggone," Daddy says. "I'm glad to hear that."

"I'll be the happiest man on the plantation," Mr. Charlie says.

"I know how you feel," Daddy says. "Yes, I know how you feel. But that three, can you lend it to me?"

"Sure, Brother," Mr. Charlie says. "Anything to bring a family back together. Nothing more important in this world than family love. Yes, indeed."

Mr. Charlie unbuttons his overall pocket and takes out the money.

"The only thing I got is five, Brother Howard," he says. "You don't happen to have change, huh?"

"I don't have a dime, Charlie," Daddy says. "But I'll be more than happy if you can let me have that five. I need some grocery in the house, too."

"Sure, Brother," Mr. Charlie says. He gives Daddy the money. "Nothing looks more beautiful than a family at a table eating something the little woman just cooked. You said Saturday, didn't you, Brother?"

"Yes," Daddy says. "I'll pay you back soon as I get paid. You can't ever guess how much this mean to me, Charlie."

"Glad I can help, Brother," Mr. Charlie says. "Hope she can do likewise."

"I hope so too," Daddy says. "Anyhow, this a start."

"See you Saturday, Brother," Mr. Charlie says.

"Soon's I get paid," Daddy says. "Hop on, Sonny, and hold tight. 'Cause I might not be able to stop and pick you up if you drop off."

IV

Daddy walks up on Madame Toussaint's gallery and knocks on the door.

"Who that?" Madame Toussaint asks.

"Me. Eddie Howard," Daddy says. He squats down so I can slide off his back. I slide down and I let Daddy hold my hand.

"What you want, Eddie Howard?" Madame Toussaint asks.

"I got three dollars," Daddy says. "I still want that advise."

Madame Toussaint's big old black dog barks three times, then I hear

Madame Toussaint coming to the door. Madame Toussaint peeps through the keyhole at me and Daddy. She opens the door and lets me and Daddy come in. We go to the fireplace and warm. Madame Toussaint comes to the fireplace and sits down in her big old rocking chair. She looks at Daddy.

"You got three dollars?" she asks.

"Yes," Daddy says. He takes out the money and shows it to her. Madame Toussaint reaches for it, but Daddy pulls it back. "This is five." he says.

"You go'n get your two dollar change," Madame Toussaint says.

"Come to think of it," Daddy says, "I ought to just owe you two and a quarter, since I done already gived you seventy-five cents."

"You want advise?" Madame Toussaint asks Daddy. Madame Toussaint looks like she's getting mad with Daddy now.

"Sure," Daddy says. "But since—"

"Then shut up and hand me your money," Madame Toussaint says.

"But I done already—"

"Get out my house, nigger," Madame Toussaint says. "And don't come back till you learn how to act."

"All right," Daddy says. "I'll give you three more dollars."

Madame Toussaint gets her pocketbook out her pocket. Then she leans close to the fire so she can look down in it. She sticks her hand in the pocketbook and gets two dollars. She looks at the two dollars a long time. She stands up and gets her eyeglasses off the mantelpiece and puts them on. She looks at the two dollars a long time, then she hands them to Daddy. She sticks the money Daddy gived her in the pocketbook; then she takes off her eyeglasses and puts them back on the mantelpiece. Madame Toussaint sits in her big old rocker and starts poking in the fire with the three switches again. Her face gets red from the fire. Her eyes gets big and white. I turn my head and hide behind Daddy's leg.

"Go set fire to your car," Madame Toussaint says.

"What?" Daddy says.

"Go set fire to your car," Madame Toussaint says.

"You talking to me?" Daddy asks.

"Go set fire to your car," Madame Toussaint says.

"Now, just a minute," Daddy says. "I didn't give you my hard-earned three dollars for that kind of foolishness. I dismiss that seventy-five cents you took from me, but not my three dollars that easy."

"You want your wife back?" Madame Toussaint asks Daddy.

"That's what I'm paying you for," Daddy says.

"Then go set fire to your car," Madame Toussaint says. "You can't have both."

"You must be fooling," Daddy says.

"I don't fool," Madame Toussaint says. "You paid for advise and I gived you advise."

"You mean that?" Daddy says. "You mean I got to go burn up my car for Amy to come back home?"

"If you want her back there," Madame Toussaint says. "Do you?"

"I wouldn't be standing here if I didn't," Daddy says.

"Then go and burn it up," Madame Toussaint says. "A gallon of coal oil and a penny box of matches ought to do the trick. You got any gas in it?"

"A little bit—if nobody ain't drained it," Daddy says.

"Then you can use that," Madame Toussaint says. "But if you want her back there, you got to burn it up. That's my advise to you. And if I was you I'd do it right away. You can never tell."

"Tell about what?" Daddy asks.

"She might be sleeping in another man's bed a week from now," Madame Toussaint says. "This man loves her and he's kind. And that's what a woman wants. That's what they need. You men don't know this, but you better learn it before it's too late."

"Can't I at least sell the car?" Daddy says.

"You got to burn it, nigger," Madame Toussaint says, getting mad with Daddy again. "How come your head so hard?"

"But I paid good money for that car," Daddy says. "It wouldn't look right if I just jump up and put fire to it."

"You, get out my house," Madame Toussaint says, looking up at Daddy and pointing her finger. "Go do just what you want with your car. It's yours. But don't you come back here bothering me any more."

"I don't know," Daddy says. "That just don't look right."

"I'm through talking," Madame Toussaint says. "Rollo? Come on, baby."

Big old black Rollo comes up and puts his head in Madame Toussaint's lap. Madame Toussaint pats him on the head.

"Come on," Daddy says. "I reckon we better be going."

Daddy squats down and I climb up on his back. I look to Madame Toussaint patting big old black Rollo on his head.

Daddy pushes the door open and we go outside. It's cold outside. Daddy goes down Madame Toussaint's three old broken-down steps and we go out in the road.

"I don't know," Daddy says.

"Hunh?"

"I'm talking to myself," Daddy says. "I don't know 'bout burning up my car."

"You go'n burn up your car?" I ask.

"That's what Madame Toussaint say to do," Daddy says. "But I don't know."

Daddy walks fast and I bounce on his back.

"God, I wish there was another way out," Daddy says. "Don't look like that's right for a man to just set fire to something like that. Look like I ought to be able to sell it for little something. Get some of my money back. Burning it, I don't get a red copper. That just don't sound right to me. I wonder if she was fooling. No. She say she wasn't. Maybe that wasn't my advise she seen in that fireplace. Maybe that was somebody else advise. Maybe she gived me the wrong one. Maybe it belongs to the man coming back there after me. They go there three times a day, she can get them mixed up."

I bounce on Daddy's back and I close my eyes. When I open them I see me and Daddy going cross the railroad tracks. We go up the quarters to Grandma's house. Daddy squats down and I slide off his back.

"Run in the house to the fire," Daddy says. "Tell your mama come to the door."

Soon's I come in the yard, Spot runs down the walk and starts barking. Mama and all of them come out on the gallery.

"My baby," Mama says. Mama comes down the steps and hugs me to her. "My baby," she says.

"Look at that old yellow thing standing out in that road," Grandma says. "What you ought to been done was got the law on him for kidnap."

Me and Mama go back on the gallery.

"I been to Madame Toussaint house," I say.

Mama looks at me and looks at Daddy out in the road. Daddy comes to the gate and looks at us on the gallery.

"Amy," Daddy calls. "Can I speak to you a minute? Just one minute?"

"You don't get away from my gate I'm go'n make that shotgun speak to you," Grandma says. "I didn't get you at twelve o'clock, but I won't miss you now."

"Amy, honey," Daddy calls. "Please."

"Come on, Sonny," Mama says.

"Where you going?" Grandma asks.

"Far as the gate," Mama says. "I'll talk to him. I reckon I owe him that much."

"You leave this house with that nigger, don't you ever come back here again," Grandma says.

"You oughtn't talk like that, Rachel," Uncle Al says.

"I talk like I want," Grandma says. "She's my daughter, not yours; neither his."

Me and Mama go out to the gate where Daddy is. Daddy stands outside the gate and me and Mama stand inside.

"Lord, you look good, Amy," Daddy says. "Honey, didn't you miss me? Go on and say it. Go on and say it now."

"That's all you want say to me?" Mama says.

"Honey, please," Daddy says. "Say you miss me. I been suffering all day long."

"Come on, Sonny," Mama says. "Let's go back inside."

"Honey," Daddy says, "if I burn the car like Madame Toussaint say, you'll come back home?"

"What?" Mama says.

"She say for Daddy—"

"Be still, Sonny," Mama says.

"She say for me to set fire to it and you'll come home," Daddy says. "You'll come back."

"We going home, Mama?" I ask.

"You'll come back?" Daddy asks. "Tonight?"

"I'll come back," Mama says.

"If I sold it?" Daddy says.

"Burn it," Mama says.

"I can get about fifty for it," Daddy says. "You could get a couple of dresses out of that."

"Burn it," Mama says.

Daddy looks across the gate at Mama a long time. Mama looks straight at Daddy. Daddy shakes his head.

"I can't argue with you, honey," he says. "I'll go and burn it right now. You can come too if you want."

"No," Mama says. "I'll be here when you come back."

"Couldn't you go up home and start cooking some supper?" Daddy asks. "I ain't et since breakfast."

"I'll cook after you burn it," Mama says. "Come on, Sonny."

"Can I go see Daddy burn his car, Mama?" I ask.

"No," Mama says. "You been in that cold too long already."

"I want see Daddy burn his car," I say. I start crying and stomping so Mama'll let me go.

"Let him go, honey," Daddy says. "I'll keep him warm."

"You can go," Mama says. "But don't come to me if you start coughing tonight, you hear?"

"Uh-huh," I say.

Mama makes sure all my clothes buttoned good, then she lets me go. I run out in the road where Daddy is.

"I'll be back soon as I can, honey," Daddy says. "And we'll straighten out everything, hear?"

"Just make sure you burn it," Mama says. "I'll find out."

"Honey, I'm go'n burn every bit of it," Daddy says.

"I'll be here when you come back," Mama says. "How you figuring on getting up there?"

"I'll go over and see if George Williams can't take me," Daddy says.

"I don't want Sonny in that cold too long," Mama says. "And you keep your hands in your pockets, Sonny."

"I ain't go'n take them out," I say.

Mama looks at Daddy and goes back up the walk.

"I love your mama some, boy," Daddy says, looking at Mama. "I love her so much it makes me hurt. I don't know what I'd do if she left me for good."

"Can I get on your back, Daddy?" I say.

"Can't you walk sometime?" Daddy says. "What do you think I'm is, a horse?"

V

Mr. George Williams pulls to the side of the road, then him and Daddy get out. Daddy opens the back door and I get out.

"Look like we got company," Mr. George Williams says.

We go over where the people are. They got a little fire going and some of them's sitting on the car fender. The rest of them standing round the fire.

"Welcome," somebody says.

"Thanks," Daddy says. "Since this my car you setting on."

"Oh," the man says. He jumps up and the other two men jump up. They go over to the little fire and stand round it.

"We didn't mean no harm," one of them say.

Daddy goes over and peers in the car, then he opens the door and gets in. I go over to the car where he is.

"Go stand side the fire," Daddy says.

"I want get in with you."

"Do what I tell you," Daddy says.

I go back to the fire, and I look at Daddy in the car. Daddy passes his hand all over the car, then he just sits there quiet and sad-like. All the people round the fire look at Daddy in the car. After a while he gets out and comes over to the fire.

"Well," he says, "I guess that's it. You got a rope?"

"In the trunk," Mr. George Williams says. "What you go'n do, drag it off the highway?"

"We can't burn it out here," Daddy says.

"He say he go'n burn it," somebody at the fire says.

"I'm go'n burn it," Daddy says. "It's mine."

"Easy, Eddie," Mr. George Williams says.

Daddy is mad but he don't say no more. Mr. George Williams looks at Daddy, then he goes over to his car and gets the rope.

"Ought to be strong enough," he says. He hands Daddy the rope, and he goes and turns his car around. Everybody at the fire watch his backing up to Daddy's car.

"Good," Daddy says.

Daddy gets between the cars and ties them together. Some of the people come over and watch him.

"Y'all got a side road anywhere round here?" Daddy asks.

"Right over there," the man says. "Leads off back in the field. You ain't go'n burn up that good car for real, is you?"

"Who field this is?" Daddy asks.

"Mr. Roger Medlow," the man says.

"Any colored people got fields round here?" Daddy asks.

"Old man Ned Johnson, 'bout two miles down the road," another man says.

"Why don't we just take it on back to the quarters?" Mr. George Williams says. "I doubt if Mr. Grover'll mind if we burn it there."

"All right," Daddy says. "Might as well."

Me and Daddy get in his car. Some of the people from the fire run up to Mr. George Williams's car. Mr. George Williams tells them something, and I see three of them jumping in. Mr. George Williams taps on the horn, then we start. I set back in the seat and look at Daddy. Daddy is quiet and sad-like.

We go way down the road, then we turn and go down the quarters. Soon's we get down there, I hear two of the men in Mr. George Williams's car calling to the people. I set up in the seat and look out at them. They standing on the fenders, calling to the people.

"Come on," they saying. "Come on to the car burning. Free. Free."

We go farther down the quarters, and the two men keep on calling.

"Come on, everybody," one of them says.

"We having a car burning party tonight," the other one says. "No charges."

The people start coming out on the galleries to see what all the racket is. I look back and I see some out in the yard, and some already out in the road. Mr. George Williams stops in front of Grandma's house.

"You go'n tell Amy?" he calls to Daddy. "Maybe she want to go, too, since you doing it all for her."

"Go tell your mama come on," Daddy says.

I jump out the car and run in the yard. It's freezing almost.

"Come on everybody," one of them says.

"We having a car burning party tonight," the other one says. "Everybody invited."

I pull Grandma's door open and go in. Mama and Uncle Al and Grandma's sitting at the fireplace.

"Mama, Daddy say come on if you want to see the burning," I say.

"See what burning?" Grandma asks. "Don't tell me that crazy nigger going through with that."

"Come on, Mama," I say.

Mama and Uncle Al get up from the fireplace and go to the door.

"He sure got it out there," Uncle Al says.

"Come on, Mama," I say. "Come on, Uncle Al."

"Wait till I get my coat," Mama says. "Mama, you going?"

"I ain't missing this for the world," Grandma says. "I still think he's bluffing."

Grandma gets her coat and Uncle Al goes and gets his coat; then we go outside. Plenty people standing round Daddy's car now. I can see more people opening doors and coming out on the galleries.

"Get in," Daddy says. "Sorry I can't take but two. Mama, you want ride?"

"No, thanks," Grandma says. "You might just get it in your head to run off in that canal with me in there. Let your wife and child ride. I'll walk with the rest of the people."

"Get in, honey," Daddy says. "It's cold out there."

Mama takes my arm and helps me in; then she gets in and shuts the door.

"How far down you going?" Uncle Al asks.

"Near the sugarhouse," Daddy says. He taps on the horn and Mr. George Williams drives away.

"Come on, everybody," one of the men says.

"We having a car burning party tonight," the other one says. "Everybody invited."

Mr. George Williams drives his car over the railroad. I look back and I see plenty people following Daddy's car. I can't see Grandma and Uncle Al, but I know they back there too.

We keep going. We get almost to the sugarhouse, then we turn down another road. This road is rough, and I have to bounce on the seat.

"Well, I reckon this's it," Daddy says.

Mama don't say nothing to Daddy.

"You know it ain't too late to change your mind," Daddy says. "All I have to do is tap on this horn and George'll stop."

"You brought any matches?" Mama asks.

"All right," Daddy says. "All right. Don't start fussing."

We go a little farther and Daddy blows the horn. Mr. George Williams stops his car. Daddy gets out of his car and goes and talks with Mr. George Williams. Little later I see Daddy coming back.

"Y'll better get out here," he says. "We go'n take it down the field a piece."

Me and Mama get out. I look down the headland and I see Uncle Al and Grandma and all the other people coming. They come up where me and Mama's standing. I look down in the field and I see the cars going down the row. It's dark, but Mr. George Williams's car lights shine bright. The cars stop and Daddy gets out of his car and goes and unties it. Mr. George Williams comes back to the headlane and turns his lights on Daddy's car so all of us can see the burning. I see Daddy getting some gas out of the tank.

"Give me a hand down here," Daddy calls. That don't even sound like his voice. Sounds like somebody else doing the calling. The men run down the field where he is and start shaking on the car. I see the car leaning; then it goes over.

"Well," Grandma says. "I never would've believed it."

I see Daddy going all around the car with the can, then I see him splashing some gas inside the car. All the other people back away from the car. I see Daddy scratching a match and throwing it in the car. Then he throws another one in there. I see little fire; then I see plenty.

"I just do declare," Grandma says. "He's a man after all."

Everybody else is quiet. We stay there a long time and look at the fire. The fire burns down low and Daddy and them go look at the car. Daddy gets the can and pours some more gas on the fire. The fire gets big again. We look at the fire some more.

"Never thought that was in Eddie," somebody says.

"You not the only one," somebody says.

"He loved that car more than he loved anything."

The fire burns down again. Daddy and them go and look at the car. They stay there a little while; then they come out to the headlane where we standing.

"That's about it, honey," Daddy says.

"Then let's go home," Mama tells him. "Sonny?" she says to me.

Me and Mama go in Grandma's house and pull the big bundle out on the gallery. Daddy picks the bundle up and puts it on his head; then we go up the quarters to us house.

"You hungry?" Mama asks Daddy.

"I'm starving," Daddy says.

"You want eat now or after you whip me?" Mama says.

"Whip you?" Daddy asks. "What I'm go'n whip you for?"

Mama goes back in the kitchen. She don't find what she's looking for, and I hear her going outside.

"Where Mama going, Daddy?"

"Don't ask me," Daddy says. "I don't know no more than you."

Daddy gets some kindling out of the corner and puts it in the fireplace. Then he pours some coal oil on the kindling and lights a match to it. Me and Daddy squat down on the fireplace and watch the fire burning.

I hear the back door open and shut; then I see Mama coming in the front room. She's got a great big old switch with her.

"Here," she says.

"What's that for?" Daddy says.

"Here. Take it," Mama says.

"I ain't got nothing to beat you for," Daddy says.

"You whip me," Mama says. "Or I turn right around and walk out that door." Daddy stands up and looks at Mama.

"You must be crazy," Daddy says. "Stop all that foolishness and go cook me some supper, woman."

"Get your pot, Sonny," Mama says.

"Shucks," I say. "Now where we going? I'm getting tired walking in all that cold. I'm go'n catch pneumonia 'fore I know it."

"Get your pot and stop answering me back," Mama says.

I go to my bed and pick the pot up again. I ain't never picked that pot up so much in all my life.

"You ain't leaving here," Daddy says.

"You better stop me," Mama says, going to the bundle.

"All right," Daddy says. "I'll beat you if that's what you want."

Daddy picks up the switch and I start crying.

"Lord, have mercy," Daddy says. "Now what?"

"Whip me," Mama says.

"Amy, whip you for what?" Daddy says. "Amy, please, just go back there and cook me something to eat."

"Come on, Sonny," Mama says. "Let's get out of here."

"All right," Daddy says. Daddy hits Mama two times on the legs. "That's enough," he says.

"Beat me," Mama says.

I cry some more. "Don't beat my mama," I say. "I don't want you to beat my mama."

"Sonny, please," Daddy says. "What y'all trying to do to me? Run me crazy? I burnt up the car. Ain't that enough?"

"I'm just go'n tell you one more time," Mama says.

"All right," Daddy says. "I'm go'n beat you, if that's what you want."

Daddy starts beating Mama, and I cry some more. But Daddy don't stop this time.

"Beat me harder," Mama says. "I mean it. I mean it."

"Honey, please," Daddy says.

"You better do it," Mama says. "I mean it."

Daddy keeps on beating Mama, and Mama cries and goes down on her knees.

"Leave my mama alone, you old yellow dog," I say. "You leave my mama alone." I throw the pot at him but I miss, and the pot go bouncing across the floor.

Daddy throws the switch away and runs to Mama and picks her up. Mama's crying in Daddy's arms. Daddy takes Mama over to the bed and lies her on the bed. Daddy lies down side Mama.

"I didn't want hit you, honey," Daddy says. "I didn't want hit you. You made me. You made me hit you."

Daddy begs Mama to stop crying, but Mama keeps on crying. I get on my bed and cry in the blanket.

I feel somebody shaking me, and I must've been asleep.

"Wake up," I hear Daddy saying.

"I'm tired and I don't feel like getting up. I feel like sleeping some more."

"You want some supper?" Daddy asks.

"Uh-huh."

"Get up then," Daddy says.

I get up. I got all my clothes on and my shoes on.

"It's morning?" I ask.

"No," Daddy says. "Still night. Come back in the kitchen and get some supper."

I follow Daddy in the kitchen, and me and him sit down at the table. Mama brings the food to the table, and she sits down too.

"Bless this food, Father, which we're 'bout to receive, the nurse of our bodies, for Christ sakes, amen," Mama says.

I raise my head and look at Mama. I can see where Mama's been crying. Mama's face is swole. I look at Daddy and Daddy's eating. Mama and Daddy don't talk and I don't say nothing neither. I eat my food. We eating sweet potatoes and bread. I got me a glass of clabber, too.

"What a day," Daddy says.

Mama don't say nothing. Daddy don't say no more neither. Mama ain't eating much. She's just picking over her food.

"Mad?" Daddy says.

"Uh-huh," Mama says.

"Honey?" Daddy says.

Mama looks at him.

"I didn't beat you 'cause you did us thing with Freddie Jackson, did I?" Daddy says.

"No," Mama says.

"Well, why, then?" Daddy says.

" 'Cause I don't want you to be the laughingstock of the quarters," Mama says.

"Who go'n laugh at me?" Daddy says.

"Everybody," Mama says. "Mama and all. Now they don't have nothing to laugh about."

"Honey, I don't mind if they laugh at me," Daddy says.

"I do mind," Mama says.

"Did I hurt you?"

"I'm all right," Mama says.

"You ain't mad no more?" Daddy says.

"No," Mama says. "I'm not mad."

Mama picks up a little bit of food and puts it in her mouth.

"Finish eating your supper, Sonny," she says.

"I got enough," I say.

"Drink your clabber," Mama says.

I drink all my clabber and I show Mama the glass.

"Go get your book," Mama says. "It's on the dresser."

I go in the front room to get my book.

"One of us got to go to school with him tomorrow," I hear Mama saying. I see her handing Daddy the note. Daddy waves it back. "Here," she says.

"Honey, you know I don't know how to act in no place like that," Daddy says.

"Time to learn," Mama says, giving him the note. "What page your lesson on, Sonny?"

I turn to the page, and I lean on Mama's leg and let her carry me over my lesson. Mama holds the book in her hand. She carries me over my lesson two times; then she makes me point to some words and spell some words.

"He know it," Daddy says.

"I'll take you over it again tomorrow morning," Mama says. "Don't let me forget it now."

"Uh-huh."

"Your daddy'll carry you over it tomorrow night," Mama says. "One night me, one night you."

"With no car," Daddy says. "I reckon I'll be around plenty now. You think we'll ever get another one, honey?"

Daddy's picking his teeth with a broomstraw.

"When you learn how to act with one," Mama says. "I ain't got nothing 'gainst cars."

"I guess you right, honey," Daddy says. "I was going little too far."

"It's time for you to go to bed, Sonny," Mama says. "Go in the front room and say your prayers to your daddy."

Me and Daddy leave Mama there in the kitchen. I put my book on the dresser and I go to the fireplace where Daddy's at. Daddy puts another piece of wood on the fire and plenty sparks shoot up the chimney. Daddy helps me to take off my clothes, and I kneel down and lean on his leg.

"Start off," Daddy says. "I'll stop you if you miss something."

"Lay me down to sleep," I say, "I pray the Lord my soul to keep. If I should die before I wake, I pray the Lord my soul to take. God bless Mama and Daddy. God bless Grandma and Uncle Al. God bless the church. . . . God bless Miss Hebert. . . . God bless Bill and Juanita." I hear Daddy gasping. "And God bless everybody else."

I jump off my knees. Them bricks on the fireplace make my knees hurt.
"Did you tell Him to bless Madame Toussaint?" Daddy says.
"No," I say. "I'm scared of Madame Toussaint."
"That's got nothing to do with it," Daddy says. "Get back down there."
I get back on my knees. I don't get on the bricks because they make my
knees hurt. I get on the floor and lean against Daddy's legs.
"And God bless Madame Toussaint," I say.
"All right," Daddy says. "Warm up good."
Daddy goes over to my bed and pulls the cover back.
"Come on," he says. "Jump in."
I run and jump in the bed. Daddy pulls the cover up to my neck.
"Good night, Daddy."
"Good night," Daddy says.
"Good night, Mama."
"Good night, Sonny," Mama says.
I turn on my side and look at Daddy at the fireplace. Mama comes out of
the kitchen and goes to the fireplace. Mama warms up good and goes to the
bundle.
"Leave it alone," Daddy says. "We'll get up early tomorrow morning and
get it."
"I'm going to bed," Mama says. "You coming now?"
"Uh-huh," Daddy says.
Mama comes to my bed and tucks the cover under me good. She leans over
and kisses me and tucks the cover some more. She goes over to the bundle and
gets her nightgown; then she goes in the kitchen to put it on. She comes back
and puts her clothes she took off on a chair side the wall. Mama kneels down
and says her prayers; then she gets in bed and covers up. Daddy stands up and
takes off his clothes. I see Daddy in his big old long white BVDs. Daddy blows
out the lamp, and I hear the spring when Daddy gets in the bed. Daddy never
says any prayers.
"Sleepy?" Daddy says.
"Uh-uh."
I hear the spring. I hear Mama and Daddy talking low, but I don't know
what they saying. I go to sleep some, but I open my eyes. It's some dark in the
room. I hear Mama and Daddy talking low. I like Mama and Daddy. I like Uncle
Al, but I don't like old Grandma too much. Grandma's always talking bad about
Daddy. I don't like old Mr. Freddie Jackson. I like Mr. George Williams. We
went riding way up the road with Mr. George Williams. We got Daddy's car
and brought it all the way back here. Daddy and them turned the car over and
Daddy poured some gas on it and set it on fire. Daddy ain't got no more car
now. . . . I know my lesson. I ain't go'n wee-wee on myself no more. Daddy's
going to school with me tomorrow. I'm go'n show him I can beat Billy Joe

Martin shooting marbles. I can shoot all over Billy Joe Martin. And I can beat him running, too. He thinks he can run fast. I'm go'n show Daddy I can beat him running. . . . I don't know why I had to say, "God bless Madame Toussaint." I don't like her. And I don't like old Rollo, neither. Rollo can bark some loud. He made my head hurt. Madame Toussaint's old house don't smell good. Us house smells good. I hear the spring on Mama and Daddy's bed. I get way under the cover. I go to sleep little bit, but I wake up. I go to sleep some more. I hear the spring on Mama and Daddy's bed—shaking, shaking. It's some dark under this cover. It's warm. I feel good way under here.

The Lesson

Toni Cade Bambara

1972

Back in the days when everyone was old and stupid or young and foolish and me and Sugar were the only ones just right, this lady moved on our block with nappy hair and proper speech and no makeup. And quite naturally we laughed at her, laughed the way we did at the junk man who went about his business like he was some big-time president and his sorry-ass horse his secretary. And we kinda hated her too, hated the way we did the winos who cluttered up our parks and pissed on our handball walls and stank up our hallways and stairs so you couldn't halfway play hide-and-seek without a goddamn gas mask. Miss Moore was her name. The only woman on the block with no first name. And she was black as hell, cept for her feet, which were fish-white and spooky. And she was always planning these boring-ass things for us to do, us being my cousin, mostly, who lived on the block cause we all moved north the same time and to the same apartment then spread out gradual to breathe. And our parents would yank our heads into some kinda shape and crisp up our clothes so we'd be presentable for travel with Miss Moore, who always looked like she was going to church, though she never did. Which is just one of the things the grown-ups talked about when they talked behind her back like a dog. But when she came calling with some sachet she'd sewed up or some gingerbread she'd made or some book, why then they'd all be too embarrassed to turn her down and we'd get handed over all spruced up. She'd been to college and said it was only right that she should take responsibility for the young ones' education, and she not even related by marriage or blood. So they'd go for it. Specially Aunt Gretchen. She was the main gofer in the family. You got some ole dumb shit foolishness you want somebody to go for, you send for Aunt Gretchen. She been screwed into the go-along for so long, it's a blood-deep natural thing with her. Which is how she got saddled with me and Sugar and Junior in the first place while our mothers were in a la-de-da apartment up the block having a good ole time.

So this one day Miss Moore rounds us all up at the mailbox and it's puredee hot and she's knockin herself out about arithmetic. And school suppose to let up in summer, I heard, but she don't never let up. And the starch in my pinafore scratching the shit outa me and I'm really hating this nappy-head bitch and her goddamn college degree. I'd much rather go to the pool or to the show where it's cool. So me and Sugar leaning on the mailbox being surly, which is a Miss Moore word. And Flyboy checking out what everybody brought for lunch. And Fat Butt already wasting his peanut-butter-and-jelly sandwich like the pig he is. And Junebug punchin on Q.T.'s arm for potato chips. And Rosie Giraffe shifting from one hip to the other waiting for somebody to step on her foot or ask her if she from Georgia so she can kick ass, preferably Mercedes'. And Miss Moore asking us do we know what money is, like we a bunch of retards. I mean real money, she say, like it's only poker chips or monopoly papers we lay on the grocer. So right away I'm tired of this and say so. And would much rather snatch Sugar and go to the Sunset and terrorize the West Indian kids and take their hair ribbons and their money too. And Miss Moore files that remark away for next week's lesson on brotherhood, I can tell. And finally I saw we oughta get to the subway cause it's cooler and besides we might meet some cute boys. Sugar done swiped her mama's lipstick, so we ready.

So we heading down the street and she's boring us silly about what things cost and what our parents make and how much goes for rent and how money ain't divided up right in this country. And then she gets to the part about we all poor and live in the slums, which I don't feature. And I'm ready to speak on that, but she steps out in the street and hails two cabs just like that. Then she hustles half the crew in with her and hands me a five-dollar bill and tells me to calculate ten-percent tip for the driver. And we're off. Me and Sugar and Junebug and Flyboy hangin out the window and hollering to everybody, putting lipstick on each other cause Flyboy a faggot anyway, and making farts with our sweaty armpits. But I'm mostly trying to figure how to spend this money. But they all fascinated with the meter ticking and Junebug starts laying bets as to how much it'll read when Flyboy can't hold his breath no more. Then Sugar lays bets as to how much it'll be when we get there. So I'm stuck. Don't nobody want to go for my plan, which is to jump out at the next light and run off to the first bar-b-que we can find. Then the driver tells us to get the hell out cause we there already. And the meter reads eighty-five cents. And I'm stalling to figure out the tip and Sugar say give him a dime. And I decide he don't need it bad as I do, so later for him. But then he tries to take off with Junebug foot still in the door so we talk about his mama something ferocious. Then we check out that we on Fifth Avenue and everybody dressed up in stockings. One lady in a fur coat, hot as it is. White folks crazy.

"This is the place," Miss Moore say, presenting it to us in the voice she uses at the museum. "Let's look in the windows before we go in."

"Can we steal?" Sugar asks very serious like she's getting the ground rules squared away before she plays.

"I beg your pardon," say Miss Moore, and we fall out. So she leads us around the windows of the toy store and me and Sugar screamin, "This is mine, that's mine, I gotta have that, that was made for me, I was born for that," till Big Butt drowns us out.

"Hey, I'm goin to buy that there."

"That there? You don't even know what it is, stupid."

"I do so," he say, punchin on Rosie Giraffe. "It's a microscope."

"Whatcha gonna do with a microscope, fool?"

"Look at things."

"Like what, Donald?" ask Miss Moore. And Big Butt ain't got the first notion. So here go Miss Moore gabbing about the thousands of bacteria in a drop of water and the somethin or other in a speck of blood and the million and one living things in the air around us is invisible to the naked eye. And what she say that for? Junebug go to town on that "naked" and we rolling. Then Miss Moore ask what it cost. So we all jam into the window smudgin it up and the price tag say $300. So then she ask how long'd take for Big Butt and Junebug to save up their allowances. "Too long," I say. "Yeah," adds Sugar, "outgrown it by that time." And Miss Moore says no, you never outgrow learning instruments. "Why, even medical students and interns and—" blah, blah, blah. And we ready to choke Big Butt for bringing it up in the first damn place.

"This here costs four hundred eighty dollars," say Rosie Giraffe. So we pile up all over her to see what she pointin out. My eyes tell me it's a chunk of glass cracked with something heavy, and different-color inks dripped into the splits, then the whole thing put into a oven or something. But for $480 it don't make sense.

"That's a paperweight made of semiprecious stones fused together under tremendous pressure," Miss Moore explains slowly, with her hands doing the mining and all the factory work.

"So what's a paperweight?" asks Rosie Giraffe.

"To weigh paper with, dumbbell," say Flyboy, the wise man from the East.

"Not exactly," say Miss Moore, which is what she say when you warm or way off too. "It's to weigh paper down so it won't scatter and make your desk untidy." So right away me and Sugar curtsy to each other and then to Mercedes, who is more the tidy type.

"We don't keep paper on top of the desk in my class," say Junebug, figuring Miss Moore crazy or lyin, one.

"At home, then," she say. "Don't you have a calendar and a pencil case and a blotter and a letter opener on your desk at home where you do your homework?" And she know damn well what our homes look like 'cause she noseys around in them every chance she gets.

"I don't even have a desk," say Junebug. "Do we?"

"No. And I don't get no homework neither," says Big Butt.

"And I don't even have a home," say Flyboy, like he do at school to keep the white folks off his back and sorry for him. Send-this-poor-kid-to-camp posters is his specialty.

"I do," says Mercedes. "I have a box of stationery on my desk and a picture of my cat. My godmother bought the stationery and the desk. There's a big rose on each sheet and the envelopes smell like roses."

"Who wants to know about your smelly-ass stationery," say Rosie Giraffe fore I can get my two cents in.

"It's important to have a work area all your own so that—"

"Will you look at this sailboat, please," say Flyboy, cuttin her off and pointin to the thing like it was his. So once again we tumble all over each other to gaze at this magnificent thing in the toy store which is just big enough to maybe sail two kittens across the pond if you strap them to the posts tight. We all start reciting the price tag like we in assembly. "Handcrafted sailboat of fiberglass at one thousand one hundred ninety-five dollars."

"Unbelievable," I hear myself say and am really stunned. I read it again for myself just in case the group recitation put me in a trance. Same thing. For some reason this pisses me off. We look at Miss Moore and she lookin at us, waiting for I dunno what.

"Who'd pay all that when you can buy a sailboat set for a quarter at Pop's, a tube of glue for a dime, and a ball of string for eight cents? It must have a motor and a whole lot else besides," I say. "My sailboat cost me about fifty cents."

"But will it take water?" say Mercedes with her smart ass.

"Took mine to Alley Pond Park once," say Flyboy. "String broke. Lost it. Pity."

"Sailed mine in Central Park and it keeled over and sank. Had to ask my father for another dollar."

"And you got the strap," laugh Big Butt. "The jerk didn't even have a string on it. My old man wailed on his behind."

Little Q.T. was staring hard at the sailboat and you could see he wanted it bad. But he too little and somebody'd just take it from him. So what the hell. "This boat for kids, Miss Moore?"

"Parents silly to buy something like that just to get all broke up," say Rosie Giraffe.

"That much money it should last forever," I figure.

"My father'd buy it for me if I wanted it."

"Your father, my ass," say Rosie Giraffe, getting a chance to finally push Mercedes.

"Must be rich people shop here," say Q.T.

"You are a very bright boy," say Flyboy. "What was your first clue?" And he rap him on the head with the back of his knuckles, since Q.T. the only one he could get away with. Though Q.T. liable to come up behind you years later and get his licks in when you half expect it.

"What I want to know is," I says to Miss Moore, though I never talk to her, I wouldn't give the bitch that satisfaction, "is how much a real boat costs? I figure a thousand'd get you a yacht any day."

"Why don't you check that out," she says, "and report back to the group?" Which really pains my ass. If you gonna mess up a perfectly good swim day least you could do is have some answers. "Let's go in," she say like she got something up her sleeve. Only she don't lead the way. So me and Sugar turn the corner to where the entrance is, but when we get there I kinda hang back. Not that I'm scared, what's there to be afraid of, just a toy store. But I feel funny, shame. But what I got to be shamed about? Got as much right to go in as anybody. But somehow I can't seem to get hold of the door, so I step away from Sugar to lead. But she hangs back too. And I look at her and she looks at me and this is ridiculous. I mean, damn, I have never ever been shy about doing nothing or going nowhere. But then Mercedes steps up and then Rosie Giraffe and Big Butt crowd in behind and shove, and next thing we all stuffed into the doorway with only Mercedes squeezing past us, smoothing out her jumper and walking right down the aisle. Then the rest of us tumble in like a glued-together jigsaw done all wrong. And people lookin at us. And it's like the time me and Sugar crashed into the Catholic church on a dare. But once we got in there and everything so hushed and holy and the candles and the bowin and the handkerchiefs on all the drooping heads, I just couldn't go through with the plan. Which was for me to run up to the altar and do a tap dance while Sugar played the nose flute and messed around in the holy water. And Sugar kept givin me the elbow. Then later teased me so bad I tied her up in the shower and turned it on and locked her in. And she'd be there till this day if Aunt Gretchen hadn't finally figured I was lyin about the boarder takin a shower.

Same thing in the store. We all walkin on tiptoe and hardly touchin the games and puzzles and things. And I watched Miss Moore who is steady watchin us like she waitin for a sign. Like Mama Drewery watches the sky and sniffs the air and takes note of just how much slant is in the bird formation. Then me and Sugar bump smack into each other, so busy gazing at the toys, 'specially the sailboat. But we don't laugh and go into our fat-lady bump-stomach routine. We just stare at that price tag. Then Sugar run a finger over the whole boat. And I'm jealous and want to hit her. Maybe not her, but I sure want to punch somebody in the mouth.

"Watcha bring us here for, Miss Moore?"

"You sound angry, Sylvia. Are you mad about something?" Givin me one of them grins like she tellin a grown-up joke that never turns out to be funny.

And she's lookin very closely at me like maybe she plannin' to do my portrait from memory. I'm mad, but I won't give her that satisfaction. So I slouch around the store bein very bored and say, "Let's go."

Me and Sugar at the back of the train watchin the tracks whizzin by, large then small then gettin gobbled up in the dark. I'm thinkin about this tricky toy I saw in the store. A clown that somersaults on a bar then does chin-ups just cause you yank lightly at his leg. Cost $35. I could see me askin my mother for a $35 birthday clown. "You wanna who that costs what?" she'd say, cocking her head to the side to get a better view of the hole in my head. Thirty-five dollars could buy new bunk beds for Junior and Gretchen's boy. Thirty-five dollars and the whole household could go visit Granddaddy Nelson in the country. Thirty-five dollars would pay for the rent and the piano bill too. Who are these people that spend that much for performing clowns and a thousand dollars for toy sailboats? What kinda work they do and how they live and how come we ain't in on it? Where we are is who we are, Miss Moore always pointin out. But it don't necessarily have to be that way, she always adds, then waits for somebody to say that poor people have to wake up and demand their share of the pie and don't none of us know what kind of pie she talking about in the first damn place. But she ain't so smart 'cause I still got her four dollars from the taxi and she sure ain't gettin it. Messin up my day with this shit. Sugar nudges me in my pocket and winks.

Miss Moore lines us up in front of the mailbox where we started from, seem like years ago, and I got a headache for thinkin so hard. And we lean all over each other so we can hold up under the draggy-ass lecture she always finishes us off with at the end before we thank her for borin us to tears. But she just looks at us like she readin tea leaves. Finally she say, "Well, what did you think of F. A. O. Schwarz?"

Rosie Giraffe mumbles, "White folks crazy."

"I'd like to go there again when I get my birthday money," says Mercedes, and we shove her out the pack so she has to lean on the mailbox by herself.

"I'd like a shower. Tiring day," say Flyboy.

Then Sugar surprises me by saying, "You know, Miss Moore, I don't think all of us here put together eat in a year what that sailboat costs." And Miss Moore lights up like somebody goosed her. "And?" she say, urging Sugar on. Only I'm standin on her foot so she don't continue.

"Imagine for a minute what kind of society it is in which some people can spend on a toy what it would cost to feed a family of six or seven. What do you think?"

"I think," say Sugar, pushing me off her feet like she never done before, 'cause I whip her ass in a minute, "that this is not much of a democracy if you ask me. Equal chance to pursue happiness means an equal crack at the dough, don't it?" Miss Moore is besides herself and I am disgusted with Sugar's treachery. So I stand on her foot one more time to see if she'll shove me. She shuts up, and Miss Moore looks at me, sorrowfully I'm thinkin. And somethin weird is goin on, I can feel it in my chest.

"Anybody else learn anything today?" Lookin dead at me. I walk away and Sugar has to run to catch up and don't even seem to notice when I shrug her arm off my shoulder.

"Well, we got four follars anyway," she says.

"Uh hunh."

"We could go to Hascombs and get half a chocolate layer and then go to the Sunset and still have plenty money for potato chips and ice cream sodas."

"Uh hunh."

"Race you to Hascombs," she say.

We start down the block and she gets ahead, which is O.K. by me cause I'm going to the West End and then over to the Drive to think this day through. She can run if she want to and even run faster. But ain't nobody gonna beat me at nuthin.

The Story of a Scar

James Alan McPherson

1973

Since Dr. Wayland was late and there were no recent news magazines in the waiting room, I turned to the other patient and said, "As a concerned person, and as your brother, I ask you, without meaning to offend, how did you get that scar on the side of your face?"

The woman seemed insulted. Her brown eyes, which before had been wandering vacuously about the room, narrowed suddenly and sparked humbling reprimands at me. She took a draw on her cigarette, puckered her lips, and blew a healthy stream of smoke toward my face. It was a mean action, deliberately irreverent and cold. The long curving scar on the left side of her face darkened. "I ask *you,*" she said, "as a nosy person with no connections in your family, how come your nose is all bandaged up?"

It was a fair question, considering the possible returns on its answer. Dr. Wayland would remove the bandages as soon as he came in. I would not be asked again. A man lacking permanence must advertise. "An accident of passion," I told her. "I smashed it against the headboard of my bed while engaged in the act of love."

Here she laughed, but not without intimating, through heavy, broken chuckles, some respect for my candor and the delicate cause of my affliction. This I could tell from the way the hardness mellowed in her voice. Her appetites were whetted. She looked me up and down, almost approvingly, and laughed some more. This was a robust woman, with firm round legs and considerable chest. I am small. She laughed her appreciation. Finally, she lifted a brown palm to her face, wiping away tears. "You *cain't* be no married man," she observed. "A wife ain't worth *that* much."

I nodded.

"I knowed it," she said. "The best mens don't git married. They do they fishin' in goldfish bowls."

"I am no adulterer," I cautioned her. "I find companionship wherever I can."

She quieted me by throwing out her arm in a suggestion of offended modesty. She scraped the cigarette on the white tile beneath her foot. "You don't have to tell me a thing," she said. "I know mens goin' and comin'. There ain't a-one of you I'd trust to take my grandmama to Sunday school." Here she paused, seemingly lost in some morbid reflection, her eyes wandering across the room to Dr. Wayland's frosted glass door. The solemnity of the waiting room reclaimed us. We inhaled the antiseptic fumes that wafted from the inner office. We breathed deeply together, watching the door, waiting. "Not a-one," my companion said softly, her dark eyes wet.

The scar still fascinated me. It was a wicked black mark that ran from her brow down over her left eyelid, skirting her nose but curving over and through both lips before ending almost exactly in the center of her chin. The scar was thick and black and crisscrossed with a network of old stitch patterns, as if some meticulous madman had first attempted to carve a perfect half-circle in her flesh and then decided to embellish his handiwork. It was so grotesque a mark that one had the feeling it was the art of no human hand and could be peeled off like so much soiled putty. But this was a surgeon's office and the scar was real. It was as real as the honey-blond wig she wore, as real as her purple pantsuit. I studied her approvingly. Such women have a natural leaning toward the abstract expression of themselves. Their styles have private meanings, advertise secret distillations of their souls. Their figures, and their disfigurations, make meaningful statements. Subjectively, this woman was the true sister of the man who knows how to look while driving a purple Cadillac. Such craftsmen must be approached with subtlety if they are to be deciphered. "I've never seen a scar quite like that one," I began, glancing at my watch. Any minute Dr. Wayland would arrive and take off my bandages, removing me permanently from access to her sympathies. "Do you mind talking about what happened?"

"I *knowed* you'd git back around to that," she answered, her brown eyes cruel and level with mine. "Black guys like you with them funny eyeglasses are a real trip. You got to know everything. You sit in corners and watch people." She brushed her face, then wiped her palm on the leg of her pantsuit. "I read you the minute you walk in here."

"As your brother . . ." I began.

"How can you be my brother when your mama's a man?" she said.

We both laughed.

"I was pretty once," she began, sniffing heavily. "When I was sixteen my mama's preacher was set to leave his wife and his pulpit and run off with me to *Dee*troit City. Even with this scar and all the weight I done put on, you can still see what I had." She paused. *"Cain't* you?" she asked significantly.

I nodded quickly, looking into her big body for the miniature of what she was.

From this gesture she took assurance. "I was twenty when it happen," she went on. "I had me a good job in the post office, down to the Tenth Street branch. I was a sharp dresser, too, and I had me my choice of mens: big ones, puny ones, old mens, married mens, even D. B. Ferris, my shift supervisor, was after me on the sly—don't let these white mens fool you. He offered to take me off the primaries and turn me onto a desk job in hand-stampin' or damaged mail. But I had my pride. I told him I rather work the facin' table, *every shift*, than put myself in his debt. I shook my finger in his face and said, 'You ain't foolin' me, with your *sly self!* I know where the *wild goose went;* and if you don't start havin' some *respect* for black women, he go'n come *back!*' So then he turn red in the face and put me on the facin' table. Every shift. What could I do? You ain't got no rights in the post office, no matter what lies the government tries to tell you. But I was makin' good money, dressin' bad, and I didn't want to start no trouble for myself. Besides, in them days there was a bunch of good people workin' my shift: Leroy Boggs, Red Bone, 'Big Boy' Tyson, Freddy May—"

"What about that scar?" I interrupted her tiresome ramblings. "Which one of them cut you?"

Her face flashed a wall of brown fire. "This here's *my* story!" she muttered, eyeing me up and down with suspicion. "You dudes cain't stand to hear the whole of anything. You want everything broke down in little pieces." And she waved a knowing brown finger. "That's how come you got your nose all busted up. There's some things you have to take your time about."

Again I glanced at my watch, but was careful to nod silent agreement with her wisdom. "It was my boyfriend that caused it," she continued in a slower, more cautious tone. "And the more I look at you the more I can see you just like him. He had that same way of sittin' with his legs crossed, squeezin' his sex juices up to his brains. His name was Billy Crawford, and he worked the parcel-post window down to the Tenth Street branch. He was nine years older than me and was goin' to school nights on the GI Bill. I was twenty when I met him durin' lunch break down in the swing room. He was sittin' at a table against the wall, by hisself, eatin' a cheese sandwich with his nose in a goddamn book. I didn't know any better then. I sat down by him. He looked up at me and say, 'Water seeks its own level, and people do, too. You are not one of the riffraff or else you would of sit with them good-timers and bullshitters 'cross the room. Welcome to my table.' By riffraff he meant all them other dudes and girls from the back room, who believed in havin' a little fun playin' cards and such durin' lunch hour. I thought what he said was kind of funny, and so I laughed. But I should of knowed better. He give me a cheese sandwich and started right off preachin' at me about the lowlife in the back room. Billy couldn't stand none of 'em. He hated the way they dressed, the way they talked, and the way they carried on durin' work hours. He said if all them tried to be like him and advanced themselfs, the Negro wouldn't have no problems. He'd point out Eugene Wells or Red Bone or Crazy Sammy Michaels and tell me, 'People like them think they can homestead in the post office. They think these primaries will need human hands for another twenty years. But you just watch the Jews and Puerto Ricans that pass through here. *They* know what's goin' on. I bet you don't see none of them settin' up their beds under these tables. They tryin' to improve themselfs and get out of here, just like me.' Then he smile and held out his hand. 'And since I see you're a smart girl that keeps a cold eye and some distance on these bums, welcome to the club. My name's Billy Crawford.'

"To tell you the truth, I liked him. He was different from all the jive-talkers and finger-poppers I knew. I liked him because he wasn't ashamed to wear a white shirt and a black tie. I liked the way he always knew just what he was gonna do next. I liked him because none of the other dudes could stand him, and he didn't seem to care. On our first date he took me out to a place where the white waiters didn't git mad when they saw us comin'. That's the kind of style he had. He knew how to order wine with funny names, the kind you don't never see on billboards. He held open doors for me, told me not to order rice with gravy over it or soda water with my meal. I didn't mind him helpin' me. He was a funny dude in a lot of ways: his left leg was shot up in the war and he limped sometimes, but it looked like he was struttin'. He would stare down anybody that watched him walkin'. He told me he had cut his wife loose after he got out of the army, and he told me about some of the games she had run on him. Billy didn't trust women. He said they all was after a workin' man's money, but he said that I was different. He said he could tell I was a God-fearin' woman and my mama had raised me right, and he was gonna improve my mind. In those days I didn't have no objections. Billy was fond of sayin', 'You met me at the right time in your life.'

"But Red Bone, my co-worker, saw what was goin' down and began to take a strong interest in the affair. Red was the kind of strong-minded sister that mens just like to give in to. She was one of them big yellow gals with red hair and a loud rap that could put a man in his place by just soundin' on him. She like to wade through the mailroom, elbowin' dudes aside and sayin', 'You don't wanna mess with *me*, fool! I'll *destroy* you! Anyway, you ain't nothin' but a dirty thought I had when I was three years old!' But if she liked you she could be warm and soft, like a mama. 'Listen,' she kept tellin' me, 'that Billy Crawford is a potential punk. The more I watch him, the less man I see. Every time we downstairs havin' fun I catch his eyeballs rollin' over us from behind them goddamn books! There ain't a rhythm in his body, and the only muscles he exercises is in his eyes.'

"That kind of talk hurt me some, especially comin' from her. But I know it's the way of some women to bad-mouth a man they want for themselfs. And what woman don't want a steady man and a good provider?—which is what Billy was. Usually, when they start downgradin' a steady man, you can be sure they up to somethin' else besides lookin' out after you. So I told her, 'Billy don't have no bad habits.' I told her. "He's a hard worker, he don't drink, smoke, nor run around, and he's gonna git a *college* degree.' But that didn't impress Red. I was never able to figure it out, but she had something in for Billy. Maybe it was his attitude; maybe it was the little ways he let everybody know that he was just passin' through; maybe it was because Red had broke every man she ever had and had never seen a man with no hand holes on him. Because that Billy Crawford was a strong man. He worked the day shift, and could of been a supervisor in three or four years if he wanted to crawl a little and grease a few palms; but he did his work, quiet-like, pulled what overtime he could, and went to class three nights a week. On his day off he'd study and maybe take me out for a drink after I got off. Once or twice a week he might let me stay over at his place, but most of the time he'd take me home to my Aunt Alvene's, where I was roomin' in those days, before twelve o'clock.

"To tell the truth, I didn't really miss the partyin' and the dancin' and the good-timin' until Red and some of the others started avoidin' me. Down in the swing room durin' lunch hour, for example, they wouldn't wave for me to come over and join a card game. Or when Leroy Boggs went around to the folks on the floor of the mailroom, collectin' money for a party, he wouldn't even ask me to put a few dollars in the pot. He'd just smile at me in a cold way and say to somebody loud enough for me to hear, 'No, sir; ain't no way you can git quality folk to come out to a Saturday night fish fry.' "

"Red squared with me when I asked her what was goin' down. She told me, 'People sayin' you been wearin' a high hat since you started goin' with the professor. The talk is you been throwin' around big words and developin' a strut just like his. Now I don't believe these reports, being your friend and sister, but I do think you oughta watch your step. I remember what my grandmama used to tell me: "It don't make no difference how well you fox-trot if everybody else is dancin' the two-step." Besides, that Billy Crawford is a potential punk, and you gonna be one lonely girl when somebody finally turns him out. Use your mind, girl, and stop bein' silly. Everybody is watchin' you!'

"I didn't say nothin', but what Red said started me to thinkin' harder than I had ever thought before. Billy had been droppin' strong hints that we might git married after he got his degree, in two or three years. He was plannin' on being a high school teacher. But outside of being married to a teacher, what was I go'n git out of it? Even if we did git married, I was likely to be stuck right there in the post office with no friends. And if he didn't marry me, or if he was a punk like Red believed, then I was a real dummy for givin' up my good times and my best days for a dude that wasn't go'n do nothin' for me. I didn't make up my mind right then, but I begin to watch Billy Crawford with a different kind of eye. I'd just turn around at certain times and catch him in his routines: readin', workin', eatin', runnin' his mouth about the same things all the time. Pretty soon I didn't have to watch him to know what he was doin'. He was more regular than Monday mornings. That's when a woman begins to tip. It ain't never a decision, but somethin' in you starts to lean over and practice what you gonna say whenever another man bumps into you at the right time. Some women, especially married ones, like to tell lies to their new boyfriends; if the husband is a hard worker and a good provider, they'll tell the boyfriend that he's mean to them and ain't no good when it comes to sex; and if he's good with sex, they'll say he's a cold dude that's not concerned with the problems of the world like she is, or that they got married too young. Me, I believe in tellin' the truth: that Billy Crawford was too good for most of the women in this world, me included. He deserved better, so I started lookin' round for somebody on my own level.

"About this time a sweet-talkin' young dude was transferred to our branch from the 39th Street substation. The grapevine said it was because he was makin' woman trouble over there and caused too many fights. I could see why. He dressed like he was settin' fashions every day; wore special-made bell-bottoms with so much flare they looked like they was starched. He wore two diamond rings on the little finger of his left hand that flashed while he was throwin' mail, and a gold tooth that sparkled all the time. His name was Teddy Johnson, but they called him 'Eldorado' because that was the kind of hog he drove. He was involved in numbers and other hustles and used the post office job for a front. He was a strong talker, a easy walker, that dude was a *woman* stalker! I have to give him credit. He was the last *true* son of the Great McDaddy—"

"Sister," I said quickly, overwhelmed suddenly by the burden of insight. "I *know* the man of whom you speak. There is no time for this gutter patter and indirection. Please, for my sake and for your own, avoid stuffing the shoes of the small with mythic homilies. This man was a bum, a hustler, and a small-time punk. He broke up your romance with Billy, then he lived off you, cheated on you, and cut you when you confronted him." So pathetic and gross seemed her elevation of the fellow that I abandoned all sense of caution. "Is your mind so *dead,*" I continued, "did his switchblade slice so *deep,* do you have so little *respect* for yourself, or at least for the idea of *proportion* in this sad world, that you'd sit here and *praise* this brute!?"

She lit a second cigarette. Then, dropping the match to the floor, she seemed to shudder, to struggle in contention with herself. I sat straight on the blue plastic couch, waiting. Across the room the frosted glass door creaked, as if about to open; but when I looked, I saw no telling shadow behind it. My companion crossed her legs and held back her head, blowing two thoughtful streams of smoke from her broad nose. I watched her nervously, recognizing the evidence of past destructiveness, yet fearing the imminent occurrence of more. But it was not her temper or the potential strength of her fleshy arms that I feared. Finally she sighed, her face relaxed, and she wet her lips with the tip of her tongue. "You know everything," she said in a soft tone, much unlike her own. "A black mama birthed you, let you suck her titty, cleaned your dirty drawers, and you still look at us through paper and movie plots." She paused, then continued in an even softer and more controlled voice. "Would you believe me if I said that Teddy Johnson loved me, that this scar is to him what a weddin' ring is to another man? Would you believe that he was a better man than Billy?"

I shook my head in firm disbelief.

She seemed to smile to herself, although the scar, when she grimaced, made the expression more like a painful frown. "Then would you believe that I was the cause of Billy Crawford goin' crazy and not gettin' his college degree?"

I nodded affirmation.

"Why?" she asked.

"Because," I answered, "from all I know already, that would seem to be the most likely consequence. I would expect the man to have been destroyed by the pressures placed on him. And, although you are my sister and a woman who has already suffered greatly, I must condemn you and your roughneck friends for this destruction of a man's ambitions."

Her hardened eyes measured my face. She breathed heavily, seeming to grow larger and rounder on the red chair. "My brother," she began in an icy tone, "is as far from what you are as I am from being patient." Now her voice became deep and full, as if aided suddenly by some intricately controlled well-spring of pain. Something aristocratic and old and frighteningly wise seemed to have awakened in her face. "Now this is the way it happened," she fired at me, her eyes wide and rolling. "I want you to *write* it on whatever part of your brain that ain't already covered with page print. I want you to *remember* it every time you stare at a scarred-up sister on the street and *choke* on it before you can work up spit to condemn her. I was *faithful* to that Billy Crawford. As faithful as a woman could be to a man that don't ever let up or lean back and stop worryin' about where he's gonna be ten years from last week. Life is to be *lived*, not traded on like *dollars!* . . . All that time I was goin' with him, my feets itched to dance, my ears hollered to hear somethin' besides that whine in his voice, my body wanted to press up against somethin' besides that facin' table. I was young and pretty; and what woman don't want to enjoy what she got while she got it? Look around sometime: there ain't *no mens,* young nor old, chasin' *no older womens,* no matter how pretty they *used to be!* But Billy Crawford couldn't see nothin' besides them *goddamn books* in front of his face. And what the Jews and Puerto Ricans was doin'. Whatever else Teddy Johnson was, he was a dude that knowed how to live. He wasn't out to *destroy* life, you can believe *that!* Sure I listened to his rap. Sure I give him the come-on. With Billy workin' right up front and watchin' everything, Teddy was the only dude on the floor that would talk to me. Teddy would say, 'A girl that's got what you got needs a man that have what I have.' And that ain't all he said, either!

"Red Bone tried to push me closer to him, but I am not a sneaky person and didn't pay her no mind. She'd say, 'Girl, I think you and Eldorado ought to git it on. There ain't a better-lookin' dude workin' in the post office. Besides, you ain't goin' *nowheres* with that professor Billy Crawford. And if *you* scared to tell him to lean up off you, I'll do it *myself,* bein' as I am your sister and the one with your interest in mind.' But I said to her, 'Don't do me no favors. No matter what you think of Billy, I am no sneaky woman. I'll handle my own affairs.' Red just grin and look me straight in the eye and grin some more. I already told you she was the kind of strong-minded sister that could look right down into you. Nobody but a woman would understand what she was lookin' at.

"Now Billy wasn't no dummy durin' all this time. Though he worked the parcel-post window up front, from time to time durin' the day he'd walk back in the mailroom and check out what was goin' down. Or else he'd sit back and listen to the gossip durin' lunch hour, down in the swing room. He must of seen Teddy Johnson hangin' round me, and I know he seen Teddy give me the glad-eye a few times. Billy didn't say nothin' for a long time, but one day he pointed to Teddy and told me, 'See that fellow over there? He's a bloodletter. There's some people with a talent for stoppin' bleedin' by just being around, and there's others that start it the same way. When you see that greasy smile of his you can bet it's soon gonna be a bad day for somebody, if they ain't careful. That kind of fellow's been walkin' free for too long.' He looked at me with that tight mouth and them cold brown eyes of his. He said, 'You know what I mean?' I said I didn't. He said, 'I hope you don't ever have to find out.'

"It was D. B. Ferris, my shift supervisor, that set up things. He's the same dude I told you about, the one that was gonna give me the happy hand. We never saw much of him in the mailroom, although he was kinda friendly with Red Bone. D. B. Ferris was always up on the ramps behind one of the wall slits, checkin' out everything that went down on the floor and tryin' to catch somebody snitchin' a letter. There ain't no tellin' how much he knew about private things goin' on. About this time he up and transferred three or four of us, the ones with no seniority, to the night shift. There was me, Red, and Leroy Boggs. When Billy found out he tried to talk D. B. Ferris into keepin' me on the same shift as his, but Ferris come to me and I told him I didn't mind. And I didn't. I told him I was tired of bein' watched by him and everybody else. D. B. Ferris looked up toward the front where Billy was workin' and smiled that old smile

of his. Later, when Billy asked me what I said, I told him there wasn't no use
tryin' to fight the government. 'That's true,' he told me—and I thought I saw
some meanness in his eyes—'but there are some other things you can fight,' he
said. At that time my head was kinda light, and I didn't catch what he meant.

"About my second day on the night shift, Teddy Johnson began workin'
overtime. He didn't need the money and didn't like to work nohow, but some
nights around ten or eleven, when we clocked out for lunch and sat around in
the swing room, in would strut Teddy. Billy would be in school or at home.
Usually, I'd be sittin' with Red and she'd tell me things while Teddy was walkin'
over. "Girl, it *must* be love to make a dude like Eldorado work overtime. *He*
needs to work like *I* need to be a Catholic.' Then Teddy would sit down and
she'd commence to play over us like her life depended on gittin' us together.
She'd say, 'Let's go over to my place this mornin' when we clock out. I got some
bacon and eggs and a bottle of Scotch.' Teddy would laugh and look in my eyes
and say, 'Red, we don't wanna cause no trouble for this here fine young thing,
who I hear is engaged to a college man.' Then I'd laugh with them and look
at Teddy and wouldn't say nothin' much to nobody.

"Word must of gotten back to Billy soon after that. He didn't say nothin'
at first, but I could see a change in his attitude. All this time I was tryin' to git
up the guts to tell Billy I was thinkin' about breaking off, but I just couldn't.
It wasn't that I thought he needed me; I just knew he was the kind of dude that
doesn't let a girl decide when somethin' is over. Bein' as much like Billy as you
are, you must understand what I'm tryin' to say. On one of my nights off, when
we went out to a movie, he asked, 'What time did you get in this mornin'?' I
said, 'Five-thirty, same as always.' But I was lyin'. Red and me had stopped for
breakfast on the way home. Billy said, 'I called you at six-thirty this morning,
and your aunt Alvene said you was still out.' I told him, 'She must of been too
sleepy to look in my room.' He didn't say more on the subject, but later that
evenin', after the movie, he said, 'I was in the war for two years. It made me
a disciplined man, and I hope I don't ever have to lose my temper.' I didn't say
nothin', but the cold way he said it was like a window shade flappin' up from
in front of his true nature, and I was scared.

"It was three years ago this September twenty-second that the thing happened. It was five-thirty in the mornin'. We had clocked out at four-forty-five,
but Red had brought a bottle of Scotch to work, and we was down in the swing
room drinkin' a little with our coffee, just to relax. I'll tell you the truth: Teddy
Johnson was there too. He had come down just to give us a ride home. I'll never
forget that day as long as I live. Teddy was dressed in a pink silk shirt with black
ruffles on the sleeves, the kind that was so popular a few years ago. He was
wearin' shiny black bell-bottoms that hugged his little hips like a second coat
of skin and looked like pure silk when he walked. He sat across from me, flashin'
those diamond rings every time he poured more Scotch in our cups. Red was

sittin' back with a smile on her face, watchin' us like a cat that had just ate.

"I was sittin' with my back to the door and didn't know anything, until I saw something change in Red's face. I still see it in my sleep at night. Her face seemed to light up and git scared and happy at the same time. She was lookin' behind me, over my shoulder, with all the smartness in the world burnin' in her eyes. I turned around. Billy Crawford was standin' right behind me with his hands close to his sides. He wore a white shirt and a thin black tie, and his mouth was tight like a little slit. He said, 'It's time for you to go home,' with that voice of his that was too cold to be called just mean. I sat there lookin' up at him. Red's voice was even colder. She said to me, 'You gonna let him order you around like that?' I didn't say nothin'. Red said to Teddy, 'Ain't *you* got something to say about this?' Teddy stood up slow and swelled out his chest. He said, 'Yeah. I got somethin' to say,' looking hard at Billy. But Billy just kept lookin' down at me. 'Let's go,' he said. 'What you got to say?' Red Bone said to Teddy. Teddy said to me, 'Why don't *you* tell the dude, baby?' But I didn't say nothin'. Billy shifted his eyes to Teddy and said, 'I got nothing against you. You ain't real, so you don't matter. You been strutting the streets too long, but that ain't my business. So keep out of this.' Then he looked down at me again. 'Let's go,' he said. I looked up at the way his lips curled and wanted to cry and hit him at the same time. I felt like a trigger bein' pulled. Then I heard Red sayin', 'Why don't you go back to bed with them *goddamn books, punk!* And leave decent folks *alone!*' For the first time Billy glanced over at her. His mouth twitched. But then he looked down at me again. 'This here's the *last time* I'm asking,' he said. That's when I exploded and started to jump up. 'I ain't goin' *nowhere!*' I screamed. The last plain thing I remember was tryin' to git to his face, but it seemed to turn all bright and silvery and hot, and then I couldn't see nothin' no more.

"They told me later that he sliced me so fast there wasn't time for nobody to act. By the time Teddy jumped across the table I was down, and Billy had stabbed me again in the side. Then him and Teddy tussled over the knife, while me and Red screamed and screamed. Then Teddy went down holdin' his belly, and Billy was comin' after me again, when some of the dudes from the freight dock ran in and grabbed him. They say it took three of them to drag him off me, and all the time they was pullin' him away he kept slashin' out at me with that knife. It seemed like all the walls was screamin' and I was floatin' in water, and I thought I was dead and in hell, because I felt hot and prickly all over, and I could hear some woman's voice that might of been mine screamin' over and over, 'You devil! . . . You *devil!*' "

She lit a third cigarette. She blew a relieving cloud of smoke downward. The thin white haze billowed about her purple legs, dissipated, and vanished. A terrifying fog of silence and sickness crept into the small room, and there was no longer the smell of medicine. I dared not steal a glance at my watch, although by this time Dr. Wayland was agonizingly late. I had heard it all, and now I waited. Finally her eyes fixed on the frosted glass door. She wet her lips again and, in a much slower and pained voice, said, "This here's the third doctor I been to see. The first one stitched me up like a turkey and left this scar. The second one refused to touch me." She paused and wet her lips again. "This man fixed your nose for you," she said softly. "Do you think he could do somethin' about this scar?"

I searched the end table next to my couch for a news magazine, carefully avoiding her face. "Dr. Wayland is a skilled man," I told her. "Whenever he's not late. I think he may be able to do something for you."

She sighed heavily and seemed to tremble. "I don't expect no miracle or nothin'," she said. "If he could just fix the part around my eye I wouldn't expect nothin' else. People say the rest don't look too bad."

I clutched a random magazine and did not answer. Nor did I look at her. The flesh around my nose began to itch, and I looked toward the inner office door with the most extreme irritation building in me. At that moment it seemed a shadow began to form behind the frosted glass, signaling perhaps the approach of someone. I resolved to put aside all notions of civility and go into the office before her, as was my right. The shadow behind the door darkened, but vanished just as suddenly. And then I remembered the most important question, without which the entire exchange would have been wasted. I turned to the woman, now drawn together in the red plastic chair, as if struggling to sleep in a cold bed. "Sister," I said, careful to maintain a casual air. "Sister . . . what is your name?"

Soldiers

Ellease Southerland

1973

He was out on the deck in his undershirt. Slippers. Way out at sea. Nobody but him. The sea. The dark so close to him he could see nothing. Just hear a hollow whistling sound. Like this: woooooooooo. Wooooooooo. Radio came on in the dark. And like he could hear all those strange languages. And he listened. Couldn't think of anything that could give him a greater sense of peace than the ship yawling and cutting. Yawling and cutting. And the dark next to him. The ship coming into port, and not knowing what the women look like. Is the street cobblestone? How does the place smell? (He fingers his bushy, trimmed mustache, gently squeezing the soft flesh of his upper lip.)

He used to stare at that grayish-brown photograph of his grandfather and laugh! He couldn't see it. Old gray-haired relatives he didn't even know would look at his face and chuckle. There's granddaddy, they would say, rubbing his head when he was eight or nine. He couldn't see it until the day when he barely glanced at the mirror and the face from the photograph jumped out! Granddaddy! The same long (handsome) face, small, squinting eyes. Now he could see it. Remembering. Way out on the ocean at night.

At first, after enlistment, they worked him so hard he couldn't see his hands. He couldn't see straight, let alone see the world. His muscles hurt from all the pulling and stretching, sometimes so tight that when he awoke in the mornings, he could barely take baby steps. Then one day, three or four months later, he was just resting his hands on his thighs and almost like magic, he discovered his muscles were hard, arms and legs. His thighs flat and tight. Nice! Very nice. Riding this ship way out at sea.

His imagination was thrown wide open in the dark. Familiar things seemed unreal. Like a dream. Along the distant imaginary shore, he pictured people inside their houses, in their everyday routine. Overseas back home it was late afternoon. His mom probably leaving the office, probably thinking of him as she headed home. Probably alone. She had begged him not to enlist. I don't mind paying your school fees, she said, tears building in her eyes. But that's not right, he said. Veteran's benefits will pay college fees. The more she cried, the more he knew he needed to go.

He always called her after they pulled into port. He called even if he broke into her night. After a while she said son, I appreciate hearing your voice. But these bills! I would truly appreciate a letter. But he didn't write. He planned to, but he didn't write. And he felt strange just walking into a foreign country and making plans to be with a woman before he dialed home. He'd call. Collect. Then hold his breath just in case this time his mother refused to accept. She would always accept.

The pure black night hugs the ocean dark with a solitude that dissolves and distinguishes, throws light on forgotten things. When he was a restless inquisitive kid, some days, nothing moved. That's how it felt. Each day he rushed to the window. He was always rushing to the windows, looking out. Sometimes nothing moved. And he wanted to ride his bike with his friends. Or ride the Silver Streak racing south. All those school days he glanced out the window and saw the days rapidly disappearing outside. The glass held him captive inside.

Young man, you did not write this composition. That's how the teacher spoke to him, with that tone. And he said what is it about this composition that makes you think I didn't write it? You think because I can get comfortable with the language when I'm talking that I can't be correct when I'm writing? Which one of these words have you prejudged me incapable of writing? Palpable? Pejorative? Egregious? By the way he said them, she could tell he knew the words. So he said, is there something about the composition or about me? She didn't say anything. Put an A on the paper. Gave him his A for the course. Young man! And he was twenty years old.

Three years ago. He had stepped outside the school window. No glass between him and the pure black sea. The hollow whistling sound. Woooooooooo. And the ship yawling and cutting.

He was trying to pick up his arm, but got no reaction. He was lying there on the ground. In all the noises. Listening . . . trying to identify the type of mortar. Felt soft, dry stuff sprinkle his face. Spit into the dust and noise. So many bullets in the air at one time that bullets split bullets. He rested against the solid noise until he saw the blood. And he was calm; he was dying. Then the sudden red pains cutting through the heat. One hundred and ten degrees.

He was lying in the heat, thirsty and dying. And he said to his friend, "Hey man, shoot me."

And he said, "Okay. . . . No!"

And the sergeant heard and said, "Dammit, man, you ain't hurt. You don't know what real pain is. That's your ticket home."

Yeah. He wanted to get up and kill him. Tried to pull up and water spilled from his skin. His mouth and nose felt dry. And his friend had some orange Kool

Aid. You know people mail Kool Aid in envelopes. With the letters. He hated cherry, but this time it was orange. And he said, "Hey, man, give me some of your Kool Aid."

He knew he wasn't supposed to, but he said, "All right. But just a little."

When he tasted the sweet, wet Kool Aid, he held on to it and kept drinking. And his friend tried to pull it away, but he kept on holding.

When the helicopter came, he was thrown in. Remembered trying to hold onto his leg. And then they threw someone else into the helicopter. Boot landed in his face. And he flew all the way to the hospital in the Philippines with the boot mashed against his face.

He kept trying to pick up his arm, but got no reaction.

One thing he had to say: when they landed in the Philippines, they were ready for him. They were ready. Team of doctors and nurses had a huge pair of scissors to cut his clothes off. He remembered some days later that the lock was broken on his pack. They do that. And take out clothes that some other soldier can use. But his books were there. And it was really a good feeling to see his books. They had sent them all that way to the hospital.

He kept begging the nurse for morphine. He got some from one and then begged the other. And she'd say, "Didn't you get your painkiller?"

And he'd say, "No." Act like he was going to die. That's how bad the pain was. But he had to pay for that later on: taking all that morphine.

The sky is made of wind. The wind blows the sun between the earth and the sky. Between the States and Asia. You thought you heard his voice but that was really somebody else's laugh.

Anyway, when he got to Philadelphia, he became friends with an older man who liked to talk about Havana in the mid-forties. He forgets his name. Taventilo, or something like that, who called him "Youngblood." Anyway, he had a chuckle in his eye. And liked to talk about Havana. In the mid-forties.

He kept trying to move his hand, tied against his chest. He pinched it, but got no reaction. So when they told him that he would have to have it cut off, he didn't care. It was that much pain. He didn't care if they wanted to amputate his head. He used to think that this man who had a hook had it screwed right into his arm. What he used to think.

He left the hospital and went to visit a friend. He didn't have any money and had to eat cheese sandwiches every day. He was AWOL. But he didn't care. And when he went back to the hospital they said to him did he realize that he was AWOL? He didn't care. And they didn't do anything.

If you're fighting in Vietnam and they send you a telegram telling you that your mother is dead and the Red Cross lends you the money so that you can go home and see your mother, it's a very long ride. Only you on the plane. The stewardess. And too much time.

His right hand, plastic, was hanging at his side. Painted almost the exact color of his skin. He held the cane in his left hand. To help him walk.

Even after the amputation, he had his hand. Psychological hand shrinking into his arm. Little by little. Each day it shrank a little more. More. Until the whole hand was in his arm.

Then he had to come back. Back to South Jamaica, New York. The buses and subways. People he knew in school. Back to curbs and streets filled with fast traffic. Couldn't care less drivers.

He got off the train at 168th. Everybody got off at the end of the line. Rushed for the steps. But he took his time. Wanted to be sure everybody was gone before he started to climb the stairs.

The conductor talked to him. "Lost, Buddy?"

"No. Thank you. Thank you."

The conductor waved. Pulled out.

Then he began to climb. One foot, and then the next, bending only the leg that would bend.

When he came outside, it was October. And in Asia, a kid, a woman, a soldier, walking with an empty sleeve. And there are so many young men walking around without their feet and hands. Some not even walking. Some not even around.

Roselily

Alice Walker

1973

Dearly Beloved,

She dreams; dragging herself across the world. A small girl in her mother's white robe and veil, knee raised waist high through a bowl of quicksand soup. The man who stands beside her is against this standing on the front porch of her house, being married to the sound of cars whizzing by on highway 61.

we are gathered here

Like cotton to be weighed. Her fingers at the last minute busily removing dry leaves and twigs. Aware it is a superficial sweep. She knows he blames Mississippi for the respectful way the men turn their heads up in the yard, the women stand waiting and knowledgeable, their children held from mischief by teachings from the wrong God. He glares beyond them to the occupants of the cars, white faces glued to promises beyond a country wedding, noses thrust forward like dogs on a track. For him they usurp the wedding.

in the sight of God

Yes, open house. That is what country black folks like. She dreams she does not already have three children. A squeeze around the flowers in her hands chokes off three and four and five years of breath. Instantly she is ashamed and frightened in her superstition. She looks for the first time at the preacher, forces humility into her eyes, as if she believes he is, in fact, a man of God. She can imagine God, a small black boy, timidly pulling the preacher's coattail.

to join this man and this woman

*   *   *

She thinks of ropes, chains, handcuffs, his religion. His place of worship. Where she will be required to sit apart with covered head. In Chicago, a word she hears when thinking of smoke, from his description of what a cinder was, which they never had in Panther Burn. She sees hovering over the heads of the clean neighbors in her front yard black specks falling, clinging, from the sky. But in Chicago. Respect, a chance to build. Her children at last from underneath the detrimental wheel. A chance to be on top. What a relief, she thinks. What a vision, a view, from up so high.

in holy matrimony.

Her fourth child she gave away to the child's father who had some money. Certainly a good job. Had gone to Harvard. Was a good man but weak because good language meant so much to him he could not live with Roselily. Could not abide TV in the living room, five beds in three rooms, no Bach except from four to six on Sunday afternoons. No chess at all. She does not forget to worry about her son among his father's people. She wonders if the New England climate will agree with him. If he will ever come down to Mississippi, as his father did, to try to right the country's wrongs. She wonders if he will be stronger than his father. His father cried off and on throughout her pregnancy. Went to skin and bones. Suffered nightmares, retching and falling out of bed. Tried to kill himself. Later told his wife he found the right baby through friends. Vouched for, the sterling qualities that would make up his character.

It is not her nature to blame. Still, she is not entirely thankful. She supposes New England, the North, to be quite different from what she knows. It seems right somehow to her that people who move there to live return home completely changed. She thinks of the air, the smoke, the cinders. Imagines cinders big as hailstones; heavy, weighing on the people. Wonders how this pressure finds its way into the veins, roping the springs of laughter.

If there's anybody here that knows a reason why

But of course they know no reason why beyond what they daily have come to know. She thinks of the man who will be her husband, feels shut away from him because of the stiff severity of his plain black suit. His religion. A lifetime of black and white. Of veils. Covered head. It is as if her children are already gone from her. Not dead, but exalted on a pedestal, a stalk that has no roots. She wonders how to make new roots. It is beyond her. She wonders what one does with memories in a brand-new life. This had seemed easy, until she thought of it. "The reasons why . . . the people who" . . . she thinks, and does not wonder where the thought is from.

* * *

these two should not be joined

She thinks of her mother, who is dead. Dead, but still her mother. Joined. This is confusing. Of her father. A gray old man who sold wild mink, rabbit, fox skins to Sears, Roebuck. He stands in the yard, like a man waiting for a train. Her young sisters stand behind her in smooth green dresses, with flowers in their hands and hair. They giggle, she feels, at the absurdity of the wedding. They are ready for something new. She thinks the man beside her should marry one of them. She feels old. Yoked. An arm seems to reach out from behind her and snatch her backward. She thinks of cemeteries and the long sleep of grandparents mingling in the dirt. She believes that she believes in ghosts. In the soil giving back what it takes.

together,

In the city. He sees her in a new way. This she knows and is grateful. But is it new enough? She cannot always be a bride and virgin, wearing robes and veil. Even now her body itches to be free of satin and voile, organdy and lily of the valley. Memories crash against her. Memories of being bare to the sun. She wonders what it will be like. Not to have to go to a job. Not to work in a sewing plant. Not to worry about learning to sew straight seams in workingmen's overalls, jeans, and dress pants. Her place will be in the home, he has said repeatedly, promising her rest she had prayed for. But now she wonders. When she is rested, what will she do? They will make babies—she thinks practically about her fine brown body, his strong black one. They will be inevitable. Her hands will be full. Full of what? Babies. She is not comforted.

let him speak

She wishes she had asked him to explain more of what he meant. But she was impatient. Impatient to be done with sewing. With doing everything for three children, alone. Impatient to leave the girls she had known since childhood, their children growing up, their husbands hanging around her, already old, seedy. Nothing about them that she wanted, or needed. The fathers of her children driving by, waving, not waving; reminders of times she would just as soon forget. Impatient to see the South Side, where they would live and build and be respectable and respected and free. Her husband would free her. A romantic hush. Proposal. Promises. A new life! Respectable, reclaimed, renewed. Free! In robe and veil.

or forever hold

* * *

She does not even know if she loves him. She loves his sobriety. His refusal to sing just because he knows the tune. She loves his pride. His blackness and his gray car. She loves his understanding of her *condition.* She thinks she loves the effort he will make to redo her into what he truly wants. His love of her makes her completely conscious of how unloved she was before. This is something; though it makes her unbearably sad. Melancholy. She blinks her eyes. Remembers she is finally being married, like other girls. Like other girls, women? Something strains upward behind her eyes. She thinks of the something as a rat trapped, cornered, scurrying to and fro in her head, peering through the windows of her eyes. She wants to live for once. But doesn't know quite what that means. Wonders if she has ever done it. If she ever will. The preacher is odious to her. She wants to strike him out of the way, out of her light, with the back of her hand. It seems to her he has always been standing in front of her, barring her way.

his peace.

The rest she does not hear. She feels a kiss, passionate, rousing, within the general pandemonium. Cars drive up blowing their horns. Firecrackers go off. Dogs come from under the house and begin to yelp and bark. Her husband's hand is like the clasp of an iron gate. People congratulate. Her children press against her. They look with awe and distaste mixed with hope at their new father. He stands curiously apart, in spite of the people crowding about to grasp his free hand. He smiles at them all but his eyes are as if turned inward. He knows they cannot understand that he is not a Christian. He will not explain himself. He feels different, he looks it. The old women thought he was like one of their sons except that he had somehow got away from them. Still a son, not a son. Changed.

She thinks how it will be later in the night in the silvery gray car. How they will spin through the darkness of Mississippi and in the morning be in Chicago, Illinois. She thinks of Lincoln, the president. That is all she knows about the place. She feels ignorant, *wrong,* backward. She presses her worried fingers into his palm. He is standing in front of her. In the crush of well-wishing people, he does not look back.

White Rat

Gayl Jones

1975

I learned where she was when Cousin Willie come down home and said Maggie sent for her but told her not to tell nobody where she was, especially me, but Cousin Willie come and told me anyway cause she said I was the lessen two evils and she didn't like to see Maggie stuck up in the room up there like she was. I asked her what she mean like she was. Willie said that she was pregnant by J.T. J.T. the man she run off with because she said I treat her like dirt. And now Willie say J.T. run off and left her after he got her knocked up. I asked Willie where she was. Willie said she was up in that room over Babe Lawson's. She told me not to be surprised when I saw her looking real bad. I said I wouldn't be least surprised. I asked Willie she think Maggie come back. Willie say she better.

The room was dirty and Maggie looked worser than Willie say she going to look. I knocked on the door but there weren't no answer so I just opened the door and went in and saw Maggie laying on the bed turned up against the wall. She turnt around when I come in but she didn't say nothing. I said Maggie we getting out a here. So I got the bag she brung when she run away and put all her loose things in it and just took her by the arm and brung her on home. You couldn't tell nothing was in her belly though.

I been taking care of little Henry since she been gone but he three and a half years old and ain't no trouble since he can play hisself and know what it mean when you hit him on the ass when he do something wrong.

Maggie don't say nothing when we get in the house. She just go over to little Henry. He sleeping in the front room on the couch. She go over to little Henry and bend down and kiss him on the cheek and then she ask me have I had supper and when I say naw she go back in the kitchen and start fixing it. We sitting at the table and nobody saying nothing but I feel I got to say something.

"You can go head and have the baby," I say. "I give him my name."

I say it meaner than I want to. She just look up at me and don't say nothing. Then she say, "He ain't yours."

I say, "I know he ain't mine. But don't nobody else have to know. Even the baby. He don't even never have to know."

She just keep looking at me with her big eyes that don't say nothing, and then she say, "You know. I know."

She look down at her plate and go on eating. We don't say nothing no more and then when she get through she clear up the dishes and I just go round front and sit out on the front porch. She don't come out like she used to before she start saying I treat her like dirt, and then when I go on in the house to go to bed, she hunched up on her side, with her back to me, so I just take my clothes off and get on in the bed on my side.

Maggie a light yeller woman with chicken-scratch hair. That what my mama used to call it, chicken-scratch hair, cause she say there weren't enough hair for a chicken to scratch around in. If it weren't for her hair she look like she was a white woman, a light yeller white woman though. Anyway, when we was coming up somebody say, "Woman cover you hair if you ain't go'n' straightin' it. Look like chicken scratch." Sometime they say look like chicken shit, but they don't tell them to cover it no more, so they wear it like it is. Maggie wears hers like it is.

Me, I come from a family of white-looking niggers, some of 'em, my mama, my daddy musta been; my half daddy he weren't. Come down from the hills round Hazard, Kentucky, most of them and claimed nigger cause somebody grandmammy way back there was. First people I know ever claim nigger, 'cept my mama say my daddy hate hoogies (up north I hear they call em honkies) worser than anybody. She say cause he look like he one hisself and then she laugh. I laugh too but I didn't know why she laugh. She say when I come, I look just like a little white rat, so tha's why some a the people I hang aroun with call me "White Rat." When little Henry come he look just like a little white rabbit, but don't nobody call him "White Rabbit," they just call him little Henry. I guess the other jus' ain't took. I tried to get them to call him little White Rabbit, but Maggie say naw, cause she say when he grow up he develop a complex, what with the problem he got already. I say what you come at me for with this a complex and then she say, Nothin, jus' something I heard on the radio on one of them edgecation morning shows. And then I say Aw. And then she say, Anyway by the time he get seven or eight he probably get the pigment and be dark, cause some of her family was. So I say where I heard somewhere where the chil'ren couldn't be no darker'n the darkest of the two parent and bout the best he could do would be high yeller like she was. And then she say how her sister Lucky got the pigment when she was bout seven and come out real dark. I tell her, Well y'all's daddy was dark. And she say, "Yeah." Anyway, I guess she still think little Henry gonna get the pigment when he get to be seven or eight, and told me about all these people come out lighter'n I was and got the pigment fore they growed up.

Like I told you my relatives come down out of the hills and claimed nigger, but only people that believe 'em is people that got to know 'em and people that know 'em, so I usually just stay around with people I know and go in some joint over to Versailles or up to Lexington or down over in Midway where they know me cause I don't like to walk in no place where they say, "What's that white man doing in here?" They probably say "yap"—that the Kentucky word for honky. Or "What that yap doing in here with that nigger woman?" So I jus' keep to the places where they know me. I member when I was young me and the other niggers used to ride around in these cars, and when we go to some town where they don't know "White Rat" everybody look at me like I'm some hoogie, but I don't pay them no mind. 'Cept sometime it hard not to pay em no mind cause I hate the hoogie much as they do, much as my daddy did. I drove up to this filling station one time and these other niggers drove up at the same time, they mighta even drove up a little ahead a me, but this filling station man come up to me first and bent down and said, "I wait on you first, 'fore I wait on them niggers," and then he laugh. And then I laugh and say, "You can wait on them first. I'm a nigger too." He don't say nothing. He just look at me like he thought I was crazy. I don't remember who he wait on first. But I guess he be careful next time who he say nigger to, even somebody got blond hair like me, most which done passed over anyhow. That, or the way things been go'n, go'n be trying to pass back. I member once all us was riding around one Saturday night, I must a been bout twenty-five then, close to forty now, but we was driving around, all us drunk cause it was Saturday, and Shotgun, he was driving and probably drunker'n a skunk and drunken the rest of us hit up on this police car and the police got out and by that time Shotgun done stop, and the police come over and told all us to get out the car, and he looked us over, he didn't have to do much looking because he probably smell it before he got there, but he looked us all over and say he gonna haul us all in for being drunk and disord'ly. He say, "I'm gone haul all y'all in." And I say, "Haul y'all all." Everybody laugh, but he don't hear me cause he over to his car ringing up the police station to have them send the wagon out. He turn his back to us cause he know we wasn goin nowhere. Didn't have to call but one man cause the only people in the whole Midway police station is Fat Dick and Skinny Dick, Buster Crab and Mr. Willie. Sometime we call Buster, Crab Face too, and Mr. Willie is John Willie, but everybody call him Mr. Willie cause the name just took. So Skinny Dick come out with the wagon and hauled us all in. So they didn't know me well as I knew them. Thought I was some hoogie jus' run around with the niggers instead of be one of them. So they put my cousin Covington, cause he dark, in the cell with Shotgun and the other niggers and they put me in the cell with the white men. So I'm drunker'n a skunk and I'm yellin' Let me outa here I'm a nigger too. And Crab Face say, "If you a nigger I'm a Chinee." And I keep rattling the bars and saying "Cov, they got me in here with the white men. Tell 'em I'm a nigger too," and Cov yell back, "He a nigger too," and then they all laugh, all the niggers laugh, the hoogies they laugh too, but for a different reason, and Cov say, "Tha's what you get for being drunk and orderly." And I say, "Put me in there with the niggers too, I'm a nigger too." And then one of the white men, he's sitting over in his corner say, "I ain't never heard of a white man want to be a nigger. 'Cept maybe for the nigger women." So I look around at him and haul off cause I'm goin hit him and then some man grab me and say, "He keep a blade," but that don't make me no difrent and I say, "A spade don't need a blade." But then he get his friend to help hole me and then he call Crab Face to come get me out a the cage. So Crab Face come and get me out a the cage and put me in a cage by myself and say, "When you get out a here you can run around with the niggers all you want, but while you in here you ain't getting no niggers." By now I'm more sober so I jus' say, "My cousin's a nigger." And he say, "My cousin a monkey's uncle."

By that time Grandy come. Cause Cov took his free call but didn't nobody else. Grandy's Cov's grandmama. She my grandmama too on my stepdaddy's side. Anyway, Grandy come and she say, "I want my *two* sons." And he take her over to the nigger cage and say, "Which two?" and she say, "There one of them," and points to Cov'ton. "But I don't see t'other one." And Crab Face say, "Well, if you don't see him I don't see him." Cov'ton just standing there grinning and don't say nothing. I don't say nothing. I'm just waiting. Grandy ask, "Cov, where Rat?" Sometime she just call me Rat and leave the "White" off. Cov say, "They put him in the cage with the white men." Crab Face standing there looking funny now. His back to me, but I figure he looking funny now. Grandy says, "Take me to my other boy, I want to see my other boy." I don't think Crab Face want her to know he thought I was white so he don't say nothing. She just standing there looking up at him cause he tall and fat and she short and fat. Crab Face finally say, "I put him in a cell by hisself cause he started a ruckus." He point over to me, and she turn and see me and frown. I'm just sitting there. She look back at Crab Face and say, "I want them both out." "That be about five dollars apiece for the both of them for disturbing the peace." That what Crab Face say. I'm sitting there thinking he a poet and don't know it. He a bad poet and don't know it. Grandy say she pay it if it take all her money, which it probably did. So the police let Cov and me out. And Shotgun waving. Some of the others already settled. Didn't care if they got out the next day. I wouldn't a cared neither, but Grandy say she didn like to see nobody in a cage, specially her own. I say I pay her back. Cov say he pay her back too. She say we can both pay her back if we just stay out a trouble. So we got together and pay her next week's grocery bill.

Well, that was one 'sperience. I had others, but like I said, now I jus' about keep to the people I know and that know me. The only other big 'sperience was when me and Maggie tried to get married. We went down to the courthouse and fore I even said a word, the man behind the glass cage look up at us and say, "Round here nigger don't marry white." I don't say nothing, just standing up there looking at him and he looking like a white toad, and I'm wondering if they call him "white toad," more likely "white turd." But I just keep looking at him. Then he the one get tired a looking first and he say, "Next." I'm thinking I want to reach in that little winder and pull him right out of that little glass cage. But I don't. He say again, "Around here nigger don't marry white." I say, "I'm a nigger. Nigger marry nigger, don't they?" He just look at me like he think I'm crazy. I say, "I got rel'tives blacker'n your shit. Ain't you never heard a niggers what look like they white?" He just look at me like I'm a nigger too, and tell me where to sign.

Then we get married and I bring her over here to live in this house in Huntertown ain't got but three rooms and a outhouse, that's where we always lived, seems like to me, all us Hawks, cept the ones come down from the mountains way back yonder, cept they don't count no more anyway. I keep telling Maggie it get harder and harder to be a white nigger now specially since it don't count no more how much white blood you got in you, in fact, it make you worser for it. I said nowadays sted a walking around like you something special people look at you, after they find out what you are if you like me, like you some kind a bad news that you had something to do with. I tell em I aint had nothing to do with the way I come out. They ack like they like you better if you go on ahead and try to pass, cause least then they know how to feel about you. Cept nowadays everybody want to be a nigger, or it getting that way. I tell Maggie she got it made, cause at least she got that chicken-shit hair, but all she answer is, "That why you treat me like chicken shit." But tha's only since we been having our troubles.

Little Henry the cause a our troubles. I tell Maggie I ain't changed since he was borned, but she say I have. I always say I been a hard man, kind of quick-tempered. A hard man to crack like one of them walnuts. She say all it take to crack a walnut is your teeth. She say she put a walnut between her teeth and it crack not even need a hammer. So I say I'm a nigger-toe nut then. I ask her if she ever seen one of them nigger-toe nuts they the toughest nuts to crack. She say, "A nigger-toe nut is black. A white nigger-toe nut be easy to crack." Then I don't say nothing and she keep saying I changed cause I took to drink. I tell her I drink before I married her. She say then I start up again. She say she don't like it when I drink cause I'm quicker tempered than when I ain't drunk. She say I come home drunk and say things and then go sleep and then the next morning forget what I say. She won't tell me what I say. I say, "You a woman scart of words. Won't do nothing." She say she ain't scart of words.

She say one of these times I might not jus' say something. I might *do* something. Short time after she say that was when she run off with J.T.

Reason I took to drink again was because little Henry was borned club-footed. I tell the truth in the beginning I blamed Maggie, cause I herited all those hill man's superstitions and nigger superstitions too, and I said she didn't do something right when she was carrying him or she did something she shouldn't oughta did or looked at something she shouldn't oughta looked at like some cows fucking or something. I'm serious. I blamed her. Little Henry come out looking like a little club-footed rabbit. Or some rabbits being birthed or something. I said there weren't never nothing like that in my family ever since we been living on this earth. And they must have come from her side. And then I said cause she had more of whatever it was in her than I had in me. And then she said that brought it all out. All that stuff I been hiding up inside me cause she said I didn't hated them hoogies like my daddy did and I just been feeling I had to live up to something he set and the onliest reason I married her was because she was the lightest and brightest nigger woman I could get and still be nigger. Once that nigger start to lay it on me she jus' kept it up till I didn't feel nothing but start to feeling what she say, and then I even told her I was leaving and she say, "What about little Henry?" And I say, "He's your nigger." And then it was like I didn't know no other word but nigger when I was going out that door.

I found some joint and went in it and just start pouring the stuff down. It weren't no nigger joint neither, it was a hoogie joint. First time in my life I ever been in a hoogie joint too, and I kept thinking a nigger woman did it. I wasn't drunk enough *not* to know what I was saying neither. I was sitting up to the bar talking to the tender. He just standing up there, wasn nothing special to him, he probably weren't even lisen cept but with one ear. I say, "I know this nigger. You know I know the niggers. (He just nod but don't say nothing.) Know them close. You know what I mean. Know them like they was my own. Know them where you s'pose to know them." I grinned at him like he was s'pose to know them too. "You know my family came down out of the hills, like they was some kind of rain gods, you know, miss'ology. What they teached you bout the Juicifer. Anyway, I knew this nigger what made hisself a priest, you know turned his white color I mean turned his white collar backwards and dressed up in a monkey suit—you get it?" He didn't get it. "Well, he made hisself a priest, but after a while he didn't want to be no priest, so he pronounced hisself." The bartender said, "Renounced." "So he 'nounced hisself and took off his turned-back collar and went back to just being a plain old every day chi'lins and downhome and hamhocks and corn pone nigger. And you know what else he did? He got married. Yeah the nigger what once was a priest got married. Once took all them vows of cel'bacy come and got married. Got married so he could come." I laugh. He don't. I got evil. "Well, he come awright. He come and she come too. She come and had a baby. And you know what else? The baby come too. Ha. No ha? The baby come out club-footed. So you know what he did? He didn't blame his wife he blamed hisself. The nigger blamed hisself cause he said the God put a curse on him for goin' agin his vows. He said the God put a curse on him cause he took his vows of cel'bacy, which mean no fuckin', cept everybody know what *they* do, and went agin his vows of cel'bacy and married a nigger woman so he could do what every ord'narry onery person was doing and the Lord didn't just put a curse on him. He said he could a stood that. But the Lord carried the curse clear over to the next gen'ration and put a curse on his little baby boy who didn do nothing in his whole life . . . cept come." I laugh and laugh. Then when I quit laughing I drink some more, and then when I quit drinking I talk some more. "And you know something else?" I say. This time he say, "No." I say, "I knew another priest what took the vows, only this priest was white. You wanta know what happen to him. He broke his vows same as the nigger and got married same as the nigger. And they had a baby too. Want to know what happen to him?" "What?" "He come out a nigger."

Then I get so drunk I can't go no place but home. I'm thinking it's the Hawks' house, not hers. If anybody get throwed out it's her. She the nigger. I'm goin' fool her. Throw her right *out* the bed if she in it. But then when I get home I'm the one that's fool. Cause she gone *and* little Henry gone. So I guess I just badmouthed the walls like the devil till I jus' layed down and went to sleep. The next morning little Henry come back with a neighbor woman but Maggie don't come. The woman hand over little Henry, and I ask her, "Where Maggie?" She looked at me like she think I'm the devil and say, "I don't know, but she lef' me this note to give to you." So she jus' give me the note and went. I open the note and read. She write like a chicken too, I'm thinking, chicken scratch. I read: "I run off with J.T. cause he been wanting me to run off with him and I ain't been wanting to tell now. I'm send little Henry back cause I just took him away last night cause I didn't want you to be doing nothing you regrit in the morning." So I figured she figured I got to stay sober if I got to take care of myself and little Henry. Little Henry didn't say nothing and I didn't say nothing. I just put him on in the house and let him play with hisself.

That was two months ago. I ain't take a drop since. But last night Cousin Willie come and say where Maggie was and now she moving around in the kitchen and feeding little Henry and I guess when I get up she feed me. I get up and get dressed and go in the kitchen. She say when the new baby come we see whose fault it was. J.T. blacker'n a lump of coal.

Maggie keep saying, "When the baby come we see who fault it was." It's two more months now that I been look at her, but I still don't see no belly change.

Loimos

Edgar Nkose White

1975

I

Tonight, as yesterday, I am alone. Sitting here, sitting, sitting, under partly colored skies, under plastered ceilings.

Something important has happened, though I forget exactly what.

A new noise is upon this place. Or a new silence. Today I did not go out. I went out yesterday, though. Stepped over certain prostrate bodies, passed others.

There is a cat which has chosen my room for lounging. He or it does not mind my presence here. Dogs howl in yards, ash cans clatter.

The same dogs, the same ash cans. I do not travel at night. They say it's not safe, though there are guards almost everywhere. Their voices can be heard sometimes amid the other noises, moving beneath windows, commenting on the bodies.

At first everyone was frightened, but then those who had something to lose were only half frightened; the ritual of order kept them going. The media gave out information saying only that it was but a temporary affliction of the city caused by a series of freak accidents in several vital sewers. The result was a pestilential increase, and though but few actually saw signs of rats, rumor was fast about.

I was quite amazed to hear those I knew speak of it. The wise spoke wisely, the foolish foolishly—such is the boring way of life—but now even the foolish saw things I thought them quite incapable of. Many knew before they died (which you will have to admit was quite something).

In the beginning I heard the more learned of them say, "This pestilence will be a good thing because the rich will be hurt by this; it will bring them to reality." I heard them speaking in small cafés or outside of school buildings holding paperback books in gloved hands. But later, when the rich efficiently left the city, being followed quickly by the bourgeoisie and the friends of the bourgeoisie (comprised mainly of the aforementioned learned people), I heard nothing. Now among the dying there are only the poor, the artists, the scavengers, and the various police and guardsmen who have volunteered (for a laudable sum) to oversee us in our peculiar stages of frenzy.

Strangely enough, though, this affliction upon the city has caused little change in the various exigencies. For did I not upon the early part of the morning experience with more than a little dread the metacarpal knocking of my landlady upon my door? She, staring into my sunken and myopic brown eyes, asked with hostility for the rent. Then myself, speaking as one afraid, saying, "Mrs. Mortmain, I regret not having the rent, but my grandmother died three days ago. She raised me, you see."

For, in truth, I had gone out upon the streets some three days before, walking awkwardly through streets which had never seemed so narrow toward the hospital to acquire the false teeth, the small mirror, the slippers, and the one or two pieces of effluvia which were to be membered among her remains.

My landlady, who was clad in some gray garments to hide her now-withered and childlike sex, looked from behind her eyes, unspeaking. She told me to state the particulars of my grandmother's death. This I did successfully, I think. I ushered her in from the doorway, saying, "You see, Mrs. Mortmain, several days ago my grandmother, having reached the latter part of seventy, suffered an inroad in her health, culminating a few days after, when her heart reached the maximal point of disease and perished. They believe it to be an affliction of the heart, though it may have been the plague."

Whereupon Mrs. Mortmain stopped me and let out a series of jeremiads regarding the difficulties of maintaining Topeth House, our domicile, now that we've become gentrified. I wanted to say something clever but didn't (or couldn't). She paused a moment, involved herself in various fiscal machinations, and then said in a voice not altogether foreign, "I'll give you one more week. Next Monday, the money or you're out!"

She exited by the door, leaving death behind in the hallway. Mrs. Mortmain is a woman of unusual cruelty.

It is winter now, so if my grandmother died several days ago, she died in winter. It's better to die in winter than summer, I think, though perhaps not. I left the funeral home along with the body and the pollinctor. I entered the funeral car, which seemed sufficiently real to be entered. En route to the graveyard, we passed many young people, and older people, some on their way home, some leaving from home. I saw also several women who moved me to think of pussy. This, however, I dismissed, as I feared some might judge my action of fornication in a public streetway, or atop a hearse amid day laborers, to be asocial. Later, however, as I walked upon the too-soft earth of the graveyard ground, I had great difficulty keeping myself from thinking of the many times Jill and I had made love in dark afternoons. Making love on couches and beds and creaking floors, and her small strong thighs swelling, quivering, and myself breathing into her quite open woman's body. I like the smell of the room after we've made love. The fish smell, craven warm smell of aftersex. Then out of the window night would come.

There being no minister, the pollinctor spoke the comfortable words; the trees stood up for death. Shadows which were our shadows walking away. Some had thrown what I believe to be flowers upon the grave. Having gathered for death we departed, fingers of branches downturned. The wind backward moving.

"They say when people are buried their bones turn to snakes."

"To snakes?"

"Yes, to snakes."

"Large snakes?"

"Yes, large snakes that slither along the earth."

II

Perhaps at this point it would not be amiss to speak on the matter of my youth; my youth was an unfortunate one.

III

Perhaps it's the asymmetry of my house which causes everything here to seem so warped. There are so many mirror angles, so very much unevenness here.

When I am thrown out of sleep and wake to a lower earth, I brush my teeth with the bristles of a pig. I wash away the visible pain of the yesterday and prepare a quick identity for today. A clean body at least gives you the illusion of control.

Sitting at what I shall call a table, I note that a bit of burnt toast tastes better if dipped in lukewarm coffee. Should I use one or two teaspoons of sugar? There is a plague on; in times of extreme poverty such as these it is best to conserve resources, think of tomorrow. Fuck tomorrow, there will be no tomorrow. Even the plunderers of my food have stopped coming. I must teach myself to wait. Perhaps look at television for many hours and watch one white man's face dissolve into another. In times of plague, comedy is always requisite. Perhaps if I watch some blond bitch figure out new ways to take her husband's balls on TV, I'll forget that I'm dying. I sometimes see black faces on the screen, but none of them seem as tortured as mine for some reason. They are all happily floating into brightly lit apartments and celebrating each other's existence. The blacks of television land, people such as I've never met. Perhaps if you keep a myth constant enough it will become real. Perhaps if I stare at this television screen long enough I will become what I see. How nice.

I notice I am having more trouble with the spacing of time these days. Ellen was here some darknesses ago. It was not such a huge space of time. Taller than

Jill, more desperate with her hands. I can't remember what her nails feel like on my back. If it was two weeks ago that would be less than a month. There is something which I try to get from her which I can't get. I don't have to be careful of hurting her, thank God. She is stronger than Jill. I don't know how not to damage what I touch anymore.

With Jill I have to be slow. Slower of speech even than of action. Words slip out. Words like "kill," "plague," and "nigger." She doesn't want to deal with any of that. She comes to visit me in my lean house; she makes love with me and returns to a less vicious part of the city.

Ellen is high yellow and carries Georgia in her head and mouth. When we make love, we bring four hundred years of white-hot hate to bed with us.

She blames me for every white man that has control of life. She blames me for the sequestrated death which is New York City. She is right. Her eyes ask, "Amid the slave ships, why did you not kill them on the way? If you could not kill the masters, why did you not kill me and then yourself?" And because I will not answer, her fingers take more skin from my back. It was some space of time ago that Ellen was here.

IV

I have a neighbor named Dave; he plays music on a willing piano. Every day his fingers grow stronger. You can measure the extent of the plague by how much music he plays. Perhaps he will show me the way. He is angry at me for not making my own music instead of living off his. There will come a time to play, but first I must learn to listen better. The music is the mother. The rhythms are the poles of life which you must live between. The rhythms are unavoidable as the beating of the heart. As when my mother breathed over me with a naturalness which allowed me silence.

My mother was immense and black. She had warmness running through her, which is why I was so disappointed leaving the womb. That much I remember clearly.

I don't dream much these days; usually it's the same dream. Something about myself entering a strange city. Snow falling very carefully, laying itself down on its appointed piece of ground.

And into this city which I enter strangely, various people place themselves. I ask them the way, but they cannot understand my language, and one by one they disappear into various houses, leaving footprints only upon the snow.

I remember the way Carolyn slept. She would entwine herself in her hands or sometimes just one long thin African arm making a pillow for herself.

My room has colors now. It must be the reflection of the traffic lights on the rain-wet windows.

The infraluminescence of the outside world. The sound of garbage cans being overturned. Someone is searching. The voices of the ARABBIATI. Is that noise in the street perhaps God? No, it is just the homeless in Tompkins Square.

I can't travel today. The subways are catacombs. That woman came again seeking her rent. I sat in silence and listened to her breathing behind the door. It was a long time, and then her smell went away. I'm going to have to kill this woman, she interrupts my quiet. What is it that white people have with money, this necromancy which they have with lucre? I thought that at least now when the end is so ridiculously visible they would get away from that foolishness. I should have realized that this is all they have left, the only thing, which defines them. The bitchhound which drives them to hell and causes them to string atrocities together as beads later to be called history.

V

Jill penned the following note on an immaculate pink sheet of paper and slipped it under my door:

Dear Aunt Kosi,
Came to see you today. You were not at home. I need to see you. Are you all right? Are you missing me?

Yours,
Jill

Jill is madness and two minute breasts with nipples hard and glad and the nose of a rich girl.

Jill does not know, as she did not know, as she will not know, what's happening. She does not see the plague; she will not ever let herself.

If the world goes on at all, she will continue to slip in and out of silk panties in front of silent dead antiques. I'm willing to concede now finally that people are far better off in ignorance.

Jill floats through the streets of the Lower East Side; she is unaware of the predatory buildings and the low conspiratorial sky over her. She passes the vacant churches with all their desperate bells and odors. She passes the store-shops of the Jews, who flee like bandits when the sun gives up the sky, the sounds of their iron gates giving off the screech of animals. Jill passes it all and doesn't see. Her eyes look only for my broken building with its hallway narrow as an asylum's.

I remember taking Jill with me up to Harlem, on a Hundred Sixteenth Street and Eighth Ave. And I put her in a restaurant to wait as I went in desperate search for a connection. The drizzle of the sky and the junkie whores dying all around us. The twenty-year-old tired and aged woman who coughed into a mysterious paper bag; and her knees giving out beneath her. And Jill standing amid all those pox-marked women, completely distant as if this was merely someone else's dream wherein she was but an incident.

When I was small, I followed my grandmother through the chimera of the New York streets. Her arms were strong and had many veins, which always made me think of plants. She would pull me along by centripetal force as she shipped around corners. She moved strong through dangerous streets and defended me against dreadful metallic beasts which were called cars. When I was small, I believed that anyone who bent over me was doing so to kiss me, and I always turned my face upwards to receive it.

As I grew older the image that was always in my mind was of pursuit. It seemed that I and everyone I knew were running through backyards or over rooftops, always being chased. Preparation for the plague.

This much I know. Black bodies long and angular, asses upturned, limbs always moving. These bodies were not made for cities. Eyes which were fashioned for sunlight, eyes made easy at the sight of green. Bodies designed to outline before the moon. Have no business with concrete and do no trade with brick.

Black women turned into office girls taught to perfect a vacancy of expression. A dementia of thighs, skirts, and commerce. Men with warrior bodies carrying envelopes and pushing buttons until finally they develop that look of irrelevancy. Until there is no separation between the black bodies and the garbage in the streets. A heavy plague through the city.

VI

The newspapers now say that it is not safe to walk the streets even in daytime in sections which have been named "desperate." They mean of course my section of the city. They have made this place into an armed camp. It seems that it should be evident, even to them, that it is impossible to lock me out without locking themselves in. These fools have made a perfect prison for themselves. Perhaps the gates and locks give them some comfort at night. They seem so fearful, though. Where do they think they can go without me? Wherever they need cheap labor I am. Don't they see me driving the subways, cooking their food? I'm at every hospital in the city, and if not me, then my woman is. My woman operates their telephone, overhears everything. Anywhere in the city they can't escape us. The more frightened the city the more they need the music, our music.

And you can tell the mood of the times by the bodies you meet. The bodies have become androgynous. The women have become like men, hard, cold bodies incapable of being held. They have made the flesh into wax, into greedy capable machines. Stiff arms culminating in hands held clenched. The corpulent senility of isolation. But I have seen all this before. It is part of a total re-remembrance of another city, another plague.

Days which I have walked before. Perhaps in Europe where, too, the signs were evident. The Dutch with their grotesque faces, Holland which gave off a reek of colonialism and diamonds.

I advance on a level ground, the sun as equal before me as behind. The screams which I hear are only more constant now because I focus on them. Screams never leave the earth, they merely take up the spaces between past, present, and future, they incorporate themselves in continuity.

The androgynous bodies move on. The Ukrainians along Seventh Street, dying in their dark clothes.

The Chinese who find themselves placed in a labyrinth of ghetto streets seem more somnambular.

There is a chaos even to the process of putrefaction.

Ten thousand years to get from the cave to the tenement house, they shall have to call that progress. It's strange, though, for even these people lie at night impaled upon a pillow. As they lie awake awaiting the momentary cessation of pain from the body's engine, yet they are not willing to give up any power. They want it until the end. I can't understand these people.

They have to maintain property which is the remnant of the large dream. Property is a device of remembrance, a kind of feeble way of continuing a presence which was possibly warm, possibly loving. Finally they find themselves in a closed house filled with pictures of barren properties, and the penalty is infinite time in which they must think on themselves.

Rockefeller had land upon which he never walked and may never walk. Houses into which he never entered. The price he had to pay was his son's life sacrificed to headhunters.

But let me say it another way. I live in a city which was not built for me, a city which never noted my existence. Everything in this place was built either from my flesh or the flesh of others who do not matter. I look out from a window onto Gomorrah. I note faces darkly contorted, ashen. Men, halfmen, sidle graveward in the streets.

The Lower East Side quivers, utters up a smell like the shit of diseased animals. The almost dead of the Bowery stumble toward the Red Cross shelter to sell their polluted blood for wine.

The liquor stores are little beacons of death all run by white men who flee the city in the night. The artists move with dead eyes. The women all have one body. These are the women of the field. The women are the only light down here. Black women, black Puerto Rican women, silver cross between their thighs.

All the houses are boarded and mute. Queer toy houses filled with screams. The police who scatter darkness. They wait for us to go mad. Unnatural colors, unnatural taste, unnatural sleep.

Footsteps going directionless. Eyes which dare not look up.

Faces sometimes encountered which were once familiar and now are aged and crumbling. Young men who turn the plague inward upon themselves. The same streets which LeRoi walked hating himself. And with the passing of the day the passing out of the white powder which is dope. You sprinkle heroin in the palm of the hand, and a cross is always visible, which whispers death.

The Catholic priests when they walk go straight as the church steeples. Their collars betray a bit of public filth. They do not see me as they walk. The church is one of the last strongholds. It hopes to outlast the plague.

Then the night falls down covering up even the harlotry of the stars. A time for vagaries and inquietudes. A time which God must have put aside for men to steal and run into the swamps which are the backyards or over rooftops.

Those who are afraid always sit behind the locked door in expectation of something from outside. But what defense have they from all that which is within? They would like the old lies in a new way. They do not want to hear the word plague, they would rather hear music. There will be a time when they will come to learn survival even from us. They who have the frames but no homes, power and no life flow of culture. And I will wait watching. And everywhere and so loudly the plague. And tonight as yesterday I am alone.

The Education of Mingo

Charles Johnson

1977

Once, when Moses Green took his one-horse rig into town on auction day, he returned to his farm with a bondsman named Mingo. He went early in a homespun suit, stayed through the sale of fifteen slaves, and paid for Mingo in Mexican coin. A monkeylike old man, never married, with tangled hair, ginger-colored whiskers like broomstraw, and a narrow knot of a face, Moses, without children, without kinfolk, who seldom washed because he lived alone on sixty acres in southern Illinois, felt the need for a field hand and helpmate—a friend, to speak the truth plainly.

Riding home over sumps and mudholes into backcountry imprecise yet startlingly vivid in spots as though he were hurtling headlong into a rigid New Testament parable, Moses chewed tobacco on that side of his mouth that still had good teeth and kept his eyes on the road and the ears of the Appaloosa in front of his rig; he chattered mechanically to the boy, who wore tow-linen trousers a size too small, a straw hat, no shirt, and shoes repaired with wire. Moses judged him to be twenty. He was the youngest son of the reigning king of the Allmuseri, a tribe of wizards, according to the auctioneer, but they lied anyways, or so thought Moses, like abolitionists and Red Indians; in fact, for Moses Green's money nearly everybody in the New World from Anabaptists to Whigs was an outrageous liar and twisted the truth (as Moses saw it) until nothing was clear anymore. He was a dark boy. A wild, marshy-looking boy. His breastbone was broad as a barrel; he had thick hands that fell away from his wrists like weights and, on his sharp cheeks, a crescent motif. "Mingo," Moses said in a voice like gravel scrunching under a shoe, "you like rabbit? That's what I fixed for tonight. Fresh rabbit, sweet taters, and cornbread. Got hominy made from Indian corn on the fire, too. Good eatings, eh?" Then he remembered that Mingo spoke no English, and he gave the boy a friendly thump on his thigh. " 'S all right. I'm going to school you myself. Teach you everything I know, son, which ain't so joe-fired much—just common sense—but it's better'n not knowing nothing, ain't it?" Moses laughed till he shook; he liked to laugh and let his hair down whenever he could. Mingo, seeing his strangely unfiled teeth, laughed too, but his sounded like barking. It made Moses jump a foot. He swung round his head and squinted. "Reckon I'd better teach you how to laugh, too. That half grunt, half whinny you just made'll give a body heart failure, son." He screwed up his lips. "You sure got a lot to learn."

Now Moses Green was not a man for doing things halfway. Education, as he dimly understood it, was as serious as a heart attack. You had to have a model, a good Christian gentleman like Moses himself, to wash a Moor white in a single generation. As he taught Mingo farming and table etiquette, ciphering with knotted string, and how to cook ashcakes, Moses constantly revised himself. He tried not to cuss, although any mention of Martin Van Buren or Free-Soilers made his stomach chew itself; or sop cornbread in his coffee; or pick his nose at public market. Moses, policing all his gestures, standing the boy behind his eyes, even took to drinking gin from a paper sack so Mingo couldn't see it. He felt, late at night when he looked down at Mingo snoring loudly on his corn-shuck mattress, now like a father, now like an artist fingering something fine and noble from a rude chump of foreign clay. It was like aiming a shotgun at the whole world through the African, blasting away all that Moses, according to his lights, tagged evil, and cultivating the good; like standing, you might say, on the sixth day, feet planted wide, trousers hitched, and remaking the world so it looked more familiar. But sometimes it scared him. He had to make sense of things for Mingo's sake. Suppose there was lightning dithering in dark clouds overhead? Did that mean rain? Or the Devil whaling his wife? Or—you couldn't waffle on a thing like that. "Rain," said Moses, solemn, scratching his neck. "For sure, it's a storm. Electri-city, Mingo." He made it a point to despoil meanings with care, chosing the ones that made the most common sense.

Slowly, Mingo got the hang of farm life, as Moses saw it—patience, grit, hard work, and prayerful silence, which wasn't easy, Moses knew, because *every*thing about him and the African was as different as night and day, even what idealistic philosophers of his time called structures of intentional consciousness (not that Moses Green called it that, being a man for whom nothing was more absolute than an ax handle, or the weight of a plow in his hands, but he knew sure enough they didn't see things quite the same way). Mingo's education, to put it plainly, involved the evaporation of one coherent, consistent, complete universe and the embracing of another one alien, contradictory, strange.

Slowly, Mingo conquered knife and spoon, then language. He picked up the old man's family name. Gradually, he learned—soaking them up like a sponge—Moses' gestures and idiosyncratic body language. (Maybe too well, for Moses Green had a milk leg that needed lancing and hobbled, favoring his right knee; so did Mingo, though he was strong as an ox. His *t*'s had a reedy twang like the quiver of a ukulele string; so did Mingo's.) That African, Moses saw inside a year, was exactly the product of his own way of seeing, as much one of his products and judgments as his choice of tobacco; was, in a sense that both pleased and bum-squabbled the crusty old man, himself: a homunculus, or a distorted shadow, or—as Moses put it to his lady friend Harriet Bridgewater—his own spitting image.

"How you talk, Moses Green!" Harriet sat in a Sleepy Hollow chair on the Sunday afternoons Moses, in his one-button sack coat and Mackinaw hat, visited her after church services. She had two chins, wore a blue dress with a flounce of gauze and an apron of buff satin, above which her bosom slogged back and forth as she chattered and knitted. There were cracks in old Harriet Bridgewater's once well-stocked mind (she had been a teacher, had traveled to places Moses knew he'd never see), into which she fell during conversations and from which she crawled with memories and facts that, Moses suspected, Harriet had spun from thin air. She was the sort of woman who, if you told her of a beautiful sunset you'd just seen, would, like as not, laugh—a squashing sound in her nose—and say, "Why, Moses, that's not beautiful at all!" And then she'd sing a sunset more beautiful—like the good Lord coming in a cloud—in some faraway place like Crete or Brazil, which you'd probably never see. That sort of woman: haughty, worldly, so clever at times he couldn't stand it. Why Moses Green visited her . . .

Even he didn't rightly know why. She wasn't exactly pretty, what with her gull's nose, great heaps of red-gold hair, and frizzy down on her arms, but she had a certain silvery beauty, intangible, elusive, inside. It was comforting after Reverend Raleigh Liverspoon's orbicular sermons to sit a spell with Harriet in her religiously quiet, plank-roofed common room. He put one hand in his pocket and scratched. She knew things, that shrewd Harriet Bridgewater, like the meaning of Liverspoon's gnomic sermon on property, which Moses couldn't untangle to save his life until Harriet spelled out how being and having were sorta the same thing. "You kick a man's mule, for example, and isn't it just like ramming a boot heel in that man's belly? Or suppose," she said, wagging a knitting needle at him, "you don't fix those chancy steps of yours and somebody breaks his head—his relatives have a right to sue you into the poorhouse, Moses Green." This was said in a speech he understood, but usually she spoke properly in a light, musical voice, such that her language, as Moses listened, was like song. Her dog, Ruben—a dog so small he couldn't mount the bitches during rutting season and, crazed, jumped Harriet's chickens instead—ran like a fleck of light around her chair. Then there was Harriet's three-decked stove, its sheet-iron stovepipe turned at a right angle, and her large wooden cupboard—all this, in comparison to his own rude, whitewashed cabin, and Harriet's endless chatter, now that her husband, Henry, was dead (when eating fish, he had breathed when he should have swallowed, then swallowed when he should have breathed), gave

Moses, as he sat in his Go-to-meeting clothes nibbling egg bread (his palm under his chin to catch crumbs), a lazy feeling of warmth, well-being, and wonder. Was he sweet on Harriet Bridgewater? His mind weathervaned—yes, no; yes, no— when he thought about it. She was awesome to him. But he didn't exactly like her opinions about his education of young Mingo. Example: "There's only *so* much he can learn, being a salt-water African and all, don't-choo-know?"

"So?"

"You know he'll never completely adjust."

"So?" he said.

"You know everything here's strange to him."

"So?" he said again.

"And it'll *always* be a little strange—like seeing the world through a fun house mirror?"

Moses knocked dottle from his churchwarden pipe, banging the bowl on the hard wooden arm of his chair until Harriet, annoyed, gave him a tight look. "You oughta see him, though. I mean, he's right smart—r'ally. It's like I just shot out another arm and that's Mingo. Can do anything I do, like today: he's gonna he'p Isaiah Jenson fix some windows and watchermercallems"—he scratched his head—"fences, over at his place." Chuckling, Moses struck a friction match on his boot heel. "Only thing Mingo won't do is kill chicken hawks; he feeds 'em like they was his best friends, even calls 'em Sir." Lightly, the old man laughed again. He put his left ankle on his right knee and cradled it. "But otherwise, Mingo says just what I says. Feels what I feels."

"Well!" Harriet said with violence. Her nose wrinkled—she rather hated his raw-smelling pipe tobacco—and testily laid down a general principle. "Slaves are tools with life in them, Moses, and tools are lifeless slaves."

The old man asked, "Says who?"

"Says Aristotle." She said this arrogantly, the way some people quote Scripture. "He owned thirteen slaves (they were then called *banausos*), sage Plato, fifteen, and neither felt the need to elevate their bondsmen. The institution is old, Moses, old, and you're asking for a peck of trouble if you keep playing God and get too close to that wild African. If he turns turtle on you, what then?" Quotations followed from David Hume, who, Harriet said, once called a preposterous liar one New World friend who informed him of a bondsman who could play any piece on the piano after hearing it only once.

"P'raps," hemmed Moses, rocking his head. "I reckon you're right."

"I know I'm right, Moses Green." She smiled.

"Harriet—"

The old woman answered, "Yes?"

"You gets me confused sometimes. Abaht my feelings. Half the time I can't rightly hear what you say, 'cause I'm all taken in by the way you say it." He struggled, shaking saliva from the stem of his pipe. "Harriet, your Henry, d'ya miss him much? I mean, abaht now you should be getting married again, don't you think? You get along okay by yourself, but I been thinking I . . . sometimes you make me feel—"

"Yes?" She brightened. "Go on."

He didn't explain how he felt.

Moses, later on the narrow, root-covered road leading to Isaiah Jenson's cabin, thought Harriet Bridgewater wrong about Mingo and, strange to say, felt closer to the black African than to Harriet. So close, in fact, that when he pulled his rig up to Isaiah's house, he considered giving Mingo his farm when he died, God willing, as well as his knowledge, beliefs, and prejudices. Then again, maybe that was overdoing things. The boy was all Moses wanted him to be, his own emanation, but still, he thought, himself. Different enough from Moses so that he could step back and admire him.

Swinging his feet off the buckboard, he called, "Isaiah!" and, hearing no reply, hobbled, bent forward at his hips, toward the front door—"H'lo?"— which was halfway open. Why could he see no one? "Jehoshaphat!" blurted Moses. From his lower stomach a loamy feeling crawled up to his throat. "Y'all heah? Hey!" The door opened with a burst at his fingertips. Snatching off his hat, ducking his head, he stepped inside. It was dark as a poor man's pocket in there. Air within had the smell of boiled potatoes and cornbread. He saw the boy seated big as life at Isaiah's table, struggling with a big lead-colored spoon and a bowl of hominy. "You two finished al-raid-y, eh?" Moses laughed, throwing his jaw forward, full of pride, as Mingo fought mightily, his head hung over his bowl, to get food to his mouth. "Whar's that fool Isaiah?" The African pointed over his shoulder, and Moses' eyes, squinting in the weak light, followed his wagging finger to a stream of sticky black fluid like the gelatinous trail of a snail flowing from where Isaiah Jenson, cold as stone, lay crumpled next to his stove, the image of Mingo imprisoned on the retina of his eyes. Frail moonlight funneled through cracks in the roof. The whole cabin was unreal. Simply unreal. The old man's knees knocked together. His stomach jerked. Buried deep in Isaiah's forehead was a meat cleaver that exactly split his face and disconnected his features.

"Oh, my Lord!" croaked Moses. He did a little dance, half juba, half jig, on his good leg toward Isaiah, whooped, "Mingo, what'd you *do?*" Then, knowing full well what he'd done, he boxed the boy behind his ears, and shook all six feet of him until Moses' teeth, not Mingo's, rattled. The old man sat down at the table; his knees felt rubbery, and he groaned, "Lord, *Lord, Lord!*" He blew out breath, blenched, his lips skinned back over his tobacco-browned teeth, and looked square at the African. "Isaiah's daid! You understand that?"

Mingo understood that; he said so.

"And you're responsible!" He stood up but sat down again, coughing, then pulled out his handkerchief and spit into it. "Daid! You know what daid means?" Again, he hawked and spit. "Responsible—you know what *that* means?"

He did not; he said, "Nossuh, don't know as I know that one, suh. Not Mingo, boss. *Noss*uh!"

Moses sprang up suddenly like a steel spring going off and slapped the boy till his palm stung. Briefly, the old man went bananas, pounding the boy's chest with his fists. He sat down again. Jumping up so quick made his head spin and legs wobble. Mingo protested his innocence, and it did not dawn on Moses why he seemed so indifferent until he thought back to what he'd told him about chicken hawks. Months ago, maybe five, he'd taught Mingo to kill chicken hawks and be courteous to strangers, but it got all turned around in the African's mind (how was he to know New World customs?), so he was courteous to chicken hawks (Moses groaned, full of gloom) and killed strangers. "You idjet!" hooted Moses. His jaw clamped shut. He wept hoarsely for a few minutes like a steer with the strangles. "Isaiah Jenson and me was friends, and—" He checked himself; what'd he said was a lie. They weren't friends at all. In fact, he thought Isaiah Jenson was a pigheaded fool and only tolerated the little yimp in a neighborly way. Into his eye a fly bounded. Moses shook his head wildly. He'd even sworn to Harriet, weeks earlier, that Jenson was so troublesome, always borrowing tools and keeping them, he hoped he'd go to Ballyhack on a red-hot rail. In his throat a knot tightened. One of his eyelids jittered up, still itchy from the fly; he forced it down with his finger, then gave a slow look at the African. "Great Peter," he mumbled. "You couldn'ta known that."

"Go home now?" Mingo stretched out the stiffness in his spine. "Powerful tired, boss."

Not because he wanted to go home did Moses leave, but because he was afraid of Isaiah's body and needed time to think things through. Dry the air, dry the evening down the road that led them home. As if to himself, the old man grumped, "I gave you thought and tongue, and looka what you done with it—they gonna catch and kill you, boy, just as sure as I'm sitting heah."

"Mingo?" The African shook his long head, sly; he touched his chest with one finger. *"Me?* Nossuh."

"Why the hell you keep saying that?" Moses threw his jaw forward so violently muscles in his neck stood out. "You kilt a man, and they gonna burn you crisper than an ear of corn. Ay, God, Mingo," moaned the old man, "you gotta act responsible, son!" At the thought of what they'd do to Mingo, Moses scrooched the stalk of his head into his stiff collar. He drilled his gaze at the smooth-faced African, careful not to look him in the eye, and barked, "What're you thinking *now?*"

"What Mingo know, Massa Green know. Bees like *what* Mingo sees or don't see is only what Massa Green taught him to see or don't see. Like Mingo lives through Massa Green, right?"

Moses waited, suspicious, smelling a trap. "Yeah, all that's true."

"Massa Green, he owns Mingo, right?"

"Right," snorted Moses. He rubbed the knob of his red, porous nose. "Paid good money—"

"So when Mingo works, it bees Massa Green workin', right? Bees Massa Green workin', thinkin', doin' *through* Mingo—ain't that so?"

Nobody's fool, Moses Green could latch onto a notion with no trouble at all; he turned violently off the road leading to his cabin and plowed on toward Harriet's, pouring sweat, remembering two night visions he'd had, recurrent, where he and Mingo were wired together like, say, two ventriloquist's dummies, one black, one white, and there was somebody—who he didn't know, yanking their arm and leg strings simultaneously—how he couldn't figure, but he and Mingo said the same thing together until his liver-spotted hands, the knuckles tight and shriveled like old carrot skin, flew up to his face and, shrieking, he started hauling hips across a cold black countryside. But so did Mingo, *his* hands on *his* face, pumping his knees right alongside Moses, shrieking, their voice inflections identical; and then the hazy dream doorwayed luxuriously into another where he was greaved on one half of a thrip—a coin halfway between a nickel and a dime—and on the reverse side was Mingo. Shaking, Moses pulled his rig into Harriet Bridgewater's yard. His bowels, burning, felt like boiling tar. She was standing on her porch in a checkered Indian shawl, staring at them, her book still open, when Moses scrambled, tripping, skinning his knees, up her steps. He shouted, "Harriet, this boy done kilt Isaiah Jenson in cold blood." She lost color and wilted back into her doorway. Her hair was swinging in her eyes. Hands flying, he stammered in a flurry of anxiety, "But it wasn't altogether Mingo's fault—he didn't know what he was doin'."

"Isaiah? You mean Izay-yah? He didn't kill Izay-yah?"

"Yeah, aw no! Not really—" His mind stuttered to a stop.

"Whose fault is it then?" Harriet gawked at the African picking his nose in the wagon (Moses had, it's true, not policed himself as well as he'd wanted). A shiver quaked slowly up her left side. She sloughed off her confusion and flashed, "I can tell you whose fault it is, Moses. Yours! Didn't I say not to bring that wild African here? Huh? Huh? Huh? You both should be—put to sleep."

"Aw, woman! Hesh up!" Moses threw down his hat and stomped it out of shape. "You just all upsetted." Truth to tell, he was not the portrait of composure himself. There were rims of dirt in his nails. His trouser legs had blood splattered on them. Moses stamped his feet to shake road powder off his boots. "You got any spirits in the house? I need your he'p to untangle this thing, but I ain't hardly touched a drop since I bought Mingo, and my throat's pretty dr—"

"You'll just have to get it yourself—on the top shelf of the cupboard." She touched her face, fingers spread, with a dazed gesture. There was suddenly in her features the intensity found in the look of people who have a year, a month, a minute only to live. "I think I'd better sit down." Lowering herself onto her rocker, she cradled on her lap a volume by one M. Shelley, a recent tale of monstrosity and existential horror; then she demurely settled her breasts. "It's just like you, Moses Green, to bring all your bewilderments to me."

The old man's face splashed into a huge, foamy smile. He kissed her gently on both eyes, and Harriet, in return, rubbed her cheek like a cat against his gristly jaw. Moses felt lighter than a feather. "Got to have somebody, don't I?"

In the common room, Moses rifled through the cupboard, came up with a bottle of lukewarm bourbon, and, hands trembling, poured himself three fingers' worth in a glass. Then, because he figured he deserved it, he refilled his glass and, draining it slowly, sloshing it around in his mouth, considered his options. He could turn Mingo over to the law and let it go at that, but damned if he couldn't shake loose the idea that killing the boy somehow wouldn't put things to rights; it would be like they were killing Moses himself, destroying a part of his soul. Besides, whatever the African'd done, it was what he'd learned through Moses, who was not the most reliable lens for looking at things. You couldn't rightly call a man responsible if, in some utterly alien place, he was without power, without privilege, without property—*was*, in fact, property—if he had no position, had nothing, or virtually next to nothing, and nothing was his product or judgment. "Be damned!" Moses spit. It was a bitter thing to siphon your being from someone else. He knew that now. It was like, on another level, what Liverspoon had once tried to deny about God and man: *If* God was (and now Moses wasn't all that sure), and *if* He made the world, then a man didn't have to answer for anything. Rape or murder, it all referred back to who-or-whatever was responsible for that world's makeup. Chest fallen, he tossed away his glass, lifted the bottle to his lips, then nervously lit his pipe. Maybe . . . maybe they could run, if it came to that, and start all over again in Missouri, where he'd teach Mingo the difference between chicken hawks and strangers. But, sure as day, he'd do it again. He couldn't change. What was *was*. They'd be running forever, across all space, all time—so he imagined—like fugitives with no fingers, no toes, like two thieves or yokefellows, each with some Godawful secret that could annihilate the other. Naw! Moses thought. His blood beat up. The deep, powerful stroke of his heart made him wince. His tobacco maybe. Too strong. He sent more whiskey crashing down his throat. *Naw!* You couldn't have nothing and just go as you pleased. How strange that owner and owned magically dissolved into each other like two crossing shafts of light (or, if he'd known this, which he did not, particles, subatomic, interconnected in a complex skein of relatedness). Shoot him maybe, reabsorb Mingo, was that more merciful? *Naw!* He was fast; fast. Then manumit the African? Noble gersture, that. But how in blazes could he disengage himself when Mingo shored up, sustained, *let be* Moses' world with all its sores and blemishes every time he opened his oily black eyes? Thanks to the trouble he took cementing Mingo to his own mind, he could not, by thunder, do without him now. Giving him his freedom, handing it to him like a rasher of bacon, would shackle Mingo to him even more. There seemed, just then, no solution.

Undecided, but mercifully drunk now, his pipe bowl too hot to hold any longer, Moses, who could not speak his mind to Harriet Bridgewater unless he'd tied one on, called out, "I come to a decision. Not about Mingo, but you'n' me." It was then seven o'clock. He shambled, feet shuffling, toward the door. "Y'know, I was gonna ask you to marry me this morning"—he laughed; whiskey made his scalp tingle—"but I figured living alone was better when I thoughta how married folks—and sometimes wimmin with dogs—got to favoring each other . . . like they was wax candles flowing tergether. Hee-hee." He stepped gingerly, holding the bottle high, his ears brick red, face streaky from wind-dried sweat, back onto the quiet porch. He heard a moan. It was distinctly a moan. "Harriet? Harriet, I ain't put it too well, but I'm asking you now." On the porch her rocker slid back, forth, squeaking on the floorboards. Moses' bottle fell— *bip!*—down the stairs, bounced out into the yard, rolled, and bumped into Harriet Bridgewater. Naw, he thought. Aw, naw. By the wagon, by a chopping block near a pile of split faggots, by the ruin of an old hand pump caked with rust, she lay on her side, the back fastenings of her dress burst open, her mouth a perfect O. The sight so wounded him he wept like a child. It was then seven-fifteen.

October 7 of the year of grace 1855.

Midnight found Moses Green still staring down at her. He felt sick and crippled and dead inside. Every shadowed object thinging in the yard beyond, wrenched up from its roots, hazed like shapes in a hallucination, was a sermon on vanity; every time he moved his eyes he stared into a grim homily on the deadly upas of race and relatedness. Now he had no place to stand. Now he was undone. "Mingo . . . come ovah heah." He was very quiet.

"Suh?" The lanky African jumped down from the wagon, faintly innocent, faintly diabolical. Removed from the setting of Moses' farm, the boy looked strangely elemental; his skin had the texture of plant life, the stones of his eyes an odd, glossy quality like those of a spider, which cannot be read. "Talky old hen daid now, boss."

The old man's face shattered. "I was gonna marry that woman!"

"Naw." Mingo frowned. From out of his frown a huge grin flowered. "You say—I'm quoting you now, suh—a man needs a quiet, patient, uncomplaining woman, right?"

Moses croaked, "When did I say that?"

"Yesstiday." Mingo yawned. He looked sleepy. "Go home now, boss?"

"Not just yet." Moses Green, making an effort to pull himself to his full height, failed. "You lie face down—heah me?—with your hands ovah your head till I come back." With Mingo hugging the front steps, Moses took the stairs back inside, found the flintlock Harriet kept in her cupboard on account of slaves who swore to die in the skin of freemen, primed it, and stepped back, so slowly, to the yard. Outside, the air seemed thinner. Bending forward, perspiring at his upper lip, Moses tucked the cold barrel into the back of Mingo's neck, cushioning it in a small socket of flesh above the African's broad shoulders. With his thumb he pulled the hammer back. Springs in the flintlock whined. Deep inside his throat, as if he were speaking through his stomach, he talked to the dark poll of the boy's back-slanting head.

"You ain't never gonna understand why I gotta do this. You a saddle across my neck, always will be, even though it ain't rightly all your fault. Mingo, you more me than I am myself. Me planed away to the bone! Ya understand?" He coughed and went on miserably: "All the wrong, all the good you do, now or tomorrow—it's me indirectly doing it, but without the lies and excuses, without the feeling what's its foundation, with all the polite make-up and apologies removed. It's an empty gesture, like the swing of a shadow's arm. You can't never see things exactly the way I do. I'm guilty. It was me set the gears in motion. Me . . ." Away in the octopoid darkness a wild bird—a nighthawk maybe—screeched. It shot noisily away with blurred wings askirring when the sound of hoofs and wagons rumbled closer. Eyes narrowed to slits, Moses said—a dry whisper—"Get up, you damned fool." He let his round shoulders slump. Mingo let his broad shoulders slump. "Take the horses," Moses said; he pulled himself up to his rig, then sat, his knees together beside the boy. Mingo's knees drew together. Moses's voice changed. It began to rasp and wheeze; so did Mingo's. "Missouri," said the old man, not to Mingo but to the dusty floor of the buckboard, "if I don't misremember, is off thataway somewheres in the west."

Scat

Clarence Major

1979

"Just take us to the city, I'll tell you where to stop," I said to the taxi driver.

Now we were spurting in fumes of gas and metal from JFK through the complex night. Colored objects dashing zooming by. This ground-level entrance was so sensuous and ritual-like. Up ahead, through the windshield, I could see the comforting persistent lights of the great city.

But how about this driver? Could we trust him? I kept looking at his audacious name: *Gunman.* A warped scheme in his mind? Is he simply a man of routine, simply doing his job?

And Baby, from the very beginning, injured like a lonely ovary in a vacant woman, simply refused to think, to make decisions, which left me with the colossal load of not only my mismanaged self, but slightly cringing, restless and pummeled under the load of her spirit. Though I wasn't fully aware of it yet, I was desperately, wildly, happy.

I watched the back of the driver's head. Then he gave a quick boorish laugh and called over his shoulder, "Popular impulses at special human rates?" "What'd he say?" "Baby, listen—" I began, slightly weary, showing my ill-breeding already. And we had been together only since October twenty-eighth, and this was like the day after the Plot, I mean the Sacrifice, December twenty-sixth; but, I decided to control my usually unveiled but mystifying tongue, which, in any case, was tired. "What were you going to say?" But the cabby thought Cathy was addressing him and retorted: "I only was trying to remind you folks that I haven't the slightest idea where I should take you. How about Brooklyn?"

I thought of asking several questions at once but all of them jammed up in me and nothing came out for a moment anyway. "You see," I began, "the problem, mac—" and I threw my weight forward, elbows on my knees so that he could catch the body of each word in at least the ear on *this* side of his head, over the roar of the expressway traffic, the heavy groaning of trucks and buses and the swift oozing metal sounds of the glittering modern buggy-wagons that still had horsepower for some mysterious reason: ". . . the problem is *this*—" Suddenly, while still focusing his cumbersome head forward like any good driver he shamelessly cut into my sentence. "The only reason I suggested Brooklyn is there's a lot of superstitious people in other parts of the city. I live in Brooklyn myself; you'd never know it, though, because I don't have a Brooklyn accent— did you notice? Well, you folks are obviously from outta town so you didn't notice. Even grew up there, and I don't talk like your ordinary taxicab driver—if you know what I mean—"

Cathy, in a furiously cheerful voice, broke his dialogue, announcing: "Didn't you use the word, superstition?"

"Yeah, lady, that's what I said, but I'll explain to you what I mean by that, if you give me a moment—*can you both hear me?*—" A little too loudly we assured him but he cranked up his voice anyway and pumped on: "Like the gentleman called me *mac*"—and now, directly to me—"I know you didn't mean nothing by doing that, but it just proves a point; the same thing I'm talking about, the way I talk. I mean, I never call people mac, you know what I mean?" I could feel his passionate desire to turn around to witness my reaction to his clouded question, but he didn't and because he was obviously such an excellent driver I never saw his face. After awhile it was like his voice was coming out of the backside of his head and it seemed so natural for him. "That's the way cab drivers talk, you know—hey mac, mac this and mac that." His pause was very stingy. "Well, the young lady ask me about superstitions. Now, I ain't—I mean *am not*—no expert on the real nature of these kinds of things, and I don't know anything about you people. I mean whether or not you two are married or just friends or what have you, but I know this, that—except for in Brooklyn—a mixed couple, and as I say, I don't know if you are a mixed couple, I mean if you two are—you know what I mean, married or going together—for all I know, you could be a couple of civil rights workers. Right? Right! And I really don't care, I mean I don't even care to know, but in case youse in some way roman-tic"—for the quickest and most tense moment of his speech he suddenly and automatically took his fat, reddened hands from the wheel to form the beautiful word romantic; he just threw his palms up, facing each other, as though he were holding something round and invisible—"then I'd suggest Brooklyn, because there's less hard feelings there against . . . Well, you know what I mean. In Brooklyn, you'll never find people going around using bedbugs, for example, as a cure for sore eyes. But in Manhattan—oh Christ! there're folks who do this kind of thing—they actually mix bedbugs, all crushed up, with salt and the human milk of a pregnant woman, if they can find one, and not only for sore eyes but the poorer people, in the ghetto, you know, they're even dumber than just the average guy, they even take it internally, they claim it cures urban hysteria. It's witchcraft, is what it is . . ."

O merciful wrathful gods. I was too tired to laugh but this was about to get to me. And to make matters worse, Cathy in her usual innocent manner flatly stated: "Are you saying that this is generally true of *everybody* who lives in Manhattan?"

And the driver, really excited now, defensively snapped: "Do you know what *literal* means, young lady? Yeah, you do, huh. Well, that's the way I mean it. I wouldn't tell you anything that isn't true." He hunched his shoulders.

I was still leaning forward to hear better. Cathy now anxiously joined me. I was looking straight ahead, fearful suddenly at his lack of concentration on his driving but trying to keep my composure. I must have been peering for some indication of our destiny—signs to Manhattan?—or at least my own, as I listened to the sovereign voice of our volunteer tour guide.

"There certainly ain't nothing in it for me, I mean for me to lie to you, deliberately," he said. "Ask yourself. What could I get out of it? Just trying to be a decent fellow and tell you how it is in Manhattan since you both are obviously from no parts of New York. It's the worst part of the city. But I can tell you everything you want to know about the Bronx, Queens and Staten Island too. Now, you find some kind of superstitious practices, but to a lesser degree, because, well, those people out there they've had a little more education, but Manhattan is the worst of all."

I could feel Cathy's excitement and frustration and confusion. She obviously wanted to argue with the man but didn't know how to begin. His voice was so coolly antiseptic, so sure: "My son-in-law, he's a lawyer, told me just the other day, believe it or not, that a Manhattan lady came to him to file for a divorce from her husband. Want to hear the reason she wanted a divorce?" By all means, I smoothly assured him. "This husband of hers, the poor guy, he dropped a black ace of spades—*accidentally*—while just playing a normal game of cards"—he pronounced the word *cads*—"in their living room. You know, just sitting around with the fellas. *That's why* she wanted a divorce. And before you call me a liar, I'll tell you this, my son-in-law is, first, a good Catholic, a Harvard man, a responsible gentleman who maintains his ethics, and a decent husband to my daughter. They're even buying a home in Brooklyn Heights. And if you knew anything about the city here at all you would know what *that* means."

"Mister Lawman," Cathy shot, "you *must* be putting us on—"

This of course steamed him up again. *I* wanted to hear what he had to say; I was ready to believe anything. And everything he said, so far, sounded perfectly logical to me.

"Look—" he snapped ambitiously, "do you know anybody, in your hometown, wherever you come from, who hangs garlic around in their home? I mean to keep evil spirits away?"

"No," Cathy admitted.

"Do you know or have you ever heard of people who go around rubbing bald-headed old helpless men on their heads just to try to improve *their own* memory? Or how about this theory that water is fattening? Have you ever known anybody to stop drinking water because it's fattening? Well, there're a lot of Manhattaners who are right now, I mean this very minute, on a *water* diet. I mean a lot of them don't drink the stuff at all, and nothing that contains it, not even liquor. And furthermore, all over Manhattan there are like thousands and thousands of voodoo rites. And I don't mean concealed in some basement. Right out in the open. Certain people are put under spells by certain other people for certain reasons, and they're actually held like that, as victims. They use everything from rotten apple roots to certain kinds of perfumes to get certain effects, cause people to go insane or walk around crazy-like, you know—restless, can't sit down or nothing, just going on and on until they drop dead. You've heard of the hippies, haven't you? Sure you have. That's what's happened to those poor kids. They're all under a spell. They've been hexed. And, believe me, I'm not trying to scare you folks. I'm just trying to inform you. Actually, there're a lot of cab drivers who won't even go into Manhattan, especially way uptown, the farther you get uptown the worse it is—" He coughed and now speaking directly to me: "Nothing personal to you sir—but the colored peoples are the worst of all. But it's not just *them.* I don't want to give you that impression. It's all of New York City. Like I say, except for Brooklyn. It's really funny sometimes. You can be driving around in Manhattan and see people strutting and just ah strolling along and everybody, I mean *everybody* is carrying an umbrella—"

Cathy cut in: "But why?"

"Well, you see, they have this belief, it's like part of Manhattan culture, you know. They believe that if you carry an umbrella that *that* will forestall rain."

"But what have they got against rain?" Cathy is about to lose her temper.

"Search me!" His shoulders lifted and fell again. "All I can tell you is what I see!"

I cut in: "But you *are* still taking us to Manhattan?"

He pondered the hugely serious and complex question for several moments. "You see, it's a long drive in, and right now you still got a chance to choose. Like they say on television, when they're talking politics, you know an *alternative*—" He chuckled, his shoulders rocking. "That's a nice big word, huh?" He stopped laughing, then said: "I don't mean to dwell on this subject. If anything I hate is somebody who dwells on a subject. But while you're making up your minds, let me ask you a question? You sir, *or* the lady. Have either one of you heard of the art of capnomancy?"

"The art of what?" I cleared my throat, hoping my mind would also defog.

"It's an evil art that's practiced, very commonly practiced, in Manhattan; some people call it pollution—"

Cathy cut in: "But how about the Village, certainly the Village—"

He cut her off: "The Village is no different. Of course you may find some strange people there, you know, they're all weird down there. Really weird people. And as I say, some of them might call it pollution but the true name of it is capnomancy. It's an art. It's done with smoke. And it's very deadly. So, if you decide on Manhattan *anyway,* remember that. Because you're going to come up against it."

"But if it's smoke, certainly it would drift to Brooklyn too." Cathy pleaded.

He answered her swiftly, very curtly: "Nope. We don't have that sort of thing in Brooklyn." His tone was absolutely self-righteous.

After a moment of silence, I said, "I won't ask you what *do* you have in Brooklyn." This statement obviously bewildered and confused him.

He said, "But why not?"

I said, "Because I've heard that, aside from other more private reasons, they haven't started body snatching yet, in Brooklyn." We were shooting straight ahead eighty-six miles per hour on the expressway and for the first time he turned completely around. He was so perplexed he looked like the Ambassador of Confusion. He also looked like Jackie Gleason.

"What're you talking about?"

Well, I was a little surprised that he hadn't heard but I faked more astonishment than I felt. "You *mean* you haven't heard?"

"No, but I'm all ears—"

I relaxed and quickly cleared up his confusion. "Don't go around talking about this to anybody you don't know because you could easily get into trouble. But already in certain parts of the world—I'm not saying where—people are being *snatched* off the streets under the shadowy cover of night and taken to certain places, usually hospitals, where very rich or important people who have heart trouble are in critical condition, about to die. They call these captured people—who're always poor and defenseless—*donors.* They're especially interested in pregnant women because their hearts are in better shape."

"No!" said the cabby. He chuckled, obviously not taking me very seriously.

Cathy, by the way, was listening intently. She should have been because I had never before told her this secret information that had come my way, quite by accident (and even now I'm not at liberty to reveal the source). He now was truly puzzled and seemingly more seriously intent on what I was saying.

"You see, the only way the operation can succeed is if you catch a person who is healthy, walking around with good blood circulation—and you have to *act* swiftly like they say where I come from. And they use very sharp instruments, have everything all ready. Then *shuph!* cut out the donor's ticker and get it into the other person's chest pronto."

"Holy Christ! in Heaven! What *are* you talking about?" The man is truly alarmed.

For the first time since we'd left Wayne at the airport in Chicago Cathy laughed, though it wasn't a happy laugh.

As an afterthought I thought it only fair to add: "Of course, they use antiseptics and all kinds of—"

He cut me off: "Just hold on a second will you. Answer me this. What has this got to do with Manhattan?"

"Nothing—" I said, so thrilled that he had finally gotten the point. "That's *why* I've decided we're going to Manhattan. Just head for the Village and I'll decide where you can let us out when we get there."

"Look!" the driver said in an offended tone. "If you're talking about what I *think* you're talking about, which is murder, *and* if you think for one minute that we have that sort of stuff going on in Brooklyn, then you're dead wrong. You got another thought coming."

It always makes me feel joyful to know what I'm going to do next. So, by now, I was quite overjoyed when I reached up and gave our friend the driver a friendly slap on the shoulder. "Well, pal, I certainly wasn't referring to Brooklyn and I'm mighty happy to have your word that Brooklyn is still safe, at least to that degree."

At the same time I could see the huge black mouth of the midtown tunnel up ahead, specked with yellow lights. I had the distinct feeling that we were making an exit rather than an entrance.

Now Is the Time

Cecil M. Brown

1981

I will admit that reason is a good thing. No argument about that. But reason is only reason, and it only satisfies man's rational require-ments. Desire, on the other hand, is the manifestation of life itself— of all of life—and it encompasses everything from reason down to scratching oneself. And although, when we're guided by our desires, life very often turns into a messy affair, it's still life and not a series of extractions or square roots.

—Dostoyevsky, Notes from Underground

I parked my car in the courtyard just in front of the guest house. Facing west and looking beyond the guest house I could see the tennis court and bathhouses; to my right were the boxing gym, the dogs, and the cars. To my left was the main house. I remembered all this because I'd been to one of Billy's parties, where Billy entertained most of the party-goers in Hollywood. The comics have told me and I've observed it for myself that he liked nothing better than sharing his wealth with others and got the biggest pleasure out of seeing other people enjoying his estate.

I knocked at the back door of the main house and a Chicano maid opened it, greeted me politely, and said Billy was waiting for me upstairs. After leading me into the room, where I got a glimpse of the spacious kitchen with its slacked hardwood floors and stark simplicity, she led me up some stairs covered with two-inch carpeting to Billy's study.

When I entered the room I immediately saw Billy seated behind a large, modern Danish-style desk of books and mementoes and photos in an orderly hodgepodge. He was wearing a red T-shirt with *Hana* written across it, a pair of white ducks, and tennis shoes. On his head he wore one of those Hermes hats with silver wings. As I slowly sunk into the cushion and made my way to him he leaped up and started laughing. His infectious laughter seduced me immediately and though I wasn't aware of it, I realize, now that I look back on it, I was laughing too.

"Sit down, Partner," he said in a Western cowboy voice, "and rest your feet."

He'd done the voice so well that he rewarded himself with a chuckle.

"What you want to drink?" he asked me as I dropped into the chair adjoining his desk.

I knew he drank vodka, and I asked for it myself. He told this to the maid, who was still standing waiting for her orders, and she went away.

"Do you like fights?" my host asked and turned to the color video television of the Muhammad Ali–Frazier fight. Every time the champ hit Frazier, Billy would jump up and laugh like an excited child.

"Get 'im, Champ! Look at that! Look! The champ's got 'im down. He's knocked the shit out of Frazier! Sonabitch! Is that it? That's it!"

He clicked the television off with a remote control and announced to me, "That's it!" and then he said, almost to himself, "I've seen this fight a million times and each time I act just like a damn fool! It fucks me up to see anything that beautiful. I don't know why but it does!"

When he was watching the fight I took the time to drink in the room. It was the sort of room that could easily be an office when the occasion arose, and with the carpeting and soft-cushioned leather sofas and the video sets and sound systems (large impressive speakers stood ominously in the corners) it could easily be a playpen, a place to kick back in, entertain a half dozen intimate friends. A long glass window ran along the wall, just behind Billy's desk, and overlooked the courtyard, the guest house, gym, and garage; on the opposite wall a window overlooked moorish arches, a Spanish-styled fountain, a moorish plaza. This gave me an ancient, dark, soothing state of mind, like a bit of fantasy. This fantastic element seemed balanced with the realistic everywhere in the room itself. African sculptures, some standing in one corner as tall as an average man, added to this fantastic mood.

Along the walls perpendicular and adjacent to the two walls just described were the many plaques given to him commemorating his genius in comedy, movie posters advertising his cinematic pantomine, pictures and photographs capturing his social life at parties, his personal life in Hawaii, and his family life with his children. Then right in the middle of these (on the east wall) this touch of fantasy: a beautiful picture of an incredibly beautiful woman in an ancient Greek costume holding a spear and shield. This picture, though small, dominated the room. Who was the girl? And what role was she playing? And in what play? Did Billy also have an interest in drama? Was he in love with an actress, some true beauty of the drama stage? Was there a fantastic, hidden dimension to this already protean girl-crazy shape-shifter?

Making her entrance and exit as quietly as an unearthly sprite, the Chicano maid brought my vodka. It was like some weird, spooky magic. One moment I'm looking at the wall and the next there's this glass of vodka sitting right in front of me. I had to turn my head quick—real quick too—to see the last of her white, starched uniform disappearing behind the closed door. One day, I promised myself silently, I'll have servants fast like that. One minute they're here, the next minute they're gone. Off to some mysterious island to bring me back some strange, fantastic pleasure in the form of a drug which I'd serve as a vodka.

"Do you do this?" Billy asked and offered me the piece of paper with the White Girl on it.

"Of course," I said and accepted it, and, in the manner of an adept accepting from his guru some hip potion, a token of their deep and heavy pondering over the spiritual presences in life and death, I took a ceremonial snort. The thing about White Girl is that it just puts me to sleep. But not when I am doing it with my moral mentor! It was like smoking your first cigarette with your father: you are now taking the same moral assumptions about life that he has—you are, for better or worse, on the same level somehow and he knows you know this now and that's what is communicated between you by the smoking of the verboten cigarette or the snorting of the illegal White Girl.

At least that's the way I saw it that afternoon as all the light was leaving the sky. I was, after all, looking for help: I felt washed up as a comic, but I didn't want to face up to the truth. *I wasn't funny any more.* Even with jokes that I'd previously gotten laughs off, audiences would now, when I told them, look at me uncomprehendingly like I was a fool. Nobody would laugh at me. I was ashamed of my routine, my "show."

And then, as if he possessed a clairvoyant sense, Billy said, "I saw your show."

Oh, God, now! He had said it! With one word of condemnation he could make me a show-biz cripple for life! Don't you—the greatest comedian since the beginning of the world, not you whom I admire more than my very own father, not you whose records I listened to and admired when only three years old! Not you whom I compared to Dionysus in the *Bacchantes,* comparing your comedy to his savage divinity of wine in my college senior thesis, not you who is like a god to me—don't you be the one to tell me how unfunny my "show" was, please.

Quickly I interrupted him and condemned myself before he could. I'd much rather hear it from my own mouth, the lesser mouth, as it were, than his.

"I was lousy," I confessed. "I was terrible! I—"

"Yes," he said, "you were pretty bad."

"I don't know why I was so lousy," I went on in this pitiful voice, in a voice, now that I look back on it, not unlike one of Billy's typical heroes, an utter loser, "Nobody laughed at me."

"You weren't funny. That's why," he said in a tone of voice that indicated that I'd offended him and his profession by declaring that I belonged to it. I kept shaking my head and looking depressed. When I wasn't shaking my head in self-loathing I'd hang it down between my legs like a rock on the end of a string which I was about to drop into some dismal chasm below. Except I couldn't drop my head! If only I could disappear! If only I could become a fly! And buzz off!

"In fact," Billy went on, "I don't think I've ever seen anybody as bad as you were. There's something irritating about your work."

"That's the best thing anybody ever said to me," I confessed.

"Have you ever thought of giving it up?" he asked, peering into my face in such a manner as to suggest somebody searching into a dark, empty room and, finding nothing, closing the door.

Have I ever thought of giving it up? You mean, have I ever thought of killing myself?

How could I give it up? When there were so many funny people in the world to talk about, how could I not be a comic? When the corruption I saw all around me every day at the Beverly Hills Hotel, on the street corners, in the Polo Lounge, how could I not be a comic? And yet how could I explain this to him? Could he understand?

"Yes, I've thought of giving it up," I lied. "Right after this meeting with you I'm going to give it up and then kill myself."

"Why not?" He laughed. "You're already dead."

The pun didn't escape me and I rewarded his shrewdness with a laugh.

"So you've thought of giving it up?" he asked again.

"Yes," I lied again.

"Don't," he said.

"Don't . . . what?" I asked.

"Give it up," he muttered.

"But I'm living in misery," I challenged.

"I know, so did I. When I said a few minutes back that your show was the worst I'd ever seen I wasn't telling the complete truth. The worst show I'd ever seen was my first show. I was just like you. I was so bad I felt I'd offended the audience by just showing up. First I tried to be a singer, but the more I tried to be a singer, the worse I got. So I'd tell little jokes between songs. The people would boo my songs and laugh at my jokes. Clubs started hiring me for my jokes, and club managers would tell me, 'Billy, lay off the songs. Do more jokes,' until pretty soon I'd dropped the songs and was doing all jokes. Except, as soon as I started thinking hard about comedy, suddenly I wasn't funny. I started doing jokes from jokebooks, and other comics' jokes I'd heard get laughs, until I couldn't live with myself anymore. I wasn't being honest. I did one show once in Las Vegas that was worse than the show I saw you do at the Comedy Club. I'm not trying to pull rank on you by saying my show was worse than yours. But it was."

"It's hard to imagine a show worse than mine," I admitted to him without shame.

"You remind me of myself. I wasn't always funny when I *first* started."

I didn't believe this, but I went on nodding my head in agreement. Could anybody who'd ever seen Billy Badman believe he wasn't born funny?

"I know a little bit about comedy," he said in this typical understated manner. "To be funny, you have to learn to laugh at yourself. Laugh at your troubles!"

I know a little bit about comedy—under-fucking-statement of the century! Does he know a little bit about comedy!

Suddenly, silently, there stood this tall, svelte, attractive woman beside Billy. I recognized her lovely face as belonging to the girl holding the shield and sword in the picture. She was wearing a considerable bit more than a Grecian loincloth, dressed as she was in blue shorts and a pink tank top.

"Oh, this is my girlfriend, Tina," Billy said by way of introduction. "Tina, this is Jonah. He works at the Comedy Club."

"Hello." She smiled and extended a frail, suntanned hand for me to shake, which I did.

"We were talking about something," Billy said in a voice that succeeded in both informing her and dismissing her at once.

"I want to be with you, darling," Tina said and put her arm around his neck. I made a move in my chair that said, If you want to be alone I can leave, but Billy made a gesture with his hand that said, Don't move, I know how to handle this.

"I'm talking to a friend," Billy said with a slight annoyance in his voice.

"Nice meeting you, Jonah," Tina said and went back downstairs.

"Comedy," Billy went on, as if Tina hadn't interrupted him, "is about trouble. Everybody's in trouble, everybody's got to die. Death makes comedy possible! A comic makes people laugh at their problems and troubles, even though for that particular expression of the trouble, death is not so obvious, but it's always there. When somebody slips on a banana peel we laugh because he could also fall and kill himself."

Bert Williams! Bert-fucking-Williams! Did he know about Bert Williams or did he develop independently from him? Surely he knew they were kin, belonging to the same family? But even as I thought these thoughts, what I'm doing, see, is I'm leaned all over like a student or something. *Not one word* was going to escape my talking brain-box, is what I'm trying to get over by my pose.

And I'm going to spend the balance of my days trying to live up to the wisdom that I'm about to receive from this great master!

"What about Bert Williams?" I finally had the courage to say.

"Bert Williams, the old mime artist? Ah, my friend Randell Young who lives in Berkeley told me about him. Somebody showed me a film about him once. He was able to come out and just stick his white-gloved hand out and make the audience laugh for forty minutes!"

"Were you influenced by him?"

"No, I was already a comic before I knew about him."

"But you belong to the same family, the same kin. I have this theory—well, it's not important."

"No, go on. Theory. I want to hear it."

"Well, first there was Williams. He studied black people. He was the first scientist of black culture. He said he looked at blacks as if he wasn't one of them! He learned their humor and their dialect. He studied with Petro in Europe to get the timing right. Because of his aesthetic distance, as it were, he became popular with whites like Al Jolson, Will Rogers, and W.C. Fields, who made money and career out of Negro impersonations. Then came the black side of his lineage: Ernest Hogan, Billy Kersands, Sam Lucas, Bailey and Fletcher, Coles and Johnson. They were the coon shouters. They were the early satirists who took the word 'coon' and turned it back on whites. Then came World War I. Then Stepin Fetchit and his gang. Then after World War II and the sixties, Dick Gregory, Bill Cosby, Redd Foxx. Then Richard Pryor. Then you. Don't you see? You're one family, but Bert stands at the head of the family."

"What about you?" he asked slyly.

"Me? I don't count. I'm nobody. I'm not even funny."

"*Nobody.* Isn't that the most famous of Bert Williams' songs?"

"Yes, yes it is."

"Isn't that the song that made him famous?"

"Yes."

"Then maybe you would be better off by being nobody. People like to laugh at a nobody. Especially a nobody that ain't funny. Maybe you should start laughing at what a nobody you are."

"I agree that I'm nobody," I said. I just remembered something. When I did that college senior paper the main point of comparison between the Greek god Dionysus and Bill's humor was first of all the divinity element, and second— the most important thing—was that Dionysus had taken the form of a human being. Billy often gave me the impression, especially in this part of our meeting, of being a spirit who had incarnated himself into the physical person of Billy Badman.

"Be a good nobody then," he said in the manner that suggested a guru speaking.

A God incarnate—like when I looked over the tall African statue that seemed to be guarding the portal against evil spirits, he seemed to have been reading my thoughts. I was thinking, *I've never been to Africa!*

"Have you ever been to Africa?" he asked.

"No."

"Go, Jonah. Go. It'll make you proud. Even the snakes hold their heads up in Africa."

I looked at the picture of Tina in the shield and sword.

"What play is that from?" I asked.

"I don't know," he said. "It's written down on the bottom of it," he said. "Look and see what it's from."

Crossing the room I looked at the picture frame: *Springfield College. Antigone, Summer, 1967.*

"Antigone," I said.

"Means nothing to me." He laughed.

"She rebels against her father and society and tradition."

He shook his head in the direction in which Tina had left and said, "That's her all right!"

"You don't think living with a white woman is a problem anymore?" I asked suddenly.

"No," he said, "I think we're beyond that now. Everybody feels that a black man and a white woman can have as many problems as anybody else."

"And as much happiness as anybody else," I bravely commented.

"That's right," he said.

"But-but-but everything you do, records, concerts, films, are all about black people, yet—and yet you don't live like a nigger, like the black people in your records or films. You don't live in a ghetto."

"Don't be naïve, Jonah! Don't think like a white boy! You have a lot more at stake than that! And a lot less to lose than you think! Listen, you're about to fall into their trap of making you think that you can be safe in America! You can't, brother! Do you think for a moment that if you are successful and live like Billy Badman you've escaped being black and are therefore safe? *Jesus!* I see now why you're not funny! Nobody can be funny who lives an illusion! Do you think I'm safe? All this you see"—he waved to his room and the swimming pool and guest house and gym—"is the price I've had to pay to do my work! I keep this bullshit going so they'll leave me the fuck alone! Sure, I'm happy, but not because of what I am but in spite of it."

"But you've at least escaped the ghetto!"

"The biggest ghetto in the world is show business."

"But you don't have to suffer in obscurity as millions of blacks still do."

"That's why I feel committed to them and why, I suppose, they don't feel so committed to me."

"At least the police leave you alone!"

"Says who? If I do the slightest thing it's in the newspaper. If I shit in the street, tomorrow the headlines'll say BILLY BADMAN SHITS IN THE STREET! and on top of that they're making money off it too!"

"But the studios will protect you."

"They do protect superstars, but since I'm a black superstar they could just change the rules. You see the situation I'm in—we're in?"

As with the statue and the picture of Tina as Antigone, so it was when I looked at the chess set on his desk: he read my mind.

"You like that chess set?" he asked.

"Where's it from?" I asked, impressed, for each of the pieces had been hand carved from wood like a miniature tribe of Zulu warriors, each piece representing somebody in the tribal army, with the King and Queen in these little skirts made out of straw and spears made out of toothpicks.

"We picked that up in Africa," he said. "Do you want to play some chess?"

"Sure."

"You have any money?"

"I got some. Not much."

"How much you got?"

I took out all of my money and put it on the table. It came to something like five dollars and some change.

"Pick up the change," he said. "I'll bet you a thousand dollars against the five I'll beat you."

"Okay," I said, accepting the challenge as if it were fair. My role as ingenu was to pretend that anything he said or did was perfectly normal.

There was nothing braggadocio about his challenge—what he meant by this was what he thought was fair.

"Hello, baby," Billy said to Tina as she came into the room. "We are playing a game of chess. Would you like some cocaine, dearie?"

She was so really pissed she was trembling. "You've ignored me all evening! And I'm fed up with it, goddam it!" Tina shouted, standing right over Billy.

"Baby, I'm sitting here enjoying a game of chess with my friend. Now what's the problem?"

"The problem is that you spend all your goddam time with your fucking friends and I wanna be with you!"

Her eyes were red with anger and it looked as if she'd been crying.

In a calm voice so different from the madman reputation his well-publicized fits of anger had earned him, Billy inquired into the origin of her dissatisfaction.

"All goddam evening, you've ignored me!" Tina stammered out, "And I'm sick of it!"

Billy turned to me and explained they'd had a big party just that afternoon and she was understandably tired. I nodded in agreement. With the same calm voice, he turned to Tina.

"Tina, we had a party. Many people were here. Now you were downstairs talking with the ladies and I was upstairs—"

"That's just it. I hated being downstairs talking with the ladies. You spend all of your goddam time up here enjoying yourself—"

She interrupted herself and picked up a box of cookies that were lying on the table and emptied them on Billy's head. Some of the cookies spilled over onto the chessboard.

"Now why did you do that?" Billy asked in a subdued voice. I expected, to be quite honest, for him to hit her upside her head, but he simply nodded his head.

"Because I wanted to! Damn you!"

Billy said, "Listen, I have a friend here and we are playing chess. Now if you wanted to tell me something that I did wrong, why can't you wait until my friend leaves, and then you can cuss me out or kick my ass or whatever. But I think you've gone too far."

"Fuck you, motherfucker, I'm leaving." She turned and started for the door.

"Wait a minute," Billy called out, still in that cool voice. "If you want to leave, why don't you do it right?"

He got up and went over to the wall and took down the picture of Tina in the role of Antigone, where she had a toga draped over her shoulder in the picture.

He took it down.

"This is the only thing you've given me in all the time we've been together."

He threw it across the room, and the glass shattered at her feet.

"Take that with you, if you want to leave," he said calmly, sitting back down in front of the chess game.

At this point I thought, This is a trick! a joke they both are playing on me! Any minute they'll turn to me and say, Ha! We caught you, didn't we? Knowing Billy's reputation as a prankster and remembering Dionysus as Euripides portrayed him (as a god who maliciously tricked mortals who didn't honor him by getting drunk and dressing up like a woman and worshiping him), I pictured some weird put-on. But if this was what was happening, they deserved the Academy Award for their acting, so convincing it was.

Tina picked the picture up and started for the door, but Billy picked up a photo on the desk.

"Oh, I forgot something." He threw it against the wall. "Take all the shit you gave me, okay. And get out of my life. I don't love you anymore. Do you understand?"

Tina stood there looking at him, her face red and streaked with tears and anger.

"You've fucked up our chess game, you've poured cookies all over my head. Look, Tina, you don't have to abuse me like that. I know how to abuse Billy. I'm very good at self-abuse. After all, I've done that all my life: Abuse myself.

"Look," Billy said, taking up a pencil can and knocking it against his head. "Look, I'm very good at self-abuse!"

Is this not comedy? I thought. I was dying with laughter but I held it in.

"Bastard!" Tina spat at him and went out the door again.

He turned his attention back to the chess board.

All the pieces had been covered with cookies. I started to pick the pieces of crumbs away from the pieces.

"Just look at that? What kind of person would do that?" he asked me.

"I think I should be leaving," I said.

"Leaving? Why? Because she's acting a fool? No, man, you're my friend. I want you to stay. I need for you to stay, Jonah. This bitch is trying to make me hit her. If I hit her the police will be up here in a minute. I don't want that. If the police come up here I'm going to the penitentiary. She knows this. She is trying to—"

Tina reappeared in the door.

Both Billy and I sat silent and watched her. She came across the room and over to us and swept the chess pieces off the board.

"Bastard!" she announced and started back for the door.

"No. Tina, I've had it with you. You took your clothes off in front of my son. My son came to me and he was crying and I said what's wrong but he wouldn't say anything. I made him tell me, Tina. He said you came out of your bedroom naked. You showed my son your pussy, woman."

"And you beat my face in," Tina accused him right in front of me.

"And you spit in my face and called me a nigger!" he shot back.

She came back. "And you beat me up."

"Well, just leave. I told you to leave. Now leave. I've done all I could for you, just leave. You would never treat Warren Beatty like you treated me. Or any of those other white boys you star-fucked."

He turned to me.

"Man, can you imagine her doing that to Warren Beatty?"

I said, "No!"

"That's right, because she doesn't respect me. I'm still a nigger to her. She told me so herself."

"No!" I replied incredulously—as I figured my part called for. I was like some weird straight man. "She called you a what? Where?"

"We were in Africa. I told her, I said, 'Tina, look up at the sky.' They got some skies in Africa that are a motherfucker, man! The stars glitter like diamonds on a piece of black velvet. I said, 'Look up at the sky,' I said. 'Do you see any star up there called nigger?' She got sassy on me and said, 'Yeah, there's one!' Do you think she do that to any of those white boys she fucked?"

In spite of all this—or perhaps because of it—Billy insisted on a drink. Trailing along behind him, I followed my host into the kitchen, where he took down from the cabinet a fifth of Stolichnaya vodka. No sooner had he poured us out a good portion in two tumblers than Tina appeared in the doorway. This time she was carrying a broom. With the broom as a weapon, she attacked us. We fell backwards through the dining room, falling and holding onto the vodka; we managed to make it back to the bedroom, where Billy locked the door.

"That bitch was trying to kill us." He laughed. "But we were trying to be cool, huh? Look," he said as if he'd thought my thoughts, "you're still holding your glass! Ha, ha, ha!" He laughed in that particular way he has. "You didn't even spill a drop!"

He was so busy telling me about my glass that he had forgotten his. He was holding his high over his head like Charlie Chaplin did in one of his films, as the waiter with the precariously balanced tray that keeps its equilibrium despite a knock-down-and-drag-out fight that takes place in the saloon.

"You know we some funny motherfuckers," he said, laughing deep inside his chest. "We try to be cool out here in Hollywood, but where we come from we've been hurt and abused, man. We never had a lot of liquor to spill. If we'd been white boys, we would've dropped the glasses and poured the liquor out. But we niggers, although we don't want to be, but way down deep in our souls we are still niggers who can't afford to spill the vodka. If Tina had a gun and had shot and killed us, we would've fell over each other and died, but when the undertaker came to get our dead asses, he'd have to take the vodka glasses out of our hands and pour the vodka out because there'd still be vodka in them. And some other nigger assistant undertaker would sneak up to our bodies when the white undertaker wasn't looking and steal that vodka. *'That's good vodka,'* the nigger'd say. *'Gonna take that vodka home! Sheet, them niggers dead, they don't know no difference.'* "

Billy was up, faking the part of the white undertaker, the black assistant undertaker, and the two stiffs (us with the vodka glasses) all at once. 'Mister White Man, hehehe, you think we oughta take dese glasses outa these niggers' hands?' 'Naw, fool, I believe these boys' family gonna pay fo' the vodka, niggers gonna die with liquor on they bref!' "

I laughed hard, feeling relief briefly from the insistent, pounding, urgent knocking at the door. Apparently she'd taken off her shoe and was applying the heel of it to the wooden door. But Billy went on talking as if nobody was there, and I went on pretending that I didn't hear anybody either. His genius for making humor out of any situation, I learned that night, was his protection against hurt; it was his camouflage technique, the yellow and black spots on the butterfly's back that allows him to blend into the yellow leaves and black tree bark and prevents the predator from seeing him and devouring him in one hysterical gulp. His humor was his mimicking device, his cloud of black ink that the octopus uses to hide behind when an enemy attacks.

"Who is Randell?" I finally had the nerve to say.

"Randell?" he said, and his face lighted up. "That's a motherfucking genius. A literary genius. We would be fucking some bitches together and you know what he'd do, he'd turned over to me and say I was 'literary.' I'd say, 'What's literary about fucking a bitch?' and he'd say, 'You do it metaphorically.' "

"Was he there that night at the Hollywood Bowl?" I asked. I didn't have the nerve to ask him directly about the famous night when he told the gay community to kiss his rich, happy, black ass. I just didn't have the nerve and also I suppose I realized that there was really nothing he could say about it that he hadn't said on the stage that night.

"Was Randell there?" he asked himself. "Yes, Randell was there. He was there, now that I remember. He goes everywhere, man. He is the freest person I know. He never has any money but he just goes where he wants. He has curiosity. Real curiosity. I have that too. When I'm somewhere he just shows up. I was in Cannes at the Film Festival when my first big film came out and I got this note in my box one afternoon and the note said, *You better get out of France fucking our white women,* and I looked at the note and I said to myself, Who would send me a note like this? And I looked at the note again and at the bottom of it was this signature, *KKK,* and I said to myself, If this is not a joke played on me by Randell then my ass is in real trouble! I said this to myself as a prayer because at the time, man, I believed that the Ku Klux Klan had written it; it was the sort of prayer you sent up if you're Daniel in the lion's den, because I knew that Randell was still in Berkeley. The last time I saw him he was in Berkeley enjoying the royalties he made on his novel. *How could he get to Cannes and how did he know that I was here?* It turned out that the motherfucker knocked on my door later that night, and, man, was I glad to see him! When you leave America you're, at first, glad to be away from niggers, but then the first one you see, especially if he's a friend, you jump pass yourself with excitement. Man, me and Randell got some of the finest bitches in Cannes. He didn't have a nickel, he'd been living in Paris, man, with all the famous writers like James Jones, Irwin Shaw, James Baldwin, Carlos Fuentes, and the nigger didn't have a French franc on him, I'm not kidding—"

Boom! Boom! Boom! Tina was knocking on the door with something else. We couldn't figure out what it was she was knocking with this time but Billy, momentarily forgetting that he was supposed to be ignoring her ass, tilted his head back into a listening stance like the famous doe deer in one of his imitations, and I saw the origin of the doe deer imitation then, saw his curiosity he so much admired in his friend Randell.

Boom! Boom! Boom!—and Billy looked at me with an expression on his face that said, What the fuck is she hitting the door with now? But he silently let the question drop and took another hit of the coke and passed it to me and I took a hit.

"—Nigger was broker than a motherfucker, but it never bothered him any. He'd be talking shit just like he had a pocketful of money. Anyway, I gave him a whole handful of French money because French money don't look like real money, you know what I'm talking about? It's like play money. Big, oversized money, with no green in it. Who ever seen money with no green in it? This French money had a picture of a Frenchman on it, de Gaulle or one of them motherfuckers, and it was like a painting. So I gave half of what I had to Randell. He told me later that I gave him two thousand dollars! And I didn't know it. He told me that about two years later. And I told him—"

Boom! Boom! Krack! Now she had picked up something else to hit it with. Billy looked at the door again.

"If I opened that door—" He cut himself off. "That door is the door to the penitentiary."

I looked at the wooden door, at the fashionable woodwork around the handle, at the door of a famous rich superstar. How did he mean that? Suddenly I saw what he meant and the wooden door dissolved into the gray iron bars of a jail cell. *I am tired of beating her, man, I don't love her anymore, I don't want to beat her anymore, she wants me to beat her!* I thought of Tina as a vampire, a ghoulish vampire back from the dead, straight out of Edgar Allan Poe, beating at the door, I thought of the image of the door being knocked down and Tina, like Ligeia, appearing before us with the greenish, rotten flesh falling from her face, from her skull, rats and worms crawling out of her skin, back from the— fresh from the grave.

Krack! Krack! Krack!

"What about the Hollywood Bowl?" I started again. "I mean, Randell was there—"

Krack! Krack! Krack!

Tina's knocking was gathering momentum now.

"Yeah, Randell was there," Billy said. "Sent me this telegram. I'll never forget that. 'Cause I came home, I was scared a little. When they interviewed me in the gay press later, I said I wasn't scared. But I was scared. I was scared about what I'd done but I was so happy because I knew I'd done the right thing, I'd said what was in my heart. Somebody asked me, said, 'Do you fear your career is over?'" and I said—I don't know what I said, but what I thought was this: 'If my career is over because I said what was in my heart, then I didn't have a career to start with. So fuck it!'"

We both laughed, genuinely, like friends, like brothers, and I felt very close to him then, and it was not with an effort, or pretext, or pretense that I ignored Tina's knocking at the door.

"Randell," he said, lighting a cigarette. I took one too, "Randell sent me a telegram. It said, CLASSIC JUVENAL SATIRE. But I was too ignorant to ask him who Juvenal was. Who is this motherfucker called Juvenal?"

"He was a writer that lived in Rome around the time of one of those evil emperors."

"Oh?" he answered and stretched and yawned with boredom.

Krack! Krack! Krack!

Billy said, "I had a dream about Tina. In this dream she's all in white and leads me with a blindfold on into hell. I take off the blindfold and see I'm in hell. I say to her, 'Why did you lead me here. I've been in hell before, and I'm used to it. I expected better from you—' "

"That was Dante's trip," I said. "Beatrice leads Dante out of hell."

"Dante?"

"The thirteenth-century poet. He wrote his dream up as a poem called the *Divine Comedy* in three parts. He had this broad, Beatrice, that led him around through places, except he wasn't blind."

"But a fool like me?"

"Yeah."

"Dante, eh? Well, I had the same dream. I'm going to use it in my movie, too."

He got up and went to the door, put his ear to it quietly.

"I think she's gone," he said, opening it just a little.

I expected to see Tina dead at the door from having committed suicide. But when he opened it she wasn't even there.

"Let's take a walk," he said.

As we came down the long hallway, Billy peeped into one of the rooms, then another.

He came to one door that was half closed, pushed the door open quietly, and walked in. He turned and beckoned silently for me to come see. I went over to the door and looked in. It was a bedroom and on the bed was Tina. What she'd done, she'd curled up in the bed without taking her clothes off. Her face was as quiet and calm and as beautiful as a sleeping child.

Billy reached down and kissed her on the cheek so softly that she didn't wake up. In her clenched hands was the Sukuma African sculpture she had been using to bang against the door with. Now we knew what she had been using.

We walked out by the swimming pool and he looked over at the tennis court. (I remember Randell telling me how avid a tennis player Billy was and how he was impressed by anybody who could beat him and since almost anybody could beat him he was impressed a lot. In fact, Randell said, one of the sure ways that white boys got to Billy was to beat him at a game of tennis.) As we passed it, Billy said, "I don't know why I built that tennis court. I can't stand the game now."

We walked around the swimming pool. The morning light was beginning to glow, a morning bird chirped, a rooster crowed.

Billy looked at his watch. "That rooster," he said laughing, "is never on time."

I felt very close to him now, and I'd lost a lot of my overearnestness.

"Let's talk about our business," he said. "I want you to warm them up for me tomorrow night, because you have a natural style. Don't worry about not being funny, just be natural and don't get pretentious. It's okay if you're not funny. I believe you understand what I mean by that. If you can master this about yourself you'll be the funniest person in this business. Except me."

We laughed.

"All the kidding aside," he said, "I need you for this. You have a voice in what you say to an audience that takes them into your confidence and speaks the truth. I need you to warm them up for me. Can I count on you?"

"Yes," I said.

"Meeting closed," he said and put something in my hand.

"I lost the game." He laughed. "I had to forfeit it."

We walked on toward my car. "Do you realize we stayed up all night?" I asked.

As a reply he suddenly laughed.

"I'm laughing at myself," he said. "I'm trying to figure out how to clean up the fact that you've seen my old lady pour cookies on my head."

We both laughed.

"You don't have to explain it to me," I said, like a man.

And he treated me like a man, too.

"I've been wondering how I was going to explain to you, how I could say what I said to her and then say I loved her, but I see I don't need to explain it to you."

He looked into my eyes and gave me a hug.

"We're friends now," he said.

"I know," I said. "Good morning."

"Good morning to you, Jonah."

I got in the car and pulled out of the yard. He was going into the house. He waved, I waved, and I went out of the gate.

The world was just waking up when I pulled out of the gate and onto the highway. A blueness was giving way to a light gray haze. A few more cars hit the road carrying people to work. I felt exhilarated, not tired. Looking back on this now, I realize that that evening was the first time I'd laughed in a long time. True, I had laughed at my friend's misfortune, but I had laughed at it with my friend; and he had laughed at my misfortune with me. What this meant for me was that I was developing my sense of humor; what it meant for my friend was that he was learning to master his.

And what a guy that Billy was! How he could abuse himself. I laughed, thinking about him hitting himself across the head with that can. And the way he so sincerely cast himself as more sinned against than sinning! And Tina? What an actress! But who could write a script big enough for the two of them? Only God, probably. And when Billy told me comedy was based on real trouble and tragedy, he wasn't kidding! And me! What an impostor! But what could I do: I loved him but was afraid of her. He was right about her, she would make him hurt her, but she knew that the greatest damage he could do to her would be what he would do to himself.

It was from this evening that I began to develop a sense of what it meant to be funny.

Damballah

John Edgar Wideman

1981

Orion let the dead, gray cloth slide down his legs and stepped into the river. He picked his way over slippery stones till he stood calf deep. Dropping to one knee he splashed his groin, then scooped river to his chest, both hands scrubbing with quick, kneading spirals. When he stood again, he stared at the distant gray clouds. A hint of rain in the chill morning air, a faint, clean presence rising from the far side of the hills. The promise of rain coming to him as all things seemed to come these past few months, not through eyes or ears or nose but entering his black skin as if each pore had learned to feel and speak.

He watched the clear water race and ripple and pucker. Where the sun cut through the pine trees and slanted into the water he could see the bottom, see black stones, speckled stones, shining stones whose light came from within. Above a stump at the far edge of the river, clouds of insects hovered. The water was darker there, slower, appeared to stand in deep pools where tangles of root, bush, and week hung over the bank. Orion thought of the eldest priest chalking a design on the floor of the sacred obi. Drawing the watery door no living hands could push open, the crossroads where the spirits passed between worlds. His skin was becoming like that in-between place the priest scratched in the dust. When he walked the cane rows and dirt paths of the plantation he could feel the air of this strange land wearing out his skin, rubbing it thinner and thinner until one day his skin would not be thick enough to separate what was inside from everything outside. Some days his skin whispered he was dying. But he was not afraid. The voices and faces of his fathers bursting through would not drown him. They would sweep him away, carry him home again.

In his village across the sea were men who hunted and fished with their voices. Men who could talk the fish up from their shadowy dwellings and into the woven baskets slung over the fishermen's shoulders. Orion knew the fish in this cold river had forgotten him, that they were darting in and out of his legs. If the whites had not stolen him, he would have learned the fishing magic. The proper words, the proper tones to please the fish. But here in this blood-soaked land everything was different. Though he felt their slick bodies and saw the sudden dimples in the water where they were feeding, he understood that he would never speak the language of these fish. No more than he would ever speak again the words of the white people who had decided to kill him.

The boy was there again hiding behind the trees. He could be the one. This boy born so far from home. This boy who knew nothing but what the whites told him. This boy could learn the story and tell it again. Time was short but he could be the one.

"That Ryan, he a crazy nigger. One them wild African niggers act like he fresh off the boat. Kind you stay away from less you lookin for trouble." Aunt Lissy had stopped popping string beans and frowned into the boy's face. The pause in the steady drumming of beans into the iron pot, the way she scrunched up her face to look mean like one of the Master's pit bulls, told him she had finished speaking on the subject and wished to hear no more about it from him. When the long green pods began to shuttle through her fingers again, it sounded like she was cracking her knuckles, and he expected something black to drop into the huge pot.

"Fixin to rain good. Heard them frogs last night just a singing at the clouds. Frog and all his brothers calling down the thunder. Don't rain soon them fields dry up and blow away." The boy thought of the men trudging each morning to the fields. Some were brown, some yellow, some had red in their skins, and some white as the Master. Ryan black, but Aunt Lissy blacker. Fat, shiny blue-black like a crow's wing.

"Sure nuff crazy." Old woman always talking. Talking and telling silly stories. The boy wanted to hear something besides an old woman's mouth. He had heard about frogs and bears and rabbits too many times. He was almost grown now, almost ready to leave in the mornings with the men. What would they talk about? Would Orion's voice be like the hollers the boy heard early in the mornings when the men still sleepy and the sky still dark and you couldn't really see nobody but knew they were there when them cries and hollers came rising through the mist?

Pine needles crackled with each step he took, and the boy knew old Ryan knew somebody spying on him. Old nigger guess who it was, too. But if Ryan knew, Ryan didn't care. Just waded out in that water like he the only man in the world. Like maybe wasn't no world. Just him and that quiet place in the middle of the river. Must be fishing out there, some funny old African kind of fishing. Nobody never saw him touch victuals Master set out and he had to be eating something, even if he was half crazy, so the nigger must be fishing for his breakfast. Standing there like a stick in the water till the fish forgot him and he could snatch one from the water with his beaky fingers.

A skinny-legged black waterbird in the purring river. The boy stopped chewing his stick of cane, let the sweet juice blend with his spit, a warm syrup then whose taste he prolonged by not swallowing, but letting it coat his tongue and the insides of his mouth, waiting patiently like the figure in the water waited, as the sweet taste seeped away. All the cane juice had trickled down his throat before he saw Orion move. After the stillness, the illusion that the man was a tree rooted in the rocks at the riverbed, when motion came it was too swift to follow. Not so much a matter of seeing Orion move as it was feeling the man's eyes inside him, hooking him before he could crouch lower in the weeds. Orion's eyes on him and through him boring a hole in his chest and thrusting into that space one word, *Damballah.* Then the hooded eyes were gone.

On a spoon you see the shape of a face is an egg. Or two eggs because you can change the shape from long oval to moons pinched together at the middle seam or any shape egg if you tilt and push the spoon closer or farther away. Nothing to think about. You go with Mistress to the chest in the root cellar. She guides you with a candle and you make a pouch of soft cloth and carefully lay in each spoon and careful it don't jangle as up and out of the darkness following her rustling dresses and petticoats up the earthen steps each one topped by a plank which squirms as you mount it. You are following the taper she holds and the strange smell she trails and leaves in rooms. Then shut up in a room all day with nothing to think about. With rags and pieces of silver. Slowly you rub away the tarnished spots; it is like finding something which surprises you though you knew all the time it was there. Spoons lying on the strip of indigo: perfect, gleaming fish you have coaxed from the black water.

Damballah was the word. Said it to Aunt Lissy and she went upside his head, harder than she had ever slapped him. Felt like crumpling right there in the dust of the yard it hurt so bad but he bit his lip and didn't cry out, held his ground and said the word again and again silently to himself, pretending nothing but a bug on his burning cheek and twitched and sent it flying. Damballah. Be strong as he needed to be. Nothing touch him if he don't want. Before long they'd cut him from the herd of pickaninnies. No more chasing flies from the table, no more silver spoons to get shiny, no fat old woman telling him what to do. He'd go to the fields each morning with the men. Holler like they did before the sun rose to burn off the mist. Work like they did from can to caint. From first crack of light to dusk when the puddles of shadow deepened and spread so you couldn't see your hands or feet or the sharp tools hacking at the cane.

He was already taller than the others, a stork among the chicks scurrying behind Aunt Lissy. Soon he'd rise with the conch horn and do a man's share, so he had let the fire rage on half his face and thought of the nothing always there to think of. In the spoon, his face long and thin as a finger. He looked for the print of Lissy's black hand on his cheek, but the image would not stay still. Dancing like his face reflected in the river. Damballah. "Don't you ever, you hear me, ever let me hear that heathen talk no more. You hear me, boy? You talk Merican, boy." Lissy's voice like chicken cackle. And his head a barn packed with animal noise and animal smell. His own head but he had to sneak round in it. Too many others crowded in there with him. His head so crowded and noisy lots of time don't hear his own voice with all them braying and cackling.

Orion squatted the way the boy had seen the other old men collapse on their haunches and go still as a stump. Their bony knees poking up and their backsides resting on their ankles. Looked like they could sit that way all day, legs folded under them like wings. Orion drew a cross in the dust. Damballah. When Orion passed his hands over the cross the air seemed to shimmer like it does above a flame or like it does when the sun so hot you can see waves of heat rising off the fields. Orion talked to the emptiness he shaped with his long black fingers. His eyes were closed. Orion wasn't speaking but sounds came from inside him the boy had never heard before, strange words, clicks, whistles, and grunts. A singsong moan that rose and fell and floated like the old man's busy hands above the cross. Damballah like a drumbeat in the chant. Damballah a place the boy could enter, a familiar sound he began to anticipate, a sound outside of him which slowly forced its way inside, a sound measuring his heartbeat then one with the pumping surge of his blood.

The boy heard part of what Lissy saying to Primus in the cooking shed: "Ryan he yell that heathen word right in the middle of Jim talking bout Sweet Jesus the Son of God. Jump up like he snake bit and scream that word so everybody hushed, even the white folks what came to hear Jim preach. Simple Ryan standing there at the back of the chapel like a knot poked out on somebody's forehead. Lookin like a nigger caught wid his hand in the chicken coop. Screeching like some crazy hoot owl while Preacher Jim praying the word of the Lord. They gon kill that simple nigger one day."

Dear Sir:
The nigger Orion which I purchased of you in good faith sight unseen on your promise that he was of sound constitution, "a full grown and able-bodied house servant who can read, write, do sums, and cipher," to recite the exact words of your letter dated April 17, 1852, has proved to be a burden, a deficit to the economy of my plantation rather than the asset I fully believed I was receiving when I agreed to pay the price you asked. Of the vaunted intelligence so rare in his kind, I have seen nothing. Not an

English word has passed through his mouth since he arrived. Of his docility and tractability I have seen only the willingness with which he bares his leatherish back to receive the stripes constant misconduct earn him. He is a creature whose brutish habits would shame me were he quartered in my kennels. I find it odd that I should write at such length about any nigger, but seldom have I been so struck by the disparity between promise and performance. As I have accrued nothing but expense and inconvenience as a result of his presence, I think it only just that you return the full amount I paid for this flawed *piece of the Indies.*

You know me as an honest and fair man and my regard for those same qualities in you prompts me to write this letter. I am not a harsh master, I concern myself with the spiritual as well as the temporal needs of my slaves. My nigger Jim is renowned in this county as a preacher. Many say I am foolish, that the words of scripture are wasted on these savage blacks. I fear you have sent me a living argument to support the critics of my Christianizing project. Among other absences of truly human qualities I have observed in this Orion is the utter lack of a soul.

She said it time for Orion to die. Broke half the overseer's bones knocking him off his horse this morning and everybody thought Ryan done run away sure but Mistress come upon the crazy nigger at suppertime on the big house porch naked as the day he born and he just sat there staring into her eyes till Mistress screamed and run away. Aunt Lissy said Ryan ain't studying no women, ain't gone near to woman since he been here, and she say his ain't the first black butt Mistress done seen all them nearly grown boys walkin round summer in the onliest shirt Master give em barely come down to they knees and niggers man nor woman don't get drawers the first. Mistress and Master both seen plenty. Wasn't what she saw scared her less she see the ghost leaving out Ryan's body.

The ghost wouldn't steam out the top of Orion's head. The boy remembered the sweaty men come in from the fields at dusk when the nights start to cool early, remembered them with the drinking gourds in they hands scooping up water from the wooden barrel he filled, how they throw they heads back and the water trickles from the sides of they mouth and down they chin and they let it roll on down they chests, and the smoky steam curling off they shoulders. Orion's spirit would not rise up like that but wiggle out his skin and swim off up the river.

The boy knew many kinds of ghosts and learned the ways you get round their tricks. Some spirits almost good company and he filled the nothing with jingles and whistles and took roundabout paths and sang to them when he walked up on a crossroads and yoo-hooed at doors. No way you fool the haunts if a spell conjured strong on you, no way to miss a beating if it your day to get beat, but the ghosts had everything in they hands, even the white folks in they hands. You know they there, you know they floating up in the air watching and counting and remembering them strokes Ole Master laying cross your back.

They dragged Orion across the yard. He didn't buck or kick but it seemed as if the four men carrying him were struggling with a giant stone rather than a black bag of bones. His ashy nigger weight swung between the two pairs of white men like a lazy hammock but the faces of the men all red and twisted. They huffed and puffed and sweated through they clothes carrying Ryan's bones to the barn. The dry spell had layered the yard with a coat of dust. Little squalls of yellow spurted from under the men's boots. Trudging steps heavy as if each man carried seven Orions on his shoulders. Four grown men struggling with one string of black flesh. The boy had never seen so many white folks dealing with one nigger. Aunt Lissy had said it time to die, and the boy wondered what Ryan's ghost would think dropping onto the dust surrounded by the scowling faces of the Master and his overseers.

One scream that night. Like a bull when they cut off his maleness. Couldn't tell who it was. A bull screaming once that night and torches burning in the barn and Master and the men coming out and no Ryan.

Mistress crying behind a locked door and Master messing with Patty down the quarters.

In the morning light the barn swelling and rising and teetering in the yellow dust, moving the way you could catch the ghost of something in a spoon and play with it, bending it, twisting it. That goldish ash on everybody's bare shins. Nobody talking. No cries nor hollers from the fields. The boy watched till his eyes hurt, waiting for a moment when he could slip unseen into the shivering barn. On his hands and knees hiding under a wagon, then edging sideways through the loose boards and wedge of space where the weathered door hung crooked on its hinge.

The interior of the barn lay in shadows. Once beyond the sliver of light coming in at the cracked door the boy stood still till his eyes adjusted to the darkness. First he could pick out the stacks of hay, the rough partitions dividing the animals. The smells, the choking heat there like always, but rising above these familiar sensations the buzz of flies, unnaturally loud, as if the barn breathing and each breath shook the wooden walls. Then the boy's eyes followed the sound to an open space at the center of the far wall. A black shape there. Orion there, floating in his own blood. The boy ran at the blanket of flies. When he stomped, some of the flies buzzed up from the carcass. Others too drunk on the shimmering blood ignored him except to join the ones hovering above the body in a sudden droning peal of annoyance. He could keep the flies stirring but they always returned from the recesses of the high ceiling, the dark corners of the building, to gather in a cloud above the body. The boy looked for something to throw. Heard his breath, heavy and threatening like the sound of the flies. He sank to the dirt floor, sitting cross-legged where he had stood. He moved only once, ten slow paces away from Orion and back again, near enough to be sure, to see again how the head had been cleaved from the rest of the body, to see how the ax and tongs, branding iron and other tools were scattered around the corpse, to see how one man's hat and another's shirt, a letter that must have come from someone's pocket, lay about in a helter-skelter way as if the men had suddenly bolted before they had finished with Orion.

Forgive him, Father. I tried to the end of my patience to restore his lost soul. I made a mighty effort to bring him to the Ark of Salvation but he had walked in darkness too long. He mocked Your Grace. He denied Your Word. Have mercy on him and forgive his heathen ways as you forgive the soulless beasts of the fields and birds of the air.

She say Master still down slave row. She say everybody fraid to go down and get him. Everybody fraid to open the barn door. Overseer half dead and the Mistress still crying in her locked room and that barn starting to stink already with crazy Ryan and nobody gon get him.

And the boy knew his legs were moving and he knew they would carry him where they needed to go and he knew the legs belonged to him but he could not feel them, he had been sitting too long thinking on nothing for too long and he felt the sweat running on his body but his mind off somewhere cool and quiet and hard and he knew the space between his body and mind could not be crossed by anything, knew you mize well try to stick the head back on Ryan as try to cross that space. So he took what he needed out of the barn, unfolding, getting his gangly crane's legs together under him and shouldered open the creaking double doors and walked through the flame in the center where he had to go.

Damballah said it be a long way a ghost be going and Jordan chilly and wide and a new ghost take his time getting his wings together. Long way to go so you can sit and listen till the ghost ready to go on home. The boy wiped his wet hands on his knees and drew the cross and said the word and settled down and listened to Orion tell the stories again. Orion talked and he listened and couldn't stop listening till he saw Orion's eyes rise up through the back of the severed skull and lips rise up through the skull and the wings of the ghost measure out the rhythm of one last word.

Late afternoon, and the river slept dark at its edges like it did in the mornings. The boy threw the head as far as he could and he knew the fish would hear it and swim to it and welcome it. He knew they had been waiting. He knew the ripples would touch him when he entered.

Kiswana Browne

Gloria Naylor

1982

From the window of her sixth-floor studio apartment, Kiswana could see over the wall at the end of the street to the busy avenue that lay just north of Brewster Place. The late-afternoon shoppers looked like brightly clad marionettes as they moved between the congested traffic, clutching their packages against their bodies to guard them from sudden bursts of the cold autumn wind. A portly mailman had abandoned his cart and was bumping into indignant window shoppers as he puffed behind the cap that the wind had snatched from his head. Kiswana leaned over to see if he was going to be successful, but the edge of the building cut him off from her view.

A pigeon swept across her window, and she marveled at its liquid movements in the air waves. She placed her dreams on the back of the bird and fantasized that it would glide forever in transparent silver circles until it ascended to the center of the universe and was swallowed up. But the wind died down, and she watched with a sigh as the bird beat its wings in awkward, frantic movements to land on the corroded top of a fire escape on the opposite building. This brought her back to earth.

Humph, it's probably sitting over there crapping on those folks' fire escape, she thought. Now, that's a safety hazard. . . . And her mind was busy again, creating flames and smoke and frustrated tenants whose escape was being hindered because they were slipping and sliding in pigeon shit. She watched their cussing, haphazard descent on the fire escapes until they had all reached the bottom. They were milling around, oblivious to their burning apartments, angrily planning to march on the mayor's office about the pigeons. She materialized placards and banners for them, and they had just reached the corner, boldly sidestepping fire hoses and broken glass, when they all vanished.

A tall copper-skinned woman had met this phantom parade at the corner, and they had dissolved in front of her long, confident strides. She plowed through the remains of their faded mists, unconscious of the lingering wisps of their presence on her leather bag and black fur-trimmed coat. It took a few seconds for this transfer from one realm to another to reach Kiswana, but then suddenly she recognized the woman.

"Oh, God, it's Mama!" She looked down guiltily at the forgotten newspaper in her lap and hurriedly circled random job advertisements.

By this time Mrs. Browne had reached the front of Kiswana's building and was checking the house number against a piece of paper in her hand. Before she went into the building she stood at the bottom of the stoop and carefully inspected the condition of the street and the adjoining property. Kiswana watched this meticulous inventory with growing annoyance but she involuntarily followed her mother's slowly rotating head, forcing herself to see her new neighborhood through the older woman's eyes. The brightness of the unclouded sky seemed to join forces with her mother as it highlighted every broken stoop railing and missing brick. The afternoon sun glittered and cascaded across even the tiniest fragments of broken bottle, and at that very moment the wind chose to rise up again, sending unswept grime flying into the air, as a stray tin can left by careless garbage collectors went rolling noisily down the center of the street.

Kiswana noticed with relief that at least Ben wasn't sitting in his usual place on the old garbage can pushed against the far wall. He was just a harmless old wino, but Kiswana knew her mother only needed one wino or one teenager with a reefer within a twenty-block radius to decide that her daughter was living in a building seething with dope factories and hangouts for derelicts. If she had seen Ben, nothing would have made her believe that practically every apartment contained a family, a Bible, and a dream that one day enough could be scraped from those meager Friday night paychecks to make Brewster Place a distant memory.

As she watched her mother's head disappear into the building, Kiswana gave silent thanks that the elevator was broken. That would give her at least five minutes' grace to straighten up the apartment. She rushed to the sofa bed and hastily closed it without smoothing the rumpled sheets and blanket or removing her nightgown. She felt that somehow the tangled bedcovers would give away the fact that she had not slept alone last night. She silently apologized to Abshu's memory as she heartlessly crushed his spirit between the steel springs of the couch. Lord, that man was sweet. Her toes curled involuntarily at the passing thought of his full lips moving slowly over her instep. Abshu was a foot man, and he always started his lovemaking from the bottom up. For that reason Kiswana changed the color of the polish on her toenails every week. During the course of their relationship she had gone from shades of red to brown and was now into the purples. I'm gonna have to start mixing them soon, she thought aloud as she turned from the couch and raced into the bathroom to remove any traces of Abshu from there. She took up his shaving cream and razor and threw them into the bottom drawer of her dresser beside her diaphragm. Mama wouldn't dare pry into my drawers right in front of me, she thought, as she slammed the drawer shut. Well, at least not the *bottom* drawer. She may come up with some sham excuse for opening the top drawer, but never the bottom one.

When she heard the first two short raps on the door, her eyes took a final flight over the small apartment, desperately seeking out any slight misdemeanor that might have to be defended. Well, there was nothing she could do about the crack in the wall over that table. She had been after the landlord to fix it for two months now. And there had been no time to sweep the rug, and everyone knew that off-gray always looked dirtier than it really was. And it was just too damn bad about the kitchen. How was she expected to be out job-hunting every day and still have time to keep a kitchen that looked like her mother's, who didn't even work and still had someone come in twice a month for general cleaning. And besides—

Her imaginary argument was abruptly interrupted by a second series of knocks, accompanied by a penetrating, "Melanie, Melanie, are you there?"

Kiswana strode toward the door. She's starting before she even gets in here. She knows that's not my name anymore.

She swung the door open to face her slightly flushed mother. "Oh, hi, Mama. You know, I thought I heard a knock, but I figured it was for the people next door, since no one hardly ever calls me Melanie." Score one for me, she thought.

"Well, it's awfully strange you can forget a name you answered to for twenty-three years," Mrs. Browne said, as she moved past Kiswana into the apartment. "My, that was a long climb. How long has your elevator been out? Honey, how do you manage with your laundry and groceries up all those steps? But I guess you're young, and it wouldn't bother you as much as it does me."

This long string of questions told Kiswana that her mother had no intentions of beginning her visit with another argument about her new African name.

"You know I would have called before I came, but you don't have a phone yet. I didn't want you to feel that I was snooping. As a matter of fact, I didn't expect to find you home at all. I thought you'd be out looking for a job." Mrs. Browne had mentally covered the entire apartment while she was talking and taking off her coat.

"Well, I got up late this morning. I thought I'd buy the afternoon paper and start early tomorrow."

"That sounds like a good idea." Her mother moved toward the window and picked up the discarded paper and glanced over the hurriedly circled ads. "Since when do you have experience as a fork-lift operator?"

Kiswana caught her breath and silently cursed herself for her stupidity. "Oh, my hand slipped—I meant to circle file clerk." She quickly took the paper before her mother could see that she had also marked cutlery salesman and chauffeur.

"You're sure you weren't sitting here moping and daydreaming again?" Amber specks of laughter flashed in the corner of Mrs. Browne's eyes.

Kiswana threw her shoulders back and unsuccessfully tried to disguise her embarrassment with indignation.

"Oh, God, Mama! I haven't done that in years—it's for kids. When are you going to realize that I'm a woman now?"

She sought desperately for some womanly thing to do and settled for throwing herself on the couch and crossing her legs in what she hoped looked like a nonchalant arc.

"Please, have a seat," she said, attempting the same tones and gestures she'd seen Bette Davis use on the late movies.

Mrs. Browne, lowering her eyes to hide her amusement, accepted the invitation and sat at the window, also crossing her legs. Kiswana saw immediately how it should have been done. Her celluloid poise clashed loudly against her mother's quiet dignity, and she quickly uncrossed her legs. Mrs. Browne turned her head toward the window and pretended not to notice.

"At least you have a halfway decent view from here. I was wondering what lay beyond that dreadful wall—it's the boulevard. Honey, did you know that you can see the trees in Linden Hills from here?"

Kiswana knew that very well, because there were many lonely days that she would sit in her gray apartment and stare at those trees and think of home, but she would rather have choked than admit that to her mother.

"Oh, really? I never noticed. So how is Daddy and things at home?"

"Just fine. We're thinking of redoing one of the extra bedrooms since you children have moved out, but Wilson insists that he can manage all that work alone. I told him that he doesn't really have the proper time or energy for all that. As it is, when he gets home from the office, he's so tired he can hardly move. But you know you can't tell your father anything. Whenever he starts complaining about how stubborn you are, I tell him the child came by it honestly. Oh, and your brother was by yesterday," she added, as if it had just occurred to her.

So that's it, thought Kiswana. That's why she's here.

Kiswana's brother, Wilson, had been to visit her two days ago, and she had borrowed twenty dollars from him to get her winter coat out of layaway. That son-of-a-bitch probably ran straight to Mama—and after he swore he wouldn't say anything. I should have known, he was always a snotty-nosed sneak, she thought.

"Was he?" she said aloud. "He came by to see me, too, earlier this week. And I borrowed some money from him because my unemployment checks hadn't cleared in the bank, but now they have and everything's just fine." There, I'll beat you to that one.

"Oh, I didn't know that," Mrs. Browne lied. "He never mentioned you. He had just heard that Beverly was expecting again, and he rushed over to tell us."

Damn. Kiswana could have strangled herself.

"So she's knocked up again, huh?" she said irritably.

Her mother started. "Why do you always have to be so crude?"

"Personally, I don't see how she can sleep with Willie. He's such a dishrag."

Kiswana still resented the stance her brother had taken in college. When everyone at school was discovering their blackness and protesting on campus, Wilson never took part; he had even refused to wear an Afro. This had outraged Kiswana because, unlike her, he was dark-skinned and had the type of hair that was thick and kinky enough for a good "Fro." Kiswana had still insisted on cutting her own hair, but it was so thin and fine-textured, it refused to thicken even after she washed it. So she had to brush it up and spray it with lacquer to keep it from lying flat. She never forgave Wilson for telling her that she didn't look African, she looked like an electrocuted chicken.

"Now that's some way to talk. I don't know why you have an attitude against your brother. He never gave me a restless night's sleep, and now he's settled with a family and a good job."

"He's an assistant to an assistant junior partner in a law firm. What's the big deal about that?"

"The job has a future, Melanie. And at least he finished school and went on for his law degree."

"In other words, not like me, huh?"

"Don't put words into my mouth, young lady. I'm perfectly capable of saying what I mean."

Amen, thought Kiswana.

"And I don't know why you've been trying to start up with me from the moment I walked in. I didn't come here to fight with you. This is your first place away from home, and I just wanted to see how you were living and if you're doing all right. And I must say, you've fixed this apartment up very nicely."

"Really, Mama?" She found herself softening in the light of her mother's approval.

"Well, considering what you had to work with." This time she scanned the apartment openly.

"Look, I know it's not Linden Hills, but a lot can be done with it. As soon as they come and paint, I'm going to hang my Ashanti print over the couch. And I thought a big Boston fern would go well in that corner, what do you think?"

"That would be fine, baby. You always had a good eye for balance."

Kiswana was beginning to relax. There was little she did that attracted her mother's approval. It was like a rare bird, and she had to tread carefully around it lest it fly away.

"Are you going to leave that statue out like that?"

"Why, what's wrong with it? Would it look better somewhere else?"

There was a small wooden reproduction of a Yoruba goddess with large protruding breasts on the coffee table.

"Well"—Mrs. Browne was beginning to blush—"it's just that it's a bit suggestive, don't you think? Since you live alone now, and I know you'll be having male friends stop by, you wouldn't want to be giving them any ideas. I mean, uh, you know, there's no point in putting yourself in any unpleasant situations because they may get the wrong impression and uh, you know, I mean, well . . ." Mrs. Browne stammered on miserably.

Kiswana loved it when her mother tried to talk about sex. It was the only time she was at a loss for words.

"Don't worry, Mama." Kiswana smiled. "That wouldn't bother the type of men I date. Now maybe if it had big feet—" And she got hysterical, thinking of Abshu.

Her mother looked at her sharply. "What sort of gibberish is that about feet? I'm being serious, Melanie."

"I'm sorry, Mama." She sobered up. "I'll put it away in the closet," she said, knowing that she wouldn't.

"Good," Mrs. Browne said, knowing that she wouldn't either. "I guess you think I'm too picky, but we worry about you over here. And you refuse to put in a phone so we can call and see about you."

"I haven't refused, Mama. They want seventy-five dollars for a deposit, and I can't swing that right now."

"Melanie, I can give you the money."

"I don't want you to be giving me money—I've told you that before. Please, let me make it by myself."

"Well, let me lend it to you, then."

"No!"

"Oh, so you can borrow money from your brother, but not from me."

Kiswana turned her head from the hurt in her mother's eyes. "Mama, when I borrow from Willie, he makes me pay him back. You never let me pay you back," she said into her hands.

"I don't care. I still think it's downright selfish of you to be sitting over here with no phone, and sometimes we don't hear from you in two weeks—anything could happen—especially living among these people."

Kiswana snapped her head up. "What do you mean, *these people*? They're my people and yours, too, Mama—we're all black. But maybe you've forgotten that over in Linden Hills."

"That's not what I'm talking about, and you know it. These streets—this building—it's so shabby and rundown. Honey, you don't have to live like this."

"Well, this is how poor people live."

"Melanie, you're not poor."

"No, Mama, *you're* not poor. And what you have and I have are two totally different things. I don't have a husband in real estate with a five-figure income and a home in Linden Hills—*you* do. What I have is a weekly unemployment check and an overdrawn checking account at United Federal. So this studio on Brewster is all I can afford."

"Well, you could afford a lot better," Mrs. Browne snapped, "if you hadn't dropped out of college and had to resort to these dead-end clerical jobs."

"Uh-huh, I knew you'd get around to that before long." Kiswana could feel the rings of anger begin to tighten around her lower backbone, and they sent her forward onto the couch. "You'll never understand, will you? Those bourgie schools were counterrevolutionary. My place was in the streets with my people, fighting for equality and a better community."

"Counterrevolutionary!" Mrs. Browne was raising her voice. "Where's your revolution now, Melanie? Where are all those black revolutionaries who were shouting and demonstrating and kicking up a lot of dust with you on that campus? Huh? They're sitting in wood-paneled offices with their degrees in mahogany frames, and they won't even drive their cars past this street because the city doesn't fix potholes in this part of town."

"Mama," she said, shaking her head slowly in disbelief, "how can you—a black woman—sit there and tell me that what we fought for during the Movement wasn't important just because some people sold out?"

"Melanie, I'm not saying it wasn't important. It was damned important to stand up and say that you were proud of what you were and to get the vote and other social opportunities for every person in this country who had it due. But you kids thought you were going to turn the world upside down, and it just wasn't so. When all the smoke had cleared, you found yourself with a fistful of new federal laws and a country still full of obstacles for black people to fight their way over—just because they're black. There was no revolution, Melanie, and there will be no revolution."

"So what am I supposed to do, huh? Just throw up my hands and not care about what happens to my people? I'm not supposed to keep fighting to make things better?"

"Of course you can. But you're going to have to fight within the system, because it and these so-called 'bourgie' schools are going to be here for a long time. And that means that you get smart like a lot of your old friends and get an important job where you can have some influence. You don't have to sell out, as you say, and work for some corporation, but you could become an assembly-woman or a civil liberties lawyer or open a freedom school in this very neighborhood. That way you could really help the community. But what help are you going to be to these people on Brewster while you're living hand-to-mouth on file-clerk jobs waiting for a revolution? You're wasting your talents, child."

"Well, I don't think they're being wasted. At least I'm here in day-to-day contact with the problems of my people. What good would I be after four or five years of a lot of white brainwashing in some phony prestige institution, huh? I'd be like you and Daddy and those other educated blacks sitting over there in Linden Hills with a terminal case of middle-class amnesia."

"You don't have to live in a slum to be concerned about social conditions, Melanie. Your father and I have been charter members of the NAACP for the last twenty-five years."

"Oh, God!" Kiswana threw her head back in exaggerated disgust. "That's being concerned? That middle-of-the-road Uncle Tom dumping ground for black Republicans!"

"You can sneer all you want, young lady, but that organization has been working for black people since the turn of the century, and it's still working for them. Where are all those radical groups of yours that were going to put a Cadillac in every garage and Dick Gregory in the White House? I'll tell you where."

I knew you would, Kiswana thought angrily.

"They burned themselves out because they wanted too much too fast. Their goals weren't grounded in reality. And that's always been your problem."

"What do you mean, my problem? I know exactly what I'm about."

"No, you don't. You constantly live in a fantasy world—always going to extremes—turning butterflies into eagles, and life isn't about that. It's accepting what is and working from that. Lord, I remember how worried you had me, putting all that lacquered hair spray on your head. I thought you were going to get lung cancer—trying to be what you're not."

Kiswana jumped up from the couch. "Oh, God, I can't take this anymore. Trying to be something I'm not—trying to be something I'm not, Mama? Trying to be proud of my heritage and the fact that I was of African descent. If that's being what I'm not, then I say fine. But I'd rather be dead than be like you—a white man's nigger who's ashamed of being black!"

Kiswana saw streaks of gold and ebony light follow her mother's flying body out of the chair. She was swung around by the shoulders and made to face the deadly stillness in the angry woman's eyes. She was too stunned to cry out from the pain of the long fingernails that dug into her shoulders, and she was brought so close to her mother's face that she saw her reflection, distorted and wavering, in the tears that stood in the older woman's eyes. And she listened in that stillness to a story she had heard as a child.

"My grandmother," Mrs. Browne began slowly in a whisper, "was a full-blooded Iroquois, and my grandfather a free black from a long line of journeymen who had lived in Connecticut since the establishment of the colonies. And my father was a Bajan who came to this country as a cabin boy on a merchant mariner."

"I know all that," Kiswana said, trying to keep her lips from trembling.

"Then know this." And the nails dug deeper into her flesh. "I am alive because of the blood of proud people who never scraped or begged or apologized for what they were. They lived asking only one thing of this world—to be allowed to be. And I learned through the blood of these people that black isn't beautiful and it isn't ugly—black is! It's not kinky hair and it's not straight hair—it just is.

"It broke my heart when you changed your name. I gave you my grand-mother's name, a woman who bore nine children and educated them all, who held off six white men with a shotgun when they tried to drag one of her sons to jail for 'not knowing his place.' Yet you needed to reach into an African dictionary to find a name to make you proud.

"When I brought my babies home from the hospital, my ebony son and my golden daughter, I swore before whatever gods would listen—those of my mother's people or those of my father's people—that I would use everything I had and could ever get to see that my children were prepared to meet this world on its own terms, so that no one could sell them short and make them ashamed of what they were or how they looked—whatever they were or however they looked. And Melanie, that's not being white or red or black—that's being a mother."

Kiswana followed her reflection in the two single tears that moved down her mother's cheeks until it blended with them into the woman's copper skin. There was nothing and then so much that she wanted to say, but her throat kept closing up every time she tried to speak. She kept her head down and her eyes closed, and thought, Oh, God, just let me die. How can I face her now?

Mrs. Browne lifted Kiswana's chin gently. "And the one lesson I wanted you to learn is not to be afraid to face anyone, not even a crafty old lady like me who can outtalk you." And she smiled and winked.

"Oh, Mama, I . . ." and she hugged the woman tightly.

"Yeah, baby." Mrs. Browne patted her back. "I know." She kissed Kiswana on the forehead and cleared her throat. "Well, now, I better be moving on. It's getting late, there's dinner to be made, and I have to get off my feet—these new shoes are killing me."

Kiswana looked down at the beige leather pumps. "Those are really classy. They're English, aren't they?"

"Yes, but, Lord, do they cut me right across the instep." She removed the shoe and sat on the couch to massage her foot.

Bright red nail polish glared at Kiswana through the stockings. "Since when do you polish your toenails?" she gasped. "You never did that before."

"Well"—Mrs. Browne shrugged her shoulders—"your father sort of talked me into it, and, uh, you know, he likes it and all, so I thought, uh, you know, why not, so . . ." And she gave Kiswana an embarrassed smile.

I'll be damned, the young woman thought, feeling her whole face tingle. Daddy's into feet! And she looked at the blushing woman on her couch and suddenly realized that her mother had trod through the same universe that she herself was now traveling. Kiswana was breaking no new trails and would eventually end up just two feet away on that couch. She stared at the woman she had been and was to become.

"But I'll never be a Republican," she caught herself saying aloud.

"What are you mumbling about, Melanie?" Mrs. Browne slipped on her shoe and got up from the couch.

She went to get her mother's coat. "Nothing, Mama. It's really nice of you to come by. You should do it more often."

"Well, since it's not Sunday, I guess you're allowed at least one lie."

They both laughed.

After Kiswana had closed the door and turned around, she spotted an envelope sticking between the cushions of her couch. She went over and opened it up; there was seventy-five dollars in it.

"Oh, Mama, darn it!" She rushed to the window and started to call to the woman, who had just emerged from the building, but she suddenly changed her mind and sat down in the chair with a long sigh that caught in the upward draft of the autumn wind and disappeared over the top of the building.

"Recitatif"

Toni Morrison

1983

My mother danced all night and Roberta's was sick. That's why we were taken to St. Bonny's. People want to put their arms around you when you tell them you were in a shelter, but it really wasn't bad. No big long room with one hundred beds like Bellevue. There were four to a room, and when Roberta and me came, there was a shortage of state kids, so we were the only ones assigned to 406 and could go from bed to bed if we wanted to. And we wanted to, too. We changed beds every night and for the whole four months we were there we never picked one out as our own permanent bed.

It didn't start out that way. The minute I walked in and the Big Bozo introduced us, I got sick to my stomach. It was one thing to be taken out of your own bed early in the morning—it was something else to be stuck in a strange place with a girl from a whole other race. And Mary, that's my mother, she was right. Every now and then she would stop dancing long enough to tell me something important and one of the things she said was that they never washed their hair and they smelled funny. Roberta sure did. Smell funny, I mean. So when the Big Bozo (nobody ever called her Mrs. Itkin, just like nobody ever said St. Bonaventure)—when she said, "Twyla, this is Roberta. Roberta, this is Twyla. Make each other welcome," I said, "My mother won't like you putting me in here."

"Good," said Bozo. "Maybe then she'll come and take you home."

How's that for mean? If Roberta had laughed I would have killed her, but she didn't. She just walked over to the window and stood with her back to us.

"Turn around," said the Bozo. "Don't be rude. Now Twyla. Roberta. When you hear a loud buzzer, that's the call for dinner. Come down to the first floor. Any fights and no movie." And then, just to make sure we knew what we would be missing, "*The Wizard of Oz.*"

Roberta must have thought I meant that my mother would be mad about my being put in the shelter. Not about rooming with her, because as soon as

Bozo left she came over to me and said, "Is your mother sick too?"

"No," I said. "She just likes to dance all night."

"Oh." She nodded her head and I liked the way she understood things so fast. So for the moment it didn't matter that we looked like salt and pepper standing there and that's what the other kids called us sometimes. We were eight years old and got F's all the time. Me because I couldn't remember what I read or what the teacher said. And Roberta because she couldn't read at all and didn't even listen to the teacher. She wasn't good at anything except jacks, at which she was a killer: pow scoop pow scoop pow scoop.

We didn't like each other all that much at first, but nobody else wanted to play with us because we weren't real orphans with beautiful dead parents in the sky. We were dumped. Even the New York City Puerto Ricans and the upstate Indians ignored us. All kinds of kids were in there, black ones, white ones, even two Koreans. The food was good, though. At least I thought so. Roberta hated it and left whole pieces of things on her plate: Spam, Salisbury steak—even Jell-O with fruit cocktail in it, and she didn't care if I ate what she wouldn't. Mary's idea of supper was popcorn and a can of Yoo-Hoo. Hot mashed potatoes and two weenies was like Thanksgiving for me.

It really wasn't bad, St. Bonny's. The big girls on the second floor pushed us around now and then. But that was all. They wore lipstick and eyebrow pencil and wobbled their knees while they watched TV. Fifteen, sixteen, even, some of them were. They were put-out girls, scared runaways most of them. Poor little girls who fought their uncles off but looked tough to us, and mean. God, did they look mean. The staff tried to keep them separate from the younger children, but sometimes they caught us watching them in the orchard where they played radios and danced with each other. They'd light out after us and pull our hair or twist our arms. We were scared of them, Roberta and me, but neither of us wanted the other one to know it. So we got a good list of dirty names we could shout back when we ran from them through the orchard. I used to dream a lot and almost always the orchard was there. Two acres, four maybe, of these little apple trees. Hundreds of them. Empty and crooked like beggar women when I first came to St. Bonny's but fat with flowers when I left. I don't know why I dreamt about that orchard so much. Nothing really happened there. Nothing all that important, I mean. Just the big girls dancing and playing the radio. Roberta and me watching. Maggie fell down there once. The kitchen woman with legs like parentheses. And the big girls laughed at her. We should have helped her up, I know, but we were scared of those girls with lipstick and eyebrow pencil. Maggie couldn't talk. The kids said she had her tongue cut out, but I think she was just born that way: mute. She was old and sandy-colored and she worked in the kitchen. I don't know if she was nice or not. I just remember her legs like parentheses and how she rocked when she walked. She worked from early in the morning till two o'clock, and if she was late, if she had too much cleaning and didn't get out till two-fifteen or so, she'd cut through the orchard so she wouldn't miss her bus and have to wait another hour. She wore this really stupid little hat—a kid's hat with ear flaps—and she wasn't much taller than we were. A really awful little hat. Even for a mute, it was dumb—dressing like a kid and never saying anything at all.

"But what about if somebody tries to kill her?" I used to wonder about that. "Or what if she wants to cry? Can she cry?"

"Sure," Roberta said. "But just tears. No sounds come out."

"She can't scream?"

"Nope. Nothing."

"Can she hear?"

"I guess."

"Let's call her," I said. And we did.

"Dummy! Dummy!" She never turned her head.

"Bow legs! Bow legs!" Nothing. She just rocked on, the chin straps of her baby-boy hat swaying from side to side. I think we were wrong. I think she could hear and didn't let on. And it shames me even now to think there was somebody in there after all who heard us call her those names and couldn't tell on us.

We got along all right, Roberta and me. Changed beds every night, got F's in civics and communication skills and gym. The Bozo was disappointed in us, she said. Out of 130 of us state cases, 90 were under twelve. Almost all were real orphans with beautiful dead parents in the sky. We were the only ones dumped and the only ones with F's in three classes including gym. So we got along—what with her leaving whole pieces of things on her plate and being nice about not asking questions.

I think it was the day before Maggie fell down that we found out our mothers were coming to visit us on the same Sunday. We had been at the shelter twenty-eight days (Roberta twenty-eight and a half) and this was their first visit with us. Our mothers would come at ten o'clock in time for chapel, then lunch with us in the teachers' lounge. I thought if my dancing mother met her sick mother it might be good for her. And Roberta thought her sick mother would get a big bang out of a dancing one. We got excited about it and curled each other's hair. After breakfast we sat on the bed watching the road from the window. Roberta's socks were still wet. She washed them the night before and put them on the radiator to dry. They hadn't, but she put them on anyway because their tops were so pretty—scalloped in pink. Each of us had a purple construction-paper basket that we had made in craft class. Mine had a yellow crayon rabbit on it. Roberta's had eggs with wiggly lines of color. Inside were cellophane grass and just the jelly beans because I'd eaten the two marshmallow eggs they gave us. The Big Bozo came herself to get us. Smiling she told us we looked very nice and to come downstairs. We were so surprised by the smile we'd never seen before, neither of us moved.

"Don't you want to see your mommies?"

I stood up first and spilled the jelly beans all over the floor. Bozo's smile disappeared while we scrambled to get the candy up off the floor and put it back in the grass.

She escorted us downstairs to the first floor, where the other girls were lining up to file into the chapel. A bunch of grown-ups stood to one side. Viewers mostly. The old biddies who wanted servants and the fags who wanted company looking for children they might want to adopt. Once in a while a grandmother. Almost never anybody young or anybody whose face wouldn't scare you in the night. Because if any of the real orphans had young relatives they wouldn't be real orphans. I saw Mary right away. She had on those green slacks I hated and hated even more now because didn't she know we were going to chapel? And that fur jacket with the pocket linings so ripped she had to pull to get her hands out of them. But her face was pretty—like always—and she smiled and waved like she was the little girl looking for her mother, not me.

I walked slowly, trying not to drop the jelly beans and hoping the paper handle would hold. I had to use my last Chiclet because by the time I finished cutting everything out, all the Elmer's was gone. I am left-handed and the scissors never worked for me. It didn't matter, though; I might just as well have chewed the gum. Mary dropped to her knees and grabbed me, mashing the basket, the jelly beans, and the grass into her ratty fur jacket.

"Twyla, baby. Twyla, baby!"

I could have killed her. Already I heard the big girls in the orchard the next time saying, "Twyyyyyla, baby!" But I couldn't stay mad at Mary while she was smiling and hugging me and smelling of Lady Esther dusting powder. I wanted to stay buried in her fur all day.

To tell the truth I forgot about Roberta. Mary and I got in line for the traipse into chapel and I was feeling proud because she looked so beautiful even in those ugly green slacks that made her behind stick out. A pretty mother on earth is better than a beautiful dead one in the sky even if she did leave you all alone to go dancing.

I felt a tap on my shoulder, turned, and saw Roberta smiling. I smiled back, but not too much lest somebody think this visit was the biggest thing that ever happened in my life. Then Roberta said, "Mother, I want you to meet my roommate, Twyla. And that's Twyla's mother."

I looked up it seemed for miles. She was big. Bigger than any man and on her chest was the biggest cross I'd ever seen. I swear it was six inches long each way. And in the crook of her arm was the biggest Bible ever made.

Mary, simpleminded as ever, grinned and tried to yank her hand out of the pocket with the raggedy lining—to shake hands, I guess. Roberta's mother looked down at me and then looked down at Mary too. She didn't say anything, just grabbed Roberta with her Bible-free hand and stepped out of line, walking quickly to the rear of it. Mary was still grinning because she's not too swift when it comes to what's really going on. Then this light bulb goes off in her head and she says "That bitch!" really loud and us almost in the chapel now. Organ music whining; the Bonny Angels singing sweetly. Everybody in the world turned around to look. And Mary would have kept it up—kept calling names if I hadn't squeezed her hands as hard as I could. That helped a little, but she still twitched and crossed and uncrossed her legs all through service. Even groaned a couple of times. Why did I think she would come there and act right? Slacks. No hat like the grandmothers and viewers, and groaning all the while. When we stood for hymns she kept her mouth shut. Wouldn't even look at the words on the page. She actually reached in her purse for a mirror to check her lipstick. All I could think of was that she really needed to be killed. The sermon lasted a year, and I knew the real orphans were looking smug again.

We were supposed to have lunch in the teachers' lounge, but Mary didn't bring anything, so we picked fur and cellophane grass off the mashed jelly beans and ate them. I could have killed her. I sneaked a look at Roberta. Her mother had brought chicken legs and ham sandwiches and oranges and a whole box of chocolate-covered grahams. Roberta drank milk from a thermos while her mother read the Bible to her.

Things are not right. The wrong food is always with the wrong people. Maybe that's why I got into waitress work later—to match up the right people with the right food. Roberta just let those chicken legs sit there, but she did bring a stack of grahams up to me later when the visit was over. I think she was sorry that her mother would not shake my mother's hand. And I liked that and I liked the fact that she didn't say a word about Mary groaning all the way through the service and not bringing any lunch.

Roberta left in May when the apple trees were heavy and white. On her last day we went to the orchard to watch the big girls smoke and dance by the radio. It didn't matter that they said, "Twyyyyyla, baby." We sat on the ground and breathed. Lady Esther. Apple blossoms. I still go soft when I smell one or the other. Roberta was going home. The big cross and the big Bible was coming to get her and she seemed sort of glad and sort of not. I thought I would die in that room of four beds without her and I knew Bozo had plans to move some other dumped kid in there with me. Roberta promised to write every day, which was really sweet of her because she couldn't read a lick so how could she write anybody? I would have drawn pictures and sent them to her but she never gave me her address. Little by little she faded. Her wet socks with the pink scalloped tops and her big serious-looking eyes—that's all I could catch when I tried to bring her to mind.

I was working behind the counter at the Howard Johnson's on the Thruway just before the Kingston exit. Not a bad job. Kind of a long ride from Newburgh, but okay once I got there. Mine was the second night shift, eleven to seven. Very light until a Greyhound checked in for breakfast around six-thirty. At that hour the sun was all the way clear of the hills behind the restaurant. The place looked better at night—more like shelter—but I loved it when the sun broke in, even if it did show all the cracks in the vinyl and the speckled floor looked dirty no matter what the mop boy did.

It was August and a bus crowd was just unloading. They would stand around a long while: going to the john, and looking at gifts and junk-for-sale machines, reluctant to sit down so soon. Even to eat. I was trying to fill the coffeepots and get them all situated on the electric burners when I saw her. She was sitting in a booth smoking a cigarette with two guys smothered in head and facial hair. Her own hair was so big and wild I could hardly see her face. But the eyes. I would know them anywhere. She had on a powder-blue halter and shorts outfit and earrings the size of bracelets. Talk about lipstick and eyebrow pencil. She made the big girls look like nuns. I couldn't get off the counter until seven o'clock, but I kept watching the booth in case they got up to leave before that. My replacement was on time for a change, so I counted and stacked my receipts as fast as I could and signed off. I walked over to the booth, smiling and wondering if she would remember me. Or even if she wanted to remember me. Maybe she didn't want to be reminded of St. Bonny's or to have anybody know she was ever there. I know I never talked about it to anybody.

I put my hands in my apron pockets and leaned against the back of the booth facing them.

"Roberta? Roberta Fisk?"

She looked up. "Yeah?"

"Twyla."

She squinted for a second and then said, "Wow."

"Remember me?"

"Sure. Hey. Wow."

"It's been awhile," I said, and gave a smile to the two hairy guys.

"Yeah. Wow. You work here?"

"Yeah," I said. "I live in Newburgh."

"Newburgh? No kidding?" She laughed then, a private laugh that included the guys but only the guys, and they laughed with her. What could I do but laugh too and wonder why I was standing there with my knees showing out from under that uniform. Without looking I could see the blue-and-white triangle on my head, my hair shapeless in a net, my ankles thick in white oxfords. Nothing could have been less sheer than my stockings. There was this silence that came down right after I laughed. A silence it was her turn to fill up. With introductions, maybe, to her boyfriends or an invitation to sit down and have a Coke. Instead she lit a cigarette off the one she'd just finished and said, "We're on our way to the Coast. He's got an appointment with Hendrix." She gestured casually toward the boy next to her.

"Hendrix? Fantastic," I said. "Really fantastic. What's she doing now?"

Roberta coughed on her cigarette and the two guys rolled their eyes up at the ceiling.

"Hendrix. Jimi Hendrix, asshole. He's only the biggest—Oh, wow. Forget it."

I was dismissed without anyone saying good-bye, so I thought I would do it for her.

"How's your mother?" I asked. Her grin cracked her whole face. She swallowed. "Fine," she said. "How's yours?"

"Pretty as a picture," I said and turned away. The backs of my knees were damp. Howard Johnson's really was a dump in the sunlight.

James is as comfortable as a house slipper. He liked my cooking and I liked his big loud family. They have lived in Newburgh all of their lives and talk about it the way people do who have always known a home. His grandmother has a porch swing older than his father and when they talk about streets and avenues and buildings they call them names they no longer have. They still call the A&P Rico's because it stands on property once a mom-and-pop store owned by Mr. Rico. And they call the new community college Town Hall because it once was. My mother-in-law puts up jelly and cucumbers and buys butter wrapped in cloth from a dairy. James and his father talk about fishing and baseball and I can see them all together on the Hudson in a raggedy skiff. Half the population of Newburgh is on welfare now, but to my husband's family it was still some upstate paradise of a time long past. A time of ice houses and vegetable wagons, coal furnaces and children weeding gardens. When our son was born my mother-in-law gave me the crib blanket that had been hers.

But the town they remembered had changed. Something quick was in the air. Magnificent old houses, so ruined they had become shelter for squatters and rent risks, were bought and renovated. Smart IBM people moved out of their suburbs back into the city and put shutters up and herb gardens in their backyards. A brochure came in the mail announcing the opening of a Food Emporium. Gourmet food, it said—and listed items the rich IBM crowd would want. It was located in a new mall at the edge of town and I drove out to shop there one day—just to see. It was late in June. After the tulips were gone and the Queen Elizabeth roses were open everywhere. I trailed my cart along the aisle tossing in smoked oysters and Robert's sauce and things I knew would sit in my cupboard for years. Only when I found some Klondike ice cream bars did I feel less guilty about spending James's fireman's salary so foolishly. My father-in-law ate them with the same gusto little Joseph did.

Waiting in the checkout line I heard a voice say, "Twyla!"

The classical music piped over the aisles had affected me and the woman leaning toward me was dressed to kill. Diamonds on her hand, a smart white summer dress. "I'm Mrs. Benson," I said.

"Ho. Ho. The Big Bozo," she sang.

For a split second I didn't know what she was talking about. She had a bunch of asparagus and two cartons of fancy water.

"Roberta!"

"Right."

"For heaven's sake. Roberta."

"You look great," she said.

"So do you. Where are you? Here? In Newburgh?"

"Yes. Over in Annandale."

I was opening my mouth to say more when the cashier called my attention to her empty counter.

"Meet you outside." Roberta pointed her finger and went into the express line.

I placed the groceries and kept myself from glancing around to check Roberta's progress. I remembered Howard Johnson's and looking for a chance to speak only to be greeted with a stingy "wow." But she was waiting for me and her huge hair was sleek now, smooth around a small, nicely shaped head. Shoes, dress, everything lovely and summery and rich. I was dying to know what happened to her, how she got from Jimi Hendrix to Annandale, a neighborhood full of doctors and IBM executives. Easy, I thought. Everything is so easy for them. They think they own the world.

"How long," I asked her. "How long have you been here?"

"A year. I got married to a man who lives here. And you, you're married too, right? Benson, you said."

"Yeah. James Benson."

"And is he nice?"

"Oh, is he nice?"

"Well, is he?" Roberta's eyes were steady as though she really meant the question and wanted an answer.

"He's wonderful, Roberta. Wonderful."

"So you're happy."

"Very."

"That's good," she said and nodded her head. "I always hoped you'd be happy. Any kids? I know you have kids."

"One. A boy. How about you?"

"Four."

"Four?"

She laughed. "Step kids. He's a widower."

"Oh."

"Got a minute? Let's have a coffee."

I thought about the Klondikes melting and the inconvenience of going all the way to my car and putting the bags in the trunk. Served me right for buying all that stuff I didn't need. Roberta was ahead of me.

"Put them in my car. It's right here."

And then I saw the dark blue limousine.

"You married a Chinaman?"

"No." She laughed. "He's the driver."

"Oh, my. If the Big Bozo could see you now."

We both giggled. Really giggled. Suddenly, in just a pulse beat, twenty years disappeared and all of it came rushing back. The big girls (whom we called gar girls—Roberta's misheard word for the evil stone faces described in a civics class) there dancing in the orchard, the ploppy mashed potatoes, the double weenies, the Spam with pineapple. We went into the coffee shop holding on to one another and I tried to think why we were glad to see each other this time and not before. Once, twelve years ago, we passed like strangers. A black girl and a white girl meeting in a Howard Johnson's on the road and having nothing to say. One in a blue-and-white triangle waitress hat, the other on her way to see Hendrix. Now we were behaving like sisters separated for much too long. Those four short months were nothing in time. Maybe it was the thing itself. Just being there, together. Two little girls who knew what nobody else in the world knew—how not to ask questions. How to believe what had to be believed. There was politeness in that reluctance and generosity as well. Is your mother sick too? No, she dances all night. Oh—and an understanding nod.

We sat in a booth by the window and fell into recollection like veterans.

"Did you ever learn to read?"

"Watch." She picked up the menu. "Special of the day. Cream of corn soup. Entrées. Two dots and a wriggly line. Quiche. Chef salad, scallops. . . ."

I was laughing and applauding when the waitress came up.

"Remember the Easter baskets?"

"And how we tried to *introduce* them?"

"Your mother with that cross like two telephone poles."

"And yours with those tight slacks."

We laughed so loudly heads turned and made the laughter hard to suppress.

"What happened to the Jimi Hendrix date?"

Roberta made a blow-out sound with her lips.

"When he died I thought about you."

"Oh, you heard about him finally?"

"Finally. Come on, I was a small-town country waitress."

"And I was a small-town country dropout. God, were we wild. I still don't know how I got out of there alive."

"But you did."

"I did. I really did. Now I'm Mrs. Kenneth Norton."

"Sounds like a mouthful."

"It is."

"Servants and all?"

Roberta held up two fingers.

"Ow! What does he do?"

"Computers and stuff. What do I know?"

"I don't remember a hell of a lot from those days, but Lord, St. Bonny's is as clear as daylight. Remember Maggie? The day she fell down and those gar girls laughed at her?"

Roberta looked up from her salad and stared at me. "Maggie didn't fall," she said.

"Yes, she did. You remember."

"No, Twyla. They knocked her down. Those girls pushed her down and tore her clothes. In the orchard."

"I don't—that's not what happened."

"Sure it is. In the orchard. Remember how scared we were?"

"Wait a minute. I don't remember any of that."

"And Bozo was fired."

"You're crazy. She was there when I left. You left before me."

"I went back. You weren't there when they fired Bozo."

"What?"

"Twice. Once for a year when I was about ten, another for two months when I was fourteen. That's when I ran away."

"You ran away from St. Bonny's?"

"I had to. What do you want? Me dancing in that orchard?"

"Are you sure about Maggie?"

"Of course I'm sure. You've blocked it, Twyla. It happened. Those girls had behavior problems, you know."

"Didn't they, though. But why can't I remember the Maggie thing?"

"Believe me. It happened. And we were there."

"Who did you room with when you went back?" I asked her as if I would know her. The Maggie thing was troubling me.

"Creeps. They tickled themselves in the night."

My ears were itching and I wanted to go home suddenly. This was all very well but she couldn't just comb her hair, wash her face, and pretend everything was hunky-dory. After the Howard Johnson's snub. And no apology. Nothing.

"Were you on dope or what that time at Howard Johnson's?" I tried to make my voice sound friendlier than I felt.

"Maybe, a little. I never did drugs much. Why?"

"I don't know, you acted sort of like you didn't want to know me then."

"Oh, Twyla, you know how it was in those days: black—white. You know how everything was."

But I didn't know. I thought it was just the opposite. Busloads of blacks and whites came into Howard Johnson's together. They roamed together then: students, musicians, lovers, protesters. You got to see everything at Howard Johnson's, and blacks were very friendly with whites in those days. But sitting there with nothing on my plate but two hard tomato wedges wondering about the melting Klondikes it seemed childish remembering the slight. We went to her car and, with the help of the driver, got my stuff into my station wagon.

"We'll keep in touch this time," she said.

"Sure," I said. "Sure. Give me a call."

"I will," she said, and then, just as I was sliding behind the wheel, she leaned into the window. "By the way. Your mother. Did she ever stop dancing?"

I shook my head. "No. Never."

Roberta nodded.

"And yours? Did she ever get well?"

She smiled a tiny sad smile. "No. She never did. Look, call me, okay?"

"Okay," I said, but I knew I wouldn't. Roberta had messed up my past somehow with that business about Maggie. I wouldn't forget a thing like that. Would I?

Strife came to us that fall. At least that's what the paper called it. Strife. Racial strife. The word made me think of a bird—a big shrieking bird out of 1,000,000,000 B.C. Flapping its wings and cawing. Its eye with no lid always bearing down on you. All day it screeched and at night it slept on the rooftops. It woke you in the morning, and from the *Today* show to the eleven o'clock news it kept you an awful company. I couldn't figure it out from one day to the next. I knew I was supposed to feel something strong, but I didn't know what, and James wasn't any help. Joseph was on the list of kids to be transferred from the junior high school to another one at some far-out-of-the-way place and I thought it was a good thing until I heard it was a bad thing. I mean I didn't know. All the schools seemed dumps to me, and the fact that one was nicer looking didn't hold much weight. But the papers were full of it and then the kids began to get jumpy. In August, mind you. Schools weren't even open yet. I thought Joseph might be frightened to go over there, but he didn't seem scared so I forgot about it, until I found myself driving along Hudson Street out there by the school they were trying to integrate and saw a line of women marching. And who do you suppose was in line, big as life, holding a sign in front of her bigger than her mother's cross? MOTHERS HAVE RIGHTS TOO! it said.

I drove on and then changed my mind. I circled the block, slowed down, and honked my horn.

Roberta looked over and when she saw me she waved. I didn't wave back, but I didn't move either. She handed her sign to another woman and came over to where I was parked.

"Hi."

"What are you doing?"

"Picketing. What's it look like?"

"What for?"

"What do you mean, 'What for?' They want to take my kids and send them out of the neighborhood. They don't want to go."

"So what if they go to another school? My boy's being bussed too, and I don't mind. Why should you?"

"It's not about us, Twyla. Me and you. It's about our kids."

"What's more *us* than that?"

"Well, it is a free country."

"Not yet, but it will be."

"What the hell does that mean? I'm not doing anything to you."

"You really think that?"

"I know it."

"I wonder what made me think you were different."

"I wonder what made me think you were different."

"Look at them," I said. "Just look. Who do they think they are? Swarming all over the place like they own it. And now they think they can decide where my child goes to school. Look at them, Roberta. They're Bozos."

Roberta turned around and looked at the women. Almost all of them were standing still now, waiting. Some were even edging toward us. Roberta looked at me out of some refrigerator behind her eyes. "No, they're not. They're just mothers."

"And what am I? Swiss cheese?"

"I used to curl your hair."

"I hated your hands in my hair."

The women were moving. Our faces looked mean to them of course and they looked as though they could not wait to throw themselves in front of a police car or, better yet, into my car and drag me away by my ankles. Now they surrounded my car and gently, gently began to rock it. I swayed back and forth like a sideways yo-yo. Automatically I reached for Roberta, like the old days in the orchard when they saw us watching them and we had to get out of there, and if one of us fell the other pulled her up and if one of us was caught the other stayed to kick and scratch, and neither would leave the other behind. My arm shot out of the car window but no receiving hand was there. Roberta was looking at me sway from side to side in the car and her face was still. My purse slid from the car seat down under the dashboard. The four policemen who had been drinking Tab in their car finally got the message and strolled over, forcing their way through the women. Quietly, firmly they spoke. "Okay, ladies. Back in line or off the streets."

Some of them went away willingly; others had to be urged away from the car doors and the hood. Roberta didn't move. She was looking steadily at me. I was fumbling to turn on the ignition, which wouldn't catch because the gearshift was still in drive. The seats of the car were a mess because the swaying had thrown my grocery coupons all over and my purse was sprawled on the floor.

"Maybe I am different now, Twyla. But you're not. You're the same little state kid who kicked a poor old black lady when she was down on the ground. You kicked a black lady and you have the nerve to call me a bigot."

The coupons were everywhere and the guts of my purse were bunched under the dashboard. What was she saying? Black? Maggie wasn't black.

"She wasn't black," I said.

"Like hell she wasn't, and you kicked her. We both did. You kicked a black lady who couldn't even scream."

"Liar!"

"You're the liar! Why don't you just go on home and leave us alone, huh?"

She turned away and I skidded away from the curb.

The next morning I went into the garage and cut the side out of the carton our portable TV had come in. It wasn't nearly big enough, but after a while I had a decent sign: red spray-painted letters on a white background—AND SO DO CHILDREN****. I meant just to go down to the school and tack it up somewhere so those cows on the picket line across the street could see it, but when I got there, some ten or so others had already assembled—protesting the cows across the street. Police permits and everything. I got in line and we strutted in time on our side while Roberta's group strutted on theirs. That first day we were all dignified, pretending the other side didn't exist. The second day there was name calling and finger gestures. But that was about all. People changed signs from time to time, but Roberta never did and neither did I. Actually my sign didn't make sense without Roberta's. "And so do children what?" one of the women on my side asked me. Have rights, I said, as though it was obvious.

Roberta didn't acknowledge my presence in any way, and I got to thinking maybe she didn't know I was there. I began to pace myself in the line, jostling people one minute and lagging behind the next, so Roberta and I could reach the end of our respective lines at the same time and there would be a moment in our turn when we would face each other. Still, I couldn't tell whether she saw me and knew my sign was for her. The next day I went early before we were scheduled to assemble. I waited until she got there before I exposed my new creation. As soon as she hoisted her MOTHERS HAVE RIGHTS TOO I began to wave my new one, which said, HOW WOULD YOU KNOW? I know she saw that one, but I had gotten addicted now. My signs got crazier each day, and the women on my side decided that I was a kook. They couldn't make heads or tails out of my brilliant screaming posters.

I brought a painted sign in queenly red with huge black letters that said, IS YOUR MOTHER WELL? Roberta took her lunch break and didn't come back for the rest of the day or any day after. Two days later I stopped going too and couldn't have been missed because nobody understood my signs anyway.

It was a nasty six weeks. Classes were suspended and Joseph didn't go to anybody's school until October. The children—everybody's children—soon got bored with that extended vacation they thought was going to be so great. They looked at TV until their eyes flattened. I spent a couple of mornings tutoring my son, as the other mothers said we should. Twice I opened a text from last year that he had never turned in. Twice he yawned in my face. Other mothers organized living room sessions so the kids would keep up. None of the kids could concentrate, so they drifted back to *The Price Is Right* and *The Brady Bunch*. When the school finally opened there were fights once or twice and some sirens roared through the streets every once in a while. There were a lot of photographers from Albany. And just when ABC was about to send up a news crew, the kids settled down like nothing in the world had happened. Joseph hung my HOW WOULD YOU KNOW? sign in his bedroom. I don't know what became of AND SO DO CHILDREN****. I think my father-in-law cleaned some fish on it. He was always puttering around in our garage. Each of his five children lived in Newburgh, and he acted as though he had five extra homes.

I couldn't help looking for Roberta when Joseph graduated from high school, but I didn't see her. It didn't trouble me much what she had said to me in the car. I mean the kicking part. I know I didn't do that, I couldn't do that. But I was puzzled by her telling me Maggie was black. When I thought about it I actually couldn't be certain. She wasn't pitch-black, I knew, or I would have remembered that. What I remember was the kiddie hat and the semicircle legs. I tried to reassure myself about the race thing for a long time until it dawned on me that the truth was already there, and Roberta knew it. I didn't kick her; I didn't join in with the gar girls and kick that lady, but I sure did want to. We watched and never tried to help her and never called for help. Maggie was my dancing mother. Deaf, I thought, and dumb. Nobody inside. Nobody who would hear you if you cried in the night. Nobody who could tell you anything important that you could use. Rocking, dancing, swaying as she walked. And when the gar girls pushed her down and started roughhousing, I knew she wouldn't scream, couldn't—just like me—and I was glad about that.

We decided not to have a tree, because Christmas would be at my mother-in-law's house, so why have a tree at both places? Joseph was at SUNY New Paltz and we had to economize, we said. But at the last minute, I changed my mind. Nothing could be that bad. So I rushed around town looking for a tree, something small but wide. By the time I found a place, it was snowing and very late. I dawdled like it was the most important purchase in the world and the tree man was fed up with me. Finally I chose one and had it tied onto the trunk of the car. I drove away slowly because the sand trucks were not out yet and the streets could be murder at the beginning of a snowfall. Downtown the streets were wide and rather empty except for a cluster of people coming out of the Newburgh Hotel. The one hotel in town that wasn't built out of cardboard and Plexiglas. A party, probably. The men huddled in the snow were dressed in tails and the women had on furs. Shiny things glittered from underneath their coats. It made me tired to look at them. Tired, tired, tired. On the next corner was a small diner with loops and loops of paper bells in the window. I stopped the car and went in. Just for a cup of coffee and twenty minutes of peace before I went home and tried to finish everything before Christmas Eve.

"Twyla?"

There she was. In a silvery evening gown and dark fur coat. A man and another woman were with her, the man fumbling for change to put in the cigarette machine. The woman was humming and tapping on the counter with her fingernails. They all looked a little bit drunk.

"Well. It's you."

"How are you?"

I shrugged. "Pretty good. Frazzled. Christmas and all."

"Regular?" called the woman from the counter.

"Fine," Roberta called back and then, "Wait for me in the car."

She slipped into the booth beside me. "I have to tell you something, Twyla. I made up my mind if I ever saw you again, I'd tell you."

"I'd just as soon not hear anything, Roberta. It doesn't matter now, anyway."

"No," she said. "Not about that."

"Don't be long," said the woman. She carried two regulars to go and the man peeled his cigarette pack as they left.

"It's about St. Bonny's and Maggie."

"Oh, please."

"Listen to me. I really did think she was black. I didn't make that up. I really thought so. But now I can't be sure. I just remember her as old, so old. And because she couldn't talk—well, you know, I thought she was crazy. She'd been brought up in an institution like my mother was and like I thought I would be too. And you were right. We didn't kick her. It was the gar girls. Only them. But, well, I wanted to. I really wanted them to hurt her. I said we did it, too. You and me, but that's not true. And I don't want you to carry that around. It was just that I wanted to do it so bad that day—wanting to is doing it."

Her eyes were watery from the drinks she'd had, I guess. I know it's that way with me. One glass of wine and I start bawling over the littlest thing.

"We were kids, Roberta."

"Yeah. Yeah. I know, just kids."

"Eight."

"Eight."

"And lonely."

"Scared, too."

She wiped her cheeks with the heel of her hand and smiled. "Well, that's all I wanted to say."

I nodded and couldn't think of any way to fill the silence that went from the diner past the paper bells on out into the snow. It was heavy now. I thought I'd better wait for the sand trucks before starting home.

"Thanks, Roberta."

"Sure."

"Did I tell you? My mother, she never did stop dancing."

"Yes. You told me. And mine, she never got well." Roberta lifted her hands from the tabletop and covered her face with her palms. When she took them away she really was crying. "Oh, shit, Twyla. Shit, shit, shit. What the hell happened to Maggie?"

Girl

Jamaica Kincaid

1984

Wash the white clothes on Monday and put them on the stone heap; wash the color clothes on Tuesday and put them on the clothesline to dry; don't walk barehead in the hot sun; cook pumpkin fritters in very hot sweet oil; soak your little cloths right after you take them off; when buying cotton to make yourself a nice blouse, be sure that it doesn't have gum on it, because that way it won't hold up well after a wash; soak salt fish overnight before you cook it; is it true that you sing benna[1] in Sunday school?; always eat your food in such a way that it won't turn someone else's stomach; on Sundays try to walk like a lady and not like the slut you are so bent on becoming; don't sing benna in Sunday school; you mustn't speak to wharf-rat boys, not even to give directions; don't eat fruits on the street—flies will follow you; *but I don't sing benna on Sundays at all and never in Sunday school;* this is how to sew on a button; this is how to make a buttonhole for the button you have just sewed on; this is how to hem a dress when you see the hem coming down and so to prevent yourself from looking like the slut I know you are so bent on becoming; this is how you iron your father's khaki shirt so that it doesn't have a crease; this is how you iron your father's khaki pants so that they don't have a crease; this is how you grow okra—far from the house, because okra tree harbors red ants; when you are growing dasheen, make sure it gets plenty of water or else it makes your throat itch when you are eating it; this is how you sweep a corner; this is how you sweep a whole house; this is how you sweep a yard; this is how you smile to someone you don't like too much; this is how you smile to someone you don't like at all; this is how you smile to someone you like completely; this is how you set a table for tea; this is how you set a table for dinner; this is how you set a table for dinner with an important guest; this is how you set a table for lunch; this is how you set a table for breakfast; this is how to behave in the presence of men who don't

[1]Calypso music.

know you very well, and this way they won't recognize immediately the slut I have warned you against becoming; be sure to wash every day, even if it is with your own spit; don't squat down to play marbles—you are not a boy, you know; don't pick people's flowers—you might catch something; don't throw stones at blackbirds, because it might not be a blackbird at all; this is how to make a bread pudding; this is how to make doukona;[2] this is how to make pepper pot; this is how to make a good medicine for a cold; this is how to make a good medicine to throw away a child before it even becomes a child; this is how to catch a fish; this is how to throw back a fish you don't like, and that way something bad won't fall on you; this is how to bully a man; this is how a man bullies you; this is how to love a man, and if this doesn't work there are other ways, and if they don't work don't feel too bad about giving up; this is how to spit up in the air if you feel like it, and this is how to move quick so that it doesn't fall on you; this is how to make ends meet; always squeeze bread to make sure it's fresh; *but what if the baker won't let me feel the bread?;* you mean to say that after all you are really going to be the kind of woman who the baker won't let near the bread?

[2]A spicy plantain pudding.

Chitterling

Henry Van Dyke

1985

I first heard the fat ladies scream in the spring of my twelfth year. I'd come downtown from Harlem that spring to carry off an ill-fated crime at Mrs. Liebman's. Mrs. Sophie Liebman's. On West Fifty-eighth Street. Around the corner from the Plaza.

I rang her buzzer.

"Lambkin," she squealed as she scooped up the yapping dog, the puff of white fur at my feet. "Lambkin, my lambkin, oh, Mama's missed you so." The dog's tongue darted maniacally about the woman's large face; then she said to me, "Well, come in, come in, do."

Mrs. Sophie Liebman had a busy face; some part of it was always in motion. From her forehead to her nose she looked like Claude Rains, with brows both sinister and sophisticated; the lower part of her face, however, was large and horsy and clumsy and it appeared as if she tried every now and then to push this part of her face in alignment with the top part. In addition to her busy face, she wore too much rouge and too much powder and too much perfume, and she said "lambkin" too much.

"I suppose you want," Mrs. Liebman said, fingering the brooch on her bosom, "the reward."

"Yes ma'am," I said meekly, shifty-eyed with shame. Actually, I was more frightened than ashamed; I wasn't experienced in the ways of crime.

"Off! Off!" Mrs. Liebman shouted to her dog, who'd plopped in a fluffy ball upon a red velvet settee. "Lambkin, you *know* Mama's told you not to . . ." She trailed off into an affectionate gurgle as the dog (its name was Adrian) jumped to the floor and she went over to the rosewood desk near the window. "Where," she asked me, "do you live, lambkin?"

I'd been called many things during my twelve years, but never lambkin, and I didn't like it. "Harlem," I told her.

"I mean, where in Harlem exactly."

"Up. On a Hundred Eighteen. Near Eighth Avenue."

Her jeweled fingers did a sluggish twirl in the air. "Really, now? Near the Victoria Bar and Grill?"

I was suddenly alert. I couldn't believe it. "You *know* where the Victoria Bar and Grill is at?"

"No, no, not really. I mean, I've—I've heard of it." She sat at her rosewood desk. "Now, let's see," she said, poking fat, ringed fingers about the clutter on the desktop.

(Weeks later, many weeks later, I learned that Mrs. Liebman was the landlord of a number of tenement buildings around One Hundred Seventeenth and Eighteenth streets and it was not unlikely at all that she'd perhaps heard of the Victoria Bar and Grill—even if it was a rundown, dinky place where number runners hung out.) At that moment, in her lemon and rose apartment, my only thoughts were those of finishing up my business of crime and getting the hell out of there.

Crime, I say. I do not exaggerate. It was not by accident I appeared at Mrs. Liebman's door with her dog (whose name was not lambkin) to seek a reward. I wasn't clever enough to cook up the scheme myself but I certainly was dumb enough to go along with it. Leroy's scheme. And Melvin's. It was, I suppose, largely Leroy's idea, for it was he who'd said, "It's easy, man. These here rich white folks need they dogs walked, see. So we walk 'em, see. Then split."

But I didn't see, I told Leroy. Both he and Melvin were going on sixteen and they both bragged about having spent time in a boys' reformatory upstate. Melvin was the quiet one and the meanest. Leroy was less mean, and he did most of the talking, and he was the one who told me (impatient with my denseness) that once you could convince somebody to walk their dog, you did it—you did it until they trusted you. Then one day, one-two-three, the dog would be stashed away in an apartment up in Harlem. After that, the business part began. The lost-and-found stuff. The negotiating. Leroy and Melvin, expert dog-snatchers, needed me, a younger accomplice, and they told me over and over, "You ain't gonna git in no trouble if you act stupid, stupid."

And it seemed to be working, my stupid act, except—except Mrs. Liebman was writing a check! Neither Leroy nor Melvin could cash a check. And to make matters worse, I could see from her front windows facing Fifty-eighth Street, three stories below, both Leroy and Melvin pacing back and forth on the sidewalk waiting for me and the loot. It occurred to me (as it had only vaguely before) that Leroy and Melvin were capable of grabbing all the money, boxing my ears, and leaving me unrewarded for my troubles.

"Lambkin?" The wiggling of Mrs. Liebman's rhinestone fountain pen stopped and she raised her Claude Rains eyes. "My dear, what is the matter with you?"

Leroy and Melvin had seen me at the window. They'd begun to make obscene and impatient gestures down there on the sidewalk below.

"What is it that—" Mrs. Liebman came over and looked out on the street to see what had made me so fidgety. At first she smiled, and even seemed pleasantly surprised. "Why, those are the very same kids who—" Then she turned to me, the smile gone, and her granite jaw jutted out in anger.

I dashed toward the door, but mounds of chiffon and tulle blocked my exit. Rubies and diamonds and sapphires flashed before me as she pummeled and flung fat hands at my head. "You filthy little beast! You filthy little beast!"

I cried less from the pain than I did out of shame. "They put me up to it," I pleaded. "Honest to God. Honest to God, lady."

She got in a good number of stinging smacks before she stopped, still blocking my exit, and stuck her ringed fingers on her chiffon hips. "I ought to have you put away. All this time my poor lambkin—"

"Please, I'm sorry, lady. I—please, lady . . ."

Whether she saw that my tears were real or whether she suddenly thought of all those acres of slum buildings she owned up on a Hundred and Eighteenth Street, I don't know, but she let her hands fall from her hips and then reached out and drew me to her. "You poor thing . . . poor, poor dear . . . what on earth brought you to this? Hmmm?" She patted my head as if to ease the pain she'd only seconds before inflicted. "Now, come. Come along." She pulled me into her long kitchen and made me sit at a glossy red-topped table.

Soup. With no meat and potatoes in it. It was all right, the soup, but I liked a nice hefty soup like my Aunt Ernestine and Aunt Willa fixed for me at home.

More than anything, I was glad to be able to kill some time: I'd been beaten up once that day and I didn't want another smacking from Melvin and Leroy downstairs. It was the certain knowledge that my partners-in-crime were waiting outside that prompted me to talk and talk and answer her questions—anything to kill time. And questions she did ask. There was no end to them. She wanted to know about my two aunts I lived with, and about my big brother who hung out with the Morningside Heights gang and kept getting into trouble, and about what I learned in school, and about what I wanted to be when I grew up. About everything. I'd never met anybody who could ask so many questions about things I'd always thought to be dull and ordinary. In truth, I wanted to know about *her*—things like why she lived alone, and what she did all day long, and where she got so much money. Years later I've more than once regretted I wasn't aggressive along these lines, for it now strikes me odd how little I really know about Mrs. Liebman, Mrs. Sophie Liebman.

It was getting dark outside and she told me I'd better go. "Surely your aunts will wonder what's happened to you."

"No, they won't," I replied quickly, which was true, but I was thinking more about Melvin and Leroy than I was about my aunts. "Aunt Willa maybe a little bit," I added. "Aunt Ernestine, she don't pay me no never mind anyhow."

Mrs. Liebman suddenly became businesslike. She said, "Come on, don't worry. I'm sure those awful old boys have gone on home by now." She went to the window, looked out, and closed the venetian blinds. "Anyway, I'll give you taxi money."

"But I never done took a taxi in my life, Mrs. Liebman."

"Never taken," she corrected me. "Your language is atrocious. Utterly. Come," she said, kicking off her fluffy slippers (the same color as Adrian's fur) and slipping into a pair of brown sandals, "I'll show you down." Then, after a pause, with her head cocked as if she were listening to something, she said, "There's one condition."

I waited for that condition. She didn't say anything. She moved around over the thick lemon carpet like a soft bear in slow motion; finally she said she'd put me in a taxi if I promised to come back, two days later, to visit her. As an added inducement, she whispered, "I'll have a little present for you." Then, with greater speed than I imagined her capable, she guided me out to the elevator and downstairs, where she told the doorman to fetch a cab.

Before I reached Columbus Circle I paid the driver, got out, pocketed the remaining money, and walked the rest of the way home.

Thursday, after school let out, I walked down Central Park West to Mrs. Liebman's. There was no sign of Leroy and Melvin. The edges of the park were their preying ground, but I did not see them and I crossed my fingers they'd given me up as being hopeless as a go-between and that they'd found another sucker to aid them in their extortion schemes.

When I rang Mrs. Liebman's buzzer, 3E, she opened the door and a cyclone of perfume struck me. She had on a hat. "I told Max to let you come up. You have any trouble?"

Max was her doorman. I had no trouble from him but he'd sniffed a lot and stared at me with cold blue eyes. Adrian barked. He looked as if he'd just been washed. Quickly, I looked around to see if I could spy the present she'd promised.

"Come, then, lambkin, we're off," she said, checking her purse to see if she had her keys, and before I could get my breath or ask any questions, we were flying downtown in a yellow cab to Young Boys Outlet on Fourteenth Street. Her present turned out to be a complete set of clothes, including undershorts. The jacket and pair of pants were okay, I guess, but I thought they looked dumpy and old-fashioned. I downright hated the Buster Brown shoes. Over a cheeseburger and a strawberry milkshake, in a Village café, I began to wonder what Aunt Ernestine and Aunt Willa would say about the clothes Mrs. Liebman had bought; sure as anything, they'd accuse me of stealing them; they'd never believe the truth. I finally spoke up and told Mrs. Liebman I'd have trouble at home.

"Hmmm, I suppose." She toyed with the salt at the rim of her cocktail glass. Her eyebrows turned into bird wings and threatened to fly off her powdered face. "Yes, yes . . . I never thought of that." Then, suddenly, the bird wings above her eyes came to roost and she, with a spurt of energy, lifted her glass and took a deep sip. (Many weeks later I learned that her drink was called a margarita; many years later I went back to try one myself but the little café had turned into a Chinese laundry.) It was, though, at that moment, if I can at all pinpoint it, that I became attached to Mrs. Liebman; I'd found a cohort, for I discovered she was capable of as much duplicity as I. No mere nice old lady she! That Thursday, in the tiny Village café, like espionage agents trading state secrets, we put our heads together—hers over a second margarita, mine over a strawberry milkshake—and mapped out the ground rules, concocted our lie. It amounted to this: I'd keep my new clothes at her apartment; I'd come to visit her each Tuesday and Thursday; she'd give me a small allowance to show my aunts in order to explain my biweekly disappearance; I'd pretend I had a part-time job walking her dog and running errands (which turned out not to be a lie, in any case); and I'd say nothing about riding around in taxis and having cheeseburgers and milkshakes (I didn't know about the snails then) and going to picture galleries.

I soon found the game of it was exciting, and the milieu—such a far cry from my aunts' cockroach-ridden apartment with its odor of urine and collard greens—was as exotic as I imagined Baghdad or Kalamazoo to be. I could hardly wait to leave my drab-penny world of One Hundred Eighteenth Street and enter Mrs. Liebman's realm of thick lemon carpets, porcelain doodads, heavy perfume, and rides in yellow taxicabs.

The night I heard the fat ladies scream I told Aunt Willa a lie: I said Mrs. Liebman's dog was ailing and I had to go to the vet with him and I'd be late getting home. Inasmuch as my school grades had improved (Mrs. Liebman helped me with geography and math) and I brushed my teeth and combed my hair more frequently, I was on the good side of Aunt Willa and she seldom made a fuss. (Also, I suspect both Aunt Willa and Aunt Ernestine had more important things to worry about than my comings and goings: they were worried, I think, that my older brother, Beauregard, had begun to use drugs.)

"Now, just remember," Mrs. Liebman told me as we settled down into the comfortable red seats at the opera house, "Wotan is the father and Brünhilde is his daughter. Okay? She sings the most, Brünhilde does."

As far as I could tell, everybody sang a lot. Screamed really. At one point there were seven or eight ladies, all of them fat, screaming at the same time. The name of the opera Mrs. Liebman had to pronounce for me; it was called *Die Walküre.*

Occasionally, whenever Mrs. Liebman saw that my attention had strayed and I'd begun to squirm in my seat, she bent down and whispered, "It's the *ring,* dear. You see, it's about the *ring.* "

I never saw a ring. Nobody wore one. And it was confusing, too: I knew Hunding was the villain, but I could not get it straight in my mind who Sieglinde was. At intermission I said, "Mrs. Liebman, who is this Fricka?" I pointed to the list of characters on the program.

"Lambkin," she replied—I had the feeling she was speaking to the crowd around us as well as to me—"she's Mrs. Wotan. The king's wife."

"And this one?" I asked, pointing to the program again.

She bent over. She owned glasses but never wore them. "That's Brünhilde, dear. She's the main daughter. She's the one who sings the most."

Her explanation wasn't particularly edifying, but I said brightly, "Oh," as if the mystery were solved, and bent to tie the lace of my Buster Brown shoe. I did not dare ask her about Siegmund, for I knew she'd tell me something that would mix me up more than I already was.

To kill time during the next act, I played silent word games and counted as many heads as I could in front of me. I tried not to fall asleep. Once, I glanced up at Mrs. Liebman and noticed a hazy glaze over her eyes; I knew her mind was not on the opera any more than mine was. I believed her to be imagining that she was Brünhilde herself, marching through the streets of Harlem, with her head high, banishing all the winos and junkies and slum buildings in sight, leaving in her wake a trail of Goodness and Light. . . .

She took pity on me—or herself?—and left the opera house at the next intermission. It was late and I was so tired that I did not bother to go to her place and get out of my Downtown Clothes. As luck would have it, Aunt Willa and Aunt Ernestine were deep in a battle with Beauregard. I sneaked by them, went to my corner of the bedroom, slipped out of my clothes, and hid them. I fell asleep, dreaming of fat ladies screaming.

In early summer when school was over two things happened: Beauregard was sent upstate to a correctional institution, and Mrs. Liebman had a nervous breakdown. I felt guilty that I cared less about Beauregard than I did about Mrs. Liebman. Max, the doorman, who'd become more friendly during the course of my Tuesday and Thursday visits, told me Mrs. Liebman had gone to stay with her daughter in Brooklyn Heights.

"Forever and ever?" I asked, trying not to show my panic.

"Now, now, laddie," Max said, "I guess not forever. It's happened before. She—"

"But *when,* then? When'll she be back?"

Max shrugged. "Her stuff is still up there. She'll probably be back sooner or later." A man in a dark suit and a woman in a lime dress stepped out of the elevator, giggling. The woman said, "Maxie, do be a doll and get us a cab, won't you?" As Max darted toward the curb he said to me, "Okay, kid. Off with you. Run along."

I hurried home and the moment I got into the apartment I asked Aunt Willa, "What's a nervous breakdown? What happens when you get a nervous breakdown?"

Of late, Aunt Willa had become accustomed to my odd inquiries and the dropping of—what must have seemed to her—fancy names. (When I said—not showing off, really—that the graffiti on Brad Johnson's barbershop wall looked like a Max Ernst painting, she replied with *"A who?"*; when I said once—and that time I *was* trying to show off—"Beauregard's behavior is getting most obstreperous," she blinked her large brown eyes and said, "Chile, what kind of talk is that? You pick up that from that white woman you work for downtown?")

This time, though, when I asked Aunt Willa exactly what a nervous breakdown was, she said, not missing a beat, "Honey, it's what I got right now. It's what I've always got. I get up in the morning with my nerves broke down and I go to bed at night with my nerves broke down. You ate? There's some collards in the kitchen if you want."

So Aunt Willa was of no help. Aunt Ernestine had moved back in with her man friend over on St. Nicholas Avenue, but I wouldn't have asked her anyway. Fourteen days went by before I found out what a nervous breakdown really was and that was from Mrs. Liebman herself. (I'd gone down to Fifty-eighth Street every Tuesday and Thursday, only to see Max shaking his head in a quiet "no," even before I reached him, half a block away. Then one day, as he saw me approach, his dour mouth turned into a smile and I knew everything was all right.)

"Don't fret about it, lambkin," Mrs. Liebman told me. "Dr. Sterne gave me some wonderful pills. Divine little pills." She looked as if she'd lost weight, and I noticed she was not wearing any of her rings, but other than that she was exactly the same—her face did busy work, she fluttered around over her lemon carpet, and she picked up Adrian and plopped him down every two seconds or so. "Now. Let's celebrate. I've an idea."

I was so happy to see her, so pleased that my double life had resumed, I might have done anything she requested. And at first I did honestly try to eat them—the snails. We sat in the Plaza. In the Oak Room. We caused quite a stir. Everybody looked at us. Mrs. Liebman loved the attention.

"Es-car-gots," she said, making me repeat the word. I was a little embarrassed because, as was the case in the lobby at the *Die Walküre* intermission, she seemed to be speaking to other people as well as to me.

The piece of rubbery meat looked like a swollen blackhead. I got it down. Just.

"Hmm," she said, extracting with a silver prong the hideous goody from its shell and dipping it into a puddle of garlic and butter. "Celestial, aren't they?

Absolute bliss. Waiter, waiter," she called, pressing butter from her lip, "another margarita, please."

It was during her instructions to the tall, solicitous waiter that I managed (with a sleight of hand I've not ever in my life managed since) to get the snail out of my mouth and into the big soft napkin. I was a bit resentful, too, that I didn't have a frosty-salty drink to wash down the little uglies. I did however have a potted plant at my elbow and I made good use of it: when Mrs. Liebman glanced around the room to see who was watching us, I surreptitiously removed the unchewed snail from my napkin and slung it into the plant. A potted palm, I think it was. This operation was by no means easy, for it apparently gave Mrs. Liebman pleasure to watch me partake of the esoteric delights before us, and she took in my every movement. With a cunning born of sheer necessity, I knew I had to get her mind off me and get her to talk about herself. Without preparation, without finesse, I asked, "Mrs. Liebman, why do you live all alone? Why aren't you married?"

She was startled. She took a margarita sip. "But I am, lambkin. I was. I mean, Jay and I don't get along anymore." She pressed her napkin to her lips and the bird wings above her closed eyes threatened to set out in flight.

Another squiggly went into the potted plant. Three down, three to go.

"You see," she said, "it happens with grown-ups like that sometimes." Then she opened her eyes and I saw for a moment more anger in them than remorse. Then she smiled. "Now, eat up, my dear. You needn't ration them out like that. We can get oodles more if we like."

"No, no." To avert that catastrophe, I quickly said, "They're yummy, Mrs. Liebman, but they're so rich. They fill you up quick, don't they? I never had anything to fill me up so quick—'cept chitlins."

"Chitlins?"

"Yeah, you know, chitlins. Ain't you ever had no chitlins?"

"Haven't you ever had any," she corrected me.

"Haven't you ever had any?" I repeated.

"No, I've never had—and they're chitterlings, my dear. *Chitterlings.* You really must learn to—"

"No, they ain't—aren't. They're chitlins." She was on my turf and I contradicted her, without malice aforethought, without disrespect.

She gave me her Claude Rains look and said evenly, "Chit-ter-lings."

I shook my head. I knew she didn't know what she was talking about because I'd seen "chitlins" written all over the place in stores in Harlem and I'd heard all kinds of people saying "chitlins" all my life. I was angry, and in some vague and obscure way I knew that in the course of the clash our relationship had altered; I was no longer a child and she was no longer a grown woman; we were two people; we'd had, muffled and guarded as it was, our first fight. She must have sensed and understood the transformation of our relationship even more than I, for, after a moment of stiff hesitation, she reached across the table—without humoring me, without placating me—and gently gave my arm a reconciliatory squeeze. To all the world, we might well have been lovers.

I said ungraciously, in my new manhood, "I don't want any more of these." When I saw that I'd hurt her, I quickly added, regretting my cruelty, "They're so *rich*, Mrs. L. They're so *rich.*"

The "Mrs. L." business was a stroke of genius; I'd made amends in aces.

"Of course, darling, of course," she said, and quickly finished off the remaining escargots on my plate.

Naturally, I could not tell her that I was still hungry and wanted more than anything a cheeseburger and a strawberry milkshake, nor did I grumble even once when she took me around the corner to the Paris Cinema to see a French film with subtitles I did not understand one bit.

There was no problem in finding chitlins in Harlem, but I wanted to buy some in a box with the name written on it. Tuesday, before I went downtown again, I found what I needed: LOUELLA'S HOME COOKED CHITLINS. They smelled of butter and garlic. I thought Mrs. Liebman would like them. More important, the square white box had the word *chitlins* printed on it, clear as day.

"I don't think Mrs. Liebman can see you now," Max told me when I arrived at Fifty-eighth Street.

"But it's Tuesday," I protested, the box of chitlins still warm in my hands and reeking of butter and garlic.

"I know, I know, laddie, but—" He pushed back his cap and stood there in silence for a few seconds. "Mrs. Hoffman is—her daughter's up there now." He acted embarrassed and kept fussing with his cap. "Whatcha got in the box?"

"A—a present," I told him.

Max took the box of chitlins and tapped me on the shoulder. "I'll get it to her."

"But—"

Max left me as if he had no time for an argument. I went to the pay telephone on the corner and got no satisfaction there either; a high-pitched voice said, "No, this is Anna Hoffman. Mother is—Mother is indisposed. I'll have her call you." She hung up. I replied to the voice, which had disappeared, "Lady, I ain't got no telephone."

That afternoon I sat in Morningside Heights Park and stared at the shadows in the sunlight. At night I lay awake in bed. Wednesday I did the same thing. When I got downtown on Thursday, Max said, "She doesn't live here anymore." He had changed back into his uppity ways I remembered from our first meetings. "Wait. Here's a package for you."

It was wrapped in brown paper. A string was around it. There was an envelope on top.

"Okay, kid, you can't loll around here in the lobby." The elevator door opened. Some people came out. "All right, run along, I tell you."

My Downtown Clothes and Buster Brown shoes were in the package. The note was from Mrs. Liebman. It said, *Lambkin, thank you for the chitterling. Mrs. L.*

Chitterling! If my throat had not been so tight, I'd have cursed more than I did. In some irrational attempt to get even, I dumped the clothes and shoes in a Central Park trash basket.

I took the note to the library with me.

But Webster's dictionary turned out to be a traitor as well; it offered me three choices: over and over, I read *chitterlings or chitlings or chitlins.* Had Mrs. Liebman been as right as Aunt Willa and all of Harlem? I looked at the note again: *Lambkin, thank you for the chitterling. Mrs. L.* Maybe she'd had only one bite. Was one bite a chitterling?

Now, many years later, I've acquired a taste for escargots, and somewhere along the way I've lost interest in chitlins, and I even own four Kirsten Flagstad recordings, but I've not told Mrs. Liebman this; I was never again to see her after that afternoon at the Plaza.

Jesus and Fat Tuesday

Colleen J. McElroy

1987

Plaisance had stomped past the double RECEIVING doors and down the hall when the cops brought Maggie Boujean into ARC. We'd only been on duty for half an hour when Maggie arrived, and aside from a soldier they'd snatched off a Greyhound bound for Gulf Port, a D-and-D who had messed over a whole bus load of passengers and was still sleeping after being pulled in during the afternoon shift, Maggie was the first casualty on the ward that night. Before she arrived, I figured to have an easy night of it, so I'd let Plaisance make the waiting room his center stage. Then the cops burst through the doors, noisy as usual—sometimes noisier than the drunks they dragged in behind them. Not that Maggie Boujean needed any additional racket, but all the hoo-ha the cops made trying to get her out of the car and into the lobby had forced Plaisance to cut his conversation short.

He had been in the middle of one of his man-to-man talks with me; that is, I was the dude listening and he was the fool talking. The problem with Plaisance was that he believed all that shit folks told him about Blacks and Cajuns being great lovers, so every time I turned around, he was trying to get me to slip him the skinny on what women needed so he could score. Like the other day when he said, "Touti, I was doing this piece when she put the squeeze on me so tight, I think my balls they gonna fall off. This happened to you sometime, Touti?" I said, "Man, how come you always got to be asking me some shit about screwing? Black folks don't want to be talking about screwing all the time, man."

Now and again, I'd let him talk me into cruising with him. It didn't make any difference that most times when we'd tried hustling together, women had all but laughed in our faces. Plaisance wasn't a quitter. Mostly I kept to myself. But if he wasn't talking tail, he was talking fast money and how it must be that I know where the two of us could make some of it. That was the one thing he had in common with my mother. She was a woman who didn't want nobody to bring her no bad news. Didn't matter if her bad news was somebody else's good news, she still didn't want to hear it. So when half of Pointe Coupee Parish struck it rich with oil, and we didn't own enough land to even sink a dry hole, my mama wouldn't let us mention the VasCo Corporation in the house. *Don't make no difference if we can't smell money, Toulouse. That money be in the ground. Ain't nobody gone give you nothing. What you want, you got to take it, boy. It's right here in Pointe Coupee, Touti. Right here in front of your nose. You got to make the good times roll. Listen to you mama, Touti.*

Next to my mother, Plaisance was the only person I knew who thought it was a God-given duty to talk some sense into me. The night Maggie Boujean showed up at the ARC, Plaisance's "good sense" had to do with trying to make me turn slick so we could hit it big during Mardi Gras. He'd been working on that idea for nearly two weeks, and he had a week left before New Orleans went on its annual ape-shit spree. I wasn't buying, but that didn't stop Plaisance. To him, New Orleans was Mardi Gras, and Mardi Gras was a good way to make money off a bunch of fools trying to be hot shots with nothing in their pockets but chicken scratch. He claimed it was easy pickings if you got bold enough. That was surely another thing he had in common with my mama. *Standing there smiling won't even catch you a toothache,* she'd tell me. But I hadn't left Pointe Coupee Parish to dance jim-jack on some New Orleans street corner. A good job was good enough until I could figure my own ways and means.

Still, I let him talk. His noise was no skin off my nose. And before Maggie arrived, all the noise had belonged to Plaisance. I would have had no luck trying to tell him I'd already heard most of the nonsense he was spouting, so I had just been letting him eat up some time until he got tired. Mostly, I didn't trouble myself with his words; I simply watched his face, contented myself with noting how he fit his lips around the words he made. *Lip service,* Mama had called it. *You can tell a lot about folks that way.* I had figured out what kind of dude Plaisance was before he opened his mouth. Three years I'd been working with him, and I wasn't impressed one diddley-damn with what I'd seen in that time. His face full of bad skin gave me all the history I needed to tell me why he resented having been born on that skinny stretch of Delta he called home. Now, the way he told it, he was out, in the big city, but I knew he spent most of his time scared that he'd have to go back.

"They always ready for to take you home, Touti," he'd say. Didn't matter how many times I told him he had to have something to go back to, he simply didn't see the world my way. He viewed working in the alcoholic recovery ward as a sign of failure. That had been his pitch before the cops busted through the door.

"They gone keep you here till the Bayou been sucked back to the sea, man. Folks like us—Cajun folks, black folks, even big-time Creoles—we all the same to them. Me and you, we got nothing. They make money, Touti, but all we gone get is white hairs." He'd patted his belly. "Mardi Gras coming. We make it our day, eh, Tooti? We get a scam, eh? They make Lent come Fat Tuesday, and we make like fat cats come Lent."

I'd let him have his fill of saying that shit, then tried to change the subject away from that same argument I'd heard back home. Even after VasCo pulled in three wells in two months, folks around my neighborhood had ragged about getting the short end of the stick. Even after they could stop picking pecans and start stuffing croker sacks with hard cash, they were still scared some white man was going to come along and rip them off. That's the problem with being born black and poor in a country that expects you to stay black and poor. Folks see your color long before they see your money. I had to shake my head to keep from thinking about it, but if I closed my eyes, Plaisance's ragging didn't sound much different from what I'd always heard. *Make something of yourself, boy.* The same-old same-old, just a change of names, I thought.

Plaisance had been on my case all night, and right when the cops shoved open the doors, he'd pumped his fist into the air and said, "You don't watch it, Touti, they hump you like some ol' stray dog. Take your stuff from you when your back is turned." He was still pumping air when the cops burst in. They stared, but Plaisance flashed his brown-toothed grin and left the lobby. And while I listened to the protesting stomp of Plaisance's departing feet, Maggie Boujean, bleary-eyed and clothed like a bat out of hell, came lurching into my life.

And she started on me as soon as she reached the desk. "Jesus done been here and gone," she slurred. Then both patrolmen let her slip to the floor, the two of them so eager to release her into my custody, they simultaneously reached for the admitting papers.

"Been here and *gone,*" she repeated in a louder voice. One of the officers attempted to pull her upright, and Maggie thanked him by spewing a thin stream of bile onto his shirt. The cop yelled, *"Shit!"* and let her go, while I looked anxiously toward the RECEIVING doors that seconds before had held big-butt Plaisance, the only person who was bound by job description to clean up behind Maggie. At least I could make him clean up unless his objections to doing dirty work forced me to grab bucket and mop rather than hear one more explanation of, "This one Cajun they got to pay twice fore spring till he work so hard."

I quickly walked around the desk and lifted Maggie to her feet. "Let me get you a chair," I coaxed. The cop wiped his shirt as I steered clear of the brown spittle that trailed off the end of Maggie's left arm, but he made no attempt to help me raise her off the floor. Not that I needed his help.

"Where's the doctor?" he asked.

Maggie heaved again and I tilted her bony shoulders away from me, wincing as the motion hurled vomit against the connecting rim of the counter and the floor. This would certainly bring some bit of unwelcome philosophy from Plaisance, I thought. I turned my head as the liquid spread in a thin line along the Rubbermaid rim of the baseboard—an expensive donation from some fee-bleminded politician in lieu of more staff and, by Plaisance's calculation, the hardest place to clean in the entire damn hospital. Yeah. I was destined to hear a few of Plaisance's choice words.

"Can't you get a doctor?" the cop insisted.

"Doctor ain't here," I told him. "This time of night, all you got is orderlies. This time of night, any doctor with sense is home in bed."

Maggie slid from the chair and whacked her head against the counter before I could catch her.

"It's a sin what a body can do to itself," the cop muttered. His buddy, the one who had escaped Maggie's reconstituted booze, grunted an eager, "Un-huh," then asked me how to spell *delirium.* I plopped Maggie into the seat a final time and signed Dr. Ann Garcia's name to the forms, blessing the good doctor with the insight of never once, in ten years of my employment, having checked to see where I placed her signature. Then I wordlessly handed them their route copies of the admittance papers. As the cops left, I overheard one of them say, "Either that nigger is a dummy or he's got a stick up his ass. Put a white coat on some colored folks and they forget their place." I knew my place enough to keep Maggie from throwing up all over me, I thought, as I buttoned my lab jacket.

"Eh, Touti. How they make us work now, eh?"

I silently swore this would be the last time I'd let Plaisance sneak up on me. I usually had to swear that at least twice a week. "Don't call me Touti," I said.

"Big Toot." He laughed. "When we gonna bust out of here? We get somebody with dice, eh? With cards? I know your people roll the snake eyes like that." He snapped his fingers.

I said, "Buzz off, man," and stretched Maggie across two chairs. "Just get that crap cleaned off the floor, Plaisance. I'm gonna check the ward for bed space."

"You think we need to call Garcia?" he asked. "They don't like it if we take this old bag's clothes off and we got no female interning."

"Don't sweat it," I told him. "Let Dr. Garcia stay at home. This old bag can sleep with her clothes on. By the looks of her, she's used to it."

Maggie was snoring almost before the blanket settled around her. And she would have been comfortably situated in the ward if the next half hour had run smoothly, but ten minutes after the first two cops disappeared, another team brought in a kid yelling and screaming about bats and vampires, and we never got a chance to put Maggie in a room. Both Plaisance and I had our hands full tying the kid down and mopping up after him. The newcomer was a thin-faced boy about twenty-two, and so pretty he could have been a girl, except his silk slacks were tight and full in all the right places, and he had enough muscles to carry his own weight with any man: that is, if he stayed sober and off the streets long enough. He had the kind of body some movie type could turn into a hot property and fast money. I looked at the tightness of his biceps as he pulled both me and Plaisance off balance and decided he was probably into fancy weights and jogging. He was the kind of kid who could bust a French Quarter party and make the host apologize for the trouble he'd gone through to get in.

"Just be cool," I said as he arched his back and tried to buck free of us. "The party's over, kid." I almost had him down when he grabbed my arm and pulled himself up until his face was inches away from mine. His lips moved, wordlessly, but his eyes were closed. Suddenly his eyes opened, flat and unfocused, and he began a howl that I swore was going to last longer than any man could hold his breath. His pupils were so wide, all I could see in the panic of his eyes was my own reflection. "Just be cool, kid. Go to sleep," I said, then ducked as he took a swipe at me.

"Cajun," Plaisance grunted. "Somebody been giving him thin drinks." Then he sniffed the kid's breath and looked at the lower rim of his eyes. "Little bit of smack too, eh? Uptown," he snarled as the boy fought us again. Plaisance straddled the kid's legs and removed his shoes. "Italian leather," he said and grunted again.

Even his toes had been manicured. "Mardi Gras gonna be good to him if he sobers up." I laughed. "He's so bad, betcha they match those shoes and don't put nothing but Italian olives in that booze they feeding him. Nothing but the best for this custom model."

Plaisance gave me a look he reserved for doctors and middle-class drunks. I decided to make myself scarce.

I was in no mood to show Plaisance the connection between one thought and another. That would take more time than we had left on the shift. He deliberately wouldn't understand what olives had to do with a good-looking Cajun drunk any more than he really understood what Mardi Gras had to do with Lent. Like most white folks, he got thick-skinned if he had to hear the truth from the black side of the fence. If I pinned him to the wall on some of that hokey crap about black folks that he'd learned in school, he'd beg off talking. "So much thinking make it hurt," he'd say, then let his eyes turn into little hard black dots and he'd look like one of those bull-mouthed river-bottom fish stacked face up in the open market.

What saved Plaisance from being really ugly was his Clark Gable mustache. You know, that kind of slick, bad-dude gambler's dust mop that looked like it was painted on. The way he kept it shaped, some folks overlooked that mess of thick black hair on his head . . . and chest, and arms, and neck. Plaisance was just one hairy dude. Ape-man, I called him when we hosed down after the shift.

Without his clothes, you could really say that Plaisance was into hair shirts. And the hair on his head was clumped up like lumps of overcooked spaghetti. Thinking about his hair made me rub my own head. When my fingers got tangled, I decided I'd better get a haircut soon. Hair and gut. We were a pair, all right. Both of us fat and unable to sleep nights—that's why we made such a good ward team—but Plaisance's mustache made him look smarter than he was. Underneath all that Hollywood front, he was dumb and stubborn. I had a better chance of watching the wind whip up his greasy hair than I did of seeing him change his opinion. And he always thought he could wear me down by talking.

In a pinch, I could throw him off guard. I'd tell him his problem was that he didn't understand jazz. I'd say, "Plaisance, jazz is something you got to listen to. Lookit, it ain't what they play, it's what they don't play that makes the music rock. You know . . . not just some loud keyboard shit, but how they let you wait for the next sound, then don't play what you expect. You got to fill in for yourself. You got to learn to wait, to ride with it. Slip in and over what you hear." But Plaisance said he wanted regular music, that old country thump-thump Delta banjo music. "So you know where you going and where you been," he'd say.

I was back at the desk when I heard Plaisance leaving the boy's room. The ward grew quiet again. It was surely a slow night. I thought about the jazz concert that was coming up that next weekend and hitched my belt a notch tighter. I'd been on duty for nearly two hours. Six more shifts and four hours on this desk before I could lose myself in Freddie Hubbard's sounds. I reached for papers I had to fill out before the night was over. If I'd had Plaisance's view of the world, I'd have been able to disappear in a trail of bad words and reappear only when the situation reached disaster, but as it was, my timing had never been under my control. I'd just settled down to work at the desk when Maggie woke up.

Some patients I never really get to know, and some I know too well—drunk or sober, whether I want to know them or not. Maggie Boujean selected the chair with the busted bottom and fixed me with her eyes, two bleary headlights centered in a face that was so boozy yellow, her skin looked like a beeswax mask or an old onion peel. But her expression suggested she knew too much about me already. I tried fixing my own face with a look that said I was bored with drunks who had nothing better to do than test my good manners. I found myself wishing for a mustache like Plaisance's, or maybe even a beard, anything to hide from Maggie's shrimp-eyed stare.

"I seen Jesus tonight," she announced.

"We got a kid in there seeing vampires. Maybe you ought to talk to him," I said.

She leaned forward and began to speak slowly, shaping every word as if, by being deliberate, she could fool me into thinking she was also sober. "I-said-*Jesus,*" she repeated. "In-Heavenly-light," she said. Then she leaned back, smiling as if she'd just discovered sentences, and satisfied that she had kept a string of sounds from tumbling into the wrong words.

I shook my head. I wasn't fooled. Her voice was soft and quiet. Too soft. I'd never known a woman to go soft in voice unless she had something directly in mind. I watched her trying to keep her expression attached to the loose flesh of her face, then her features lost some of their alcoholic fuzziness and turned accusing, like a cop about to give a ticket when a warning would have served the same purpose. Or like she was thinking of some Marie Laveau voodoo spell to put on me.

"I seen Jesus," she chanted. "Seen him."

I waited.

"Standing in front of his flying saucer and it all golden with light."

I'd been suckered again! Years of working on this job, and I'd been suckered like a catfish baited on cornbread, like a tourist buying an original Basin Street tambourine. Then I heard Plaisance behind me.

"If I could see Jesus . . ." he sang, "could see him walk . . ."

I hoped that by not turning around, he'd think I wasn't listening, but Plaisance was still warmed by the idea of calming down that Cajun kid, so he walked over and put his arm on my shoulder.

"Could see Jesus make all the good folks talk . . ."

I found a reason to pick a wad of paper off the floor. Next to having him sneak around all the time, my second problem with Plaisance was his need to always touch me—grab my hand, slap my shoulder, or pat my ass. He claimed it was in his blood, but Cajun or not, folks don't have to get that close all the time.

"She needs a ward bed," I told him before he could start singing again.

"She get the best one, eh, Touti?" He grinned as if we'd been waiting the whole night for Maggie Boujean.

"Don't make no never mind if it's the best one or not. Just get one," I said.

". . . could nat'chully make folks down here walk," Plaisance sang, then slapped the floor with his mop and whanged through the swinging doors. "I see you in a minute, Big Toot," he said.

Maggie watched me take a deep breath. "I had a husband like that." She laughed. "Stubborn and no-carrified. Had to paint him white."

"*White?*" I knew I'd heard the word, but I repeated it anyway. It was like looking for a sock or something you'd lost that was supposed to be only in one place. You figure if you keep looking in that place, you'll change what you see and find that sucker. I figured if I said the word again, I could keep Maggie from making some kind of stupid racist remark. "*White?*" I said again.

"I told him." She grinned. "I said: Mess with me one more time and I'll make sure you get your just rewards. Woulda painted him red, but didn't have no red paint."

Well, shit, I thought, that ain't exactly racist. Not yet anyway. But I still wasn't winning. "Red?" I whispered.

"Yeah," she said, like she was telling me what any fool would know about red. "Well, what the hell," she said. "Don't you think red would have been better, seeing as how my old man wasn't going nowhere but down there with Lucifer nohow? But I couldn't find me no red, so . . . white it was."

For a moment, I actually had tried to follow her, then I realized I'd been leaned into the deadly combination. "Booze and logic," Dr. Garcia would say. "Put them together and the whole world goes to shit." I glared at Maggie, but I finally managed to close my mouth and point my finger at her the way my mother used to do when I had fat-mouthed once too often. There are only two ways you can talk to a drunk: you can either play charades and say the magic word or you silence them with death threats. Maggie understood my threat right away and leaned back in her chair. I knew my night would not return to normal until I got her into a ward, but I could hear that dime-a-dance Cajun kid screaming into the alcohol that was stuck in his system, and I knew that right now Plaisance would be too busy to find Maggie a bed. I started shuffling papers, looking official while I brought myself under control.

I pulled a blank chart from the files and settled down to pass the time. "If they're talking in here, they can't be drinking out there in the street," Dr. Garcia would say. "That's our job. Keeping them off the street and getting them sober." I watched Maggie as I straightened the papers in the clipboard. Garcia must have gotten her patience from growing up in Casper, Wyoming, because what I read in Maggie's New Orleans eyes told me sober hadn't been a part of her vocabulary for a long time.

"You're my best intern, Toulouse. You know how to listen," Dr. Garcia would say.

I told myself that one day I was going to have to explain to that lady doctor that all I knew to do was not say anything. That wasn't the same as listening. That wasn't the same as that blue-eyed patience she used when folks opened up to her. What I had was what most Southern folks have, especially black folks. I'd had time to learn how to close my eyes on what was really happening and let all kinds of secrets slip by me. But with Maggie sitting there, I picked up my pen and readied myself with the questions the good doctor had taught me to use.

"You fill out your papers yet?" I asked.

Maggie looked stupid. "Did you slip me some when I come in here?"

"I got some forms here," I said, holding up the clipboard. "I got some questions to ask."

Maggie smiled. "Ain't met many colored folks ask me nothing, but I don't mind if you ask me some. Pretty black man like you could ask me anything."

I stroked my chin and thought again of growing a mustache. "Well, I got some questions for you."

"I'm ready," Maggie said, and that was the last time I had to urge her on. Once she got the hang of it, no official forms could have held the answers she gave to any one question.

She was a farm girl, if you could call sandbag bayou country farmland. Took care of chickens, she said. "When I gathered eggs, I'd cluck. *Chee*-chick-chick-*chee*. Could cluck them eggs right out of their asses." She laughed.

Maggie's laugh damn near rocked the walls. I cocked my ear to make sure the boy in the ward was finally going under, but the only sound I heard was the faint scratch of cicadas snapping away at the sweet March night that seeped under the outside doors. And I could smell Plaisance's evening meal heating up on the burners in the back room—cayenne peppers and bay in day-old fish stock. Somewhere near the south end of the ward, I heard Plaisance's mop slapping as he dipped it from his bucket of pine-blue water and flung it against the corridor's walls. But nothing seemed to be reacting to Maggie's laughter. I eased back to the questionnaire and chose another one of those red tape standards, the bit about next of kin and permanent address. Maggie took it to heart.

Her father beat her, she told me. Came back to the farm every night with his string of fish and his gut ready for drinking. He'd raped her too, she added. More than once, and afterwards, if I could believe her, took her to church to say confession. "Got the booze from my mama," she said. "But didn't get nothing from my old pappy but shit. Still, I'm luckier than some. Seen a lot worse off than me. You know that's the truth, don't you?"

I grunted. More because I'd learned to grunt no matter what the question. I grunted and let her talk. Sometimes I listened; sometimes I didn't. I already knew the story and a dozen versions like it, but when my attention wandered, she'd fix me with her eyes.

It was Maggie's shifting gaze that let me know someone had entered the waiting room.

For a second, I didn't understand Maggie's signal. I thought she was punctuating some seamy part of her story about her daddy, or her old man, and how she'd sent him painted on his way to hell and glory. Then I heard a voice, and though I could not understand the words, I turned. I was still trapped in Maggie's world of dirt farmers and home brew, but I began to focus until finally I realized the woman staring back at me was my sister, Lacey.

"Weasel," I said, as if I'd been calling out to her every day for the last ten years. "You're here," I said, as if I'd unlatched a door and all the shit I thought I'd stored away had started falling toward me. I hadn't heard the ward doors open, hadn't heard her footsteps or any change in the way the air smelled. She was just there, staring at me. Her face made the memories of all those years I had in my head seem like something that had happened yesterday. It was like looking into my own face—a little smoother, a little older than my thirty-four years, but mine—the same dark brown skin, the same long nose and heavy eyebrows. Mama's face. The face of Pointe Coupee Parish.

I would have been less surprised to see Dr. Garcia standing there in housecoat, hair curlers, and hiking boots, carrying a fishing rod baited with one of her famous hand-tied flies. I would have even accepted Plaisance's latest woman leaning on the arm of a red-necked sheriff, or better yet, his woman come to tell the truth about all those Saturday nights he'd claimed. But no, I faced my own dear sister, standing there looking like swamp bait with her hair as ratty as an unmade bed and her clothes rumpled from sitting on a Greyhound. And if I knew my sister at all, her knees and hands rough from doing day work. Lacey had been born old and bent into habit, and, like Mama, she'd kept to it, pulling her hour wages no matter how many wells VasCo struck for folks lucky enough to own land. *The luck of the draw,* Mama had laughed when the money passed us by. *Lincoln gave colored folks forty acres and a mule. All I got was the goddamn mule,* she'd said, laughing at me. The only time she hadn't laughed was when I'd left home. With that thought, I went from Mama to money to all the reasons I'd put ten years between me and my family. "Weasel," I said again, this time, whispering her name as if the sound would make her disappear.

I looked down at the clipboard. None of the questions covered this, so I placed it carefully on the counter and hitched up my pants. Nothing could have brought Lacey here except Mama. I knew I hadn't summoned her up, had not called her by letter or Vieux Carré voodoo spirit. So surely the only way she'd arrived to see me was because of Mama. Here was my sister come to track down the renegade, the no-account runaway son. I looked up. Looking into Lacey's face was harder than sidestepping a drunk who was bursting through the fog of a minus blood-sugar count. Except I wasn't nearly ready to see through the fog that covered Lacey's eyes.

"Ain't you got enough trouble without coming here?" I asked.

"Mama's dead," she said in a flat voice.

"She's where?" I asked, and we both heard the stupidity in that question.

"Mama's dead," Lacey repeated.

"Dead?"

"Mama's dead so you can come home now, Toulouse," she added.

I shrugged and straightened up the papers in the clipboard again. For a second, Lacey was silent, but when she opened her mouth to speak, I spread out my arms. I had to say something, but I needed to remember more than what you say when a drunk goes off on you. Still the best I could do was, "Home is where you hang your hat. Home is where people want to see you when you get there. Home . . ." My mouth dried up.

"Folks need to get home," Maggie interrupted.

"Who's that?" Lacey asked.

Lacey's voice was still flat, as if she were ready to fill it with accusations. I leaped at the chance to divert her attention. "That's Maggie," I told her. "Maggie Boujean, lately of the ARC." I said it as if Maggie were more family than Lacey, as if saying Maggie's name might keep me from saying the wrong name, keep the ARC in focus, keep Lacey from telling me again what she'd just said.

When Lacey said Maggie's name, she added a soft curl to her voice. "Maggie Boujean, eh? Your new lady friend, brother? Something you want to tell me about?"

It was the last question that stopped me, the tone of it, the way she made her voice turn into Mama's in just a few words. *I ain't gone never act like Mama,* she'd once told me. But then, she'd also said, *Mama's dead,* saying *Mama* as if she expected me to still know who that was, and *dead . . .*

Ten dogs for every boy like you, Mama had laughed. I was ten years old, in the tree outside her bedroom window. *Come on in here, boy,* she'd said. *You can stay out there all night and tomorrow, and that dog ain't never gonna come back. It's dead. Say it. Say That dog done died, and come on in here.* I'd put my head down, gulping air, holding onto the tree as if it would keep me alive. *Come on down from there, you hear me? Come on down. A black man ain't got that much time to be making up his mind, so you get on down from that tree.* My head was full of drowning but my mother stretched out her arms to help me to safety. At the bottom of the tree, there was Lacey.

"What you gone do?" Lacey asked. She was talking louder now. Almost shouting to cover Maggie's sobbing.

I stared at both of them. Women. I shook my head.

"I got two boys out there somewheres," Maggie sputtered. "Cutest damn babies you ever saw."

I knew drunks cried over everything and nothing at all. Half of what you did in D-tox was waiting out a drunk's need to cry. But Maggie had been sitting there, talking so easily, looking so much a part of ARC, like a piece of equipment, her crying seemed out of place. "Don't," I pleaded.

"Damn it, man," Lacey snapped. "I said your mama's dead and you begging this white woman not to cry. Don't you understand me?"

"Mama sent me away. Told me not to come back," I said.

"Well, she's dead now," Lacey said, and Maggie cried, "Dead. Dead."

"Told me I wasn't nothing to speak of. Said I couldn't hold my own. Wanted to stay in my room too much. Let folks tell me what to do. Said I was scared. Said—"

"Will you shut the hell up!" Lacey shouted.

"My babies," Maggie wept. "My babies. Send them letters when I can. Gone now. Gone. . . ."

Lacey and I stared at each other and Maggie began to seriously howl. At least somebody was crying, I thought.

"You tell me right now what you gonna do," Lacey demanded.

She waited, but I couldn't bring myself to form the right words. Now Maggie was blubbering about God and her family and how a woman's got to do what she'd got to do to keep going in this world. I remembered my mama talking, loud and full of herself—my daredevil of a mother, my double-dog-dare-you and I'm-disappointed mother. Always pushing but always there to help, even when I didn't need it. Reciting *Hiawatha* to me and Lacey when we couldn't get past some bullshit story about the antebellum South for a seventh grade test. She'd memorized the first part and all we did was to fall asleep giggling about our half-Indian neighbors. And Mama doing the Charleston on Saturday nights in the living room, just before the fire burned out, her big frame loose with the movement of dancing and drinking, and some dude come in from the mill on False River with a pocket full of money and a weekend to spend it. I thought of her catching the snake I needed for fifth grade show-and-tell. Catching it in a pickle jar and sealing the jar tight until the snake turned pale in the moonshine gin, thin and papery like the vegetables she canned one summer and left too long on the back porch. My daredevil mother. My don't-need-you mother.

"Bus for Pointe Coupee leaves at seven. You tell me what you gonna do, brother." Lacey waited. "You got family back home, like it or not," she added.

Between them two women, that boy don't need no father.

"Don't seem I got much to speak of by way of family now," I said.

"Faith ain't nothing for a woman," Maggie muttered. "Look at the Bible. Turned the wife into a pillar of salt just cause the lady had curiosity. What kinda God turns people to salt cause they got the balls to look for something?"

"I guess I better tell them you ain't coming home," Lacey said.

I still couldn't get my mouth to work.

Maggie snorted. "Who's to say? Specially since the husband was the one who told the wife not to look back. Well, hell, don't that make sense? Course she had to look back. What kinda wife would let her old man tell her what to see?"

Lacey looked around the waiting room, then narrowed her eyes at me. "You still playing that same old game, huh? Stuck in this rat hole with some fools cause you can't flash no dollar bills. I thought when you left home, you was gonna get rich overnight. Thought you was gonna be some black Horatio Alger. Some big superstar with Motown albums and suede underwear."

"What you talking about? That's Mama's talk."

Lacey shrugged. "Could be, but I still see you stuck in this dump, poor as ever." She looked at the way my belly bulged against my belt buckle. "Thought you was gonna be the next Fats Waller, gonna do the boogie-woogie piano like Big Maceo."

"I'm working here," I said. "Got me a job and don't have to *be* nothing but working. You see me working here, don't you?"

"I didn't ask you about no job. I'm asking you about all that big-time dreaming you did back home. You remember all that dreaming about the good life, don't you? Told me it was the American way."

"I got nothing to say."

Lacey pursed her lips. "That's always been your trouble, brother. You always got nothing to say and won't listen to folks who try to talk some sense into you."

"Why I got to listen? Wasn't nowhere for me to go, back home. Always on top of me. Acting like I got to make up for what they ain't never had. I told her: You ain't responsible for my happiness. I told her: I got to make my own way. But she was always on me, asking for something. I couldn't hear myself think for listening to her mouth. And half the time, I didn't even know what she wanted from me." I stopped. My own voice was beginning to fill up too much of my head.

"Mama never asked you for nothing, Toulouse. She never asked cause she knew she was never gonna get it."

"Men always leaving women to do by themself," Maggie cried.

"Shut up," Lacey told her. Then she turned on me. "You ain't changed, brother. Everybody's fault but yours. I just come to see for myself. I knew you'd find out she was dead sooner or later, but I just wanted to see if you had any forgiving in you. Should've saved myself the trip, Toulouse. You still holed up like always." She looked around the room. "Seems fitting for you. A place to sack out and crazy folks to waste your time. But don't you worry none. Pointe Coupee can bury Mama without you. Ain't no reason for you to come home now."

I sorted forms, and the noise of the papers almost drowned out Maggie's crying.

If Plaisance hadn't entered the room at that moment, I wouldn't have known Lacey was near the door. "Somebody go home now, eh, Touti?" Whatever Lacey saw in Plaisance made her lips tight. He tried brushing aside her look. "You stay," he told her. "We make him show you a good time. Find us some easy money, eh?"

"I had all the good times I need," Lacey said, and turned again, but she stood there for a moment when I called out to her.

"Weasel, I can try to make it home next week," I said.

She shrugged. "Don't bother on my account," she said, then she walked into the sweet-smelling spring night. This time she shoved the doors open wide and the antiseptic air of the ARC fought with the night flowers for a while before the doors choked off their scents. Then the latches clicked and the outside world no longer existed. I breathed again.

Plaisance was laughing. When he saw my expression, he stopped. *Half a mind,* Mama had said. *Half a mind makes half a mouth.*

I nodded toward Maggie. "Get her into a ward, Plaisance."

"Touti, how come you never ask this boy, eh? Shee-et! For you, Cajun just work." Then he motioned Maggie toward the south ward.

"What kinda God won't let you turn back?" Maggie asked. "What kinda God turn you to salt?"

The World of Rosie Polk

Ann Allen Shockley

1987

I

The hot afternoon sun, inflating the summer sky of 1952, made a sheath of flat, scorching heat rise and fall against her with the jerking movements of the truck. Rosie had been riding all day and night with the others crammed against her, the smell of unwashed bodies and acrid breaths piercing her nostrils like a privy. She knew it was worse for the ones in the middle, cramped in by more heat and odors. Because she had been among the first to join Big Ernest's crew back in Virginia, she had a choice place at the side of the truck, where nothing was in front of her except the wooden railing that fenced them in like cattle. Between the makeshift bars, she could see the asphalt of Highway 13, lanced on each side with sprawling farmland. The fields were ripe for picking now. The migrant season was in full bloom.

She twisted her head to look through the rear window of the truck to see how Big Ernest was doing, driving all that distance by himself. He was bent hard over the wheel of the ancient Chevy, as if his clinched position would certainly keep the truck moving. The black derby hat, which he always wore, was cocked low over his eyes, and the usual unlit cigar was clamped wetly in his wide mouth. She often wondered why he just didn't chew tobacco instead of a lifeless tube. Someone once told her that he kept a gun in the truck to keep anybody dissatisfied from jumping off. As far as she knew, nobody ever tried to jump off, and nobody messed with Big Ernest.

Rosie pulled her large straw hat lower over her face to shield the lined brownness of it against the sun. She was only thirty-four, but her stiff, crinkled hair was graying rapidly, and the jaws of a previously handsome, strong face now had sunken hollows from the absence of teeth removed long ago and never replaced. She had once been tall and straight as an oak tree. Now, from the stoopwork of picking, lifting, and dragging in the fields, her shoulders were rounded, but not so much as those of some of the women on the truck. Lord, she thought, trying to exercise her stiff muscles in the limited body space, what the fields that birth beans, tomatoes, peas, and corn can do to a person. Somehow, she had still managed to hold on, due to the strength in her back, if nothing else. She had to, for this was her life: the few weeks in the year when she earned her living bent to pick the food from the land.

"God, it's hot!" a female voice complained, startling her, reminding her that these humans beside her did speak.

"Sho' is," Rosie agreed, looking down at Maybelline sprawled heavily on a stool much too small for her obese size. On account of being unable to stoop any longer in the fields, Maybelline went along to cook the food, wash clothes, and mind children too young to become field weeds arched like sickles in the images of their parents. Everybody liked jovial, yellow Maybelline. They liked her booming laughter rising straight and honest from her guts, her raucous manner with the men, and knowledgeableness with the women. Maybelline could stop fights, wipe away tears, and bring the sunshine of the Lord into the private pits of hell. Since they wanted Maybelline to ride in comfort, they found her a stool from a trash heap to sit on, while they slumped upon the piles of blankets, crates, and cardboard suitcases that housed their possessions, or stood until they could stand no more—the children, women, and men.

"I hope it don't rain. I didn't make but twelve dollars last week pickin' them strawberries on old man Grimes's farm. He's too stingy to pay more'n ten cents a quart. And him sellin' 'em for more. After I paid for food and the rent, wasn't nothin' hardly left for Charlie and me," Rosie fretted.

"Un-huh, I know. It's mighty hard," Maybelline replied, pulling a red polka-dot handkerchief out of her dress pocket to wipe her face. She had begun to sweat a lot, even when it wasn't hot. The heat just went through her in the winter as well as summer, causing water to form drops the size of peas on her face. The unhealthy sweat went along with the pains in her legs and back.

Rosie turned around to see where Charlie was. Charlie looked a lot like her with his flat features, but not about his too old, vacant, staring eyes. He was piled atop the brown army blanket bulging with their belongings. His chest was bare, and the oversized, worn-out jeans he had on were drawn with a cord under his protruding navel. The whorls of tight hair covering his oblong-shaped head were tangled and needed combing.

When Charlie saw his mother looking at him, he shouted across to her, "Mama, I'm thirsty. I want some sweetin' water!"

Rosie looked away. She had bought him pop at the last stop, an endless distance in her memory somewhere down the road. Twenty cents for a grape soda. Big Ernest wrote it down in that dirty notebook he kept in his hip pocket. The notebook was always showing, always reminding them about owing him. Big Ernest was a sonofabitch. But what could *she* do? With the money he cheated out of them, he could at least buy a good truck that had a top on it to haul them around. It was by the grace of God they hadn't run into any rain on this trip. All Big Ernest wanted to do was gyp them and sip on his cheap red wine. When the wine got to telling on him, he would get mean and nasty and cuss them all out just to be cussing. Call them a bunch of ignorant niggers. Sometimes, it was a wonder one of those strapping young men didn't draw back and knock the shit out of him. But they needed Big Ernest like he needed them. He needed workers, and they a crew boss to carry them where the work was and to take care of them like children. They couldn't do it alone.

Numbness entombed her feet and legs. Lord, she was tired of riding. Big Ernest turned off the highway, and now they were traveling back roads. This meant they must be nearing Ridgeville, where the snap beans were and the factory that wanted them for canning.

Charlie shouted again to her, "Mama—I'm thirsty!"

Worrisome just like his daddy, Floyd, she thought. Although she was never sure if it was Floyd or Pete that time. She giggled, remembering. Both were sure hot after her. In those days, she was really something. She had more hair and young tender meat on her bones. She hadn't started having all them children yet. The first time had been Mary when she was fifteen. Mighty young to be having a baby, but there has to be *some* love in a person's life, especially when there is nothing else. Her family had strayed apart long before. She had had a hard time with Mary. Wasn't no midwife in that camp, or woman who knew much about trouble in childbirth. She had lain alone in fear and pain and blood until, in desperation, someone went into town for a doctor, who refused to come because he didn't wait on nigger patients, least of all, nigger migrant workers. A week later, Mary died.

Afterward, having the others wasn't too bad, since she had already been torn open. The second was Lula, born in Florida; Lonnie in Georgia; and, last, Charlie in Maryland during tomato-picking time. She didn't know where Lula was. Lula had gone off with a boy three years ago. Poor Lonnie was dead—killed in Fruitland, Maryland, over sixty cents in a crap game. His death put a real hurting on her, for Lonnie worked right beside her and gave her money. The law didn't even want to go into the camp and get the man who did it. Just niggers killing niggers. And, too, some were just scared to go into a camp nicknamed Bloodsville, for there people were as used to killing as breathing.

The loud blaring of a car's horn passing them untangled the coil of her thoughts. A long, sleek blue car went by them recklessly. She could see the staring eyes in the white children's faces leaning far out of the windows to gape back at all the niggers jammed in the back of the noisy old truck. She watched the car until it was no more. The truck rumbled on down the narrow road into the stark hot desert of the day.

II

By twilight time, the truck ended its journey on the land of John Tilghman. The work crew, twenty-five of them, tried to straighten up and put life into their stiff muscles. They dropped slowly off the truck, the feel of the hard, firm ground almost coming as a shock. Arms reached up to help women with sleeping children.

"Thank God, we're here at last!" Maybelline breathed the sigh of relief for them all.

The camp was five miles outside of town on a barely used dirt road. To Rosie, the place was similar to the others; only it didn't appear to be as bad as the one they had just left. The decrepit rows of unpainted shanty houses, with jagged metal roofs and sagging boards for steps, were propped up on concrete blocks. Some still had windows and doors intact. A pump for water was at the end of the houses which faced each other across a dusty path, strewn with the debris of cans, bottles, and crates left over from whoever was there last. The outdoor toilet sat in the distance behind the houses, and back of it was a graveyard of rusted washtubs, wheelbarrows, and flabby tires.

As if attempting to hide the living quarters from the front, where the highway bordered the farm, acres and acres of planted corn, snap beans, and tomatoes stretched beneath the sky. This broad expanse of land had been amassed by John Tilghman's family through generations in Sussex County. The Tilghman family lived in town and made its money off crops grown and harvested by migrants and shipped in Tilghman trucks to wholesalers in Philadelphia and Wilmington. John Tilghman rarely came near the camp. This he left to his longtime friend and field boss, who took care of the things Tilghman had no stomach for. To the field workers, John Tilghman was merely a name.

Rosie looked around at the place like all the many others she had seen and lived and worked on. "My Lord," she murmured to herself, "don't nothin' ever change for me?"

"Com'on, you people. Let's git a move on!" Big Ernest shouted, stumbling out of the truck, eyes bloodshot. His old khaki army shirt was soaking wet in the back, the shirttail hanging out over baggy green cotton pants. It was rumored he had been a corporal in the army once. Steadying himself, he straightened up before them, planting his short, squat legs apart, hands on hips, eyeing them beneath the brim of the derby hat. This stance had given him the name Big Ernest.

"Now git yourselves one of them places to stay in. Tomorrow, we start real early in the fields. Done wasted 'nough time on the road."

"Hey—Big Ernest. I'm in a real bad way for some smokes—" a man called out to him.

"Fuck them cigarettes now and let's git this shit off'n this truck!" Big Ernest snapped back, pointing a finger at the vehicle still loaded with possessions.

A white Buick came careening down the side road, kicking up dust and coming to a squealing stop beside the truck. A middle-aged white man with thinning blond hair looked out of the car at them.

"There's Mista Todd," Big Ernest muttered low, teeth biting hard on the soggy cigar.

The man gave a long, beckoning sound on his horn, and Big Ernest moved away from them, bracing himself to walk evenly over to the car. The group quietly watched the men talking, the white man's lips moving the most, while Big Ernest kept nodding his head up and down. Out of deference or because it was hot, Big Ernest had taken his hat off and Rosie could see his smooth, nut-brown head.

Charlie tugged at her dress. "Mama, I'm thirsty!"

The white man in the Buick turned his attention back to the crew again, scrutinizing the workers with speculative, hard work eyes. Then he gunned the powerful motor to turn around in the dust and drive hurriedly out of the yard.

"All right, you niggers, listen to me—" Big Ernest began, slapping his hat on again while walking back to them. "That was Mista Todd—the field boss. He says that he don't want no one leaving here until these fields are picked clean and all the money owed him for rent and such is paid off. I'm goin' into town to the store for you and git your eatin's or anythin' else you want. If you ain't got the money, I'll put it down in the book. Tomorrow, we start *work*. Mista Todd said you better do a good job, for he's thinkin' mighty hard *and* long 'bout gittin' some Puerto Ricans to come in and do the work. Y'all don't want *that* to happen, do you, or your black asses'll be out of work!"

Why's he always talkin' 'bout our black asses and his'n is just as black too? Rosie pondered to herself. She felt Charlie's movements clinging to her skirt, as though he too understood Big Ernest's threat.

Then, out of the openness, a man's deep voice shouted out: "Aw, Ernest, cut out that talk 'bout Puerto Ricans. That ain't nothin' but to make these people work harder and cheaper."

A startled hush fell over the group as the man who had spoken up to Big Ernest approached them, seemingly from nowhere out of the dwindling, dusky twilight.

Before Rosie realized it, the words came out over the tiredness and anger submerged within her, bred from the long trip and the insensitiveness of Big Ernest. "Mista, you sure done spoke the God's awful truth!"

The stranger's gaze fell hard upon her for a moment, and then back again to focus on Big Ernest. "You know I'm right, Ernest, so cut that tryin' to scare these people."

"Now you just wait a minute there, Jackson," Big Ernest snapped back, reaching into his shirt pocket for a new cigar. "Nobody asked *you* to git into this. You just mind *your* business and I'll take care of *mine*—these people here. Now y'all haul ass and git that stuff off'n my truck!"

As the crew scattered at the lash of the order, Rosie squinted to see Jackson better—the man who had come out of the dark holes of the shacks to challenge Big Ernest. He loomed tall and black and ugly as sin before her. The more she stared at the strongly built stranger with the jagged knife scar making a split from the corner of his right eye down to his upper lip, she knew this was a man to be feared and respected. His ears stuck out like jutting cliffs, and unlike all the other men here, he had a beard covering most of his lower face. It was hard for her to tell how old Jackson was; for him and the rest, time had made a quick swath in their lives, like the Grim Reaper hurrying death through decay.

"Jackson"—Big Ernest was still standing there looking at him too—"don't you start no trouble with me," he warned, chewing hard on the unlit cigar. "You just be glad I'm lettin' you work with this crew."

"You ain't got nothin' to do with me, Ernest, and you know it!" the man, Jackson, said evenly, grit edging the words.

"Hey, we got things to do." Maybelline's voice interrupted, coming loud from the tangled knot of weary people pausing to listen. "Can't git nothin' done standin' 'round like this."

"Yeah, g'wan, *git,*" Big Ernest echoed, relieved to regain his authority.

Charlie tugged on her again, "Mama, I'm thirsty!"

"Thirsty myself, son. Let's go see what kind of water that pump's givin' up."

"Don't want no pump water. Want sweetin' water!" Charlie bellowed.

At that moment, Jackson's eyes settled upon them, dark, piercing, amused as he looked at her and the boy. She felt the others moving around and against her as they carried their blankets, suitcases, crates, and brown paper bags stuffed with all they owned to the vacant houses. For some reason, she found herself rooted there, until Jackson's gigantic frame came over to her. He walked slowly, with a slight limp in his left leg. The cast-off khaki army trousers he wore, like Big Ernest did sometimes, fit snugly to his well-muscled thighs. There was power in him, and for a sensitive moment while watching him approach her, she felt a sensuous response she hadn't known in a long time warmly stroke her body, settling in the V-angle of her legs. She rebuked herself. She was too old to be feeling like that again. *That* feeling had died with Charlie's coming—eight years ago. Hadn't it?

"You sure got spunk, lady," he said, softly, standing in front of her. "Out of all these people, you got spunk! I like people like that." Then, looking down at Charlie, he grinned. "Boy's thirsty. I got some nice cold water in my place and a piece of ice to go in it."

"I don't want no *water!*" Charlie persisted, sensing an ally in this man who was taking time to talk to him. "I want sweetin' water."

"We'll git that some other time," Jackson promised. "Right now, I'll give you what's on hand. Water!"

"I got to git my stuff off'n the truck," Rosie said.

"I'll git it for you," Jackson offered. "And I'm goin' to show you a right nice place hidden by a clump of trees past the rest. Got a cookstove and two beds."

"*Two* beds?" Rosie sighed. "Me and Charlie just been sleepin' together the best way we can."

"Which one is your'n?" Jackson asked, following her back to the truck.

"The big brown blanket over there." She pointed.

He climbed on the truck and reached for her bundle, lifting the weight of it with ease. "Com'on 'fore somebody else finds that place."

The one-room house was in better condition than the others, with simulated brick siding and the two windows unbroken. The beds were iron with old straw mattresses. A kerosene stove sat in a corner by a sink that did not have running water. The center of the room was occupied with a rickety, scarred brown table surrounded by three mismatched chairs.

"Used to be a crew leader's place long time ago," he explained, watching her show pleasure at the surroundings. "I'm in back of you a little piece." He stopped, frowning. "What's your name?"

"Rosie," she said quietly, "Rosie Polk."

"All right, Rosie Polk. While you gittin' things together, I'll take the boy and give him his water."

"His name's Charlie."

"Let's go, Charlie. You can bring your mama some water back, too."

She watched them leave—the big man with her son. Then she turned to untie the knot of the blanket and unpack to stay in what was home, at least for now.

III

Early morning of the next day, Rosie, with Charlie beside her, began the long stretching hours in the fields picking snap beans. The heat was oppressive, bearing down on figures going through the puppetlike down and up movements of picking the beans and putting them into hampers, then dragging them along the parallel rows to the checker.

Rosie, like the other women, wore a wide-brimmed straw hat on top of a handkerchief covering her head and ears, and pants, beneath the shapeless dress, to protect her legs from the insects. Dresses distinguished the women from the men stooped in the fields. There was little talking between the workers harvesting the crops. Too much of an exchange of words would impede the progress of filling the hampers whose numbers meant pay.

Rosie stopped for a moment to straighten up, taking the tail end of her dress to fan her face. At the far end of the row, she could distinguish Jackson with his belt of tickets. He was the checker and examined the hampers to see if there were any bad beans picked; he gave the workers a ticket for each full hamper. This was a good job and showed that Jackson was favored by the white field boss. Rosie smiled, thankful that the checker was Jackson. She knew some who were meaner than hell, dumping full loads on the ground just because one or two bad beans or tomatoes were in them. Jackson saw her looking at him and waved. She waved back, blinking in the glare of the sun. The friendly gesture in the open fields brightened her spirits.

"Wonder where *he* come from?" She had forgotten Leroy was picking on the other side of her. He had paused to rest too, taking off his tattered shirt to wipe the sweat off his face and chest. Leroy had been with the crew all the way too. He was a burnt-orange color and looked as if he had some Indian mixed up in him.

"Don't know, since he was already here. Big Ernest sure don't like him!" she replied, chuckling.

"Maybe he knows somethin' 'bout Big Ernest *we* don't know," Leroy scoffed, putting the sweat-dampened shirt back on.

"Maybe." Rosie grunted, stooping again to the beans.

Leroy looked down at her form like an overdressed scarecrow. "Which place you stayin' in, Rosie?"

She straightened up again to see his face grinning at her meaningfully. "Not your'n," she flared back.

Leroy threw back his head, laughing loudly. "Just thought you might like some comp'ny some night."

"All right, you people over there. Stop all that yakkin' and git to work!" They saw Mister Todd shouting at them menacingly. "Can't git no beans picked like that."

"Damn white sonofabitch," Leroy muttered, under his breath.

"Stoopin' and pickin'," Rosie said, shaking her head. " 'Fore I die, I'd sure like to know how it feels to do somethin' else in this life."

"Well, you ain't ever goin' to know," Leroy said, spitting into the dirt. " 'Cause that's all you can do."

IV

Until Saturday of the next week, which was payday, nine days off, Rosie and Charlie ate baloney stew and drank grape sodas. Going home in the evening past Maybelline's house, she could smell the big pot of greens and fatback cooking for those who bought meals from her. Charlie would eat his food quickly, sopping up the stew juice with day-old bread, then curl up on the bed and go to sleep, tired from the fields.

One evening after she had cleaned up the plates and lit the kerosene lamp, a knock sounded on the door, and she heard someone calling her name.

"Rosie?" It was Jackson standing outside in the darkness. "Just thought I'd come by and see how you and the boy are doin'."

"Charlie's gone to sleep. Ain't easy workin' in the fields for a little boy."

"Ain't no kind of life for a boy *or* woman," Jackson added, entering the dim, smoky shadows of the room.

"Man much neither." Rosie went on sadly. "I've seen some ole men just fall right over and die in the field. That's the only way you can leave it—free."

Jackson sat down in one of the chairs by the table. A clothesline was strung across the room with her clothes and Charlie's hanging on it. The washing gave the room a wet-damp smell. Some of the grimy dirt and insecticide used for spraying the crops still stubbornly stained the pant legs. All the washboard scrubbings in the world wouldn't get them out.

Rosie sat down at the table with him. His clean white T-shirt and blue pants made her aware that she hadn't washed or changed her field clothes. When all you did was live to work from morning to night, you didn't think about nothin' else—not even yourself.

Jackson took out a pack of cigarettes and offered her one. She shook her head. She had given up smoking a long time ago. Somehow, the smoke didn't mix with the dust and spray and heat from the sun bursting her lungs. She watched him drag deeply on the cigarette, like he enjoyed it so much. She tried to remember the last time she sat with a man like this—talking and watching him smoke, the cigarette starkly white between his black fingers.

"Where you from, Jackson?" she asked, thinking that he must be from someplace afar that made good, strong black men.

"Georgia. But I live 'round here now. Came to these parts two years ago following the crops. Got tired of movin', movin', and movin', so I just stayed. Man gits tired." He flicked the cigarette ashes in the empty soda bottle left on the table. "Mista Todd let me stay on to do odd jobs 'round here. Said I was dependable and a good worker. You know how white folks like to have a special nigger." He winked at her. "Anyways, he's got some cows and chickens down the road a piece, and planting time, I runs the tractor here."

She watched him out of the corner of her eye, not wanting to look directly at him. For some reason, she felt shy around him. He sat leaned back in the chair with his legs spread wide. Furtively, she glanced at the crotch of his pants. Warmth stole over her like a heated spring. He grinned, as if knowing her thoughts.

"You live by yourself?" Quickly, her hand covered her mouth, ashamed of the question that had slipped out. It was the same as asking if he had a woman.

Now he laughed, and she saw his teeth, even and bright. She ran her tongue unconsciously around the inside of her mouth where her back jaws were ragged with teeth and spaces in between. She wanted to laugh back, respond to him, but dared not.

"Yeah, I live by myself. Can cook right good too. You and the boy come over for supper Sat'day. I'll show you."

Surprise transfigured her face into almost childishness. No one had ever cooked for her except her mother; then after she got old enough, she took over the chores.

"*Cook* for us!" This time, she forgot the missing teeth and laughed aloud at the thought. A *man* cooking for her and Charlie!

"Sure. You two com'on over and see. I'll show you. I learnt to cook when I was ten. My mama died when we was little. My daddy tried to keep all five of us younguns together—somehow. He worked in the factory and fields and put *us* to work. Made us go to school too," he said proudly, putting out the cigarette butt in the bottle. "Up to the fifth grade. Then he got hisself a woman who just moved right in and took over. By then, I knew it was time for me to leave. Started gittin' crowded after *she* started havin' babies."

She listened quietly, amazed that he had gone to the fifth grade. She had hardly made it to the third. She glanced over at Charlie, still sleeping soundly, curled into a ball. Poor Charlie. He was like her, never staying in a place long enough to finish anything.

"Well, Rosie, I'm goin' so's you can git to sleep. It's been a long day," he said, getting up.

"All our days are long," she murmured wearily.

"Don't forget—Sat'day," he called back, closing the door softly to keep from awakening the boy.

No, she wouldn't forget. Thinking about it would help her to get through the rest of the days that were alike in their unvaried sameness.

V

The following day was clouded with threats of rain. They worked harder, faster, feverishly to fill as many baskets as they could before the rain started. Rain meant no work, no work meant no pay, and no pay was being indebted for living.

By noon, the dreaded rain came in a furious torrent, as if the devil were in the sky mocking them. It rained all day and night, and continued on into the next morning. Boredom set in and, with it, frustration. To occupy time, the women washed clothes that refused to dry in the dampness that crept into the shanties from cracks and holes in the floors and walls. The children became restless, cooped up in the cramped quarters where there was nothing else to do but take care of the younger ones, while impatient parents took it out on them by screaming epithets. The men spent the time gambling with promises until payday and sending Big Ernest back and forth into town for wine bought on credit.

Rosie used up her time trying to scrub away the encrusted dirt left over by those before her. The thought of Saturday night helped to brighten the gloom of the rain. She had just put a bucket under the spot where the roof was leaking when the door swung open and Leroy entered without knocking. He came in dripping wet, dressed in an old black rubbery raincoat, smelling of wine and grinning like a fool.

"Hey, Rosie." He smirked, hanging his coat on a nail by the door. "Thought maybe you'd be lonesome on a day like this." Swaying, he slumped down in the chair where Jackson had sat before.

"No time to git lonesome." She frowned at him. "Got things to do."

"Oh, hell. Forgit them things to do. Here," he invited, pulling a pint bottle of wine out of his pocket, "have a li'l taste. Make you feel like a new woman."

She moved to pull the blanket closer around Charlie, asleep on the bed. "Naw, Leroy."

He swigged noisily from the bottle, wiping his mouth with the back of his hand. "What's the best thing to do on a day like this with the rain fallin' and ever'thin'?"

Ignoring him, Rosie sat down to darn Charlie's underwear. That was the best way to get rid of Leroy, she decided, pretend like he wasn't there.

Brushing aside her disdainful silence, he went on garrulously. *"Lovin'!* That's the best thing to do when it's rainin'. Takes away all your worries—makes the sun shine again."

She heard his chair scrape the floor as he moved closer to reach over and squeeze her breast. "That's exactly what you need!"

"Git your hands off'n me, Leroy!" She slapped angrily at him.

"Aw, now, Rosie," he began, voice low, wheedling. "I ain't never seen a woman yet who wasn't interested in a little lovin' now and then. And *I'm* the one who can give it like the doctor ordered. Your man, Leroy. Right here!"

"G'on home, Leroy, and leave me alone," she said, getting up to go back to the box of clothes where others needing patching were.

In one quick motion, he sprang out of the chair, grabbing her from behind. She felt the push of his hard body against her and smelled his sour cigarette smell. She tried to twist out of his grasp as he began kissing the back of her neck and side of her cheek. His breath came faster as he half pulled and pushed her to the bed. Here, he threw her down, falling on top of her, while his hand ran paths under her dress and up her legs, touching her body.

"Com'on, Rosie," he pleaded, "you know you want it."

She stiffened against him, tightening her legs together, reaching beneath the mattress for what would stop him. "You better let go of me, Leroy, 'fore I stick this knife clean up your behind!"

He let go of her, rolling over to the side of the bed and getting up. "Since when'd *you* git so touchy?" he sneered. "I heard that, one time, all somebody had to do was tap you on the shoulder and your dress'd fly up!"

"Git out of here, Leroy."

Charlie awakened, stared at them sleepily, then closed his eyes again. He had seen his mother and men before.

"Okay, I'm goin'. But you ought to be glad I'm even in-ter-ested. Ugly as *your* black ass is!"

The words tore through her more ravishing than pain. "Look who's got the nerve to call somebody ugly!" she flung back weakly at the sound of his leaving.

She stayed on the bed with her eyes tightly closed, refusing to open them until she was certain he was gone. Outside, the rain thrashed ominously against the thin walls of the house. The sound of fate.

VI

It rained for three days. When the sun finally came out, they went back into the muddy fields, feet sinking into the soft ground. By the time Saturday came, Rosie owed for the rent and the food bought on credit. In the pay line, she heard a woman grumbling, "Always owin', owin', owin'. After owin', ain't nothin' left. One of these days, I ain't goin' to owe nothin' 'cept to the Lord."

Later that evening, she bathed Charlie in the big round tub that she washed clothes in. Then she dressed him in a clean pair of pants patched at the knees and a faded yellow shirt. She combed and brushed his hair, applying Vaseline to make the tight curls softer. Afterward, she got herself ready, putting on the one good dress she had, a cotton print with a wide skirt, and tied her hair up in a bandanna. Holding Charlie by the hand, she walked self-consciously over to Jackson's.

On the way, she saw Maybelline sitting on her stoop. "Jackson tolt me y'all were comin' over to dinner. Just be sure eatin's all!" She guffawed, slapping her heavy thigh.

"Maybelline, you got a nasty mind!" Rosie laughed back good-naturedly, hurrying Charlie along.

Jackson's house was different. It had electricity and two rooms. The front room had a stove with an old brown icebox beside it, a sink, and sagging upholstered chairs with grease-stained backs. The table was set and covered with a red plastic cloth that almost matched the curtains at the windows. One large light bulb hung on a wire down over the table. The second room was small, with a pine bed and a chest of drawers with the bottom drawer missing. A curtain separated the rooms.

"Supper's all ready," he announced proudly, gesturing toward the stove.

"I'm hungry!" Charlie said, running over to bounce up and down on a chair. He hadn't seen a chair with springs before.

"He's always hungry," Rosie said, apologetically.

"Growin' boys got appetites. I cooked some black-eyed peas, rice, and ham hocks."

"Hum-m-m. Sure smells good."

"Y'all sit down and help yourselves. You goin' to git brownskin service."

"Uh-huh! Ain't nothin' I like better'n brownskin service!" Rosie breathed, sitting down.

When dinner was over, they talked and Jackson played piggyback with Charlie. When the evening sky deepened, she began to feel a twinge of regret, hating to go back to her place, which wasn't as bright and cheerful as this.

"Like my cookin'?" he asked, smiling.

"Real good." She smiled back, forgetting the hole of her mouth.

"You need to smile more, Rosie," he said gently.

"Takes happenin's to make a person smile."

"I know we got it rough. It's our luck. But we might as well try to git a little pleasure out of life while we can. We only come this way once."

From afar, they could hear children playing. A woman cursed and a man laughed. The sound of a bottle being flung out of a window splintered the evening like cracked ice.

"Let's go into town," Jackson said, abruptly.

"Into *town?*" she repeated, the idea completely foreign to her. She looked down at what she wore: the long, shapeless dress bought at a rummage sale, where clothes still held the odor of their owners, and shoes run over from wear.

"Sure. We goin' to take a ride. Look at the sky and see other folks. Right, boy?"

Charlie jumped up eagerly, happy with the thought of leaving this place. All he did was work. He went nowhere and saw nothing but the same old people all the time.

"Big Ernest don't let us go into town," Rosie said, hesitantly.

Jackson stood up, his full length stretching almost to the ceiling. "Rosie, Big Ernest don't rule *me.* I knew him *when.* Back there in the army in Alabama when all we did to fight the war was clean up the mess hall and polish white officers' boots. You see this scar on my face?" he asked, running a finger down the length of the crooked line. "That's when Big Ernest thought he could try to boss me but found out diff'rent. He thought being a corporal made him Jesus. Treated us like dirt. I showed him one night off base that he wasn't no black God 'cause of a coupla stripes. Only he ain't got no scars to show for it—'ceptin' when he sees me and 'members. He had a knife and I just had my fists." Jackson took Charlie's hand. "Okay, boy, let's all go for that ride."

Jackson had an ancient, rusty blue Plymouth without a right fender. Somehow, through nursing and amateur tampering, he kept it running. The back seat was torn out and only the springs remained.

"Ain't much," he said modestly, "but I bought it for almost nothin' from Mista Todd. He's got a junkyard down the road. It'll git us into town." He laughed, opening the door for them.

When they got into town, Main Street was busy with people shopping or milling around talking. There was a five-and-dime store, Acme, drugstore, clothing shop, bank, bowling alley, and liquor store with a noisy barroom in the rear.

Jackson, Rosie, and Charlie made a strange trio, walking slowly down the street. Charlie was wide-eyed and speechless, gaping at the lighted windows and storewares. The people on the street stared at them in anger and repugnance, giving them plenty of space to pass. They were outsiders—migrant workers—drifting flotsam on Tilghman's place. These people were known to be ignorant and mean with it. The townspeople wished that they didn't have to be there, but they were needed. Even the town's blacks moved over as they passed, branding them as dumb nigger field hands. Two or three of the townsmen recognized Jackson, and their gaze softened. They *knew* him.

Jackson bought Charlie his first ice-cream cone, which he ate very slowly, savoring the strange chocolate flavor. They passed George Kleen's Clothing Shop, and Rosie stopped to peer in at the dresses displayed on white mannequins.

"My, ain't they pretty? That green one's sure nice. If I can pick 'nough next week and it don't rain no more—" She said nothing else, knowing she wouldn't ever pick enough.

They walked on into and against the fading, long summer night. Cars honked horns, neighbors shouted to each other, children ran boisterously ahead of parents down the street. Rosie didn't know when she had felt this good before—like a person. When they got back to the camp, she slept well and without dreams.

VII

Sunday morning, she was awakened by a knock on her door. "Rosie, got somethin' for you and the boy."

"Just a minute," she called, quickly pulling on the old work pants and shirt over her gown.

Upon hearing the knock, Charlie sprang out of the bed. "Mama, it's Jackson!"

Jackson came in carrying two packages under his arms. Charlie ran over to him, grabbing his legs. "What'cha got?" he asked excitedly.

"This one's for you. And the big one's your mama's."

"What'd you go and buy somethin' for us for?" Rosie questioned, confusion and surprise clouding her face.

"Person who works all the time ought to have somethin' for themselves—*sometimes.*" Jackson looked away from what he saw in her eyes.

Shakily she opened the box and took out the green dress nestled between tissue paper. "Jackson—you went and bought the dress in the window!"

"Yeah. Went back last night just 'fore the store closed. Got Charlie some new pants and a ball. Can't 'spect a boy to grow up without havin' a ball once in his life. Can you?"

Charlie tore open his package, exposing the pants and the bright red ball. Rosie watched him happily bouncing the ball up and down. The last toy he had was a miniature fire truck with one wheel off given to him for Christmas by a church group.

"Jackson, you spent all your money on *us*," Rosie chastised him softly.

"Not quite all. And what if I did? I'm makin' somebody happy."

Rosie held the dress up before her, smiling, forgetting her almost empty mouth.

"We goin' into town in style next Sat'day night. So don't forget to wear that dress!"

The next Saturday, they dressed up in their new clothes and went once again into town with Jackson. This time, Rosie didn't mind the stares and whispers.

Later, in the darkness of his room, he enfolded her in his arms and made slow love to her. She discovered the tenderness of him, the massive power of his giving and taking. She felt wanted again and needed, and shuddered at the flow of warmth within her. She had had many men before, but because Jackson was the most gentle of them all, she now knew what it meant to really have a man. Patiently, he helped her to climb with him and reach the summit of passion. Afterward, she slept in the protection of his mountainous frame.

Working in the fields wasn't as bad now for her. She had Jackson to fill her day thoughts and be with her at nights. She lived the days as they came, treasuring each, for she knew they soon would have to move to follow the crops. Leaving men and having them leave her had been woven into the pattern of her existence.

Finally, when the fields were picked clean, Big Ernest told them to get ready to move out. They were going on up Route 13 north to Pennsylvania. Big Ernest had contracted work on another farm.

In the early grayness of Sunday's dawn, she awakened Charlie. "We got to leave here now. Work's all done."

Charlie turned over sleepily, rubbing his eyes. "Why we gotta go, Mama? Always goin'. Why can't we stay here with Jackson?"

" *'Cause we got to go!*" she cried out angrily, not wanting to be reminded. "Git your things and put 'em in the blanket."

Outside, she could hear the movements of people preparing to leave: the talk, grumbling, cries of still-sleepy children. Big Ernest's shouts rose high above the other sounds. "Hustle it up. Crops gotta be picked. Git the lead outa your asses!"

Rosie knotted the blanket with their things and dragged it out the door. She was abandoning the house occupied by her and those before her and the ones who would come after her. It was now just another place in the backwash of her life.

The morning sky was sullen with clouds. She didn't want rain. Not while riding in that truck. Someone threw her bundle on the truck for her. Silently Charlie climbed up and took his place on the blanket, which he protected and which protected him. His life was now molded into acceptance. She found a place beside him near the rail.

Maybelline, planted precariously on her stool, looked at her quietly. "Kind of looks like rain, don't it, Rosie?"

Rosie nodded. She didn't want to talk now. She looked at the line of shanties and strained to see Jackson's place where she was leaving a piece of her behind. She looked down to see Charlie looking at it too.

"Everybody in!" Big Ernest called, climbing into the cabin of the truck, derby low over his eyes, cigar stationed in his mouth. The truck's motor started and stopped.

"Oh, Lordy, don't tell me the thing ain't goin' to move?" Someone giggled.

The motor coughed, sputtered, and finally turned over. Rosie stared out of her mind's eye into nothing.

"Ever' place we go, we leave a little sumpin' behind, honey," Maybelline said gently. "And we takes a little sumpin' with us."

Suddenly the truck jerked to a stop, toppling some of the standing bodies against each other. They saw Big Ernest getting out of the truck cursing. "Goddam crazy nigger! You want to git killed? Standin' there in the middle of the road like a dumb-assed fool!"

"There he is, honey." Maybelline chuckled, raising herself up laboriously to look over the side of the truck. "Standin' there big as a giant."

Rosie peered over the railing to see Jackson looming tall, naked to the waist, barefooted in the road, looking like he had just gotten out of bed.

"Rosie! Com'on down from there!"

"G'wan," Maybelline urged, laughing. "Can't you hear that man yellin' his fool head off for you?"

She felt immobile among the bodies around her, remembering other men in the past who had called her name, men with whom it always turned out to be the same. Why should she? Nothing was ever any different in this gray world of hers.

"Nigger," Big Ernest snarled at Jackson, "you keepin' my crew from gittin' on the road. Time counts in this biz'ness."

Jackson's eyes darted back at Big Ernest, then returned to the truck as swiftly as a fly could light and leave. "Rosie!"

Her words were not intended to be spoken aloud, but somehow they slipped out. "Ain't no use. Goin' to be just like with the rest of 'em."

"You don't know that, honey," Maybelline soothed, squeezing her hand. "Things *do* change sometimes for some of us—for the best."

"Mama," Charlie tugged pleadingly at her skirt, "Jackson wants you."

She moved slowly at first, feeling all eyes upon her. Then faster over the crates, boxes, and people, with Charlie trying to drag their blanket that she had forgotten. She jumped off the truck straight into the vise of his arms, the blanket landing at her feet.

"Just where in hell you think *you* goin'?" Big Ernest confronted her, hands on his hips. "Git back up there in that truck."

"Ain't gittin' back up there," Rosie shot back, anger rising within her. There he was giving orders, always giving orders. "Sick of trucks," she went on, letting her longtime pent-up frustrations cascade out at him. "All my life, I been doin' nothin' but gittin' on and off trucks. Ridin' and gittin' no place."

A flicker of surprise crossed Big Ernest's face. None of the crew had ever talked back to him like that before. Not even a man. Incensed, he threw her a mean look. "You my worker. 'Sides, you owe me money," he added triumphantly.

"Money?" Jackson repeated, stepping between them. "How much?"

"A hundred dollars."

Rosie frowned in bewilderment. How could crackers, baloney, sweetin' water for Charlie, beans, and kerosene for cooking come to that much? Especially when she had been repaying him.

"I don't believe you," Jackson said coldly.

"Oh? Well, look. See, it's right here in the book." Big Ernest extracted a greasy note pad from his pocket. "I 'member 'cause she's been owin' since we started out."

Jackson's face hardened, the scar quivering like something alive. "I knows all 'bout how you keeps them books, Big Ernest," he said warningly. "You keeps 'em so's you can have the people owin' all the time."

"Now you wait a minute, Jackson." Big Ernest edged forward menacingly. "You callin' me a cheat?"

Rosie watched Big Ernest's hands. He could be mighty quick with a knife or gun. She moved nearer to Jackson. Big Ernest had better not try anything.

"I'm goin' to give you fifty dollars," Jackson stated firmly, reaching into his wallet. "And that's all. Now git and leave us be."

The people in the truck watched in silence, straining to hear, to see, to know. Someone snickered, and a man coughed mockingly.

Big Ernest stared hard and long at Jackson, whose eyes locked unwaveringly with his. Finally he muttered low, "Damn crazy nigger." Spitting in the dust, he wheeled around to go back to the truck.

" 'Bye, Rosie!" Maybelline shouted over the roar of the motor. " 'Member what I tolt you!"

"One less body on this old heap takin' up space!" a voice called back teasingly.

"You didn't think I was goin' to let you go, did you?" Jackson grinned, holding her close. "You goin' to stay here with me. Be my wife."

Wife! Not woman. She felt a wave of giddiness. None in the past had offered her that. Tears streamed down her cheeks. Ashamed and happy, she smiled as the thought overtook her. "Why, I don't even know your whole name." Those who worked in the fields didn't bother with more than one name—Joe, Pete, Lucy. Wasn't no need. "A wife ought to know that."

"You goin' to be Mrs. Joe Louis Jackson."

"Hum-m-m, I likes that." Suddenly she laughed. "My, my, somebody sure knew what to name *you!*"

"Suits you fine too." He smiled, taking her hand and Charlie's. "Com'on, let's go home."

Mali Is Very Dangerous

Reginald McKnight

1988

In my first few days in Senegal I quickly learned to fend off illness, culture shock and flies, but I had no prophylactic against M.D.—Moustapha Diole, a very gentle but underhanded soul who peddled to tourists on N'Gor Beach. I met M.D. on my second day in the country near N'Gor Village, a labyrinthine stone crab surrounded by hotels, bush, and endless cobalt blue water. On that day he stripped me of one hundred dollars in less than ten minutes for some very chintzy-looking "authentic African art." Fortunately for me, one hundred dollars was all the cash I carried that day.

There I was, a twenty-six-year-old graduate anthropologist, relatively well read in the folklore, history, art, and contemporary literature of West Africa. I had been given a very handsome chunk of research money by a reputable, if not redoubtable, East Coast university in order to study African market systems. In less than thirty-six hours in-country, I found myself bamboozled by a snaggletoothed, illiterate old man into buying trinkets a kleptomaniac would scorn. It wasn't my squandering the money that disturbed me so much as it was M.D.'s deftness at convincing me that junk was jewelry, trash was treasure, up was down. A lesson in smart shopping I won't soon forget.

I ran into M.D. again one night several weeks later on N'Gor Beach while strolling, repeating French phrases to myself. I suppose, because M.D. had had such tremendous luck with me at our first meeting, he seemed expressly happy to see me. "Ahhh, here comes the original mark," he must have been thinking. He took my hand, shook it like we were old school chums, and without letting go, told me in his most eloquent Franco-American pidgin he wanted to introduce me to his wife and kids. I figured his intent was to let his family meet, up close, the sap who had tripled his monthly income in seconds flat. His wife was very sick, he told me, but he wanted me to meet her just the same. He led me down the beach, clutching my hand as if I were his steady.

What's funny about Islamic countries like Senegal is that you rarely see men holding women's hands. You see men hold men's hands, and women hold women's hands. It's an oddly pleasant custom, man and man, woman and woman, strolling hand in hand—not that I personally cared for the custom though. The best I could muster was an aesthetic, and distant, appreciation.

M.D. tried pulling me toward his place as if I'd heartily agreed to come along. I told him I was busy, that I had a lot of research to attend to, that I was tired, wanted to turn in early. He grinned, pretending not to understand. Then he told me he wanted me to meet a "young girl" before going to his home in N'Gor. I felt myself put up a little less resistance, but resisted nevertheless. I simply wasn't interested in meeting his young girl, his old wife, or anybody else. I told him so. He gave me this long, hurt-looking face with sad-dog eyes. "You are my friend?" he asked. "Yes," I said. "The best friend I ever had."

"Please, my friend, come. Come see my wife. She very sick."

A dozen snappy comebacks occurred to me, but I couldn't bring myself to say anything nasty. "Please come with me," he said. And I relented, thinking, I need an enemy out here like I need a sand sandwich. So, I let M.D. lead me by the hand to a bar at the Diarama Hotel. Once there he introduced me to the young girl, his sister, he told me. He then, very casually, asked me whether I wanted her. I guess any normal man would have. Tall, big butt, mahogany eyes and skin, rice-white teeth, breasts Solomon couldn't describe. A killer dame. I wasn't the least bit interested. At the time, I was trying to remain faithful to my girlfriend Lillian, which ended up, ten months later, like waiting for an order of fish and chips at a Taco Bell.

I wasn't interested in M.D.'s "sister," but I was certainly intrigued. Maybe mystified would be a better word, for it seemed to me that M.D. was offering me the whore for nothing. Now, Senegalese whores go for a lot less than they do in the States. Two, three bucks a round when I was in Senegal. I kept asking M.D. how much this one would cost and he kept saying, "You are my friend. You are my friend." I wasn't sure whether he was talking discount, COD, or marriage. But the issue wasn't vital to me. I only expressed interest so as not to offend anyone.

M.D. remained vague, so I made to leave. He gave me another long/dog look. "You no want meeting my wife?" he said. Rather than answer, I offered to buy him and the whore a beer. I came back to the table with a couple of Heinekens.

"Hinkin!" said M.D. "He bring us Hinkin. Oh, you very big man. You are as boss." Oh cripes, I thought. I am as fool. Rule number thirty-two for getting by in Senegal: *never try to buy yourself out of a pain in the ass.* M.D., steadily tapping my leg, giving me a sinner's grin, said, "You like my sister?" He said this the way Millie Jackson would say, "You like my sweet thang, don't you, baby?" And for some reason still a mystery to me today, I said, "Yes-M.D.-I-really-like-your-sister-but-you-see-I-am-married." He looked at me as if I'd said, "I-am-in-Senegal," and without blinking, twitching, flinching, said, "You like my sister?"

"Yeah, she's very nice, but I'm married."

"I am marry too."

"Well, yeah right, so you understand what I'm trying to say to you." M.D. shrugged, sipped his beer, said, "You no like my sister I get 'nother sister." He turned toward the bar, waved, and a quarter of a minute later a woman in a green boubou billowed to our table. She was shorter than the first one, shorter on looks, and wasted. Wordlessly, she sat next to M.D.'s big sister, leaned toward the woman, buried her face between those indescribable breasts and nuzzled them for a long time. I mean a long time. M.D. told me it was supposed to make me horny. I don't believe it did.

Again I tried to shove off. Again I got the long/dog face and sat down. Not knowing what to do, I bought another round of beer, and tried to make small talk to Big Sister. I leaned toward her, and in my best Berlitz French, said, "Votrage?" She looked at me as if I'd spoken Hebrew, so I said, "Votre nom?" She sat blink-blink-blinking at me vacantly. I said, "Well, then do you give good skull?" She sat there. I sat there. I ordered four more beers and clammed up.

M.D. sucked down the last few clouds of foam from his beer glass and said, "You are very big man. You meet my wife now."

He took me straightaway to his little bantam-weight home in the village. His wife was indeed very ill. She lay in bed, dull-eyed and ugly as sin. A small, brown sack lay on its side next to the bed. Its contents—medicines of all sorts, pills, liquids, oils—were spilled onto the floor horn-of-plentylike. M.D. introduced me to his wife. I couldn't catch her name. Her smile looked delicate enough to be blown away by the wind stirred up by moth wings. She gave me her hand; it was hot, the skin dry, tough, and her grip strong. As I held her hand and smiled back at her, two little boys slid from behind a curtain separating the bedroom from another room. M.D. beckoned them, told them to take my hand. They did so. The both of them looked less than healthy. They stood grim-faced, penguinlike. The smaller of the two, a boy about five, whistled out his nose, wheezed and gurgled out his throat. I stood there wondering what dark, exotic disease I might be contracting.

M.D. offered me food. "Come and chop," he put it. I gravely told him I myself was very sick, married, and pressed for time, that I was homeward bound. He probably looked hurt here too, but as the room was lit only by a single candle, I was impervious to the crook and curve of his face in the semidarkness. He offered to walk me home. As much as I wanted to, I couldn't refuse his offer, as N'Gor is a maze, a tight sheepshank on the tip of the Cap Vert. The village is older than Western history. You could walk into N'Gor alone and pop out somewhere in the eighteenth century.

As we walked, it became apparent to me that M.D. was blitzed. We made slow progress as he had to stop to piss here and there. Moreover, he added to our mileage by sloshing side to side, or rearing two or three steps in order to pick up forward momentum. As we neared the hotel complex, he sidled up to me, and took my hand. "I have for you something I want give you," he said. I didn't know what to say, so I said, "Why?"

"Is because you are very big man. I give this no other man. You only. You—you are my brother, and very big man." The way he leaned against me, whispered deep in my ear, squeezed my hand to punctuate his words, made me want to slap the black off him. "You know juju?" he said. Here we go, I thought, and told him I'd heard of it, but knew very little about it. He licked his lips. "Juju," he said, "is very strong, very good. It make you protection. If a man he put you knife anywhere, anywhere on you is no cut or pain you."

"Oh yeah?" I said. I didn't know what else to say.

"Oh yes. Is true."

"And you want to give me this juju?"

"Is true. If man he put gun *or* knife for you is no pain." I wasn't the goddamnedest interested, moved, impressed. All I could think of was shucking the old boy and getting back to the soothing drabness of my bungalow. And as we neared the bungalow area, I turned to M.D. and thrust my hand at him, saying goodnight. He seemed shocked by this, said, "I want give you him this night." I stopped dead and eased my hand from his. "This very important," he said. "Too important. If a man gun he knife is no killing you. *Tu comprendre?*"

"Look, M.D., I'm very honored, you know, happy? that you've offered me your sister, and your juju and everything, but it's OK. I just want to be your friend.

"You are my friend, no?"

"You are my friend, yes, M.D., but I really don't need any juju."

We were near a hotel security guard when I said this, and because I'd spoken rather loudly, M.D. grabbed my arm and shushed me. "Is secret," he whispered. I was so flustered it took me nearly ten minutes to find my room. I must admit I was becoming intrigued. I ushered him into my room, offered him some gin and a seat.

After I listened to him rattle on about his sister's beauty, honesty, and breasts, the puissance of his juju and the bigness of me, Idi, Idrissa Ndaiye, my interpreter, stepped in without knocking. "Hey, Berd, What's happening?"

When I think about it, I've got to admit that *interpreter* is too fancy a word to attach to my friend Idi. We met on my fourth day in Senegal and immediately hit it off. And, since my French was virtually nonexistent, and my Wolof absolutely so, Idi usually would end up interpreting for me. I never paid him a dime, but because he loved speaking English, and perhaps because I could afford to buy and share with him things he loved but couldn't afford—Nigerian weed, American and British and Canadian cigarettes, good French bread, canned meats, and café au lait—I was pretty sure he felt fairly recompensed.

I liked him very much. His *moutoneux* head and skinny frame are all I truly miss about Senegal. I was so relieved to see him step through my door that night, it took me a moment to note M.D.'s transition from English to Wolof. When I did notice, I became suspicious that M.D. might be filling Idi's head with propaganda, telling my companion to be a brother and help M.D. skin me for a few dollars more. So I put up my mental dukes and suspended all belief in everything while Idi explained things to me. "No, no, no," said my interpreter, "the girl is really not a whore. She just wants to be like your girlfriend while you are here. She could live with you if you like, or you could just you-know-what with her whenever you want to." He wore a grin that would make Jack Kennedy look like a pyorrhea victim. A hero's grin. One of those grins journalists are fond of calling "winning smiles." I struggled to remain wary. "How much is it supposed to cost me?" I said.

"That's up to you, boy. How much do you give Lillian for making love?"

"I don't pay Lillian for sex. She's my wife, not my whore."

"Your wife?"

"Well, I told him that so he'd lay off, but it didn't make a dent."

"Well of course not." Idi frowned. "What does this mean to a Muslim who could have three or four wives? Look, wife, girlfriend—really this does not matter. My point is that even if you don't give her money, you give her things. You give her jewelry and clothes. You take her to dinner or buy her a little makeup."

"Be serious, Idi, I don't even know the woman."

"Who knows women?"

"Tell him I'll think about it." M.D. cocked an eyebrow at whatever Idi told him, which seemed to take longer than your standard, He'll give it some thought. M.D. nodded and said something to me. Idi turned to me, said, "He wants to know if you are still interest in the juju." I could read nothing in Idi's face. He looked Buddha-tranquil. "I don't know about the juju," I said. "I'm not sure what he means." Idi took a chair, folded his arms, crossed his legs and spoke to M.D. M.D. sipped his drink, set it on the nightstand, then spoke in Wolof. I listened to him as if his voice were music. I strained to hear something familiar in his voice, truthfulness or deceit, mockery or gravity. But it was useless, for I wasn't even certain whom he was addressing. He seemed to recede into the steamy night air. It was as if his voice came from stereo speakers, or wafted in through the windows. And then, slow and easy, like skillful counterpoint, came Idi's translation. It sent chills through me. Idi's English seeped into M.D.'s

Wolof so perfectly that I couldn't tell whether his translation was for my benefit, or a sign of symbiosis between M.D. and himself.

" 'This juju I want to give you was given me by my father more than twenty-five years ago. You must remember, my friend, that the juju cannot be bought or sold or it will lose the power in it. For the past twenty-five years, I fear no man or creature. With this juju, I can walk anywhere with no fear or hesitation. As long as I wear it, nothing can penetrate my skin. Bullets cannot harm me; knives cannot harm me.

" 'Many years ago I was a trader in Bamako. Perhaps you are not aware of all the dangers that wait inside Mali for a boy with stuff and money. There are many, my friend. So many that Death stands wherever your back is turn. Life has a tight, tight fist there, and not a week pass when there is no talk of some young, unprotec-teh fool found slaughter and free of all his worldly things, in the cold of early morning.

" 'I was young, but not a fool. I carry this with me wherever I went.' " M.D. stood and lifted his boubou, grinned as if he were flashing. Looped round his flabby belly was a tubular leather belt, the ends of which were held together by a simple loop and a crude leather button. There was also a second button and a second loop, but these were left unfastened. M.D. dropped his head and looked at the belt, his bottom lip poking. He was sitting between me and the rickety lamp on the nightstand between the beds. His silhouette strikes me now as having looked like a shriveled Alfred Hitchcock's, although at the time no such simile came to me. I just wanted him to finish his story and go home. I was very uneasy.

He squinted down at me, said in English, "Mali is very dangerous," then sat down, dropped the hem of his boubou, and turned to Idi.

" 'It was winter, and there I was, a young boy of twenty-five in the finest markets of Bamako with fine stuff to sell. I made, on my first day, a twenty-thousand CFA profit. There was nothing I could not sell. And I had everything. Did you want scissors? American perfume? Right here, I got 'em right here. Watches, you say? *Rouge à lèvres,* you say? Come to Moustapha Diole.

" 'My second day gave me another profit of twenty thousand CFA, and my next day brought me three times this much. By the end of one month only I was ready to return home. Imagine this. Here I was doing in one month what it usually take other to do in six.

" 'On the night I was to leave there, I decide I should taste a little whiskey and a few women. I made my way to the night market not far from the airport to find those things. Before Independence, it was possible to find these markets. During the day, these markets appear to be simply regular markets, and as far as anybody knew, the day business was all they did. But at night, Berd, at night, *Wyyo!* many, many sweet and bad things could be bought in those places. Do you want a woman? No problem. Do you want a Russian rifle? *Voilà!* Human flesh, you say?' "

I was growing uncertain as to whose story this was. It seemed that Idi was on the verge of racing ahead of M.D. M.D. looked a bit baffled as Idi told me about the night markets. Even after Idi (evidently) explained to M.D. what he'd told me, I noted a shade of bewilderment sweep across M.D.'s face. He nodded once, twice, then asked Idi a question. *"Si, si,* No problem." M.D. resumed:

" 'Yes, my friend. This was not a place for children, my friend. Here is a place where the spirit is too happy to leave from the body. Here is a place where money flies faster than airplanes?' " M.D. bugged his yellow eyes and thrust one bony finger toward the ceiling. He turned to me with the finger still stiff in the air and said, "Mali is very dangerous." He brought the finger down slow and easy as if drawing a curtain down on the English parenthetical. He turned to Idi.

" 'I was in this place searching for what I wanted, when all of the sudden I heard a familiar voice call to me. I have the eyes of a village man. I can see coins at the bottom of the sea, but I saw no person this night. I turn around, and jump when I see to find myself face-to-face with a big and huge Mauritanian that I did business with some days before. Ah! he was a big, big, big. 'Hello, my friend,' he say. *'Asalaam aleikum,'* I say to him. 'You don't remember me, my good friend?,' say this *nar.* 'I certainly hope you do,' he say, 'because we made business together a few days ago only.' As he say this I slip my hand in my boubou, and close the second button of my belt. This I did, you see, to bring power to it. The *nar* continue speaking like this; 'You see my brother, I have change my mind about our bargain. I would like to return you these sunglasses. You see they are not the quality you promise.'

" 'I don't know what you mean,' I say. 'I am arrive in Bamako yesterday only.'

" 'You remember me and I remember you.'

" 'Perhaps you met my brother,' I respond.

" 'My money, nigger, give it to me.' Before I could move I saw the *nar's* arm fall to me like a shadow. He hit me two hard times on my head with a knife. Before I could reach for my knife, he was on me again. He stab on my arm, head, and neck very crazily and angry. It was not until the fourth time he hit me that I realize that I was feeling no pain. Not one pain at all. The juju was working!

" 'Suddenly, the *nar* stop his attack. His knife drop to the ground with a loud sound, and I hear him back away from me slowly. Then my hand found the handle of not my knife, but of my machete. I had it out at the same time he turn to run. I close my eyes and swing with the power of Mohammed almost. When I open my eyes I expect to see his big *nar* head rolling on the ground. Instead I was disappoint to see him run away like a baboon. I drop down to my hands and knees to feel for blood, but find only his right hand and most of his bottom lip.' "

Nice story, I thought. I looked at Idi for a good long while, trying to read his face. Nothing. The mastery he held over his face rivaled the Mona Lisa. It held balanced, soft, almost fuzzy, like one might hold a ball of light in the palm of one's hand. I wanted to throw something at him. M.D.'s eyes were yellow-yellow. They told me very little. They were as unreadable as Idi's eyes, but outlined with drunken nonchalance.

Then M.D. said something to Idi. "He wants to know," said Idi, "if you have a knife."

"What for?" I said, as if I'd just stumbled into the room. Idi looked at me as if I knew damned well what for, but nevertheless said, "He wants to prove the belt works."

"Is he serious?"

"I think."

"You mean he's going to stab himself?"

"Yes, I think."

"Tell him he doesn't have to. Tell him I believe him, but I'm just not interested."

"Doesn't matter, Berd. He wants to show you anyway."

"How do you know? Did you ask him?" I looked at M.D. He sat gravely nodding, bottom lip poking big as Texas, looking just as cool as cool can.

Now look. My little pocket knife is no kabar. The blade, at best, is a mere three or four inches long. It's sharp enough to pierce an orange with but slight pressure. With medium pressure, it's sharp enough to pierce the flesh. I often use it to punch new holes in my belts. I slipped the knife from my pocket, and, oddly enough, tossed it across the room to Idi, as if he were a member of the studio audience and M.D. the Amazing Kreskin. Idi cocked his head, opened the knife, got up, and handed the knife to M.D., who took the knife, uncovered his beer belly, fastened the belt's second button and peppered himself about two dozen times. He beckoned me, asking me to inspect his work. I did. There were about two dozen pin pricks on his belly, each holding the faintest droplets of blood. Otherwise, his stomach was fine. "*Aam,*" M.D. said, and handed me the knife. "Now you must stab him," said Idi.

"Tell him I believe him," I said.

"Won't do any good."

"Is true," M.D. said. "Is no pain you."

I looked from Idi's eyes to M.D.'s and back. Idi seemed rather bored. M.D. looked stoned, eager and somewhat supercilious. With one arm akimbo, bottom lip poking, he smacked himself on the belly, said, "Is strong. Very good." "I don't want to hurt him," I said to no one in particular. "I don't think you will," said Idi. I touched the knife point to the palm of my hand in order to gauge its sharpness. It seemed to me that one moderate poke would sink the blade an inch or two into the old man's stomach. I folded the blade. "Tell him to fuckin' forget it," I said. But Idi argued that it had become "a thing of honor," that I couldn't back out. "He say," Idi went on, "that you have brought him good luck. He say his wife has medicine because of you."

"That's because of the mark-up on the garbage I bought from him. It hasn't got a damned thing to do with luck. I was just too stupid to bargain with him." And then I went on about how I too was being honorable by pledging my belief in M.D.'s word. But Idi just stared at me as if I'd said something stupid. "You want me to tell him that?" said Idi. M.D. weaved and bobbed, daintily holding up the hem of his boubou. "No. Hell with it," I said, opening up the knife. I gently pushed the point into M.D.'s soft belly. I increased the pressure bit by bit. The knife depressed his stomach like a finger poke. I withdrew the knife, drew back and jabbed hard, then harder. I looked up and grinned at Idi. He was at the dresser fixing himself a drink. I shrugged and pounded M.D.'s stomach so hard the blade folded across my index finger and M.D. fell backward onto the bed.

Not a scratch. I turned toward Idi, who was now intently watching me. "Is true," I said.

So.

As Idi explained it, M.D., indeed, wanted to give me the juju, but this is the kind of giving he'd had in mind. I was to have named one price—any price—in exchange for the belt. All I had to do was name one price and the price would stick. Haggling would negate the belt's power. And according to Idi, the only reason M.D. brought up the matter of money was because it was a ritual way of showing respect for the power of the juju, M.D., and M.D.'s poor dead dad. So there I was. I'd seen what M.D.'s miraculous belt could do, or more objectively, what his miraculous stomach could do, or what my eyes could not do, or whatever. I didn't know what to say. I vacillated between what was and what wasn't was.

Having the belt meant either going through the rest of my life essentially unafraid of another human being, or making a complete and very perforated ass of myself. I alternately envisioned myself single-handedly stopping crime in the United States, and winding up dead from self-inflicted wounds in my little Senegalese bungalow. I didn't know who how from nothing. And one matter, completely aside from the question of the belt's efficacy, was that of the money. If I'd offered him five dollars, think of the statement I'd have been making about M.D. and his father. On the other hand, what if I'd offered him fifty, or five hundred dollars? You just don't go around ready to hand out big simolea for things in which you don't believe. I wanted to say, Look, Idi, tell this yutz to go wax himself. He's a huckster. Tell him I'm a goddamn American and I don't believe in shit. I wanted to say, No, no, on second thought, I really don't believe this motherjumper works. Tell him to get me a goddamn gun I can poke in his eye. Then we'll see about this he-no-kill-no-pain hooey. I wanted to say, Get me back to Boston. I wanted to say, Help! Mr. Wizard, I don't wanna be an anthropologist no more! Instead I said, and quite soberly I might add, "Tell him," I said, "Tell him I'll think about it."

Anyway, Idi, who'd sat through the whole affair with his disengaged, beatific mug, told me next morning over café au lait and bread, that M.D. was more than likely trying to pull a fast one. He said the juju Moustapha Diole had offered me probably wasn't the one actually protecting him.

"He's not a stupid man," said Idi.

Her Mother's Prayers on Fire

Don Belton

1989

she's not a bad girl because
she wants to be free

—*song*

The bandleader gave the signal. The drummer kicked hard on the bass drum.
It sounded like a gunshot. In the audience, ageless pretty boys in box-back suits
stopped talking. "Bring it on," shouted a woman seated at a table near the stage.
She finished her drink and stabbed out her cigarette. "Take over!"

The eight-piece band laid down the opening bars of "Check Yourself." The
horns let loose with a wail. The guitars answered in sharp arpeggios. The
drummer washed the air with thunder.

A spotlight fell on Frances. She stood there a moment, tensed, the muscles
visibly throbbing in her bared arms and legs. The light came up on Beryl,
Lucinda, and Marie, to the right of Frances, forming a pyramid with Beryl
downstage at the apex. Their images bled through colored smoke.

Frances went to work, growling the song's bitter news, dancing out to the
edge of the hard rhythm. Her voice was a springing sex sound. Beryl, Lucinda,
and Marie fell into a coordinated dance routine, jerking and pumping in place.
Their voices sparked one another. Soon, their faces were greasy with sweat and
paint. Their big earrings shook.

It was Frances who held the audience. Her mouth looked like an electric-
pink wound. Her waterfall eyelashes eclipsed her startled eyes. Her voice threatened to drown out the horns. When the drummer took a solo, Frances did the
"pony" back and forth from the microphone stand, stealing his fire. She began

to whirl. She turned herself into a pyrotechnic blur of noise, flesh, and color. Relentlessly, she worked her spell, pushing energy to the breaking point, backing off an instant, then driving again. She did this over and over, until a man at one of the tables said, "Have mercy." And a woman cried, "Tell the truth!"

The song ended, and she jerked herself still like a toy switched off suddenly. Beryl, Lucinda, and Marie stepped back from the stage lights. Frances leaned forward to cloak herself in the eerie armor of applause.

They were backstage in the narrow storeroom that Doll, when he told them he had them booked at Mr. Wonderful's Supper Club, called a dressing room. Frances was shaking out her long-haired wig. She brushed the wig and set it on a Styrofoam head.

Beryl looked at the wig enviously. "That is a pretty wig, Fran. That's one hundred percent human hair. European hair. You can tell. That wig cost a nice piece a change. You oughta let me borrow it next week when Preston take me to New York City for my birthday."

Lucinda said, "You think you into something because you going to New York. Where all is he taking you?"

"We going to this Spanish restaurant in the Village called El Faro. Then we going to see Ornette Coleman and Don Cherry at the Five Spot. You know how Preston is about jazz—even on my birthday."

Lucinda sucked her teeth. "You think you big time."

Marie was in the dark far corner of the room, putting on street clothes. Marie said, "She big time even if she ain't going no farther than Jersey City. Beryl, you lucky and don't even know it. A lot of fellas wouldn't think no more of a girl on her birthday than to take her to a rock-and-roll movie at the Branford and think she's wrong if she won't let him put his hand down her bra setting up in the balcony. Preston has class."

Lucinda said, "Eldridge took me to the Crystal Room at Bamberger's for my birthday."

"I told Preston I would rather die," said Beryl, "than be stuck in Newark, tryna have a romantic birthday dinner in some department store cafeteria. That's for sure. I see enough of Newark the rest of the year. At least I deserve to go some place halfway decent for my birthday."

"Well, I'd never let you put your nasty head in a wig of mines. I'll tell you that much," said Lucinda, retouching the long Egyptian lines along her eyelids with an eyebrow pencil. "You don't need no wig anyway. You got good hair, if you would take care of it. Your hair could be long enough to whup your behind every time you walk. You got that wild Geechee hair. You need to cultivate your hair. That's all. You too cheap to buy a twenty-five-cent jar of Dixie Peach and a five-cent comb."

Beryl lifted a comb off the makeshift dressing counter and waved it like a baton. "I got my comb right here. So just shut up, Lucy."

"That's *my* comb," snapped Frances, "that you *supposedly* borrowed when we played the union party last month. I just know you forgot."

Lucinda told Beryl, "You want everything you see Frances with. You so jealous. You want a wig so bad, order yourself one out the *Ebony* magazine like everybody else. They got this mean wig, I seen in there last month for twenty-nine ninety-five called the Polynesian. So don't order that one. That one's mines."

"Frances ain't get *that* wig out no magazine. That ain't no damn mail-order glamour she got." Beryl turned on Frances suddenly. "Is it, Sister?"

Frances opened her cosmetics case and started rubbing Noxzema on her face.

Beryl hated Noxzema. She swore the smell of the eucalyptus oil that gave the cream its distinctive odor made her sick to her stomach.

"I'm not your sister," Frances said in a voice as cool as Noxzema. "So don't ride me. And stay out my business."

"I ain't tryna ride you. If I wanted to ride you I woulda asked you where you stayed all week. I woulda asked you how come you been cutting out on rehearsal early. How come don't nobody see you around the way no more."

Frances smoothed the cream on her face, staring into the reflection of her own eyes. "Go to hell, hear me, Beryl?"

"Damn, I was only admiring your wig."

"Forget you."

"Well, that's it!" Marie zipped herself into her slacks and patted her hips. She was wearing a black jersey and tight black jeans. She stepped into her sling-back sandals. "I'm going outside and smoke me a reefer. Anybody else want to come? Or yall just want to stay in here and fight over some simple shit? And, in case you don't get it, Fran, what Beryl tryna to tell you is, she's pissed cause Doll bought you that wig."

"Beryl can kiss my natural behind," Frances said politely, sliding her head-band into place before applying cream to her forehead.

Marie put on her jacket, used Frances' white lipstick, and left the room.

"Who says Doll bought Frances a wig?" asked Lucinda, offended that everyone seemed to know about this but her.

"Yeah, Doll bought it, all right," Beryl shouted, jumping to the middle of the tight room so hard her breasts shook in her bodice. "That ain't all he doing for her."

"Keep it up, hear, Beryl? Keep fucking with me, hear? I done told you don't ride me."

"I ain't got to ride you. You got that process-haired nigger riding your velvet ass, you think you a queen now. You better not let that man's pigmeat go to your head, baby. I'm tryna warn you. Doll will stomp you and think nothing of it. He won't even look back."

Lucinda had been twisting into a pleated skirt. Now she was as still as a folded bat. The look on her face was fearful and grave. "If she messing with Doll," Lucinda ventured, "she'll be lucky to get up and walk off from just an ass-beating. She'll be lucky if he *don't* look back—if he don't kill her. Everybody on Springfield Avenue know the kinda man Doll Jefferson is."

"Look, Lucy, shut up. You don't know what you talking about. I'm talking to Frances."

Lucinda sounded like she was working herself up to cry. "How come I'm the one got to shut up? You think I'm not hip no more just because my family moved to Montclair. I *hear* things. We should have never agreed to let him manage the Jewelettes."

"We thought we knew what we was doing when we let him manage us. But what did we say? Wasn't none of us going for his talk. Okay. Frances said Doll got the connections we need. We tryna get over. Fine. But we ain't got to be nasty to do it. Frances, even your mother will tell you what a man like Doll will do to you, and her mind so wrapped up in Jesus and the church she ain't even studying these streets."

"Don't tell me nothing about my mother. I don't want to hear it. Mind your own business. Both of you. And don't say *nothing* to me about my mother."

"What you mean I can't say nothing to you about your mother? Frances, you must be crazy or high, one. I know you *and* your mother since I was in the first grade. What you telling me: Don't say nothing about Mother Deal and mind my business? You wrong, Fran. Your nose full of Doll now. You feeling huffy. *Somebody* got to talk to you."

It was true she and Beryl had been girls together. All of them. Lucinda and Marie too. They had braided one another's hair and rhythmically scratched each other's scalps with big-handled combs to soothe the tension of summer evenings as adolescence came on. Together, they observed the seasons of boys turning into men—boys who, one season, sounded like mourning doves and, the next, like noisy new car motors and who looked fierce and fine in two-toned Italian sweaters, chinos, and alligator shoes.

They had raised one another. They dressed one another. They jumped into one another's business, corrected and fought for one another. They loved each other with a love that was too hungry, at the same time it was too full, for any boy or any man. They taught each other to dance and to swear. They learned to sing together, sparking one another's voices to forge a new language adequate for the mystery of their experience, producing a sound as sassy and rich as girl talk.

The first time Frances saw her, Beryl was riding a bicycle down Stratford Place. Beryl was an amazing sight with her streaming hair ribbons and ruffled romper suit, gliding on a jewel-red bike, all that thick hair sailing along with her.

Frances' mother had been standing at the tall living room window of 42 Stratford.

"That is one pretty black child," Frances heard her mother say. She left her paper dolls to see who her mother was talking about, and there was Beryl moving with the energy of a baby panther.

Mother and daughter had watched through the window, awed by that black, shining energy. Then Odessa said to Frances, "Put on your sweater, baby, and go see if she'll give you a ride."

Beryl had a human gift that even Odessa Deal approved. Not before or since had she encouraged her daughter to play with any of the neighborhood children.

Now, Frances felt her resolve weaken an instant, as she went to the tiny basin to rinse her face. She returned from the sink, dabbing her face with a towel.

Beryl came up on her. She told Frances, "You oughta be glad you got friends, Frances, while you still got them. I'm going to tell you where it's at, whether you like it or not. A lot of people will look right at you messing yourself up and won't say nothing to you. But you can tell by their look they thinking you ain't right."

Frances put her wig inside its box. She began repacking her cosmetics case. "I don't want nothing from you, Beryl. I don't want no preaching. There ain't a thing you can say to me. I don't care about looks or your opinion or anybody else's opinion about my life."

"What you think your life is? You ain't the only person with a life. You think your life something that come scot-free of everybody else? Listen to me, Frances. I will scream. I will curse you out. I will kick your ass if it come to that. I love you. And you ain't right, girl. You ain't but fifteen years old. Whatever you doing, it ain't right. Why you acting the way you been acting?

"Okay. You and your mother wasn't getting along, so you moved out. Okay. First, you asked me to see if my parents would let you stay with us for a while till you get your thing together. Fine. You stay at my house three days, next thing I know you staying at Lucinda's. You there a few days. Then we don't know where you staying. We see you at rehearsal, and that's all. Next thing I know so-and-so saying, 'I saw Frances driving around with Doll.' I hear, 'Frances living with Doll.' Your mother asking us about you, and we don't know what to say. Long as we been hanging together, I feel bad I don't know what's going on with you—where you are, who you with, if you all right. I know you, Fran. We been through . . . *everything*. This shit ain't right."

Lucinda sat down on the only chair in the room. She looked as frail as a child's ghost. "She's telling you the truth. You're our girl, Frances. You're our *heart*. If Doll hurts you I don't know what I'd do."

Frances closed the cosmetic bag and tossed it into the flight bag she used for her stage costume. "You don't understand. You don't really know Doll. He is *not* a killer or whatever else you think. He's a man—a good man—out here tryna *do* something instead of just laying on his back crying about the white man. Doll has done a lot for us, including getting us this gig. I don't know about you, but I'm sicka lip-synching to records at basement parties. How long we wanted to get a gig at Mr. Wonderful's before Doll took over managing us? We couldn't even get *in* Mr. Wonderful's, much less do a show here."

Marie was back in the room, smelling like reefer. They heard the jangle of her earrings near the door. "Why don't yall get offa Fran's case. Beryl, you worse than somebody's mother. God knows I was tireda the Jewelettes going nowhere. I ain't just singing and dancing for my health. How long was we supposed to go on with nothing to show for our struggling? Doll bought us costumes. We rehearse with a band. Plus, now he talking about getting us a show at the Glitter Club. Can you get us a show at the Glitter Club, Beryl?"

"The Glitter Club!" Lucinda said with a ribald squeal. "Ain't nobody told me nothing about no Glitter Club, baby. We really be into something at the Glitter Club. They had the Shirelles there last month." She was dancing in the small space, caught up in a fantasy of glamour and expression. "We going to turn that place *out.*"

"No." Beryl shook her head as if the force of her shaking head could wake the four of them from a deadly dream. "No. Frances always digging up some man to manage the group. Frances act like she can't do nothing without a man at the crown of it, running the whole show. Look, you think I don't want the Jewelettes to get over? I want us to get over. I know we can. But not like this. . . . And not with Doll Jefferson. You think he doing so much for us. He messed up a lot of deals for us too. We coulda sang at the Terrace Ballroom with the Inez and Charlie Fox Show, but they wouldn't pay us the amount *Doll* wanted. He messed that up, instead of letting us decide among ourselves—as a group—if we would perform for their amount."

It don't work that way, Frances wanted to tell her, but repented.

"Yeah," Beryl went on, "he getting us fifty dollars apiece each show now, but we don't know what he get. We don't know what deals he's making on us."

Frances understood Beryl, and that was what made everything so hard. She remembered how, when the group was formed, the four of them would congregate in Beryl's bedroom because she had the full-length mirror. They would crowd the mirror, trying on outlandish getups, hairstyles, and makeup styles. They listened to stacks of 45 singles: "It's in His Kiss," "Gee Whiz," "A Change Is Gonna Come." Marie worked them through dance steps. The twist. The chicken. The twine. Frances and Marie drank Nehi sodas, listening to Beryl whisper scandals from the pages of *Tan Confessions* or *Bronze Thrills,* while Lucinda sat hunched by the phonograph listening to a record over and over, writing down the words. Then they would all copy out the lyrics in theme books bought by their parents for the intended purpose of keeping algebra or history notes. They would listen together to the record with the volume turned to a hiss and find their individual parts. They soon realized they had their own special harmony. Soon they preferred their versions to the recorded versions. Marie filled out their sound with an all-stops-out blues way of singing. Beryl had that church feeling. Lucinda's singing bird voice gave the music a shimmery wistfulness. Frances was jazzy. She had the natural lead sound; the way she acted out a song like a dramatic star and leaned on her vowels and word endings. She had the power to pronounce a word so distinctly it made you remember what the word was all about.

They made themselves believe they could be as big as the Shirelles or the Supremes. The Jewelettes' success would not only mean escaping high school and adolescence into a grown-up world of furs, cars, and fame. For Frances, it meant getting out of Newark and finally shedding her Holy Ghost-believing mother.

They had made Beryl the group spokeswoman. Beryl kept them together. She was the stable one. She used to tell them, "We're a group. Can't nobody do this but us. We're a family." Everyone agreed on that. If they were having a rehearsal and someone messed up or was late or cursed, that member was fined a quarter. "I want us to make it to the top and stay there," Beryl used to say. *I* want *us* was the way all of them, even Frances, had talked about the group then.

Now Marie was saying, "Give me a break. How else we going to make it? Frances is realistic. And if she want to sleep with Doll, it's her business. It sure ain't hurting us."

"Yall." Frances was surprised at how tired her own voice sounded. "I got to go."

"Ain't you going to hang out and wait for Doll to bring us our money?" asked Lucinda, worried.

"Don't be a fool," Beryl told her. "She can get hers anytime she want."

Frances gave Marie a cold but gentle kiss on the side of the face. She had the slick flight bag on her arm. She put on her coat, cracker-shaped with a jut-out collar.

"Gimme a cigarette before you go," Marie said, moving away from the door.

Frances went in her bag, gave her a Kool, and lit it. Returning the cigarettes, she fingered the inside of her bag.

Lucinda noticed the panicked look on her face. "What's wrong, Fran?"

Beryl said, "This what she looking for." Beryl flung a dome-shaped diamond ring out onto the room. The ring tumbled on the floor and stopped short of Frances' feet. It glowed in the room's semidarkness.

They looked at the ring, stunned. Even Frances, who had been in constant motion all night, was suddenly arrested by the jewel's spell, her restless hands stilled.

Finally, Lucinda walked up and knelt before the ring. She picked it up reverently and carefully, as if plucking a star from the sky in an elementary school play. Then she looked up at Frances.

"You are sure a sister with a plan," Marie said, impressed.

At length, Lucinda's mouth formed a letter O.

Frances said, "Give me my ring."

Lucinda moved toward her, holding the ring in front of her, spellbound.

All eyes were on Frances, as she put the ring on her finger. She threw the flight bag and purse on the floor. Her rage lit up the room. She walked up to Beryl. "You had the nerve to go in my bag," she said.

"Frances, I—"

She leapt on Beryl with all her strength, tearing at her hair and clothing. Her knees were on Beryl's back. Beryl fought wildly to get loose, screaming into the floor.

Marie and Lucinda pulled Frances off. Beryl jumped up and slammed her against the door. The doorknob struck her side. She doubled over on the floor near her flight bag. She gathered her things and put the door between herself and the room.

As she shut the door on them, she glimpsed Beryl's face. It was a face where outrage, like a thick mucus, had entirely drowned out the eyes. It was a face for something terrible and exquisite in herself she was already sorry she had betrayed.

She heard Beryl calling after her as she went down the hall. "Get outa here. I know what you doing. You ain't fooling nobody. I'm going to tell your mother everything. Run. Keep on running. Just don't come back here when Doll finish wiping his feet on you."

But she was not running. She was walking through the congested backstage area of the supper club and down Avon Avenue, calm and spent.

Though she had not seen her mother in fourteen days now, she still sensed Odessa rising each morning before the first light and praying to get her hold back on her daughter's life. Frances felt her mother's rebukes against the Devil. She could hear, whenever she slowed down too long, her mother's voice: "I call you in, in the name of Jesus."

The temperature dipped to thirteen below zero that night. The streets iced over and sparkled like rivers of frozen light. She was standing near the courthouse when she saw the hulking Coup de Ville come streaming up Market Street and stop for her. The driver came out and opened the door for her. She threw her things into the backseat and jumped in. Ray Charles was on the radio singing

"Baby What I Say." The music sounded so free. She snuggled against Doll and kissed him with her eyes closed and her mouth open. He smelled like J&B, cigarettes, and After Dark cologne. The door closed behind her. The driver got back in and took off.

She opened her coat and hiked up her skirt to let the car's heater bathe her long legs. They had just hit the interstate when Doll ordered the driver to stop on the side of the road so they could set up a bar.

Doll handed her a metal cup full of Scotch. The driver beat out a bubbling rhythm on the steering wheel. She sipped the Scotch. It burned her throat. Then she felt the warmth fill her body. She handed the Scotch back to Doll. Doll handed it to the driver. He had to poke him in the shoulder blade to get his attention, he was so lost in his drumming. That boy was beat-crazy. She polished up her ring on the sleeve of her coat. Then she took out a cigarette and placed it between her lips.

She wondered how long her girlfriends would wait in the dressing room for their money before realizing Doll was not coming. Beryl would be the first to figure things out. Lucinda would refuse to believe it. Marie would be cool.

Doll told Frances he liked a woman who could quit a town just like that.

"Let me fire that up for you, sugar," Doll said.

The sound the match made, as it burst into blue fire on the side of the Glitter Club matchbox, gave her a rush of exhilaration. She felt energized and clean like light set free. It was a supernatural sound. That sound, the energized *pop* and *whoosh*, Frances knew, as she inhaled on the cigarette against the burning match, was more than the sound of a match head bursting into flame: It was the sound of all her mother's prayers on fire.

Wings of the Dove

Hal Bennett

1989

Old Susanna Jackson dying down the street, and White Preacher eat Sunday dinner at our house. Pale September sun wobble in and out the kitchen ever since he come. He slouch at the table strewn with gnawed chicken bones and greasy napkins, liberally picking his teeth. He use his own gold toothpick instead of our old common ones. He look stuffed, happy, and hopeful, like he expect some man to pop from the salt shaker and claim responsibility for us ten children.

Fluvanna, our mama, she announce the event like Nancy Reagan herself coming to the ghetto. "White Preacher'll be here at two pee-em Sunday," she say. Come that time, half the children scatter. But Roy, he definitely stay. He want to write everything down, he say. Fluvanna turn to him with her finger like a spear. "We's *Virginia,*" she say emphatically, screwing up her face. She mean he can write all he want to, but impoliteness is always unwelcome wherever Virginians congregate, especially to guests of whatever color. We even call White Preacher that out of politeness so's not to confuse him with Black Preacher, who exercises his civil rights by eating at white houses nowadays.

Anyway, old Susanna Jackson down the street dying. She the mother of our most famous militant, Hardy Lee Jackson. He an old man now in a California prison for crimes none of us hardly remember. White Preacher and other liberals like him practically live here with us and Hardy Jackson in the ghetto in the sixties. Then something happen. "Civil rights is *accom-pli-shed!*" Roy say he remember somebody saying, probably after Jimmy Carter get elected and choose a jailbird black woman to be his daughter's nanny. Then all the white people go away, Hardy get arrested, and that old iron curtain fall back down around the ghetto, as Roy say.

Until White Preacher discover Fluvanna in his congregation the other day, over there across the railroad tracks. Her name come from a county and a river in Virginia next to Charlottesville where the University of Virginia is, designed by Thomas Jefferson. She out on some errand for her madam and she go into White Preacher's church unsuspecting. "Child, my feet hurt me like the dickens! And the sun so hot, the sidewalk even hotter. I surely thought I'd faint. So I go into this great big church to sit down in the cool." She tell us that later. Roy stand around, grinning, nodding, wrinkles in his forehead. He going to be our *chronicler* some day, he say, but he waiting for money to buy him a word processor, so he say.

So White Preacher with his yellow hair, he come down and look at Fluvanna hard, probably seeing hisself back in the sixties again. "I thought you come to *integrate* the church," he tell Fluvanna later, and she see he scared to death of that. She see a copy of *The Color Purple* on his desk, along with the Bible and some pamphlets about Come to Jesus. Fluvanna feel real good when she see *The Color Purple* on his desk; that show he still a real liberal. That book's like a Bible in the ghetto now, all them things Alice Walker say about black men being rapists. Which black women and white folks do dearly love to hear.

"Y'all ain't integrated yet?" Fluvanna ask, unconsciously accusing, then bite her devilish tongue. After all, she *is* from Virginia, named after a county and a river there.

"Well, we are *now,*" White Preacher say, trying to laugh. Then he excuse hisself and go out somewhere, perhaps to the toilet. Fluvanna pick up *The Color Purple* and thumb through it, although she know it most by heart. The way that woman suffer in *The Color Purple* make Fluvanna feel good and somehow triumphant when the woman triumph too.

Also, something there remind her of Hardy, she tell us later, make her feel kind of peculiar up between her legs. Sometime I wonder if Hardy Lee Jackson be our father, but Roy say we too intelligent for Hardy to be that. Furthermore, Hardy been locked up so long they would've had to do it long distance, Roy say.

Anyway, Fluvanna don't have time to read no more because White Preacher come back with a hammer in his hand. She get real scared, thinking he going to kill her to keep the church from being integrated after all. But he laugh when he see the look on her face.

"This here hammer belong to Hardy Lee Jackson," he say, and his face grow solemn. "He did some work for me around the church here, back in the sixties," he say, "and he left his hammer with me." It a real hammer, too, just like any ordinary hammer to Fluvanna. She can't tell whether it's Hardy's or not. And she still got a suspicion White Preacher going to murder her to hold back integration. She remember that Rosa Parks woman in Montgomery, Alabama, the way her hurting feet start that whole Civil Rights Movement in the sixties. A Virginia woman would die first before she let everybody carry on so about *her* feet, and on television at that.

But White Preacher go on talking about Hardy and what a sin and a shame it is California won't let him go. "We have our Rudolf Hess and we have our

Spandau, too," he say, kind of dark like, and Fluvanna wonder what in the world he talking about. She remember what she read in *The Color Purple* and it make her feel real warm and lonesome for Hardy, who used to be her love way back when. He must be an old man by now, like Fluvanna practically an old lady.

Then she remember how everybody seem young back in the Civil Rights Movement, so young and so full of hope. But Roy say, "We come face to face with our own prejudices in the sixties," and he write that in white chalk on a red brick wall one day. Fluvanna don't understand but she say she learn a whole lot about herself after reading *The Color Purple*. About what it really mean to be a black woman, she say. All black women like that book, white women too, but they got better excuses for being ignorant. All black men despise it, including fags, except them that dress up like women. Roy say he going to write that Alice Walker a piece of his mind one of these days, soon as he get his word processor. Her picture all over the ghetto on postcards, like she the Lincoln Monument or something.

"Anyway," White Preacher go on, "I recently got a communication from Miss Susanna, Hardy's sainted mother," he say. "She informs me that she is dying, and I'm going to visit her, with some of the other militants from the sixties, those who aren't already dead. I want you to tell her so, Fluvanna, and to return Hardy's hammer to her as well, in case she wants to leave a legacy."

Well, Fluvanna get the giggles. She don't figure then that White Preacher know what a hammer signify in the ghetto. Or maybe only in Virginia where we got dirtier minds. *John Henry had him a hammer,* the song go, or, *How your hammer hanging, boy?* all the men say to each other. *Hammer* is a word that got a whole lot to do with black men's manhood, what's left of it after *The Color Purple* get through hacking at it. So Fluvanna giggle, and White Preacher think it's nerves, which it probably was, his holding Hardy's hammer in his hand.

So she say anything to get out of there. Her feet feel fine by then, and she say, "That's mighty nice of you, Preacher, and I want you to come to dinner tomorrow night. We got pig feet soaking in salt water to take that awful smell away, and I going to make some Aunt Jemima cornbread mix, and we going to have some real soul food, potato salad and collard greens and all that."

Which make White Preacher smile with fond remembrance, Fluvanna say. "I have not really *eaten* since Selma," he say, referring to Selma, Alabama, where all that civil rights stuff went on back in the sixties with Martin Luther King. She wonder what White Preacher been eating all this time, being married and everything. His wife live away in an ivory tower, so Roy say. She a little pale white thing, look bewildered all the time, like White Preacher probably do terrible things to her when he get the appetite.

"But I intended to go see Miss Susanna tomorrow night," he say, "along with some of the other ex-militants. We want to pay her a special homage, seeing that she's on her deathbed and Hardy's still in jail. Maybe you could make the dinner for Sunday?" he say hopefully. And Fluvanna start suspecting that being a white preacher and everything, maybe he can't digest black folk's food except on the Sabbath.

So she say all right and go home, after dropping Hardy's hammer off with Miss Susanna Jackson, who's dying propped up in her bed, looking out the window at the falling leaves. Fluvanna tell Miss Susanna that White Preacher coming with the ex-militants tomorrow night, and Miss Susanna say, "It's sure going to be hard for me, honey, talking to them. I been thinking that the sixties caused a lot of flurry on top—you know what I mean?—but it didn't convert the people. So they soon started falling back to their old ways, black and white alike. As for me, I'm awfully interested in Reagan, you know? He sent a black man up into space, two or three, less I'm mistaken. That's more than any Democrat ever done for us, don't you see, honey?"

But Fluvanna of course don't see the difference between poverty programs and outer space. She think Miss Susanna just raving out of her head since she's dying. She give her Hardy's hammer and a peck on the forehead, then come on home to us.

The first thing Roy say, after she tell us how was her day, is that he know where to steal him a word processor, he got to begin his chronicles. Fluvanna whack his head in. We all get together and ask our usual question, "Mama, who our daddy is?" I get this terrible feeling sometime that *her* daddy is our daddy, that old, stinking, smelling black man in overalls there in Fluvanna County in Virginia.

But she answer like she always do. "The Lord God in heaven is all of our Father," she say unctuously, like God personally come down from up yonder and carry her off to bed ten times. If that be true, Roy ask me sometime, then why ain't we gods instead of niggers? Or is God a nigger Hisself and heaven that Big Ghetto in the Sky? But nobody ask Fluvanna because she hit with a real heavy hand sometime.

So we get through the next few days somehow. Old black women leaning in windows reading *The Color Purple,* calling out dirty passages to each other. Black men all drugged up and out in droves, raping everybody. Roy nearly get arrested, trying to steal his word processor. Fluvanna turn the pig's feet in the brine, to make sure they white all over. Then White Preacher and the other ex-militants pull up in four or five cars at Miss Susanna's house, and we all go down to the homage. Roy take his notebook, and this is what he write:

Ornery as she is, Miss Susanna get up for the occasion. Death just have to wait, she say, seeing she's going to have an homage. I look up the word in my pocket dictionary I steal from Woolworth's. It say, "hom-age," in black letters, "1. respect or reverence paid or rendered," and so forth. The first thing White Preacher and them others do is kneel and pray. Then Miss Susanna serve Apple Zapple and everybody get swashed.

"I'm terribly interested in Reagan," Miss Susanna say. She all dolled up in some kind of purple dress with a white collar and a kind of face carved in a white stone tied on a red ribbon around her neck. "Reagan send two or three black men out into space," she say. "How can anybody reasonably say we're inferior after that? Furthermore, I have not read *The Color Purple,* which some thoughtful black people consider slander."

The ex-militants look at each other and kind of smile slyly. They figure Miss Susanna's not right in the head, since she going to die anyway. She sitting in a big rocking chair, and they file past her, kissing the back of her hand, like she some kind of queen.

"That's all right, Sugar," one of the men say, pacifying. "President Reagan's got his points, even if they is all sharp." He wear an Afro that's twenty years old, and somebody's hand-me-down dashiki. He look himself like somebody bought him at the Salvation Army. Some of his colleagues snuffle down in their throats and hide smiles behind their hands.

There about fifteen or twenty people there, white and black, most of them as old as Fluvanna is, some of them older, but no Jews at all. I calculate. (NOTE— Examine the Jewish absence. Contrast with Jewish presence in the sixties. QUES-TIONS—Was it wise to alienate them? Is it reasonable that America's two most despised groups should despise each other? CHECK THIS OUT.)

"We went to the mountain, and now we in the valley," some of them say. That's an *allegory,* according to my dictionary: "*al-le-go-ry* 1. figurative treatment of one subject under the guise of another." Which I suppose mean most of them had to drive down from Eagle Rock in the mountains to get here to the ghetto. And also that all of them pretty swashed on Apple Zapple under the guise of being sober.

Anyway, Miss Susanna seem to be reading my mind about the mountains. "It sure getting dark," she say, "and I'm told that Halley's Comet can be seen from Eagle Rock. I'd sure like to see it before I die." And White Preacher, he clap his hand to his forehead and say, "What a capital idea!" So we all pack into the cars and drive up to Eagle Rock so Miss Susanna can see Halley's Comet before she die.

It is cold and dark up there. Looking down into the valley, we can see Cousinville sprawled at our feet. Further away is Newark, then the black space where the river runs, then all the flashing lights of New York City.

"It sure is pretty," Miss Susanna say. Then she move closer to the railing and start searching the sky. The wind blowing so hard it make her wig rise, like something under it peeping out. White Preacher and them other ex-militants grab hands and start singing "We Shall Overcome," like we already had.

Then, Miss Susanna straighten up and point. "There it is!" she cry. "Oh, there it is!" Then she fall down. We all think she dead. But Fluvanna step up and feel her. "She still breathing," Fluvanna say. All them ex-militants say,

"Praise be the Lord," or something like that. So we put Miss Susanna in somebody's car and head on back to the ghetto.

Fluvanna and the rest of us ride with White Preacher. He crying, tears like clear plastic on his cheek when car lights hit them. He turn once and say to Fluvanna and the rest of us squeezed in the back seat, "Praise be to God," he say. "She did see the comet, although none of the rest of us could."

I don't say a word. But I seen the same thing Miss Susanna see. And it wasn't the comet at all. It was a jet plane flying low over the horizon with all them red and white lights flashing. But if they want to believe she see the comet, let them. Roy hunched over scribbling in his seat by the window, and I busy trying to figure out if God's our father after all.

So we get through the next day or two until White Preacher show up for Sunday dinner. "You didn't bring your missus?" Fluvanna ask, which is a decided breach of good manners, unless White Preacher got his missus in his pocket. He look bewildered, like he just remember he is married. He mumble something about his missus not being well, and touch his yellow hair.

I suppose she still up in that ivory tower of hers, probably looking for comets, if not for something more dire. (Roy's dictionary: "dire—causing or attended with real fear or suffering; dreadful; awful: a dire calamity.") Then White Preacher ask if Miss Susanna still dying, and Fluvanna say she is, insofar as she know. Then he sit down to eat. But not pig's feet, since they went bad from all that soaking.

So Fluvanna fried three good-sized chickens, the same as she'd do in Virginia if the preacher is coming to eat. They dearly do love their fried chicken, black ministers do, and that is one stereotype that is true, so Roy say. He say you take all black preachers, even the famous ones—Adam Clayton Powell, Martin Luther King (father and son), Ralph Abernathy, Andy Young, Jesse Jackson (no kin to Miss Susanna), and all the rest, Roy say—and he bet you a dollar to a donut that every one of them freak out on fried chicken.

White Preacher ain't no different, seem to me. Roy say he sit at the table with that same air of *careless authority* that black preachers carry about them like some people carry pigskin briefcases. He prop his elbows up and eat the good parts without the slightest hesitation. Especially the juicy legs and breasts, like we'd fried him up some woman or something, the grease squishing in his mouth as he chew.

Like this is something too good to miss, the sun come out, sneak through the window past the curtains, and sit on the floor, watching White Preacher gnaw the bones and suck them for good measure. Roy say they teach them how to do that in seminary. Fluvanna and the girls going back and forth to the kitchen like ants, stuffing White Preacher. He turn red in the face from exertion.

The chicken feet and neck and wings fall to the rest of us, as always. And I get the wings, as always, which is Fluvanna's way of trying to make me into an angel, so she say. White Preacher go through everything—cornbread, collard greens, potato salad, and candied yams. Then loosen his collar and start picking his teeth very liberally, he feel that comfortable with us this fall day.

Roy writing in his notebook:

White Preacher's blue eyes seem full of that special satisfaction of accomplished gluttons. Good manners require us to treat him like he the Pope. Face flushed, jowls quivering, grease on his chin and even the tip of his nose, he look more like a fox that just eat up all the hens than he do like an ex-militant. (QUESTIONS: Just what is an ex-militant? And is Miss Susanna right about the sixties, when she say surfaces were stirred but not men's souls? CHECK THIS OUT.)

Then, while we eating strawberries and whipped cream for dessert, a little pickaninny come busting in with a note from Miss Susanna. Which I read, since Roy's ducked out to see about his word processor. *I have decided not to die after all,* Miss Susanna write. *I think I'll hang around to see the consequences of Reagan.*

Fluvanna laugh and shovel strawberries into her mouth. "That Susanna," she say, and slap another chicken wing on my plate, although I am enjoying my dessert. "Brave woman," White Preacher say, real smug, like he know everything all the time.

I eat the chicken wing along with my strawberries, and it taste real good, the mixture. I'm thinking of how Miss Susanna been on the verge of death ever since I know her. Fluvanna laugh and say Miss Susanna tough as white leather, she ain't never going to die.

Also, it Miss Susanna who plunk me on the head when I complain about always getting the chicken wings. "They're the wings of the dove, honey," she tell me, part in fun, part her own special kind of truth. Roy say Miss Susanna see life as one long struggle between beauty and absurdity, something no preacher ever could understand.

Still, looking at White Preacher's face shining with grease and hope at our dinner table, I wonder if what Miss Susanna see at Eagle Rock was a plane after all. I see an airplane, but who know what she see? Whatever it was sure make her postpone dying again.

Come down to that, who know what *I* see? I look at Roy just as he come shagging in, the setting sun a *dire* shimmering glow behind him in the doorway, and Roy look at me and grin.

Zazoo

Larry Duplechan

1989

I can still remember the smells of that summer. More than anything else about it, the scents of that years-ago summer cling to my soft inner tissues like the cold I am nursing today. I recall the smells of wetness, the perpetual, all-pervading, endless Louisiana wet, that suffocatingly hot wet that fell as warm rain, only to dissipate into steam just above the ground. The scent of the damp grasses that grew thigh-high to my father around the muddy little lake where we went crawfishing once—my father, my brother Dalton, my cousin Curtis, and me— using bits of pork rind on a string. The dark semisweet scent of the mud, mud that seemed nearly as omnipresent as the wetness and the heat, clay-red and seemingly alive in its power to suck your shoes under.

I remember the sickening sweet-sweet smell of the Off insect repellent that Duchess liked to say was like whiskey to the mosquitoes that relentlessly bit our arms and necks and faces, no matter how slick and shiny and smelly with bug spray. I remember the odor of Curtis's teenage sweat, sharp and pungent, an odor that no amount of Right Guard deodorant could entirely mask.

Even now, as L.A. rains one of its all too infrequent spring rains, making the backyard muddy and soft (at least I assume it's soft—I haven't been out today), making it smell as much like the Louisiana bayou country as it ever does; as I sit up in bed with the new Vidal in my lap and an ugly head cold pressing against the backs of my eyes, the smell of the rain-soaked Bermuda grass takes me all the way back to the summer of 1968. It was the summer before I turned eleven, the summer Great-Grandma Eudora died, the summer my cousin Curtis showed me. Showed me how.

It was the summer Mom and Dad finally allowed me to go hunting with Curtis. Mom insisted I was still too young to go hunting, as if Curtis felled great brown bears with double-barreled shotguns, instead of picking off wild birds and small game with a BB gun. My father hesitated only on the grounds that Great-Grandma Eudora's funeral had been less than twenty-four hours earlier, wondering whether it might not be disrespectful of the recently dead for any of us to go hunting so soon after the burial of Duchess's mother, my mother's beloved grandmother. Unlike our annual Christmas visits, this was not, after all, a pleasure trip.

Still, I begged and pleaded and whined—I didn't resort to whining often, but when I did I was expert at it—and not only did my parents finally acquiesce, but they even decided to allow Dalton (a full two and a half years younger than I) to go along. Even though I considered it the height of unfairness that Dalton should reap the benefits of my begging, pleading, and whining, in my joy at the prospect of finally accompanying Curtis into the woods that began just across the muddy dirt road from Duchess's house, I let it slide and ran immediately into the back room (the "extra room," as Duchess always called it) to pull on my high-top tennis shoes—I owned no boots.

The mud smells and moist green smells of the heavy-branched trees (what varieties of tree grew in the little forest I didn't know at the time and, frankly, still wouldn't know) mixed with the stronger scents of wet fur and animal droppings as we walked with some difficulty through the woods. The mud suctioned at my shoes as if it meant to keep them, and the mosquitoes hummed bebop solos in both my ears as I followed behind Dalton (though younger, he was just as tall, much more robust, and a good deal more adventurous than I), who followed Curtis. Curtis and Dalton each carried a BB-shooting air rifle. I had agreed to let Dalton carry the second gun, which made me look like Mr. Nice Guy in front of the folks, when actually I simply hadn't the smallest desire even to hold a gun. I shoved distastefully at mossy low-hanging tree branches that brushed against me as I walked. Although we had not been gone ten minutes, already the steamy heat had rendered my sweatshirt sticky wet and uncomfortable; the insect repellent was doing me no good—indeed, it seemed to lure the mosquitoes—and I was beginning to doubt the wisdom of coming out at all. I had no taste for the hunt itself, anyway. My only desire was to be with Curtis.

I had a crush on my cousin Curtis bigger than the State of Louisiana and a goodly chunk of Texas. Curtis was three years my senior. He had a voice nearly as deep as my father's and a smile that made my toes curl: a smile full of so many teeth that they stacked on top of one another on one side, a smile that deeply dimpled his handsome mahogany-brown cheeks. He also had one of the most beautiful bodies I had ever seen outside of a Hercules movie or a Charles Atlas Dynamic Tension ad in the back of a comic book. Curtis wasn't very tall (only an inch or two taller than I), but he owned an ancient iron barbell set, black and rusted and noisy, and he exercised every day.

I'd seize every opportunity to sit on Curtis's bed, my back against the whitewashed plaster wall, and watch him, shirtless and barefoot, pressing the barbell up from his chest (exhaling with an audible *pshoop*), and then lowering the bar back (inhaling slowly, *sssssp*); up and down, again and again, Curtis's face a mask of concentration, the veins in his big arms distended, one blood vessel throbbing rhythmically in the center of his forehead, his muscles seemingly capable of bursting his glossy brown skin. I'd sit, watching him as if he were my favorite TV show, my legs pulled up and crossed tightly around my hard penis. I often got hard watching Curtis; but then, I often got hard sitting in math class, or at the dinner table, or just sitting. Dalton often sat with me, but I'd ignore him as completely as I could, pretending to be alone with Curtis, that Curtis was performing for me, only me.

After he finished lifting, Curtis would stand in front of the slightly warped full-length mirror bolted to the bathroom door, flexing his muscles and studying the imperfect reflection of his perfect body. Then he'd turn to me, smile (each of his cheeks indented with a long, deep dimple), and say, "Boy, ah'm built, yeah!" Usually, I could only smile—he was so beautiful I could hardly speak.

Before we had gone deep enough into the woods to lose sight of the house, I looked down to find that the mud had lapped over the tops of both my shoes, ruining them—the stubborn red clay would never wash out. A huge, long-limbed mosquito swooped at my face, just missing my right eye, and I stopped and swatted wildly at the winged nuisance with both hands, and cried out a high-pitched little "Ah!" Dalton turned, quickly sizing up my predicament, rolled his eyes, and made a little tapping sound with his tongue. And I knew I'd done a sissy thing. Whenever I did a sissy thing—made a wild, futilely short throw of a softball, or hid my eyes during a scary movie, or cried when angry—Dalton would give me one of those looks, and I'd know he was wondering to himself what he could possibly have done to deserve such a big brother.

I hoped Curtis hadn't noticed what I'd done. Curtis seemed to like me— possibly (I thought) even more than he liked Dalton—and it was of the utmost importance to me that his affection and respect for me not be diminished by some inadvertent sissified action on my part. I looked toward Curtis and was relieved to find he was not looking at me but had run on ahead, obviously having heard some significant sound deeper into the woods.

"C'mon, y'all," he called over his shoulder.

I don't really remember what hit me first, but it was probably the smells: wet fur and blood, fear and pain.

"Lookadat!" Curtis gestured toward the ground with the barrel of his gun. There on the wet mossy ground, a large brown rabbit was caught by the hind foot in one of the traps Curtis kept set for raccoons, muskrats, and other rodents, whose hides he expertly removed from the carcasses and sold, and whose stringy flesh Duchess often stewed with canned tomatoes for supper. (Oh, how my L.A. stomach spasmed at the scent of simmering coon. While my family's collective lips smacked over the oily meat, I preferred a supper of Rice Krispies and milk.) The rabbit's eyes were big and shiny as brown marbles. The fur of its trapped foot was matted with blood; I could see the startling white of bare bone where the animal had obviously gnawed through its own flesh in a wild attempt to free itself. Its other three limbs scraped furiously at the ground as if on a treadmill gone berserk, its instinct for escape far outweighing its power.

The rabbit's mouth was open far wider than I would have imagined possible. And it was screaming. An impossible sound, at once high-pitched and guttural. I had never before heard a rabbit make any sound at all—I had no idea one could scream.

I could feel my morning meal (pancakes and Duchess's homemade pork sausage) rising toward my throat. I turned and ran blindly, only managing to go a few feet before colliding with the trunk of a tree, at the roots of which my stomach unquestionably offered up my breakfast. The pounding of my head nearly obscured the sound, the clean, hard *phttt* of the BB gun shooting the rabbit dead. I assumed at first the gun had been Curtis's; then I heard Dalton's voice calling, "I *shot* it! I *shot* it!"

I leaned against the tree, crying and puking, until I felt Curtis's hand touch me (with surprising gentleness) on my back.

"Hey, Zazoo, you all right?" Curtis often called me Zazoo. To this day, I don't know why. No one else called me that, no one ever had. Maybe there was something in my often nervous, jittery, hands-aflying manner that reminded Curtis of Zazu Pitts (who was still very much in evidence through daily reruns of *My Little Margie*). Maybe I just looked Zazoo to him. At any rate, it gave me such a feeling of specialness that Curtis had this strange little name for me—he always called Dalton Dalton—that I never questioned it.

"I—I—" I stammered through hiccuping sobs. Who knows what I might have been trying to say? I stood against that tree, mud and vomit splattered across the tops of my sneakers, my face streaked with tears and snot, while, in my tear-blurred peripheral vision, I could just see Dalton, shaking his head in utter disgust, his right hand clutching the rabbit's carcass—limp and bloody and minus a hind foot—by its long ears. I wiped at my running nose with the side of my arm. My degradation seemed complete. I had shown myself for the sniveling sissy crybaby I truly was, and I had done so in grand style.

"Aw, c'mon, Zazoo," Curtis crooned on one note, his hand making little downward stroking motions between my shoulder blades. He reached into his back jeans pocket, retrieved a wrinkled wad of a red bandanna, and offered it to me. I brought the cloth to my face (it was full of Curtis's smells), wiped at my mouth, blew my nose, and pocketed the bandanna.

"You all right, Zazoo?"

I sniffed snot and said Yes (sniff), thank you, still looking down at the puddle I had left at the base of the tree, not daring to look at Curtis's face, noticing how my vomit seemed to blend into the colors of the fungus-covered ground.

"Zazoo," I heard Dalton repeat in a mocking stage whisper. "Heck!" I turned quickly toward Dalton, filled with temporary fraternal hatred, but turned back just as quickly at the sight of the bloody animal clutched in Dalton's fist.

"We better get on back," Curtis said. "Have Duchess give you some'm fuh yuh stomach."

"But we just *got* here," Dalton protested.

"We come back another time," Curtis said.

"But we're *leaving* tomorrow! Shoot!"

"C'mon." Curtis ignored Dalton, put his arm around my shoulders, and we started back.

"Shoot!" Dalton shouted from behind us. "You big baby. You always ruin *everything.* Big baby!" I could hear the loud wet slaps of Dalton's stomping steps behind us. And I didn't care. Curtis kept his arm around me all the way back to the house, and that was well worth Dalton's wrath. It was even worth throwing up for.

"Duchess," Curtis called as the screen door slapped shut behind us, "Zazoo got sick to his stomach."

"Big baby," Dalton grumbled, "ruin everything. Duchess, can I have a tea cake?"

Mom, Dad, and Duchess were seated at the kitchen table having strong black coffee and Duchess's tea cakes.

"What's the matter, baby?" Duchess said, putting down her cup.

"Now," Mom said, "I knew you shouldn't o' gone out there. You always had a weak stomach."

"Dalton, don't be callin' yuh gran'ma Duchess," Dad said. "Call her Gran'ma."

"But Daddy," Dalton said, grabbing three big tea cakes from the plate on the table, "Curtis calls her Duchess and she's his gramma, too."

"I'll fix you some chamomile tea," Duchess said, taking the big old black kettle off the stove to fill.

"I didn't *say* Curtis," Dad said. "I say *you.*"

"You best go wash your face, Zazoo," Curtis said, patting me on the small of the back.

"Thass all right if he call me Duchess—everybody do." And almost everybody did. According to my mother, Grandpa Sherman had given her that name, and it was all I had ever heard him call his wife to the day he died, though no one (not even Grandma) could seem to remember when he began calling her Duchess, or why.

"Naw, iss *not* all right, Miz Mary," I heard Dad saying as I shut the bathroom door behind me.

The boy in the mirror smiled at me. His face was stained with tears and snot, but he was smiling. I had shown my true self—sissy, crybaby, the works—and Curtis had not forsaken me.

My heart threatened to explode with love.

I spent the rest of the afternoon in the spare room, with the big old Philco console radio on, rereading *Tom Sawyer* (I had found a tattered copy in Curtis's room), my embarrassment wrapped around me like a big old sweater. I wondered at my own reaction to the sight of the trapped rabbit. I had cried less at Great-Grandma Eudora's funeral, and even that had been more a reaction to my mother, sobbing loudly from beneath Dad's big, comforting arm, and Duchess, her tear-beaded eyes closed, rocking herself and moaning My Lord, my Lord, than any real sense of loss at the death of Eudora, whose large, warm, kitchen-smelly presence I knew relatively little. In fact, upon viewing Eudora's remains, it had occurred to me that I had never before seen my great-grandmother's hair (now at last revealed as short as my own and entirely white); she had worn a checkered kerchief around her head Aunt-Jemima-style on every other occasion I could remember having seen her.

I was amazed that the rabbit's death, loud and bloody and right before my eyes, was so much more real to me than Eudora's: a silent, painless expiration in her sleep nearly a week before, while I too had slept, nearly half the country away.

As I pondered this, staring toward if not exactly at the opposite wall, fingers tucked between the pages of *Tom Sawyer,* Curtis burst into the room, wearing only his baggy once-white boxer shorts, dancing a silly head-down, hip-shaking dance across the hardwood floor, singing out of tune with Otis Redding on the radio, "HOLD huh, SQUEEZE huh, nevah LEAVE huh!" And I laughed, as uncontrollably as I had cried before.

Curtis stopped dancing and stood, fists on hips, screwing his face into a parody of anger, looking beautiful and ridiculous.

"You laughin' at me, boy?" he said, lowering his voice a gruff octave. I shook my head no, convulsed with laughter.

Curtis fell to the floor, tickling me in the ribs and belly, making me laugh until I nearly peed my pants. Then he did a quick tippy-toe from the room, leaving me in a spasming heap, tears in my eyes and giggles leaking from between my lips, my penis stiff as a popsicle stick.

The afternoon had about exhausted me. Shortly following a supper of Duchess's okra gumbo (during which Dalton made an obvious point of not speaking to me), I crawled into bed early without being asked to. I shared Curtis's bed on our visits, a turn of events which I considered a privilege far surpassing Dalton's having a bed to himself. Most nights I purposely kept myself awake, feigning sleep until I was sure Curtis was sleeping. Then I would slowly reach out my hand and touch Curtis's humid back. Or lean toward him and smell the grassy scent of his hair. Or, if I was feeling particularly adventurous,

I would tickle the sole of his foot with my toes, just enough to make him grunt in his sleep and kick out at the sheets.

That evening, I remember, Curtis had gone out to visit some friends of his from school, so I slid over to the far side of the old spring-twangy bed, pressed my back against the cool wall, and allowed the ever-present swamp cooler to hum me quickly to sleep. I dreamed of Curtis and me sitting in the corner of the spare room, both of us with our shirts off, Curtis's arm around me, both of us smiling and laughing. The feeling was sweet and warm, and it was still with me when I suddenly awoke, hot and covered with sweat, my penis so hard it hurt. It was pitch dark, and I had no idea how long I had been asleep. Curtis had not yet come to bed, but I could hear Dalton's snoring from the opposite side of the room, over the sound of the swamp cooler.

My pajama bottoms were twisted and bunched around my thighs, lodged securely up the cleft of my behind: I shinnied them down past my knees. I continued the movement of my hips even after pulling down my p.j.s, enjoying the feeling of the slightly damp sheets against my skin. It was something I'd been doing quite often for a year or so, this rubbing-against-the-sheets thing. Not every single night, but often. Suddenly, an image of Curtis pressing his barbell up from his chest popped into my mind uninvited; I welcomed it in, and it added to my enjoyment.

I didn't hear Curtis come in. When I felt the weight of him on the bed, I stopped suddenly, breathlessly, embarrassed at being caught in my private pleasure. I lay completely still for a long moment, not knowing what, if anything, to say. Curtis was silent for several breaths, long enough for my eyes to become accustomed to the darkness, so that I could just make out his form, dark against dark, his shorts looking so white they seemed to glow. Curtis finally whispered, "I know why you're doing that."

"What?" I was genuinely surprised. Did this mean Curtis did it too? I had assumed I'd invented it, or at least discovered it.

"I know what you're doing," Curtis rephrased, a bit louder.

"I just," I stammered, raising myself up on my elbows, not easily accomplished with my pajama bottoms wadded around my calves. "It just feels—I dunno, it's—"

"You don't even know, do you?" Curtis said. "I bet you don't even know."

"Know what?"

"Know how."

"How?" I said.

"Shoot," Curtis said. I could see his smile in the dark. "You don't even know."

"What do you mean?" I said. I kicked free of my pajamas and sat up, pulling the sheet up around my waist.

"Here," he said, pulling his legs up onto the bed. "I'll show you, if you want. I'll show you how."

And to my amazement, Curtis reached into the long opening of his boxer shorts and fished out his penis. I could almost feel my pupils dilate. I was not, I hasten to mention, one of those boys with a long history of playing Doctor with the neighborhood girls, or touching wienies with little boyhood chums around somebody's swimming pool while Mom and Dad are out playing Pinochle. I had, in fact, never engaged in any sort of sexual play with another child, not even with Dalton. This was a first. And I was fascinated.

I watched in rapt attention as Curtis's penis stirred, then grew beneath his fingers; its head, purple-brown like his gums when he smiled, peeked out like a turtle from a collar of skin my own organ did not have. His penis seemed impossibly large; my own seemed small and babyish by comparison.

I wanted to touch it. I leaned forward slightly, toward it. Curtis whispered, "Go ahead." He'd probably meant it as a direction to mimic his slow stroking motion on myself, but instead I reached out (my heart pounding loud enough to deafen me) and stroked up the underside of Curtis's big thing with trembling fingers. It was startlingly hot, and it moved at my touch like some strange little animal.

"Do yours," Curtis said, pushing my hand gently away.

I moved my hand from him reluctantly, and began to mirror Curtis's hand motion as best I could, finding the sensation neither more nor less pleasurable than my usual sheet dance. Watching Curtis, though, was wonderful. I gazed enraptured (is that too strong a word, I wonder—no, I think not), as Curtis's head finally fell back against the wall, his eyes closing as if falling asleep. And then his penis was spewing long white ribbons that fell in bright contrasting stripes against his dark brown thighs and belly and fingers; and he was humming low in his throat. My first climax was much less dramatic, merely a long head-to-heels shudder, like a sudden chill, and a drop of clear liquid (it looked like Karo syrup) that dripped slowly from my penis and down the back of my hand.

This moment, this thing that Curtis had somehow chosen to share with me on this night, was like nothing I'd ever before experienced—wonderful, frightening, mysterious. I could not have felt closer to my cousin if we had shared our darkest secrets or mingled our blood. I loved Curtis at that moment like never before, with a terrible aching love the likes of which I have yet to recapture in any or all of the loves that have followed (and there have been two or three).

When he had finished, Curtis opened his eyes, looked at me through the dark, smiling what seemed to be a secret sort of smile, and said, "See?" Then he tiptoed the three or four steps to the bathroom. I heard the water running for a bit, and then Curtis came out, wiping his hands on a towel, which he then handed to me. I wiped myself off, pulled up my pajamas, and lay back, my heart racing as if I'd been running for blocks, feeling somehow different, wondering if I might look different now. I fell asleep almost instantly.

When I awoke, it crossed my mind that I might have dreamed it. But I knew better. Curtis was gone; he had set off hunting on his own. "Before day in the morning," Duchess said. He had not returned by the time we were ready to leave for the train station, and I didn't get to say good-bye to him. It felt terribly important that I see Curtis before we left, though for what reason I couldn't say. Maybe I expected some sign—a look, another secret smile, some reconfirmation of my sense that Curtis and I had in the night become special to one another, joined somehow.

I craned my neck toward the woods in search of Curtis even as we lit out, Dad behind the wheel of Duchess's huge old '60 Chevy; the weight of it, us, and our luggage digging twin trenches in the muddy road before finally taking off. As the car lurched away, I squirmed completely around in the car seat— "Hey, cut it out!" said Dalton, his first words to me in nearly twenty-four hours—hoping to see Curtis running from the woods, having forgotten the time, wanting as much as I wanted to say good-bye. Or at least to catch a glimpse of him walking that big-stepping walk with some carcass or other slung over his wide shoulder. But no. I turned forward in the seat ("Cut it *out!*" whined Dalton), my fists clenched with all my strength.

"Bless yo' li'l heart," Duchess said when she noticed the tears coming down my face. "You gon' miss yo' gran'ma, yeah."

"Big baby," Dalton mumbled.

I didn't see much of Curtis after that summer. We all got the Hong Kong flu that December and did not return until the following July. By that time, I found the three years that separated Curtis and me had become a wider, deeper valley than it had ever seemed before. Curtis was dating and had little time to spend with younger cousins, and (it seemed) little desire to spend it. I wondered at first if he felt ashamed for what we had done together the summer before, but it became obvious to me (by then twelve years old and fancying myself reasonably sophisticated) that Curtis was becoming a man, while I was still very much a boy. In any case, we never again did the thing together. But no matter. I had adopted it as my own, and enjoyed it often.

Shortly after he turned eighteen, Curtis got a girl pregnant (no one ever told me this—I overheard it); and some months following the birth of their child (a boy they named Curtis), he married the girl and they moved to Oklahoma, where Curtis went to work in the oil fields. And I never saw him again.

By the time Dalton called to tell me Curtis had died of colon cancer somewhere in Tennessee at the age of thirty-four, I hadn't even spoken to Curtis in over fifteen years. When I heard Dalton's voice on the telephone, I knew it was death—since we had grown up and grown apart, Dalton seldom called me for anything less.

"I got some bad news," he said, and took in a deep, audible breath. "Cousin Curtis passed." The short sentence seemed to take the whole breath.

Tears fell as he told me the when and where of the funeral, but I wasn't listening. I knew I wouldn't go; I have never understood the practice of viewing remains. It reminds me of the animals Curtis used to carry back from the woods—hides, carcasses.

"Remember that name he used to call you?" Dalton said. "Zazzy or something."

"Zazoo," I said.

"Yeah, right. Zazoo. Where'd that come from, anyway?"

"I never asked."

I thanked Dalton for the call; said, Yes, I'll see you at the funeral—Dalton went to them all. I hung up the telephone and immediately poured myself a brandy.

Strange. I'd been thinking of Curtis that very day. You see, it was raining.

Guess Who's Coming to Seder

Trey Ellis

1989

What?

Shhhhh.

So now you, my son, my only son, shush me? The one who took all your vicious kicks? Like a Nazi bastard you goose-stepped in my belly and now with the shush?

Buba.

So now with the Yiddish? I thought you'd forgotten in front of your pretty shiksa wife and your goyim friends, call me Mammy or something?

Mrs. Cohen's son, Alan, explodes his eyes overwide at his mother's bifocal lenses. Hidden absolutely are her eyes; instead, the weighty glasses only televise the two candle flames next to the two platefuls of matzoh in front of her.

It's getting late, Alan, Megan. Donnel Washington eyes first his wife, Carlene, then Vietta, his little girl. Their six palms push on the tablecloth, raising their asses off the cane geometry of the Cohens' chairs' seat bottoms simultaneously.

Donnel, please. My mother's from New York and she's lost almost all her hearing and her mind too. She doesn't mean anything by it. Carlene, I'm sorry.

You call *this* wine? Does *she* think French is kosher now that she's an expert on our religion or something?

Heather, *please* pass your grandmother the Mogen David. Megan Cohen, Heather's mother, starts to throw her hands at her mother-in-law's trachea but snatches them back to wring her own blond bun.

Heather slides the now wet curl of brown hair from the soft crack between her lips, latches it behind an ear. Pouring, her right nipple, through her bra and her blouse, jostles a liver spot on her grandmother's bare triceps. The noise of a car's wheels rolling, its engine screwing through missed gears to stop near the house, pulls Heather's eyes, her head, to the door.

Such large, firm roses. I had such firm roses when I was young and sweet too, back when grandfather was alive . . . but what use are they to anyone now that they hang over the fat of my belly like dead things. Heatherchick, if you go a day in your life without wearing a brassiere, so help me God I'll chop yours off.

Drink the first cup of wine, and fill Elijah's cup. Pass around a basin to wash the hands. Take parsley or spring onion, dip them in vinegar or salt water, pass them around the table, and say:
"Blessed are you YHWH our God, Ruler of the Universe who create the fruit of the earth."
"Barukh atay YHWH elohenu melekh ha-olam boray p'ri ha a-da-mah."

It's a shame Derrick isn't here for this part of the ceremony. I think he would have liked it. Heather, you're sure you told him eight o'clock?

Yes, Dad. I told you already he has a big paper due. But I don't know where he is *all* the time. You *could* ask Mister and Miz Washington.

Carlene and Donnel Washington smile with Alan and Megan Cohen at the new pink on Heather's face.

We must apologize for him. I left a note on the kitchen table, but that boy's so willful no telling what mess he's into now. As she speaks about her son, Carlene reties the bow that her daughter has again untied in the burnt offering of her hot-combed hair.

Mah nishtanah ha-lai-lah? Mah nishtanah ha-lai-lah? Who's going to say it already? Billy, you're the baby, so tell me what is it that holds you so quiet?

Billy Cohen slurps the dangling lunger of saliva back through his lips but not before the last inch and three-quarters detaches, dives through the red surface of his Paschal wine, floats back white bubbles.

Actually, Buba, Vietta Washington is the youngest. Vietta, could you please read from the top of page 72. Where it says, Why is this night . . .?

Vietta looks hard at her mother. Ma, can't I just eat the crackers? I feel stupid.

Go on, baby. Don't be bashful. Carlene pets her neck.

Let Derrick do it, if he ever makes it. This is all his fault anyway.

Don't make me tell you twice.

[Huff] "Whyisthisnightdifferentfromallothernights? On all, other, nights we may—"

What? I'm sure she's not speaking Hebrew. Then let me help for God's sake: She-b'khol ha-le-lot a-nu okh-lin sh'ar y'ra-kot, ha-lai-lah ha-zeh ma-ror. She-b'khol ha-le-lot eyn anu mat-bilin a-fi-lu p-am a-chat, ha-lai-lah ha-zeh sh-tay f'a-mim. She-b'khol ha-le-lot a-nu okh-lin beyn yosh-vin u-veyn m'su-bin, ha-lai-lah ha-zeh ku-la-nu m'su-bin.

Thank you, Buba. Continue reading, Vietta, please?

The teaching invites us to meet and to teach four children: one wise and one wicked, one innocent and one who does not relate by asking.
What does the wise one say? "What are the testimonies, and the statutes, and the rules which . . .?"

. . . which, Y-H-W . . .?
Yahweh, Vietta. It's a sin for Jews to pronounce the real name of Him or Her.
You mean you can't say *God-God-God-God!*
I'll slap the black off you, girl, when we get home. Apologize.
That's okay, Carlene, my mother started it. Alan's eyes flick to their corners to watch his mother.
So now with the killer looks? At your own mother even? I wish I could've heard what terrible things you've all been spitting at me now that I'm deaf, more dead than alive, my last seder in all probability.

Invite and wait for discussion on these questions: Who are the four children? Are they among us? Are they within each of us? Are these good answers?

It must be time to talk about the four children now and of course they are still with us, especially the wicked one who's lost the language, doesn't even get bat mitzvahed like my beautiful granddaughter next to me, or who marries out of the religion like my only son, so technically my two grandchildren here aren't even really Jewish. Back in olden times these would have been the ones saying, Freedom, shmeedom, I'd rather stay here with this bunch of greasy Arabs as their dirty slave . . . no offense.
Carlene crinkles the skin around her eyes, raising weakly her cheeks and upper lip from her teeth.
Why should anyone be offended, Buba? All of us, blacks and Jews, have been enslaved, there's no hiding from it, right?
Come on, Alan, *our* emancipation was a tad more recent, don't you think? Were your great-grandparents born slaves? Hmmm? The knife in Donnel's left hand, coated in haroseth (ritualized mortar made of diced apples and nuts, wine and raisins), disintegrates the matzoh (representing the brick), in his right hand. Haroseth and matzoh flakes stucco his palm, then the napkin.
Yes, but . . . Heather, honey, what's your take on all this?
I don't know.
Come on now, sweetie, is tonight really that bad?
Heather handles the bottle of kosher French by its neck, jams its nose into the bottom of her glass until the rising choppy waves of wine redden her knuckles, then overflow and wound the white tablecloth.
Heatherchick! You know that it's not yet that we toast. I swear before your

grandfather's ghost you even *sip* before the right time and *ping!* there again goes my blood clot and half of my face will die like your Aunt Estelle's in the home.

Lifting the glass to her mouth, Heather looks at no one. Noisily, gulp after gulp of wine bubbles back around her mouth's corners.

Young lady, that wasn't too nice. Megan turns a bit from her daughter, tilts her face into her hand, milks her rising smile from her cheeks into her palm.

Mrs. Cohen whistles "Dai Dai Enu" at the Hockney lithograph on the wall.

Buba, we're still trying to discuss the four children As the B'nai B'rak rabbi's instructed.

Now it's getting very late, Megan, Alan; and Vietta has school tomorrow.

So they're leaving in the middle of seder? They hate Jewish so that they want calamity to strike us all down?

Uh, Donnel, I'm so sorry. My mother thinks if anyone leaves, gets up from their chair before the last cup of wine is drunk, all the Jews in the house will be slain. See, in 1583, there was this thing in Istanbul.

Maybe they're Farrakhan Mooslims.

I'll have you know that the Washingtons' son, Derrick, and our Megan have been seeing each other all through U of M, so they might very soon be "family."

Ma!

After discussion, all sing.

Go tell it on the mountain,
over the hills and everywhere.
Go tell it on the mountain—
Let my people go!

Who are the people dressed in white?
Let my people go!
Must be the children of the Israelite—
Let my people go!

Where did you get this hippie seder from anyhow?

Cousin Naomi found it at the Rainbow Reformed Temple in New York.

[A moment of silence. Then a reader says:]

"But let us also question the plagues: Can the winning of freedom be bloodless? It was not bloodless when Nat Turner proclaimed, 'I had a vision, and I saw white spirits and black spirits engaged in battle, and the sun was darkened—the thunder rolled in the heavens and blood flowed in streams—and I heard a voice saying, Such is your luck, such you are called to see, and let it come rough or smooth, you must surely bear it.' "

I-lu i-lu ho-tzi-a-nu, ho-tzi-a-nu mi-mitz-ra-yim, ho-tzi-a-nu mi-mitz-ra-yim dai-ye-nu. DAI-DAI-YE-NU, DAI-DAI-YE-NU, DAI-DAI-YE-NU, dayenu, dayenu!
[All drink the third cup. Refill glasses, but not to the top.]
[The door is opened.]

Alan returns Vietta's bow from the floor to her lap, slouches down to her as she confetties her paper napkin. It's almost over, sweetheart, then Billy can show you his Nintendo. He just got Donkey Kong. We're just waiting a little bit for the ghost of Elijah to come down and drink his cup of wine. If you leave milk and cookies out for Santa Claus, it's sort of like that. Alan stretches to pat Vietta's shoulder, but she flinches.

Miss Thing, I raised you better than acting up like this outside the house.
Dingdingding-dong.

Billy's curtains of matzoh-flaked lips pull back, reveal teeth behind braces. Heather's back straightens, red reclaims her face.

Did I hear the doorbell go off? At least this you did right, my little Alan. Mrs. Cohen laughs. The messiah rings the doorbell! My uncle's half-brother, Arkady, the Shostakovich of indoor plumbing, used to rig a pump to Elijah's cup to make it look like the spirit was drinking it. Oh how I always fell for that as a girl.
Dingdingding-dong.

Heather, get the door, it's okay.

Top of the Game

John McCluskey, Jr.

1989

They were standing at a snack shop in O'Hare, a midafternoon snack of jumbo hot dogs and colas on the counter in front of them, when Roberta Tolbert turned to her son and said, "Junior, this is the end of the line. That man better break Alvin's scoring record tonight, because I won't go another step further."

It was not the first time she had said something like this. Just four days earlier at Boston's Logan Airport she had turned to him as they neared the security check station. "We go from one arena to the next. Then they march us from one TV station to the next, just a-marching, just a-marching." She had smiled then, pumped her arms several times.

"No, son, I'm tired of all those grinning reporters asking about your daddy's scoring records and wanting to know about his appetite and habits and things." Alvin, Jr., remembered that a security guard, a balding Cape Verdean, had waited patiently for her to place her purse on the slow-moving belt.

"I simply don't need all those cameras up in my face while I'm trying to watch the game, especially when I can't give a kitty who wins. They don't give me time to blow my nose. And I don't—I mean, really don't—need to shake the hand of the first vice-president of this and the second vice-president of that. I need to be back home with my third graders." She had waved her hand then, shaken her head, and stepped through the security arch without a beep. Then they had flown on to Cleveland for a three-day stand and more interviews.

Now a group of arriving passengers was headed from a nearby gate. Tanned and in their wrinkled pastels or florals, they talked loudly to those meeting them. They must have landed from Florida, Alvin, Jr., guessed, the rush of waves and bright tropical light close to their memories. They would be ambushed by the Chicago cold, breaths stolen. He shook his head slowly, turned to his mother.

"Mama, I can't blame you one bit, you know that. Who could have guessed that the man would go into a slump right in the middle of the season with us following him from town to town? If anybody had told me that we'd be on this . . . this caravan so long, I would have called him crazy."

"Plus they're always asking silly questions," she said, using her straw to swirl the ice in her cup.

"What?"

"The reporters and the television folks. It's always, uh, 'Well, how do you feel now that Hurdie-Birdie is about to break your husband's record?' What do they expect me to say—I'm the happiest woman in the world to know my husband's name will be erased from the record books? What do they want me to say? It's silly is what it is. You got your good job with the city and me just one year from retirement. We don't need this, really." Then with two hands, she picked up her jumbo hot dog as if a sacred flute and turned it slowly to her lips.

Alvin, Jr., had seen it all coming. They had joined the Chicago Middies some ten days before. Alvin Tolbert's record as all-time American Basketball Federation scorer was to have been broken at Madison Square Garden, then Boston Garden before Cleveland Coliseum. Tonight the Middies were returning home to play the New Jersey Majors, and the Middies' aging forward, Clarence "Thunderin' " Hurd, was due again to smash the record that very night, if not tomorrow night or the next, before a wildly cheering crowd and a fleet of cameras. AFA officials thought it would be a good idea to have the Tolberts on hand for the occasion and practically begged them to join the team. "See it as a short vacation on us," someone had told them on a conference call. But they were losing patience.

Of course, the travel had its comforts and special pleasures. All their expenses were paid. They stayed in the best hotels with the team. Their steaks were most tender, their lobster tails most succulent. A limousine, usually off-white with smoked windows, maneuvered them soundlessly through traffic. A smiling front-office staff member, in obligatory gray pinstripes, sat with them at courtside, and their seats were just behind the Middies' bench, close enough for them to lean forward and tap one of the players on the shoulder, if they cared to. Thousands would gladly change spaces with them, and they knew it.

Chewing slowly, Roberta looked at her son and, raising her chin, tapped a corner of her mouth twice. As reflex he dabbed at the corners of his mustache, catching beads of mustard against his napkin. Then she started again, resolute, "I was doing just fine until all this came along. Just fine, thank you. Now they've brought us out here to all this cold weather and, Lord knows, I didn't bring along that many wool dresses." She sighed, glanced around quickly as if she had just discovered that they were among hundreds of strangers trading places.

"Let's go," she said after they had finished. "You can do all the talking this time, though. I'm talked out."

* * *

A machine from a dream, the limousine delivered them to a television station five blocks from the hotel. Passersby slowed to watch as they got out, the wind nearly taking Roberta's hat. They were whisked past cool-eyed secretaries to a studio set breezy in ferns and blond furniture. By now they no longer wondered about the small size of the sets. They knew well the quick movements of the staff, movements as precise as those of a surgery team. The lights, the tiny microphones, and the assured manner of a host with a ready smile—yes, they knew it all well.

For this taping, the Tolberts were seated on a low-backed couch. As their mikes were fitted on, Roberta leaned toward her son and whispered, "What's this show called again?"

"*Chicago Dateline*, I think."

He had been watching a young, richly brown woman in headphones working one of the cameras. She wore tight jeans and a bright-red oversized sweater. Her headband matched her sweater. He smiled at her. She smiled back. Stroking a corner of his mustache and bold with the energy of the newly famous, he winked. She winked back, then laughed aloud, a warm and throaty laugh. He wanted to hear it closer, to lean slowly against it.

What now? he wondered. Invite her to the game, to breakfast the next morning? Or would she prefer the celebration party Hurd would plan for after the game? Back in Dayton, his shyness would have stopped him at the wink. He rubbed his hands together and wove feeble plots.

But they were already in the middle of the countdown, the host (Fred, Dan, Jerry?) clearing his throat and straightening his tie. As the final act, mouth closed, he slowly slid his tongue around his top row of teeth. Roberta Tolbert fidgeted.

". . . four, three, two, one." The camera light blinked red and the show began.

The man spoke easily, turning from the camera to the Tolberts and back during the introduction. The questions were the expected ones, the same ones asked in New York, Boston, Cleveland. They summoned the familiar parade of memories that needed to be compressed into a few sentences with no pauses, no stutters, and please look straight into the camera.

WHAT WAS HE LIKE AS A FATHER?

Late springs and early summers were his releases. The Baltimore Barons made it to the playoffs only twice during his twelve years on the team. So, from early April through mid-September he would be planted at home, cutting grass or painting or standing out front swapping tales with other fathers. The youngest of three children, Alvin, Jr., was the only son. The day after his twelfth birthday, he jogged with his father to a nearby cinder track. There his father began to train him to be a world-class sprinter. After every workout, Junior would return home exhausted, slumped and straining for air, while his father fingered a stopwatch and talked about the feats of Jesse Owens. ("They tell me ol' Jesse could have outrun Man o' War, if he had a mind to.") It was not until Junior had made the junior high sprint relay team and was in the care of a coach his father respected that he stopped the training sessions with his son.

But you should have been there the time I told him I was going to try out for the high school swim team and maybe rest through the track season. He just fell on the couch and laughed.

"A swimmer? My son, the swimmer?" he was asking the ceiling. My father had grown up in Detroit where there had been few pools available for blacks, and he had never learned to swim.

"A black man swimming in the Olympics. Now ain't this a blip? You'll be the first." Everything had to be Olympics, world class. Baltimore was too small; America was too small, you see. He said it over and over again, getting used to it like the notion was a new candy.

And why not swimming? It was all in the learning or, as his father always taught him, in the breathing and the balance, the concentration and the love. Besides, had his father been born shooting hook shots from fifteen feet from the basket? Though Junior did make the swim team at Howard University, he never got to the Olympic trials. Still, it was hard for him even now to pass up any water without plunging in—serene lakes, rivers, whole oceans invited him. As late as five years ago, at the age of twenty-seven, he thought briefly about starting training to swim the English Channel. You didn't need to be fast, just strong, steady.

To the invisible thousands watching, Roberta remembered him as the children's ally. Until they were teenagers, it seemed, he could carry two of his children, especially the daughters who curled like kittens, in a single arm. He soothed them after she had taken a switch or leather strap to their behinds. He would discipline them only rarely and, even then, more out of disappointment than anything else. Like the time Junior took $5 from the kitchen table and lied about never having seen it.

Once we drove out to California and stopped in Columbus. Alvin thought it would be fun to show the kids where he played college basketball. There was a summer camp for high school players or something like that going on at the Arena. Anyway, we got in and were walking the hallways off the gym, when we saw the old team pictures, the same ones we had at home. Junior found Alvin in three of them, asking before each one, "Daddy, is that you?"

He did look different in all three—mustache, no mustache and with goatee, then clean-faced. Seeing those pictures in that strange place, miles from Baltimore, thrilled the kids. They must have thought he had simply imagined those years or that his past was in a world they would never see. They might as well have seen his baby shoes.

WHAT WAS IT LIKE LIVING WITH A SUPERSTAR?

She glanced off, then back to the camera. She spoke proudly of the fact that he was recognized everywhere—the bank, the post office, the hardware store. Grown men pushed their way to him for autographs. She suggested how women batted their eyes and touched the ends of their hair while they talked—oh, he was a handsome man, my Alvin. Then she spoke of other things.

First, there's the phone, the calls of congratulations after the victories, and can you speak to the thus-and-so group next week, and could you please talk to my boy who's down on himself for missing that last-second shot against Douglas High? When the team lost and you had a bad night, the phones would be dead and you'd drag around the house. Oh, maybe one or two might call and say that the referees had the eyes of their twice-widowed aunts who were going in for cataract surgery that very day. Erskine was good for coming up with something like that, baldheaded Erskine who stuck by you through those years in Baltimore even after you retired. You can't buy a good friend like that. And you could be so cranky after you retired, even hurting people like Erskine. You found most things so dull and maybe they were, but it was Erskine who found you collapsed on the sidewalk and ran to get me, him already crying, you already dying.

Junior shifted on the couch as his mother spoke. Her thick gray hair, one thin spot at the crown, seemed to glow with a bluish tint. He was glad to have talked her out of the hair piece. It would have fooled no one. It was better this way. Her skin smooth and unblemished, she looked beautiful.

By the time he began his next answer, Junior was relaxed, the tightness easing across his stomach. For the audience, he could recall the awe which first stretched the eyes of his childhood friends. During his father's best seasons, Junior was always among the first ones picked for games during school recess period. When the professional playoffs approached, his buddies gathered shyly in one corner of his backyard, their questions given to them by curious parents and sprinkled at his feet during their football games. His imagined prowess had to be genetic like the color of his eyes, even if not handed down like a halo. It took them several seasons to realize that his jump shot was only average, that in touch football games he dropped long passes with calm regularity.

WHAT DOES IT FEEL LIKE TO WATCH THIS GREAT PLAYER MAKE THE FINAL ASSAULT ON THE RECORD WHICH YOU, THE LEAGUE, AND THE NATION HOLD SO DEAR?

Like watching a man on the last climb to the top of a great mountain who must look down to smile over the distance he has covered. Then he looks up and you watch the terror spread over his face like a shadow. The end is near. A finger slips, then a foot.

The answers given, the memories churned up, the interview ended. They shook hands with the host again and with the director who strode onto the set. Alvin, Jr., did manage to say hello to the woman handling the camera. He wanted to say something more but felt clumsy.

"Both of you were very good," she said, winding cord.

"Thank you," he said. "We've had a lot of practice lately."

"I hope the tired turkey doesn't break the record."

He blinked, trying to smile. "Records are made to be broken."

"I don't believe that," she said. "I bet you don't either." Her smile was dazzling. He rocked. Then someone tapped him on the shoulder and reminded him that the limousine was waiting. He handed her a business card.

Outside a cold rain had started, a rain they stared through over dinner, a rain the limousine purred through en route to the fieldhouse. At stops, other drivers and riders would rub out a circle on their own fogged windows and try to peer through the smoked windows of the limousine. Roberta looked straight ahead, but Junior would smile and wave, hoping someone could see. And he thought suddenly of the admiring glances he was sure to get back home from women who had seen him on national television, women who otherwise smiled only faintly when he greeted them each morning at the office. The men would ask for descriptions of the behind-the-scene personalities of wildly popular interviewers and players. On the first morning back at the office, he might take an hour to talk it all out before getting them back to work.

At the fieldhouse, they were met by a smiling, stocky man who held an umbrella for them. Junior took him for an aging outside linebacker, free-lancing with the Middie organization, a friend of a friend of a friend. The Tolberts had forgotten his name and his title by the time they settled inside.

Roberta sat between Junior and the front-office man. "Looks like a good crowd tonight," the man said. "You win three in a row, and you get a good crowd. You lose three in a row and, unless you got a superstar, people claim the weather is too bad and they stay home. Winning brings good business and good weather. By the way, Hurd's going to do all right tonight. We got him in with a sports psychologist this afternoon. Guy's the best, does wonders with some of the Bears players all the time. The prima-donna types, you know."

He tapped his forehead. "We figure Hurd got a little problem, you know, these last couple of weeks. The pressure and all is making him blow the record out of proportion. There's gotta be a name for it, but I can't remember it now. Anyway, the doc says he's over it. I bet the two of you ready to take that walk to center court."

Roberta Tolbert nodded and sat back with her son. They turned their attention to the warm-ups and Clarence "Thunderin' " Hurd. At forty-two, he was the oldest player on the court. "Thunderin' " was a high school coach's idea. Rookies flattered him by calling him "Too Smooth." Players who knew him longer called him "Old 'n Easy." Now he was loose and laughing, taking passes and gliding in for lay-ups. His shots banked softly off the glass. As he waited his turn for a rebound, he bounced lightly on his toes. He let his arms go limber at his sides. He would lean forward and say something to the player in line in front of him. They would slap palms and laugh the laugh of conspirators.

With a different club representative, the Tolberts had had dinner with Hurd that first cold night when they had arrived in New York. Hurd had spoken cautiously, sitting stiffly, as if answering a question put to him by Howard Cosell.

"Mr. Tolbert was a hero of mine, and he will always be the greatest for me. I'm fortunate to have learned so much from him on and off the court. For the two years I knew him before he retired, he was the perfect gentleman, taught plenty of us how to carry ourselves. I try to carry myself the way he did." Like a child ending his first recitation, he breathed deeply and leaned back. The executive smiled, stroked at an imaginary beard.

During that dinner, Roberta was cordial. She took Hurd's measure with a stern eye. Several times, during other less guarded moments, she started to interrupt and correct his grammar, but Junior had nudged her. Roberta softened only when he showed them pictures of his family, bragged about his daughter's grades. Junior had even thought about taking Hurd up on the early invitation to join some of the players for their afternoon bid-whist games. And he wanted to know whether there was any truth to the rumor that Hurd had planned to retire at the end of the last season, only to be talked out of it by club management. ("Think of the record, think of the crowds!" the front office must have begged.)

Tonight the stooped and jovial forward needed just 21 points, three fewer than his career game average, to break the all-time scorer's record. When the Tolberts had joined the team in New York, he had needed 36 points. An average night tonight and they could all go back to their normal lives. But only after the record-setting shot. There would be a break in the game and they would all go down to center court for the presentation of the game ball and a plaque to Hurd. He and Roberta would smile and shake Hurd's hand. Spotlights would race across the ceiling; a band would play. The cheers would be thunderous. A flock of balloons would float to the ceiling, and the President might call. Junior knew it all by heart.

Now, as if he himself were about to compete, Junior's stomach churned during the "Star-Spangled Banner" and through the introductions. Then he held his breath.

"Well, Mama, here we go."

"Yeah, I guess so," she said.

After the tip-off, Junior exhaled long and slow. When Hurd scored his first points just two minutes in, a jump shot banked in softly from six feet out, the crowd stomped and cheered. Behind them a man chanted, "Hurd, Hurd, Hurd." Junior turned, saw him slap palms with a man sitting next to him. "Tonight is the night, ba-bee!"

His mother frowned. "Your daddy didn't even bother with the backboard on a shot like that."

Hurd missed three shots in a row before he scored near the end of the quarter, a lazy hook with the defensive man well off him. In the second quarter he managed one tip-in before missing four shots in a row, four shots that hit the inside of the rim and bounced high outside or skimmed around the rim and fell off. When he came out of the game with six minutes left before half time, there was a smattering of applause and, like cruel slaps, two short boos from the seats far behind the bench. He waved to the Tolberts without smiling and took a seat on the bench. He shook his head as he toweled off his forehead, the back of his head. One or two teammates slapped him on the back. There was no gesture or posture of bright triumph. It was his antics—the waving of an arm high overhead like swinging a lasso (after a score), the jamming of an imagined spike through the floor (after blocking a shot), and the quick shimmy as if stepping into a cold shower (after a dunk)—that were copied on every play-ground in America. In his heyday this was the man who talked confusion into the men guarding him. He would whisper to them to get more sleep, eat extra bowls of cereal, forgo sex for months in order to have enough stamina to control him. When he guarded others, they would swear the rim would rise a foot, its circumference shrink. Junior knew all these stories. Hurd must be proud to know that ten or twenty years from now old and young would gather on park benches, street corners, barbershops to compare his exploits to Alvin's, then to the most recent record holder's. But now he sat as the second quarter wound down, and when the horn finally sounded, he jogged slowly off the court. His team was winning by six points.

Junior and Roberta sipped beer through the half-time show, neither of them looking for long at the high school drill team performing on the court. The front-office man had excused himself.

"What do you think is wrong with Hurd, Junior? Too much pressure?"

He shrugged. "It can't be nerves. You don't play sixteen years, make all the records that he's made, and suddenly get nervous. No, it's just a little bad luck, just a slump. We all have those."

"I guess it's better to blame luck than nerves," she said. She drew a small printed schedule from her purse. "At this rate, he won't get his record until . . ." She paused to count down the schedule. "Until Portland." She sighed and shook her head.

A man was making his way toward them from across the court. He wore a snap-brim hat, a pencil-thin mustache, and, closer in, they could see that he chewed a toothpick in a corner of his mouth. Junior could have shaved in the glassy shine off the man's knob-toed shoes. The man introduced himself as an old fan of Alvin's and politely asked to take their picture. They agreed and smiled weakly for him, their faces frozen in the flash. They also autographed his program.

"Thank you so very much, and God bless you. I got autographs of all the famous colored folks who ever came to Chicago. Got Muhammad Ali's, Lena

Horne's, Count Basie's, Martin Luther King's . . . everybody's." He smiled proudly and tapped his camera. "Got most of them on camera, too, so thank you very much, you hear?"

"Well, thank you," Roberta said, touching the ends of her hair.

The man was backing away, but stopped. "You know, the first time I saw Alvin Tolbert play I said to myself, said 'He's going to be something special. Nothing tricky, just steady, until one day everybody will look up and he will have more points than anybody.' Yep, sure did, from the very start." He slapped his chest twice. "And a regular dude, too. Remember the Barons clinched the title here in '64, and they went over to Pancho's on 56th Street and we was sipping on scotch and milk—"

"My husband didn't drink," Roberta said.

The man scratched his chin. "Must got him confused then. Yeah, yeah. Probably one of them boxers I'm thinking about. Anyway, he was my man, my main man. Y'all enjoy what's left to enjoy." He turned to Alvin, Jr. "Hurd can't do half of what your daddy could do on the court, I'm here to tell you." Then he left.

"Be patient with your public," Junior said, as if quoting from a rule book.

On the court someone was receiving a plaque and applause was starting up.

"How's the house?" Junior asked, startling himself. They had covered everything else on the trip—health, his prospects for marriage, why his sisters wrote or called so seldom. But he kept imagining his mother alone during the evenings. And wondered.

"Oh, it's fine," she said. "I got somebody to repaint the whole inside. Now, if the tulips and rosebushes act right in the spring, the house will look all right."

He had helped her move from Baltimore to Silver Spring six years ago. It was a smaller house that Roberta decorated well.

"You were thinking about a cleaning woman once a week. . . ."

"I thought better about it," Roberta said. "I can save the money and go on another sea cruise. This time to Mexico."

"Think you'll miss these bright lights back in Maryland?" Junior teased.

"Not me. But I can see it is going to your head. Grinning back at all these fast young women." She could not hide her smile. And it was true. The shapely producer in the peach knit dress in Boston, the petite flight attendant who touched his elbow and told him how much she enjoyed his last movie, the woman from the Cleveland front office whose soft hoarse laughs kept him joking all game, the one behind the camera this afternoon—he was growing irresistible.

"You do need to settle down," Roberta said. "One or two more grandchildren I wouldn't mind."

He was relieved when the teams came back on the floor. Relieved, too, when the front-office man returned with hot dogs and colas—a diet one for his mother. The man talked about inevitabilities.

"The balloons are ready, the spot man is waiting, the plaque is all shiny and under wraps. It's just up to Hurd."

When the third quarter began, Junior sat forward to watch, but soon the watching grew painful. Hurd missed his first eight shots and ran up and down the court with a bewildered expression. Once he arched a shot from the corner, a shot fans called his "money shot." Junior knew from the arc that the ball would miss the basket by four feet. On the first bounce it landed in the lap of a startled woman in the second row. A minute later, Hurd came in hard for a dunk, knocking over a defender—were the referees pulling for him, too?—before missing the shot. The crowd was poised to scream at the beauty of the soaring, the power of the stroke, the rattle of the rim. They groaned when the ball bounced out behind the foul line and the Majors started a fast break in the other direction. When he tried to compensate for too much power, the ball fell short of the rim.

His movements grew stiff. He was called for traveling twice, a rarity for "Too Smooth." He must be thinking the mechanics of his motions, Junior guessed. One could grow weary and confused just walking as if it depended upon the conscious command of each muscle and bone. Thinking can be an enemy in such moments.

He scored nothing in the third and, each time he missed, he looked, not to the bench, but to the crowd as if a child ashamed. But his team was still ahead. A boo or two could be heard as the team walked back out for the last quarter.

"I guess they figure they can do that for the price of the ticket," Roberta said.

Junior nodded. "They would faint if they had to run up and down the court six times. Most of them can barely get up the steps with their hot dogs and beer."

Hurd was soon at the foul line for two shots. Junior sweated with him. Could feel the pebbly grain of the ball and ran a finger along one of the seams. He took two deep breaths, blew the air out, relaxed the chest and stomach muscles before he shot. Missed.

"You bum, you shoulda quit already!"

Roberta turned and stared, then pointed a finger at the man standing three rows behind them. The man sat and refused to meet her look.

Junior put his arm around his mother to turn her around. "Alvin would have been climbing these seats if he heard him say something like that," she said.

Hurd made the second shot. And that would be the extent of his scoring for the night. He came out, their lead safe, with four minutes left in the game.

"I'm beginning to feel sorry for him," Roberta said. "I don't remember your daddy going through all this. If he did, he never told me."

"Don't feel sorry for him. He's got the rest of the season to score fourteen points. He endorses tennis shoes, has a street named after him in Birmingham, and, according to *Jet* magazine, will be in a spy movie next summer. He's all right."

"Well, you know what I mean."

"I don't think I do."

"The embarrassment, son. He got to have a certain amount of pride no matter how much money he makes. This is probably the only thing he knows how to do."

"The money will help ease his pain," Junior said. "Even if he never scored another basket, he's had a good career. Wish I could retire at forty-two."

"People will remember him for messing up when he could have had the record days ago."

"Why did you change your mind on him? A while ago you thought he was the boogieman, now you feeling for him."

She chuckled. She had called him "Hurdie-Birdie" and thought him as country as navy beans and cornbread, it was true. "I was just holding on to the past like a fool. Alvin was more than a record in some book or"—nodding behind her to the fan who had shouted at Hurd—"some legend for somebody like that."

Junior thought for a moment. "Yeah, this caravan's got nothing to do with us. It'll roll whether we're here or not. Nobody will miss us. They won't even miss Hurd this time next year. We've all been invented."

Junior thought to the shot his father had taken to break the old record. It was an ordinary follow-up. A guard, Smith, had missed a long and arching shot from just behind and to the right of the key. The ball hit high off the glass and to the left where Alvin was charging in. He took it waist high on one bounce and put it back up lightly as if placing a feather on the rim. Any school-aged player, after mastering the contradiction of hard charge and sudden soft release of the ball, could have made it. The record had been set by no high arching shot from the corner, no switch-handed jump shot in the faces of two charging defenders, but by a simple "bunny" shot.

Months later, he had tiptoed down from his bedroom to watch his father playing the video tape of the shot. The tape reversed, his father watched it again and again. Then he yawned and saw Junior.

"Son, you have just seen me watch this for the last time. See how easy these things happen? It's just as easy and natural as breathing. It's always that way. You just do it the way you always done it. People forget your sweat anyway." Then he turned off the recorder, not even waiting for the part where he received the game ball, waved to the crowd, and grinned. "Then you have to know when to get out. Same go for preachers and politicians, even the best of them. You got to know when you've reached your peak and when it's downhill. You got to go before you start falling. Only Jimmy Brown and Wilt Chamberlain understood that. I may not be the smartest man in the world, but I got common sense." That's when he told him that he would retire after one more season. He was true to his word, and, as far as Junior knew, he never watched that tape again.

Junior stood as the crowd counted off the last seconds. When the buzzer sounded, the Middies charged off the court in triumph. Hurd trotted off last.

The front-office man was standing and muttering, "Damn." Junior shook his hand and told him better luck tomorrow night.

"Wait here for me, Mama. I'm going to the locker room."

"What for?" she asked.

"I'll be right back. Just five minutes."

"Well, hurry up. These folk got all that beer in them and can act crazy." She waited with the dazed man.

Junior walked across center court, pausing to look at each basket, then around the arena at the highest rows. For a moment he imagined, had there been the celebration, how faces would flush in the racing lights, how balloons would touch the ceiling just above their heads. Then he waited outside the locker room for a minute or two. There was a crowd of autograph seekers, mostly young boys, pulling their fathers, or loud-laughing men in tight bright blazers, or two or three women in expensive furs and glittering high-heeled shoes. Showing their press badges, sportswriters walked right past him. He followed one in, then identified himself to a short bald man just inside the door.

"Come on in," he was told.

The writers were finishing with the head coach and the team's high scorer. Only one interviewed Hurd at his locker.

He saw Junior and smiled. Waved him over. He quickly put an end to the interview. "We didn't look too bad, hunh?"

"No, not at all. Congratulations. You keep it up and y'all will sail right into the playoffs."

"You right." Junior noticed the specks of gray and the thinning hair at the top of Hurd's head as though for the first time. As Hurd pulled off his socks, he groaned.

"I'm getting too old for this, youngblood." It was a line, half serious, that he used a lot. "One of these days I'll retire and the hardest work you'll catch me doing is sitting up in the broadcast booth spinning yarns." Then he looked around. "Just between the two of us and my shoes over yonder, I'll probably hang it up after this season. Your daddy was smart. He got out at the top of his game. I don't want to hang around. Get called a bunch of bad names."

"Mr. Hurd, we're heading back tomorrow morning."

"Come on with that 'mister' jive. The name's Clarence. But, hey, you got to stay around. We ain't even played that little game of Tonk we was supposed to play."

"Sure would like to, but I got to get back to my job. A couple more days away and the office might just float on away without me there."

"Heh-heh, boss-man, huh?" Hurd chuckled. In his voice played the various sounds of workers in large, sweltering fields far from the cities, though he claimed Birmingham as home. "Well, I guess you got to get on home. But tomorrow night's gone be the night, you know."

They shook hands. "Good luck," Junior said. "We'll read about it in the papers." He hesitated, then said, "Just remember to take it easy. You already got what you need."

Hurd looked off. "You sure got that right. I been pressing too hard, forgetting everything I know even at my age. Yeah, I'll take it easy. It's the only way *to* take it."

Near the door Junior smiled and kept walking past two reporters who asked him to comment on the game.

The next morning on a plane soaring through eight thousand feet and banking east, he noticed a boat, most likely a cabin cruiser challenging sudden winter storms, skimming the surface of Lake Michigan. He imagined himself even smaller in, say, August on that same surface stroking toward Canada. It would be for something simple—a late brunch in Ontario where he'd rest for a spell before starting back. There would be no ceremony, no crowds, no interviews—just the quiet doing of the thing.

But it was February, and he was flying home. His mother had left two hours earlier. By the time his plane would land and he drove the twenty minutes of expressway to his apartment, he guessed that his mother would have already aired out the den in Silver Spring and lingered to dust Alvin's trophies. And, for sure, Clarence "Thunderin' " Hurd, in the middle of a card game, would be boasting, unchastened, that the scoring record, the record that had withstood assaults for eleven years, would fall that very night—second quarter, y'all just watch up—with a thunderous slam dunk.

Going to Meet Aaron

Richard Perry

1989

1971

First I see the bridge like steel flesh marrying continent to island, and then I come all the way around the curve and see the river. Out in the middle it's smooth, wears the shadow of the structure high above it. The sun is down the river, hiding behind the trees. Where the leaves are thin, the trees are shining. The river is below me, the bridge above, and these kids on bikes go flying past, and they are gone, and the trucks are sailing, exploding across the bridge leaving wakes of rumbling; *You know,* Aaron said, *we might be killed.*

Yesterday we sat in my apartment. I was bitching about teaching science to eighth-grade kids in Brooklyn, we were drinking beer, the windows open, the roar of traffic to New Jersey and the Bronx continuous explosion. In the street, sixteen floors below, a truck backfired. I looked through the window and when I did George Washington Bridge surprised me. It was always there beyond the rooftops, silver, it surprised me.

"You know," Aaron said, "we might be killed."

"I know."

"I'm scared."

"It's healthy."

"Never been scared like this. You?"

"Uh-huh. Mississippi. 1964."

His eyes were brown. "You never talk about it."

"Didn't do much good."

He didn't say anything. I thought about it. "That's not exactly true. It didn't do what we expected."

"White people?"

"And black. They got tired of dying. They stopped believing in nonviolence. Split the movement."

"You?" He was smiling. "You believed in nonviolence?"

"It was the times," I said, and looked across the room at the black bag in the corner. Inside were the explosives, the detonators, and the coils of wire. Tomorrow we would go into the bank. On the back of the closet door hung the shit-colored uniforms of a cleaning company. We would get into the bank that way. I hoped Aaron would hold together. I was not afraid. There was a clenched fist in my stomach, but I was not afraid.

On the bridge the trucks are booming. At the bottom of the hill, beneath the bridge, the lighthouse, faded cylinder of red. I'm thirsty, but the fountain has no water, the handle gone, the curve of granite basin choked with mud. I cross the withered grass, step through the lighthouse door, into the garbage, the stench of dead things. The graffiti has no wit or grace or vision. I begin to climb the twisting staircase and then I'm at the top.

Nothing is any different here. The same river, the same sky with its broad markings of cirrus clouds, the same bridge suspending the detonating trucks, except that now I can see the red clay of the tennis courts, the players in white and green and blue. Except I can see the sun not bleeding that makes the river shine. Like it didn't in Mississippi. I wanted to see it, Roscoe took me there. It was big. An ocean without breakers I couldn't see across. A long flat boat in the muddy middle. "If I had a dollar," Roscoe had said, "if I had a dollar for every nigger on the bottom. . . ."

The Palisades are purple. In the marina, the alabaster sailboats, masts like minarets. A space between them, as if a boat is missing; *Tell me about Mississippi,* Aaron said.

I was going to be a leader. Free black people, change the world. Instead I lost things. Confidence. A woman who loved me. . . .

On the bridge the trucks are booming. I go back down the lighthouse stairs, step into the sunshine, the sudden breeze, the sick sweet smell of river. I take the path that curves past the benches that line the tennis courts, the Saint Bernard, mouth roped with saliva, the man with delicate hands who strokes it. The balls say *thwuck* when they are mis-hit. *Tell me,* Aaron said.

It was July, we entered in the morning. And in the Delta, cotton flanked the highway, and in the fields black bodies trailing sacks bent as though in agony. Rows of shacks like from another time, children naked, bellies curved. I felt empty.

Go on.

We passed a chain gang. Black men linked, they were not singing. Guards in motionless relief. I was scared of it all, but mostly I was scared of them. White people. We were to offer our love to them. We were to turn the other cheek. It was beautiful. The land, I mean. I'd never seen such beauty. . . .

Beyond the courts, the path divides. I bend, drink from the fountain, and then I walk. To my right, where the shore juts in a brief promontory, a black boy, arms dangling pail and pole, tiptoes across the rocks. He squats and settles himself. The red bobber rides the surface of the river, *you ain't going to Mississippi*, my father said, he took me fishing. He took the fish in his hand, he took the knife. *Like this*, he said, and when I did my hand was bleeding.

Beryl, I said. There was blood on the grass, on my hand, they began to kill us. Willie McGhee, Bobby Johnson, Schwerner, Chaney, Goodman. Willie McGhee, Bobby Johnson, Schwerner, Chaney, Goodman. Seven years, it feels like yesterday, the sore on my shoulder carrying Bobby's casket on the dry road in the brutal heat, on one side of the sky a sullen sun, a crescent moon in the other. . . .

I walk. I go past the baseball field, the backstop sags. The sun gives to the twisted metal the quality of sculpture, a huge bird, wing broken, struggling to rise. The pavement curves to stone steps descending to the underpass beneath the southbound West Side Highway, cars humming and wooshing as I move below them through the cool, dark tunnel. At the edge of the northbound lanes I stand gauging the traffic, then sprint across the asphalt to the open space where on the grass attendants sit in dazzling white, the ambulatory patients a covey of dozing quail around them. I am past them, walking the edge of Riverside Drive, up by the psychiatric wing of the hospital, the inmates behind the steel mesh on the veranda, their afternoon tea laced with Thorazine.

I was going crazy. I deserted Beryl, just left without an explanation. I'd begun to hate, all the time dreaming about dying, I didn't want to die. Bobby Johnson was sixteen, brain tissue across his open mouth like leaking.

You loved Beryl, didn't you? Aaron said.

Marcus, do you love me?

Beryl, I said.

You loved Beryl, didn't you? But she was white.

I begin to run. I run until I'm breathing hard, until the fist in my stomach opens and the street levels: the river, the sun a huge bronze coin in its center, appearing from below the hill, as if it and not I has done the rising. There had been four days of rain the past week, a sudden chill followed by a record-breaking three-day heat, and now this perfect sunshine. Potholes gape in the street, cars negotiate as if across a field mined with explosives. I think about the night before me, the bank, and how I will place the bomb just so, and I come to the street shooting off to the left and then dividing, one branch heading uptown, the other climbing to where the Museum of the American Indian sprawls in this largely black and Puerto Rican setting. Then the graveyard as I cross the street, and the feeling comes over me again, the sense that nothing lost will be recovered. Once I belonged. Someone loved me. I had great plans, a movement. There were times in Mississippi when I paused to rejoice that I was alive, in that place, a mover and a shaker, despite my fear. We made history. And though we underestimated America, we were right to believe in love. Even when they didn't love us, when they killed us, driving us to hate, we were right to believe in love.

But how could you both affirm love and deny it?

Marcus, Beryl said.

And didn't I understand that it was a question not of love but of power?

Why are you? Aaron said. *It's not the only bank. All over the country, the world, people are investing in South Africa.*

We met at a poetry reading where the theme was revolution; he'd fallen in love with the word. He was tall, intense, and very smart, a doctoral candidate in economics; he was lonely. I felt responsible for him. He had good instincts, but he didn't know who he was. He still doesn't. He's seeking definition, becoming. I'd worked with Malcolm before they gunned him down, and Aaron thought I was special. I didn't tell him about the emptiness in me, the struggle to keep from screaming. I needed to be somebody, not a thing or a profession, but a feeling. I needed to be whole, to walk the earth in peace, make babies, love somebody. Part of it was my fault, but part was that the world wouldn't let me. I tell myself all the time that it's been seven years since I went south and lost a part of me; let it go, make a normal life. Join the Y, learn a foreign language. Then I dream again about Mississippi, and when I wake up, sweating, there's no one to talk to about what happened there, no one to help me understand why I can't let go.

So when Aaron asked me why, I told him because I had to. You couldn't live in the world and not take responsibility. The world must understand that it could not forever grind black people beneath its feet, because we would not stand for it. I was passionate; my speech reverberated with conviction.

I didn't want to disillusion him, so I didn't say anything about what I knew would happen next. I didn't say that if black people took a position of defiance, retaliation would be swift and brutal; that armies would be marshaled, not only the men in uniform, but ordinary citizens, and they would move to smash us. They would do this without compunction. It would be easy, for the times are changing. King is dead, and another Kennedy. Nixon will be president again. We are bleeding in Vietnam and Cambodia, Kent State and Chicago, Watts, Jackson State, Oakland, Newark. Some have retreated, turned to drugs and religion, self-help groups and meditation. Some have been slaughtered in rooms that wept for sunlight. Once old black folks believed in us, believed that we would change things, and now they wait without belief, like cattle, the shoulders curved, the undilated nostrils. They are waiting for the children to stop dying, for the war to end, for things to get better, but it is a waiting undefined except by weariness.

I refuse to fool myself. I know that tonight will make no great difference; in the morning they'll remove the rubble and go on about the business of making money. But I have to do it. If nothing else, it will inconvenience them. And I cannot live in the world and not take responsibility.

When I reach Broadway, the street is flush with traffic. Near the cemetery gate, beneath a purple parasol, stands a man with a portable freezer, a black man in a mechanic's blue uniform, on his chest pocket the name *Morty* stitched in white. My mouth is dry. He will have something cold and sweet.

"What you selling?"

"Iceys."

"Italian?"

"African."

"No lie? Iceys from the motherland. What part of Africa they come from?"

"Why don't you tell me what flavor you want? That way you can refresh yourself while I give you the history."

"That's fine. What you got?"

"Cherry, orange, lime divine, and lemon what is both sucking sour and smacking sweet. I recommends the lemon if you can stand the contradiction."

"Cherry."

In the graveyard, an attendant is planting flowers. Morty opens the freezer, the cold air billowy, pulls the curved utensil from the coffee can, scoops once, twice, then hands me the white cup heaped with red.

"That's thirty cents, American money."

I pay. The icey is cold, delicious. A bus lumbers to the corner. The lone disembarking passenger is a pregnant black woman in a bright green dress. In the graveyard, the attendant struggles to his feet, brushes dirt from his pants.

"So, where they come from?"

Morty is a small man, wiry, a face that suggests it has never been surprised. "These here happen to be from Timbuktu. Some coming in next week from Morocco."

In the distance, east of Broadway, the boom of an explosion, another. Morty looks toward the sound.

"They're tearing down some buildings over on Audubon Avenue," I say, and I follow his eyes to the southeast corner where a couple past the bloom of youth necks flagrantly in the sun.

"Folks is always tearing down," Morty says, "and they's always building."

"I guess so. But that's how things get changed. Tear them down and build something else."

"That so?" He is looking not at me but at the couple, an expression of longing on his face. "Who told you that, youngblood?"

"Common knowledge."

"Common to who?" He turns to me, eyebrows arched.

"Everybody. What's the matter? You don't believe in change?"

"Wouldn't know. Ain't never seen none."

"You from Missouri? You only believe what you see?"

"I'm from Newark. Springfield Avenue."

In the graveyard the space the attendant departed is hushed. "What I mean," I say, "is that everything changes. *Eventually.*"

And Morty snorts and says, "Not from where I stand it don't. Might look like change. But it ain't nothing but things staying the same."

"Maybe it's where you're standing." I gesture toward the graveyard. "Maybe it's affected your vision."

"You can put that back in your pocket. These eyes sees exactly what they looks at."

"Really? What do they see?"

He stares at me, as if measuring my worth or capacity for understanding, and then he spiels. "I see you and me. This street. The cit-y. Birds, trees, and the bumblebee buzzing in the shade of the cemetery. The rhythm of music, the depth of the sea. I see the heart of all mystery. So what makes you want to fuck with me?"

"Okay." I laugh. "I see you can see. But just one more question, for real now. Why you set up here? Isn't business a little slow in front of a graveyard?"

A third explosion sounds in the east, heavy and dull, and Morty says, "Oh, everybody comes by here, youngblood. Sooner or later," and looks directly into my eyes. Despite myself, I flinch. I cover what I'm feeling with another laugh, wave what's left of my icey.

"Yeah. Well, later," thinking, yes, everybody does come by here. But don't let it be me. Not tonight.

I ignore the traffic light, cross the street on my way to meet Aaron. There's a fist in my stomach, opening and closing, but I'm not afraid. I say it out loud to convince myself, and the brother on the corner turns to check me out.

Willie Bea and Jaybird

Tina McElroy Ansa

1990

When Willie Bea first saw Jaybird in The Place, she couldn't help herself. She wanted him so bad she sucked in her bottom lip, cracked with the cold, then she ran her tongue so slowly over her top lip that she could taste the red Maybelline lipstick she had put on hours before. He looked like something that would be good to eat, like peach cobbler or a hot piece of buttered cornbread.

She had just entered the bar clutching her black purse under her arm and smiling to try to make herself look attractive among the six o'clock crowd of drinkers and dancers and socializers, every one of them glad to be done with work for the day. He was there at the end of the bar in his golden Schlitz uniform sharing a quart of Miller High Life beer with a buddy. Willie Bea noticed right away how he leaned his long frame clear across the bar, bent at the waist, his elbows resting easily on the Formica counter. There didn't seem to be a tense bone in his lean efficient body.

He look like he could go anywhere in the world, Willie Bea thought as she followed her big-butt friend Patricia as she weaved her way to a nearby table already jammed with four of her friends, two men, two women. "If somebody put him in a white jacket and a flower in his buttonhole, he could pass for an actor in a Technicolor movie."

As the jukebox started up again, playing a driving Sam and Dave number, he looked around the bar, picked up his glass of beer, and headed toward her table with his chin held high over the other patrons. When he smoothly pulled up a chair to her table and straddled it backwards, Willie Bea crossed her stick legs and pinched her friend Pat's thigh under the table to give her some Sen-Sen for her breath.

"Hey, Little Mama, you got time for a tired working man?"

She had to remember to wipe the uncomfortable moisture from the corners of her mouth with her fingertips before she could respond to him.

She still felt that way, four years after they had started going together, when she looked at him.

Nothing gave her more pleasure than to be asked her marital status with Jaybird around.

"Willie Bea, girl, where you been keeping yourself?" some big-mouthed woman would shout at her over the din of the jukebox at The Place. "I ain't seen you in a month of Sundays. You still living with your aunt, ain't you?" This last expectantly with pity.

Willie Bea would roll her shoulders and dip her ears from side to side a couple of times in feigned modesty.

"Naw, girl, I *been* moved out of my aunt's," Willie Bea would answer. "I'm married now. I live with my . . . *husband.*"

The old horse's big mouth would fall open, then close, then open as if she were having trouble chewing this information.

"Husband? Married??!!"

"Uh-huh. That's my husband over there by the jukebox. Naw, not him. My Jay is the tall light-skinned one, the one with the head full of curly hair."

Willie Bea never even bothered to look at her inquisitor when she pointed out Jay. She could hear the effect the weight of the revelation had had on the woman. And Willie Bea only glanced smugly at the old cow as she raced around the bar nearly knocking over a chair to ask her friends and companions why no one told her that skinny little shiny-faced Willie Bea had a man.

"I thought she was sitting there mighty sassy looking."

Even Willie Bea would have admitted it. Most days, she did feel sassy, and it was Jaybird who made her so. He burst into the bathroom while she was in the bathtub and pretended to take pictures of her with an imaginary camera. He teased her about flirting with Mr. Maurice, who owned the store on the corner near their boardinghouse, when the merchant sliced her baloney especially thin, the way she liked it.

Now, she really thought she was cute, with her little square monkey face and eager-to-please grin, a cheap jet black Prince Valiant wig set on the top of her head like a wool cap with her short hair plaited underneath and a pair of black eyeglasses so thick that her eyes looked as if they were in fish bowls.

Jaybird had done that to her. He even called her "fine," an appellation that actually brought tears to her eyes made huge and outlandish by the Coke-bottle-thick glasses.

"Fine." It was the one thing in life Willie Bea longed to be. She had no shape to speak of. She was just five feet tall and weighed about ninety pounds. But she did her best to throw that thing even though she had very little to throw.

"If I had me a big old butt like you, Pat," she would say to her friend, "ya'll couldn't stand me."

The pitiful little knot of an ass that she had was her sorrow, especially after noticing from Jaybird's gaze that he appreciated a full ass. His favorite seemed to be the big heart-shaped ones that started real low and hung and swayed like a bustle when the woman walked. Many mornings, Jay lay in bed watching Bea move around the room getting dressed and thought, Her behind ain't no bigger than my fist. But he didn't dare say anything, even as a joke. He knew it would break her heart.

But since she knew she didn't have a big ass, she did what she had done since she was a child when someone told her what she was lacking: She pretended she did and acted as if her ass was the prize one in town. The one men in juke joints talked about.

Wherever she went—to the market, to work cleaning houses, to The Place, downtown to shop—she dressed as if she had that ass to show off.

She wore tight little straight skirts that she made herself on her landlady's sewing machine. Skirts of cotton or wool or taffeta no wider than twelve inches across. Not that wide, really, because she wanted the skirt to "cup," if possible, under the pones of her behind and to wrinkle across her crotch in front. Using less than a yard of material and a Simplicity quickie pattern she had bought years before and worked away to tatters, she took no more than an hour to produce one of her miniature skirts.

On Sundays, when the house was empty of other boarders or quiet from their sleep, Willie Bea used her landlady's sewing machine that she kept in the parlor. The steady growl of the old foot-pedal-run Singer disturbed no one. In fact, on those Sundays she and Jaybird went out and she did no sewing, the other tenants of the large white wooden house felt an unidentified longing and found themselves on the verge of complaining about the silence.

Willie Bea looked on the ancient sewing machine, kept in mint condition by the genial landlady who always wore plaid housedresses and her thin crimpy red hair in six skinny braids, as a blessing. She didn't mind that the machine was a foot-propelled model rather than an electric one. It never occurred to her to expect anything as extravagant as that. For her, the old machine was a step up from the tedious hand-sewing that she had learned and relied on as a child. With the waist bands neatly attached and the short zippers eased into place by machine, her skirts had a finished look that would have taken her all night to accomplish by hand.

Many times, she felt herself rocking gently to the rhythm she set with her bare feet on the cold iron treadle to ease a crick in her stiff back before she realized that she had been at the job nonstop all afternoon. Just using the machine made her happy, made her think of men watching her at the bus stops in her new tight skirt and later, maybe, these same men letting some sly comment drop in front of Jaybird about her shore looking good.

She imagined Jaybird jumping in the men's faces, half angry, half proud, to let them know that was his *wife* they were talking about. Just thinking of Jaybird saying, "my wife" made her almost as happy as her being able to say "my husband."

She loved to go over in her head how it had come to pass, their marriage. They had been living together in one room of the boardinghouse at the top of Pleasant Hill for nearly three years, with him seeming to take for granted that they would be together for eternity and with her hardly daring to believe that he really wanted her, afraid to ask him why he picked her to love.

As with most of his decisions, movements, he surprised her.

One evening in August, he walked into their room and said, "Let's get married." As if the idea had just come to him, his and original. She responded in kind.

"Married? Married, Jay?" she said, pretending to roll the idea around in her head a while. Then, "Okay, if you want."

It was her heart's desire, the play-pretty of her dreams, being this man's wife.

She bought stiff white lace from Newberry's department store to make a loose cropped sleeveless overblouse and a yard of white polished cotton and sewed a tight straight skirt for the ceremony at the courthouse.

When they returned to their room for the honeymoon, Willie Bea thought as she watched him take off his wedding suit that no other man could be so handsome, so charming, so full of self-assured cockiness . . . and still love her.

He was tall and slender in that way that made her know that he would be lean all his life, never going sway-backed and to fat around his middle like a pregnant woman. He was lithe and strong from lifting cases and kegs of Schlitz beer all day long, graceful from leaping on and off the running board of the moving delivery truck as it made its rounds of bars and stores.

Once when he had not seen her, Willie Bea had spied him hanging fearlessly off the back of the beer truck like a prince, face directly into the wind, his eyes blinking back the wind tears, a vacant look on his face. His head full of curly hair quivering in the wind. The setting sunlight gleamed off the chrome and steel of the truck, giving a golden-orange color to the aura that Willie Bea felt surrounded him all the time.

Overcome by the sight, Willie Bea had had to turn away into an empty doorway to silently weep over the beauty of her Jaybird.

Jaybird even made love the way she knew this man would—sweet and demanding. When her friend Pat complained about her own man's harsh unfeeling fucking, Willie Bea joined in and talked about men like dogs. But first, in her own mind, she placed Jaybird outside the dog pack.

"Girl, just thank your lucky stars that you ain't hooked up with a man like Henry," Pat told her. "Although God knows they all alike. You may as well put 'em all in a croker sack and pick one out. They all the same. One just as good as the other. Just take your pick."

"Uh-huh, girl, you know you telling the truth," Willie Bea would answer.

"Why, that old dog of mine will just wake any time of the night and go to grabbing me and sticking his hand up my nightdress. He don't say nothing, just grunt. He just goes and do his business. I could be anything, a sack of flour, that chair you sitting on."

"What you be doing?" Willie Bea asked in her soft singsong voice, even though she already knew because Pat always complained about the same thing. But she asked because she and Pat had grown up together, she had been Pat's friend longer than anyone outside of her family. And Willie Bea knew what a friend was for.

"Shoot, sometimes I just lay there like I *am* a sack of flour. I thought that would make him see I wasn't getting nothing out of his humping. Then I saw it didn't make no difference to him whether I was having a good time or not. So, now, sometimes I push him off me just before he come. That makes him real mad. Or I tell him I got my period.

"Some nights, we just lay there jostling each other like little children jostling over a ball. I won't turn over or open up my legs and he won't stop tugging on me."

"Girl, both of ya'll crazy. That way, don't neither of you get a piece. That's too hard," Willie Bea said sincerely.

"Shoot, girl, some nights we tussle all night." Pat gave a hot dry laugh. "Henry thinks too much of hisself to fight me for it, really hit me upside my head or yell and scream, 'cause with those little paper-sheer walls, everybody next door would know our business. So while we fighting, it's real quiet except for some grunts and the bed squeaking."

Then, she laughed again.

"I guess that's all you'd be hearing anyway."

Willie Bea tried to laugh in acknowledgment. Once Pat told her, "Shoot, girl, I've gotten to liking the scuffling we do in bed better than I ever liked the screwing."

That made Willie Bea feel cold all over.

"It's like it make it more important," Pat continued. "Something worth fighting for. Some nights when he just reach for me like that, it's like he calling me out my name. And I turn over ready to fight.

"I would get somebody else, but they all the same, you may as well pick one from the sack as another. But look at you, Bea. You just agreeing to be nice. You don't believe that, do you?"

"I didn't say nothing," Willie Bea would rush to say. "I believe what you say about you and Henry. I believe you."

"That ain't what I mean and you know it. I'm talking about mens period."

"I know what you saying about men."

"Yeah, but you don't think they all alike, do you?" Pat asked.

Willie Bea would start dipping her head from side to side and grinning her sheepish closed-mouth grin.

"Go on and admit it, girl," Pat would prod.

After a moment, Willie Bea would admit it. "I don't know why he love me so good."

Then, Pat would sigh and urge her friend to tell her how sweet Jay was to her . . . in bed, at the table, after work. Especially in bed.

Willie Bea balked at first, each time the subject came up. But she always gave in, too. She was just dying to talk about Jaybird.

Most women she knew held the same beliefs that Pat did about men. They sure as hell didn't want to hear about her and the bliss her man brought her. She had found they may want to hear about you "can't do with him and can't do without him" or how bad he treat you and you still can't let him go. All of that. But don't be coming around them with those thick windowpane eyes of hers all bright and enlarged with stories of happiness and fulfillment. Those stories cut her other girlfriends and their lives to the quick.

But her friend Pat, big-butt Pat, urged Bea to share her stories with her. Sometimes, these reminiscences made Pat smile and glow as if she were there in Willie Bea's place. But sometimes they left her morose.

Willie Bea, noticing this at first, began leaving out details that she thought made Pat's love pale in comparison. But Pat, alert to nuances in the tales, caught on and insisted that Willie Bea never leave stuff out again if she was going to tell it.

And Willie Bea, eager to tell it all, felt as if she were pleasing her friend as much as herself. So she continued telling stories of love and dipping her ear down toward her shoulder in a gay little shy gesture.

"When Jaybird and me doing it, he has this little grufflike voice he uses when he talks to me."

"Talk to you? What ya'll be doing, screwing or talking?" Pat would interrupt, but not seriously.

"He says things like, 'Is that all? That ain't all. I want it all. Uh-huh.' "

At first, Willie Bea was embarrassed disclosing these secrets of her and Jaybird's passionate and tender lovemaking. But Pat seemed so enthralled by her stories that Willie Bea finally stopped fighting it and gave herself over to the joy of recounting how Jaybird loved her.

Pat never told Willie Bea that many of the women at The Place talked under their breaths when Jaybird and Willie Bea came in together.

"He may sleep in the same bed with her, but I heard he put an ironing board between 'em first," some said.

"He can't really want that little old black gal. He just like her worshiping the ground he walk on." another would add.

Pat knew Willie Bea would have tried to kill whoever said such things. But even Pat found it hard to believe sometimes that her little friend had attracted Jaybird.

Mornings, Pat watched Willie Bea step off the city bus they both took to their jobs, her too-pale dime-store stockings shining in the early light, her narrow shoulders rotating like bicycle pedals in the direction opposite the one she sent her snake hips inside her straight skirt, and thought how changed her friend was by the love of Jaybird. Now, that walk is something new, Pat thought, as the bus pulled away from the curb.

Willie Bea, who lived two blocks above Pat, got on the bus first, then alit first when she got near the white woman's house she cleaned five days a week. Pat stayed on until the bus reached downtown near the box factory where she worked. They rode to and from work together nearly every day.

So, one evening when Pat wasn't on the bus when she got on returning home, Willie Bea began to worry about her. All that one of Pat's co-workers on the bus said when Willie Bea asked was, "She left work early."

I wonder if she's sick, Willie Bea thought.

She was still thinking about her friend when the bus began making its climb up Pleasant Hill. I better stop and see 'bout her, Willie Bea thought.

She was still standing with her hand near the signal wire when the bus slowed to a stop in front of the cinder block duplex where Pat lived, and Willie Bea saw the gold of a Schlitz beer uniform slip back inside the dusty screen door of her friend's house.

The bus driver paused a good while with the bus door open waiting for Willie Bea to leave. Then he finally hollered toward the back of the bus, "You getting off or not?"

Willie Bea turned around to the driver's back and tried to smile as she took her regular seat again. When she reached her boardinghouse, she was anxious to see Jaybird and ask him who the new man was working on the beer truck. But he wasn't home.

She sat up alone on the bed in the boardinghouse room long after it grew dark.

Willie Bea didn't know how long she had been asleep when she heard the rusty doorknob turn and felt a sliver of light from the hall fall across her face. Jaybird almost never stayed out late without her or telling her beforehand.

"You okay, Jay?" she asked sleepily.

He only grunted and rubbed her back softly. "Go back to sleep, Bea," he said. "I'm coming to bed now."

Willie Bea lay waiting for Jaybird to say something more, to say where he had been, to say he saw her friend Pat that day. But he said nothing.

And when he did finally slip into bed, it felt as if an ironing board was between them.

Screen Memory

Michelle Cliff

1990

The sound of a jump rope came around in her head, softly, steadily marking time. Steadily slapping ground packed hard by the feet of girls.

Franklin's in the White House. Jump/Slap. *Talking to the ladies.* Jump/Slap. *Eleanor's in the outhouse.* Jump/Slap. *Eating chocolate babies.* Jump/Slap.

Noises of a long-drawn-out summer's evening years ago. But painted in such rich tones she could touch it.

A line of girls wait their turn. Gathered skirts, sleeveless blouses, shorts, bright, flowered—peach, pink, aquamarine. She spies a tomboy in a striped polo shirt and cuffed blue jeans.

A girl slides from the middle of the line. The woman recognizes her previous self. The girl is dressed in a pale blue starched pinafore, stiff and white in places, bleached and starched almost to death. She edges away from the other girls; the rope, their song, which jars her and makes her sad. And this is inside her head.

She senses there is more to come. She rests her spine against a wineglass elm. No one seems to notice her absence.

The rope keeps up its slapping, the voices speed their chanting. As the chant speeds up, so does the rope. The tomboy rushes in, challenging the others to trip her, burn her legs where she has rolled her jeans. Excitement is at a pitch. Franklin! Ladies! Eleanor! Babies! The tomboy's feet pound the ground. They are out for her. A voice sings out, above the others, and a word, strange and harsh to the observer's ears, sounds over the pound of feet, over the slap of rope. *Bulldagger! Bulldagger! Bulldagger! Bulldagger!* The rope sings past the tomboy's ears. She feels its heat against her skin. She knows the word. Salt burns the corners of her eyes. The rope-turners dare, singing it closer and closer. Sting!

The girl in the pinafore hangs back. The girl in the pinafore who is bright-skinned, ladylike, whose veins are visible, as the ladies of the church have commented so many times, hangs back. The tomboy, who is darker, who could not pass the paper bag test, trips and stumbles out. Rubbing her leg where the rope has singed her. The word stops.

Where does she begin and the tomboy end?

Fireflies prepare to loft themselves. Mason jars with pricked lids are lined on the ground waiting to trap them. Boys swing their legs, scratched and bruised from adventure or fury, from the first rung of a live oak tree. Oblivious to the girls, their singing—nemesis. The boys are swinging, talking, over the heads of the girls. Mostly of the War, their fathers, brothers, uncles, whoever represents them on air or land or sea.

The woman in the bed can barely make out their voices, though they speak inside her head.

Sudden lightning. A crack of thunder behind a hill. Wooden handles hit the dirt as the rope is dropped. Drops as big as an elephant's tears fall. The wind picks up the pace. Girls scatter to beat the band. Someone carefully coils the rope. Boys dare each other to stay in the tree.

The girl in the blue pinafore flies across the landscape. She flies into a window. To the feet of her grandmother.

Slow fade to black.

The woman in the bed wakes briefly, notes her pain, the dark outside.

Her head is splitting.

She and her grandmother have settled in a small town at the end of the line. At the edge of town where there are no sidewalks and houses are made from plain board, appearing ancient, beaten into smoothness, the two grow dahlias and peonies and azaleas. A rambling rose, pruned mercilessly by the grandmother, refuses to be restrained, climbing across the railings of the porch, masking the iron of the drainpipe, threatening to rampage across the roof and escape in a cloud of pink—she is wild. As wild as the girl's mother, whom the girl cannot remember, and the grandmother cannot forget.

The grandmother declares that roses are "too showy" and therefore she dislikes them. (As if dahlias and peonies and azaleas in their cultivated brightness are not.) But the stubborn vine is not for her to kill—nothing, no living thing, is, and that is the first lesson—only to train.

While the rose may evoke her daughter, there is something else. She does not tell her granddaughter about the thing embedded in her thigh, souvenir of being chased into a bank of roses. Surely the thing must have worked its way out by now—or she would have gotten gangrene, lost her leg clear up to the hip—but she swears she can feel it. A small sharp thorn living inside her muscle. All because of a band of fools to whom she was nothing but a thing to chase.

The grandmother's prized possession sits against the wall in the front room, souvenir of a happier time: when her husband was alive and her daughter held promise. An upright piano, decorated in gilt, chosen by the King of Bohemia and the Knights of the Rosy Cross, so says it. The grandmother rubs the mahogany and ebony with lemon oil, cleans the ivory with rubbing alcohol, scrubbing hard, then takes a chamois to the entire instrument, slower now, soothing it after each fierce cleaning.

The ebony and the ivory and the mahogany come from Africa—the birthplace of civilization. That is another of the grandmother's lessons. From the forests of the Congo and the elephants of the Great Rift Valley, where fossils are there for the taking and you have but to pull a bone from the great stack to find the first woman or the first man.

The girl, under the eye of the grandmother, practices the piano each afternoon. The sharp ear of the grandmother catches missed notes, passages played too fast, articulation, passion lost sliding across the keys. The grandmother speaks to her of passion, of the right kind. "Hastiness, carelessness, will never lead you to any real feeling, or"—she pauses—"any lasting accomplishment. You have to go deep inside yourself—to the best part." The black part, she thinks, for if anything can cloud your senses, it's that white blood. "The best part," she repeats to her granddaughter seated beside her on the piano bench, as she is atilt, favoring one hip.

The granddaughter, practicing the piano, remembers them leaving the last place, on the run, begging an old man and his son to transport the precious African thing—for to the grandmother the piano is African, civilized, the sum of its parts—on the back of a pickup truck.

A flock of white ladies had descended on the grandmother, declaring she had no right to raise a white child and they would take the girl and place her with a "decent" family. She explained that the girl was her granddaughter—sometimes it's like that. They did not hear. They took the girl by the hand, down the street, across the town, into the home of a man and a woman bereft of their only child by diphtheria. They led the girl into a pink room with roses rampant on the wall, a starched canopy hanging above the bed. They left her in the room and told her to remove her clothes, put on the robe they gave her, and take the bath they would draw for her. She did this.

Then, under cover of night, she let herself out the back door off the kitchen and made her way back, leaving the bed of a dead girl behind her. The sky pounded and the rain soaked her.

When the grandmother explained to the old man the circumstances of their leaving he agreed to help. To her granddaughter she said little except she hoped the piano would not be damaged in their flight.

There is a woman lying in a bed. She has flown through a storm to the feet of her grandmother, who is seated atilt at the upright, on a bench which holds browned sheets of music. The girl's hair is glistening from the wet but not a strand is out of place. It is braided with care, tied with grosgrain. Her mind's eye brings the ribbon into closer focus; its elegant dullness, no cheap satin shine.

Fifty cents a yard at the general store on Main Street.

"And don't you go flinging it at me like that. I've lived too long for your rudeness. I don't think the good Lord put me on this earth to teach each generation of you politeness." The grandmother is ramrod straight, black straw hat shiny, white gloves bright, hair restrained by a black net. The thing in her thigh throbs, as it always does in such situations, as it did in front of the white ladies, as it did on the back of the old man's truck.

The granddaughter chafes under the silence, scrutiny of the boy who is being addressed, a smirk creasing his face. She looks to the ceiling where a fan stirs up dust. She looks to the bolts of cotton behind his head. To her reflection in the glass-fronted cabinet. To the sunlight blaring through the huge windows in front, fading everything in sight: except the grandmother, who seems to become blacker with every word. And this is good. And the girl is frightened.

She looks anywhere but at the boy. She has heard their "white nigger" hisses often enough, as if her skin, her hair signify only shame, a crime against nature.

The grandmother picks up the length of ribbon where it has fallen, holds the cloth against her spectacles, examining it, folding the ribbon inside her handkerchief.

The boy behind the counter is motionless, waiting for his father's money, waiting to wait on the other people watching him, as this old woman takes all the time in the world. Finally: "Thank you, kindly," she tells him, and counts fifty cents onto the marble surface, slowly, laying the copper in lines of ten; and the girl, in her imagination, desperate to be anywhere but here, sees lines of Cherokee in canoes skimming an ice-bound river, or walking to Oklahoma, stories her grandmother told her. "They'd stopped listening to their Beloved Woman. Don't get me started, child."

The transaction complete, they leave—leaving the boy, two dots of pink sparking each plump cheek, incongruous against his smirk.

The woman in the bed opens her eyes. It is still, dark. She looks to the window. A tall, pale girl flies in the window to the feet of her grandmother. Seated at the piano, she turns her head and the grandmother's spectacles catch the lightning.

"I want to stay here with you forever, Grandma."

"I won't be here forever. You will have to make your own way."

"Yes, ma'am."

"We are born alone and we die alone and in the meanwhile we have to learn to live alone."

"Yes, Grandma."

"Good."

They speak their set-piece like two shadow puppets against a white wall in a darkened room. They are shades, drawn behind the eye of a woman, full-grown, alive, in withdrawal.

"Did something happen tonight?"

"Nothing, Grandma; just the storm."

"That's what made you take flight?"

"Yes, ma'am."

"Are you sure?"

"Yes, ma'am."

She could not tell her about the song, nor the word they had thrown at the other girl, to which the song was nothing.

She could not tell her about the pink room, the women examining her in the bath, her heart pounding as she escaped in a dead girl's clothes. They had burned hers.

Two childish flights. In each the grace which was rain, the fury which was storm chased her, saved her.

In the morning the sky was clear.

"Grandma?"

"Yes?"

"If I pay for it, can we get a radio?"

"Isn't a piano, aren't books enough for you?"

Silence.

"Where would you get that kind of money?"

"Mrs. Baker has asked me to help her after school. She has a new baby."

"Do I know this Mrs. Baker?"

"She was a teacher at the school before we came here. She left to get married and have a baby."

"Oh." The grandmother paused. "Then she is a colored woman?" As if she would even consider having her granddaughter toil for the other ilk.

"Yes. And she has a college education." Surely this detail would get the seal of approval, and with it the chance of the radio.

"What a fool."

"Grandma?"

"I say what a foolish woman. To go through all that—all that she must have done, and her people too—to get a college education and become a teacher and then to throw it all away to become another breeder. What a shame!"

With the last she was not expressing sympathy for a life changed by fate, or circumstances beyond an individual's control; she meant disgrace, of the Eve-covering-her-nakedness sort.

"Yes, Grandma." The girl could but assent.

The woman in the bed is watching as these shadows traverse the wall.

"Too many breeders, not enough readers. Yes—indeed."

"She seems like a very nice woman."

"And what, may I ask, does that count for? When there are children who depended on her? Why didn't she consider her responsibilities to her students, eh? Running off like that."

Watching the shadows engage and disengage.

"She didn't run off, Grandma."

No, Grandmother. Your daughter, my mother, ran off, or away. My mother who quit Spelman after one year because she didn't like the smell of her own hair burning—so you said. Am I to believe you? Went north and came back with me, and then ran off, away—again.

"You know what I mean. Selfish woman. Selfish and foolish. Lord have mercy, what a combination. The kind that do as they please and please no one but themselves."

The grandmother turned away to regard the dirt street and the stubborn rose.

The granddaughter didn't dare offer that a selfish and foolish woman would not make much of a teacher. Nor that Miss Elliston—whose pointer seemed an extension of her right index finger, and whose blue rayon skirt bore an equator of chalk dust—was a more than permanent replacement. The bitterness went far too deep for mitigation or comfort.

"Grandma, if I work for her, may I get a radio?"

"Tell me, why do you want this infernal thing?"

"Teacher says it's educational." Escape. I want to know about the outside.

"Nonsense. Don't speak nonsense to me."

"No, ma'am."

"And just how much do you think this woman is willing to pay you?"

"I'm not sure."

"What does her husband do, anyway?"

"He's in the navy, overseas."

"Of course." Her tone was resigned.

"Grandma?"

"Serving them coffee, cooking their meals, washing their drawers. Just another servant in uniform, a house slave, for that is all the use the United States Navy has for the Negro man."

She followed the War religiously, *Crisis* upon *Crisis*.

"Why didn't he sign up at Tuskegee, eh? Instead of being a Pullman porter on the high seas, or worse."

"I don't know," her granddaughter admitted quietly, she who was half-them.

"Yellow in more ways than one, that's why. Playing it safe, following a family tradition. Cooking and cleaning and yassuh, yassuh, yassuh. They are yellow, am I right?"

"Yes, ma'am."

"Well, those two deserve each other."

It was no use. No use at all to mention Dorie Miller—about whom the grandmother had taught the granddaughter—seizing the guns on the *Arizona* and blasting the enemy from the sky. No use at all. She who was part-them felt on trembling ground.

Suddenly—

"As long as you realize who, what these people are, then you may work for the woman. But only until you have enough money for that blasted radio. Maybe Madame Foolish-Selfish can lend you some books. Unless," her voice held an extraordinary coldness, "she's sold them to buy diapers."

"Yes, ma'am."

"You will listen to the radio only at certain times, and you must promise me to abide by my choice of those times, and to exercise discretion."

"I promise," the girl said.

Poor Mrs. Baker was in for one last volley. "Maybe as you watch the woman deteriorate, you will decide her life will not be yours. Your brain is too good, child. And can be damaged by the likes of her, the trash of the radio."

Not even when Mr. Baker's ship was sunk in the Pacific and he was lost, did she relent. "Far better to go down in flames than be sent to a watery grave. He died no hero's death, not he."

"Full fathom five thy father lies;
Of his bones are coral made;
Those are pearls that were his eyes:"

The baby with the black pearl eyes was folded into her chest as she spoke to him.

"Nothing of him that doth fade,
But doth suffer a sea-change
Into something rich and strange."

She imagined a deep and enduring blackness. Salt stripping him to bone, coral grafting, encrusted with other sea-creatures. She thought suddenly it was the wrong ocean that had claimed him—his company was at the bottom of the other.

"Sea-nymphs hourly ring his knell:
Ding-dong.
Hark! now I hear them—ding-dong, bell."

She heard nothing. The silence would be as deep and enduring as the blackness.

The girl didn't dare tell the grandmother that she held Mrs. Baker's hand when she got the news about her husband, brought her a glass of water, wiped her face. Lay beside her until she fell asleep. Gave the baby a sugar tit so his mother would not be waked.

The girl was learning about secrecy.

The girl tunes the radio in. Her head and the box are under a heavy crazy quilt, one of the last remnants of her mother; pieced like her mother's skin in the tent show where, as her grandmother said, "she exhibits herself." As a savage. A woman with wild hair. A freak.

That was a while ago; nothing has been heard from her since.

It is late. The grandmother is asleep on the back porch on a roll-away cot. Such is the heat she sleeps in the open air covered only by a thin muslin sheet.

The misery, heaviness of the quilt, smelling of her mother's handiwork, are more than compensated for by *The Shadow*. Who knows what evil lurks in the hearts of men?

The radio paid for, her visits to Mrs. Baker are meant to stop—that was the agreement. But she will not quit. Her visits to Mrs. Baker—like her hiding under her mother's covers with the radio late at night, terrified the hot tubes will catch the bed afire—are surreptitious and fill her with a warmth she is sure is wrong. She loves this woman, who is soft, who drops the lace front of her camisole to feed her baby, who tunes in to the opera from New York on Saturday afternoons and explains each heated plot as she moves around the small neat house.

The girl sees the woman in her dreams.

On a hot afternoon in August Mrs. Baker took her to a swimming hole a mile or two out in the country, beyond the town. They wrapped the baby and set him by the side of the water, "Like the baby Moses," Mrs. Baker said. Birdsong was over them and the silver shadows of fish glanced off their legs.

"Come on, there's no one else around," Mrs. Baker told her, assuring her when she hesitated, "There's nothing to be ashamed of." And the girl slipped out of her clothes, folding them carefully on the grassy bank. Shamed nonetheless by her paleness.

Memory struck her like a water moccasin sliding through the muddy water. The women who would save her had her stand, turn around, open her legs—just to make sure.

She pulls herself up and comes to in her hospital bed. The piano in the corner of the room, the old lady, the girl, the jump rope, the white ladies, recede and fade from her sight. Now there is a stark white chest which holds bedclothes.

In another corner a woman in a lace camisole, baby-blue ribbon threaded through the lace, smiles and waves and rises to the ceiling, where she slides into a crack in the plaster.

The woman in the bed reaches for the knob on the box beside her head and tunes it in; Ferrante and Teicher play the theme from *Exodus* on their twin pianos.

Her brain vibrates in a contrecoup. She is in a brilliantly lit white room in Boston, Massachusetts. Outside is frozen solid. It is the dead of winter in the dead of night. She could use a drink.

What happened, happened quickly. The radio announced a contest. She told Mrs. Baker about it. Mrs. Baker convinced her to send her picture in to the contest: "Do you really want to spend the rest of your days here? Especially now that your grandmother's passed on?" Her heart stopped. Just like that.

The picture was taken by Miss Velma Jackson, Mrs. Baker's friend, who advertised herself as v. JACKSON, PORTRAIT PHOTOGRAPHY, US ARMY RET. Miss Jackson came to town a few years after the War was over, set up shop, and rented a room in Mrs. Baker's small house. In her crisp khakis, with her deep brown skin, she contrasted well with the light-brown pasteled Mrs. Baker. She also loved the opera, and together they sang the duet from *Norma*.

When she moved in talk began. 'There must be something about that woman and uniforms,' the grandmother said in one of her final judgments.

Miss Jackson, who preferred "Jack" to "Velma," performed a vital service to the community, like the hairdresser and the undertaker. Poor people took care to keep a record of themselves, their kin. They needed Jack, and so the talk died down. Died down until another photographer came along—a traveling man who decided to settle down.

Jack's portrait of the girl, now a young woman, came out well. She stared back in her green-eyed, part-them glory against a plain white backdrop, no fussy ferns or winged armchairs. The picture was sent in to the contest, a wire returned, and she was summoned.

She took the plain name they offered her—eleven letters, to fit best on a marquee—and took off. A few papers were passed.

"Will you come with me?"

"No."

"Why not?"

"I can't."

"Why not?"

"Jack and I have made plans. She has some friends in Philadelphia. It will be easier for us there."

"And Elijah?"

"Oh, we'll take him along, of course. Good schools there. And one of her friends has a boy his age."

"I'm going to miss you."

"You'll be fine. We'll keep in touch. This town isn't the world, you know."

"No."

Now there was nothing on the papers they sent—that is, no space for RACE?

Jack said, "And what do you propose to do? Say, hey, Mr. Producer, by the way, although I have half-moons on my fingernails, a-hem, a-hem?"

She was helped to her berth by a Pullman porter more green-eyed than she. In his silver-buttoned epauleted blue coat he reminded her of a medieval knight, on an iron horse, his chivalric code—RULES FOR PULLMAN PORTERS—stuck in his breast pocket. He serenaded her.

> "De white gal ride in de parlor car.
> De yaller gal try to do de same.
> De black gal ride in de Jim Crow car.
> But she get dar jes' de same."

He looked at her as he stowed her bag. "Remember that old song, Miss?"

"No."

Daughter of the Mother Lode. The reader might recall that one. It's on late-night TV and also on video by now. She was the half-breed daughter of a Forty-Niner. At first, dirty and monosyllabic, then taken up by a kindly rancher's wife, only to be kidnapped by some crazy Apaches.

Polysyllabic and clean and calicoed when the Apaches seize her, dirty and monosyllabic and buck-skinned when she breaks away—and violated, dear Lord, violated out of her head, for which the rancher wreaks considerable havoc on the Apaches. You may remember that she is baptized and goes on to teach school in town and becomes a sort of mother confessor to the dance-hall girls.

As she gains speed, she ascends to become one of the more-stars-than-there-are-in-the-heavens, and her parts become lighter, brighter than before. Parts where "gay" and "grand" are staples of her dialogue. As in, "Isn't she gay!" "Isn't he grand!" She wears black velvet that droops at the neckline, a veiled pillbox, long white gloves.

She turns out the light next to the bed, shuts off the radio, looks out the window. Ice. Snow. Moon. The moon thin, with fat Venus beside it.

The door to the room suddenly whooshes open and a dark woman dressed in white approaches the bed.

"Mother?"

"Don't mind me, honey. I'm just here to clean up."

"Oh."

"I hope you feel better soon, honey. It takes time, you know."

"Yes."

The woman has dragged her mop and pail into the room and is now bent under the bed, so her voice is muffled beyond the whispers she speaks in—considerate of the drying-out process.

"Can I ask you something?" This soft-spoken question comes to the actress from underneath.

"Sure."

"Would you sign a piece of paper for my daughter?"

"I'd be glad to."

If I can remember my name.

The woman has emerged from under the bed and is standing next to her, looking down at her—bedpan in her right hand, disinfectant in her left.

The actress finds a piece of paper on the bedside table, asks the girl's name, signs *With every good wish for your future.*

"Thank you kindly."

She lies back. Behind her eyelids is a pond. Tables laden with food are in the background. In the scum of the pond are tadpoles, swimming spiders. Darning needles dart over the water's surface threatening to sew up the eyes of children.

A child is gulping pond water.

Fried chicken, potato salad, coleslaw, pans of ice with pop bottles sweating from the cold against the heat.

The child has lost her footing.

A woman is turning the handle of an ice-cream bucket, a bushel basket of ripe peaches sits on the grass beside her. Three-legged races, sack races, races with an uncooked egg in a spoon, all the races known to man, form the landscape beyond the pond, the woman with the ice-cream bucket, the tables laden with food.

Finally—the child cries out.

People stop.

She is dragged from the water, filthy. She is pumped back to life. She throws up in the soft grass.

The woman wakes, the white of the pillow case is stained.

She pulls herself up in the bed.

The other children said she would turn green—from the scum, the pond water, the baby frogs they told her she had swallowed. No one will love you when you are green and ugly.

She gets up, goes to the bathroom, gets a towel to put over the pillow case.

"Hello. Information?"

"This is Philadelphia Information."
"I would like the number of Velma Jackson, please."
"One moment please."
"I'll wait."
"The number is—"
She hangs up. It's too late.

"She did run away from them, Mama. She came back to you. I don't think you ever gave her credit for that."
"And look where she is now, Rebekah."
"She ran away from them, left a room with pink roses. Sorry, Mama, I know how you hate roses."
"Who is speaking, please?" The woman sits up again, looks around. Nothing.

What will become of her?
Let's see. This is February 1963.
She might find herself in Washington, D.C., in August. A shrouded marcher in the heat, dark-glassed, high-heeled.
That is unlikely.

Go back? To what? This ain't *Pinky*.
Europe? A small place somewhere. Costa Brava or Paris—who cares? Do cameos for Fellini; worse come to worse, get a part in a spaghetti western.
She does her time. Fills a suitcase with her dietary needs: Milky Ways, cartons of Winston's, golden tequila, boards a plane at Idlewild.
Below the plane is a storm, a burst behind a cloud, streak lightning splits the sky, she rests her head against the window; she finds the cold comforting.

Age Would Be That Does

Percival Everett

1990

It was with some resolve that Rosendo Lapuente put a bullet through the head of his sister's dog Grasa. Some resolve, a great deal of excitement and an admirable measure of luck as he dispatched the animal from well over forty yards. Of course it was not until Rosendo and his friend, Mauricio Rocha, were well upon the fallen prey that they realized it was a dog and not until Rosendo's face was mere inches from the canine's head that he recognized it as Grasa.

"Oh my," Rosendo said. "This is your fault."

"It was you who shot him," Mauricio said.

"You told me it was a deer."

"All I said was, 'There, there is one.' I didn't say 'deer.' "

Rosendo studied the dog. "No matter. I've killed my sister's Grasa. *Me siento mareado.*"

"*Respire hondo,*" Mauricio said and sucked much air and let it out slowly to show what he meant.

"And she's always yelling at me that I'm too old and blind to go hunting. She'll never let me forget *this.*" Rosendo sat on a log, laid the rifle on the ground between his legs.

"*No es para preocuparse,*" Mauricio said.

"How do you figure that?"

"How will she know?" Mauricio asked.

Rosendo sighed. "I suppose you're right. It would be a shame to hurt her with such news. It was a terrible pet anyway, a car chaser. Did you know that?"

"I had heard."

The two friends began their hike out of the forest, saying nothing. Rosendo gave the rifle to Mauricio to carry. They shared the gun and kept it hidden in the shed in back of the house Rosendo shared with his younger sister Maria. The men shared vision; that was how they saw it. Mauricio claiming an ability to see things some distance away and Rosendo saying he could focus on things close.

So, Rosendo did the reading and Mauricio did the driving, having managed to retain his permit by uncannily guessing correctly the letters of the eye chart, each relying on the other for constant reports. Actually, Mauricio couldn't make out things that far away and Rosendo had to hold large print an arm's length from his face, so it was a safe bet that they saw about the same things equally well, or poorly.

They came out of the canyon mouth and found Mauricio's car, a blue Datsun sedan that his daughter who lived in Albuquerque had given him when she bought one of those little vans that Mauricio said looked like a suppository. Mauricio wrapped the gun up in a blanket while Rosendo leaned against the car peering at nothing in particular, but in general back at the woods.

"Let me ask you something, Moe," Rosendo said.

Mauricio slammed shut the hatch.

"Do you think that we're old?"

Mauricio looked at the same trees. "Hell, I know for a fact we're old. But not like you're thinking. We're young men who still go hunting."

"*Si*, we hunt dogs, pet dogs. What was Grasa doing so far out here anyway?"

The fact of the matter was that they were not very far from Rosendo's home. The house was just a half-mile from the canyon, but Mauricio's driving took them repeatedly over the same dirt lanes and through the same turns. Any trip for Mauricio in his blue Datsun took three times as long as it should have. Walking through the woods was much a like matter for them. Rosendo had killed the dog no more than a hundred yards deep into the woods, but they believed themselves to have marched two or three miles, which perhaps they had but in circles. When anyone saw the blue Datsun parked at the canyon opening they spread the word to steer clear of the forest.

They parked in the back yard behind the shed and sneaked inside to hide the weapon behind the drums of corn that Maria fed the wild turkeys. The birds were actually chickens, but one day Maria had jokingly referred to them as turnkeys and Rosendo said, "And fine looking birds they are too. But, Maria, they don't sound much like turkeys."

"*Hasta luego*, Rosie," Mauricio said, back in his car and waving goodbye to Rosendo as he drove away.

Rosendo took a deep breath and walked through the back door of the house and into the kitchen where Maria was sitting and chatting with Carlita Hireles. "Hello, Maria," he said and proceded to wash his hands at the sink.

"Aren't you going to say hello to Father Ortega?" Maria said, sharing a smile and silent laughter with her friend.

"I'm sorry, Padre, I didn't see you," Rosendo said, dried his hands on a towel and reached to shake.

Carlita lowered her voice and said, "It's good to see you, Rosie."

Rosendo paused at the softness of the hand and then considered it not unlikely that a hand which had never seen manual work should feel so. "What brings you way out here?" Rosendo asked. "Somebody die?"

"No, no, just saying hello," Carlita said in her altered voice.

Rosendo nodded, knowing as he passed from the kitchen into the living room that he had just spoken to Carlita Hireles because he recognized the smell of her, perfume and make-up and fancy soap. They were having a laugh on him, but that was okay, especially today as Grasa wouldn't be showing up for dinner. It was enough that he knew it to be Carlita.

Later, as Rosendo sat eating his dinner, Maria stood at the screen of the back door looking out for Grasa. It was then that Miguel Rocha, Mauricio's nephew and Willard Garcia drove into the backyard with much loud noise from their big-wheeled pickup. They came into the house excited.

"*Qué le ocurre?*" Maria asked.

"A lion," Willard said.

"Yes, there is a cougar around. He killed two sheep over in San Cristobal," Miguel said.

Rosendo listened to them and stood. "A lion?"

"Si, Rosie." Miguel caught his breath. "From the size of the tracks a big one too."

"We're just going around and making sure everybody knows," Willard said. "You know, so people are careful and watch out for their stock and things like that."

"Well, you're doing a fine job," Maria said. "Would you boys like to take some sopaipillas with you?"

They thanked her and each took a couple and left.

"A lion," Maria said, sitting and shaking her head. "I hope that Grasa hasn't met up with him."

Rosendo chewed his dinner. "A dog would have little chance against such a beast. Poor Grasa."

The old man finished his meal and went into the living room where he sat and rocked and listened to the radio. He enjoyed particularly the call-in talk shows which had people arguing about such strange things. He was often disgusted and constantly amazed. "That there are such people," he would say, getting up to grab a bran muffin from the basket on the kitchen table. Rosendo stayed up later than Maria as was his custom, then went to the door and looked out over the yard. The moon was full and Rosendo sensed that more than he saw it. He heard a noise.

"Rosie," a voice called to him in a whisper.

"Moe? Is that you?"

"Si."

Rosendo listened for movement from Maria's room and finding none, walked outside. "Moe?"

"Rosie?"

It took the men ten minutes to locate each other by sound, but they did, by the shed.

"I didn't hear your car," Rosendo said.

"I parked down the road."

"Why have you come here so late?" Rosendo asked.

"I left early, but it was very long drive. When it got dark it became an even longer way."

Rosendo nodded.

"Did you hear about the lion?" Mauricio asked.

"Miguel was here. He told us. There hasn't been a lion around here in many years."

"Miguel and Willard and some of the others are talking about tracking the animal down," Mauricio said. "What do they know about tracking lions, about hunting them? I asked them that and they laughed at me."

"They've never even seen a lion. You and I have seen a lion. Remember?"

"I remember."

"That was a big animal," Mauricio said.

"It killed a bull, I recall that."

"I think it is we who have to get this monster," Mauricio said.

Rosendo looked back in what he thought was the general direction of the house. "I believe that you're right. We can't tell anyone though."

"They would try to stop us."

Rosendo sighed. He then invited his friend to stay the night in his house. "It will be too long a drive for you tonight. We will rise early and leave before Maria wakes up."

Mauricio agreed and retired to the sofa where he slept until first light. Rosendo made sandwiches, collected other foods, filled a couple of canteens and tied two rolled-up blankets to his knapsack. The men took their rifle from the shed, found Mauricio's blue Datsun and then, after a moderate amount of driving, found the mouth of some canyon. They wandered most of a day, putting some distance between themselves and the car by following an arroyo. They stopped once to eat and rest, but were driven by great excitement and so moved at a decent clip through the forest. They were very serious about their mission, talking little and walking with ears peeled for noises which might alert them to the cat's presence. Neither had any doubt that they would find the animal. As to what would happen when they did, they were split; Rosendo claiming the right to shoot the lion because he had paid for the shells and Mauricio claiming the same right because the hunt had been his idea. They argued the point off and on, deciding that it just mattered how far away the lion was when the moment arrived. They sat down in a clearing by the creek at dusk and built a fire, ate little weiners from a can with day-old sopaipillas.

"Just like old times, eh, Moe?"

"I can't wait to see their faces when we show up with the lion's head," Mauricio said.

"The head will be very heavy."

"Perhaps, his paw then."

"I wish I had remembered the radio," Rosendo said.

"Just something else to carry," said Mauricio as he stood. He walked some yards away from the campsite and into the trees to relieve himself.

Rosendo, who had not noticed his friend's movement, also did not notice that the cougar had come and sat quietly in his friend's place.

"It's cooler out here than I thought it would be," Mauricio called from the trees.

"You sound like you're in a tunnel," Rosendo said.

The lion just sat there and panted.

Rosendo chuckled. "You're getting old, *amigo*. A little walk has fatigued you."

"What was that?" Mauricio asked.

The lion belched.

Rosendo fanned at the odor. "Say 'excuse me.' "

"I'm sorry," Mauricio said, "I didn't know you could hear."

The cougar left.

Mauricio finished his business and returned to the fire, approaching Rosendo from the other side. "Any more of those weinies left?"

Rosendo jumped at the voice on the wrong side. "What?"

"Did I scare you?"

"How did you do that?"

"Do what?" Mauricio sat down and found the little tin of weiners, took a bite of one.

"Moe, I think that the lion was just here. Did you get up and go somewhere?"

"I took a crap back in the trees."

"Hmmm," said Rosendo, "And you were not here beside me."

Mauricio laughed. "I cannot be in two places at once."

"Let me smell your breath," Rosendo said.

"What is wrong with you?"

Rosendo leaned forward, "Just breathe and let me smell." Mauricio did and Rosendo groaned. "Just as I thought."

"Bad?"

"The lion was here, Moe. He was sitting right beside me."

Mauricio said nothing. The men sat back-to-back and covered themselves with the blankets, taking turns tossing sticks into the fire. But they did not sleep. Instead they wondered about things, asked questions like: Did state troopers shift their pistols from hip to hip periodically to avoid being lopsided? and How many yards long was the town of Red River?

"They'd have to," Mauricio said concerning the state trooper question. "Do you know how heavy those pistols are?"

"I know how heavy they are."

"It would damage their legs if they didn't switch back and forth."

Rosendo shook his head. "People are right or left-handed. You can't just wear the thing on any side. It was to be on the side of the hand they use."

"They'd end up walking in circles if they switch and even it out," Mauricio said.

"We'll have to find a state trooper and watch him over a period of time," Rosendo said.

Mauricio agreed that that was the way to clear up the matter. That's the way their arguing went and they didn't know they had gone to sleep until morning came and the birds sang loud songs and squirrels and chipmunks rattled branches.

"Do you think we should continue on up the mountain?" Mauricio asked.

Rosendo looked up the arroyo splitting the canyon and then down. "What do you think?"

"I think the lion went down."

Rosendo nodded his agreement and that was the way they began to retrace their previous day's steps.

"There is one thing," Mauricio said.

"What is that?" Rosendo asked.

"We were closer to the beast than anyone else. You were near enough to smell the lion's breath."

"Yes, I was," Rosendo said.

Going for the Moon

Al Young

1990

The first time it happened, I figured, well, chalk it up to coincidence. We'd been talking so much in science class about the connection between how you think and what actually happens to you that I figured that maybe subconsciously, like Mr. Cleveland's always saying, I might've been hallucinating or projecting or something.

I mean, when I got home and Edrick told me somebody'd actually heaved a brick in the window of the bar downstairs, I went to laughing and coughing so hard he got scared and, for a skinny minute there, musta thought I might be needing some professional attention. I even put on my coat and went down to see for myself the hole the brick'd made.

Naturally, I didn't stand right in fronta the Ivory Coast where Nate and June, the dippy bartenders, could see me. I had sense enough to go across the street. I was impressed. Whoever did it'd done a clean, righteous job. Nate and June had boarded the window up temporarily so business could go on as usual, but deep down I knew this was gonna put a hurting on those suckers. Yet and still, something about it was disturbing.

"Zee," said Edrick, "you don't seem all that happy about this."

"When did it happen?" I asked.

"Before I got up. So it musta been in broad daylight. I woke up to this big commotion down on the street. The police came out and stood around, and June was out there with her fat self, talking all loud and bad. I thought it was great!"

"I'll have to think about it," I told my brother.

"What's there to think about?"

"Don't know," I said. "It just makes me feel kinda creepy the way it all went down."

"But Zee, you yourself told me you'd been concentrating on shaking 'em up, didn't you? Or maybe I've just been imagining and making all this stuff up since you moved in?"

"No, it's true. I did sit and picture a lotta stuff, including a brick smashing out their window. That image came up a lot, I must admit."

"So now that it's popped out for real, Zee, how come you're acting so weird?"

It took a full minute for me to think through that one. I'm not into violence. At least I don't believe I ever was.

Out of all the missed sleep and raw nerves the Ivory Coast had caused us with that loud-ass jukebox of theirs, it was the bass that got to me. The damn thing pounded right under my bed like it was the Tell-Tale Heart or something. The minute my head hit the pillow, it was *boom-bip/boom-boom-bip!* I'm talking about every night of the week. And nights when I had some heavy studying to do for school or some paper or a short story to write, look like it got twice as loud.

Of course I'd call up and ask 'em to turn the music down. Usually, if it was Nate answering the phone, he'd just say something like, "Yeah, well, okay, it must be pretty rough on you, up there gotta go to school in the morning and here we are down here, rattling you all around in your bed. We'll see what we can do."

But June, she was mean, man! Cold! She'd say stuff like, "Listen, don't you think it's kinda weird, in the first place, to be living up over a bar? How come you don't move? This is a business we got going here."

"Now, wait a minute," I'd say. "What's that suppose to mean? Me and Edrick ain't running no business, so we don't count, right? Just so happens we like it here."

"Well, we do, too, and our customers got a right to be entertained."

That's the kinda changes the Ivory Coast'd been putting us through, only it was rougher on me than it was on Edrick because he worked between midnight and eight, the graveyard shift at Safeway. Why any supermarket thinks it's gotta be open twenty-four hours a day is still beyond me, but that's the way it was. Neither one of us wanted to have anything to do with the cops, so we never called 'em.

Also, the apartment, even though it was on the small side, was nice and got a lotta sun. Edrick had dragged home so many potted plants from the Safeway, the window side of the dining room was starting to look like Golden Gate Park. Okay, I'm exaggerating a little, but you know what I mean. I'm not exaggerating, though, when I tell you the rent was right. In other words we put up with all that racket and hurt feelings and hassle with the Ivory Coast because we liked being where we were, out there on Geary near Golden Gate Park.

The flip side, you understand, was being able to come home from schoo and there Edrick would be, usually just getting up and showering and shavin So even with my little part-time bookstore job, which Miz Perlstein at La

Chance High had helped me get through Community Outreach Program, my brother and me still had time to hang out together.

I really like Edrick. After I got outa detention and Moms started leaning on that vodka again, the only solution was for me to go stay with him. I never knew our father. And as much as Moms and me fought and didn't get along, especially when she was juicing *and* smoking that stuff, I still missed her something terrible. Sometime in the middle of the afternoon, while I'd be working at the bookstore or in the middle of some class, I'd remember how Moms'd spoken to me inside a dream I'd forgot I had the night before. I worried about her, and wondered how long she was gonna stay down in Texas, drying out. Even though Edrick wasn't but twenty-two, that was old enough for him to be my legal guardian.

When I told Mr. Cleveland before class about what'd gone down at the Ivory Coast, he said, "I wouldn't feel too bad about that brick through the window, Zephyr. Just because the thought rolled around in your head, that doesn't necessarily mean you endorse that sort of thing."

"But I thought about it a lot," I told him. "And the night before it happened, I sat there on the edge of the bed, waiting to hear the glass go to shattering."

I liked talking with Mr. Cleveland in his office. He asked me to call him Wayne, which I would only do every once in a while. It never felt right. I mean, the brother was straight out of the sixties, the way he talked and thought. Even that big Afro he wore and the dashikis he'd come in wearing sometime woulda looked corny on anybody else. But with Mr. Cleveland, there was something okay about that. I liked him. Somehow he automatically made you wanna show some respect.

I mean, he wasn't tryna force you into no mold or pretend like he was your buddy, like some of the people at the juvenile authority do. He was just tryna get me to do more of my own thinking for a change. Mosta the time anyway. I must admit there were days when Mr. Cleveland didn't make much sense with all that positive stuff he liked to talk. I mean, all the depressing stuff happening all around me was enough to make anybody negative.

"So you know what that means?" Mr. Cleveland was saying. "It means you weren't the only one in the building who's been bothered by the noise level of that bar. The possibility of that brick going through that window has probably been hanging out there in space in the form of a thought for a long time. It's a thought form that's been waiting for somebody to pick it up and act on it, that's all."

"You think so?" I said.

"I'd be willing to bet anything that's what occurred."

And when I looked at Mr. Cleveland, at the way the late spring sunlight was angling in through the dirty window by his desk and falling on his face, that's when I understood how much he himself believed in what he was telling me. I could tell by his eyes how excited he was.

"So," I said, "all this you're telling us about thought waves isn't just another theory?"

"Absolutely not, Zephyr. Thoughts are as real as microwaves or TV waves or radio or radiation."

It wasn't hard to see that Mr. Cleveland knew I still wasn't quite ready to buy all of this, even though we'd been kicking it around—along with atoms and biology and the universe and other mind-blowing stuff—since I got into his general science class and made it into one of my hyphenates last winter when I first came to Last Chance. A hyphenated class is when you take a regular class—like science or accounting or history or whatever—only you can make it, say, a creative writing class too. That's what I've done with Mr. Cleveland's class.

And that's what I liked about Last Chance High. It wasn't just another alternative education deal tryna help you save face; it's saving my butt. I'm learning how giving is more important than to all the time be taking and receiving.

"The mind is a sending and receiving mechanism," Mr. Cleveland went on. "You still have a problem with that, don't you?"

"Yeah."

"And what is it?"

"Well," I said, "if it really works that way, then how come we mostly go through negative experiences?"

You'd have to have your nose cut clean off to keep from smelling all through the room that strong peppermint tea Mr. Cleveland liked to sip on. "Is that how life feels to you?" he said. "Mostly negative?"

"Sure, that's the way the world is, don't you think?"

"I used to think that way," he said.

Mr. Cleveland always leaves his door cracked, maybe so the next person in line to see him could see he was already busy with somebody, so I caught a little glimpse of Marlessa Washington out there in the hall. It was just enough to make my belly go to tingling. She was sitting out there, listening to her Walkman, kinda flipping through our textbook.

"What you've got to understand," Mr. Cleveland was saying, "is that the subsconscious mind doesn't know how to take no for an answer."

"How do you mean?"

"Yes is the only answer it recognizes. It only knows how to carry out whatever instructions we give it. It's like we saw in class with seeds and what happens when you plant them in dark, fertile soil, then water and look after them. Up above ground, it might not look like much is happening. But down underneath, down below the surface, there's plenty going on. Next thing you know—*bam!* Up comes the beginning of some flower or plant. It's like magic. That's what thinking is, Zephyr—magic. It's like a magic seed you plant in your subconscious, which is like soil. Then all you have to do is keep watering and fertilizing it. That's what we're doing all the time without realizing it."

"That's the part I don't get, Mr. Cleveland—I mean, Wayne."

He smiled and said, "All it means is this: A good deal of the time we're planting negative seeds of thought, negative suggestions in our subconscious without even realizing it."

"How do we do that?"

"We're unconscious of our thinking. We forget that thoughts are real, that thinking itself is real. It isn't a fantasy or something we imagine. Thought waves are real waves traveling out into the environment, the same as any other signals. They go out and get picked up on frequencies, or wavelengths. This room right now is full of voices and music and pictures passing clean through us, or maybe bouncing off us. All we have to do to pick them up is snap on a radio or television and tune it to the right frequency."

"Whoa!" I said. "That's more than I can handle!"

"No, it isn't, Zephyr. You've been waiting to hear all this for a long time now. I only happen to be the one you've okayed to put it to you straight and clear."

"I'll still have to think about it," I said.

Mr. Cleveland stood up with a big grin on his face and said, "And check out *how* you think about it."

"Well," I said, getting up from my chair, "right now I gotta go rock and roll with a test in Miss Santiago's current affairs class."

"Last Chance might be the last of the alternative high schools," Mr. Cleveland said, "but even here T.C.B. is still in style."

And even though the way he talked sounded funny and outa date sometime, Mr. Cleveland had that one right. I did have to take care of business in Santiago's class. Either that, or lose some units. Like everybody else who'd either been kicked out of or dropped out of some other high school, I liked Last Chance. And I wanted to get high school behind me and get on with it, whatever that meant.

The second time it happened, Marlessa was with me and I, for one, got pretty shook up again, even though we both tried to make out like what'd happened wasn't any big thing.

I'd finally got up the nerve to ask her out, so that Saturday night we were just crawling up to the toll booth on the Bay Bridge on the way back from a Run-DMC concert in Oakland. Marlessa was driving her mother's car, a raggedy old Rabbit. I handed her some quarters.

Marlessa squinched her face up and said, "No, Zephyr, I got enough for the toll."

"But if you're gonna drive," I said, "the least I can do is pay for this."

"But you've already paid for the concert tickets and our refreshments."

"So?"

"So that's enough. Besides, at the rate we're moving, I figure it's costing us about a penny a minute on this bridge to get to San Francisco. And with my luck, there won't be no parking place around our building after we get there."

"You still live at home?" I asked.

"Sure," said Marlessa. "If it wasn't for my mother and her friend baby-sitting for Little David, I don't know what I'd do. Don't you stay at home?"

"Nope. Well, not exactly."

She didn't say anything.

What I like most about Marlessa is she doesn't come right out and poke and pry around in your business. It's the same as when she looks at you. It's never direct or, I guess you could say, without your permission. She always looks like she's peeking at you through a slat in a venetian blind or out the corner of a curtain. I go for that. I suppose what I'm tryna say is that she's kinda shy, but she's also, you know, respectful.

After a while she said, "Little David, after I had him, both my parents said I was gonna have to support him my own self. That's why I dropped outa school for a year and a half. But then Mama got to where she loved Little David so, she said I needed to go back to school. I thought so, too. So that's how I wound up at Last Chance, where I could make my own schedule and really do courses that did *me* some good."

"You thought much yet about what you might wanna get into?"

"Yeah, I wanna either go to Contra Costa Community College or else to the University of San Francisco."

I was amazed. I mean, it sounded like Marlessa kinda had her act together. I still didn't have even the shakiest idea of what I wanted to do. I was starting to try to think about it, though.

"But how'd you get it narrowed down to those two?" I asked.

"They both have good restaurant management training programs," she said, "and that's what I wanna do."

"You mean, like, manage a Church's Chicken or a Burger King or a McDonald's?"

Marlessa laughed.

"No, Zephyr," she said. "You don't need no schooling to run a fast food joint. One day I'd like to open up a place of my own. Something with style, you know, where food from different kindsa cultures could come together."

"Like what?"

"Like, oh, we'd have a little soul food, but I'd be careful to pick which dishes we'd do because a lotta that Southern stuff'll kill you, you know. All that grease and high cholesterol. Then maybe some Guatemalan dishes and maybe some Samoan or Chinese food. You know, it'd be like a little tastebud sampling of San Francisco, all available in one place."

I said, "I can see you've been thinking about this."

"I dream a lot," Marlessa said. "I don't think it's anything wrong with that, do you?"

"Mr. Cleveland wouldn't think so."

Marlessa rolled up the window to shut out the booming rhythm and rap the car in the next lane was blasting us with. I looked over, sure it was gonna be a car fulla brothers and sisters, but it turned out to be a bunch of wild-looking Chinese kids. The girls had Technicolor streaks in their hair, and the dudes all had 'em an earring.

Marlessa laughed again. "On second thought," she turned to me and said, "change what I said to Vietnamese food."

I was tryna picture what such a restaurant would look like: how the tables would be spaced and how the menu would look. I even thought about what Marlessa might have on the walls and how the waiters or the waitresses would dress, and what the kitchen would look like. But it wasn't easy to picture. All I knew about restaurants was from the summer I worked at a McDonald's on Market Street, so all I could imagine was funk and commotion.

"Zephyr," she asked me all of a sudden, "are you still on probation?"

"No," I said, a little surprised that Marlessa would come right out and ask anything that personal. I tried to joke to smooth over the wrinkled-up feeling I had.

"No," I went on. "You won't catch me stealing *nothing* else again."

"What'd they actually nail you for, Zephyr?"

"Oh, I had this scam. It was beautiful."

"Please don't feel you gotta tell me about it."

"Okay," I said, glad to hear Marlessa say that. "But we thought it was pretty slick. We'd go in these big stores, ask the clerk for empty boxes for moving, and wind up looting 'em blind before we came out."

"Were you doing it for money, or what?"

"No, for fun mostly. Sure, we'd sell some of the stuff on the street, but mainly it was what me and my buddies did. I used to . . . oh, I used to cop a lotta liquor that way."

"Were you one of those teenage alcoholics, too?"

"No," I said, feeling sad again. "No, I was getting it for my mother."

For a long time Marlessa fell back into her silent thing, acting like she was concentrating on making her exit from the bridge.

"You seen much of your mom lately?" Marlessa asked.

"No, just a postcard sometime. She don't call me or my brother much.

Nowhere near enough, even though we tell her it's okay for her to call collect. Sometimes it really gets to me."

"Well," said Marlessa, "I see far too much of my mother. So what we got here is a situation that needs balancing. You need to see more of yours and I need to see less of mine."

I didn't think what Marlessa said was funny, but I kinda faked a weak chuckle anyway just to let her know how much I appreciated her interest.

"Uh-uh!" she said. "Now, here's where the problem comes up."

"What problem?"

"The parking problem. If you don't get over here where I live before nine o'clock at night, ain't no way in the world these people are gonna leave you a parking space. Makes me sick!"

"Wait," I said. "Don't even think like that."

"Then what should I do, then?"

"Just picture that you're gonna get a parking place, just the right space for nobody else's car but yours. Tell you what, let's picture it together and see what happens."

"Aw, Zephyr, here you go again with all that Mr. Cleveland stuff."

"Here, let's just try it and see what happens, okay?"

While Marlessa headed up Hayes toward her place, right there across from Alamo Park, I went to picturing a big fat space right out in fronta her house almost. At first, I was scared to try to be too specific and was ready to settle for any kinda puny parking place at all. Then something inside me said no, that since it was only a mental exercise or game I was trying out, then, hell, I might as well up and go for the moon.

Before I knew it, Marlessa was driving right up to the house. I could feel all those let-down juices settling in my stomach. All that talking and picturing we'd been doing, and we might as well've been in some kinda oil painting. I mean, wasn't nothing moving!

Marlessa's jaws were starting to get tight as she circled the block. It looked to me like people were even parked bumper to bumper in red zones and by fire hydrants and in places where it was illegal for cars to be.

"What's going on?" she asked. "This is worse than usual."

"Maybe somebody's having a party," I said.

"I don't hear no music," she said, "do you?"

"Are you still picturing that perfect space?" I asked Marlessa as she rounded the block a third time.

"I'd be lying to you, Zephyr, if I said I was."

"Well, I still am," I said. "And I'm going for the big one."

"What you mean, the big one?"

"I mean right out there in fronta your house."

It was so nice to hear Marlessa laughing again until suddenly it didn't seem to matter whether we ever found another parking space or not.

"I'm gonna drive over a coupla blocks," she said.

"No, no! Marlessa, let's just give it one more try. Go around the block again."

It caused her to do a lotta sighing, but Marlessa finally chugged around the block and eased up toward her apartment house again.

"See," she said, "this is getting old pretty fast, Zephyr."

And just when she said that, a big old van parked right in fronta her place started signaling to pull out from the curb. And that's not all. At the same time, people had suddenly popped out onto the street from outa nowhere and standing at their car doors with the keys in their hands.

"I don't believe this!" Marlessa said. "This isn't something you and some of your slick buddies set up, is it?"

The trouble was, I didn't believe it either. I didn't know what to say. All I did was grunt and shake my head the whole time Marlessa was parking the car.

Then we both got to giggling.

"Zephyr," she said, "that was something. We're gonna have to tell Mr. Cleveland about this. He likes all this strange synchronicity stuff."

"Yeah, but . . . I was so busy concentrating on this parking space . . . we forgot something."

"What?"

"How do *I* get home?"

Marlessa leaned across the seat and gave me a friendly little lipstick smack on the jaw.

"Well," she said, "I guess now we'd better get busy and start picturing some transportation for you, hunh?"

"What?"

"I'm only playing with you, Zephyr," she said. "Would you like to come up and meet Little David?"

"But, uh, it's kinda late. Won't your folks mind?"

"Folk."

"Hunh?"

"My father doesn't live with us anymore. And Mama rode up to Sacramento with my cousin to visit my grandmama."

"Your mother's gone?"

"Yeah, but that doesn't mean you can come up there and show out on me."

"Then who's minding your baby?"

"Zephyr," she said, "you ever hear tella baby-sitters? I'll drop you off when I drive the baby-sitter home."

And that's exactly what Marlessa did. She let me peep in at her little boy. He was a cute little joker, too. Looked mostly like Marlessa, but he musta favored his daddy some. I still can't get over her having a kid and still a kid herself.

But when we got upstairs and Mrs. Jackson pointed to the crib where the baby was sleeping. Marlessa went over, leaned down, and kissed Little David. She kissed him in a way that was real different but sorta the same way she'd kissed on me back there in the car. Watching her do this, something clicked, and for a second, I flashed on how it used to be, a long time ago, when Dad and Moms were still together and they'd tuck me in bed for the night. That cozy feeling. You know. With a nice sleepiness pulled up around it all tight and snug like fresh-washed sheets and warm covers.

Marlessa drove Mrs. Jackson home, and I realized she only lived a few blocks from me. I sat in the back, holding the baby. He was all cute and blanketed down and everything, and it was an okay thing to do. But it still made me feel funny. I sure wasn't ready to be a father yet.

When Marlessa dropped me off, I said, "Let's do this again sometime."

"You tell me when."

"Is next Saturday too soon?"

"I'll tell you at school."

I said, "We have a telephone, you know."

She said, "Maybe the best thing would be to send you a telepathic message."

"We can try that, too," I said.

I honestly can't remember when the third time was. I mean, after that, I kinda lost count. Maybe a better way to put it would be to say I quit keeping track of my thoughts turning out to be for real. And I think that might be because my whole way of thinking is beginning to get changed around. Little by little, this idea about thoughts being magic isn't such a big, humongous thing anymore; it's just the way things are.

More and more I'm looking hard at what goes on inside my mind and how I feel about it. I'm starting to pick and choose my thoughts, the same as you'd pick a cassette to pop in the Walkman. I like being in charge of the kinda thoughts I play in my mind.

If Edrick and his sometime girlfriend Rosie have a fight, and he starts sending out all those bummed-out feelings, well, that's Edrick. I mean, I can be sympathetic, but now I know I don't have to buy into his trip. Or if down at the bookstore I'm unpacking some newspaper like the *Enquirer* or the *Globe*, and the front-page story is about how everybody on earth, by the year 2055, is gonna to be dying from AIDS, I know I got at least two choices. I can either freeze on a headline such as that and stay hung up on it, or else I can stack that information up against other things we're learning about epidemics and disease.

Fifteen, twenty times a day somebody will be tryna sell me some crack, and I'll stop and think about what smoking it is gonna do to my mind, to this thought player of mine. I already know what weed and vodka used to do to Moms, and I see what dope is doing to other people I know, so I don't have to think too hard. Every few weeks, looks like, somebody at Last Chance or one of my running buddies from the old neighborhood, over in Western Addition, would burn theirself out or catch some disease or just up and die all of a sudden.

I still felt like living for a long time, and I wish I could say there was a happy ending to this story, but I'm still living it out.

All I can report for sure right now—since mosta this is still so new to me—is that if the city keeps cutting back Last Chance's budget, pretty soon it won't exist no more. And this joint is too good a thing to lose. Mr. Cleveland keeps me up on all such as that.

"So what can we do about it?" I asked him.

"All you can do, Zephyr, is pass on anything good you think you might've picked up here. You know that rhyme of mine: 'Hold on to what's alive and forget the other jive.' "

The other day when I got home, the Ivory Coast was all boarded up. Not just the window, the whole place! There was a sign pasted on that very window the brick'd sailed through. The Board of Health was shutting 'em down. Probably for being too nasty, I guess.

As I stood out there on Geary in the rain and read it, every word on the notice was like an M&M melting on your tongue, or maybe even like sitting in the movies and chewing on a Jujyfruit. I swear, I didn't have a thing to do with that. Still, I couldn't wait till Edrick got home to see it.

It's no accident, though, that Marlessa's starting to test out some of these mind games, or whatever you wanna call 'em. Now, since so much interesting stuff has been happening to me, Edrick and his girlfriend Rosie are sort of testing it out. Last week Edrick told me Safeway was finally gonna move him out of that graveyard slot, where he's mainly been stocking shelves all night, and put him on the day shift as an apprentice checker.

When I asked Edrick how he felt about this, he said, "Well, I have been wanting a change for a long time. But I'm not sure I can make the switch all that easy. It's so peaceful there at night."

"Maybe," I said, just to get his goat, "this is the result of something Rosie's been concentrating on. She never was crazy about the hours you worked."

"Hmmm," said Edrick. "I don't know about all this brainwashing stuff."

"Let's just keep on sending Moms them good thoughts," I told him.

For the last couple of weeks, every night before I fall asleep, I been picturing Moms hard, imagining her getting well down there in Texas. I started doing this after I noticed how often somebody would either call me when I thought about 'em deep, or else I'd run into 'em. Some kinda way they'd show up. Me and Marlessa, we've been getting outrageous with it.

Guess what?

Moms called long distance from Houston this morning just when I was rushing out of the house to catch the bus to school.

"Hey, Moms," I said, all outa breath from dashing back up the steps, praying I could pick it up before that last ring.

"Hi, Zee," she said, all staticky. It wasn't the best connection in the world.

"What's going on? Is anything wrong?"

"No, are you and Edrick all right?"

"We're doing just fine. You get that last money order we sent?"

"Yeah, Zee, yeah, I got it. You're the best two boys a mother could wish for."

When she said that, I froze up a little. Moms never talked that way much, not that I can remember.

"Moms, you sound different."

"Different? How?"

"You sound better."

Even through all that long distance static and space, I could hear the little sniffling and funny breathing she was doing at the other end. So I wasn't a bit surprised when she came back on in this choked-up voice.

"Zee," she said.

"Yes, Moms."

"I'm sorry it's had to be like this. But I'll make it up to you two . . . somehow. I haven't had nothing to drink in so long, I've forgotten what it tastes like."

I didn't know what to say to this. Moms had told me and Edrick this so many times before, I wasn't sure how to react. But you know what? This time I didn't care.

"I'm into some new stuff, Moms."

"Like what?"

"Oh, just thinking more than I use to."

"Well, you never were what I'd call slow; just hard-headed like your father. Going by your letters, it sounds like you kinda like that school you're in. This teacher of yours, this Mr. Cleveland, sounds like he's on the ball."

"It's the best thing ever happened to me, Moms. I'm writing a story about it."

"Yeah?"

"Well, never mind. When you coming home?"

"Zee?" she said, like all of a sudden the connection'd gotten so bad she couldn't hear me. "Zee? Baby, you still there?"

"Yeah, Moms, I'm right here."

"Oh, there you are. I can hear you now. Zee, there's something I have to tell you."

"What is it, Moms?"

"I love you."

"I love you, too, Moms. You coming home soon?"

She didn't say nothing for a long time. I stood there, looking down at the street where the number 34 bus was just then creaking up.

"Pretty soon," she said finally. "I figured maybe right after school lets out might be the best time to come back up there and get resettled."

"Oh, that's good news."

"You and Edrick are gonna have to help me find a place to stay, though."

"Don't worry about that. You can stay here with us for a while if you have to. It'll be tight, but—"

"And Zee . . ."

"Yes, Moms."

"I even stopped smoking grass, too. But I haven't been able to cut out cigarettes yet. I'm gonna try, though."

"Don't worry about that, Moms. One thing at a time."

"I finally joined this outfit that helps drunks like me."

"Are you gonna let 'em help you, for a change?"

"Yes . . . yes, I am."

It took all the willpower I had to keep from blurting out all the stuff about thinking and thoughts Mr. Cleveland has been dropping on us. But something tells me Moms wasn't jiving this time. There was so much life in her voice, and I swear, this time I can almost feel deep down in my own gut how she wasn't as scared as she used to be. I knew there was a lotta thinking and concentrating to be done, but I was glad just the same.

"Moms," I cleared my throat and said, "me and Edrick can't wait."

Quilting on the Rebound

Terry McMillan

1991

Five years ago, I did something I swore I'd never do—went out with someone I worked with. We worked for a large insurance company in L.A. Richard was a senior examiner and I was a chief underwriter. The first year, we kept it a secret, and not because we were afraid of jeopardizing our jobs. Richard was twenty-six and I was thirty-four. By the second year, everybody knew it anyway and nobody seemed to care. We'd been going out for three years when I realized that this relationship was going nowhere. I probably could've dated him for the rest of my life and he'd have been satisfied. Richard had had a long reputation for being a Don Juan of sorts, until he met me. I cooled his heels. His name was also rather ironic, because he looked like a black Richard Gere. The fact that I was older than he was made him feel powerful in a sense, and he believed that he could do for me what men my own age apparently couldn't. But that wasn't true. He was a challenge. I wanted to see if I could make his head and heart turn 360 degrees, and I did. I blew his young mind in bed, but he also charmed me into loving him until I didn't care how old he was.

Richard thought I was exotic because I have slanted eyes, high cheekbones, and full lips. Even though my mother is Japanese and my dad is black, I inherited most of his traits. My complexion is dark, my hair is nappy, and I'm five-six. I explained to Richard that I was proud of both of my heritages, but he has insisted on thinking of me as being mostly Japanese. Why, I don't know. I grew up in a black neighborhood in L.A., went to Dorsey High School—which was predominantly black, Asian, and Hispanic—and most of my friends are black. I've never even considered going out with anyone other than black men.

My mother, I'm glad to say, is not the stereotypical passive Japanese wife either. She's been the head nurse in Kaiser's cardiovascular unit for over twenty years, and my dad has his own landscaping business, even though he should've retired years ago. My mother liked Richard and his age didn't bother her, but she believed that if a man loved you he should marry you. Simple as that. On the other hand, my dad didn't care who I married just as long as it was soon. I'll be the first to admit that I was a spoiled-rotten brat because my mother had had three miscarriages before she finally had me and I was used to getting everything I wanted. Richard was no exception. "Give him the ultimatum," my mother had said, if he didn't propose by my thirty-eighth birthday.

But I didn't have to. I got pregnant.

We were having dinner at an Italian restaurant when I told him. "You want to get married, don't you?" he'd said.

"Do you?" I asked.

He was picking through his salad and then he jabbed his fork into a tomato. "Why not, we were headed in that direction anyway, weren't we?" He did not eat his tomato but laid his fork down on the side of the plate.

I swallowed a spoonful of my clam chowder, then asked, "Were we?"

"You know the answer to that. But hell, now's as good a time as any. We're both making good money, and sometimes all a man needs is a little incentive." He didn't look at me when he said this, and his voice was strained. "Look," he said, "I've had a pretty shitty day, haggling with one of the adjusters, so forgive me if I don't appear to be boiling over with excitement. I am happy about this. Believe me, I am," he said, and picked up a single piece of lettuce with a different fork and put it into his mouth.

My parents were thrilled when I told them, but my mother was nevertheless suspicious. "Funny how this baby pop up, isn't it?" she'd said.

"What do you mean?"

"You know exactly what I mean. I hope baby doesn't backfire."

I ignored what she'd just said. "Will you help me make my dress?" I asked.

"Yes," she said. "But we must hurry."

My parents—who are far from well off—went all out for this wedding. My mother didn't want anyone to know I was pregnant, and to be honest, I didn't either. The age difference was enough to handle as it was. Close to three hundred people had been invited, and my parents had spent an astronomical amount of money to rent a country club in Marina Del Rey. "At your age," my dad had said, "I hope you'll only be doing this once." Richard's parents insisted on taking care of the caterer and the liquor, and my parents didn't object. I paid for the cake.

About a month before the Big Day, I was meeting Richard at the jeweler because he'd picked out my ring and wanted to make sure I liked it. He was so excited, he sounded like a little boy. It was beautiful, but I told him he didn't have to spend four thousand dollars on my wedding ring. "You're worth it," he'd said and kissed me on the cheek. When we got to the parking lot, he opened my door and stood there staring at me. "Four more weeks," he said, "and you'll be my wife." He didn't smile when he said it, but closed the door and walked around to the driver's side and got in. He'd driven four whole blocks without saying a word and his knuckles were almost white because of how tight he was holding the steering wheel.

"Is something wrong, Richard?" I asked him.

"What would make you think that?" he said. Then he laid on the horn because someone in front of us hadn't moved and the light had just barely turned green.

"Richard, we don't have to go through with this, you know."

"I know we don't *have* to, but it's the right thing to do, and I'm going to do it. So don't worry, we'll be happy."

But I *was* worried.

I'd been doing some shopping at the Beverly Center when I started getting these stomach cramps while I was going up the escalator, so I decided to sit down. I walked over to one of the little outside cafés and I felt something lock inside my stomach, so I pulled out a chair. Moments later my skirt felt like it was wet. I got up and looked at the chair and saw a small red puddle. I sat back down and started crying. I didn't know what to do. Then a punkish-looking girl came over and asked if I was okay. "I'm pregnant, and I've just bled all over this chair," I said.

"Can I do something for you? Do you want me to call an ambulance?" She was popping chewing gum and I wanted to snatch it out of her mouth.

By this time at least four other women had gathered around me. The punkish-looking girl told them about my condition. One of the women said, "Look, let's get her to the rest room. She's probably having a miscarriage."

Two of the women helped me up and all four of them formed a circle around me, then slowly led me to the ladies' room. I told them that I wasn't in any pain, but they were still worried. I closed the stall door, pulled down two toilet seat covers, and sat down. I felt as if I had to go, so I pushed. Something plopped out of me and it made a splash. I was afraid to get up but I got up and looked at this large dark mass that looked like liver. I put my hand over my mouth because I knew that was my baby.

"Are you okay in there?"

I went to open my mouth, but the joint in my jawbone clicked and my mouth wouldn't move.

"Are you okay in there, miss?"

I wanted to answer, but I couldn't.

"Miss." I heard her banging on the door.

I felt my mouth loosen. "It's gone," I said. "It's gone."

"Honey, open the door," someone said, but I couldn't move. Then I heard myself say, "I think I need a sanitary pad." I was staring into the toilet bowl when I felt a hand hit my leg. "Here, are you sure you're okay in there?"

"Yes," I said. Then I flushed the toilet with my foot and watched my future disappear. I put the pad on and reached inside my shopping bag, pulled out a Raiders sweatshirt I'd bought for Richard, and tied it around my waist. When I came out, all of the women were waiting for me. "Would you like us to call your husband? Where are you parked? Do you feel light-headed, dizzy?"

"No, I'm fine, really, and thank you so much for your concern. I appreciate it, but I feel okay."

I drove home in a daze and when I opened the door to my condo, I was glad I lived alone. I sat on the couch from one o'clock to four o'clock without moving. When I finally got up, it felt as if I'd only been there for five minutes.

I didn't tell Richard. I didn't tell anybody. I bled for three days before I went to see my doctor. He scolded me because I'd gotten some kind of an infection and had to be prescribed antibiotics, then he sent me to the outpatient clinic, where I had to have a D & C.

Two weeks later, I had a surprise shower and got enough gifts to fill the housewares department at Bullock's. One of my old girlfriends, Gloria, came all the way from Phoenix, and I hadn't seen her in three years. I hardly recognized her, she was as big as a house. "You don't know how lucky you are, girl," she'd said to me. "I wish I could be here for the wedding but Tarik is having his sixteenth birthday party and I am not leaving a bunch of teenagers alone in my house. Besides, I'd probably have a heart attack watching you or anybody else walk down an aisle in white. Come to think of it, I can't even remember the last time I went to a wedding."

"Me either," I said.

"I know you're gonna try to get pregnant in a hurry, right?" she asked, holding out her wrist with the watch on it.

I tried to smile. "I'm going to work on it," I said.

"Well, who knows?" Gloria said, laughing. "Maybe one day you'll be coming to my wedding. We may both be in wheelchairs, but you never know."

"I'll be there," I said.

All Richard said when he saw the gifts was, "What are we going to do with all this stuff? Where are we going to put it?"

"It depends on where we're going to live," I said, which we hadn't even talked about. My condo was big enough and so was his apartment.

"It doesn't matter to me, but I think we should wait a while before buying a house. A house is a big investment, you know. Thirty years." He gave me a quick look.

"Are you getting cold feet?" I blurted out.

"No, I'm not getting cold feet. It's just that in two weeks we're going to be man and wife, and it takes a little getting used to the idea, that's all."

"Are you having doubts about the idea of it?"

"No."

"Are you sure?"

"I'm sure," he said.

I didn't stop bleeding, so I took some vacation time to relax and finish my dress. I worked on it day and night and was doing all the beadwork by hand. My mother was spending all her free time at my place trying to make sure everything was happening on schedule. A week before the Big Day I was trying on my gown for the hundredth time when the phone rang. I thought it might be Richard, since he hadn't called me in almost forty-eight hours, and when I finally called him and left a message, he still hadn't returned my call. My father said this was normal.

"Hello," I said.

"I think you should talk to Richard." It was his mother.

"About what?" I asked.

"He's not feeling very well," was all she said.

"What's wrong with him?"

"I don't know for sure. I think it's his stomach."

"Is he sick?"

"I don't know. Call him."

"I did call him but he hasn't returned my call."

"Keep trying," she said.

So I called him at work, but his secretary said he wasn't there. I called him at home and he wasn't there either, so I left another message and for the next three hours I was a wreck, waiting to hear from him. I knew something was wrong.

I gave myself a facial, a manicure, and a pedicure and watched Oprah Winfrey while I waited by the phone. It didn't ring. My mother was downstairs hemming one of the bridesmaid's dresses. I went down to get myself a glass of wine. "How you feeling, Marilyn Monroe?" she asked.

"What do you mean, how am I feeling? I'm feeling fine."

"All I meant was you awful lucky with no morning sickness or anything, but I must say, hormones changing because you getting awfully irritating."

"I'm sorry, Ma."

"It's okay. I had jitters too."

I went back upstairs and closed my bedroom door, then went into my bathroom. I put the wineglass on the side of the bathtub and decided to take a bubble bath in spite of the bleeding. I must have poured half a bottle of Secreti in. The water was too hot but I got in anyway. Call, dammit, call. Just then the phone rang and scared me half to death. I was hyperventilating and couldn't say much except, "Hold on a minute," while I caught my breath.

"Marilyn?" Richard was saying. "Marilyn?" But before I had a chance to answer he blurted out what must have been on his mind all along. "Please don't be mad at me, but I can't do this. I'm not ready. I wanted to do the right thing, but I'm only twenty-nine years old. I've got my whole life ahead of me. I'm not ready to be a father yet. I'm not ready to be anybody's husband either, and I'm scared. Everything is happening too fast. I know you think I'm being a coward, and you're probably right. But I've been having nightmares, Marilyn. Do you hear me, nightmares about being imprisoned. I haven't been able to sleep through the night. I doze off and wake up dripping wet. And my stomach. It's in knots. Believe me, Marilyn, it's not that I don't love you because I do. It's not that I don't care about the baby, because I do. I just can't do this right now. I can't make this kind of commitment right now. I'm sorry. Marilyn? Marilyn, are you still there?"

I dropped the portable phone in the bathtub and got out.

My mother heard me screaming and came tearing into the room. "What happened?"

I was dripping wet and ripping the pearls off my dress but somehow I managed to tell her.

"He come to his senses," she said. "This happen a lot. He just got cold feet, but give him day or two. He not mean it."

Three days went by and he didn't call. My mother stayed with me and did everything she could to console me, but by that time I'd already flushed the ring down the toilet.

"I hope you don't lose baby behind this," she said.

"I've already lost the baby," I said.

"What?"

"A month ago."

Her mouth was wide open. She found the sofa with her hand and sat down. "Marilyn," she said and let out an exasperated sigh.

"I couldn't tell anybody."

"Why not tell somebody? Why not me, your mother?"

"Because I was too scared."

"Scared of what?"

"That Richard might change his mind."

"Man love you, dead baby not change his mind."

"I was going to tell him after we got married."

"I not raise you to be dishonest."

"I know."

"No man in world worth lying about something like this. How could you?"

"I don't know."

"I told you it backfire, didn't I?"

For weeks I couldn't eat or sleep. At first, all I did was think about what was wrong with me. I was too old. For him. No. He didn't care about my age. It was the gap in my teeth, or my slight overbite, from all those years I used to suck my thumb. But he never mentioned anything about it and I was really the only one who seemed to notice. I was flat-chested. I had cellulite. My ass was square instead of round. I wasn't exciting as I used to be in bed. No. I was still good in bed, that much I did know. I couldn't cook. I was a terrible housekeeper. That was it. If you couldn't cook and keep a clean house, what kind of wife would you make?

I had to make myself stop thinking about my infinite flaws, so I started quilting again. I was astonished at how radiant the colors were that I was choosing, how unconventional and wild the patterns were. Without even realizing it, I was fusing Japanese and African motifs and was quite excited by the results. My mother was worried about me, even though I had actually stopped bleeding for two whole weeks. Under the circumstances, she thought that my obsession with quilting was not normal, so she forced me to go to the doctor. He gave me some kind of an antidepressant, which I refused to take. I told him I was not depressed, I was simply hurt. Besides, a pill wasn't any antidote or consolation for heartache.

I began to patronize just about every fabric store in downtown Los Angeles, and while I listened to the humming of my machine, and concentrated on designs that I couldn't believe I was creating, it occurred to me that I wasn't suffering from heartache at all. I actually felt this incredible sense of relief. As if I didn't have to anticipate anything else happening that was outside of my control. And when I did grieve, it was always because I had lost a child, not a future husband.

I also heard my mother all day long on my phone, lying about some tragedy that had happened and apologizing for any inconvenience it may have caused. And I watched her, bent over at the dining room table, writing hundreds of thank-you notes to the people she was returning gifts to. She even signed my name. My father wanted to kill Richard. "He was too young, and he wasn't good enough for you anyway," he said. "This is really a blessing in disguise."

I took a leave of absence from my job because there was no way in hell I could face those people, and the thought of looking at Richard infuriated me. I was not angry at him for not marrying me, I was angry at him for not being honest, for the way he handled it all. He even had the nerve to come over without calling. I had opened the door but wouldn't let him inside. He was nothing but a little pipsqueak. A handsome, five-foot-seven-inch pipsqueak.

"Marilyn, look, we need to talk."

"About what?"

"Us. The baby."

"There is no baby."

"What do you mean, there's no baby?"

"It died."

"You mean you got rid of it?"

"No, I lost it."

"I'm sorry, Marilyn," he said and put his head down. How touching, I thought. "This is all my fault."

"It's not your fault, Richard."

"Look. Can I come in?"

"For what?"

"I want to talk. I need to talk to you."

"About what?"

"About us."

"Us?"

"Yes, us. I don't want it to be over between us. I just need more time, that's all."

"Time for what?"

"To make sure this is what I want to do."

"Take all the time you need," I said and slammed the door in his face. He rang the buzzer again, but I just told him to get lost and leave me alone.

I went upstairs and sat at my sewing machine. I turned the light on, then picked up a piece of purple and terra-cotta cloth. I slid it under the pressure foot and dropped it. I pressed down on the pedal and watched the needle zigzag. The stitches were too loose so I tightened the tension. Richard is going to be the last in a series of mistakes I've made when it comes to picking a man. I've picked the wrong one too many times, like a bad habit that's too hard to break. I haven't had the best of luck when it comes to keeping them either, and to be honest, Richard was the one who lasted the longest.

When I got to the end of the fabric, I pulled the top and bobbin threads together and cut them on the thread cutter. Then I bent down and picked up two different pieces. They were black and purple. I always want what I can't have or what I'm not supposed to have. So what did I do? Created a pattern of choosing men that I knew would be a challenge. Richard's was his age. But the others—all of them from Alex to William—were all afraid of something: namely, committing to one woman. All I wanted to do was seduce them hard enough—emotionally, mentally, and physically—so they wouldn't even be aware that they were committing to anything. I just wanted them to crave me, and no one else but me. I wanted to be their healthiest addiction. But it was a lot harder to do than I thought. What I found out was that men are a hard nut to crack.

But some of them weren't. When I was in my late twenties, early thirties— before I got serious and realized I wanted a long-term relationship—I'd had at least twenty different men fall in love with me, but of course these were the ones I didn't want. They were the ones who after a few dates or one rousing night in bed, ordained themselves my "man" or were too quick to want to marry me, and even some considered me their "property." When it was clear that I was dealing with a different species of man, a hungry element, before I got in too deep, I'd tell them almost immediately that I hope they wouldn't mind my being bisexual or my being unfaithful because I was in no hurry to settle down with one man, or that I had a tendency of always falling for my man's friends. Could they tolerate that? I even went so far as to tell them that I hoped having herpes wouldn't cause a problem, that I wasn't really all that trustworthy because I was a habitual liar, and that if they wanted the whole truth they should find themselves another woman. I told them that I didn't even think I was good enough for them, and they should do themselves a favor, find a woman who's truly worthy of having such a terrific man.

I had it down to a science, but by the time I met Richard, I was tired of lying and conniving. I was sick of the games. I was whipped, really, and allowed myself to relax and be vulnerable because I knew I was getting old.

When Gloria called to see how my honeymoon went, I told her the truth about everything. She couldn't believe it. "Well, I thought I'd heard 'em all, but this one takes the cake. How you holding up?"

"I'm hanging in there."

"This is what makes you want to castrate a man."

"Not really, Gloria."

"I know. But you know what I mean. Some of them have a lot of nerve, I swear they do. But really, Marilyn, how are you feeling for real, baby?"

"I'm getting my period every other week, but I'm quilting again, which is a good sign."

"First of all, take your behind back to that doctor and find out why you're still bleeding like this. And, honey, making quilts is no consolation for a broken heart. It sounds like you could use some R and R. Why don't you come visit me for a few days?"

I looked around my room, which had piles and piles of cloth and half-sewn quilts, from where I'd changed my mind. Hundreds of different-colored threads were all over the carpet, and the satin stitch I was trying out wasn't giving me the effect I thought it would. I could use a break, I thought. I could. "You know what?" I said. "I think I will."

"Good, and bring me one of those tacky quilts. I don't have anything to snuggle up with in the winter, and contrary to popular belief, it does get cold here come December."

I liked Phoenix and Tempe, but I fell in love with Scottsdale. Not only was it beautiful but I couldn't believe how inexpensive it was to live in the entire area, which was all referred to as the Valley. I have to thank Gloria for being such a lifesaver. She took me to her beauty salon and gave me a whole new look. She chopped off my hair, and one of the guys in her shop showed me how to put on my makeup in a way that would further enhance what assets he insisted I had.

We drove to Tucson, to Canyon Ranch for what started out as a simple Spa Renewal Day. But we ended up spending three glorious days and had the works. I had an herbal wrap, where they wrapped my entire body in hot thin linen that had been steamed. Then they rolled me up in flannel blankets and put a cold washcloth on my forehead. I sweated in the dark for a half hour. Gloria didn't do this because she said she was claustrophobic and didn't want to be wrapped up in anything where she couldn't move. I had a deep-muscle and shiatsu massage on two different days. We steamed. We Jacuzzied. We both had a mud facial, and then this thing called aromatherapy—where they put distilled essences from flowers and herbs on your face and you look like a different person when they finish. On the last day, we got this Persian Body Polish where they actually buffed our skin with crushed pearl creams, sprayed us with some kind of herbal spray, then used an electric brush to make us tingle. We had our hands and feet moisturized and put in heated gloves and booties, and by the time we left, we couldn't believe we were the same women.

In Phoenix, Gloria took me to yet another resort where we listened to live music. We went to see a stupid movie and I actually laughed. Then we went on a two-day shopping spree and I charged whatever I felt like. I even bought her son a pair of eighty-dollar sneakers, and I'd only seen him twice in my life.

I felt like I'd gotten my spirit back, so when I got home, I told my parents I'd had it with the smog, the traffic, the gangs, and L.A. in general. My mother said, "You cannot run from heartache," but I told her I wasn't running from anything. I put my condo on the market, and in less than a month it sold for four times what I paid for it. I moved in with my mother and father, asked for a job transfer for health reasons, and when it came through, three months later, I moved to Scottsdale.

The town house I bought feels like a house. It's twice the size of the one I had and cost less than half of what I originally spent. My complex is pretty standard for Scottsdale. It has two pools and four tennis courts. It also has vaulted ceilings, wall-to-wall carpet, two fireplaces, and a garden bathtub with a Jacuzzi in it. The kitchen has an island in the center and I've got a 180-degree view of Phoenix and mountains. It also has three bedrooms. One I sleep in, one I use for sewing, and the other is for guests.

I made close to forty thousand dollars after I sold my condo, so I sent four to my parents because the money they'd put down for the wedding was non-refundable. They really couldn't afford that kind of loss. The rest I put in an IRA and CDs until I could figure out something better to do with it.

I hated my new job. I had to accept a lower-level position and less money, which didn't bother me all that much at first. The office, however, was much smaller and full of rednecks who couldn't stand the thought of a black woman working over them. I was combing the classifieds, looking for a comparable job, but the job market in Phoenix is nothing close to what it is in L.A.

But thank God Gloria's got a big mouth. She'd been boasting to all of her clients about my quilts, had even hung the one I'd given her on the wall at the shop, and the next thing I know I'm getting so many orders I couldn't keep up with them. That's when she asked me why didn't I consider opening my own shop? That never would've occurred to me, but what did I have to lose?

She introduced me to Bernadine, a friend of hers who was an accountant. Bernadine in turn introduced me to a good lawyer, and he helped me draw up all the papers. Over the next four months, she helped me devise what turned out to be a strong marketing and advertising plan. I rented an 800-square-foot space in the same shopping center where Gloria's shop is, and opened Quilt-works, Etc.

It wasn't long before I realized I needed to get some help, so I hired two seamstresses. They took a lot of the strain off of me, and I was able to take some jewelry-making classes and even started selling small pieces in the shop. Gloria gave me this tacky T-shirt for my thirty-ninth birthday, which gave me the idea to experiment with making them. Because I go overboard in everything I do, I went out and spent a fortune on every color of metallic and acrylic fabric paint they made. I bought one hundred 100-percent cotton heavy-duty men's T-shirts and discovered other uses for sponges, plastic, spray bottles, rolling pins, lace, and even old envelopes. I was having a great time because I'd never felt this kind of excitement and gratification doing anything until now.

I'd been living here a year when I found out that Richard had married another woman who worked in our office. I wanted to hate him, but I didn't. I wanted to be angry, but I wasn't. I didn't feel anything toward him, but I sent him a quilt and a wedding card to congratulate him, just because.

To be honest, I've been so busy with my shop, I haven't even thought about men. I don't even miss having sex unless I really just *think* about it. My libido must be evaporating, because when I *do* think about it, I just make quilts or jewelry or paint T-shirts and the feeling goes away. Some of my best ideas come at these moments.

Basically, I'm doing everything I can to make Marilyn feel good. And at thirty-nine years old my body needs tightening, so I joined a health club and started working out three to four times a week. Once in a while, I babysit for Bernadine, and it breaks my heart when I think about the fact that I don't have a child of my own. Sometimes, Gloria and I go out to hear some music. I frequent most of the major art galleries, go to just about every football and basketball game at Arizona State, and see at *least* one movie a week.

I am rarely bored. Which is why I've decided that at this point in my life, I really don't care if I ever get married. I've learned that I don't need a man in order to survive, that a man is nothing but an intrusion, and they require too much energy. I don't think they're worth it. Besides, they have too much power, and from what I've seen, they always seem to abuse it. The one thing I *do* have is power over my own life. I like it this way, and I'm not about to give it up for something that may not last.

The one thing I do want is to have a baby. Someone I could love who would love me back with no strings attached. But at thirty-nine, I know my days are numbered. I'd be willing to do it alone, if that's the only way I can have one. But right now, my life is almost full. It's fun, it's secure, and it's safe. About the only thing I'm concerned about these days is whether or not it's time to branch out into leather.

Biographical Notes

TINA MCELROY ANSA, 1949–
Ansa attended Spelman College. She has worked as a journalist for the *Charlotte Observer* (North Carolina) and the *Atlanta Constitution*. Author of the novel *Baby in the Family* (1989), she has contributed stories to *Callaloo* and several other literary journals. She lives in St. Simons Island, Georgia.

JAMES BALDWIN, 1924–1987
Baldwin was born August 2 in Harlem, New York, and attended De Witt Clinton High School in the Bronx. As a teen he preached at Fireside Pentecostal Assembly. Later, he held a variety of jobs, such as dishwasher and waiter, before moving to Paris in the late forties. He published one collection of stories, *Going to Meet the Man* (1965), six novels, and several collectons of essays.

TONI CADE BAMBARA, 1939–
Bambara was born in New York City on March 25. She was educated at Queens College (CUNY), University of Florence, Ecole de Mime Etienne Decroux in Paris, and earned an M.A. from City College (CUNY). Author of *Gorilla, My Love* (1972), stories, and two novels, she has also written for television and edited several anthologies.

DON BELTON, 1956–
Belton was born August 7 in Philadelphia. He has lived in Vermont, Colorado, and Michigan, where he taught literature and creative writing at the University of Michigan at Ann Arbor. Author of the novel *Almost Midnight* (1986), he has also contributed to the *Denver Post, Newsweek,* and other periodicals.

HAL BENNETT, 1930–
Bennett was born April 21 in Buckingham, Virginia. He attended Mexico City College and later settled in Hackensack, New Jersey, where he still lives. Author of a collection of poems, five novels, and a story collection, *Insanity Runs in Our Family* (1977), Bennett has also written for *Harper's* and other periodicals.

ROBERT BOLES, 1942–
Boles was born in June in Chicago. Because his father was an architect in the State Depart-

ment's Foreign Service division, Boles spent his early years abroad. In 1960–62 he served with the U.S. Air Force in France as a medic. He has worked as a reporter, teacher, editor, and photographer. His novels, *The People One Knows* (1964) and *Curling* (1968) reflect his New England background. He has contributed short stories to *The New Yorker* and to a number of other magazines and literary journals such as *Tri-Quarterly*.

MARITA BONNER, 1899–1971
Born in Boston and educated in Cambridge, Bonner later lived in Washington, D.C., and Chicago, where she earned a living as a teacher. Her collected works, originally published primarily in *Crisis* and *Opportunity*, appear in *Frye Street and Environs: The Collected Works of Marita Bonner* (1987).

ARNA BONTEMPS, 1902–1973
Born October 13 in Alexandria, Louisiana, Bontemps lived in Huntsville, Alabama; Nashville, Tennessee; Chicago; and New Haven, Connecticut, where he worked as a university librarian. Author of many books—novels, anthologies, and history—he is perhaps best known for such anthologies as *American Negro Poetry* (1963) and for his many books for children.

CECIL M. BROWN, 1943–
Brown was born July 3 in Bolton, North Carolina. He earned a master's degree from the University of Chicago. Author of the novels *The Life and Loves of Mr. Jiveass Nigger* (1970) and *Days Without Weather* (1982), Brown has also written plays for both stage and screen and contributed to such magazines as *Partisan Review, Kenyon Review,* and *Evergreen Review*. He lives in Berkeley, California.

CHARLES WADDELL CHESNUTT, 1858–1932
Born June 20, in Cleveland, Ohio, Chesnutt grew up in Fayetteville, North Carolina. Self-educated, he began collecting folk material while working as a clerk in his father's general store. After moving north, he worked as a stock market reporter and eventually settled in Cleveland. Author of three novels and two story collections, his best-known works are *The Wife of His Youth and Other Stories of the Color Line* (1899), *The Marrow of Tradition* (1901), and *The Conjure Woman and Other Tales* (1899).

MICHELLE CLIFF, 1946–
Cliff was born November 2 in Kingston, Jamaica. She attended Wagner College and earned a M. Phil. from Warburg Institute in London in 1974. She has worked as a reporter and researcher for *Life* and as a visiting writer at various schools and institutions. Winner of several awards, she is the author of two volumes of poetry, two novels, and the story collection *Bodies of Water* (1990). She lives in Santa Cruz, California.

CYRUS COLTER, 1910–
Born January 8 in Noblesville, Indiana, Colter has spent most of his life in Chicago, where he works as a lawyer. Author of four novels, *Rivers of Eros* (1972), *The Hippodrome* (1973), *Night Studies* (1979), and *A Chocolate Soldier* (1988), he has also published a collection of short stories, *Beach Umbrella* (1970).

SAMUEL R. DELANY, 1942–
Delany was born April 1 in Harlem. His apprenticeship years as a science fiction writer during the early sixties were spent on the Lower East Side, where he met and married poet Marilyn

Hacker. Author of *Dhalgren* (1975) and numerous other science fiction novels, Delany has also published two volumes of autobiography and a "sword and sorcery" series called "Return to Neveryon."

HENRY DUMAS, 1934–1968

Born July 20 in Sweet Home, Arkansas, Dumas was a poet, novelist, and short story writer whose life ended on a Harlem station platform, when he was shot by a policeman—according to some reports—for jumping over a turnstile. He had attended the City University of New York and Rutgers University and contributed stories to a few literary periodicals. Two years after his death the first of his more than six books, *Ark of Bones and Other Stories* (1970), appeared. His other collection of stories is *Rope of Wind* (1979).

PAUL LAURENCE DUNBAR, 1872–1906

Dunbar was born in Dayton, Ohio, on June 27. His father was a fugitive slave. Sickly as a child, Dunbar attended integrated public schools but spent much time alone reading and was working as an elevator operator when William Dean Howells took an interest in him. He is the author of several outstanding novels, among them *The Uncalled* (1898), *The Fanatics* (1901), and *The Sport of the Gods* (1902). Unfortunately Dunbar—whose fiction is often first rate—is best known as a dialect poet.

LARRY DUPLECHAN, 1956–

Duplechan was born December 30 in Los Angeles. He is the author of three novels, *Eight Days a Week* (1985), *Blackbird* (1986), and *Tangled Up in Blue* (1989). His work also has appeared in *Hometowns* and other anthologies of gay literature. He lives in Los Angeles.

JUNIUS EDWARDS, 1929–

Edwards was born in Alexandria, Louisiana. He attended the University of Oslo. His short stories appeared in *The Transatlantic Review* and other magazines. Author of the novel *If We Must Die* (1963), Edwards was awarded a Eugene Saxton Fellowship in 1959.

TREY ELLIS, 1962–

Born in Washington, D.C., Ellis was a student at Phillips Academy. He later attended Stanford University and worked as a journalist and translator in Italy; he has also traveled extensively in Central America and Africa and has lived for an extended period in Greece. The author of the novel *Platitudes* (1988), he now lives in Venice, California.

RALPH ELLISON, 1914–

Ellison was born March 1 in Oklahoma City, Oklahoma, where he grew up. In New York in the late thirties, Ellison worked for the WPA. Author of one famous prize-winning novel, *Invisible Man* (1952), Ellison has published excerpts from his second novel-in-progress in various periodicals. He has also published two collections of essays, *Shadow and Act* (1964) and *Going to the Territory* (1986).

PERCIVAL EVERETT, 1956–

Everett grew up in Columbia, South Carolina, attended the University of Miami and the University of Oregon, and earned a master's degree from Brown University. He worked as a sheep-ranch hand, a musician, and a college professor at the University of Notre Dame. He is author of the novels *Suder* (1983), *Walk Me to the Distance* (1985), *Cutting Lisa* (1986), *Zulus* (1990), and other books.

JESSIE FAUSET, 1882–1961
Born in Camden County, New Jersey, Fauset grew up near Philadelphia and was educated at the University of Pennsylvania, Cornell, and the Sorbonne. She is the author of four novels, *There Is Confusion* (1924), *Pum Bun* (1928), *The Chinaberry Tree* (1931), and *Comedy, American Style* (1933). These forgotten novels were rediscovered in the seventies.

RUDOLPH FISHER, 1897–1934
Fisher was born May 9 in Washington, D.C., and earned degrees from Brown and Columbia University. He was a physician who specialized in roentgenology and worked for the New York Department of Health. Author of two novels, *The Walls of Jericho* (1928) and *The Conjure-Man Dies* (1932), he also wrote many short stories, later collected under the title *The City of Refuge* (1987).

ERNEST J. GAINES, 1933–
Born in Oscar, Pointe Coupee Parish, Louisiana on January 15, Gaines attended Vallejo Junior College and San Francisco State College and did graduate work at Stanford, where he was awarded a Wallace Stegner Fellowship in creative writing. Author of *The Autobiography of Miss Jane Pittman* (1971), four other novels, and *Bloodline* (1968), a collection of stories, he was honored in 1987 at the American Academy and Institute of Arts and Letters.

ROSA GUY, 1928–
Born September 2 in Trinidad, Guy grew up in the United States. Best known as the author of children's books and novels for young adults, such as *The Disappearance* (1979) and *Paris Pee Wee and Big Dog* (1984), Guy is also a translator and playwright.

CHESTER HIMES, 1909–1984
Himes was born in Jefferson City, Missouri, July 29. He served six years in Ohio State Penitentiary for armed robbery. While in prison he began writing and publishing short stories in such periodicals as *Coronet, Pittsburgh Courier,* and *Esquire* and is the author of eighteen novels, ten of which are detective stories originally published in France in the "Serie Noir" by Gallimard. His best-known novel is his first, *If He Hollers Let Him Go* (1945). *The Collected Stories of Chester Himes* was published in 1990. Himes died of Parkinson's disease in Moraira, Spain.

LANGSTON HUGHES, 1902–1967
Hughes was born February 1 in Joplin, Missouri. During and after college he worked at various odd jobs before shipping out as a seaman to Europe and Africa. Throughout his life he lived for extended periods in Europe and Mexico. Known primarily as a prolific folk poet, Hughes published seven collections of short fiction, six juvenile books, and two novels and edited eight anthologies.

ZORA NEALE HURSTON, 1881–1960
Hurston was born January 7 in Eatonville, Florida. She attended Howard University and Barnard College and did graduate work at Columbia University. During her lifetime she published seven books: three novels, two works of folklore, and an autobiography. Several collections of her work appeared after her death. She is perhaps best known for her second novel, *Their Eyes Were Watching God* (1937), but she also conducted pioneering anthropological research in the South and in Jamaica and Haiti.

CHARLES JOHNSON, 1948–
Johnson was born April 23 in Evanston, Illinois, and attended Southern Illinois University. He later earned a master's degree from the State University of New York at Stony Brook. He is the author of screenplays, cartoon collections, a story collection called *The Sorcerer's Apprentice* (1986), and three novels: *Faith and the Good Thing* (1974), *Oxherding Tale* (1982), and *Middle Passage* (1990), for which he won the National Book Award.

GAYL JONES, 1949–
Born January 23 in Lexington, Kentucky, Jones earned an M.A. from Brown University. Her works of fiction are *Corregidora* (1975), *Eva's Man* (1979), and *The White Rat* (1977). She is also a playwright and has published four volumes of poetry. She taught from 1975 to 1983 at the University of Michigan.

LEROI JONES/AMIRI BARAKA, 1934–
Born October 7 in Newark, New Jersey, Baraka moved to New York's Greenwich Village in the fifties and became identified with a group of poets later characterized as Beat and/or Black Mountain. In the mid-sixties he became a Black Nationalist and eventually returned to Newark, where he opened a theater. In the seventies he shifted to Marxism. He is the author of one story collection, *Tales* (1967), and numerous plays and collections of poems.

WILLIAM MELVIN KELLEY, 1937–
Kelley was born November 1 in New York City, where his father was an editor and his mother a designer. After attending Harvard University in the late fifties, he published his first novel, *A Different Drummer* (1961), and two years later his first collection of stories, *Dancers on the Shore*. These were followed by three novels, *A Drop of Patience* (1965), *dem* (1967), and *Dunfords Travels Everywheres* (1970).

JAMAICA KINCAID, 1949–
Kincaid was born May 25 in St. John's, Antigua, West Indies. She emigrated to the United States and became a U.S. citizen. In 1976 she started working as a staff writer for *The New Yorker* and began publishing her stories in its pages. She is the author of one story collection, *At the Bottom of the River* (1983), and two other books, *Annie John* (a cycle of stories) (1985) and *A Small Place* (1988).

NELLA LARSEN, 1891–1964
Larsen was born in Chicago. Her mother was Danish and her father Jamaican. She was raised by her mother and a stepfather. She attended private schools and Fisk University and spent two years at the University of Copenhagen. In 1919 she married Elmer S. Imes, a physicist. Author of two novels, *Quicksand* (1928) and *Passing* (1929), Larsen also contributed to periodicals such as *Opportunity* and *Forum*, where "Sanctuary" appeared in 1930. She lived for many years in New York City, where she worked as a librarian and later as a supervising nurse in the hospitals of the Lower East Side.

CLARENCE MAJOR, 1936–
Born December 31 in Atlanta, Major grew up in Chicago. He later earned a bachelor's degree from the State University of New York and a Ph.D. from the Union Institute in Ohio. Author of *My Amputations* (1986), *Such Was the Season* (1987), five other novels, and nine volumes

of poetry, Major teaches African-American literature and directs the creative writing program at the University of California in Davis.

PAULE MARSHALL, 1929–
Born April 9 in Brooklyn, New York, to West Indian parents, Marshall grew up feeling strong ties to the Caribbean. After college and working as a librarian, she published her first and best-known novel, *Brown Girl, Brownstones* (1959). Author of three other novels, Marshall has also published two collections of stories, *Soul Clap Hands and Sing* (1961) and *Reena and Other Stories* (1983).

JOHN MCCLUSKEY, JR., 1944–
McCluskey was born October 25 in Middletown, Ohio. He attended Harvard University and earned a master's degree from Stanford. Author of the novels *Look What They Done to My Song* (1974) and *Mr. America's Last Season Blues* (1983), McCluskey has contributed to many anthologies and periodicals and edited the collected stories of Rudolph Fisher. He is currently a professor of Afro-American Studies at Indiana University in Bloomington.

COLLEEN J. MCELROY, 1935–
McElroy was born October 30 in St. Louis, Missouri. She attended the University of Maryland and in 1973 earned a doctorate from the University of Washington, where she is now a professor of English. Author of seven volumes of poetry and two story collections, she has also contributed poems and stories to a wide range of anthologies and periodicals.

CLAUDE MCKAY, 1899–1948
McKay was born in Clarendon, Jamaica. In 1912 he moved to the United States, where he attended Tuskegee Institute and Kansas State College. He worked with Max Eastman on various left-wing periodicals. Author of three novels, *Home to Harlem* (1928), *Banjo* (1929), and *Banana Bottom* (1933), he also published a collection of stories, *Gingertown* (1932). He died penniless in Chicago.

REGINALD MCKNIGHT, 1955–
McKnight earned a master's from Denver University in 1987. He spent a year as a scholar in Senegal. Author of two novels and the story collection *Moustapha's Eclipse* (1988), he has been a contributor to many periodicals and has won several literary awards. He teaches at the University of Pittsburgh.

TERRY MCMILLAN, 1951–
McMillan was born in Port Huron, Michigan, and has lived in New York, Arizona, and California, where she attended the University of California at Berkeley. Recipient of many awards, she is the author of *Mama* (1987) and two other novels. McMillan lives in northern California.

JAMES ALAN MCPHERSON, 1943–
McPherson was born September 16 in Savannah, Georgia. He attended Morgan State University in the early sixties, Harvard and Iowa University in the late sixties. A recipient of a Pulitzer Prize, a MacArthur fellowship, and other awards, McPherson is the author of two collections of stories, *Hue and Cry* (1969) and *Elbow Room* (1977).

TONI MORRISON, 1931–
Born Chloe Anthony Wofford, on February 18 in Lorain, Ohio, Toni Morrison grew up in

Ohio and later earned a B.A. from Howard and an M.A. from Cornell. From 1955 to 1964 she was a college teacher. In 1965 she became an editor at Random House where she remained till returning full time to teaching in the early eighties. Author of *Beloved* (Pulitzer Prize, 1988) and four other novels, she is Robert F. Goheen Professor of the Humanities at Princeton.

GLORIA NAYLOR, 1950–

Naylor was born January 25 in New York and attended Brooklyn College. She earned a master's degree from Yale in 1983. Author of *The Women of Brewster Place* (1982) and two other novels, Naylor has received a Guggenheim and other awards for her fiction. She has been a visiting professor at Brandeis, Cornell, and other universities. Naylor lives in New York.

DIANE OLIVER, 1943–1966

Oliver was born in Charlotte, North Carolina. She attended the University of North Carolina at Greensboro and was a student at the Writer's Workshop of the University of Iowa. She died in an automobile accident a few days before she was to receive her master's degree.

RICHARD PERRY, 1944–

Perry was born January 13 in New York, where he grew up. He attended City College (CUNY) and earned an M.F.A., from Columbia in 1972. He teaches English at Pratt Institute in Brooklyn and lives in New Jersey. Author of the novels *Changes* (1974) and *Montgomery's Children* (1984), Perry has written for *The New York Times Book Review* and other periodicals.

ANN PETRY, 1908–

Petry was born October 12 in Old Saybrook, Connecticut, where she has lived most of her life. Her father was the local druggist and she herself worked as a pharmacist after earning a Ph.D. in 1931. But she also lived briefly in New York and did postgraduate work at Columbia while working in advertising and as a reporter during the early forties. Author of *The Street* (1946) and two other novels, Petry has also published four children's books and a short-story collection, *Miss Muriel and Other Stories* (1953).

ANN ALLEN SHOCKLEY, 1927–

Born June 21 in Louisville, Kentucky, Shockley was educated at Fisk University and Western Reserve University. She has worked as a librarian at various universities and has been an associate professor of library science at Fisk since 1970. She has edited several scholarly reference works and is the author of *Loving Her* (1974), one other novel, and a collection of stories.

ELLEASE SOUTHERLAND, 1943–

Southerland was born June 18 in Brooklyn. She attended Queens College (CUNY) and earned an M.F.A. from Columbia. She teaches black literature at Manhattan Community College and at Pace University. Author of a collection of poems and the novels *White Shadows* (1964) and *Let the Lion Eat Straw* (1979), her stories and poems appear primarily in black periodicals.

JOHN STEWART, 1933–

Stewart was born January 24 in St. Johns, Trinidad, and grew up there and in Los Angeles, California. He holds degrees in English and creative writing and earned a Ph.D. in anthropology from U.C.L.A. Stewart is the author of the novel *Last Cool Days* (1971) and the story collection *Curving Road* (1975) and several scholarly works. He is director of African-American Studies at the University of California in Davis.

JEAN TOOMER, 1894–1967
Toomer was born in Washington, D.C., and was raised by his mother in his grandparents' home in Georgetown. As a young man he enrolled in and dropped out of several universities. In his search for a philosophy to live by, he eventually became a Quaker. *Cane* (1923) is his best-known book. A collection of his previously unpublished writings, *The Wayward and the Seeking,* appeared in 1980.

HENRY VAN DYKE, 1928–
Van Dyke was born October 3 in Allegan, Michigan, and attended the University of Michigan. Author of the novels *Ladies of the Rachmaninoff Eyes* (1965), *Blood of Strawberries* (1969), *Dead Piano* (1971), and *Lunacy and Caprice* (1987), he has been a recipient of a Hopwood and a Guggenheim and was honored by the American Academy of Arts and Letters. His short works have appeared in *The O. Henry Prize Stories, Transatlantic Review, Antioch Review,* and other periodicals.

ALICE WALKER, 1944–
Born February 9 in Eatonton, Georgia, Walker attended Spelman College and earned a B.A. from Sarah Lawrence College in 1965. She is the author of five poetry and two story collections. Of her three novels, *The Color Purple* (1982), the best known one, won a Pulitzer Prize.

DOROTHY WEST, 1907–
Born June 2, West grew up in Boston, where she attended Girls' Latin School and Boston University, and then studied journalism in New York at Columbia. In the thirties she edited the literary journal *Challenge* (later *New Challenge*). Author of several short stories and many articles, she has published one novel, *The Living Is Easy* (1948). West lives on Martha's Vineyard.

EDGAR NKOSE WHITE, 1947–
White was born April 4 in Montserrat, British West Indies, moved to the United States when he was five, and later earned a B.A. from New York University. Author of more than a dozen produced plays, White is also author of *Sati, the Rastifarian* (1973), *Children of Night* (1974), and two other novels. He is the recipient of an O'Neal, a Rockefeller, and many other awards and grants.

JOHN EDGAR WIDEMAN, 1941–
Born June 14 in Washington, D.C., Wideman grew up in the Homewood section of Pittsburgh, the setting for much of his fiction. Later he earned degrees from the University of Pennsylvania and Oxford University. Author of *Reuben* (1987), *Philadelphia Fire* (1990), five other novels, and two story collections, he has contributed essays and book reviews to many periodicals. He is the recipient of many prizes and awards. Wideman is a professor of English at the University of Massachusetts.

JOHN A. WILLIAMS, 1925–
Williams was born December 5 in Jackson, Mississippi, but grew up in Syracuse, New York.

During and after college he worked in public relations, as a reporter, and for the welfare department. In the late sixties he became a college teacher. His first novel, *The Angry Ones*, appeared in 1961. By 1991 he had published ten other novels, the best known of which was *The Man Who Cried I Am* (1967). He has also published six nonfiction books and contributed to dozens of anthologies and periodicals.

CHARLES WRIGHT, 1932–

Wright was born in Franklin, Missouri, on June 4. Early on, he worked at his writing under the direction of Lowney Handy in Marshall, Illinois. Wright is the author of two novels, *The Messenger* (1963) and *The Wig: A Mirror Image* (1966); a nonfiction work, *Absolutely Nothing to Get Alarmed About* (1973); and a variety of uncollected short stories.

RICHARD WRIGHT, 1908–1960

Born September 4 near Natchez, Mississippi, Wright was the son of a millworker and a teacher. Largely self-educated, he began to write at an early age. As a young man Wright moved to Chicago, joined the Communist Party, and worked for the WPA. Later, in New York, his first books—*Uncle Tom's Children* (1938), a collection of stories, and *Native Son* (1940), a novel—were published. In the mid-forties he moved to Paris. After his death, a second collection of short stories, *Eight Men* (1961), appeared. He also wrote four other novels and five nonfiction books.

AL YOUNG, 1939–

Young was born May 31 in Ocean Springs, Mississippi, and grew up in Detroit. He attended the University of Michigan and the University of California at Berkeley. Young is the author of *Snakes* (1970) and three other novels, five volumes of poetry, and three memoirs. He has been honored with many awards and has been a visiting professor at many universities. He lives in Palo Alto, California.

Credits